GERMINAL

ÉMILE ZOLA, born in Paris in 1840, was brought up in Aix-en-Provence in an atmosphere of struggling poverty after the death of his father in 1847. He was educated at the Collège Bourbon at Aix and then at the Lycée Saint-Louis in Paris. After failing the *baccalauréat* twice and then taking menial clerical employment, he joined the newly founded publishing house Hachette in 1862 and quickly rose to become head of publicity. Having published his first novel in 1865 he left Hachette the following year to become a full-time journalist and writer. *Thérèse Raquin* appeared in 1867 and caused a scandal, to which he responded with his famous Preface to the novel's second edition in 1868 in which he laid claim to being a 'Naturalist'. That same year he began work on a series of novels intended to trace scientifically the effects of heredity and environment in one family: *Les Rougon-Macquart*. This great cycle eventually contained twenty novels, which appeared between 1871 and 1893. In 1877 the seventh of these, *L'Assommoir* (*The Drinking Den*), a study of alcoholism in working-class Paris, brought him abiding wealth and fame. On completion of the Rougon-Macquart series he began a new cycle of novels, *Les Trois Villes: Lourdes, Rome, Paris* (1894–6–8), a violent attack on the Church of Rome, which led to another cycle, *Les Quatre Évangiles*. While his later writing was less successful, he remained a celebrated figure on account of the Dreyfus case, in which his powerful interventions played an important part in redressing a heinous miscarriage of justice. His marriage in 1870 had remained childless, but his happy, public relationship in later life with Jeanne Rozerot, initially one of his domestic servants, brought him a son and a daughter. He died in mysterious circumstances in 1902, the victim of an accident or murder.

ROGER PEARSON is Professor of French at the University of Oxford and Fellow and Tutor in French at The Queen's College, Oxford. He is the author of standard critical works on Voltaire, Stendhal and Mallarmé. He has translated and edited Voltaire, *Candide and Other Stories* (1990), Zola, *La Bête humaine* (1996) and Maupassant, *A Life* (1999). He has also revised and edited Thomas Walton's translation of Zola, *The Masterpiece* (1993).

ÉMILE ZOLA

Germinal

Translated with an Introduction and Notes
by ROGER PEARSON

PENGUIN BOOKS

PENGUIN BOOKS

Published by the Penguin Group
Penguin Books Ltd, 80 Strand, London WC2R ORL, England
Penguin Putnam Inc., 375 Hudson Street, New York, New York 10014, USA
Penguin Books Australia Ltd, 250 Camberwell Road, Camberwell, Victoria 3124, Australia
Penguin Books Canada Ltd, 10 Alcorn Avenue, Toronto, Ontario, Canada M4V 3B2
Penguin Books India (P) Ltd, 11 Community Centre, Panchsheel Park, New Delhi – 110 017, India
Penguin Books (NZ) Ltd, Cnr Rosedale and Airborne Roads, Albany, Auckland, New Zealand
Penguin Books (South Africa) (Pty) Ltd, 24 Sturdee Avenue, Rosebank 2196, South Africa

Penguin Books Ltd, Registered Offices: 80 Strand, London WC2R ORL, England

www.penguin.com

First published 1885
This translation published 2004

016

Set in 10.25/12.25 pt PostScript Adobe Sabon
Typeset by Rowland Phototypesetting Ltd, Bury St Edmunds, Suffolk
Printed in England by Clays Ltd, St Ives plc

ISBN-13: 978-0-140-44742-2

www.greenpenguin.co.uk

Penguin Books is committed to a sustainable
future for our business, our readers and our planet.
This book is made from Forest Stewardship
Council™ certified paper.

MIX
Paper from
responsible sources
FSC
www.fsc.org   FSC™ C018179

ALWAYS LEARNING   **PEARSON**

Contents

Chronology

1840 2 April Émile Zola born in Paris, the son of an Italian engineer, Francesco Zola, and of Françoise-Emilie Aubert.

1843 The family moves to Aix-en-Provence, which will become the town of 'Plassans' in the Rougon-Macquart novels.

1847 Francesco Zola dies, leaving the family nearly destitute.

1848 The rule of King Louis-Philippe (the July Monarchy, which came to power in 1830) is overthrown and the Second Republic declared. Zola starts school. Karl Marx publishes *Manifesto of the Communist Party*.

1851 The Republic is dissolved after the *coup d'état* of Louis-Napoleon Bonaparte who in the following year proclaims himself emperor as Napoleon III. Start of the Second Empire, the period that will provide the background for Zola's novels in the Rougon-Macquart cycle.

1852 Zola is enrolled at the Collège Bourbon, in Aix, where he starts a close friendship with the painter Paul Cézanne.

1858 The family moves back to Paris and Zola is sent to the Lycée Saint-Louis. His school career is undistinguished and he twice fails the *baccalauréat*.

1860 The start of a period of hardship as Zola tries to scrape a living by various kinds of work, while engaging in his first serious literary endeavours, mainly as a poet. These years saw the height of the rebuilding programme undertaken by Baron Haussmann, Prefect of Paris from 1853 to 1869, which is reflected in several of Zola's novels.

1862 Zola joins the publisher Hachette, and in a few months becomes the firm's head of publicity.

1863 Makes his début as a journalist.

1864 Zola's first literary work, the collection of short stories, *Contes à Ninon*, appears. Founding of the First International.

1865 Publishes his first novel, *La Confession de Claude*. Meets his future wife, Gabrielle-Alexandrine Meley; they marry in 1870.

1866 Leaves Hachette. From now on, he lives by his writing.

1867 Publication of *Thérèse Raquin*, the story of how a working-class woman and her lover kill her husband, but are afterwards consumed by guilt. In the Preface to the second edition (1868), Zola declares that he belongs to the literary school of 'Naturalism'.

1868–9 Zola develops the outline of his great novel-cycle, *Les Rougon-Macquart*, which he subtitles 'The Natural and Social History of a Family under the Second Empire'. It is founded on the latest theories of heredity. He signs a contract for the work with the publisher Lacroix.

1870 The outbreak of the Franco-Prussian War leads in September to the fall of the Second Empire. Napoleon III and Empress Eugénie go into exile in England and the Third Republic is declared. Paris is besieged by Prussian forces. *La Fortune des Rougon* starts to appear in serial form.

1871 Publication in book form of *La Fortune des Rougon*, the first novel in the Rougon-Macquart cycle. After the armistice with Prussia, a popular uprising in March threatens the overthrow of the government of Adolphe Thiers, which flees to Versailles. The radical Paris Commune takes power until its bloody repression by Thiers in May; the events would have great importance for the Socialist Left. Zola was shocked both by the anarchy of the Commune and by the savagery with which it was repressed. He begins to think of writing a novel about radical politics, which would later become *Germinal*.

1872 Publication of *La Curée*, the second of the Rougon-Macquart novels. Part of it had appeared in serialized form (September–November 1871), but publication had been suspended by the censorship authorities.

1873 Publication of *Le Ventre de Paris*, the third of the cycle, set in and around the market of Les Halles. Mikhail Bakunin publishes *Statehood and Anarchy*.

1874 Publication of *La Conquête de Plassans*.

1875 Publication of *La Faute de l'Abbé Mouret*.

1876 *Son Excellence Eugène Rougon* follows the career of a minister under the Second Empire. Later in the same year, the seventh of the Rougon-Macquart novels, *L'Assommoir* (*The Drinking Den*), begins to appear in serial form and immediately causes a sensation with its grim depiction of the ravages of alcoholism and life in the Parisian slums.

1877 *L'Assommoir* is published in book form and becomes a bestseller. Zola's fortune is made and he is recognized as the leading figure in the Naturalist movement.

1878 Zola follows the harsh realism of *L'Assommoir* with a gentler tale of domestic life, *Une page d'amour*. Buys a house at Médan.

1879 *Nana* appears in serial form, before publication in book form in the following year. The story of a high-class prostitute, the novel was to attract further scandal to Zola's name.

1880 Publication of *Les Soirées de Médan*, an anthology of short stories by Zola and some of his Naturalist 'disciples', including Maupassant. Zola expounds the theory of Naturalism in *Le Roman expérimental*. In May, Zola's literary mentor, the writer Gustave Flaubert, dies; in October, Zola loses his much-loved mother. A period of depression follows and he suspends writing the Rougon-Macquart for a year.

1882 Zola's next book, *Pot-Bouille*, centres on an apartment house and the character of the bourgeois seducer, Octave Mouret. The novel analyses the hypocrisy of the respectable middle class.

1883 Mouret reappears in *Au Bonheur des Dames*, which studies the phenomenon of the department store. While on holiday in Brittany meets Alfred Giard, left-wing *député* for Valenciennes, who interests Zola in the miners' cause.

1884 *La Joie de vivre*. At the invitation of Giard spends a week at the end of February visiting the mining community of Anzin, near Valenciennes, and goes down a working mine to research the realities of life underground. Law passed on

21 March legalizing trade unions. 2 April Zola begins writing *Germinal*, which starts to appear in *Le Gil Blas* in November and is published in book form the following year.

1886 *L'Œuvre* provides a revealing insight into Parisian artistic and literary life, as well as a reflection of contemporary aesthetic debates, drawing on Zola's friendship with many leading painters and writers. However, Cézanne reacts badly to Zola's portrait of him in the novel, and ends their friendship.

1887 *La Terre*, a brutally frank portrayal of peasant life, causes a fresh uproar and leads to a crisis in the Naturalist movement when five of his 'disciples' sign a manifesto against the novel.

1888 Publication of *Le Rêve*. Zola begins his liaison with Jeanne Rozerot, the mistress with whom he will have two children.

1890 *La Bête humaine*, the story of a pathological killer, is set against the background of the railways.

1891 *L'Argent* examines the world of the Stock Exchange.

1892 *La Débâcle* analyses the French defeat in the Franco-Prussian War and the end of the Second Empire.

1893 The final novel in the cycle, *Le Docteur Pascal*, develops the theories of heredity which have guided *Les Rougon-Macquart*.

1894 With *Lourdes*, Zola starts a trilogy of novels, to be completed by *Rome* (1896) and *Paris* (1898), about a priest who turns away from Catholicism towards a more humanitarian creed. In December, a Jewish officer in the French Army, Captain Alfred Dreyfus, is found guilty of spying for Germany and sentenced to life imprisonment in the penal colony on Devil's Island, off the coast of French Guiana.

1897 New evidence in the case suggests that Dreyfus's conviction was a gross miscarriage of justice, inspired by anti-Semitism. Zola publishes three articles in *Le Figaro* demanding a retrial.

1898 Zola's open letter, *J'Accuse*, in support of Dreyfus, addressed to Félix Faure, President of the Republic, is published in *L'Aurore* (13 January). It proves a turning point, making the case a litmus test in French politics: for years to come, being pro- or anti-Dreyfusard will be a major component of a French person's ideological profile (with the nationalist Right leading the campaign against Dreyfus). Zola is tried for libel and sentenced to a year's imprisonment and a fine of 3,000 francs. In July, waiting for a retrial (granted on a technicality), he leaves for London, where he spends a year in exile.

1899 Zola begins a series of four novels, *Les Quatre Évangiles*, which would remain uncompleted at his death. They mark his transition from Naturalism to a more idealistic and utopian view of the world.

1902 29 September Zola is asphyxiated by the fumes from the blocked chimney of his bedroom stove, perhaps by accident, perhaps (as is still widely believed) assassinated by anti-Dreyfusards. On 5 October his funeral in Paris is witnessed by a crowd of 50,000. His remains were transferred to the Panthéon in 1908.

Introduction

*(New readers are advised that this Introduction
makes the detail of the plot explicit.)*

'This is one of those books you write for yourself, as an act
of conscience.'
(Zola, in a letter to Henry Céard of 14 June 1884[1])

Considered by André Gide to be one of the ten greatest novels
in the French language, *Germinal* is the story of a miners' strike.
Set in northern France during the 1860s, the work takes its title
from the name of a month in the Republican calendar. This
calendar, introduced by decree on 5 October 1793 and back-
dated to 22 September 1792 (which thus became the first day
of the First Republic), was a logical consequence of the ban on
the Christian religion in France following the Revolution of
1789. Replacing the Gregorian calendar, it took the autumnal
equinox as its starting point and was designed to segment time
in a non-Christian manner. Each of the year's twelve months
was divided into three ten-day periods known as *décades*, while
the five (or, in leap years, six) remaining days became national
holidays.

The months themselves were renamed to evoke the principal organic or meteorological characteristic of the moment:
Vendémiaire, Brumaire and Frimaire for the autumn months
of vintage, mist and frost; Nivôse, Pluviôse, Ventôse for the
winter months of snow, rain and storm; Germinal, Floréal,
Prairial for the spring months of seed, flowers and meadows;
and Messidor, Thermidor and Fructidor for the summer months
of harvest, heat and fruit. Derived from Latin, these names –
like those of the renamed days (*primidi, duodi, tridi*, etc.) – were
intended to evoke the Roman Republic, which revolutionary
France proudly if briefly took as its model. However, following
Napoleon Bonaparte's *coup d'état* in 1799 and his Concordat

with the Roman Catholic Church in 1801, the calendar was eventually abandoned as from 1 January 1806.

Germinal was thus the seventh month – from 21 March to 19 April during the first seven years of the calendar, but from 22 March to 20 April during the subsequent six – and its name suggests germination and renewal. Not only was the calendar itself the product of the Revolution, but the date of 12–13 Germinal in the Year Three (1–2 April 1795) is also of particular significance because of a famous uprising mounted by the Parisian populace who were facing starvation. As a title, therefore, *Germinal* neatly focuses on the novel's two central subjects: political struggle and the processes of nature. Indeed at the centre of the title is the mine itself (in French the word is pronounced like 'mean'), Zola's chosen emblem of the oppressive working conditions in which ill-paid labour makes a fortune for capital. Since the novel opens in March and ends in the April of the following year, its chronology combines one annual cycle with a symbolic passage through the month of 'germination'. Thus, more obliquely still, the title also encapsulates a profound ambiguity at the heart of Zola's narrative and perhaps at the heart of all human striving. Can there be progress – social, political, intellectual, moral progress – or is every new beginning but the repetition of an eternal cycle of growth and decay? If a revolution is one turn of the wheel, does it take us forward or bring us full circle? Are we getting somewhere or going nowhere?

Plans and Preparations

Germinal was originally published in serialized form in the newspaper *Le Gil Blas*. The first of the eighty-nine instalments appeared on 26 November 1884, the last on 25 February 1885. The completed novel was then published in book form on 2 March, and over the first five years this original French version sold some 83,000 copies. It was the thirteenth of the twenty novels comprising Zola's great family saga entitled *Les Rougon-Macquart* (1871–93): its central character, Étienne Lantier, is the son of Gervaise, a laundry-woman, in *L'Assom-*

moir (*The Drinking Den*: 1877) and brother to the eponymous heroine of *Nana* (1880), to the artist Claude Lantier in *L'Œuvre* (*The Masterpiece*: 1886) and to the psychopathic engine-driver Jacques Lantier in *La Bête humaine* (1890).

Les Rougon-Macquart was intended, as its subtitle states, to present 'The Natural and Social History of a Family under the Second Empire', and Émile Zola (1840–1902) was only in his late twenties when he submitted a book proposal to the publisher Lacroix in 1869 outlining the project. Between the ages of twenty-one and twenty-five he had been working for the major Parisian publishing house Hachette, at first in the dispatch department and then in marketing, where he quickly rose to become head of publicity. There he learned the 'business' of being a professional writer: how to write, what to write, how to sell what you write. Notoriety helps, and the racy bedroom scenes of his first novel *La Confession de Claude* (1865) soon made his name widely known. The sex and violence of *Thérèse Raquin* (1867) caused an even greater stir, and in the following year controversy was further fuelled by his uncompromising Preface to its second edition. Rejecting all charges of sensationalism and pornography he roundly defended the 'scientific' purpose of the book: namely, a physiological rather than psychological analysis of the 'love' that brings two people of differing 'temperaments' together and an attempt to present the 'remorse' which follows their murder of an inconvenient husband as an entirely physical, 'natural' process.

By the time, therefore, that Zola submitted his book proposal to Lacroix he was a distinctly marketable commodity, and the project itself did not disappoint: a series of ten novels which would trace the effects of heredity and environment on the successive generations of one family while presenting an exposé of French society under the rule of the Emperor Napoleon III. Something like Balzac's *Comédie humaine* therefore (which reflects the earlier decades of the century), but more 'scientific' – especially in its study of the effects of heredity – and also less coloured by the subjective opinions of its author. After an opening novel which traced the origins of the family and its division into a respectable and wealthy branch (the Rougons) and an illegitimate and genetically flawed branch (the Macquarts, from whom Gervaise Lantier and her children are descended), the remaining nine novels would focus in turn on the separate worlds of fashionable upper-class youth, banking and financial chicanery, government and the civil service, the Church, the army, the working class, the *demi-monde*, bohemia and the legal profession. A lucrative contract was secured.

Fortuitously the Second Empire ended – with the Franco-Prussian War and the disastrous defeat at Sedan on 1 September 1870 – just as Zola was writing the first of these ten novels, so that his new saga at once became the record of a fallen dynasty and a vanished world. At the same time his enthusiasm for the project grew, with the result that within a year or so he was already conceiving of a further seven novels for the series. Perhaps because of his experience of the Commune when republican elements took control of the city of Paris between March and May 1871, he now intended that one of these extra novels should focus on the domain of left-wing politics. In his earlier plan he had envisaged that his novel on the working class – which became *L'Assommoir* – would depict the appalling conditions in which the new urban proletariat was forced to live and work and how the demands and pressures of such an existence rendered it a prey to the alcohol which was so cheaply available and so injurious to health, resolve and marital harmony. Now he wanted to write another novel about working-class life, which would chart the contemporary manifestations of the revolutionary currents that – in France at least – had sprung to view in 1789, 1830, 1848 and 1871. *Germinal* would be that novel, the people's novel.

When *L'Assommoir* was published in 1877 (as the seventh novel in the series), it earned Zola large royalties and vociferous reviews. Those on the political Right charged him once again with being tasteless and immoral, while – more importantly for someone of his own moderate left-of-centre views – those on the Left condemned him for depicting the working class in such a negative light. Where Zola had thought he was indicting the system by showing how low human beings can be brought by background and circumstance – and often, as in Gervaise's case, despite their very best efforts – his socialist detractors saw a degrading portrait which would only reinforce bourgeois prejudice. They were unwilling to acknowledge that in so powerfully eliciting the reader's sympathy for Gervaise as the honourable victim of insuperable and malign forces Zola might have been hoping to make that reader a partisan of social and political reform.

By way of defending the honourableness of his intentions Zola let it be known that he was planning another novel about the working class, and one which would focus on its political aspirations and on the economic and social conditions in which its members lived. But which area of work should he choose? While on holiday at Bénodet in Brittany in 1883, Zola met Alfred Giard (1846–1908), the left-wing *député* for Valenciennes and a biologist with a particular research interest in the reproductive organs. Since his constituency in northern France was one of the centres of the French coal-mining industry, Giard no doubt saw a golden opportunity to secure the services of a brilliant publicist for the miners' cause; while Zola, no doubt keen to re-establish his radicalist credentials, could also see the artistic and polemical merits of taking a miners' strike as his subject. Accordingly, and characteristically, he began to document himself thoroughly, reading book after book about the mining industry, about the topography and geology of the area around Valenciennes and about radical politics: about the history of socialism and about the International Working Men's Association founded in 1864, better known as the First International. He familiarized himself with the full range of radical political theory: the libertarian socialism of Pierre-Joseph Proudhon (1809–65), who had famously declared in 1840 that property is theft (if it means the ability of one man to exploit the labour of another but not if it means the individual's right to possess his own 'means of production', be it land or a workshop full of tools); the 'Communism' or 'centralized socialism' of Karl Marx (1818–83), who had published his *Manifesto of the Communist Party* in 1848 and whose *Das Kapital* (1867) had begun to appear in French translation in 1875; the ideas of Auguste Blanqui (1805–81), the revolutionary socialist and insurrectionary who had been prominently involved in the revolutions of 1830 and 1848 and was elected President of the Commune (1870–71) while in prison, where indeed he spent long periods; and finally the anarchism, or 'nihilism', of the Russian revolutionary Mikhail Bakunin (1814–76), author of *Statehood and Anarchy* (1873).

More particularly, Zola read how Marx had been elected one of the thirty-two members of the First International's provisional General Council and then assumed its leadership; how the representatives of the national federations would meet at a congress every year in a different city; and how at The Hague in 1872 the clash between supporters of Marx's socialism and Bakunin's anarchism led to an irrevocable split in the movement. In order to prevent the Bakunists from gaining control of the Association, the General Council, at Marx's behest, moved its headquarters to New York before finally disbanding at a conference in Philadelphia in 1876. The Bakunists nevertheless took over the *de facto* leadership of the International and held their own congresses from 1873 to 1877. At the Socialist World Congress in Ghent in 1877 the Social Democrats broke away because their motion to restore the unity of the First International was rejected by the anarchist majority. But the International now began to wither, and after the Anarchist Congress in London in 1881, it ceased to represent an organized movement. Only later, four years after the publication of *Germinal* in 1885, was the Second International, the so-called Socialist International, founded at a congress in Paris. This Second International supported parliamentary democracy and finally, at its congress in London in 1896, expelled the anarchists (who opposed it) from its ranks, reaffirming the Marxist doctrine of the class struggle and the unstoppable advent of proletarian rule. *Germinal* was thus set at a time when the International was in its infancy and yet published after its (temporary) demise, and it must therefore have left its first readers with an overwhelming sense of both the ephemerality and the inevitable recurrence (1789, 1830, 1848, 1870–1 ...) of revolutionary fervour.

But by way of preparing to write *Germinal* Zola did not just read books. At first posing as Giard's secretary (but then, when his cover was blown, being shown round by Giard's brother Jules), he visited the small mining town of Anzin, near Valenciennes, on 23 February 1884. A strike had begun there four days earlier, and he remained for approximately a week, taking copious notes on what he saw and heard – a document which remains a powerful and accurate account of the realities of colliery life at that time. Zola was aware that there had been a major strike at Anzin in 1866 (as well as several since), and because *Les Rougon-Macquart* was set during the Second Empire, he chose this as the focus for his imaginative reconstruction of the past. Hence the chronology of *Germinal*, which begins in March 1866 – a date which is not given in the novel itself but which can be inferred from the reference in the opening chapter to the Emperor waging war in Mexico. But Zola drew on other strikes for his novel, notably on the strike at La Ricamarie in the mining area of Saint-Étienne, where on 16 June 1869 troops fired on the striking workers. Thirteen miners were killed, including two women, and sixty were given a prison sentence. Similarly at Aubin, in the Aveyron, fourteen striking miners were shot dead on 7 October 1869, and twenty were wounded. Working conditions in the mines had changed little in the intervening years, and so Zola could use what he saw at Anzin in 1884 for the fictional recreation of events in 1866–7. But the political situation had evolved considerably. A law passed on 19 May 1874 had made it illegal to employ women to work underground or children under twelve to work anywhere in a mine; and on 21 March 1884 a bill sponsored by René Waldeck-Rousseau (1846–1904) was passed, legalizing trade unions. The next day saw the beginning of what would have been the revolutionary month of Germinal. Twelve days later, on his very own '12 Germinal' – and indeed on the day of his forty-fourth birthday – Zola began to write the first chapter of his novel.

As he wrote in a letter to Georges Montorgueil on 8 March 1885,

Perhaps this time they'll stop seeing me as someone who insults the people. Is not the true socialist he who describes their poverty and wretchedness and the ways in which they are remorselessly dragged down, who shows the prison-house of hunger in all its horror? Those who extol the blessedness of the people are mere elegists who should be consigned to history along with the humanitarian claptrap of 1848. If the people are so perfect and divine, why try and improve their lot? No, the people are down-trodden, in ignorance and the mire, and *it is from that ignorance and that mire that we should endeavour to raise them*.[2]

People and Politics

Germinal is a novel about people and about the people: about particular human beings and about humanity at large. As the account of a miners' strike it is the story of the 10,000 workers employed by the Mining Company based in the fictional location of Montsou, a town evocatively named as the place where the sous pile up in a mountain of riches for the enjoyment of everyone but the men, women and children who actually pro-duce the coal. And it is the terrible fate of this workforce which is here traced in such well-documented and painful detail. But by extension, and as Zola wrote when he first began to draft the novel, it is the story of 'the struggle between capital and labour'. Within the context of the 1860s *Germinal* records (with a small measure of historical licence) how a recession in the United States has led to empty order-books in the French coal-mining industry, where companies which have overinvested in new plant and machinery must now economize by cutting back production and reducing their workers' pay. Bust threatens to follow boom, and it's the poor what gets the blame – for drink-ing, for promiscuity, for having more babies than they need. Meanwhile shareholders feast and demand their dividend, and the nation's ruler Napoleon III engages in quixotic warfaring in Mexico at great expense to his country's economy. For Zola this 'struggle between capital and labour' would be the 'most important issue of the twentieth century', and *Germinal* was intended as a foretaste of what lay in store. But it was also a picture of what was actually happening: thanks to the wonders

of the economic cycle the slump of the 1860s was happening
again in the 1880s. And the miners were still striking.

While the novel thus anticipates the politics of the global
economy and the global village, its narrative focus is nevertheless
much more precise: namely, the inhabitants of Village Two
Hundred and Forty, a purpose-built pit-village of no name and
no character, serried rows of cheap housing perched on a windy
plateau and overlooking a featureless plain where it always
seems to rain. At Number 16 in Block 2 lives the Maheu family,
who have worked in the mine since its creation exactly 106
years earlier. Grandpa Maheu, known as Bonnemort (literally
'good death') because death has spared him so often, is the
grandson of Guillaume Maheu, who (he likes to believe) discovered the first coal near Montsou and so led to the first mine
being sunk there. And his son and grandsons are now working
down the mine at Le Voreux, that 'voracious' pit which seems
to gobble up the workers' flesh like some ancient god demanding
human sacrifice. His son Toussaint Maheu and his daughter-in-
law, La Maheude – so called, like all the miners' wives, because
she is merely an adjunct of her (wedded or common-law) husband – have produced seven children; and the heedlessness with
which they have been conceived – at 'playtime', after the miner
has had his bath – is matched only by the casual cruelty with
which heredity and environment snatch their lives away.
Already handicapped by the genetic effects of generation after
generation of slave labour and malnutrition, they are ugly,
anaemic and variously deformed – only then to be starved,
crippled or fatally injured. Or shot, if they should dare to protest.

Love is not love but sex; and sex is not making love but
screwing, raping, having it off, in the fields, on the roof of a
shed, behind the spoil-heap where all the rubble from the mine
is piled. Not a mountain of riches nor a bed of roses but a
weed-infested dump upon which to sow the seed of yet more
wasted, worthless lives. Such human fellowship as exists is
the solidarity of 'comrades', of the men, women and teenage
children who are obliged to live and work cheek by jowl, on an
inadequate wage, a prey to illness and a miserable climate. To

live is to survive; by stealing a moment's bodily pleasure and starting another life, or by saving a life, racing to the rescue of a fellow-miner after a rock-fall or sinking new shafts through solid rock to save a comrade from drowning or starving to death hundreds of metres below the ground. Life goes on; it matters little who lives it.

Surrounding the Maheu family are other mining families: the Levaque household next door, where a slattern shares her bed with both husband and lodger, and the Pierrons', where life is good because man and wife collaborate with the bosses. Violent, predatory males roam the streets and country paths or haunt the innumerable bars, bent on oblivion or a charmless fuck. Meek and powerless girls like Catherine Maheu resign themselves to their fate; others, like La Mouquette, seek out the men themselves, 'loving' them and leaving them with hearty insouciance, and baring their buttocks to all who deserve their contempt.

So much for 'labour' and the have-nots. What of 'capital'? The haves are represented by three types: the shareholder, the independent entrepreneur and the company executive. Léon Grégoire has inherited shares in the Mining Company which, in today's terms, bring him in an annual income of £125,000–£150,000 or around $200,000. Though the capital value of his shares recently topped the £3 million mark, he was never tempted to sell and does not regret the fact that a falling stock market has now reduced this value by nearly a half. Income is income. 'Capital' is the God he worships, a sacred treasure to be left buried in the ground and dug up little by little (in his case literally) by those fine fellows who've been digging it up for him and his ancestors for over a hundred years. This is the kind of ownership that Proudhon described as 'theft', but Grégoire's defence is that (a) his great-grandfather took enormous risks in creating the Mining Company, and (b) that he and his family live soberly, without extravagance or luxury, and distribute alms to the poor (albeit in kind, for money would merely encourage them to drink). And his parasitic caution proves sadly well founded. Deneulin, his cousin, has sold his shares and invested the money in setting up as a mine-owner himself, beneficially exploiting the natural resources of his country and creating new employment in the region. But his small privately owned company is no match for the competitive muscle of the big public corporations; and when the combination of falling demand and rising costs is exacerbated by worker unrest, he goes under, losing all his capital and reduced to being a mere employee in the company of which he once owned part. 'Theft', it seems, pays better than enterprise. And better than subservience. Hennebeau, the manager of the Company's mines, is the paid lackey, rewarded with a free house and a salary that earns the contempt of his heiress wife. A company executive perhaps, with servants and an entrée to the Grégoires' drawing-room, but a servant none the less, beholden to a Board of Directors whose grace and favour he must earn with sleepless nights. Emasculated by his adulterous wife, he is also the emasculated representative of a higher power, a mouthpiece for capitalism (we employers take the financial risks; we are subject to market forces and can only pay what we can pay; we are not a charity) while envying the workers what he perceives to be their glorious sexual freedom.

In illustrating 'the struggle between capital and labour', Zola is careful above all to nuance his effects and to avoid a crass polarization of goodies and baddies. On the side of 'labour', Maheu and his wife may be the models of decency and good sense, but their neighbours the Levaques are their feckless, hot-headed opposites. Chaval is a wife-beater (like Levaque), even if his 'wife' is only a girl in her mid teens who has not yet reached puberty. He is without principle, a violent, jealous man, a trimmer ready to call the comrades out to impress his girl and no less ready to send them back to work again at the first hint of promotion. The Pierrons are collaborators, selfish enough to lock their daughter in the cellar and send her grandmother on a fool's errand while they stuff themselves on rabbit and drink wine before a roaring fire. On the side of 'capital', the Grégoires are doting parents and benevolent employers. It is, of course, easy to be both these things when you have the money, but Deneulin manages it in straitened circumstances, and his daughters are no less resourceful in their penny-pinching than the

beleaguered La Maheude. Mme Hennebeau is the model of
the blithe bourgeoise, oblivious to the reality of the miners'
suffering, but her husband is intended to evoke sympathy as the
victim of a sexless and unhappy marriage; and the current cause
of his cuckoldry, his young nephew Paul Négrel, is not without
his merits as an engineer and a leader of men, professionally
and genuinely concerned for the miners' safety and a devoted
and courageous participant in their rescue. Maigrat, the shop-
keeper – whose name in French suggests the presence of a rat in
the midst of fasting and lean times – is the fat and unacceptable
face of capitalism, at once a usurer charging exorbitant rates of
interest and a man for whom a woman's body is but part of a
universal barter system regulated by the exigencies of supply
and demand. But his silent, suffering wife, chained to her ledgers
from morning till night, may become the focus of the reader's
compassion and illicit glee as she looks down from a window at
the terrible mutilation of her dead husband's very own means
of (re)production.

Just as he illustrates the different faces of capitalism, so too
Zola takes pains to represent the wide variety of ways in which
'labour' reacts politically and practically to the impossibilities
of its situation. Clearly the Catholic Church is of no use, be it
in the form of cuddly Father Joire who is all things to all men
and wants only a quiet life, or in the form of his replacement,
Father Ranvier, a skeletal fanatic who exploits the miners' suffering to try and convert (or return) them to the Catholic faith
with false promises of a meritocracy and universal happiness.
No, labour must find its own solution; and the options occupy
a spectrum which runs from passive – and pacifist – acceptance
to the most extreme anarchism. The older ones, like Bonnemort
(aged fifty-eight) or his inseparable friend Mouque, have seen it
all before. They have fought and protested and struck, but all
to no avail. Why bother? Resistance is pointless and always ends
in tears – and bullets. But in *Germinal* the situation becomes so
extreme that even Bonnemort is eventually goaded into an act
of barbarous 'revolutionary' vengeance. Those aged about forty,
like Maheu and his wife, have learned from the events of 1848
twenty years earlier that 'revolution' can leave the revolution-

aries destitute and the political situation unchanged. But these pragmatists are still young enough to feel anger and the longing for justice, and a combination of hunger-induced light-headedness and intoxicating political oratory still has the power to make them substitute aspiration for caution and to render them the most ardent and determined participants in the strike. Such are the bitter lessons of previous resistance that passive acquiescence has become almost a congenital flaw, and a young girl like Catherine is as dutiful in the workplace as she is submissive to the male. But even she ends up wanting to 'slaughter the world', much like La Brûlé, another skeletal fanatic, whose husband has been killed in the mine and who has never lost her passionate desire to wreak vengeance on the bosses.

For most of the miners resistance to oppression is an emotional and instinctive response, and few have the ability to articulate their feelings, let alone the social and economic realities of the situation in which they find themselves. Even Maheu, elected as their spokesman, is no orator. Tongue-tied and intimidated by the conventional hierarchy of worker and boss, he represents none the less the voice of genuine grievance, and when the miners' delegation confronts the management in the person of M. Hennebeau, Maheu is inspired to fluent articulacy by his own, acute experience of the sheer impossibility of supporting a family on the meagre wage which he and its members are paid. Quite simply they are living below subsistence level. But just what this level should rightly be was then known in France – as it is in *Germinal* – as the 'social question': in a society which had only relatively recently been industrialized, what was a fair level of pay, and what sort of living and working conditions was it reasonable to provide for the new working class?

For some, like Rasseneur, the ex-miner and now owner of a public house, it was important (and supposedly feasible) to divorce this 'social question' from wider political issues relating to power, governance and representation. For him – as for La Maheude in the earlier part of the novel – strikes only make matters worse for the poverty-stricken workers. Much better to negotiate with the bosses and, little by little, through compromise and persistence, secure gradual improvements in pay and conditions. Political protest or 'agitation' is counter-productive in that it alienates the bosses and delays change. But the authenticity of Rasseneur's position is undermined by his own self-interestedness: by his vanity in seeking to be the miners' leader and by his commercial motive in stirring up unrest so as to attract miners to his bar. His wife, more radical than he, scorns his moderation, which she sees as muddle-headed cowardice, and opts for the Marxist solutions proposed by Pluchart. No less in love with the sound of his own voice than Rasseneur, Pluchart is a member of the newly founded International and seeks both to propagate its ideas and to raise money through the subscriptions of new members. Opposed to strikes, he nevertheless advocates this one so that the normally placid and politically apathetic miners will have need of the International's financial support and will, in their frustration, become more receptive to its revolutionary agenda.

From a post-twentieth-century perspective Pluchart's Marxist programme may seem dated and, in some respects, even uncontroversial. Rather than being powerless and divided within their own workplace, the workers of the world need to unite and rise up against the bourgeois men of property, seizing the means of production – or rather taking them back into their own rightful ownership – and replacing a class-based political system with the rule of the collective. Patriarchal family structures shall be replaced by relationships based on equality, between men and women, between parents and children; marriage shall be abolished, as shall the right to inherit. But even Pluchart's Marxism is not enough for someone like Souvarine, a young Russian aristocrat who has given up training to be a doctor in order to learn a manual trade – to be more in touch with the people – and who is a convert to the anarchism, or 'nihilism', of Bakunin. For the anarchists, the only way forward is to start again from scratch, *ex nihilo*. All attempts at rationally conceived reform, and even the Marxist overthrow of the bourgeois State, are anathema, for they will not extirpate the underlying canker of inequality and injustice. Only by beginning with an absolutely clean sheet – even if this were to mean wiping out most of the human race – can we hope to establish a just society on a permanent and secure basis. Within the novel Souvarine's philosophy is the most chilling and, as it turns out, the most destructive. But with characteristic subtlety Zola makes Souvarine, of all the characters in *Germinal*, the most acute commentator on the situation facing the miners. He sees that in an unregulated capitalist economy the minimum wage is actually determined by capital's need for labour and that it will fluctuate in such a way as to allow workers to produce more workers (that is, live and raise families) but at the cheapest possible cost. And he sees that during a slump it is financially in the interests of the Montsou Mining Company to provoke a strike rather than to lay off its workers: that way it avoids the odium of a lockout, and it weakens its opponents by exhausting their nascent provident fund.

But Souvarine represents the ultimate paradox: inhumanity in the service of humanity. He has severed all ties of blood and affection, save only for his obsessive stroking of a plump rabbit whom, with Russian wit, he has christened Poland. Just as the Bear looks down on its neighbour as a mere political satellite, so the anarchist cuddles a pet in his lap and dreams of holding the fate of the whole world in his hands. His is the conviction of the religious fanatic or of a Robespierre ushering in the Reign of Terror. But Zola is no terrorist.

Enter the Hero

So where does Zola stand on the issue of people and politics? Is *Germinal* a blueprint for revolution or reform? Or neither? Is it perhaps a reactionary demonstration of the impossibility of change? Should we read it as a largely impersonal, non-committal documentary which happens to end with the vaguely optimistic prospect that the seeds of a better future lie buried in the mud and muddle of today? Or does it offer the more considered and authentic vision of a Darwinian evolution in which nature nurtured becomes a second nature?

Just as Souvarine dreams of a *tabula rasa* upon which to start afresh, so Zola begins his novel from scratch: 'Dans la plaine rase, sous une nuit sans étoiles . . .' Out on the open plain, on a starless, ink-dark night . . . Emerging from this featureless void and into the world of mining strides the figure of Étienne Lantier, a handsome 21-year-old mechanic, intelligent but poorly educated, and bearer of a fatal flaw: a predisposition to murderous, alcoholic rage, which he carries in his blood. And *Germinal* is the story of Étienne's refusal to accept what he finds.

Unlike Grandpa Maheu, who has joined many strikes and been shot at by the King's troops, Étienne scorns the mute acceptance of the ways of the world. Unlike La Maheude, who has known the danger and loss that come from stepping out of line, it will take little to rouse him to action. For Étienne is by nature rebellious, and the novel traces his education – in the classroom of experience as well as from books – as he struggles for a way of improving the lot of his fellow human beings, his 'comrades'. His journey begins in his instinctive insubordination, of the sort which has seen him fired from his job as a railway mechanic in nearby Lille; and his untutored mind provides a propitious seedbed where the ideas and opinions of Rasseneur, Pluchart and eventually Souvarine may germinate and grow. At first he is simply intoxicated by the prospect of overthrowing the oppressor, but as yet he has no idea how to achieve this nor what political system to put in the oppressor's place. As with the commercial opportunist Rasseneur and the political careerist Pluchart, his raised political consciousness stimulates personal ambition, and he becomes as much interested in his own image as a young leader of the people and in becoming the first working man to address the National Assembly in Paris. More insidiously he begins to aspire to some of the refinements of bourgeois living, and the reek of poverty soon nauseates him. Gradually his political ideas become more sophisticated, and he oscillates (healthily) between delirious moments of conviction and gloomy periods of doubt. But the question of what to put in place of the status quo is answered by the collectivism of Pluchart, which he espouses with a new glibness and fanaticism, and his moment of glory comes in the forest of Vandame as he is acclaimed by an assembled throng of some 3,000 people. But when, as Rasseneur bitterly predicts, the people turn on him and blame him for their defeat, his disgust at their poverty increases, and he becomes more and more tempted by the taste for final solutions manifested by Souvarine.

But he is 'saved' by reading Charles Darwin (1809–92), whose *On the Origin of Species by Means of Natural Selection* was first published in 1859 and translated into French in 1865. His reading of Darwin makes him question Souvarine's *tabula rasa*: what if the old injustices just spring up again in the vacuum left by the 'total destruction' which the Russian anarchists seek? And so Étienne reverts to Pluchart's collectivism, except that now his disgust at the reek of poverty is exceeded by an even greater hatred of the bourgeois. Blending Marx and Darwin, he comes to see the bourgeoisie as a worn-out and superannuated class which, in the battle for the survival of the fittest, can be replaced by a 'young' and vigorous proletariat who will renew the world and its ways for the better. With organized trade unions and bigger provident funds, progress *can* be made. Above all Étienne steps back from the allure of violence and destruction and comes to place his faith in legality. Though the strike has been defeated, there is a new political awareness among the miners at large, together with a new preparedness to abandon their age-old passivity and a readiness to organize their resistance. And this is what informs the famous image of germination with which the novel ends:

> Beneath the blazing rays of the sun, on this morning when the world seemed young, such was the stirring which the land carried in its womb. New men were starting into life, a black army of vengeance slowly germinating in the furrows, growing for the harvests of the century to come; and soon this germination would tear the earth apart.

This is not the trite or spuriously optimistic image which some readers have thought, for in 1885 Zola knew what the future – as seen from 1867 – actually held in store: the legalization of trade unions and, slowly but surely, a better deal for organized labour. But also the Commune. Reform *was* possible – and urgently needed. For during the Commune and later at Anzin Zola had also witnessed first hand the pent-up anger which might indeed one day tear the earth apart. The Russian Revolution of 1917 would not have surprised him had he lived to see it, nor the Stalinist totalitarianism which later ensued. And nor would the taste for final solutions which brought the Holocaust, although perhaps he could not have predicted the way in which the seeds of that particular whirlwind were sown.

The Truth about Humanity: Nature and Naturalism

For these reasons *Germinal* bears out some of the claims which Zola made when he was writing his book proposal for *Les Rougon-Macquart* at the end of 1868. Then he argued that in depicting modern France he would have particular regard to the social upheaval consequent upon the gradual erosion of class barriers. His proposed novels, he noted, 'would have been impossible before 1789'. In depicting this social upheaval he did not intend to gloss over the baser aspects of human behaviour, and he fully planned to depict the 'moral monstrosities' thrown up by the 'turbulence' of the contemporary world. While he conceded that there was a perceptible movement in the social and political life of contemporary France towards a fairer and more democratic society, he nevertheless stressed that 'we are still beginners when it comes to improving our lot': 'men will be men, that is to say animals which are good or bad depending on the circumstances'. For Zola progress was less a matter of trying to change human nature than of *knowing* human nature and, slowly but surely, trying to make the world a better place on the basis of that knowledge. He thought that this move towards a freer and fairer society 'would take a long time to come to fruition, even supposing that it ever could'. But what he really believed in was 'the possibility of ongoing progress towards the *truth*': 'a better society can come only from knowing the truth'. And his own novels were intended to shed this light: 'to tell the *truth about humanity*, to take the machine apart and show the hidden workings of heredity and the ways in which people are influenced by their surroundings. The law-makers and the moralists will then be free to draw whatever conclusions they wish from my work and to patch the wounds which I shall have revealed.'[3]

Zola's preoccupation with heredity began as a way of going one better than Balzac, his major rival as a chronicler of French society, who had focused exclusively on the ways in which human behaviour is determined by habitat. To the modern eye the preoccupation may seem at once prescient and quaint. As the Human Genome Project decodes the formulae by which human beings are physiologically created and governed, the ancient notion of destiny is being given a new lease of life, and it seems appropriate that the health and behaviour of succeeding members of the Rougon and Macquart families should be dictated by their forebears. Moreover, recent research has confirmed that the predisposition to alcoholism evinced by Étienne Lantier can indeed be genetically transmitted. And yet the crude insistence with which Zola depicts the malign effect of gin on his hero, not to mention the wolf-like appearance he develops as he drunkenly measures up to Chaval, can easily remind us more of the world of melodrama and Gothic horror films. But here we see Zola the Naturalist. On the one hand – and this is perhaps his greatest claim to originality in the history of the French novel – he does wish to depict human beings as subject to nature and natural processes. On the other, he wants to take the natural process and lend it a symbolic value which powerfully illustrates the 'truth about humanity'.

The term 'naturalist' was first used in the literary context by the Positivist philosopher and cultural historian Hippolyte Taine (1828–93), who applied it to Balzac as a term of praise for his quasi-scientific appraisal of the human animal kingdom. Zola adopted the term as a label for the newer and more thoroughgoing brand of Realism which he (and, as he saw it, the Impressionists) were evolving. Like Balzac he, too, wanted to enhance the prestige of the novel by conferring on it the intellectual status of scientific inquiry; and he borrowed Taine's own Positivist categories of *race*, *milieu* and *moment* as his blueprint for the Rougon-Macquart saga. While he compared his novels to experiments (in the essay 'The Experimental

Novel', first published in 1879), the role of the novelist was as
much that of a demonstrator as of a discoverer. He recognized
quite explicitly that, unlike the experimental scientist, the novelist cannot let the ingredients in his test-tube take over and react
independently of his intervention. Rather, the novelist infers the
'truth about humanity' from his observations of the world about
him and then creates a story which will demonstrate his conclusions in action. If he considers, for example, that human
mental processes are physiologically determined, he will depict
the revolutionary zeal of a man like Étienne Lantier as the result
of an innate aggression which is exacerbated by the circumstances of arduous labour and sexual rivalry. Even where the
evidence of the real world is against him – sexual promiscuity,
for example, is not attested in any of the contemporary accounts
of mining communities – he may yet posit a phenomenon in
order to 'demonstrate' a larger truth: here, that cramped living
conditions and financial hardship combine to dehumanize and
uncivilize, reducing men and women to the level of animals
rather than raising them up to a level where 'finer feelings' might
plausibly exist.

For it is all very well believing that human beings have a soul
and that we are complex psychological entities who 'fall in
love' and enjoy all sorts of intricate emotional and intellectual
experiences. But we also eat and drink, wake and sleep, defecate
and copulate. And we fear, we hate. How better to highlight
these realities than to set your novel in a world of poverty where
the most essential and not at all straightforward activity is
finding something to eat; where drinking (alcohol) is at once
paradise and hell; where sleeping is no antidote to exhaustion;
where accommodation is so limited that bodily functions must
be performed without privacy; where copulation is the only
pleasure that doesn't cost money (at least initially). All the basic
features of human existence which the bourgeois novel so gaily
takes for granted are here, quite literally, a matter of life and
death. Human beings are animals, in need of warmth and rest
and safety; and the opening pages of *Germinal* offer an arresting
portrait of one human being who is completely *deprived*, on the
verge of ending up 'like a stray dog, a dead carcass lying behind

some wall or other'. Homeless, jobless, penniless, friendless, he has nowhere to go and nowhere to hide from the bitterly cold winds blowing across the empty plain. Life itself is a *tabula rasa* on which we must construct shelter and purpose.

Throughout *Germinal*, as elsewhere in *Les Rougon-Macquart*, Zola constantly dispels our fond illusions by making a concerted attempt to break down the barriers between human beings and other animals, and between animals and plants or objects. The miners display the dumb submissiveness of the herd; the mob is like a river in spate. Horses like Battle and Trumpet are best friends, with memories and longings every bit as powerful as those of their supposed masters. The mine itself is a voracious beast, or a living network of veins and arteries which retaliates when injured. Whether it be the water flooding the mine or the alcohol-tainted blood pumping through Étienne's brain, fundamental – even cataclysmic – natural processes are at work which render the distinctions of the world into animal, vegetable and mineral at best irrelevant and at worst deceptive. Seen in this light Zola's Naturalist world is an entropic world, in which nature inevitably reverts to a state of chaos, despite all human effort to create order and to dominate its course. What is natural can no more be withstood or reversed than, it seems, one can protect a mine like Le Voreux from the great underground sea known as the Torrent.

And yet Le Voreux is destroyed, first and foremost, by human agency. The Torrent is unleashed by a crazed and perverted application of human reason. The mine, on the contrary, has become a safer place since the days when young girls would plunge down its shaft to their death with the merest loss of footing. If being part of the natural process means being shaped by heredity and environment and being assimilated to dumb animals and plants, by the same token it also means being part of a process of evolution. Where historically there is hope at the end of *Germinal*, because the future contains the legalization of trade unions, then 'naturally' there is hope also. For we carry within us the seeds of eventual betterment. Education – which the miners lack but are gradually receiving, which Étienne lacks but gradually acquires – is the key. Human beings can learn, and what they learn is genetically transmissable. The aristocracy and the bourgeoisie call this 'breeding'; Zola calls it 'progress'.

This central Zolian tenet is more plainly illustrated in *La Bête humaine*, published five years later, where the central psychopathic character finds himself unable to kill in cold blood because of the 'accumulated effect of education, the slowly erected and indestructible scaffolding of transmitted ideas'. His hand is stayed by 'human conscience', an 'inherited sense of justice': only when his mind is overwhelmed by atavistic dark forces of primordial bloodlust at the sight of a woman's white flesh does Jacques Lantier kill. But Zola's idea of 'civilization' as a process of intellectual and moral evolution is already present in *Germinal*, where the novel ends on an optimistic note because human conscience has clearly taken a step forward. Though defeated, the miners have become more aware of their situation and of the possibility of improving it. The strike may have seemed like all the strikes before it: born of fond hope and killed by cruel reality. But with each strike the hopes become less fond and the reality slightly less cruel. For Zola it is possible to envisage that in demonstrating the 'truth about humanity' – as Étienne in his way has just done for the mining community of Montsou – the novelist is himself educating his reader and contributing to the gradual 'evolution' of a more civilized, less inhuman society. Indeed perhaps Zola is the real hero of *Germinal*, for as a consciousness-raiser his rhetoric is far superior – and far more insidious – than that of his leading character.

Presentation and Progress

As a revolutionary leader Étienne tends to talk in clichés, borrowing ideas and phrases from Marx and others or relying on the familiar vistas of the promised land and the city on a hill. But Zola's moral landscape is a flat, open plain, a level playing-field on which to enact a Darwinian struggle in which humanity itself is fighting for survival. Not for him the quasi-mystical perpectives which beguile Souvarine and Father Ranvier so that these ideological opposites are united in their murderous obliviousness to the realities of human experience. Rather, a powerful symbolic vision of life itself in which the forces of creation and destruction are waging an eternal war and in which human beings might, just might, be able to help the cause of creation.

Following completion of the novel and its publication in book form, Zola was quoted in the Paris newspaper *Le Matin* on 7 March 1885 as saying that as far as he was concerned a novel consisted of two things: the material and the process of creation ('les documents et la création'). Two weeks later he elaborated in a letter to Henry Céard:

> We [novelists] are more or less liars, but how do our lies work and what are the thoughts behind them? . . . For my own part, I still believe that my lies lead in the direction of the truth. I have enlarged upon the facts and taken a leap towards the stars on the trampoline of precise observation. Truth soars upon the wing of the symbolic.[4]

Zola's symbolic vision is certainly a 'Naturalist' vision in that it presents human beings as subject to nature, and it is also Darwinian in its emphasis on life as a battle of the food chain. Ours is a voracious universe, and images of eating and devouring and consuming and gobbling up abound. Human antagonisms – the class struggle, sexual rivalry, even the sexual act itself – are all presented in terms of eating. Mealtimes structure the narrative and demonstrate the central and fundamental divide between the miner's 'prison-house of hunger' and the groaning tables of centrally heated bourgeois dining-rooms. Even the daily alternation of day and night becomes a dialectic of eating and being eaten. And Zola's vision is also, to use David Baguley's term, an 'entropic vision', in which individuality and orderly difference give way to the chaos of the mob and an orgy of undifferentiated desire. Take for example the several accounts of the rampaging mob in Part V, or the astonishing description of Widow Desire's dance-hall in Part III, the scene of a Bosch-esque bacchanalia of mingling limbs and liquid dissolution with beer flooding through the human body as the Torrent will later inundate the mine. The thirst for beer, sex and justice seems one and the same.

But even here there is emphasis also on regeneration, on collapse as being merely part of a broader cycle of integration and disintegration. The mass drinking-binge at Widow Desire's at once builds to an orgasm of contentment ('God! This is the life, eh?') and precedes a multitude of innumerable private orgasms: 'From the fields of ripe corn rose warm, urgent breath: many a child must have been fathered that night.' Similarly, the destructive debauches of the rampaging mob will sow the seed of a heightened political awareness. In fact these 'entropic' elements are part of the broader picture of an epic struggle between human beings and nature, and indeed of the epic struggle going on within nature itself. To sink a mine-shaft is a human assault upon nature, but, as with the disused mine at Réquillart, nature soon reclaims its territory as shrub and bramble grow back and two trees appear to have sprung from the very depths of the earth. The ant-like activities of human beings digging up the earth are as nothing compared with the vast and eternal forces of nature, where today's flooded mine offers 'a reminder of the ancient battles between earth and water when great floods turned the land inside out and buried mountains beneath the plains'.

This sense of a 'broader picture' is given also by the quasi-mythological portrayal of the human condition in *Germinal*. The quite unnaturalistically named Widow Desire is herself like some Mother Earth, a fount of fertility and indirect progenitrix of every miner in the region. For a desire whose permanent partner is always dead and in the past is a desire that cannot rest. Similarly, the women laying waste the boilers at a mine are participants in a witches' sabbath. The succeeding generations of the Maheu family seem like a dynasty of slaves who have worked for the 'hidden god' of capital since time immemorial, this 'squat and sated deity' who demands human sacrifice – like a latter-day Moloch – but remains constantly out of sight. The mine itself, and especially the unquenchable fires of Le Tartaret, are evocative of a Christian hell in which the damned live out an eternity of torture and irredeemable subjugation. At the same time the mine is suggestive of the 'hidden' forces at work not only in capitalist society but also in the human body and the human psyche, a subterranean network of 'pathways' in which blockage means disaster and the accumulated pressures of desire and trauma may explode with all the fatal consequences of firedamp. It is a place in which to confront the past, as when Étienne remembers his own in Part I, Chapter IV, or a place, as Étienne, Chaval and Catherine discover at the end, to plumb the violent reality of lust and sexual rivalry. In short, the mine is what lies beneath the surface: dark, monstrous and frightening.

But that is indeed Zola's purpose: to reveal, to bring to light what lies – literally and metaphorically – beneath the surface. At one level Zola goes to great lengths to allow us to visualize the action of the novel, which is no doubt why there have been so many successful film versions of *Germinal*. Thanks to his own on-the-spot investigations he knows exactly what the inside of a mine or a pitman's house actually looks and feels like, and the role which he adopts as the narrator of the story is essentially that of a dispassionate and anonymous cameraman focusing his lens on some powerful and eloquent evidence. But he is not merely a documentarist. He is also a demystifier. Where some myths disguise and obfuscate – like the picture of the happy worker which Mme Hennebeau blindly peddles to her Parisian visitors – his novels are intended to demonstrate the truth and thus contribute towards the creation of a better society. While such an ambition may itself seem quaint in a postmodernist world where all discourse is suspect, it is not necessarily a risible or a nugatory aim. Moreover, the Zola of *Germinal* – and indeed of *Les Rougon-Macquart* as a whole – is alive to the insidious and corrosive power of what is now called 'spin' or 'media management'. Throughout the novel we see how 'capital' covers up the truth, playing down the extent of the damage to its mines in order not to worry the shareholders and attempting to 'bury' the news of miners being shot in order to deflect public outrage. The readiness of the uneducated to cross their fingers or to believe in the existence of ghosts is seen as part of their submissiveness, as part of their understandable but fatal inability to confront, assess – and change – the reality of their situation. But if the uneducated have every excuse, how much worse it is that a benign couple like the Grégoires can be quite so blind to this reality, or that Deneulin's pleasant and capable daughters should be so appallingly content to view the murderous destruction of Le Voreux as a 'thrilling' aesthetic experience.

Just as Zola catalogues, through Étienne's 'education', the various political responses which it might be possible to have towards the actualities of mining and working-class life, so too he is careful to record a wide spectrum of 'interpretative' responses in order to highlight quite where he himself stands as a novelist writing about this subject. If he had to masquerade as Giard's secretary in order to research this subject at Anzin, that was no doubt because he feared the charge to which the bourgeois and indeed many members of the mining community are open at the end of *Germinal*: namely, that they are tourists. It has become fashionable to visit the scene of disaster, be it the collapse of Le Voreux or the rescue attempt going on to save the trapped miners. But Zola is no gawping rubberneck or heartless aesthete. Above all he is not simply the professional novelist doing the research for his latest, money-spinning bestseller, exploiting human suffering before he returns to his house in the country to write it up before a four-course lunch. Perhaps indeed that is why his documentation at Anzin was quite so thorough, and so valuable: he had a guilty conscience.

And his only saving grace can be that of 'education'. As Étienne walks along the road from Marchiennes to Montsou at the beginning of the novel, he is not only destitute, he is also ignorant. The world of mining is a closed book to him, and the plain itself is a barren, windswept wasteland. His only hope is that sunrise may bring a modest rise in temperature. At the end, as he walks along the same road in the opposite direction, he has become knowledgeable, and he has a job to do. He is a man with a train to catch. The new dawn means progress. The world of mining – and the workers' struggle for justice – has become an open book, and the plain is now a teeming, 'germinating' surface from beneath which the truth is just waiting to spring into view: 'a whole world of people labouring unseen in this underground prison, so deep beneath the enormous mass of rock that you had to know they were there if you were to sense the great wave of misery rising from them'.

Buried beneath our own ignorance and incarcerated within our own prejudice, we readers of *Germinal* have similarly been provided with a map to the unknown. But we have not been lectured or subjected to the 'humanitarian claptrap' of the kind which Étienne himself still foolishly rehearses in his head: 'Discomfited by the workers' reek of poverty, he felt the need to raise them up to glory and set a halo on their heads; he would show how they alone among human beings were great and unimpeachably pure, the sole font of nobility and strength from which humanity at large might draw the means of its own renewal.' Rather we have been given a warning:

> *Germinal* is about compassion, not about revolution. What I wanted was to say loud and clear to the fortunate of this world, to its masters: Take heed. Look beneath the surface. See how these wretched people work and suffer. There may still be time to avoid total catastrophe. But hasten to be just, or else disaster looms: the earth will open at our feet and all nations will be swallowed up in one of the most terrible upheavals ever to take place in the course of human history.[5]

It could be argued that when Zola wrote those words in December 1885 (to David Dautresme, editor of *Le Petit Rouennais*) he was simply demonstrating the cynical pragmatism of a successful bourgeois who did not want his new-found wealth taken away from him. But it might more persuasively be argued that *Germinal* is a piece of shrewd propaganda, the work of a man of genuine compassion who was appealing to the cynical pragmatist in his fellow bourgeois in order to improve the lot of his fellow human beings.

Is Zola's warning still of relevance? It may seem not. In some so-called developed countries the mining industry itself has almost ceased to exist, and even the manufacturing worker is an endangered species. Social and economic conditions have changed enormously since the second half of the nineteenth century. But the fundamental issue in *Germinal* perhaps has not. Shoot the miners or pay them a fair wage? That question now seems simple. But it might not seem so simple – even if today's reader of *Germinal* still wished to give the same answer – if the issue were put more broadly. Should 'the fortunate of this world', its 'masters', stamp out the expression of grievance or seek to eradicate its cause? What if the choices were different, more contemporary? Tiananmen Square or a measure of democracy? A War on Terror or an autonomous State of Palestine?

When Zola was asphyxiated by the fumes from his bedroom fire on 29 September 1902, it was discovered that his chimney had been capped during repair work. Was this an accident or did someone on the political Right who objected to his defence of the Jewish army officer, Captain Alfred Dreyfus, plan his death? Already he had accepted a prison sentence and exile in England as the price of his defence of this innocent man. Had he now paid with his life for his belief in the truth? The answer to that question is not known. But on 5 October some 50,000 people followed his funeral procession through the streets of Paris, including a delegation of miners from the Denain coalfield. And from the single word they chanted during the procession it is evident that they at least believed in the authenticity of their champion – and in the power of that one word to symbolize protest against injustice wherever and whenever throughout the history of human affairs that injustice may be found: 'Germinal! Germinal! Germinal! . . .'

NOTES

1. Émile Zola, *Correspondance*, ed. B. H. Bakker (10 vols, Montreal and Paris, 1978–95), vol. 5, p. 126.
2. Ibid., pp. 240–41.
3. Quotations from 'Notes sur la marche générale de l'œuvre' in Émile Zola, *Les Rougon-Macquart* (5 vols, Paris: Gallimard, Bibliothèque de la Pléiade, 1960–67), vol. 5, pp. 1738–41.
4. Zola, *Correspondance*, vol. 5, p. 249.
5. Ibid., p. 347.

Further Reading and Filmography

In English

All twenty novels in the Rougon-Macquart cycle have been translated into English, and the principal ones are available in Penguin Classics, as is *Thérèse Raquin*.

BIOGRAPHIES

Frederick Brown, *Zola. A Life* (New York, 1995; London, 1996)

F. W. J. Hemmings, *The Life and Times of Émile Zola* (London, 1977)

Graham King, *Garden of Zola* (London, 1978)

Alan Schom, *Émile Zola. A Bourgeois Rebel* (London, 1987)

Philip Walker, *Zola* (London, 1985)

CRITICAL STUDIES

David Baguley, *Naturalist Fiction. The Entropic Vision* (Cambridge, 1990)

— (ed.), *Critical Essays on Émile Zola* (Boston, 1986)

Elliot M. Grant, *Émile Zola* (New York, 1966)

—, *Zola's 'Germinal'. A Critical and Historical Study* (Leicester, 1962)

F. W. J. Hemmings, *Émile Zola* (2nd edn, Oxford, 1966; reprinted with corrections, 1970)

Irving Howe, 'Zola: The Genius of *Germinal*', *Encounter* 34 (1970), pp. 53–61

Robert Lethbridge and Terry Keefe (eds), *Zola and the Craft of Fiction. Essays in Honour of F. W. J. Hemmings* (Leicester, 1990; paperback edn, 1993)

Brian Nelson, *Zola and the Bourgeoisie* (London, 1983)

Naomi Schor, *Zola's Crowds* (Baltimore, 1978)

Colin Smethurst, *Émile Zola. 'Germinal'* (London, 1974; repr. Glasgow, 1996)

Philip Walker, *'Germinal' and Zola's Philosophical and Religious Thought* (Amsterdam, 1984)

Angus Wilson, *Émile Zola. An Introductory Study of his Novels* (New York, 1952)

Richard H. Zakarian, *Zola's 'Germinal'. A Critical Study of its Primary Sources* (Geneva, 1972)

In French

CRITICAL EDITIONS

Germinal, ed. Colette Becker (Paris, 1989)

Germinal, ed. Henri Mitterand (Paris, 1978)

BIOGRAPHY

Henri Mitterand, *Zola. I. Sous le regard d'Olympia (1840–1871), II. L'Homme de 'Germinal' (1871–1893), III. L'Honneur (1893–1902)* (Paris, 1999–2002)

CRITICAL STUDIES

Colette Becker, *Émile Zola: 'Germinal'* (Paris, 1984)

—, *La Fabrique de 'Germinal'* (Paris, 1986)

Philippe Hamon, *Le Personnel du roman: le système des personnages dans les 'Rougon-Macquart' d'Émile Zola* (Geneva, 1983)

Henri Mitterand, *Le Regard et le signe* (1987)

—, *Zola: L'Histoire et la fiction* (1990)

—, *Zola et le naturalisme* (1986)

Michel Serres, *Feux et signaux de brume: Zola* (Paris, 1975)

FILMOGRAPHY

La Grève [*The Strike*], dir. Ferdinand Zecca (France, 1903)

Au pays noir [*In the Black Country*], dir. Lucien Nonguet (France, 1905)

Au pays des ténèbres [*In the Land of Darkness*], dir. Victorin Jasset (France, 1912)

Germinal, dir. Albert Capellani (France, 1913)

Germinal, anonymous direction (France, 1920)

Germinal, dir. Yves Allégret (France, 1963)

Germinal, dir. Claude Berri (France, 1993)

Note on the Translation

This translation is based on the text of *Germinal* edited by Henri Mitterand and published in vol. iii (1964) of Émile Zola, *Les Rougon-Macquart* (5 vols, Paris: Gallimard, Bibliothèque de la Pléiade, 1960–67) and as a separate volume (Gallimard, Folio, 1978).

Germinal was first translated into English in a pirated, American edition published by Belford, Clarke & Co. in Chicago in 1885. Given the extensive mistranslations and omissions of this version (by 'Carlynne'), it might be fairer to say that the first English translation was that undertaken by the journalist Albert Vandam, Paris correspondent of the London newspaper the *Globe*. This appeared in instalments in the *Globe* from 30 November 1884 to 26 April 1885 and was afterwards purchased and published in book form in June 1885 by Henry Vizetelly, father of Ernest (who subsequently edited and/or translated many of the Rougon-Macquart novels). But Vandam's version was bowdlerized. The first complete and unexpurgated translation of *Germinal* into English, privately published in London in 1894 by the Lutetian Society, was by Havelock Ellis (1859–1939), the celebrated authority on sex. Ellis's translation, prepared in collaboration with his wife Edith Lees (1861–1916), was first published in the Everyman Library in 1933. It was revised and edited by David Baguley for Everyman Paperbacks in 1996.

The present translation replaces that of Leonard Tancock for Penguin Classics, first published in 1954. Since then there have been at least two American translations: by Willard R. Trask for Bantam Books (New York, 1962) and by Stanley and Eleanor

Hochman (New American Library, New York, 1970). The most recent translation is that by Peter Collier in the Oxford World's Classics (1993), which is helpfully annotated by the translator and has an informative and well-judged Introduction by Robert Lethbridge

Germinal poses none of the problems of *L'Assommoir* where the central characters employ the colloquialisms and slang of the contemporary urban working class. Zola chose not to repeat that experiment (which has been cleverly reconstructed by Margaret Mauldon in her 1995 translation for Oxford World's Classics). When an early reviewer of *Germinal* complained that its characters were unrealistic because they did not speak the local dialect of the Département du Nord, its author replied that if they had, no one would have bothered to read his novel. In translating the language of the miners of Montsou, therefore, I have respected the predominantly polite and literate register of the original French. As to the colloquialisms and 'bad language' with which their language is nevertheless laced, I have tried to render this in a modern English which will seem neither too squeamish nor like a pastiche of working-class 'speak'. I have sought to use four-letter (and six-letter) words as sparingly as Zola uses the French equivalents (notably 'foutre' and 'bougre') but with an equivalent measure of the shock value (in a literary context) which I suppose these words to have had in 1885. In particular, Zola makes a point of using such terms when his characters are under exceptional pressure, whether drunk, as in Étienne's case on one occasion, or having finally lost patience, as in La Maheude's case later in the novel. Hence my own usage at these points in the narrative.

As to the technical vocabulary associated with mining, I have endeavoured, like Zola, to do my research. This vocabulary is explained in the Glossary of Mining Terms.

GERMINAL

PART I

Out on the open plain, on a starless, ink-dark night, a lone man was following the highway from Marchiennes to Montsou,[1] ten kilometres of paved road that cut directly across the fields of beet. He could not make out even the black ground in front of him, and he was aware of the vast, flat horizon only from the March wind blowing in broad, sweeping gusts as though across a sea, bitterly cold after its passage over league upon league of marsh and bare earth. Not a single tree blotted the skyline, and the road rolled on through the blinding spume of darkness, unswerving, like a pier.

The man had left Marchiennes around two o'clock in the morning. He walked with long strides, shivering in his thread-bare cotton jacket and his corduroy trousers. A small bundle, tied up in a check handkerchief, was evidently an encumbrance; and he pressed it to his side, first with one arm, then with the other, so that he could thrust both hands – numb, chapped hands lashed raw by the east wind – deep into his pockets. Homeless and out of work, he had only one thing on his vacant mind: the hope that the cold would be less severe once day had broken. He had been walking like this for an hour when, two kilometres outside Montsou, he saw some red fires over to his left, three braziers burning out in the open as though suspended in mid-air. At first he hesitated, suddenly afraid; but then he could not resist the painful urge to warm his hands for a moment.

A sunken path led away from the road, and the vision vanished. To the man's right was a wooden fence, more like a wall, made from thick planks and running alongside a railway line; to his left rose a grass embankment topped by a jumble of gables, apparently the low, uniform roof-tops of a village. He walked on a further two hundred paces or so. Abruptly, at a turn in the path, the fires reappeared close by him, but he was still at a loss to explain how they could be burning so high up in this dead sky, like smouldering moons. But at ground level something else had caught his attention, some large, heavy mass, a huddled heap of buildings from which rose the outline of a factory chimney. Gleams of light could be seen here and there through grime-coated windows, while outside five or six paltry lanterns hung from a series of wooden structures whose blackened timbers seemed to be vaguely aligned in the shape of gigantic trestles. From the midst of this fantastical apparition, wreathed in smoke and darkness, rose the sound of a solitary voice; long, deep gasps of puffing steam, invisible to the eye.

And then the man realized that it was a coal-mine. His misgivings returned. What was the point? There wouldn't be any work. Eventually, instead of heading towards the buildings, he ventured to climb the spoil-heap to where the three coal fires stood burning in cast-iron baskets, offering warmth and light to people as they went about their work. The stonemen must have worked late, because the spoil was still being removed. He could now hear the banksmen pushing their trains of coal-tubs along the top of the trestles, and in the light from each fire he could see moving shadows tipping up each tub.

'Hallo,' he said, as he walked towards one of the braziers.

Standing with his back to it was the driver, an old man in a purple woollen jersey and a rabbit-skin cap. His horse, a large yellow animal, stood waiting with the immobility of stone as the six tubs it had just hauled up were emptied. The workman in charge of the tippler, a skinny, red-headed fellow, was taking his time about it and looked half asleep as he activated the lever. Above them the wind was blowing harder than ever, gusting in great icy blasts like the strokes of a scythe.

'Hallo,' the driver replied.

There was a silence. Sensing the wariness with which he was being observed, the man introduced himself at once.

'I'm Étienne Lantier, I'm a mechanic. I don't suppose there's any work here?'

The fire lit up his features; he must have been about twenty-one, a handsome, swarthy sort, thin-limbed but strong-looking all the same.

The driver, reassured, shook his head.

'No, no work for a mechanic . . . We had two of them come by yesterday. There's nothing to be had.'

A sudden squall interrupted the two men. Then, pointing down at the dark huddle of buildings at the foot of the spoil-heap, Étienne asked:

'It is a coal-pit, isn't it?'

This time the old man was unable to reply, choked by a violent fit of coughing. At length he spat, and his spittle left a black stain on the crimson ground.

'Yes, it's a pit all right. Le Voreux[2] ... Look, the miners' village is just over there.'

It was his turn to point, and he gestured through the darkness to the village whose roof-tops Étienne had glimpsed earlier. But the six tubs were empty now, and so the old man followed after them on his stiff rheumatic legs, not even needing to crack the whip: his big yellow horse had set off automatically and was plodding forward between the rails, hauling the tubs behind it. A fresh gust of wind ruffled its coat.

Le Voreux was now emerging as though from a landscape of dream, and while he lingered at the brazier warming his sore, chapped hands, Étienne took in the scene. He was able to locate each part of the pit: the screening-shed with its asphalt roof; the headgear over the pit-shaft; the huge engine-house; and the square tower containing the drainage-pump. Hunkered in a hollow in the ground, with its squat brick buildings and a chimney that poked up like a menacing horn, the pit looked to him like some monstrous and voracious beast crouching there ready to gobble everyone up. As he stared at it, he began thinking about himself and the vagrant life he had been living for the past week in search of work: he saw himself back in Lille, in his railway workshop, hitting his boss and being fired and then getting turned away wherever he went. On Saturday he had arrived in Marchiennes. He had heard there was work at Les Forges, the ironworks; but there'd been nothing, neither at Les Forges nor at Sonneville's, and he'd had to spend the Sunday hidden under a woodpile in a cartwright's yard, from where the watchman had just evicted him at two o'clock that morning. He had nothing, not a penny to his name, not even a crust of bread. So what was he supposed to do now, wandering the highways and byways like this with nowhere to go and not even the slightest idea where to find shelter from the wind? Yes, it was a pit all right: he could see the paved yard in the light of the few lanterns hanging there, and the sudden opening of a door had allowed him a glimpse of the boiler fires blazing with light. Gradually he worked out what everything was, even that noise of the pump letting off steam, a slow, deep, insistent puffing that sounded as though the monster were congested and fighting for breath.

Hunched over his machine, the tippler-operator had not even looked up at Étienne, who was just going over to pick up his small bundle where he had dropped it when a fit of coughing signalled the return of the driver. He and his yellow horse could be seen slowly emerging from the darkness, having hauled up six more tub-loads.

'Are there any factories in Montsou?' Étienne asked.

The old man spat black phlegm and shouted back above the wind:

'Oh, we've got the factories all right. You should have seen them three or four years ago. Things were humming then. You couldn't find enough men to work in them, and folk had never earned as much in their lives . . . And here we all are having to tighten our belts again. Things are in a bad way round these parts now, what with people being laid off and workshops closing down all over the place . . . Well, maybe it isn't the Emperor's fault, but what does he want to go off fighting in America[3] for? Not to mention the animals that are dying of cholera,[4] and the people too for that matter.'

Both men continued to share their grievances in short, breathless bursts of speech. Étienne described his week of fruitless searching. What was he supposed to do? Starve to death? The roads would soon be full of beggars. Yes, the old man agreed, things weren't looking good at all. In God's name, it just wasn't right turning so many Christian souls out on to the streets like that.

'There's no meat some days.'

'Even bread would do!'

'That's true. If only we had some bread!'

Their voices were lost in the bleak howl of the wind as squalling gusts snatched their words away.

'It's like this,' the driver continued at the top of his voice, turning to face south. 'In Montsou over there . . .'

Stretching out his hand once more, he indicated various invisible points in the darkness, naming each one as he did so. Over in Montsou the Fauvelle sugar-refinery was still working, but the Hoton refinery had just laid off some of its men, and of the remainder only the Dutilleul flour-mill and the factory at Bleuze that made cables for the mines were managing to keep going. Then, with a broad sweep towards the north, his arm took in a whole half of the horizon: the Sonneville construction works had received only a third of its usual number of orders; of the three blast-furnaces at the ironworks in Marchiennes only two were lit; and at the Gagebois glass factory there was the threat of a strike because there'd been talk of reducing the men's wages.

'I know, I know,' said the young man as each place was identified. 'I've just been there.'

'The rest of us are all right so far,' the driver added. 'But the pits have cut their production. And look at La Victoire over there. Only two batteries of coke-ovens still going.'

He spat and departed once more behind his sleepy horse, having harnessed it to the empty tubs.

Étienne now looked out over the whole region. It was still pitch black, but the driver's hand seemed to have imbued the darkness with misery and suffering, and the young man intuitively felt its presence all around him in the limitless expanse. Was that not the cry of famine he could hear being borne along on the March wind as it swept across this featureless countryside? The gale was blowing even more furiously now, and it was as though it were bringing the death of labour in its wake, a time of want that would take the lives of many men. And Étienne scanned the horizon trying to pierce the gloom, at once desperate to see and yet fearful of what he might find.

Everything remained sunk in darkness, concealed by the obliterating night; all he could make out, in the far distance, were the blast-furnaces and the coke-ovens. These last, batteries of a hundred slanting chimneys, stood all in a line like ramps of red flame; while the two towering furnaces, further over to the left, blazed with a blue light like giant torches in the middle of the sky. It was a melancholy sight, like watching a building on fire; and the only suns to rise on this menacing horizon were these, the fires that burn at night in a land of iron and coal.

'Are you from Belgium, then?' Étienne heard the driver asking behind him when he next returned.

This time he had brought up only three tubs. They might as well be emptied: there was a problem with the extraction cage, where a nut had broken off a bolt, and work would be held up for a quarter of an hour or more. At the foot of the spoil-heap silence had fallen, and the trestles no longer shook with the constant rumble of the banksmen's tubs. All that could be heard was the distant sound of metal being hammered somewhere down in the pit.

'No, I'm from the south,' the young man replied.

Having emptied the tubs, the man in charge of the tippler had sat down on the ground, delighted by the hold-up; but he remained fiercely taciturn and simply looked up at the driver with wide, expressionless eyes as though somehow put out by so much talking. For indeed the driver was not usually given to such expansiveness. He must have liked the look of this stranger and felt one of those sudden urges to confide that sometimes make old people talk to themselves out loud.

'I'm from Montsou,' he said. 'The name's Bonnemort.'

'Is that some kind of nickname?' asked Étienne in surprise.

The old man chuckled contentedly and gestured towards Le Voreux:

'Yes, it is . . . They've dragged me out of there three times now, barely in one piece. Once with my hair all singed, once full to the gills with earth, and once with my belly full of water, all swollen like a frog's . . . So when they saw that I just refused to pop my clogs, they called me Bonnemort, for a laugh.'[5]

His mirth came louder still, like the screech of a pulley in need of oil, and eventually degenerated into a terrible fit of coughing. The light from the brazier was now shining fully on his large head, with its few remaining white hairs and a flat, ghostly pale face that was stained with bluish blotches. He was a short man, with an enormous neck; his legs bulged outwards, and he had long arms with square hands that hung down to his knees.

Otherwise, just like his horse standing there motionless and apparently untroubled by the wind, he seemed to be made of stone and appeared oblivious to the cold and the howling gale that was whistling round his ears. When finally, with one deep rasping scrape of the throat, he had finished coughing, he spat by the foot of the brazier, and the earth turned black.

Étienne looked at him and then at the stain he had just made on the ground.

'So,' he went on, 'have you been working at the pit for long?'

Bonnemort spread his arms wide.

'Long? I should say! . . . I wasn't even eight years old the first time I went down a mine. It was Le Voreux, as it happens. And today I'm fifty-eight. You work it out . . . I've done every job there is down there. Simple pit-boy to start with, then putter once I was strong enough to push the tubs, and then hewer for eighteen years. After that, because of my damned legs, they put me on maintenance work, filling in seams, repairing the roads, that sort of thing, until the day they had to bring me up and give me a surface job because the doctor said otherwise I'd 'ave stayed down there for good. So five years ago they made me a driver . . . Not bad, eh? Fifty years working at the pit, and forty-five of them underground!'

As he spoke, flaming coals would now and again fall from the brazier and cast a gleam of blood-red light across his pallid face.

'And then they tell me to call it a day,' he went on. 'Not likely. They must think I'm daft! . . . I can manage another two years all right, till I'm sixty, so I get the pension of a hundred and eighty francs. If I was to pack it in now, they'd turn round and give me the one at a hundred and fifty. Cunning buggers! . . . Anyway, I'm as fit as a fiddle, apart from my legs. It's the water that's got under my skin, you see, what with getting soaked all the time down at the coal-face. Some days I can't even put one foot in front of the other without screaming the place down.'

He was interrupted by another fit of coughing.

'And that's what makes you cough as well?' asked Étienne.

But he shook his head fiercely. When he could speak, he continued:

'No, no, I caught a cold, last month. I never used to cough, but now I just can't get rid of it . . . And the funny part is I keep coughing this stuff up. More and more of it.'

A rasp rose in his throat, and he spat black phlegm.

'Is it blood?' Étienne asked, eventually daring to put the question.

Slowly Bonnemort wiped his mouth with the back of his hand.

'It's coal . . . I've got enough coal inside this carcass of mine to keep me warm for the rest of my days. And it's five whole years since I was last down the mine. Seems I was storing it up without even knowing. Ah well, it's a good preservative!'

There was silence; the distant, rhythmic sound of hammering could be heard coming from the pit, and the moan of the wind continued to sweep past, like a cry of hunger and exhaustion rising from the depths of the night. Standing beside the startled flickering of the flames, the old man went on, lowering his voice as he revisited his memories. Oh yes indeed! He and his family were old hands at cutting the coal! They'd been working for the Montsou Mining Company ever since the beginning, and that was a long time ago, one hundred and six years to be precise. It was his grandfather, Guillaume Maheu, then a lad of fifteen, who had discovered soft coal at Réquillart, which had become the Company's first pit but was now just an old disused shaft, over near the Fauvelle sugar-refinery. That much was common knowledge, and proof was that the new seam had been called the Guillaume seam, after his grandfather's Christian name. He hadn't known him himself, but he'd been a big man by all accounts, and very strong. Died in his bed at the age of sixty. Then there was his father, Nicolas Maheu, known as Maheu the Red. He'd died when he was barely forty, at Le Voreux, back when they were still sinking the shaft; a rock-fall it was, completely flattened him, swallowed him whole, bones, flesh, blood, the lot. Two of his uncles and then, later on, his own three brothers had all lost their lives down there. As for him, Vincent Maheu, he'd managed to escape more or less unscathed, apart from his gammy legs, that is, and everyone thought him a clever bastard for doing so. But what else could you do? You had to work, and this was simply what they did, from father to

son, the same as they'd have done any other job. And now here
was his own son, Toussaint Maheu, working himself to death
down the pit, and his grandsons too, and everybody else who
lived over there in the village. A hundred and six years of cutting
coal, first the old men, then the kids, and all for the same boss.
There weren't many bourgeois, were there, who could trace
their ancestry for you quite so neatly?

'So long as we've got something to eat!' Étienne muttered
again.

'That's just what I say. As long as there's bread to eat, we'll
survive.'

Bonnemort fell silent, his gaze directed towards the village
where gleams of light were beginning to appear one after the
other.

Four o'clock was chiming on the Montsou clock-tower. The
cold was getting even sharper.

'So it's rich then, is it, this Company of yours?' Étienne went
on.

The old man's shoulders rose in a shrug and then sagged as
though beneath an avalanche of gold coins.

'Oh, yes, it's rich all right . . . though maybe not as rich as the
one next door, the one at Anzin.[6] But it's got millions and
millions all the same . . . They've lost count. Nineteen pits they
have, with thirteen producing coal – like Le Voreux, La Victoire,
Crèvecœur, Mirou, Saint-Thomas, Madeleine, Feutry-Cantel
and the others – and then six for drainage or ventilation, like
Réquillart . . . Ten thousand workers, concessions stretching
over sixty-seven communes, a production level of five thousand
tons a day, a railway linking all the pits, and workshops, and
factories! . . . Oh, yes, there's plenty of money around all right!'

The big yellow horse pricked his ears at the sound of tubs
rumbling across the trestles. They must have fixed the cage down
below, the banksmen had returned to work. As he harnessed
his horse for the downward journey, the driver added softly,
addressing the animal:

'Mustn't get into the habit of standing about nattering, eh,
you lazy old thing! . . . If Monsieur Hennebeau knew how you
were wasting your time!'

Étienne was staring pensively into the night.

'So the mine belongs to Monsieur Hennebeau, does it?' he asked.

'No,' the old man explained. 'He's only the colliery manager. He gets paid just like the rest of us.'

The young man pointed towards the vast expanse of darkness: 'So who owns all this, then?'

But Bonnemort was temporarily seized by another coughing fit of such violence that he could not catch his breath. At length, having spat and wiped the black spittle from his lips, he answered above the strengthening wind:

'What's that? Who owns it all? . . . Nobody knows exactly . . . People just . . .'

And with a wave of his hand he gestured towards an indeterminate point in the gloom, a remote, unknown place inhabited by these 'people' on whose behalf the Maheu family had been working the seams for over a century.

His voice had assumed a tone of almost religious awe, as though he were talking about some forbidden temple that concealed the squat and sated deity to whom they all offered up their flesh but whom no one had ever seen.

'But if we at least had enough to eat,' Étienne said for the third time, without apparent connection.

'That's true enough! If there was always enough bread to eat, we'd be laughing!'

The horse had set off, and the driver in turn disappeared, dragging his ailing limbs. The tippler-operator had not stirred and continued to sit there hunched in a ball, his chin thrust between his knees, staring into the void with wide, expressionless eyes.

Étienne picked up his bundle but lingered a while longer. He could feel the icy blasts of wind on his back while his chest roasted in the heat from the fire. Perhaps he should try at the pit all the same, the old man might be mistaken; and anyway he was past caring now, he'd take whatever they gave him. Where else could he go, what else could he do, when so many people round about were starving and out of work? Was he to end up like a stray dog, a dead carcass lying behind some wall or other?

And yet something made him hesitate, a fear of Le Voreux itself, out here in the middle of this open plain that lay buried in thick darkness. With each gust the force of the wind seemed to increase, as if it were blowing in from an ever-widening horizon. No dawn paled the dead sky; there was only the blaze of the tall blast-furnaces and the coke-ovens, turning the darkness blood red but shining no light into the unknown. And Le Voreux, crouching like some evil beast at the bottom of its lair, seemed to hunker down even further, puffing and panting in increasingly slow, deep bursts, as if it were struggling to digest its meal of human flesh.

II

Surrounded by the fields of corn and beet, the mining village called Two Hundred and Forty[1] lay sleeping beneath the black sky. One could just make out the four huge blocks of little back-to-back houses, all geometrically arranged in parallel lines like the blocks of a barracks or a hospital and separated by three broad avenues of equal-sized gardens. And across the deserted plateau all that could be heard was the moaning of the wind as it blew through the broken lattice fences.

At the Maheus' house, Number Sixteen in the second block, nothing stirred. Thick darkness filled the one and only first-floor room: it bore down like a crushing weight on the people sleeping there, whose presence could be felt rather than seen as they lay crowded together, their mouths open, stunned by exhaustion. Despite the bitter cold outside, the air was heavy with the warmth of the living, that stuffy heat to be found in even the best-kept bedrooms, with its reek of the human herd.

The cuckoo clock downstairs struck four, but still nothing, only the faint whistle of breathing and the deeper sound of two people snoring. And then, all of a sudden, it was Catherine who rose first. In her tiredness she had counted the four chimes as usual, through the floorboards, but without finding the strength to rouse herself completely. Then, having swung her legs out of bed, she groped about and finally struck a match to light the candle. But she remained seated, her head so heavy that it slumped back between her shoulders, yielding to an irresistible desire to fall back on to the bolster.

The candle now lit up the square room, which had two windows and was filled with three beds. There was a wardrobe, a table and two chairs made of seasoned walnut whose smoky-brown colour stood out starkly against the walls, which were painted bright yellow. And that was all, apart from some clothes hanging on nails and a jug standing on the tiled floor next to a red earthenware dish that served as a basin. In the bed on the left, Zacharie, the eldest, a lad of twenty-one, lay beside his brother Jeanlin, who was nearly eleven; in the bed on the right, two little ones, Lénore and Henri, the first aged six, the other four, lay in each other's arms; while the third bed was shared by Catherine and her sister Alzire, aged nine, who was so puny for her age that Catherine wouldn't even have felt her next to her had it not been for the sickly child's hunchback, which kept digging into her. The glass-panelled door to the bedroom stood open, and one could see the landing beyond, a kind of alcove in which their father and mother occupied the fourth bed. Next to it they had had to install the cradle of the latest addition to the family, Estelle, who was barely three months old.

Catherine made a supreme effort to force herself awake. She stretched and then ran her taut fingers through the tousled red hair that fell over her forehead and down the nape of her neck. She was of slight build for a fifteen-year-old, and all that could be seen outside the tight sheath of her nightshirt were her bluish feet, which looked as though they had been tattooed with coal, and her delicate arms whose milky whiteness stood out against her sallow complexion, itself already ruined by constant scrubbings with black soap. Her mouth, which was a little large, opened in a final yawn to reveal a fine array of teeth set in pale, anaemic gums. Her grey eyes watered as she struggled to stay awake, and they held such an expression of pain and exhaustion that her whole body seemed to be swelling with fatigue.

But a growling sound came from the landing as, in a voice thick with sleep, Maheu muttered:

'God! Is it that time already . . . Is that you, Catherine?'

'Yes, Dad . . . The clock downstairs has just struck.'

'Hurry up then, you lazy girl! If you hadn't spent all Sunday night dancing, you could have got us up earlier . . . Anyone would think we didn't have a job of work to go to!'

He grumbled on, but gradually sleep overtook him again; his reproaches became muddled and eventually subsided to be replaced by a new bout of snoring.

The girl moved about the room in her nightshirt, barefoot on the tiled floor. As she passed Henri and Lénore's bed, she covered them with the blanket, which had slipped off the bed; neither woke up, since both were lost to the world in the deep sleep of children. Alzire had opened her eyes and rolled over without a word to occupy the warm spot left by her elder sister.

'Come on, Zacharie! You, too, Jeanlin,' Catherine repeated, standing by her two brothers who each lay sprawled on his front with his nose in the bolster.

She had to grab the older of the two by the shoulder and shake him; and then, while he was muttering insults under his breath, she decided to strip the sheet off the bed. She thought this was a great joke and began to laugh at the sight of the two of them flailing about with bare legs.

'Stop messing about. Leave me be!' grumbled Zacharie crossly after he had sat up. 'It's not funny . . . And now we've bloody got to get up!'

He was a thin, gangling type of fellow, with a long face smudged by the beginnings of a beard and with the same yellow hair and anaemic pallor as the rest of his family. His nightshirt had ridden up round his stomach and he pulled it down, not for decency's sake but because he was cold.

'The clock downstairs has gone four,' Catherine repeated. 'Come on, get a move on! Father's getting angry.'

Jeanlin, who had curled up again in a ball, shut his eyes and said:

'Get lost. I'm asleep.'

Once more she gave a good-natured laugh. He was so small, with his frail limbs and huge joints swollen from scrofula,[2] that she gathered him up in her arms. But he tried to wriggle free, and his face – a wan, wrinkled, monkey-like mask pierced by two green eyes and widened by two large ears – was white with rage at his own weakness. He said nothing, and bit her on the right breast.

'Little bastard!' she muttered, stifling a cry and putting him down.

Alzire had not gone back to sleep but lay there silently with the sheet pulled up to her chin. With her clever, sick-child eyes she watched as her sister and brothers now got dressed. Another quarrel broke out over by the basin when the two boys shoved Catherine aside because she was taking too long to wash. Nightshirts were abandoned as, still half asleep, they relieved themselves, without embarrassment, as easy and natural with each other as a litter of puppies who have grown up together. In the end Catherine was ready first. She slipped on her miner's trousers, donned her cloth jacket, and fastened her blue cap[3] over her hair-bun; and in her clean Monday clothes she looked just like a little man. Nothing of her own sex remained, only the gentle sway of the hips.

'The old man's going to be really pleased to find the bed unmade when he gets back,' Zacharie said grumpily. 'I'll tell him it was you, you know.'

The 'old man' was Bonnemort, their grandfather, who worked nights and so slept by day, with the result that the bed never got cold. There was always someone snoring away in it.

Without a word of reply Catherine had already begun to straighten and smooth the blanket. By now noises could be heard coming from the neighbouring house, on the other side of the wall. These brick constructions put up by the Company were cheaply built, and the walls were so thin that one could hear the slightest sound. Everyone lived cheek by jowl, from one end of the village to the other; and none of life's intimacies remained hidden, not even from the children. Stairs shook with heavy footsteps, and then there was a gentle thud, followed by a contented sigh.

'As usual!' said Catherine. 'Down goes Levaque, and up comes Bouteloup. La Levaque here we come!'

Jeanlin sniggered, and even Alzire's eyes shone. Each morning they shared the same joke about the threesome next door, where a hewer was renting a room out to one of the stonemen, which meant that the wife could have two men, one for the night and one for the day.

'Philomène's coughing,' Catherine went on, after listening for a moment.

She was talking about the Levaques' eldest daughter, a tall girl of nineteen, who was Zacharie's girlfriend and had already had two children by him. As if that was not enough, she had such a weak chest that she had never been able to work down the mine and worked instead in the screening-shed.

'Pah! Philomène!' Zacharie retorted. 'Fat lot she cares, she's asleep! . . . It's disgusting, it really is, lying in like that till six in the morning.'

He was in the middle of pulling on his trousers when suddenly an idea occurred to him and he opened the window. Outside in the darkness the village was waking, and lights were going on one by one, visible between the slats of the shutters. There was another argument: as Zacharie leaned out to see if he could spot the overman from Le Voreux emerging from the Pierrons' house opposite, where people said he was sleeping with Pierron's wife, his sister shouted at him that Pierron had been working on the day shift at pit-bottom since yesterday and that therefore Dansaert would obviously not have been able to spend the night there. Gusts of icy-cold air were blowing into the room, and the two of them were angrily insisting on the accuracy of their information when there was a sudden wailing and screaming. It was Estelle in her cot, who had been disturbed by the cold.

Maheu woke up at once. What on earth was the matter with him? Here he was going back to sleep like some good-for-nothing layabout. And he swore so savagely that the children in the next room did not breathe another word. Zacharie and Jeanlin finished washing, slowly, for both of them were already weary. Alzire kept staring, wide-eyed. The two little ones, Lénore and Henri, still lay wrapped in each other's arms, both of them breathing in the same short breaths; neither had stirred an inch, despite the racket.

'Catherine! Bring me the candle!' shouted Maheu.

She was just finishing buttoning up her jacket, and she carried the candle into her parents' room, leaving her brothers to hunt for their clothes in the modicum of light coming through the door. Her father jumped out of bed. Catherine did not wait but groped her way downstairs in her thick woollen stockings and lit another candle in the parlour, in order to make the coffee. The family's clogs were lined up under the dresser.

'Will you be quiet, you little brat!' Maheu shouted again, infuriated by Estelle's continual screaming.

He was short like Grandpa Bonnemort, of whom he offered a stouter version, with the same large head and flat, pallid face, topped by close-cropped yellow hair. The baby was wailing even more loudly now, terrified by the big, gnarled arms swinging about above her.

'Leave her be! You know she won't be quiet,' said La Maheude, stretching out in the middle of the bed.

She, too, had just woken up, and she began to complain about how ridiculous it was that she never seemed to get a proper night's sleep. Why couldn't they all leave quietly? Buried beneath the blanket, all that could be seen of her was her long face with its broad features, which had a certain heavy beauty but which, at the age of thirty-nine, had already been disfigured by her life of poverty and the seven children she had borne. With her eyes fixed on the ceiling she spoke slowly as her husband got dressed. Neither of them heeded the little girl who was crying so hard that she was nearly choking.

'Look, I'm down to my last sou, you know, and it's still only Monday. There are another six days to go till the fortnight's up[4] ... We just can't go on like this. You bring in nine francs[5] between you, all told. Well, how am I supposed to manage on that, I ask you? There are ten of us living here.'

'What d'you mean, nine francs?' Maheu objected. 'Me and Zacharie get three, which makes six ... Catherine and Father get two, which makes four; four and six make ten ... And Jeanlin, he gets one, which makes eleven.'

'Eleven, yes, but then there are the Sundays and the days when there's no work ... It's never more than nine, believe me.'

Busy searching for his leather belt on the floor, he made no reply. Then, as he stood up, he said:

'You can't grumble, though. At least I'm still fit. There's a few of them at forty-two who get transferred to doing maintenance work.'

'That's as may be, love, but it doesn't earn us any more, does it? . . . So what on earth am I going to do? You haven't got anything, have you?'

'Two sous.'

'Oh, keep them, buy yourself a beer . . . But my God, seriously, what am I going to do? Six days? That's ages. We owe Maigrat sixty francs. He threw me out of his shop the other day . . . which won't stop me going back there, but if he insists that no means no . . .'

And La Maheude went on in the same gloomy tone, never moving her head but closing her eyes from time to time to blot out the sorry light of the candle. She told him how there was no food in the cupboard, and how the little ones kept asking for bread and butter, how there was no coffee left, and how the water gave you colic, and about the long days spent trying to cheat their hunger with boiled cabbage leaves. Bit by bit she had been obliged to raise her voice to make herself heard above Estelle's wailing, which was becoming intolerable. Maheu seemed suddenly to hear her again and, quite beside himself, he grabbed the little girl out of her cradle and threw her down on her mother's bed, spluttering with rage:

'Here, take her, before I throttle the living daylights out of her! . . . Bloody child! It has all it wants, it's got a breast to feed it, and then it complains louder than all the rest!'

Estelle had indeed begun to feed. Having vanished beneath the blanket, she was soothed by the warmth of the bed, and all that could be heard of her now was the faint sound of greedy sucking.

'Didn't the bourgeois at La Piolaine tell you to go and see them?' Maheu continued after a while.

His wife pulled a face as if to say she didn't hold out much hope there.

'Yes, they know me. They give clothes to the children of the poor . . . All right, I'll take Lénore and Henri round to see them this morning. If only they'd just give me five francs[6] instead.'

Silence fell once more. Maheu was now dressed and ready. He stood there motionless for a moment, and then finally he muttered:

'Well, what *can* we do? It's how things are. See what you can manage for the soup . . . Standing here talking about it isn't going to do any good. I'd do better to get to work.'

'You're right,' La Maheude replied. 'Blow the candle out, will you? I'd rather not see things too clearly just now!'

He blew out the candle. Zacharie and Jeanlin were already on their way down, and he followed them; the wooden staircase creaked beneath their heavy, wool-clad feet. Behind him, the landing and the bedroom were once more sunk in darkness. The little ones slept on, and even Alzire's eyelids were shut. But their mother lay there in the dark with her eyes open, and Estelle purred away like a kitten as she continued to suck on the exhausted woman's sagging breast.

Down below Catherine had begun by seeing to the fire. The cooking range, of cast-iron, had a grate in the middle, with ovens to either side, and a coal fire was kept burning in it day and night. Every month the Company gave each family eight hectolitres of *escaillage*, a type of hard coal collected off the roadway floors. It was difficult to light but, having damped down the fire the night before, the girl had only to rake it in the morning and add a few carefully chosen pieces of softer coal. Then she placed a kettle on the grate and crouched in front of the kitchen dresser.

The room, which was quite large and occupied the whole of the ground floor, was painted apple green and had the spick-and-span look of a Flemish kitchen, with flagstones that were sluiced regularly and strewn with white sand. Apart from the varnished pine dresser, the furniture consisted of a table and chairs, also in pine. Stuck to the walls were a number of garish prints, portraits of the Emperor and Empress[7] as provided by the Company, as well as various soldiers and saints, heavily daubed with gold, which all looked crude and out of place in the bright bareness of the room. The only other forms of decoration were a pink box made of cardboard that sat on the dresser and the cuckoo clock with its multicoloured dial, whose loud ticking seemed to fill the empty reaches of the ceiling. Beside the door to the staircase another door led down to the cellar. Despite the cleanliness, an aroma of fried onion left over from the night before hung in the stuffy, fetid air that was already heavy with the acrid smell of coal.

In front of the open dresser Catherine was pondering. All that was left was the remains of a loaf, plenty of cottage cheese and a mere sliver of butter; and it was her job to produce sandwiches for all four of them. Having eventually made up her mind, she sliced the bread, covered one slice with cheese and smeared another with butter and then pressed them together: this was their 'piece',[8] the double slice of bread and butter that they took with them to the mine each morning. Soon the four 'pieces' were lined up on the table, the size of each having been gradated with rigorous fairness, from the thick one for Maheu down to the small one for Jeanlin.

Though she seemed completely absorbed in her domestic tasks, Catherine must nevertheless have been mulling over what Zacharie had said about the overman and La Pierronne because she opened the front door slightly and peeped out. It was still windy. Up and down the streets, along the low façades, lights were constantly appearing and disappearing, as candles were lit in one house or blown out in another; and one could hear the faint stir of people waking to a new day. Already there was the sound of doors being shut, and the shadowy outlines of workers could be seen filing off into the night. But what was she thinking of standing here getting cold like this? Pierron was bound to be asleep still, he wasn't due to start his shift till six o'clock! And yet she waited, watching the house on the other side of the gardens. The door opened, and her interest quickened. But it must have been the Pierrons' daughter, Lydie, leaving for the pit.

The whistle of steam made her turn round. She shut the door and rushed across the room: the kettle was boiling over and putting out the fire. There was no coffee left, so she had to make do with pouring the water over last night's grounds; then she added some brown sugar to the pot. At that moment her father and two brothers came downstairs.

'God!' said Zacharie, having sniffed his bowl of coffee. 'That's hardly going to put hairs on our chest, is it!'

Maheu shrugged resignedly.

'Pah! It's hot, it'll do fine.'

Jeanlin had gathered up the crumbs from the bread and put them in his bowl, where they made a kind of sop. Having drunk some coffee, Catherine emptied the remainder of the pot into their tin flasks. The four of them stood there in the dim light of the smoking candle and hurried to finish.

'Come on, then. Are we all ready?' said her father. 'Anyone would think we were the idle rich, standing about like this.'

But a voice could be heard coming from the staircase, where they'd left the door open. It was La Maheude, shouting:

'Take all the bread. I've still got a bit of vermicelli left for the children.'

'Yes, all right!' Catherine answered.

She had damped down the fire again and left the remains of some soup in a pan wedged up against the corner of the grate: it would be warm for her grandfather to eat when he came home at six. They each grabbed their clogs from under the dresser, slung the cord of their flask over their shoulder, and tucked their 'piece' down their back, between shirt and jacket. And off they set, the menfolk first, the girl behind, blowing out the candle and locking the door behind them. The house fell into darkness once more.

'Hallo there!' said a man who was just leaving the house next door. 'We can go together.'

It was Levaque, with his son Bébert, a lad of twelve who was a great friend of Jeanlin's. Catherine was astonished and stifled a giggle as she whispered in Zacharie's ear: How about that, eh? Didn't Bouteloup even wait for the husband to leave any more!

Throughout the village the lights were going out. A last door slammed shut, and the whole place went back to sleep as the women and small children resumed their rest in beds where there was now more room. Meanwhile, from the dark, silent

village to the puffing steam of Le Voreux, a long line of shadows
moved slowly forward in the gusting wind, the miners on their
way to work, shoulders hunched and superfluous arms folded
across their chests. On their backs the 'pieces' bulged like humps.
Shivering with cold in their thin clothes they made no effort to
hurry but quietly tramped along, strung out like a straggling
herd of animals.

III

Étienne, having finally come down from the spoil-heap, had just
walked into Le Voreux; and whenever he asked if there was
work, everyone just shook their head and told him to wait for
the overman. He was left to wander about the dimly lit buildings
that were full of black, empty spaces and a disturbingly complex
array of different rooms and levels. Having climbed a dark,
half-derelict staircase he had found himself on a rickety overhead gangway and then made his way across the screening-shed
where it was so completely dark that he had to stretch out his
arms in order to avoid bumping into anything. Suddenly, right
in front of him, two enormous yellow eyes appeared, like holes
in the blackness. He was now standing under the headgear, at
the very mouth of the mine-shaft, where the coal was unloaded
after it had been brought up.

One of the older deputies, called Richomme, a large fellow
with the face of a friendly policeman and a wide grey moustache,
happened to be passing on his way to the checkweighman's
office.

'Don't suppose you could do with another pair of hands
round here, could you? I'll take whatever there is,' Étienne asked
once more.

Richomme was about to say 'no'; but then he paused and
gave the same answer as the others, before walking on:

'Wait for Monsieur Dansaert. He's the overman.'

Four lanterns had been installed here, and the reflectors,
which were designed to throw all the light back down towards

the shaft, shone brightly on the iron railings, on the levers, which operated the signals and the cage keeps, and on the wooden guides between which the two cages moved up and down. Everything else in the vast, nave-like hall was lost in darkness, and huge shadows seemed to float back and forth. Only the lamp-room at the far end was ablaze with light, while a lamp in the checkweighman's office glowed weakly, like a star on the verge of extinction. Production had just resumed. The flooring of cast-iron plates rumbled like permanent thunder beneath the unceasing passage of the coal-tubs; and as the banksmen rolled them across, the human outline of their long, curved spines stood out amid the ceaseless commotion of these black and noisy things.

Étienne stood for a moment, deafened and blinded, and chilled to the bone by the draughts coming from every direction. Then he moved forward a few paces, drawn by the gleaming steel and brass of the winding-engine, which had now become visible. It was set back some twenty-five metres from the shaft and housed at a higher level; and there it sat so securely fixed on its base of solid brick that even when it was working at full steam and producing every one of its four hundred horse-power, the walls did not so much as quiver with the action of its huge crank rod as it rose and plunged in gentle, well-oiled motion. The engineman standing by the operating lever was listening out for the signal bells while his eyes were fixed on the indicator panel where the different levels of the mineshaft were marked on a vertical groove. Beside this groove, lead weights attached to strings moved up and down representing the cages. The engine would start up each time a cage departed, and the spools – two enormous wheels measuring ten metres in diameter, around the hubs of which two steel cables wound and unwound in opposite directions – would begin to spin so fast that they faded into a grey blur.

'Mind out!' shouted three banksmen who were dragging a gigantic ladder.

Étienne had almost been crushed. His eyes were beginning to get used to the darkness, and he watched the cables as they vanished upwards, more than thirty metres of steel ribbon rising

straight up into the headgear and over the winding-pulleys
before plunging back down into the mine-shaft to connect with
the cages. A cast-iron frame, like the beams in the roof of a
bell-tower, supported the pulleys. With the noiseless, unim-
peded swoop of a bird, the cable – which was enormously heavy
and could lift up to one thousand two hundred kilograms at a
speed of ten metres per second – pursued its rapid, ceaseless
course, up and down, up and down.

'Mind out, for Christ's sake!' the banksmen shouted again,
as they raised the ladder on the other side of the engine to inspect
the left-hand pulley.

Slowly Étienne turned back towards the pit-head. The spectacle of this giant swooping above his head made him feel dizzy;
and, still shivering in the draughts, he watched the cages come
and go, deafened by the rumble of the coal-tubs. Next to the
shaft was the signal, a heavy hammer on a lever attached to
a rope which, when pulled from below, caused the hammer
to fall on a block. Once to stop, twice to descend, three times to
come up: it never stopped, great cudgel-blows that could be
heard above the din, accompanied by the bright ring of a bell.
Meanwhile the banksman in charge added to the general racket
by shouting orders to the engineman through a loudhailer.
Amid all this commotion the cages rose and vanished, emptied
and filled, leaving Étienne none the wiser as to the whys and
wherefores of these complex manœuvres.

One thing he did grasp: the pit could swallow people in
mouthfuls of twenty or thirty at a time, and with such ease that
it seemed not even to notice the moment of their consumption.
The miners began descending at four. They arrived barefoot
from the changing-room, each carrying a lamp, and waited in
small groups until there was a sufficient number. Without a
sound, springing gently up from below like some creature of the
night, the cage would emerge from the darkness and lock into
its keeps, each of its four decks containing two tubs full of coal.
Banksmen on each deck would drag the tubs out and replace
them with others, which were either empty or already loaded
with timber props. And the workers would pile into the empty
tubs, five at a time, up to a maximum of forty. An order would

issue from the loudhailer in the form of a muffled, unintelligible bellow, while the signal-rope was pulled four times to indicate a 'meat load', warning those below that a cargo of human flesh was on its way down. Then, after a slight jolt, the cage would plummet silently below, falling like a stone and leaving only the quivering trail of its cable.

'Is it a long way down?' Étienne asked a sleepy-looking miner who was waiting beside him.

'Five hundred and fifty-four metres,' the man replied. 'But there are four loading-bays on the way down. The first one's at three hundred and twenty metres.'

They both fell silent, gazing at the cable which was now coming back up.

'And what if that breaks?'

'Ah well, if that breaks . . .'

The miner gestured by way of an answer. It was his turn now, the cage having reappeared with its usual, tireless ease. He squatted in a tub with some of his comrades, down the cage went, and up it came again scarcely four minutes later, ready to devour a further load of humans. For half an hour the shaft continued to gorge itself in this way, with greater or lesser voracity depending on the level to which the men were descending, but without cease, ever famished, its giant bowels capable of digesting an entire people. It filled and it filled, and yet the darkness gave no sign of life, and the cage continued to rise up, noiselessly, greedily, out of the void.

At length Étienne was overtaken by a renewed sense of the misgivings he had felt up on the spoil-heap. Why bother anyway? This overman would send him away just like all the others. A sudden feeling of panic decided the matter and he rushed out, stopping only when he had reached the building that housed the steam-generators. Through the wide-open door seven boilers could be seen, each with a double fire-grate. Surrounded by white steam and whistling valves, a stoker was busy stoking one of these grates, whose burning coals could be felt from the doorway; and Étienne, grateful for the warmth, was just walking towards them when he bumped into a new group of colliers arriving at the mine. It was the Maheus and the Levaques. When he caught sight of Catherine, at the front of the group, with her gentle, boyish demeanour, some impulse or other made him try his luck one last time.

'Er, comrade, I don't suppose they're looking for another pair of hands round here, are they? I'll do whatever's required.'

She looked at him in surprise, startled by this sudden voice coming from the shadows. But, behind her, Maheu had heard and stopped to respond with a brief word. No, they didn't need anyone. But the thought of this poor devil of a worker being left to roam the countryside stayed with him; and as he walked away, he said to the others:

'There you are! That could be us, you see . . . So we mustn't grumble. It's not everyone who gets the chance to do an honest day's work.'

The group walked in and made straight for the changing-area, a huge room with roughly plastered walls and padlocked cupboards along each side. In the middle stood an iron stove, a kind of doorless oven ablaze with red embers and so fully stoked that lumps of coal kept splitting and tumbling out on to the earthen floor. The only light in the room came from this grate, and blood-red reflections played along the grimy woodwork and up on to a ceiling that was coated with black dust.

As the Maheus came in, peals of laughter could be heard amid the stifling heat. Some thirty workers were standing with their backs to the flames, roasting themselves with an air of profound contentment. Everyone came here like this before going down and got themselves a good skinful of warmth so that they could face the dampness of the mine. But that morning there was even more merriment than usual because they were teasing La Mouquette, one of the putters, a good-natured girl of eighteen with huge breasts and buttocks that were almost bursting out of her clothes. She lived at Réquillart with her father, old Mouque, who looked after the horses, and her brother Mouquet, who was a banksman, except that since they didn't all work the same hours she would go to the mine on her own; and, whether in the cornfields during summer or up against a wall in wintertime, she would take her pleasure with the lover of the moment. The whole pit had taken its turn; it was simply

a case of 'after you, comrade, and no harm done'. When somebody once suggested she'd been with a nailer from Marchiennes,
she had almost exploded with anger, screaming about how she
was a respectable girl and how she'd sooner cut off her own arm
than for anybody to be able to say they'd ever seen her with
anyone but a colliery worker.

'So what about that tall fellow, Chaval, then? He's had his
day, has he?' one of the miners said with a snigger. 'Helped
yourself to that other little chap instead, have you? But he'd
need a ladder, he would! . . . I've seen the pair of you round the
back of Réquillart, and sure enough, there he was standing on
a milestone.'

'So?' La Mouquette answered cheerfully. 'What's that to you?
At least nobody asked you to come and give him a push.'

The men laughed even louder at this good-natured coarseness
as they stood there flexing their shoulders, already half roasted
by the fire; and meanwhile La Mouquette, also roaring with
laughter, continued to move among them, flaunting the in-
decency of her dress and offering a spectacle that was at once
comic and disturbing as she displayed lumps of flesh so
excessively huge that they seemed almost a deformity.

But the merriment ceased as La Mouquette began to tell
Maheu how Fleurance, the tall Fleurance, would not be coming
any more: they'd found her stone dead in her bed the night
before. Some said she'd died of a heart condition, others of
downing a litre of gin too fast. Maheu was in despair. More bad
luck! Now he'd lost one of his putters and there was no way of
finding an immediate replacement! He worked on a subcon-
tracted basis, and four of them worked the seam together,
himself, Zacharie, Levaque and Chaval. If there was only Catherine to put the tubs, their rate of production would be affected.
Suddenly he shouted:

'Wait a minute! What about that fellow that was looking
for work?'

At that moment Dansaert was passing the changing-room.
Maheu told him what had happened and asked permission to
take the man on; and he played on the fact that the Company
was keen to replace the female putters with lads, like at Anzin.

The overman smiled at this, since normally the policy of exclud-
ing women from working below the surface was anathema to
the miners, who worried about their daughters finding a job
and didn't much care about questions of hygiene or morality.
Eventually, after some hesitation, he gave his permission,
but on condition that this had to be ratified by the engineer,
M. Négrel.

'Anyway,' said Zacharie, 'at the rate he was going, he'll be
miles away by now.'

'No,' said Catherine, 'I saw him stop at the boilers.'

'What are you standing there for, then? Go and fetch him!'
Maheu shouted.

The girl shot off as a sea of miners moved up towards the
shaft and left the fire clear for others. Without waiting for his
father, Jeanlin moved away also to go and fetch his lamp, along
with Bébert, a big immature lad, and Lydie, a puny little girl of
ten. Ahead of them La Mouquette could be heard protesting
loudly in the dark staircase, calling them filthy brats and threatening to give them a slap in the face if they pinched her again.

Sure enough, Étienne was in the boiler-house talking to the
stoker as he shovelled coal into the grates. It made him feel very
cold to think of the black night into which he now had to return.
Nevertheless he was on the point of resolving to leave when he
felt a hand on his shoulder.

'Come with me,' said Catherine. 'There *is* something for you.'

At first he did not understand. Then he was overwhelmed
with joy and energetically clasped the girl's hands.

'Thanks, comrade . . . You're a decent bugger!'

She began to laugh, gazing at him in the red light gleaming
from the grates. She found it amusing that he should take her
for a boy, with her slim figure and her bun hidden under her
cap. He, too, laughed happily; and they remained like that for
a moment, laughing together, face to face, their cheeks flushed.

In the changing-room Maheu was crouched in front of his
locker taking off his clogs and his thick woollen stockings.
When Étienne arrived, everything was quickly settled: thirty
sous a day, it was tiring work but he'd soon get the hang of it.
Maheu advised him to keep his shoes on, and he lent him an old

leather skullcap designed to protect the top of the head, a precaution which both father and children nevertheless scorned to adopt. They took their tools from the locker, which also contained Fleurance's shovel. Then, after Maheu had locked away their clogs and stockings, as well as Étienne's bundle, he grew suddenly impatient:

'But where the hell's that animal Chaval got to now? Screwing some girl on a pile of spoil somewhere, I'll bet . . . We're half an hour late today.'

Zacharie and Levaque were quietly toasting their backs. Eventually the former said:

'You're not waiting for Chaval, are you? . . . He got here before we did and went straight down.'

'What? You knew and didn't say anything? . . . Come on, come on, let's get going then.'

Catherine, who was warming her hands, was obliged to follow the group. Étienne let her pass and then climbed the steps behind her. Once more he found himself wandering in a labyrinth of dark stairs and corridors, where the tramp of bare feet sounded like the slap of old slippers. But the lamp-room was still blazing away behind its glass partition. It was full of shelves stacked with row upon row of Davy lamps, hundreds of them, which had been inspected and cleaned the night before and now burned like candles in a memorial chapel. As they passed the counter, each miner would take his lamp, which had his number stamped on it, examine it, and then close it himself; while the lamp-clerk, seated at a table, would record the time of descent in a register.

Maheu had to request a lamp for his new putter. Then came one last safety measure: the miners were required to file past a man who checked that all the lamps were securely closed.

'Blimey! It's not very warm in here,' Catherine muttered, shivering.

Étienne simply shook his head. He was standing in front of the pit-shaft, in the middle of the huge, draughty hall. He considered himself as brave as the next man, but he was unnerved by the rumble of the tubs, the dull thud of the signals, the muffled bellowing of the loudhailer, and the sight of the constantly whirring cables as they were wound and unwound at full steam by the spools of the winding-engine. Up and down the cages went, like stealthy beasts of the night, swallowing men by the mouthful as they disappeared down the black throat of the mine. It was his turn now. He was very cold and said nothing as he waited anxiously, which made Zacharie and Levaque snigger; for they both disapproved of the stranger being taken on like this, Levaque especially, who felt hurt at not being consulted. So Catherine was pleased to hear her father explaining things to the young man.

'Can you see, up there, above the cage? There's a safety brake, iron hooks that dig into the guides if the cable breaks. It works. Well, most of the time anyway ... The shaft itself is divided vertically into three sections by wooden planks. In the middle are the cages, on the left is the emergency shaft where there are ladders –'

He broke off to complain, though without raising his voice too loudly:

'What's the hold-up, for God's sake! It's bloody freezing in here!'

Richomme, the deputy, was waiting to go down also, with his open lamp fixed on to a stud in his leather cap, and he heard Maheu complaining.

'Careful! Walls have ears!' he muttered paternally with the voice of one who used to be a coal-getter and whose sympathies still lay with his comrades. 'All in good time ... Anyway, here we go. In you get with the rest of your team.'

The cage was indeed now waiting for them, locked into its keeps, its thin wire mesh clamped in bands of sheet metal. Maheu, Zacharie, Levaque and Catherine slipped into a tub at the back and, since this took five people, Étienne climbed in also; but the best places had been taken, and he had to squash in next to the girl, whose elbow stuck into his stomach. His lamp was getting in the way, and they told him to hang it from a buttonhole in his jacket. But he didn't hear, and continued to hold on to it awkwardly. The loading continued, above and below them, as though a herd of animals was being shovelled pell-mell into a furnace. Why hadn't they left? What was happening? Étienne felt as if they'd already been waiting for hours.

Finally there was a jolt, and they were engulfed; his surroundings took flight, and a giddy sensation clutched at his stomach as they fell. This lasted for as long as they could still see, down past the two levels where the coal was off-loaded, with the shaft lining whizzing past in a blur. As they plunged down the pit into total darkness, he became dizzy and lost all sense of reality.

'We're away,' Maheu said simply.

Everyone was calm. Occasionally Étienne wondered if he was going up or down. There were moments when they seemed not to be moving at all as the cage went straight down without touching the guides on either side; and then suddenly these wooden beams would start vibrating, as though they had come loose, and he would be afraid that some disaster was about to strike. As it was, he couldn't see the sides of the shaft even though his face was pressed to the mesh of the cage. The bodies huddled at his feet were barely visible in the light from the Davy lamps. Only the deputy's open lamp, in the next tub, shone out like a lighthouse.

'The shaft's four metres across,' Maheu continued to inform him. 'It could do with being retubbed, the water's coming in everywhere . . . Listen! We're just getting there now. Can you hear it?'

Étienne had indeed just begun to wonder why it sounded as though it were raining. At first a few heavy drops of water had splattered on to the cage roof, as though a shower were beginning; and now the rain was falling faster, streaming down in a veritable deluge. Presumably the roof must have had a hole in it because a trickle of water had landed on his shoulder and soaked him to the skin. It was becoming icy cold, and they were plunging down into the damp and the dark when suddenly they passed through a blaze of light and caught a flashing glimpse of a cave with men moving about. Already they had resumed their descent into the void.

Maheu was saying:

'That was the first level. We're three hundred and twenty metres down now . . . Look at the speed.'

He raised his lamp and shone it on to one of the beams that guided the cages; it was tearing past like a railway line beneath a train travelling at full speed. But still that was all they could see. Three more levels flashed past in a startled burst of light. The deafening rain continued to teem down in the darkness.

'My God, it's deep,' Étienne muttered under his breath.

It was as if they had been falling like this for hours. He was suffering from the awkward position he'd taken up in the tub, and especially from the painful presence of Catherine's elbow, but he didn't dare move. She didn't say a word; he could simply feel her next to him, warming him. When the cage finally reached the bottom, five hundred and fifty-four metres down, he was astonished to learn that the descent had taken exactly one minute. But the sound of the cage locking into its keeps and the accompanying sense of having something solid underfoot made him suddenly euphoric; and he joked familiarly with Catherine:

'What have you got under there that keeps you so warm? . . . I hope that's only your elbow that's sticking into my ribs!'

It was her turn to speak frankly. After all, what a stupid idiot he was, still thinking she was a boy! Couldn't he see straight?

'Or making you go blind, more like!' she replied, which provoked a gale of laughter that left an astonished Étienne completely at a loss.

The cage was emptying, and the miners crossed pit-bottom, a cavity hewn out of the rock, which was reinforced with masonry vaults and lit by three large, open lamps. The onsetters were busy wheeling the full tubs roughly across the cast-iron flooring. A smell of cellars oozed from the walls, a cool, damp reek of saltpetre mixed with the occasional waft of warmth from the nearby stable. Four roadways led off from this point, their mouths gaping.

'This way,' Maheu told Étienne. 'We're not there yet. We've still got a good two kilometres to go.'

The miners split up into groups and vanished into these four black holes. Fifteen of them had just entered the one on the left; and Étienne followed, walking behind Maheu, who was behind Catherine, Zacharie and Levaque. It was an excellent haulage roadway running at right angles to the seam and hollowed out of such solid rock that it had needed very little timbering. Along they walked in single file, on and on, silently, by the tiny light of their lamps. Étienne kept tripping over the rails. For a little while now a particular muffled sound had been worrying him, the distant tumult of a storm rising from the bowels of the earth and which seemed to be getting increasingly violent. Did this thunderous rumbling presage a rock-fall that was going to bring the huge mass of earth overhead crashing down on them all? A patch of light pierced the darkness, he felt the rock vibrate, and, having pressed his back flat to the wall, like his comrades, he saw a large white horse go past his face, pulling a train of coal-tubs. On the first tub, holding the reins, sat Bébert, while Jeanlin ran barefoot behind the last, hanging on to its rim with both hands.

On they trudged. Presently they came to a crossroads, where two further roadways led off, and the group divided again as the miners gradually dispersed among the various workings in the mine. Here the haulage roadway was timbered: oak props supported the roof and retained the crumbling rock behind a wooden framework through which one could see the layers of shale sparkling with mica and the solid mass of dull, rough sandstone. Trains of tubs went by all the time, full or empty, thundering past each other before being borne off into the darkness by phantom beasts at a ghostly trot. On a double track in a siding a long black snake lay sleeping: it was a stationary train, and its horse snorted in the darkness, which was so thick that the dim outline of the horse's quarters looked like a lump of rock that had fallen from the roof. Ventilation doors opened with a bang and then slowly closed again. As they walked on, the roadway gradually got narrower and lower, and they kept having to stoop to pass beneath its uneven roof.

Étienne banged his head, hard. Without his leather cap he would have split his skull. And yet he had been keeping his eyes firmly fixed on Maheu in front of him, following his every movement as his dark shape loomed against the light of the lamps beyond. None of the miners banged their heads, since each of them no doubt knew every bump along the way, whether it was a knot in the wood or a bulge in the rock. Étienne also found the slippery ground difficult, and it was getting wetter and wetter. From time to time they crossed what were virtually pools of water, as they could tell from the muddy squelch of their feet. But what surprised him most of all were the sudden changes in temperature. At the bottom of the shaft it had been very cold, and in the haulage roadway – through which all the air in the mine passed – an icy wind blew, whipped to a storm by the narrowness of the space between the walls. Then, as they penetrated deeper into the other roads, which each received only a meagre ration of air, the wind dropped and the temperature rose, to the point where the air became suffocatingly hot and as heavy as lead.

Maheu had made no further comment. He turned right into another roadway, simply saying 'the Guillaume seam' to Étienne but without bothering to turn round.

This was the seam where they were working one of the coal-faces. A few steps further and Étienne banged his head and elbows. The roof now sloped down so low that they had to walk for whole stretches of twenty or thirty metres bent double. Water came up to their ankles. They continued on for two hundred metres like this; and then suddenly Étienne saw Levaque, Zacharie and Catherine disappear, as though they had vanished through a thin cleft in the rock in front of him.

'We have to climb,' Maheu continued. 'Hang your lamp from your buttonhole and grab hold of the timbering.'

He, too, vanished, and Étienne was obliged to follow. A kind of chimney had been left in the seam so that the miners could reach all the subsidiary roads. It was the same width as the coal-seam itself, scarcely sixty centimetres. Fortunately the young man was slim, for being as yet unpractised it took him an excessive amount of muscular effort to hoist himself aloft, which he did by squeezing his shoulders and hips in tight, then clinging to the timbers and dragging himself up by his wrists. Fifteen metres up they came on the first of the secondary roads; but they had to keep going because the face worked by Maheu and his team was the sixth road in 'Hell', as they called it. At intervals of fifteen metres came further roads, each one running exactly above the last; and the climb seemed never-ending as they scrambled up through this crack in the rock and felt the skin being scraped off their backs and their chests. Étienne was

gasping for breath, as if the weight of the rock had crushed his
limbs; his legs were bruised, his hands felt as though they had
been torn from his arms, but above all he was desperate for air,
to such an extent that his blood felt as though it were ready to
burst from his veins. Dimly, in one of the roads, he made out
the hunched shapes of two animals, one small and one large,
pushing coal-tubs: it was Lydie and La Mouquette, already at
work. And still he had the height of two coal-faces to climb! He
was blinded by sweat and despaired of keeping pace with the
others as he heard their supple limbs slithering smoothly up the
surface of the rock.

'Keep going, we're there!' he heard Catherine say.

But as indeed he reached the spot, another voice shouted from
the coal-face:

'What the hell's this, then? Some kind of joke or what? I have
to come a whole two kilometres from Montsou, and I'm bloody
here first!'

This was Chaval, a tall, thin, bony man of twenty-five with
strong features. He was cross at having had to wait. When he
caught sight of Étienne, he asked in scornful surprise:

'And what have we got here, then?'

When Maheu had told him what had happened, he added
through clenched teeth:

'So now the boys are stealing the girls' bread out of their
mouths.'[1]

The two men exchanged a look, their eyes blazing with the
kind of instinctive hatred that flares in an instant. Étienne had
sensed the insult, but without yet fully understanding its meaning. There was a silence, and everyone set to work. All the seams
had gradually filled up, and all the faces were being worked, on
each level, at the end of each road. The gluttonous pit had
swallowed its daily ration of men, nearly seven hundred miners
who were now at work inside this giant anthill, all burrowing
into the earth and riddling it with holes, like an old piece of
wood being eaten away by woodworm. And in the heavy silence
created by the crushing mass of earth it was possible to put an
ear to the rock and hear the teeming activity of human insects
on the march, from the whirr of the cables rising and falling as

the cages took the coal to the surface to the grinding of tools as they bit into the seam deep within each working.

As he turned, Étienne once more found himself pressed up close against Catherine. But this time he could discern the nascent curves of her breasts, and at once he understood the nature of the warmth he had felt:

'So you're a girl, then?' he murmured in amazement.

Unabashed, she replied with her usual cheerfulness:

'Of course I am . . . Dear me! That took you some time!'

IV

The four hewers had just taken up position, stretched out at different levels one above the other and covering the entire height of the coal-face. Wooden planks, secured by hooks, stopped the coal from falling after they had cut it, and between these planks each man occupied a space of about four metres along the seam. This particular seam was so thin,[1] barely fifty centimetres at this point, that they found themselves virtually crushed between roof and wall; they had to drag themselves forward on their elbows and knees and were quite unable to turn round without banging their shoulders. In order to get at the coal they had to lie on one side, twist their necks, and use both arms in order to raise their *rivelaine*, a short-handled pick, which they wielded at an angle.

Zacharie was at the bottom; then came Levaque and Chaval above him, and finally Maheu at the very top. Each man hacked into the shale bedrock, digging it out with his pick. Then he would make two vertical cuts in the coal, insert an iron wedge into the space above, and prise out a lump. The coal was soft, and the lump would break into pieces which then rolled down over his stomach and legs. Once these pieces had piled up against the boards put there to retain them, the hewers disappeared from view, immured in their narrow cleft.

Maheu had the worst of it. Up at the top the temperature reached thirty-five degrees; there was no circulation of air, and the suffocating atmosphere was potentially fatal. In order to see what he was doing he had to hang his lamp from a nail, just by his head; and the continued heat of the lamp on his skull eventually raised his body temperature to fever level. But it was the wetness that made life particularly difficult. The rock above him, just a few centimetres from his face, was streaming with water, and large drops of it would keep falling in regular, rapid succession, always landing with stubborn insistence on exactly the same spot. Try as he might to twist his neck or bend his head back, they splattered remorselessly against his face and burst. After a quarter of an hour he would be soaked through, and with his body also bathed in sweat he steamed like a wash-tub. That particular morning a drop of water was continually hitting him in the eye, and it made him curse. He didn't want to stop hewing, and as he continued to hack fiercely at the rock, his body shook violently in the narrow space, like a greenfly caught between the leaves of a book and about to be squashed completely flat.

Not a word was exchanged. Everyone was tapping away, and all that could be heard was the irregular clunk-clunk of the picks, which seemed to come from far away. There were no echoes in this airless place, and sounds were more like a dull rasping. The darkness itself seemed to consist of an unfamiliar blackness that was thick with flying coal-dust and filled with gases that made the eyelids heavy. The wicks in the lamps were no more than reddish pinpricks of light beneath their gauze mantles. One could see almost nothing, and the coal-face simply rose into a pitch-black void, like a broad, flat, sloping chimney piled high with the soot of a dozen winters. Ghostly shapes moved about in it, and chance gleams of light picked out the curve of a hip, or a sinewy arm, or a wild-looking face blackened as though in readiness for a crime. From time to time, lumps of coal would gleam in the darkness as they came away, suddenly illuminated – a flat surface here, a sharp edge there – by the glint of light on crystal. Then it would all be dark again, and apart from the loud thudding of the picks all that could be heard were gasping lungs and the occasional groan of discomfort and fatigue caused by the thick air and the water raining down from the underground springs.

Zacharie was not feeling strong – the consequence of a heavy night – and he soon stopped hewing on the pretext that some timbering needed to be done, which meant he could take it easy for a while and whistle softly to himself as he stared absently into space. Behind the hewers nearly three metres of the seam had been dug out and still they had not taken the precaution of shoring up the rock, being at once careless of the danger and jealous of their time.

'Hey, you there, with your nose in the air!' Zacharie called to Étienne. 'Pass me some props.'

Étienne, who was being taught by Catherine how best to use his shovel, had to carry the props to the coal-face. There was a small amount left over from the day before, the usual practice being to bring down each morning some that had been cut exactly to the dimensions of the seam.

'Come on, hurry up, you lazy bastard!' Zacharie continued, as he watched the new putter hoist himself awkwardly up through the loose coal with his arms full of four lengths of oak.

With his pick he cut a notch in the roof and another in the wall, and then wedged the two ends of the beam in place so that they served as a support. Each afternoon the shifters came and fetched the rubble left at the end of each tunnel by the hewers and then disposed of it in the cavities where the seam had already been mined. They made no effort to remove the timbering, and simply kept the uppermost and lowermost roads free for haulage.

Maheu stopped grunting. He had finally managed to prise out his block of coal. He wiped his streaming face on his sleeve and began to concern himself with what Zacharie had climbed up behind him to do.

'No, leave that for now,' he said. 'We'll see about it after lunch . . . Better we keep hewing if we want to fill our usual number of tubs.'

'Yes, but look,' replied Zacharie, 'it's sagging. There's a crack there. I'm worried it's going to fall in.'

But his father merely shrugged. Let it fall in, then! Anyway, it wouldn't be the first time. They'd survive all right. Eventually he grew angry and ordered his son back to the coal-face.

In fact they were all taking a breather now. Levaque was lying on his back cursing as he examined his left thumb where the skin had been taken off by a piece of falling sandstone. Chaval was furiously removing his shirt, stripping to the waist to try and get cool. They were already black with coal, covered in a layer of fine dust that dissolved in their sweat and trickled down them and collected in pools. Maheu was the first to set to again, tapping away at the coal lower down so that his head was flush with the rock. The dripping water now landed on his forehead and with such stubborn regularity that he felt as though it were boring a hole through the bone in his skull.

'Don't mind them,' Catherine said to Étienne by way of explanation. 'They're always arguing about something.'

And, in her usual helpful way, she went on with the lesson.

Each full tub reached the surface just as it had left the coal-face, marked with a special token[2] so that the checkweighman could credit it to the appropriate team of miners. It was important to make sure, therefore, that it was properly full, and with clean coal, otherwise the checkweighman would not record it.

Étienne's eyes were becoming accustomed to the dark, and he looked at her, with her white, anaemic skin. He could not have said how old she was: perhaps twelve, he thought, so slight of build was she. Yet he sensed that she was older than that, noting her boyish lack of inhibition and her directness, which made him feel a little awkward. He didn't find her attractive – the pale, Pierrot face framed in its tight-fitting cap made her look too much like a young urchin – but he was amazed by the child's strength, which seemed to derive from a mixture of wiry sinews and considerable dexterity. She could fill the tub quicker than he could, in a fast, regular succession of small shovelfuls; and then, slowly and steadily, she would push it along to the top of the incline in such a way that it never got stuck and that both she and it passed easily under the low rocks. He, on the other hand, suffered all manner of cuts and bruises and kept coming off the rails and needing assistance.

It was not, in fact, the easiest of haulage roads. It was sixty metres from the coal-face to the incline; and the road itself, which had not yet been widened by the stonemen, was no more than a narrow tube. The roof was very uneven, with large bumps all along it, and at certain points a full tub could only just pass underneath, with the putters having to get down on their knees and push so as not to crack their skulls open. Moreover the timber supports were already sagging and beginning to crack. Long, pale gashes could be seen in some of them where they had already split through the middle, like crutches unequal to the task. They had to be careful not to get caught on the jagged edges; and as this slow collapse proceeded overhead, crushing the round oak props that were as thick as a man's thigh, they had to crawl forward on their bellies while all the time wondering anxiously if they were suddenly going to hear their own spines snap in two.

'Not again!' laughed Catherine.

Étienne's tub had just come off the rails at the most awkward spot. He couldn't manage to get the tubs to go straight because the rails were warped by the dampness in the ground; and he was in a rage, swearing and cursing as he wrestled furiously with the wheels, which refused, despite his extravagant efforts, to go back into place.

'Wait, wait,' said Catherine. 'If you get cross, you'll never get it to move.'

Nimbly she slid down and backed her bottom in under the tub; and then she lifted it with her hips back on to the rails. It weighed seven hundred kilograms. Étienne was astonished, and shamefully stammered his apologies.

She had to show him how to spread his legs in an arch and wedge his feet against the timbers, on both sides of the roadway, so as to give himself points of purchase. The trick was to lean forward, with your arms out straight, so as to be able to use all the muscles in your shoulders and hips simultaneously. He followed her for one trip and watched her as she moved forward with her bottom in the air and her fists so low down that she seemed to be trotting on all fours like one of those dwarf animals that work in circuses. She was sweating and panting, and her joints cracked, but she worked without complaint, with the indifference of habit, as if it was everyone's wretched lot to live like this beneath the yoke. But he simply could not manage to do the same; his shoes were an encumbrance, and his body ached as he tried to move forward like that with his head down. After a few minutes the position was agony, and he felt such intolerable pain and discomfort that he had to kneel down for a moment to straighten his back and catch his breath.

When they got to the incline, a further ordeal lay in store, and she taught him how to dispatch his tub quickly. At the top and bottom of an incline, which served all the coal-faces between any two levels in the mine, a pit-boy was posted, with the one above acting as brakeman and the one below as seizer. These scallywags, aged anywhere between twelve and fifteen, were in the habit of shouting to one another in foul language, and if anyone wanted to attract their attention they had to shout even louder and use even coarser language. Then, as soon as there was an empty tub ready to be sent up, the one at the bottom would give the signal, the putter would load her full tub on to the incline, and the weight of it would pull the other tub up once the pit-boy at the top had released the brake. Down in the roadway below, trains of tubs were gradually assembled and then hauled off to the main shaft by horses.

'Hey there, you filthy bastards!' Catherine shouted down the incline, which was entirely enclosed in wood along its hundred-metre length and boomed like a gigantic loudhailer.

The pit-boys must have been having a rest because neither of them replied. On each level the tubs stopped rolling. Eventually the shrill voice of a girl said:

'I expect one of 'em's having it off with La Mouquette!'

Loud rumbles of mirth could be heard, and every putter in the seam was in fits of laughter:

'Who was that?' asked Étienne.

Catherine told him it was young Lydie, a slip of a girl who knew more than she ought and who could put a tub as well as any grown woman, despite her doll-like arms. As for La Mouquette, she was quite capable of having both pit-boys at once.

But then the one at the bottom could be heard shouting up to them to load their tubs. A deputy must have been passing. The tubs began to roll again on all nine levels, and soon all that could be heard were the regular cries of the pit-boys and the snorting breaths of the putters as they reached the incline, steaming like overburdened mares. And whenever a miner encountered one of these girls down on all fours, with her backside in the air and her hips bulging from her boy's breeches, there would be a sudden whiff of animal lust in the air, the scent of male arousal.

After each trip Étienne returned to the stifling atmosphere of the coal-face, to the dull, irregular clunk of the picks and the strained grunts of the hewers as they stubbornly stuck to their task. All four of them had stripped to the waist, and since they were now covered in black grime right up to their caps they were indistinguishable from the loose coal surrounding them. At one point they had to dig Maheu out when he started choking for breath, and they lifted the planks to let the coal roll down on to the roadway floor. Zacharie and Levaque were complaining furiously about the seam and said it was getting hard to work, which meant it would be difficult to make it pay. Chaval turned over and lay on his back for a moment, insulting Étienne, whose presence he now found decidedly irritating.

'Little worm! Hasn't even got the strength of a girl! . . . And make sure you fill that tub! What's the matter with you, then? Don't want to hurt your arms or what? . . . I bloody warn you, I'll have that ten sous off you if you get one of ours rejected!'

Étienne was careful not to reply, being so far only too happy to have found this forced labour and quite ready to acquiesce in the brutal hierarchy of the skilled and the unskilled worker. But he was at the end of his tether: his feet were bleeding, his arms and legs were contorted with horrible cramps, and his upper body seemed to be wrapped in a tight band of iron. Fortunately it was ten o'clock, and the team decided to stop for lunch.

Maheu had a watch with him, though he never bothered to look at it. Down in this starless night he could tell the time to the nearest five minutes. Everyone put their shirts and jackets back on and came down from the coal-face. Now they squatted on their heels, elbows tight against their sides, in the position that is so habitual for miners that they adopt it even when outside the mine, which means they never feel the need of a stone or a beam to sit on. Having each taken out their piece, they solemnly bit into the thick slice of bread and exchanged a desultory word about that morning's work. Catherine, who had remained standing, at length went over to Étienne, who was stretched out across the rails a short distance away from them, leaning his back against the timbering. There was a spot there which was almost dry.

'Aren't you eating?' she asked with her mouth full, her piece in her hand.

Then she remembered that the lad had been wandering about on a dark night without a penny to his name and perhaps even without any food.

'Would you like some of mine?'

And when he refused, swearing to her that he wasn't hungry, his voice trembling from the griping pain in his stomach, she insisted cheerfully:

'Oh well, if it puts you off! . . . But look, I've only eaten out of this side. You can have the other bit.'

Already she had broken the piece in two. Taking his half, he had to stop himself from devouring it in one gulp; and he placed his elbows on his thighs so as to hide his trembling from her. Calmly treating him as simply another fellow-worker, she had just lain down on her front beside him, and with her chin cupped in one hand she was slowly eating her bread with the other. Their two lamps were on the ground between them, lighting them up.

Catherine watched him for a moment in silence. She must have found him good-looking, with his delicate features and black moustache. She had a vague smile on her face, a smile of pleasure.

'So you're a mechanic then, and the railway sacked you? . . . Why was that?'

'Because I hit my boss.'

She was astonished to hear this: it offended her own inbred belief that one should be subordinate and do what one's told.

'To be honest, I'd been drinking,' he continued, 'and when I drink, I just get mad, with myself, with everybody . . . It's a fact. I can't even have two tiny glasses of the stuff without wanting to have a go at someone . . . And then I'm ill for the next couple of days.'

'Then you mustn't drink,' she said in a serious voice.

'Oh, don't worry, I know what I'm like!'

And he shook his head; he hated alcohol with the hatred of one who was the last in a long line of drunks and who suffered in his flesh from this wild, drink-sodden inheritance, to such an extent that the merest drop had become the equivalent of poison for him.

'But it's because of Mother that I'm fed up at being sacked,' he said, having swallowed a mouthful of bread. 'She's not in a good way, and I used to be able to send her a five-franc piece from time to time.'

'Where does your mother live, then?'

'Paris . . . She's a laundry-woman, in the rue de la Goutte d'Or.'[3]

There was a silence. When he thought of these things, a pale gleam flickered across his dark eyes, a brief moment of apprehension at the lesion whose unknown consequences he harboured within his young, healthy body.[4] For a moment he was lost in contemplation of the dark reaches of the mine; and as he sat there, deep beneath the crushing weight of the earth, his mind went back to his childhood, to his mother, when she was still pretty and game for the struggle, to how she'd been abandoned by his father who'd then come back to her after she'd married someone else, and how she'd divided herself between these two men who had both exploited her, and how she'd ended up rolling in the gutter with them, in all the wine and the filth. His childhood . . . he could see the street now, and memories came flooding back: the dirty washing in the middle of the shop, the drinking sessions that made the whole house reek, the slaps across the face that could have broken a person's jaw.

'But now,' he went on slowly, 'there'll be nothing left to give her out of thirty sous . . . She'll die of poverty, for sure.'

He shrugged in resigned despair and took another bite of his piece.

'Do you want a drink?' Catherine asked, uncorking her flask.

'Oh, don't worry, it's coffee, it won't do you any harm . . . You need something to wash that down.'

But he refused: it was bad enough depriving her of half her piece. However, she insisted in a good-natured way and eventually said:

'All right, I'll go first, seeing as you're so polite . . . But now you can't refuse. It'd be rude.'

And she held out her flask. She had hoisted herself on to her knees, and he could see her up close to him in the light of the two lamps. Why had he found her unattractive? Now that she was all black and her face covered in a thin layer of coal-dust, she had a strange charm. Surrounded by the encroaching darkness of this grime, her teeth shone with dazzling whiteness in a mouth that was too large, and her eyes dilated and gleamed with a greenish tinge, like those of a cat. A wisp of reddish hair had escaped from under her cap and was tickling her ear, making her laugh. She no longer looked quite so young, she might even be fourteen.

'Since you insist,' he said, taking a swig and handing her back the flask.

She downed a second mouthful and made him have one too: she wanted them to share, she said. They found it amusing to pass the thin spout of the flask from mouth to mouth. Suddenly he wondered if he shouldn't grab her in his arms and kiss her on the lips. She had thick, pale-pink lips, their colour heightened by the coal-dust, and they tortured him with a growing desire. But he didn't dare, he felt intimidated. In Lille he had only ever been with prostitutes, and of the cheapest kind at that, which meant that he had no idea how one went about things with a young working girl who had not yet left her family.

'You must be about fourteen?' he inquired, taking another bite of his bread.

She was taken aback, almost cross.

'What do you mean "fourteen"? Fifteen, if you please! . . . I know I'm not very big for my age. But girls round here don't grow very fast.'

He continued to question her, and she told him everything, neither brazen nor embarrassed. There was evidently nothing she did not know about the ways of men and women, even though he could sense that she was still physically a virgin, a virgin child who had been prevented from maturing into full womanhood by the poor air and state of exhaustion in which she habitually lived. When he returned to the subject of La Mouquette, to try and embarrass her, she told him the most horrendous stories in a perfectly even voice and with considerable relish. Oh, that Mouquette was a one, all right! The things she got up to! And when Étienne asked her if she didn't perhaps have a boyfriend herself, she replied jokingly that while she didn't want to upset her mother, she no doubt one day would. She sat with her shoulders hunched, her teeth chattering a little from the cold on account of her sweat-drenched clothes, and wearing the gentle, resigned expression of one who is ready to submit to all things and all men.

'With everyone living so close together, there's never any shortage of boyfriends, is there?' Étienne continued.

'That's true.'

'And anyway, it doesn't do anyone any harm . . . Just best not to tell the priest, that's all.'

'Oh, the priest! I don't care about him! . . . But there's the Black Man.'

'What do you mean, the "Black Man"?'

'The old miner who haunts the pit and strangles girls who've been bad.'

He looked at her, fearing that she might be having him on.

'You don't believe that rubbish, do you? Didn't they teach you anything?'

'Of course they did. I can read and write, I'll have you know . . . Which is useful in our house, cos in Mother and Father's day you didn't learn such things.'

She really was very nice: once she had finished eating, he would take her in his arms and kiss those plump, pink lips. It was the resolve of a shy man, and the prospect of this direct approach prevented him from being able to speak further. These boyish clothes, this jacket and trousers on a young girl's flesh, excited and disturbed him. He had by now swallowed the last of his bread. He drank from the flask and handed it back for her to finish it. The moment for decisive action had arrived, and he was just casting a nervous glance in the direction of the other miners further along the tunnel when a large shadow blocked his view.

For some moments Chaval had been standing watching them from a distance. He came forward and, making sure that Maheu couldn't see him, grabbed Catherine by the shoulders where she sat, pulled her head back and pressed a brutal kiss down on to her lips, matter-of-factly and seemingly unaware of Étienne's presence. This kiss constituted an act of taking possession, and a decision born of jealousy.

Catherine, meanwhile, had sought to resist.

'Leave me alone, do you hear?'

He was holding her head and staring into her eyes. His red moustache and small pointed beard were like blazing fires in the blackness of his face, and his large nose had the look of an eagle's beak. Finally he let go of her and departed without a word.

Étienne's blood ran cold. How stupid to have waited. And now, of course, he simply couldn't kiss her, in case she thought he was simply trying to imitate Chaval. His pride was wounded, and he felt even a sense of despair.

'Why did you lie to me?' he whispered to her. 'So *he*'s your boyfriend.'

'No, he's not, I swear to you!' she cried. 'There's nothing like that between us. Sometimes he fools around but . . . And anyway he doesn't even come from round here. He arrived from the Pas-de-Calais[5] six months ago.'

They had both got to their feet: work was about to resume. When she saw how distant Étienne had become, it seemed to upset her. She must have found him more attractive than the other man, might even have preferred him. She cast about desperately for some means of showing him kindness, in order to make it up to him; and while Étienne stared in astonishment at his lamp, in which the flame was now blue and encircled by a broad ring of pale light, she tried at least to take his mind off what had happened.

'Come, let me show you something,' she murmured in a friendly way.

She led him to the end of the coal-face where she pointed to a crevice. A gentle bubbling noise could be heard coming from it, the tiniest of sounds, like the peep of a bird.

'Put your hand there. Can you feel the draught . . . ? That's firedamp.'

He was surprised. So that's all it was? This was the terrible thing that could blow them all up? She laughed and said there must be a lot of it in the air that day since the lamps were burning so blue.

'When you two layabouts have quite finished your chat!' Maheu shouted roughly.

Catherine and Étienne hurried to fill their tubs and push them towards the incline, their backs braced as they crawled along the road beneath the bumpy roof. By the second trip they were already bathed in sweat and their bones were cracking once more.

At the coal-face the men had returned to work. They often cut their break-time short like this, so as not to get cold; but their meal, devoured with mute voracity far from the sunlight, sat like lead on their stomachs. Stretched out on their sides, they were now tapping away harder than ever in their single-minded determination to fill a decent number of tubs. They became oblivious to all else as they gave themselves up to this furious pursuit of a reward so dearly won. They ceased to notice the water streaming down and causing their limbs to swell, or the cramps brought on by being stuck in awkward positions, or the suffocating darkness that was making them go pale like vegetables in a cellar. As the day wore on, the atmosphere became even more poisonous and the air grew hotter and hotter with the fumes from their lamps, and the foulness of their breath, and the asphyxiating firedamp, which clung to their eyes like cobwebs and which would clear only when the mine was venti-lated during the night. But despite it all, buried like moles beneath the crushing weight of the earth, and without a breath of fresh air in their burning lungs, they simply went on tapping.

V

Without looking at his watch, which was still in his jacket, Maheu stopped and said:

'Nearly one o'clock . . . Have you finished, Zacharie?'

Zacharie had been timbering for a while, but then he had stopped in the middle of the job and lain back gazing into space and remembering the games of *crosse*[1] he had played the previous day. He roused himself and replied:

'Yes, that'll do for now. We can check again tomorrow.'

He returned to his place at the coal-face, where Levaque and Chaval also downed tools. It was time for a break. They wiped their faces on their bare arms and looked up at the rock above them and the crazed surface of the shale. Work was almost all they ever talked about.

'Typical,' muttered Chaval. 'Just our luck to hit loose earth . . . They don't take account of that, do they, when they fix the rates?'

'Bastards,' grumbled Levaque. 'They want to bloody bury us alive.'

Zacharie began to laugh. He didn't give a damn about their work or anything else for that matter, but he liked to hear people having a go at the Company. Maheu pointed out in his quiet way that the nature of the terrain changed every twenty metres and that, to be fair, it was impossible to say in advance what sort they might find. Then, as the other two men continued to sound off about the bosses, he began to glance round uneasily:

'Shh! That's enough of that!'

'You're right,' said Levaque, also lowering his voice. 'Walls have ears.'

Even at this depth they were obsessed about the possibility of informers, almost as if the coal in the seam might actually hear them and tell the shareholders.

'All the same,' Chaval added defiantly at the top of his voice, 'if that pig Dansaert speaks to me again the way he did the other day, I'll bloody throw a brick at him . . . I mean, it's not as if I was trying to keep him from all those luscious blondes of his.'

This had Zacharie in fits. The overman's affair with Pierron's wife was a standing joke throughout the pit. Even Catherine, leaning on her shovel at the foot of the coal-face, was shaking with laughter as she briefly put Étienne in the picture. Maheu, meanwhile, was getting angry and no longer sought to conceal his anxieties:

'Hold your damned tongue, will you? . . . If it's trouble you're after, then wait till you're on your own.'

He was still talking when they heard the sound of footsteps in the roadway above them. Almost immediately young Négrel – as the miners called him among themselves – appeared at the top of the coal-face accompanied by Dansaert, the overman.

'What did I tell you!' Maheu muttered under his breath. 'There's always one of them about the place, appearing out of nowhere.'

Paul Négrel, the nephew of M. Hennebeau, was a young man of twenty-six, slim and good-looking, with curly hair and a brown moustache. His pointed nose and sharp eyes gave him the look of an amiable ferret, an intelligent, sceptical air which became one of curt authority when he was dealing with the workers. He dressed like them and was, as they were, smeared with coal; and in order to command their respect he demonstrated an almost foolhardy courage, negotiating the most awkward spots in the mine, always the first on the scene when there was a rock-fall or a firedamp explosion.

'Here we are at last. Am I right, Dansaert?' he asked.

The overman, a Belgian with a podgy face and a large, sensual nose, replied with exaggerated politeness:

'Yes, Monsieur Négrel, this is the man we took on this morning.'

They both slithered their way halfway down the coal-face, and Étienne was asked to climb up to them. The engineer raised his lamp to take a look but did not question him.

'All right,' he said finally. 'It's just that I don't like the idea of taking complete strangers in off the street, that's all . . . So make sure this doesn't happen again.'

He paid no heed to the various arguments that were put to him, about the requirements of the job and the wish to have men rather than women putting the tubs. As the hewers were taking up their picks again, he had begun to examine the roof. All at once he shouted:

'What the hell's going on, Maheu? Don't you give a damn what anyone says? . . . You'll all be buried alive, for God's sake.'

'Oh, it's solid enough,' Maheu replied calmly.

'What do you mean "solid"? . . . But the rock's already sagging, and the way you're putting the props in every two metres, anyone would think you'd rather not bother! Ah, you're all the same, you lot. You'd rather have your skulls crushed to smithereens than leave the seam for a single second and spend the necessary time on timbering! . . . Kindly shore that up at once. And with twice the number of props. Do you understand?'

When he saw that the miners were going to be uncooperative and start arguing the point, claiming that they were perfectly good judges of what safety measures were necessary, he let fly:

'Look here! When you all get your skulls smashed in, it's not you that's going to have to answer for the consequences, is it? Of course not. It's the Company that'll have to fork out for pensions for you or your wives . . . I've told you before and I'll tell you again. We know what you're like. For the sake of two more tubs a day you'd all rather get yourselves killed.'

Despite his growing anger Maheu still managed to say evenly:

'If we were properly paid, we'd do better timbering.'

The engineer shrugged but made no reply. He had now reached the bottom of the coal-face and simply called up to them:

'You have one hour left. You'd better all help. And I'm fining this team three francs.'

There was much muttering and grumbling among the miners at this. Only their sense of hierarchy held them in check, the quasi-military hierarchy from overman down to pit-boy, which made them each subordinate to the person above. Nevertheless Chaval and Levaque both made an angry gesture while Maheu tried to calm them with a look. Zacharie simply shrugged his shoulders in dismissive mockery. But of all of them Étienne was perhaps the most outraged. Ever since he had found himself down in this hell-hole, the spirit of resistance had gradually been growing within him. He looked at Catherine and saw her resigned air, as she bent to the yoke. Was it possible that people could work themselves to death at such terrible labour, down here in this mortal darkness, and still not earn even enough for their daily bread?

Négrel, meanwhile, was departing with Dansaert, who had been content to keep nodding his approval. Once more their raised voices could be heard; they had stopped again and were inspecting the timbering along the roadway where the hewers were responsible for the maintenance along the first ten metres back from the coal-face.

'I told you, they simply don't give a damn!' the engineer shouted. 'And what the bloody hell have you been doing? Aren't you supposed to supervise them?'

'Yes, yes, of course,' stammered the overman. 'But I might as well talk to a brick wall –'

'Maheu! Maheu!' Négrel bellowed.

They all came down, and he continued:

'Look at it. Do you really think that's going to hold? . . . It's completely botched. Look at that cross-timber there, the uprights aren't even supporting it any more. And all because the whole thing was done in such a hurry. It's obvious . . . God! No wonder the timbering's costing us so much. Just as long as everything holds firm while you're responsible, isn't that it? And then it all collapses and the Company has to bring in an army of men to fix it . . . Just look over there! It's a total mess!'

Chaval was about to speak, but Négrel cut him short.

'No, don't bother, I know what you're going to say. Why don't we pay you more, eh? Well, I can tell you now, you'll leave management with no alternative. Yes, we'll have to pay you separately for the timbering, and we'll reduce the rate for a tub accordingly. Then we'll soon see if you're better off . . . In the meantime, replace those props immediately. I'll be back tomorrow to check.'

And off he went, leaving them in silent shock at his threat. Dansaert, so humble in Négrel's presence, remained behind for a few moments and spoke to them in no uncertain terms:

'You'll bloody get me into trouble, you lot . . . I warn you now. You'll get more than a three-franc fine from me, I can tell you.'

After he had gone, it was Maheu's turn to explode:

'God damn it! It's simply not fair. I'm all for remaining calm, because that's the only way to get anywhere, but in the end they just drive you mad! . . . Did you hear what he said? A reduced rate for the tubs and the timbering paid separately! It's just another way of paying us less! . . . Lord God Almighty!'

He looked round for someone to take his anger out on and caught sight of Catherine and Étienne standing there idly.

'Just get me some props, will you? As if you bloody care anyway! . . . Hurry up, or you'll feel my foot you know where.'

As he went to fetch some, Étienne felt no resentment at this rough treatment and was so angry with the bosses himself that he thought the miners were being much too easygoing.

Levaque and Chaval for their part had vented their fury in a string of oaths, and all of them, including Zacharie, were now timbering away like men possessed. For almost half an hour all that could be heard was the creaking of wooden props being sledge-hammered into position. Breathing heavily with their mouths now firmly shut, the men waged their desperate battle against the rock, which, had they been able, they would have raised or shoved to one side with a simple heave of the shoulder.

'That'll do!' Maheu said finally, spent from anger and exhaustion. 'Half past one . . . Huh! Some day's work! We'll not make fifty sous! . . . Well, I'm off, I've had quite enough.'

Although there was still half an hour to go, he put his clothes back on. The others did likewise. It made them angry now just to look at the coal-face. Catherine had gone back to rolling her tub, and they had to call her, irritated by her zeal: the coal could remove itself for all they cared. And so the six of them departed, with their tools under their arms, and walked the two kilometres back to the shaft by the route they had followed that morning.

Inside the chimney Catherine and Étienne lingered for a moment as the four hewers slid down to the bottom. They had chanced on little Lydie, who had stopped in the middle of her road to let them pass and was now telling them how La Mouquette had been absent for an hour after having such a bad nose-bleed that she'd had to go off to wash her face. After they had gone, the child, exhausted and covered in grime, returned to pushing her tub, straining forward with her matchstick arms and legs like some thin black ant struggling with a load that is too big for it. Meanwhile Catherine and Étienne slithered down the chimney on their backs, pressing their shoulders flat so as not to graze their foreheads; and such was the speed of their descent down the rock-face, worn smooth by every backside in the mine, that from time to time they had to catch on to the timbering to slow themselves – so their bums didn't catch fire, they jokingly said.

Down at the bottom they found themselves alone. In the distance red stars were disappearing round a bend in the road-way. Their merriment ceased and they began to walk, with a heavy, tired tread, Catherine in front, Étienne behind. The lamps were smoking and he could barely see her through the foggy haze. It disturbed him to know that Catherine was a girl because he felt he was stupid not to kiss her and to let the memory of Chaval having done so prevent him. But there could be no doubt that she had lied to him: that man was her lover, they must be at it all the time on every available spoil-heap, for she already knew how to swing her hips like a slut. He sulked, quite without reason, as if she had been unfaithful to him. She, on the other hand, kept turning round to warn him about obstacles in his path, as though encouraging him to be more friendly. They were completely lost, they could have had such fun together! But eventually they came out into the main haulage roadway. Étienne felt released from his agony of indecision, while Catherine gave him one last look of sadness, full of regret for a moment of happiness that might never come their way again.

They now found themselves surrounded by the commotion of life underground, as deputies passed at regular intervals and tub-trains came and went, hauled along at the trot by the horses. An endless succession of Davy lamps pricked the darkness. They had to press themselves against the rock to let the shadowy presences of man and beast go past, feeling their breath on their faces as they did so. Jeanlin, running barefoot behind his train, yelled some piece of wickedness at them, but it was lost amid the rumble of the wheels. On they went, she now silent, he unable to recognize a single fork or junction from that morning's journey and imagining that she was leading him further and further astray beneath the earth. What ailed him most was the cold: it had felt increasingly chilly ever since they had left the coal-face, and the closer they came to the shaft, the more he shivered. Once again the air being funnelled between the narrow walls was blowing like a gale. They were beginning to despair of ever reaching the shaft when suddenly they found themselves at pit-bottom.

Chaval looked at them askance, his lips pursed in suspicion. The others, similarly silent, were standing there sweating in the icy draughts and busy trying to swallow their sense of grievance. They had arrived too early and were not being allowed up for another half-hour, especially as some elaborate operation was under way to bring down a horse. The onsetters were still loading tubs into the cages, with a deafening noise of clanking metal, and the cages would vanish up into the driving rain falling from the black hole. Down below, the *bougnou* – a sump ten metres deep where all the water gathered – gave off its own slimy dampness. Men were milling about constantly in the vicinity of the shaft, pulling signal-ropes, pressing levers, their clothes drenched by the spray. The reddish glow from the three open lamps cast huge moving shadows and lent this underground chamber the air of a robbers' den, like a bandit forge beside a mountain stream.

Maheu made one last attempt. He approached Pierron, who had begun his shift at six, and said:

'Come on, surely you could let us go up?'

But the onsetter, a handsome fellow with strong limbs and a gentle face, refused with a gesture of alarm:

'I just can't. Ask the deputy . . . I'd get fined.'

There was further muttering. Catherine leaned over and whispered in Étienne's ear:

'Come and see the stable. It's nice and warm in there.'

And they had to slip away without being seen, because it was forbidden to go in there. The stable was situated on the left, at the end of a short roadway. Hollowed out of the rock and measuring twenty-five metres long by four metres high, it had a vaulted brick ceiling and could accommodate twenty horses. It was indeed nice and cosy in there, warm with the heat of living animals and smelling sweetly of fresh, clean straw. The one single lamp shone steadily like a nightlight. The horses resting there turned to look, with wide, childlike eyes, and then went back to munching their oats, unhurriedly, the picture of well-fed workers whom everybody loves.

But as Catherine was reading out the names on the metal labels above the mangers, she gave a little cry when a human form suddenly rose up in front of her. It was La Mouquette emerging startled from the pile of straw where she had been sleeping. On Mondays, when she was too tired to work after her exertions on Sunday, she would give herself a punch on the nose, leave the coal-face on the pretext that she needed to bathe it, and then come here and snuggle down with the animals in their warm bedding. Her father, who had a very soft spot for her, would let her be, at the risk of getting into trouble.

And at that very moment old Mouque walked in. He was a short, bald man, battered-looking but still with plenty of flesh on him, which was unusual for an ex-miner who had turned fifty. Ever since he had been put in charge of the horses, he had taken to chewing tobacco so much that his gums bled and his mouth was all black. When he saw the pair of them with his daughter, he was furious.

'What the hell are you all doing in here? Come on, out you go! Little trollops, bringing a man in here like this! . . . And using my nice, clean straw for your dirty deeds!'

La Mouquette thought this hilarious and laughed helplessly. But Étienne was embarrassed and left, while Catherine simply gave him a smile. Just as the three of them were making their way back to pit-bottom, Bébert and Jeanlin also arrived on the scene, bringing a tub-train. There was a pause as the tubs were loaded into the cage, and Catherine went up to their horse and stroked it as she told her companion all about him. This was Battle, a white horse with ten years' service[2] and something of an elder statesman. He had spent the ten years down the mine, occupying the same corner of the stable and doing the same job every day up and down the roadways; and not once in that time had he seen daylight. Very fat, with a gleaming coat and a good-natured air, he seemed to be living the life of a sage, sheltered from the misfortunes of the world above. Moreover, down here in the darkness, he had become very crafty. The roadway in which he worked had now grown so familiar to him that he could push the ventilation doors open with his head, and he knew where to stoop and avoid getting bumped at the places where the roof was too low. He must have counted his journeys too because when he had completed the regulation number, he flatly refused to start another and had to be led back to his manger. Old age was now approaching, and his cat-like eyes sometimes clouded over with a look of sadness. Perhaps he could dimly remember the mill where he had been born, near Marchiennes, on the banks of the Scarpe, a mill surrounded by broad expanses of greenery and constantly swept by the wind. There had been something else, too, something burning away up in the air, some huge lamp or other, but his animal memory could not quite recall its exact nature. And he would stand there unsteadily on his old legs, head bowed, vainly trying to remember the sun.

Meanwhile the operation was continuing in the shaft. The signal-hammer had struck four times and they were bringing the horse down, which was always an anxious moment because occasionally the animal would be so terrified that it would be dead on arrival. Up on the surface it would struggle wildly as they wrapped it in a net; then, as soon as it felt the ground vanish from under its feet, it would go quite still, petrified with fear, and disappear from view, its eyes wide and staring, without so much as a quiver along its coat. This particular horse had been too big to fit between the cage guides, and when they had hooked its net below the cage they had been obliged to tie its head back against its flanks. The descent took nearly three minutes, as they had to slow the winding-engine for safety's sake. The tension mounted, therefore, as they waited for it below. What was happening? Surely they weren't going to leave him there dangling in the dark? Finally he appeared, as motionless as stone, his staring eyes dilated with terror. It was a bay, hardly three years old, called Trumpet.

'Mind out, mind out!' shouted old Mouque, whose job it was to receive him. 'Bring him over here. No, don't untie him yet.'

Soon Trumpet was lying in a heap on the cast-iron floor. He did not stir, seemingly still caught up in the nightmare of the dark, bottomless hole and this noisy chamber deep beneath the earth. They were beginning to untie him when Battle, who had just been unharnessed, came over and stretched out his neck to sniff this new companion who had dropped from the earth above. The workers made a circle round them and began to joke. Mmm, now then, what lovely smell was that? But Battle was becoming more excited, impervious to their mockery. He must have caught the scent of good fresh air and the long-forgotten smell of sun-drenched grass. And suddenly he gave a loud whinny, a song of gladness that could also have been a sob of tender pity. This was his way of welcoming a newcomer: with joy at the fragrant reminder of former days and with sadness at the sight of yet another prisoner who would never return to the surface alive.

'Come and look at Battle!' the workers called to each other, entertained by the antics of their old favourite. 'He's having a chat with his new comrade!'

Now untied, Trumpet still did not move. He continued to lie on his side, garrotted by fear, as if he could still feel the net tightening round him. Eventually they got him to his feet with the flick of a whip, and he stood there dazed, his legs quivering. And as old Mouque led them away, the two horses pursued their fraternal acquaintance.

'Well? Now can we go up?' Maheu inquired.

The cages had to be emptied first, and in any case there were still ten minutes to go before it was time for the ascent. Gradually the coal-faces were emptying, and all the miners were making their way back along the roadways. Some fifty men had already gathered, soaked to the skin and shivering, their lungs a prey to the pneumonia that threatened from every side with every draught of air. Pierron, for all his smooth exterior, slapped his daughter Lydie for leaving the coal-face early. Zacharie slyly pinched La Mouquette – for the warmth, he said. But unrest was growing as Chaval and Levaque spread word of the engineer's threat to lower the rate per tub and pay them separately for timbering; noisy protests greeted the proposal, and the spirit of rebellion began to germinate here in this tiny space some six hundred metres below the surface of the earth. Soon they could contain themselves no longer, and these men who were filthy with coal and frozen stiff from waiting now accused the Company of killing half its workers underground while they let the other half die of starvation. Étienne listened to them, trembling with outrage.

'Hurry up! Hurry up!' the deputy called Richomme kept shouting at the onsetters.

He was trying to hasten preparations for the ascent, not wanting to have to reprimand the men and pretending not to hear them. However, the protests became so loud that he was obliged to intervene. Behind him people were shouting that things couldn't go on like this for ever and that one fine day the whole bloody lot would go up with a bang.

'You're a sensible fellow,' he told Maheu. 'Tell them to be quiet. When you haven't got the fire-power, it's always best to hold your peace.'

But Maheu, who had calmed down and was beginning to grow nervous, was spared having to intervene, for all at once everyone fell silent. Négrel and Dansaert were emerging from one of the roadways on their way back from their inspection, and both were covered in sweat like everyone else. Habit and discipline meant that the men stood back as the engineer walked through the group without a word. He climbed into one tub, the overman into another, and five pulls on the signal-rope followed – for a 'special meat load', as they called it when it was the bosses themselves. And amid the sullen silence the cage vanished upwards into thin air.

VI

In the cage taking him to the surface, squashed into a tub with four other people, Étienne made up his mind to take to the open road once more and continue his hungry search for work. He might as well die straight away as go back down that hell-hole and not even earn enough to live on. Catherine was in a tub higher up, so he could not now feel that lovely, soothing warmth against his body. Anyway he would rather not start getting any silly ideas. It was much better he left. He'd had more of an education than the rest of them, which meant he didn't share their herd-like sense of resignation, and he'd only end up strangling the life out of one boss or another.

Suddenly he was blinded. The ascent had been so swift that he was left stunned by the daylight, and his eyelids quivered in the brightness to which he had already grown so unaccustomed. But it was a relief all the same to feel the cage lock into its keeps. A banksman opened the gate, and a stream of workmen poured out of the tubs.

'Hey, Mouquet,' Zacharie whispered in the banksman's ear. 'Are we off to the Volcano tonight?'

The Volcano was a café in Montsou which offered musical entertainments. Mouquet winked with his left eye, and a broad grin spread across his face. Short and stocky like his father, he had the cheeky look of a fun-loving lad who grabs what's going without a thought for the morrow. La Mouquette was just then coming out of the cage, and he gave her an enormous whack across the bottom as a mark of brotherly affection.

Étienne hardly recognized the tall nave of the pit-head, which had previously seemed so sinister in the eerie, flickering light of the lanterns. Now it just looked bare and dirty. A grubby light filtered through the dusty windows. The one exception, at the far end, was the winding-engine with all its gleaming brasswork; otherwise the greasy steel cables flew up and down like ribbons that had been steeped in ink, while the pulleys up above in their enormous iron framework, the cages and the tubs, the whole prodigal array of metal, made the place seem dingy by lending it the harsh grey tones of old scrap. The sheets of cast-iron flooring shook beneath the ceaseless rumble of the wheels, and from the coal in the tubs rose a fine dust which turned everything black, the floor, the walls, even the beams high up in the headgear.

Meanwhile Chaval had gone to find out how many tokens had been marked up for them on the board in the checkweighman's little glass-fronted office, and he came back furious. He had seen that two of their tubs had been refused, one because it hadn't contained the regulation amount of coal, the other because some of the coal had been dirty.

'The perfect end to a perfect day!' he fumed. 'Another twenty sous docked! . . . But of course we have to take on bloody layabouts who don't know their arse from their elbow.'

He shot a meaningful glance at Étienne, who was tempted to reply with his fists. But why bother, he thought, if he was leaving? In fact this decided the matter for him.

'The first day's always difficult,' Maheu said diplomatically. 'He'll manage it better tomorrow.'

No one was placated, and in their bitterness they were all still spoiling for a fight. As they were leaving their lamps in the lamp-room, Levaque had an altercation with the lamp-man, accusing him of not having cleaned his lamp properly for him. They only began to calm down a little when they reached the changing-room, where the fire was still burning. In fact somebody must have stoked it too much because the stove was red hot and casting blood-red reflections on to the wall, which made it seem as though the vast windowless room were ablaze. There were grunts of pleasure as backs were toasted from a distance, steaming like bowls of soup. Once the back was done, it was time for the front. La Mouquette had calmly pulled her breeches down to dry her shirt. Some boys were making fun of her, and there was a burst of laughter when she suddenly showed them her bottom, which for her was the ultimate expression of contempt.

'I'm off,' said Chaval, who had put his tools away in his locker.

Nobody moved. Only La Mouquette hurried after him, on the pretext that they were both heading in the direction of Montsou. But the joking continued, for everyone knew he didn't fancy her any more.

Meanwhile Catherine's thoughts had been elsewhere, and she had just whispered something to her father. He looked surprised, and then nodded with approval. He called Étienne over to give him back his bundle and muttered softly:

'Look, if you haven't got any money, you'll not last the fortnight . . . So if you want, I could try and get someone to sell you things on credit?'

For a moment Étienne was not sure how to respond. He had simply been going to ask for his thirty sous and then leave. But he felt ashamed to do so in front of the girl. She was staring at him, she might think he was work-shy.

'I'm not promising, mind,' Maheu went on. 'But there's no harm in asking.'

So Étienne offered no objection. People would refuse. Anyway, it didn't put him under any obligation, he could always leave after he'd had something to eat. But then he was cross with himself for not saying no when he saw how delighted Catherine was, with her pretty laugh and that look of friendship and happiness at having been able to come to his assistance. For where was the future in it?

Once they had collected their clogs and shut their lockers, the Maheus left the changing-room and followed their comrades, who were departing one by one after they had warmed themselves. Étienne went with them, while Levaque and his young lad also joined the group. But as they were passing through the screening-shed, a violent scene stopped them in their tracks.

They were in a vast shed, with beams blackened by flying coal-dust and large shutters that let in a constant draught. The tubs of coal came here directly from the pit-head and were then emptied out by tipplers on to the screens, which were long chutes made of sheet-metal. To the right and left of these chutes, the women and girls who did the screening stood on tiered steps equipped with a rake and shovel; they would rake in the stones and push the clean coal along so that it fell through funnels down into the railway wagons standing on the line beneath the shed.

Philomène Levaque was one of them, a thin, pale-looking girl with the sheeplike face of a consumptive. Her head was covered by a scrap of blue woollen scarf, and her hands and arms were black up to her elbows. She was working on the next step down from La Pierronne's mother, whom everyone called La Brûlé, an old witch of a woman who was terrifying to look at, with screech-owl eyes and a mouth as pinched as a miser's purse. The

pair of them were at each other's throats, with the younger of
the two accusing the older of raking away her stones so that it
was taking her more than ten minutes to fill one basket. They
were paid by the basket, so there were endless fights of this kind.
Pins would fly, buns would tumble and red faces would bear
the mark of black hands.

'Go on, give her one!' Zacharie shouted down to his girlfriend.

All the screeners burst out laughing.

But La Brûlé rounded on him and snarled:

'As for you, you dirty bastard! You'd do better to own up to
those two kids you gave her! . . . Did you ever hear the like! And
her a poor slip of a thing, just eighteen and barely able to stand
on her own two feet!'

Maheu had to stop his son from going down there and then
and, as Zacharie put it, seeing what the old bag was made of.
But a supervisor was coming, and rakes began rummaging in
the coal again. All that could be seen now, down the whole
length of the chute, were the women's rounded backs as they
competed desperately for each other's stones.

Outside the wind had suddenly dropped, and damp, cold air
was falling from a grey sky. The colliers hunched their shoulders,
folded their arms across their chests and departed, in ones and
twos, walking along with a roll of the hips that made their thick
bones stick out under their thin clothing. As they passed by in
the broad daylight they looked like a band of negroes who had
been knocked flat in the mud. A few had not finished their piece,
and as they brought the remains of it home wedged between
shirt and jacket, they had the air of hunchbacks.

'Look, there's Bouteloup,' Zacharie said with a snigger.

Without stopping, Levaque exchanged a few words with his
lodger, a big, dark-haired fellow of thirty-five with a placid,
honest expression.

'Soup ready, Louis?'

'Yes, I think so.'

'So the wife's in a good mood today?'

'Yes, I'd say so.'

Other stonemen were arriving, and successive groups of them
gradually disappeared into the pit one by one. This was the

three o'clock shift, yet more men for the mine to devour as new teams went down to replace the hewers at their coal-faces at the end of each roadway. The mine never lay idle: night and day human insects were always down there burrowing into the rock six hundred metres beneath the fields of beet.

Meanwhile the youngsters walked on ahead. Jeanlin was letting Bébert into the secret of a complicated scheme for obtaining four sous' worth of tobacco on credit, while Lydie followed respectfully at a distance. Then came Catherine with Zacharie and Étienne. Nobody spoke. It was only when they got to the public house called the Advantage that Maheu and Levaque finally caught up with them.

'Here we are,' Maheu said to Étienne. 'Are you coming in?'

They split up. Catherine had paused for a moment and took one last look at the young man, her big eyes as limpidly green as a mountain spring and of a crystal clarity made all the deeper by the surrounding blackness of her face. She smiled and then departed with the others along the road that led up to the miners' village.

The public house stood at the crossroads midway between the village and the pit. It was a two-storey house of whitewashed brick, and each of its windows was framed by a gaily painted border of sky blue. On a square sign nailed above the front door it read in yellow lettering: *The Advantage – Licensee: M. Rasseneur*. Behind the house was a skittle-alley enclosed by a hedge. For the Company, which had done everything in its power to buy up this tiny enclave at the heart of its own vast domains, it was a matter of much regret that a public house should have sprung up in the middle of the beetfields right next to the entrance to Le Voreux.

'Come on in,' Maheu insisted.

The room was small, bare and bright: its walls were white, and it contained three tables, twelve chairs and a pinewood counter no bigger than a kitchen dresser. There were some ten beer glasses on it at most, as well as three bottles of liqueurs, a jug and a small zinc chest with a tin tap, which contained the beer; and that was all, no pictures, no shelves, no games. In a gleaming, highly polished fireplace of cast-iron a mound of coal-slack was burning gently. On the flagstone floor a thin layer of white sand absorbed the dampness that was a constant feature of this rain-soaked region.

'Give us a beer,'[1] Maheu called to a plump, blonde-haired girl, a neighbour's daughter who sometimes minded the bar. 'Is Rasseneur about?'

The girl turned the tap and replied that the landlord would be back shortly. Slowly Maheu drained half the glass in one go to remove the dust clogging his throat. He did not offer his companion a drink. One other customer, a wet, dirty miner like himself, was sitting at a table and drinking his beer in silence, deep in thought. A third man came in, beckoned to be served, paid and left, all without saying a word.

But then a large man of thirty-eight appeared, with a round, clean-shaven face and an easy smile. This was Rasseneur, a one-time hewer who had been dismissed by the Company three years previously following a strike. He had been an excellent worker, and he was articulate, always taking the lead when it came to protesting and eventually ending up as the leader of the malcontents. His wife already ran a beer-shop, as did many miners' wives; and when he found himself out on his ear, he became a full-time landlord, scraped together some money, and set up in business directly opposite Le Voreux as an act of provocation towards the Company. The business was prospering now: his bar had become something of a meeting-place, and this allowed him to cash in on the anger he had been gradually inciting in the hearts of his erstwhile comrades.

'This is the lad I took on this morning,' Maheu explained at once. 'Is either of your rooms free? And could you let him have things on tick for the first fortnight?'

A sudden look of deep distrust passed over Rasseneur's broad features. He glanced at Étienne and replied, without even bothering to look sorry:

'Both my rooms are taken. I can't help you.'

Étienne was expecting this refusal, but it hurt him all the same, and he was surprised suddenly to feel disappointed at the prospect of leaving. No matter. Leave he would, as soon as he had his thirty sous. The miner who had been drinking at another

table had now departed. Others came in, one by one, to clear
the grime from their throats before setting off once more with
the same rolling gait. It was like a mere ablution, bringing
neither joy nor stimulus, only the mute satisfaction of a need.

'So. Nothing to report, then?' Rasseneur inquired in a meaningful way as Maheu sipped what was left of his beer.

Maheu looked around him and, seeing only Étienne, said:

'Only that there's been another bloody row . . . Yeah, about
the timbering.'

He related what had happened. The blood had rushed to
Rasseneur's face, which seemed to swell as burning excitement
blazed in his eyes and cheeks.

'Well, now! The minute they decide to cut the rate, they're
sunk.'

The presence of Étienne made him uneasy. Nevertheless he
continued, watching him out of the corner of his eye as he did
so. He spoke obliquely, leaving certain things unsaid. Without
naming them he talked about the manager, Monsieur Hennebeau, and his wife, and his nephew, young Négrel, and he said
how things could not go on like this, how one fine morning the
lid would blow off. The poverty and suffering had spread too
far, and he alluded to all the factories that were closing down
and all the workers that were being laid off. He'd been giving
away over six pounds of bread a day for the past month.
Only yesterday he'd heard that Monsieur Deneulin, a local
mine-owner, doubted whether he could survive. What's more
he'd just received a letter from Lille full of worrying news.

'You know,' he muttered under his breath, 'from that person
you met here one evening.'

But he was interrupted. His wife now appeared, a tall, thin,
intense woman with a long nose and purple cheeks. When it
came to politics, she was much more radical than her husband.

'You mean the letter from Pluchart,' she said. 'Ah now, if he
were in charge, we'd soon see some improvements round the
place.'

Étienne had been listening for some time. He understood fully
what was being said, and he was becoming increasingly excited
by all this talk of poverty and revenge.

Hearing this name suddenly blurted out like that gave him a start.

'I know Pluchart,' he said out loud, as though having not quite meant to.

All eyes were upon him, and so he was obliged to add:

'Yes, I'm a mechanic, and he was my foreman at Lille . . . A very capable man. I often used to have chats with him.'

Rasseneur studied him again; his expression rapidly changed, and at once he became friendly. Eventually he said to his wife:

'Maheu's brought along Monsieur here, who's one of his putters. He wondered if we had a room for him and could give him a fortnight's credit.'

The matter was then settled in a moment. One room was in fact free, the occupant had left that morning. Now thoroughly roused, Rasseneur warmed to his theme and kept saying that he was only asking the bosses for what was possible,[2] that he wasn't like all the others who demanded things that were too difficult to achieve. His wife shrugged: they should insist on their rights, no more, no less.

'Good night. I'm off,' Maheu broke in. 'None of that's going to stop people working down the pit, and as long as they do there'll be those that die of it . . . Look at you, for example. You've been as fit as a fiddle ever since you left three years ago.'

'It's true. I do feel a lot better,' declared Rasseneur complacently.

Étienne walked to the door to thank Maheu as he left; but the latter simply nodded silently, and the young man watched him trudge back up the road to the village. Mme Rasseneur was serving customers and asked him to wait a moment so that she could take him to his room where he could get cleaned up. Should he stay? He was having doubts again, a sinking feeling that made him look back fondly on the freedom and fresh air of the open road where the pain of hunger was mixed with the joy of being one's own boss. He felt as though he had already been living there for years, from the moment of his arrival on the spoil-heap in the middle of a howling gale to the hours spent underground lying flat on his belly in those black roads. He was loath to go down again: it was unjust and the work was too hard, and his pride as a human being revolted at the thought of being treated like some animal that can be blinded and crushed.

As Étienne was debating what to do, his eyes wandered over the immense plain and gradually began to take in what they saw. He was surprised, he hadn't pictured a panorama like this when old Bonnemort had gestured towards it in the darkness. In front of him, certainly, he again saw Le Voreux, tucked away in a hollow with its buildings of brick and timber, its pitch-covered screening-shed, the headgear with its slate roof, the winding-house and the tall, pale-red chimney, all squatting there with a malevolent air. But the pit-yard spread out much further around the buildings than he had imagined, seemingly transformed into a pool of ink by the lapping waves of stockpiled coal. It was bristling with the tall trestles that carried the overhead rails, and at one end it was completely taken over by piles of timber, which lay there like the harvest from a forest newly razed to the ground. Over to the right, the view was obstructed by the spoil-heap, which looked like some colossal barricade placed there by giants. The oldest part of it was already covered in grass, while at the other end it was being eaten away by an internal fire, which had been smouldering for a year now and gave off a thick pall of smoke. Long rust-red streaks oozed like blood from its ghost-grey surface of sandstone and shale. Beyond it stretched the fields, endless fields of corn and beet, which were bare at this time of the year, and marshes covered in rough vegetation and punctuated with a few stunted willows, and then the distant meadows divided by thin rows of poplar. In the far distance, tiny patches of white indicated towns, Marchiennes to the north, Montsou to the south; while over to the east the forest of Vandame marked the edge of the horizon with the purple line of its denuded trees. And beneath the wan sky, in the dull light of a winter's afternoon, it seemed as if all the blackness of Le Voreux and its swirling coal-dust had settled on the plain, like powder on the trees, like sand on the roads, like seed upon the earth.

As Étienne continued to gaze, what surprised him most was a canal, which he had not seen during the night. Constructed out of the river Scarpe, this canal ran in a straight line from Le

Voreux to Marchiennes, a ribbon of matt silver some two leagues long. Like an avenue raised above the low-lying ground and lined with trees, it stretched away into the distance in an endless vista of green banks and pale water, of gliding barges and vermilion sterns. Next to the pit was a landing-stage where boats were moored ready to be filled directly from the tubs that ran along the overhead rails. There the canal took a sharp turn before cutting diagonally across the marshes; and this geometrically precise stretch of water seemed to represent the very soul of the empty plain, cutting across it like a major highway and bearing away its iron and coal.

Étienne's gaze travelled from the canal back up to the village, which had been built on a plateau, but he could make out only the red tiles of the roofs. Then it moved back down towards Le Voreux and came to rest at the bottom of the muddy slope, lingering on two enormous piles of bricks which had been cast and baked on site. Here a branch of the Company's railway line passed behind a fence and led into the pit. By now the last batch of stonemen would be going down. A solitary wagon being pushed by some workmen gave a piercing screech. But the darkness and the mystery had gone, and with them the inexplicable rumblings and the sudden flaring of unfamiliar stars. In the distance the tall blast-furnaces and the coke-ovens had been pale since dawn. All that remained from before was the ceaseless panting of the drainage-pump; but as he listened to the long, deep gasps of the ogre whose hunger could never be satisfied, this time he could see the grey steam rising.

Then, suddenly, Étienne made up his mind. Perhaps he imagined he'd caught another glimpse of Catherine's bright eyes, up there at the entry to the village. Or perhaps it was the wind of revolt beginning to blow from the direction of Le Voreux. He could not tell. He simply wanted to go down the mine again, to suffer and to struggle; and he thought angrily of those 'people' Bonnemort had told him about, and of the squat and sated deity to whom ten thousand starving men and women daily offered up their flesh without ever knowing who or what this god might be.

PART II

The Grégoire property, La Piolaine, was to be found two kilometres east of Montsou, on the road to Joiselle. It was a tall,
square house of no particular style, dating from the beginning
of the previous century. Of the vast estates that had originally
belonged to it only some thirty hectares remained, which were
surrounded by walls and easy to maintain. The orchard and
kitchen garden enjoyed especial renown, since their fruit and
vegetables were celebrated as the finest in the region. For the
rest, there was no parkland, but a little wood served in its stead.
The avenue of old limes, a vault of foliage running three hundred
metres from the gate to the front steps, was one of the sights on
this bare and empty plain, where the number of large trees to
be found between Marchiennes and Beaugnies was sufficiently
small to be calculated exactly.

That morning the Grégoires had risen at eight o'clock. Generally they did not stir until one hour later, for they were devoted
to sleep; but the storm during the night had left them too restive.
After her husband had gone out at once to see if the high wind
had caused any damage, Mme Grégoire had simply come down
to the kitchen in her slippers and flannel dressing-gown. She
was short and plump, and although she was already fifty-eight,
she still had a big baby face; and beneath the dazzling whiteness
of her hair she wore an expression of wide-eyed surprise.

'Mélanie,' she said to the cook, 'you might perhaps make that
brioche this morning, since the dough is ready. Mademoiselle
Cécile will not be up for another half-hour yet, and she could
have some with her chocolate . . . It would be a nice surprise for
her, don't you think?'

The cook, a thin, elderly woman who had been with them for
thirty years, began to laugh.

'Yes, indeed, that would be a lovely surprise for her . . . My
stove's burning nicely, and the oven must be warm by now. And
Honorine can give me a hand.'

Honorine was a girl of twenty whom they had taken in as a
child and brought up, and she now worked as a housemaid.

Apart from these two women, the only other servants were the coachman Francis, who did the heavy work, and a gardener and his wife, who looked after the flowers, the fruit and vegetables, and the farmyard animals. And since the household was run on patriarchal lines in a spirit of gentle informality, this small community lived together on the best of terms.

Mme Grégoire, who had planned the brioche surprise while she was lying in bed, now waited to see the dough placed in the oven. The kitchen was huge, and judging by its extreme cleanliness and the great battery of dishes, saucepans and utensils with which it was filled, it was evidently the most important room in the house. It smelled deliciously of good food. The shelves and cupboards were overflowing with provisions.

'And make sure it's nice and golden brown, won't you?' Mme Grégoire reminded them as she departed into the dining-room.

Despite the presence of a central-heating system, which warmed the whole house, a coal fire was burning cheerfully in the grate. Otherwise there was no sign of luxury; just a large table, some chairs and a mahogany sideboard. Two deep armchairs alone bore witness to a desire for comfort and to long hours of tranquil digestion. They never used the drawing-room and preferred to sit here surrounded by cosy domesticity.

M. Grégoire had just returned. He was wearing his thick, fustian jacket, and he looked pink himself for his sixty years, with his strong features and an honest, kindly face wreathed in curls of snowy white hair. He had spoken to the coachman and the gardener; no major damage to report, just one chimney-pot down. Every morning he liked to cast an eye over La Piolaine, which was not large enough to give much cause for concern and yet afforded him all the pleasures of ownership.

'What's the matter with Cécile?' he inquired. 'Isn't she getting up today?'

'I really don't know,' his wife replied. 'I did think I heard her moving about.'

The table had been laid with three bowls on the white tablecloth. Honorine was sent to see what had become of Mademoiselle. But she came back down almost at once, stifling her giggles and lowering her voice as if she were still up in the bedroom.

'Oh, if Monsieur and Madame could only see Mademoiselle now! . . . She's sleeping like . . . oh, just like a little baby Jesus . . . Really, you can't imagine. She looks such a picture!'

Father and mother exchanged affectionate glances.

'Are you coming?' he said with a smile.

'Oh, the poor little darling!' she murmured. 'Yes, I'm coming.'

And together they went upstairs. Cécile's bedroom was the one luxurious room in the house: it had blue silk hangings and white lacquer furniture picked out in blue, the whim of a spoiled child who had been indulged by her parents. Bathed in the half-light coming through a small gap in the curtains, the girl lay sleeping in the shadowy whiteness of the bed, one cheek propped on a bare arm. She was not pretty; she looked too wholesome and full of health for that, being already fully grown at the age of eighteen. But she had wonderful, milk-white skin, as well as chestnut-brown hair, a round face and an obstinate little nose buried between two plump cheeks. The bedcover had slipped down, and her breathing was so gentle that her already ample bosom neither rose nor fell.

'That cursed wind will have kept her awake all night,' her mother said softly.

Father gestured to her to hush. They both leaned over and gazed adoringly at her innocent, unclothed form, at this daughter they had wanted for so long and whom they had conceived when they had ceased to hope. In their eyes she was perfect, not at all too fat, indeed never adequately fed. And she slept on, oblivious to their presence by her side, to their faces next to hers. But a slight tremor ruffled her impassive features. Concerned in case she should wake, they departed on tiptoe.

'Shh!' M. Grégoire said when they reached the door. 'If she hasn't slept, we mustn't disturb her.'

'The poor darling can sleep as long as she likes,' Mme Grégoire concurred. 'We can wait for her.'

They went downstairs and ensconced themselves in the armchairs in the dining-room. Meanwhile the maids were happy to keep the chocolate warm on the stove, entertained by the thought of Mademoiselle having such a long lie-in. M. Grégoire had picked up a newspaper; his wife was knitting a large woollen

bedspread. It was very warm in the room, and not a sound was
to be heard coming from the silent house.

The Grégoire fortune brought in an annual income of some
forty thousand francs[1] and derived entirely from a holding in
the Montsou mines. They loved telling the story of its origins,
which went back to the earliest days of the Company itself.

Towards the beginning of the previous century, from Lille as
far as Valenciennes, there had been a mad rush to discover coal.
The success of the concession-holders who were later to found
the Anzin Mining Company had turned the heads of one and
all. In every district people were busy taking soil samples; companies were set up, and concessions materialized overnight. But
among all the determined pioneers of the day it was the Baron
Desrumaux who was most remembered for his shrewdness and
courage. He had persevered for forty years, never faltering,
overcoming obstacle after obstacle: an initial lack of success
during his early prospecting, the new mines that had to be
abandoned after long months of toil, mine-shafts blocked by
rock-falls, miners drowned by sudden floods, hundreds of thousands of francs draining away down a few holes in the ground;
and then later the problems of managing the business, the panicking shareholders, the tussles with the hereditary landowners
of ancient estates who were determined not to recognize royal
concessions unless people came and negotiated with them first.
Finally he had established Desrumaux, Fauquenoix and Company to exploit the Montsou concession, and the pits were just
beginning to yield meagre returns when the two neighbouring
concessions, the one at Cougny, which belonged to the Comte
de Cougny, and the one at Joiselle, belonging to the Company
of Cornille and Jenard, had almost ruined him with the ferocity
of their competition. Fortunately, on 25 August 1760, a settlement had been reached between the three concessions and they
were amalgamated. The Montsou Mining Company thus came
into being in its present form. To effect a distribution of shares,
the total assets had been divided into twenty-four sous, the
standard currency unit of the day;[2] and each sou was subdivided
into twelve deniers, giving two hundred and eighty-eight deniers;
and since each denier was worth ten thousand francs, the total

capital value represented a sum of nearly three million francs. Desrumaux, near to death but none the less victorious, had received six sous and three deniers as his share.

At that time the Baron owned La Piolaine, together with three hundred hectares of land, and he employed as his steward one Honoré Grégoire, a lad from Picardy, who was the great-grandfather of Léon Grégoire, father of Cécile. At the time of the Montsou settlement, Honoré, who had been hoarding his savings of fifty thousand francs in a stocking, nervously yielded to his master's unswerving conviction. He took out ten thousand francs' worth of beautiful écus and bought a denier, terrified that he was thereby robbing his children of this part of their inheritance. Indeed his son Eugène received extremely small dividends; and since he had set himself up as a bourgeois and been foolish enough to squander the remaining forty thousand francs of his paternal legacy in a disastrous business partnership, he lived in rather reduced circumstances. But the income from the denier was gradually rising, and the family fortune dated from the time of Félicien, who realized the dream that his grandfather, the former steward, had instilled in him as a child: the purchase of La Piolaine, now shorn of its land, which he bought from the State for a derisory sum.[3] Nevertheless, the years that followed were bad ones, and they had to wait for the catastrophic events of the Revolution to run their course and for the rule of Napoleon to meet its bloody end. And so it was Léon Grégoire who benefited, after an astonishing rise in values, from the investment that his great-grandfather had so nervously and tentatively made. Those paltry ten thousand francs grew and grew with the prosperity of the Company. By 1820 they were yielding a hundred per cent, ten thousand francs. In 1844 they were earning twenty thousand; in 1850, forty thousand. Finally, just two years previously, the dividend had grown to the prodigious figure of fifty thousand francs: the value of a denier was quoted on the Lille stock exchange at one million francs, a hundredfold increase in the course of a century.

M. Grégoire had been advised to sell when the share price reached one million, but he had refused with a benign and tolerant smile. Six months later, when the industrial crisis began, the value of a denier fell back to six hundred thousand francs. But he kept smiling and had no regrets, for the Grégoires now believed steadfastly in their mine. The value would rise again; why, God Himself was not more reliable! At the same time, mixed with this religious faith in the mine, they felt a profound sense of gratitude towards a stock which had now fed and supported an entire family for over a century. It was like a private god whom they worshipped in their egotism, a fairy godmother who rocked them to sleep in their large bed of idleness and fattened them at their groaning table. And so it would continue, from father to son: why tempt fate by doubting it? And deep within their constancy lay a superstitious terror, the fear that the million francs would suddenly have melted away if they had realized their asset and placed the proceeds in a drawer. To their mind it was safer left in the ground, from whence a race of miners, generation after generation of starving people, would extract it for them, a little each day, sufficient unto their needs.

Fortune had also smiled on this house in other respects. At a very young age M. Grégoire had married the daughter of a pharmacist in Marchiennes, a plain-looking girl without a penny to her name whom he adored and who had repaid him with happiness in full measure. She had closeted herself within her domestic life, ecstatically devoted to her husband and with no other desire but his. Never once did a difference in taste come between them, as their desires merged in the pursuit of one and the same ideal of comfort and well-being; and they had been living like this for the past forty years in one long, tender exchange of affection and attentiveness to each other's needs. They lived a well-regulated life: their forty thousand a year was spent without ostentation and what they saved went on Cécile, whose late arrival had momentarily disrupted their budgeting. Even now they continued to pander to her every whim: a second horse, two more carriages, dresses from Paris. But for them this was simply one further source of joy; nothing was too good for their daughter, even though they themselves were so profoundly averse to show that they continued to wear the fashions of their youth. Any expense which did not serve a purpose seemed to them foolish.

Suddenly the door opened, and a loud voice exclaimed:

'What's this? You haven't had breakfast without me, have you!'

It was Cécile, who had come straight from her bed, her eyes still puffy with sleep. She had merely put her hair up and pulled on a white woollen dressing-gown.

'No, of course we haven't,' said her mother. 'Can't you see? We've been waiting for you ... My poor darling, that wind must have kept you awake.'

The girl looked at her in great surprise.

'It's been windy? ... I had no idea. I've been fast asleep all night.'

They found this funny, and the three of them began to laugh; and the servants bringing in the breakfast burst out laughing also, so hilarious did everyone in the household consider the fact that Mademoiselle had just slept for a whole twelve hours. The appearance of the brioche added the final touch to their general merriment.

'What? You've baked it already?' Cécile kept saying. 'Well, this *is* a surprise. Oh, it's going to taste so good, all lovely and warm in the chocolate!'

They finally took their places at the table; the chocolate was steaming in the bowls, and for some time the sole subject of conversation was the brioche. Mélanie and Honorine remained in the room, talking about how the baking had gone and watching them all tuck in with buttery lips. What a pleasure it was to cook, they said, when you saw your master and his family eating with such relish.

But then the dogs started barking loudly, and they thought it must be the lady from Marchiennes who came to give Cécile her piano lesson every Monday and Friday. There was a man also who came to teach her literature. The girl's entire education had been conducted in this manner at La Piolaine, fostering a state of happy ignorance punctuated by childish whim, with books thrown out of the window the moment she found any subject boring.

'It's Monsieur Deneulin,' Honorine announced on her return.

Behind her, M. Deneulin, a cousin of M. Grégoire's, entered

without ceremony. At once decisive in manner and forthright in expression, he walked with the gait of a former cavalry officer. Although he was over fifty, his close-cropped hair and thick moustache were still jet black.

'Yes, it is I. Good-morning . . . No, no, please don't get up.'

While the family were still busy exclaiming at his arrival, he took a seat. At length they returned to their chocolate.

'Is there something you wished to tell me?' M. Grégoire asked.

'No, nothing at all,' M. Deneulin replied hastily. 'I was out for a ride – I like to keep my hand in, you know – and since I was passing your gate, I just thought I'd call and say hallo.'

Cécile asked him how his daughters Jeanne and Lucie were. They were very well. Jeanne was forever painting, and Lucie, the elder, was always at the piano practising her singing from morning till night. There was a slight catch in his voice, an uneasiness which he was endeavouring to hide beneath his hearty good humour.

'And is everything all right at the pit?' M. Grégoire continued.

'Ah, this damned slump. The men and I are not having an easy time of it . . . We're paying for the good years, I'm afraid! Too many factories were put up, too many railways were built, and everyone was so eager to achieve enormous levels of output that too much capital was invested at once. And now the money's all tied up and there isn't any left to keep the whole thing turning . . . Still, fortunately all is not lost. I'll get by somehow.'

Like his cousin he had inherited a denier in the Montsou mines. But in his case, being an engineer and a man of enterprise, he had been consumed with the ambition to make a royal fortune and he had been quick to sell when the denier had reached the million mark. For months he had been hatching a plan. His wife had inherited the small concession of Vandame from an uncle, but only two pits in the concession were still open, Jean-Bart and Gaston-Marie, and both of them were in such a poor state of repair and had such defective equipment that it scarcely paid to work them. Well, his dream was to modernize Jean-Bart. He wanted to restore its winding-engine and widen its shaft for better access while keeping Gaston-Marie for drainage purposes only. There was gold to be had by the shovelful, as he put it. The idea was a good one. Except that the million had now been spent on the renovations, and this damned slump had come just at the very moment when high yields were about to prove him right. Added to which he was a poor businessman. He was generous to his workers in his own gruff sort of way, and since the death of his wife he had allowed himself to be swindled by various means. Also he had been letting his daughters have a free rein; the elder one talked of going on the stage, while the younger had already had three landscapes rejected by the Salon Hanging Committee.[4] The two girls neverthless remained cheerful in the face of their adversity, and the growing threat of poverty had revealed them to be very astute housekeepers.

'You see, Léon,' he went on in a hesitant voice, 'you were wrong not to sell when I did. Now everything's on the slide and your chance has gone ... Whereas if you'd entrusted your money to me, you'd soon have seen what we could have achieved at Vandame, and in our very own mine!'

M. Grégoire calmly finished his chocolate. He replied evenly:

'Never! ... You know perfectly well that I don't wish to speculate. I live a peaceful life, it would be just too silly to go bothering my head over business matters. And as far as Montsou is concerned, the shares can keep on going down, we'll still always have enough to meet our needs. You mustn't be so greedy, for goodness sake! Anyway, mark my words, you're the one who'll be feeling the pinch some day, because Montsou will start going up again and the children of Cécile's children will still be getting their daily bread from it.'

Deneulin listened to him with an awkward smile.

'So,' he said quietly, 'if I asked you to put a hundred thousand francs into my business, you would refuse?'

But at the sight of the Grégoires' worried faces he immediately regretted having gone so far. He decided to save the possibility of a loan for later, in case he was ever desperate.

'Oh, things aren't that bad! I'm just joking . . . Heavens above, you're probably right. The easiest way to make money is to let other people make it for you.'

They changed the subject. Cécile returned to the matter of her cousins, whose interests she found as fascinating as she found them shocking. Mme Grégoire promised to take her daughter to see the two dear girls on the first. fine day that presented itself. M. Grégoire, meanwhile, wore an absent expression, his thoughts elsewhere. He added loudly:

'You know, if I were you, I wouldn't persevere. I'd negotiate with Montsou . . . They're extremely keen, and you'd get your money back.'

He was referring to the long-running feud that existed between the concessions at Montsou and Vandame. Despite the latter's small size, it exasperated its powerful neighbour to have this square league of territory that didn't belong to it stuck bang in the middle of its own sixty-seven area divisions. Having tried in vain to put it out of business, the Montsou Mining Company was now plotting to buy it on the cheap as soon as it showed any signs of going under. The battle continued to rage unabated, with each mine's tunnels ending a mere two hundred metres short of the other's. Though the managers and the engineers might behave perfectly civilly to one another, it was a fight to the death.

Deneulin's eyes had blazed.

'Never!' he shouted in his turn. 'Montsou shall never get its hands on Vandame so long as I live . . . I had dinner at Hennebeau's on Thursday, and I could see him sniffing around me. Indeed last autumn, when the big guns on the Board of Directors had their meeting, they were already falling over themselves to be nice to me . . . Oh, I know their sort all right! The dukes and the marquises, the generals and ministers! Highway robbers, the lot of them, just lurking round the corner ready to have the shirt off your back!'

And so he went on. Not that M. Grégoire was going to defend the Board. Its six directors, whose posts had been created under the terms of the settlement in 1760, ran the Company like despots, and when one of them died, the five remaining directors chose the new member of the Board from among the shareholders who were rich and powerful. In the view of the owner of La Piolaine, as a man careful in his ways, these gentlemen

sometimes lacked a certain moderation in their excessive desire
for money.

Mélanie had come to clear the table. Outside the dogs began
to bark again, and Honorine was just on her way to the front
door when Cécile, needing air after all this warmth and food,
left the table.

'No, let me. It must be for my lesson.'

Deneulin, too, had risen to his feet. He watched the girl leave
the room and then asked with a smile:

'Well, and what about this marriage with young Négrel?'

'Nothing's been decided,' said Mme Grégoire. 'It's just an
idea at this stage . . . It needs some proper thought.'

'I have no doubt,' he replied, with a knowing laugh. 'I understand that the nephew and the aunt . . . But what I can't get over
is the way Madame Hennebeau makes such a fuss of Cécile all
the time.'

M. Grégoire was indignant. Such a distinguished lady, and
fully fourteen years older than the young man! It was monstrous,
such things were beyond a joke. Deneulin, still laughing, shook
him by the hand and took his leave.

'It's still not her!' said Cécile, who came back into the room.
'It's that woman with her two children. You know, Mummy,
the miner's wife we met . . . Do they have to be shown in here?'

They hesitated. Were they very dirty? No, not too dirty,
and they would leave their clogs on the front steps. Father and
mother were already settled in their two large armchairs and
digesting their breakfast. The unwelcome prospect of having
to move decided the matter.

'Show them in, Honorine.'

And so in came La Maheude and her little ones, frozen,
starving, and filled with nervous apprehension at the sight of
this room which was so warm and smelled so deliciously of
brioche.

II

Up in the bedroom, where the shutters were still closed, grey bars of daylight had filtered through and spread like a fan across the ceiling. The close atmosphere had grown even stuffier as everyone continued with their night's sleep: Lénore and Henri in each other's arms, Alzire lying on her hump with her head lolling back; while old Bonnemort, who now had Zacharie and Jeanlin's bed all to himself, was snoring away with his mouth open. Not a sound was to be heard from the recess on the landing where La Maheude had dropped off again in the middle of feeding Estelle, with her breast hanging to one side and her daughter lying across her stomach, replete with milk and likewise fast asleep, half suffocating amid the soft flesh of her mother's breasts.

Downstairs the cuckoo clock struck six. From along the village streets came the sound of doors slamming and then the clatter of clogs along the pavement: it was the women who worked in the screening-shed setting off for the pit. And silence fell once more until seven. Then shutters were thrown back, and the sound of yawning and coughing could be heard through partition walls. For a long time a coffee-mill could be heard grinding away, but still no one stirred in the bedroom.

But suddenly a distant sound of slapping and screaming made Alzire sit up in bed. Realizing what the time was, she ran barefoot to rouse her mother.

'Mummy, Mummy, it's late. Remember, you've got to go out . . . Careful! You'll crush Estelle.'

And she retrieved the child, who was nearly smothered beneath a huge molten mass of breast.

'Heaven help us!' La Maheude spluttered, rubbing her eyes. 'We're all so exhausted we could sleep the whole day long . . . Dress Lénore and Henri for me, will you? I'll take them with me. And you'd better look after Estelle. I don't want to drag her out in this dreadful weather, in case she catches something.'

She washed in a hurry and then pulled on an old blue skirt,

the cleanest she had, and a loose-fitting jacket of grey wool, which she had put two patches in the day before.

'And then there's the soup, for heaven's sake!' she muttered again.

While her mother rushed downstairs, Alzire went back to the bedroom with Estelle, who had begun to scream. But she was used to the little girl's tantrums, and although only eight she already had a woman's knowledge of the tender wiles that would soothe and distract her. Gently she laid her down in her own bed, which was still warm, and lulled her back to sleep by giving her a finger to suck. Not before time, moreover, because another racket broke out: and she had at once to go and make the peace between Lénore and Henri, who had finally woken up. These two children did not get on, and the only time they would gently put their arms round each other was when they were asleep. The moment she woke, Lénore, aged six, fell on Henri, who was two years younger and let himself be hit without hitting back. Both of them had the same oversized head, which looked as though it had been inflated and was covered in yellow hair that stuck up. Alzire had to drag her sister off him by the legs and threaten to give her a good hiding. Then there was much stamping of feet as she washed them and at each item of clothing she tried to put on them. They left the shutters closed so as not to disturb old Bonnemort while he slept. He was still snoring, despite the terrible hullabaloo the children were making.

'It's ready! Are you nearly all done up there?' shouted La Maheude.

She had pulled back the shutters, raked the fire and put on some more coal. Her one hope was that the old man had not finished off all the soup, but she found the saucepan wiped clean, and so she cooked a handful of vermicelli she'd been saving for the last three days. They could eat it plain, without butter, since the small piece that was left the day before would now be gone; but she was surprised to see that Catherine had somehow managed miraculously to leave a small knob of it after making their pieces. This time, however, the kitchen dresser was well and truly bare: there was nothing, not a crust or a leftover or even a bone to gnaw. What would become of them if Maigrat was still determined to stop their credit, and if the bourgeois at La Piolaine didn't give her a hundred sous. And yet when her menfolk and her daughter came back from the pit they would have to eat, for, sad to relate, no one had yet invented a way of living without eating.

'Come down this instant,' she shouted crossly. 'I should be gone by now.'

Once Alzire and the children had come down, she shared the vermicelli out on to three small plates. She wasn't hungry, she said. Although Catherine had already used yesterday's coffee grounds a second time, she poured more water on to them and downed two large mugfuls of coffee that was so thin that it looked like rusty water. Still, it would keep her going.

'Now remember,' she told Alzire once more. 'You're to let your grandfather sleep, and you're to keep an eye on Estelle and see she doesn't come to any harm. If she wakes up and starts screaming the place down, here's a sugar lump. Dissolve it in water and give her little spoonfuls . . . I know you're a sensible girl and you won't eat it yourself.'

'But what about school, Mum?'

'School? Well, that'll have to wait for another day . . . I need you here.'

'And the soup? Do you want me to make it if you're not back in time?'

'Ah, the soup, the soup. No, better wait till I come back.'

Alzire had the precocious intelligence of a sickly child, and she knew exactly how to make soup. But she must have understood the situation, for she did not insist. The whole village was awake now and groups of children could be heard leaving for school, dragging their clogs as they walked. Eight o'clock struck, and the sound of people chatting next door in La Levaque's house was steadily getting louder. The women's day had begun, as they gathered round their coffee-pots, hands on hips, tongues wagging, like millstones grinding away in circles. A wizened face with thick lips and a squashed nose suddenly pressed itself against the window-pane and shouted:

'You'll never guess what I've heard.'

'No, no, later!' La Maheude answered. 'I've got to go out.'

And just in case she succumbed to the offer of a glass of hot coffee, she shovelled the food into Lénore and Henri and left. Upstairs old Bonnemort was still snoring away, with a rhythmic snore that seemed to rock the house itself to sleep.

Once outside La Maheude was surprised to see that the wind had dropped. A sudden thaw was under way: beneath a dun-coloured sky all the walls looked clammy and green with damp and the roads were coated in mud, the thick, glutinous mud of coal-mining regions that looks as black as liquid soot and can so easily remove a shoe. She immediately had to smack Lénore because the little girl was having fun trying to collect the mud on her clogs as though she were digging it out with a shovel. On leaving the village they skirted the spoil-heap and followed the path along the canal, taking short cuts along pot-holed streets and across stretches of waste ground enclosed by rotting fences. There followed a succession of large sheds and long factory buildings with tall chimneys that belched out soot and filthied what remained of the countryside amid these sprawling industrial outskirts. Behind a clump of poplars stood the old Réquillart pit and its crumbling headgear: only its thick beams remained standing. Then, having turned right, La Maheude came out on to the main highway.

'Just you wait, you dirty little scamp. I'll teach you to make mud-pies indeed!'

This time it was Henri, who had grabbed a handful of mud and was busy moulding it in his hands. Having both been smacked without fear or favour, the two children stopped misbehaving and began peering sideways at the small holes their feet were making in the lumps of earth. Along they squelched, already exhausted by the effort of prising their feet out of the sticky mud with each step they took.

In one direction the road ran dead straight towards Marchiennes, two leagues of paved cobblestone road unravelling across the reddish earth like a ribbon dipped in engine-grease. But in the opposite direction it zigzagged its way down through Montsou, which had been built on the side of a broad slope in the plain. In the Département du Nord there has been a steady proliferation of roads of this kind, which are designed to proceed directly from one manufacturing town to the next, pushing forward in smooth curves and gentle gradients, and all the while turning the entire Département into one big industrial city. To the right and left of the road as it wound its way down to the bottom stood little brick houses that had been painted in bright colours to make up for the dreary climate; some were yellow, some blue, others black, these latter no doubt by way of immediate anticipation of their eventual and inevitable hue. One or two large detached two-storey houses, occupied by factory managers, interrupted the serried rows of narrow house-fronts. A church, also built in brick, looked like the latest design for a blast-furnace, and its square tower was already filthy from the soot that flew about. But among all the sugar-refineries and the rope-works and the flour-mills what really caught the eye was the number of dance-halls, taverns and beer-shops, which were so plentiful that there were over five hundred of them to every thousand houses.

As she reached the Company's yards, with its vast array of workshops and warehouses, La Maheude thought it best to take Henri and Lénore each by the hand, one on her left and one on her right. Ahead lay the large house where M. Hennebeau, the manager, lived, a sort of vast chalet set back from the road behind an iron gate and a garden with some scraggy-looking trees. At that moment a carriage had drawn up outside the front door bearing a lady in a fur coat and a gentleman who wore a medal ribbon in his buttonhole. They were evidently visitors from Paris who had just arrived at Marchiennes station, for Mme Hennebeau, who had now appeared in the half-light of the hallway, gave a cry of joyful surprise.

'Come on, you two lazybones, keep going!' La Maheude scolded, dragging the two children forward as they floundered in the mud.

She was nearing Maigrat's shop and beginning to feel very apprehensive. Maigrat lived right next to M. Hennebeau, with just a wall separating his small house from the manager's residence; and he ran a wholesale store, a long building which opened on to the road like a shop but without the shop-front. He stocked everything, groceries, cold meats, fruit, and sold anything from bread and beer to pots and pans. Having previously worked as a supervisor at Le Voreux, he had started out with a modest little shop; then, with some assistance from his former bosses, his turnover had grown and gradually driven the retailers of Montsou out of business. He was able to bring a whole range of goods under one roof, and the substantial customer base in the mining villages allowed him to cut prices and extend more generous credit. But he remained in the Company's pocket, for they had built his little house and shop for him.

'It's me again, Monsieur Maigrat,' La Maheude said humbly, for he happened at that moment to be standing at his door.

He looked at her and made no reply. He was a fat man, with a cold, polite manner, and he prided himself on never going back on a decision.

'Please, you can't send me away again like you did yesterday. We've simply got to have bread to eat between now and Saturday ... Yes, I know, we've owed you sixty francs for the past two years.'

She explained the situation in short, halting sentences. The debt was a long-standing one, which they had incurred during the last strike. Twenty times or more they had promised to pay it off, but it was impossible, they simply could not manage to spare the forty sous to give him every fortnight. Added to which she'd had a spot of bad luck the day before yesterday; she'd had to pay a cobbler twenty francs because he'd threatened to call the bailiffs in. And that was why they hadn't a penny to their name at the minute. Otherwise they could have managed till Saturday just the same as everyone else.

Maigrat stood there, arms crossed above his bulging paunch, and shook his head each time she pleaded:

'Just two loaves, Monsieur Maigrat. I'm a reasonable woman, I'm not asking for coffee or anything ... Just two three-pound loaves a day.'

'No!' he shouted finally, at the top of his voice.

His wife had appeared on the scene, a scrawny creature who

spent her days bent over the ledger not so much as daring to
lift her head. She darted away, alarmed by the sight of this
unfortunate woman turning towards her with a desperate,
beseeching look in her eyes. People said that she regularly
vacated the marital bed when the putters came shopping. Indeed
it was common knowledge: when a miner needed more credit,
he had only to send round his daughter or his wife, no matter
whether they were pretty or plain, just as long as they were
obliging.

La Maheude, who was still staring imploringly at Maigrat,
felt embarrassed to be subjected to the pale gleam of his little
eyes as they undressed her. It made her angry. Fair enough,
perhaps, when she was still young, before she'd had seven
children, but now . . . And she left, dragging Lénore and Henri
away from the walnut shells they were collecting from the gutter
where they'd been thrown.

'This will bring you bad luck, Monsieur Maigrat. Just you
wait and see.'

Now her only chance was the bourgeois at La Piolaine. If they
didn't part with a hundred sous, then she and her family might
as well all lie down and die. She had turned left on to the track
that led to Joiselle. The Board's office stood here, at the corner
of the road, a veritable palace of brick where the bigwigs from
Paris all came to hold their grand dinners every autumn, together
with princes and generals and various people in the government.
As she walked along she was already mentally spending the
hundred sous: first bread, then some coffee; after that, a quarter
kilo of butter, and a bushel of potatoes for the morning soup
and the vegetable stew in the evening; and lastly perhaps a little
brawn, because Maheu needed his meat.

The priest at Montsou, Father Joire, was passing by, holding
up his cassock with the fastidiousness of some large and well-
nourished cat that does not wish to get itself wet. He was a
gentle sort and affected to take no interest in anything in the
hope that he might anger neither the workers nor their bosses.

'Good-morning, Father.'

He kept on walking, smiling at the children and leaving her
stranded in the middle of the road. She had no religion, but she

had momentarily imagined that this priest might be about to give her something.

And off they went again, through the black, sticky mud. They still had two kilometres to go, and the little ones, rather put out and no longer finding this fun, needed more and more to be dragged. To the right and left of the road followed a succession of yet more derelict patches of waste ground surrounded by rotting fences and yet more smoke-stained factory buildings bristling with tall chimneys. When they reached open country, the vast, flat earth spread out before them, an ocean of brown, upturned soil stretching away to the purple line of the Vandame forest on the horizon and without even a single tree to suggest the presence of a mast upon its waves.

'Mummy, Mummy, carry me.'

And she carried them each in turn. There were puddles in the pot-holed road, and she had to hitch up her skirt so as not to be all dirty when they arrived. Three times she nearly fell, the damned cobblestones were so slippery. And when they finally came out at the front steps of the house, two enormous dogs rushed at them, barking so loudly that the little ones started screaming with fright. The coachman had to use his whip.

'Leave your clogs here and come in,' said Honorine.

In the dining-room mother and children stood stock-still, dazed by the sudden warmth and feeling very uncomfortable at being stared at by this old gentleman and this old lady stretched out in their armchairs.

'My child,' said the latter, 'it's time for your little deed.'

The Grégoires delegated the distribution of alms to Cécile. It was their idea of giving her a good education. One had to be charitable, they said, their house was God's house. Moreover, they flattered themselves that they were intelligent about their charity, being forever concerned that they should not be duped and encourage evil ways. Hence they never gave money, never! Not so much as ten sous, not even two sous, because, of course, as everyone knew, the moment you gave the poor so much as two sous, they drank them. And so their alms were always given in kind, and particularly in the form of warm clothing, which they distributed to destitute children during the winter.

'Oh, the poor little darlings!' cried Cécile. 'Just look how pale they are after their long walk in the cold! . . . Honorine, quick, go and fetch the parcel. It's in my wardrobe.'

The servants, too, looked at these poor wretches with that compassion tinged with guilt which is felt by those who know where their next meal is coming from. While the chambermaid went upstairs, the cook, not thinking, set the remainder of the brioche down on the table and stood there aimlessly.

'As it happens,' Cécile said, 'I've still got two wool dresses and some scarves. Oh, the little darlings will be lovely and warm in them, you'll see.'

La Maheude found her tongue at last and stammered:

'Thank you very much, Mademoiselle . . . You are all very kind . . .'

Her eyes had filled with tears. She thought the five-franc piece was now secure, and her only worry was how she should ask for it if it wasn't offered. The maid had still not returned and there was a moment of embarrassed silence. The little ones clung to their mother's skirts and gazed wide-eyed at the brioche.

'Are these your only two?' asked Mme Grégoire, for something to say.

'Oh no, Madame. I have seven.'

M. Grégoire, who had gone back to reading his newspaper, gave an indignant start:

'Seven children? But whatever for, in God's name?'

'It's unwise,' the old lady said softly.

La Maheude gestured vaguely by way of apology. What could you do? It wasn't something you thought about, a child just came along, naturally. And then when it was grown, it brought in some money and generally kept things going. In their house, for example, they could have managed if it weren't for Grandpa who was getting all stiff and for the fact that out of the whole bunch of them only her eldest daughter and two of her sons were yet old enough to work down the mine. But you still had to feed the little ones all the same, even though they didn't do anything.

'So,' Mme Grégoire continued, 'have you all been working in the mine for long?'

La Maheude's wan face lit up in a grin:

'Oh, yes, indeed we have . . . Myself, I worked down the mine till I was twenty. When I had my second, the doctor said it would be the death of me, because apparently it was doing something nasty to my bones. Anyway, that's when I got married, and then there was enough for me to do round the house . . . But on my husband's side now . . . They've been working down the mine since for ever. As far back as my grandfather's grandfather . . . well, no one knows exactly, but since the very start anyway, when they began digging for coal over at Réquillart.'

M. Grégoire gazed pensively at this woman and her pitiful children, at their waxen flesh and their colourless hair, at the process of degeneration evident in their stunted growth, at the anaemia that was gradually eating away at them, at the baleful ugliness of the starving. There was another silence, and all that could be heard was the sound of the coal burning and releasing the occasional spurt of gas. The moist, warm air in the room was heavy with the cosiness of domestic ease that brings peaceful slumber to contented bourgeois hearths.

'What can she be doing?' cried Cécile impatiently. 'Mélanie, do go up and tell her that the parcel is at the bottom of the wardrobe, on the left.'

Meanwhile M. Grégoire voiced aloud the conclusions to which he had been brought by the sight of these hungry people.

'Life can be hard, it is very true; but, my good woman, it must be said that the workers are not always sensible . . . I mean, for example, instead of putting a few sous to one side the way countryfolk do, the miners just drink and run up debts, so that in the end there's nothing left for them to feed their families on.'

'Monsieur is quite right,' La Maheude replied evenly. 'We don't always follow the straight and narrow. That's what I keep telling those good-for-nothings when they start complaining . . . But I'm one of the lucky ones, my husband doesn't drink. Mind you, sometimes, when there's a party on a Sunday night, he'll have a few too many; but it never goes any further than that. And what's so good about him is that before we married he used to drink like a bloody fish, if you'll pardon the expression

. . . And yet, you know, his being sensible like that doesn't really get us any further. There are days, like today for instance, when you could turn out every drawer in our house and you wouldn't find a single coin.'

She wanted to get them thinking about the five-franc piece, and she continued in her flat monotone, explaining to them how they had come to be in such serious debt, how it had all begun, in small stages at first, and then grown to the point where it consumed everything they had. They'd make their regular repayments every fortnight, but then one day they'd find themselves behind with the instalments, and that was it, they never managed to catch up again. The gap got wider and wider, and then the men got fed up working when it didn't even allow them to pay off their debts. Stuff that for a lark, they'd say! If things went on like this, they'd never be clear till the day they died. Anyway, people needed to see the whole picture: a collier needed his beer simply to clear the soot from his throat. That was how it started, and then when things went badly he'd never be out of the bar. So perhaps, not that anyone was to blame, mind, but all the same, perhaps the workers were just not paid enough.

'But,' said Mme Grégoire, 'I thought the Company paid for your rent and heating.'

La Maheude cast a sideways glance at the coal blazing in the fireplace.

'Oh, yes, they give us coal all right. It's not wonderful, but at least it burns . . . As for the rent, it's only six francs a month, which may not seem very much but sometimes it's mighty hard to find . . . Like today, for example, you could search me till the cows come home but you wouldn't find a single sou on me. Where there's nothing, there's nothing.'

The lady and gentleman fell silent, and as they reclined comfortably in their armchairs they began to find this display of poverty increasingly tiresome and upsetting. Afraid that she had offended them, La Maheude added with the calm and equitable air of a practical woman:

'Not that I'm complaining, of course. That's how things are, one's got to make the best of it. Especially as even if we were to try and do something about it, we probably wouldn't manage to change anything anyway . . . The wisest thing in the end, don't you think, Monsieur, Madame, is to try and go about your business honestly and accept the place where the good Lord has put you.'

M. Grégoire agreed heartily.

'With such sentiments as those, my good woman, one can rise above misfortune.'

Honorine and Mélanie finally brought the parcel. Cécile undid it and produced the two dresses. She added some scarves and even some stockings and mittens. They would all fit just beautifully, and hastily she bid the maids wrap the selected garments, for her piano teacher had just arrived and she was beginning to usher mother and children towards the door.

'We really are very short,' stammered La Maheude. 'If you could just spare a five-franc piece . . .'

The words stuck in her throat for the Maheu family were proud and did not beg. Cécile looked anxiously towards her father; but he refused point blank with the air of one called upon to perform a painful duty.

'No, it is not our custom. We simply cannot.'

Then, moved by the look of distress on the mother's face, Cécile wanted to give the children something extra. They hadn't taken their eyes off the brioche, so she cut two slices which she handed to them.

'Here, these are for you.'

Then she took them back and asked for an old newspaper.

'Wait, you can share them with your brothers and sisters.'

With her parents looking on affectionately, Cécile finally bundled them out. And these poor mites who had no bread to eat went on their way, respectfully bearing this brioche[1] in tiny hands that were numb with cold.

La Maheude dragged her children along the cobblestone road, seeing neither the empty fields nor the black mud nor the huge, pale sky curving overhead. On her way back through Montsou, she strode purposefully into Maigrat's shop and begged him so hard that she finally left with two loaves, some coffee and butter, and even the five-franc piece she had been wanting, since the man also lent money at an extortionate rate of interest. In fact it wasn't herself he was after, it was Catherine, as La Maheude understood when he told her to send her daughter to collect the rest of the provisions. They would soon see. Catherine would slap him the minute he laid a finger on her.

III

Eleven o'clock struck at the little church in Village Two Hundred and Forty, a brick chapel in which Father Joire came to say Mass on Sundays. From the school next door, which was also built of brick, the sound of children reciting their lessons could be heard even though the windows were shut to keep out the cold. Between the four great blocks of uniform housing, the broad avenues of tiny back-to-back gardens lay deserted; ravaged by winter, they made a sorry sight with their marly soil and the bumps and smudges of their last remaining vegetables. Indoors, soup was being prepared; smoke rose from the chimneys, and here and there along the rows of houses a woman would emerge, open another door, and disappear again. Even though it wasn't raining, the grey sky was so heavy with moisture that drain-pipes dripped steadily into the water-butts that stood all along each pavement. This village had simply been plonked down in the middle of the vast plateau, surrounded by black roads as though by a border of condolence, and the only cheerful note was provided by the regular bands of red roof tiles, constantly washed clean by the rain.

On her return La Maheude made a detour to buy some potatoes from the wife of a supervisor, who still had some of last year's crop left. Behind a row of scraggy poplars, which were the only trees to be seen in this flat terrain, a group of buildings stood apart from the rest, a series of houses arranged in fours and each surrounded by its own garden. Since the Company had reserved this new development for the deputies, the workers had dubbed this corner of their hamlet the First Estate, just as they called their own part of the village Never-

Never-Land by way of cheerful, ironic comment on their debt-ridden penury.

'Oof. Here we are at last,' said La Maheude as, laden with parcels, she bundled Lénore and Henri into their house all covered in mud and now thoroughly walked off their feet.

In front of the fire Estelle lay screaming in Alzire's arms. The latter, having run out of sugar and not knowing how to keep Estelle quiet, had decided to pretend to offer her her breast. This often did the trick. But she was just a sickly eight-year-old, and when she opened her dress this time and pressed the child's mouth to her emaciated chest, it merely made Estelle cross to suck the skin and find that nothing came.

'Here, give her to me!' her mother shouted as soon as her hands were free. 'We shan't be able to hear ourselves think.'

Once she had drawn from her bodice a breast as heavy as a swollen wineskin and the bawling child had latched on to the spout, there was immediate quiet, and they could finally talk. Everything else was fine, the little housewife had kept the fire going and swept and tidied the room. And in the silence they could hear Grandpa snoring away upstairs, with the same rhythmic snore that had not faltered for an instant.

'Goodness, look at all these things!' Alzire said softly, smiling at the sight of the groceries. 'I can make the soup if you want, Mum.'

The table was covered: one parcel of clothes, two loaves of bread, potatoes, butter, coffee, chicory and half a pound of brawn.

'Oh, yes, the soup,' said La Maheude wearily. 'We'd need to go and pick some sorrel and pull up some leeks . . . No, I'll make some later for the men . . . Put some potatoes on to boil just now, and we'll have them with a bit of butter . . . And some coffee, too, eh? Don't forget the coffee!'

But then she suddenly remembered the brioche. She looked at Lénore and Henri, who were now fighting on the floor, for they had already recovered their strength and their spirits, and she saw that their hands were empty. The greedy little things had quietly eaten the lot on the way home! She gave them a smack just as Alzire, who was hanging the cooking-pot over the fire, tried to mollify her.

'Leave them be, Mum. If you're thinking of me, I really don't mind about the brioche. They were hungry, what with walking all that way.'

Midday struck, and the sound of clogs could be heard as the children came out of school. The potatoes were ready, and the coffee, to which more than an equivalent amount of chicory had been added to supplement it, was gurgling through the filter in large drops. They cleared a corner of the table, but only La Maheude took her food there, since the three children were happy to eat off their knees; and as the little boy ate with mute intent, he kept turning round to look at the brawn, excited by the greasepaper wrapping but not saying a word.

La Maheude was sipping her coffee, her hands clenched round the glass to warm them, when old Bonnemort came downstairs. Usually he got up later, and his lunch would be waiting for him on the stove. But today he started grumbling because there was no soup. Then, after his daughter-in-law had told him that beggars can't be choosers, he ate his potatoes in silence. From time to time he would get up and go and spit into the ashes, by way of keeping the place clean. Then he would return to his chair and sit there in a slumped heap, rolling the food round at the back of his mouth, with his head bowed and a vacant expression on his face.

'Oh, Mum, I forgot, next door came round –'

Her mother cut her short:

'I'm not talking to that woman.'

She was still seething with resentment against La Levaque, who had pleaded poverty the day before and refused to lend her a sou, whereas she happened to know that La Levaque had plenty of money just then, seeing as Bouteloup, her lodger, had paid her his fortnight in advance. People in the village rarely lent money to each other.

'But that reminds me,' La Maheude continued. 'Put a millful of coffee in some paper, and I'll take it round to La Pierronne. She lent me some the day before yesterday.'

When her daughter had prepared the package, she told Alzire

that she would be back at once to start cooking the men's soup. Then off she went with Estelle in her arms, leaving old Bonnemort slowly chewing his potatoes, and Lénore and Henri fighting over the peelings that had fallen on the floor.

Rather than go round by the street, La Maheude cut straight across the gardens just in case La Levaque should try to speak to her. As it happened, her own garden backed on to the Pierrons', and there was a hole in the dilapidated trellis through which they were able to visit each other. The shared well was located there, serving four households. Next to it, behind a sorry clump of lilac, was the *carin*, a low shed full of old tools where they also reared a succession of rabbits to be eaten on special occasions. One o'clock struck, coffee-time, when not a soul was to be seen at window or door – except for one man, one of the stonemen, who was digging his little vegetable patch until it was time to go to work. He did not look up. But as La Maheude reached the row of houses on the other side, she was surprised to see a gentleman and two ladies come past the church. She stopped for a moment and then recognized them: it was Mme Hennebeau, who was showing her guests round the village, the man with the ribbon in his buttonhole and the lady in a fur coat.

'Oh, you really shouldn't have bothered!' La Pierronne exclaimed when La Maheude handed her the coffee. 'There was no hurry.'

She was twenty-eight and considered the prettiest woman in the village, with brown hair, a low forehead, big eyes and a small mouth – and always well turned out, as clean and dainty as a cat. Moreover, since she had not had any children she still had a fine bust. Her mother, La Brûlé, the widow of a hewer who had been killed in the mine, had sent her daughter to work in a factory, determined that she should not marry a collier; and so she had still not got over her fury that, rather late in the day, this same daughter had gone and married Pierron, who was a widower to boot and already had a girl of eight. And yet it was a happy marriage, despite all the stories and gossip about the husband's obliging ways and the lovers his wife had taken: they had not a penny of debt, they ate meat twice a week, and their house was so spick and span that you could have seen your face in the saucepans. As if that were not enough, they knew the right people, and the Company had authorized La Pierronne to sell sweets and biscuits, which she displayed in jars along two shelves behind her window. This made her a profit of six or seven sous a day, and sometimes twelve on Sundays. The only exceptions to this general felicity were La Brûlé herself, a revolutionary of the old school who ranted and raved and demanded revenge on the bosses for killing her husband, and little Lydie, who got smacked rather too often as a consequence of the family's more lively exchanges.

'What a big girl we are already!' said La Pierronne, cooing at Estelle.

'Oh, the trouble they cause! Don't get me started!' La Maheude said. 'You're lucky you don't have any. At least you can keep things clean and tidy.'

Even though everything was tidy in her own house and she did the washing every Saturday, she cast an envious housewifely eye round this room that was so bright and cheerful, stylish even, with its gilt vases on the sideboard, its mirror and its three framed prints.

She had found La Pierronne drinking coffee on her own, since the rest of her family was at the pit.

'You will stay and have a glass with me, won't you?' she said.

'No, thanks, I've just had mine.'

'What does that matter?'

And nor did it matter. Quietly the women sipped their coffee. As they looked out between the jars of biscuits and sweets, their gaze fell on the houses opposite and on the row of windows, each with its own little curtains, whose varying degrees of whiteness bespoke differing degrees of domestic virtue. The Levaques' curtains were very dirty and looked more like tea-towels that had been used to clean the saucepans.

'How can people live in such filth!' muttered La Pierronne.

That was enough for La Maheude: there was no stopping her now. Oh, if she'd had a lodger like Bouteloup, she'd soon have shown them how to make ends meet! As long as you went about it the right way, having a lodger could be a great advantage. Except that you should never sleep with them. Though in this

case the husband drank and beat his wife and was forever
chasing the girls who sang at the cafés in Montsou.

La Pierronne assumed an expression of profound disgust.
You could catch all sorts of things from those singers. There
was one at Joiselle who'd infected an entire pit.

'But I'm surprised you've let your son go with their daughter.'

'Well, I know, but you try and stop them! . . . Their garden is
right next to ours. Every summer Zacharie was always behind
the lilac with Philomène, or else on top of the shed and not
caring a blind bit who saw them. You couldn't draw water from
the well without catching them at it.'

In a crowded village where everyone lived cheek by jowl it
was a common story. Flung together at a young age, its boys
and girls soon went to the bad, having their end away, as they
put it,[1] on the low sloping roof of the shed as soon as darkness
fell. This was where the putters conceived their first baby, that
is if they couldn't be bothered to go as far as Réquillart or the
cornfields. It didn't matter, though, they got married eventually.
It was only the mothers who were cross when their sons started
too early, because once the lad was married he stopped bringing
money home to his family.

'If I were you, I'd sooner they got it over with,' La Pierronne
observed in her wisdom. 'Your Zacharie's put her in the family
way twice already, and they'll simply go somewhere else to do
it . . . Whichever way you look at it, the money's gone.'

La Maheude was furious and spread her hands wide:

'What an idea! I'd sooner put a curse on them if they went and
did it again . . . Zacharie should show us a bit of consideration,
shouldn't he? He's cost us money after all, and it's time he
paid some of it back before he saddles himself with a wife . . .
What would become of us, I ask you, if our children all started
working for other people straight away? We might as well curl
up and die!'

Gradually she calmed down.

'As a general rule, I mean. We'll just have to wait and see . . .
It's good and strong, this coffee of yours. You obviously put the
right amount in.'

After a quarter of an hour of further gossiping she made her escape, lamenting that she hadn't yet made the men their soup. Outside the children were returning to school, and one or two women had appeared on their doorsteps and were watching Mme Hennebeau walking along a row of houses pointing things out to her guests. This visit was beginning to create something of a stir throughout the village. The stoneman stopped digging for a moment, and across the gardens a pair of hens started clucking anxiously.

On her way home La Maheude ran into La Levaque, who was standing outside ready to pounce on Dr Vanderhaghen, the Company doctor, as he went past. He was a harrassed little man who had too much to do and tended to conduct his consultations on the run.

'Doctor, I can't sleep,' she said, 'I ache all over . . . I really need to see you about it.'

It was his habit to address all the women with brusque familiarity, and he replied without stopping:

'Don't bother me now. Too much coffee, that's your problem.'

'And my husband, Doctor' – it was La Maheude's turn now – 'you really must come and see him . . . He's still got those pains in his legs.'

'You're the one who's wearing him out! Now let me get on.'

The two women were left stranded, gazing after the doctor as he made his escape.

'Won't you come in,' La Levaque continued, after they had shrugged at each other in despair. 'I've got something to tell you . . . And I'm sure you'd like a spot of coffee. It's freshly made.'

La Maheude wanted to say no but was powerless to do so. Oh well! Perhaps just a mouthful all the same, to be polite. And in she went.

The parlour was black with dirt: there were greasy stains on the floor and walls, and the table and dresser were thick with grime. The stench of a slatternly household caught at La Maheude's throat. Sitting beside the fire, with his elbows on the table and his nose in a plate, was Bouteloup, still young-looking at thirty-five, a big, placid fellow with broad, square shoulders.

He was finishing off the remains of some stew. Standing close beside him was little Achille, the elder of Philomène's pair, who was already two, and he was staring at Bouteloup with the mute entreaty of a greedy animal. From time to time the lodger, a thoroughly soft-hearted sort in spite of his imposing brown beard, would put a piece of meat in the boy's mouth.

'Wait till I sweeten it a bit,' said La Levaque, as she put some brown sugar straight into the coffee-pot.

Six years older than Bouteloup, she looked terrible, like used goods. Her breasts sagged round her belly and her belly round her thighs. Her face was squashed-looking, with grey whiskers, and she never combed her hair. He had accepted her the way she was and inspected her no more closely than he did his soup to see if it had hairs in it or his bed to see if the sheets had been changed in the last three months. She was included in the rent and, as her husband was fond of repeating, honest dealings made honest friends.

'Anyway, here's what I wanted to tell you,' she continued. 'Apparently La Pierronne was seen out and about last night near the First Estate. The gentleman in question – and you know who I mean! – was waiting for her behind Rasseneur's, and off they went together along the canal . . . How about that, eh? And her a married woman!'

'Heavens!' said La Maheude. 'Pierron used to give the over-man rabbits before he was married, but now it's obviously cheaper to lend him his wife.'

Bouteloup guffawed loudly and tossed a crumb of gravy-soaked bread into Achille's mouth. The two neighbours continued to vent their feelings about La Pierronne: a flirt, they said, no prettier than the next woman, always inspecting her various orifices, and forever washing and anointing herself with creams. Still, it was her husband's business. If that's how he wanted things. Some men were so ambitious they'd wipe their boss's backside just to hear him say 'thank you'. And so they would have continued had they not been interrupted by the arrival of a neighbour who was returning a nine-month-old baby. This was Désirée, Philomène's second. Philomène herself, who ate her lunch at the screening-shed, had arranged for the woman to bring the little girl to her there so that she could suckle it while she sat down for a moment on a pile of coal.

'I can't leave my one for a single minute or she howls the place down,' La Maheude said, looking at Estelle, who had gone to sleep in her arms.

But there was no escaping the moment of reckoning which she had seen looming in La Levaque's eyes for a while now.

'Look here, it's time we did something.'

At the beginning, without a word being said, the two mothers had agreed not to have a marriage. Just as Zacharie's mother wanted to have his fortnight's wages coming in for as long as possible, so Philomène's mother was equally incensed at the idea of giving up her daughter's. There was no hurry. La Levaque had even preferred to look after the baby herself, while there was only one of them; but as soon as he started getting older and eating proper food, and then another one had arrived, she found herself getting the worst of the bargain, and she was pushing for the marriage with the urgency of a woman who has no intention of remaining out of pocket.

'Zacharie has avoided being called up for military service,' she continued, 'so there's nothing left to stop them . . . When shall we say?'

'Let's wait for the better weather,' La Maheude replied awkwardly. 'This whole business is a nuisance! If only they could have waited till they were married before going together like that . . . ! You know, honestly, I think I'd strangle Catherine if I found out she'd done anything silly.'

La Levaque shrugged.

'Oh, don't you worry. She'll go the same way as all the others.'

Bouteloup, with the calm air of one who is free to do as he pleases in his own house, rummaged in the dresser in search of bread. Vegetables for Levaque's soup were lying on the corner of the table, half-peeled leeks and potatoes which had been picked up and put down a dozen times or more in the course of this ceaseless chatter. Having just set to once more, La Levaque now proceeded to abandon them yet again and posted herself at the window.

'And what have we here? . . . My goodness, it's Mme Hennebeau with some people or other. They're just going into La
Pierronne's.'

At once the pair of them started in again on La Pierronne. Oh,
but of course, wouldn't you know! The minute the Company
wanted to show people round the village, they took them straight
to her house because it was so spick and span. No doubt they
weren't told about all the goings-on with the overman. Anyone
can be spick and span if they've got lovers who earn three
thousand francs and get their accommodation and heating free,
not to mention all the other perks. Spick and span on the surface
maybe, but underneath . . . And all the time the visitors were in
there, the two women rattled on about La Pierronne.

'They're coming out now,' La Levaque said eventually. 'They
must be doing the rounds . . . Look, love, I think they're coming
over to your place.'

La Maheude was aghast. What if Alzire hadn't wiped the
table? And what about her own soup? She hadn't made it yet!
With a rapid goodbye she rushed round to her own house
without a glance to right or left.

But everything was spotlessly clean. When she saw that her
mother was not coming back, Alzire had donned a tea-towel for
an apron and solemnly begun to make the soup. She had pulled
up the last leeks from the garden and picked some sorrel, and
now she was carefully washing the vegetables; over the fire a
large cauldron of water was heating up for the men's bath when
they got home. Henri and Lénore happened to be quiet, since
they were busy tearing up an old calendar. Bonnemort sat
silently smoking his pipe.

La Maheude was still trying to catch her breath when Mme
Hennebeau knocked on the door.

'May we, my good woman?'

Tall, blonde, a little full in the figure having reached her
matronly prime at the age of forty, Mme Hennebeau smiled
with forced affability and endeavoured to conceal her fear that
she might dirty the bronze silk outfit she was wearing under a
black velvet cape.

'Come in, come in,' she urged her guests. 'We shan't be in

anyone's way ... Well, now! Look how clean everything is again. And this good woman has seven children! All our households are like this ... As I was explaining, the Company lets the house to them for six francs a month. One large room on the ground floor, two bedrooms upstairs, a cellar and a garden.'

The man with the ribbon in his buttonhole and the lady in the fur coat, having arrived by the Paris train that morning, gazed about them blankly and seemed rather dazed by this sudden exposure to unfamiliar surroundings.

'And a garden, too,' the lady kept saying. 'Really one could live here oneself it's so charming.'

'We give them all the coal they need and more,' Mme Hennebeau continued. 'A doctor visits them twice a week; and when they're old, they're paid a pension even though no deduction is ever made from their wages towards it.'

'It's Eldorado. A land of milk and honey!' the gentleman muttered, quite entranced.

La Maheude had hastened to offer them all a seat. The ladies declined the offer. Mme Hennebeau was already growing tired of this visit, happy one minute to alleviate the tedium of her exile by playing this role of zoo guide, and then immediately repulsed by the vague odour of poverty that hung everywhere, despite the cleanliness of the carefully selected houses she dared to enter. In any case all she did was to repeat a series of stock phrases; she never otherwise bothered her head about all these workers toiling and suffering at her gates.

'What lovely children!' the lady in the fur coat said softly, while thinking them perfectly frightful with their excessively large heads and their mops of straw-coloured hair.

La Maheude had to say how old each of them was, and then they politely asked her about Estelle too. As a mark of respect old Bonnemort had taken the pipe from his mouth; but he still presented a rather worrying sight, ravaged as he had so clearly been by forty years of working down the mine, with his stiff legs, crumpled body and ashen face; and when he was seized by a violent coughing fit, he thought he had better go and spit outside, thinking that his black phlegm might upset people.

Alzire was the star of the show. What a pretty little housewife, with her tea-towel for an apron! They complimented her mother on having a little girl who was so grown-up for her age. And though nobody mentioned the hump, they could not help staring at the poor little cripple with uneasy sympathy.

'Now,' said Mme Hennebeau, resting her case, 'if anyone in Paris asks you about our villages, you can tell them. Never noisier than it is now, people living proper family lives, with everybody healthy and happy as you can see. It's the sort of place where you could come for a holiday, with clean air and lots of peace and quiet.'

'It's wonderful, wonderful!' the gentleman exclaimed in one last burst of enthusiasm.

They left the house with the spellbound air of people emerging from a freak show; and La Maheude, having shown them out, lingered on the doorstep to watch them slowly depart, talking at the top of their voices. The streets had filled, and they had to make their way through knots of women who had been drawn by the news of their visit and had passed the word from house to house along the way.

Indeed La Levaque had intercepted La Pierronne outside her own doorway when the latter arrived to see what was going on. Both women professed surprise and disapproval. Well, really, were these people perhaps proposing to spend the night at the Maheus'? It wouldn't be much fun for them, though!

'Never a penny to their name, despite all the money they earn! But what can you do? If you've got bad habits . . . !'

'Someone just told me that she went to beg from the bourgeois at La Piolaine this morning, and that Maigrat gave her food even though he'd refused her before . . . Of course, we know how Maigrat gets paid, don't we?'

'With her? No, no! That would take more courage than he's got . . . No, it's Catherine he gets paid with.'

'Well, would you believe it? And her with the nerve to tell me just a few moments ago that she'd sooner strangle Catherine if she did that sort of thing! . . . As if that tall fellow Chaval hadn't already had her on the shed roof many moons ago!'

'Shh! . . . Here they come.'

Whereupon, with quiet and unobtrusive curiosity, La Levaque

and La Pierronne had been content to watch out of the corner of their eyes as the visitors left the house. Then they quickly beckoned to La Maheude, who was still carrying Estelle round on her arm, and the three of them stood there together and watched the well-dressed backs of Mme Hennebeau and her guests as they departed. When they had gone thirty paces, the gossiping began again in renewed earnest.

'That's some money those women are wearing. Worth more than them, at any rate!'

'You're telling me . . . I don't know who the other one is, but I wouldn't give tuppence for the one from round here, despite all that meat on her. There are stories . . .'

'Oh? What stories?'

'About all the men she's had, of course! . . . First, there's the engineer . . .'

'That scrawny little runt! . . . Pah! there's nothing on him, she'd lose him between the sheets.'

'What's it to you if that's how she likes it? . . . But I don't trust ladies like them, with that look of disgust on their face as though they'd always rather be somewhere else . . . Look at the way she waggles her backside as if she despised the lot of us. It's just not decent.'

The visitors were continuing to stroll along at the same leisurely pace, still chatting away, when a barouche drew up on the road outside the church. A gentleman in his late forties stepped down, dressed in a tight-fitting black frock-coat. He had very dark skin, and his face bore the look of an authoritarian and a stickler.

'The husband!' murmured La Levaque, lowering her voice as if he could have heard her from where he stood, and gripped by the same deferential fear that the manager inspired in his ten thousand workers. 'It's true, though, isn't it? The man looks like a cuckold!'

By now the whole village was out on the streets. As the women's curiosity grew, the various little groups of them gradually merged into a crowd, while gaggles of snotty-nosed children stood about gawping on the pavements. For one brief moment even the pale head of the schoolteacher could be seen peering over the school fence. The man digging in the gardens rested his foot on his spade and stared, wide-eyed. And the rasping whispers of muttered gossip grew louder and louder, like a gust of wind whistling through dry leaves.

People had congregated in especially large numbers outside La Levaque's house. Two more women had joined them, then ten, then twenty. La Pierronne thought it prudent to remain silent for now too many ears were listening. La Maheude, being one of the more sensible among them, was also content just to watch. In order to quieten Estelle, who had woken up and begun to scream, she had calmly exposed a breast like an obliging animal ready to give suck, and this now hung down and lolled from side to side, as though elongated by the steady supply of milk welling like a spring within. After M. Hennebeau had helped the ladies into the back of the carriage and it had departed in the direction of Marchiennes, there was a final burst of chatter, with all the women gesticulating and shouting in each other's faces like an anthill that has been turned upside down.

But then the clock struck three. Bouteloup and the other stonemen had left for work. Suddenly, at the corner by the church, the first miners could be seen returning from the pit, faces black, clothes sopping wet, with their arms folded across their chests and their shoulders hunched. Whereupon all the women rushed off home, a stampede of panic-stricken housewives caught out by too much gossiping and too much coffee. And soon all that could be heard was one single cry, fraught with the remonstrations to come:

'Oh my God! The soup! I haven't made the soup!'

IV

When Maheu returned home, having left Étienne at Rasseneur's, he found Catherine, Zacharie and Jeanlin seated at the table finishing their soup. They were so hungry after they got back from the pit that they ate as they were, in their wet clothes, without even bothering to wash. Nobody waited for anyone else; the table was permanently laid from morning till night, and there was always someone sitting there having a meal as and when the working day permitted.

From the door Maheu caught sight of the groceries. He said nothing, but his worried face lit up. All morning the thought of the empty dresser and a house without coffee or butter had been troubling him, and as he tapped away at the seam in the stifling, airless heat of the coal-face, he kept having sharp pangs of anxiety. How would his wife have got on? And what were they going to do if she came back empty-handed? But here they were with everything they needed. She would tell him all about it later. He laughed with relief.

Already Catherine and Jeanlin had got up from the table and were drinking their coffee standing; while Zacharie, still hungry after his soup, was cutting himself a large slice of bread, which he spread with butter. He could perfectly well see the brawn laid out on a plate, but he didn't touch it; if there was only one portion, it meant the meat was for Father. They had all washed their soup down with a large swig of fresh water, that clear, refreshing liquid that serves so well when money is short.

'I haven't got any beer,' said La Maheude, after Father had sat down in his turn. 'I wanted to keep a bit of money back . . . But if you want, Alzire can go and fetch you a pint.'

He beamed at her. What, she had money left over, too!

'No, no,' he said. 'I've had some already. That'll do me fine.'

And Maheu slowly began, spoonful by spoonful, to devour the soggy mass of bread, potatoes, leeks and sorrel piled up in the small basin he used for a plate. Still holding Estelle, La Maheude helped Alzire make sure that her father had everything he wanted, passing him the butter and the brawn too, and putting his coffee back on the stove so that it would be nice and hot for him.

Meanwhile beside the fire the ablutions began, in a half-barrel that had been turned into a bath-tub. Catherine, who went first, had filled it with warm water; and she calmly undressed, removing her cap, her jacket, her trousers and finally her shirt, just as she had since she was eight years old and having grown up to see no harm in it. She would simply turn away and, with her front towards the fire, rub herself vigorously with black soap. Nobody took any notice of her, even Lénore and Henri were no longer curious to see how she was shaped. Once she was clean she went upstairs completely naked, leaving her wet shirt and the rest of her clothes in a heap on the floor. But then a quarrel broke out between the two brothers. Jeanlin had quickly jumped into the tub, on the grounds that Zacharie was still eating; and now his brother was shoving him out of the way, claiming that it was his turn and shouting that just because he was kind enough to let Catherine get washed first, that didn't mean he was going to wash in the dirty water left by little boys, especially as you could have filled every inkwell in the school each time this particular little boy had been in it. Eventually they had a bath together, also facing the fire, and they even helped each other get clean and rubbed each other's backs. Then, like their sister, they disappeared upstairs completely naked.

'The mess they make!' muttered La Maheude, picking the clothes off the floor in order to hang them up to dry. 'Alzire, mop up a bit, will you?'

But she was interrupted by a row going on on the other side of the wall. A man was cursing and swearing, a woman was crying, and there were sounds of a battle going on, with a shuffling and stamping of feet and a dull thumping sound as though someone were punching an empty marrow.

'The usual song and dance,' Maheu observed calmly, as he scraped the bottom of his basin with his spoon. 'Funny, though. Bouteloup said the soup was ready.'

'Ready indeed!' said La Maheude. 'I saw the vegetables still sitting on the table, not even peeled yet.'

The shouting grew louder, and there was a terrible thud, which shook the wall, followed by a long silence.

Then, swallowing a last spoonful, Maheu said with an air of calm and judicial finality:

'If the soup wasn't ready, it's understandable.'

And having downed a full glass of water he attacked the brawn. He cut small squares off it, which he speared with the end of his knife and ate off his bread, without a fork. Nobody spoke while Father was eating. He preferred to eat in silence; he didn't recognize it as Maigrat's usual brawn, it must have come from elsewhere, but he asked no questions. He simply inquired whether the old man was still asleep upstairs. No, Grandpa had gone out for his usual walk. Then silence once more.

But the smell of meat had attracted the attention of Lénore and Henri, who were having fun making streams on the floor with the spilled bathwater. They both came and stood next to their father, the little boy in front of his sister. Their eyes followed each piece, watching expectantly as it left the plate and staring in consternation as it disappeared into his mouth. Seeing how they turned pale and licked their lips, their father eventually realized how desperate they were to have some.

'Have the children had any?' he asked.

When his wife hesitated:

'You know I don't like it. It's unfair. And it puts me off my food to have them hanging round me begging for scraps.'

'Of course they've had some!' she shouted angrily. 'But if you listened to them, you could give them your share and everyone else's and they'd still be stuffing themselves till they burst . . . Tell him, Alzire. We've all had some brawn, haven't we?'

'Of course we have, Mummy,' replied the little hunch-backed girl, who in such circumstances could lie with truly adult aplomb.

Lénore and Henri stood there shocked, outraged by such a barefaced fib, when they themselves got thrashed if they didn't tell the truth. Their little hearts rose up, and they longed to protest that they had not been present when the others had eaten theirs.

'Off you go now,' their mother repeated as she herded them to the other end of the room. 'You should be ashamed of yourselves, always sticking your nose in your father's plate like that. And anyway, what if he *were* the only one who could have some? He's been out working, hasn't he, whereas all you good-for-nothing little scamps do is cost money. And cost more than you ought to boot!'

Maheu called them back. He sat Lénore on his left knee, Henri on his right; then he finished off the brawn with them as though they were having a doll's party. He cut each of them their share, in little pieces. The children devoured them with glee.

When he had finished, he said to his wife:

'No, don't pour my coffee just yet. I'll have a wash first . . . Here, give me a hand with this dirty water.'

They grabbed hold of the tub by its handles and were emptying it into the drain outside the front door when Jeanlin came down dressed in dry clothes. He was wearing trousers and a woollen jacket, which were both too big for him, tired and faded hand-me-downs from his brother. Seeing him try to sneak out of the open door, his mother stopped him.

'Where are you off to?'

'Out.'

'Out where? . . . You just listen to me. I want you to go and pick some dandelions for tonight's salad. Do you understand? And if you don't come back with that salad, you'll have me to reckon with.'

'Yes, yes, all right.'

Jeanlin departed, hands in pockets, dragging his feet and, though he was only a skinny ten-year-old, rolling his puny shoulders like an old miner. Then Zacharie came down rather more carefully dressed, wearing a tight-fitting black woollen jumper with blue stripes. His father shouted at him not to be late back; and off he went with a silent nod of the head, his pipe clenched between his teeth.

Once more the tub was full of warm water. Slowly Maheu removed his jacket. One glance, and Alzire was already taking Lénore and Henri away to play outside. Father didn't like washing in front of his family, which was the practice in many other households throughout the village. Not that he had anything against it; he just felt that splashing about together was fine for children.

'What are you doing up there?' La Maheude called up the stairs.

'I'm mending the dress I tore yesterday,' Catherine replied.

'All right . . . But don't come down. Your father's having his wash.'

So Maheu and his wife were alone. La Maheude had finally brought herself to perch Estelle on a chair, and, by a miracle, finding herself next to the fire, the child didn't wail and simply turned to gaze at her parents with the vague expression of a little creature that does not yet have thoughts. Maheu, now fully undressed, had crouched in front of the tub and dipped his head in the water before rubbing it with the black soap that, after centuries of use, had taken the colour out of these people's hair and turned it yellow. Then he got into the water and soaped his chest, stomach, arms and legs, scrubbing them energetically with both hands. His wife stood watching.

'I saw that look,' she began, 'when you came home . . . You were wondering how on earth we'd manage, eh? Those groceries certainly put a smile back on your face . . . Can you believe it, the bourgeois at La Piolaine didn't give me so much as a sou. Oh, they're kind all right, they gave me clothes for the little ones, but I was ashamed to be begging from them. It sticks in my throat when I have to ask like that.'

She paused for a moment to wedge Estelle more securely on her chair in case she fell off. Maheu continued to scrub away at his skin. He didn't seek to anticipate her account with a question, for the story interested him and he was waiting patiently to learn what had happened.

'And of course – sorry, I should have said – Maigrat had already refused me, oh yes, flatly refused me, the way you kick a dog out the door . . . So you can see what fun I was having! Woollen clothes are all very well for keeping you warm but they don't exactly fill your stomach, do they?'

He looked up but still remained silent. Nothing at La Piolaine, nothing from Maigrat: so then, how? But already she had rolled up her sleeves as usual to wash his back and the other parts of him he found it difficult to reach. And he liked her to soap him and rub him all over as hard as she could. She picked up the soap and, as she started scouring his shoulders, he braced himself against her movements.

'So I went back to Maigrat's and told him what I thought of him! Oh yes, did I tell him what I thought of him! . . . How he must have a heart of stone, and how he'd come to a bad end if there were any justice in the world . . . He didn't like it. He wouldn't even look me in the face. I'm sure he wished he was somewhere else . . .'

From his back she had moved down to his buttocks. Now completely absorbed in her task she pressed on into the clefts, scouring every inch of his body and making it gleam the way her three saucepans gleamed following one of her Saturday cleaning sessions. But she was sweating profusely after all this ferocious scrubbing, as if she had been pummelled herself, and she was so breathless that she could hardly get the words out.

'He accused me of being a parasite in the end . . . Still, we'll have enough bread to see us through to Saturday, and the best of it is that he lent me a hundred sous . . . He let me have the butter as well, and the coffee and chicory, and I was even going to ask for the brawn and the potatoes, but I could see he was starting to look unhappy . . . So I spent seven sous on the brawn and eighteen on the potatoes, which leaves me three francs seventy-five sous for a stew and a pot roast . . . How about that, eh? Not what you'd call a wasted morning, I think.'

She was drying him now, patting away with a rag at the last obstinate patches of moisture. Maheu, happy and without a thought for the morrow, gave a loud laugh and grabbed her in his arms.

'Let go of me, you brute! You're all wet, you're soaking me . . . But I just hope Maigrat hasn't got the wrong idea –'

She was about to tell him about Catherine but stopped. Why bother Father with it? They'd never hear the end of it if she did.

'What wrong idea?' he asked.

'The idea he can rip us off, of course. Catherine had better have a careful look at the bill.'

He grabbed hold of her again, and this time he didn't let go. His bath always ended like this: her rough scrubbing would excite him, and when she towelled him down it made the hair on his arms and chest tingle. Moreover, as for all the comrades in the village, it was their 'playtime', the hour of the day when more babies than enough were started into life. For at night there was always family present. Roguishly he pushed her towards the table: couldn't a fellow enjoy his one good moment in the day, what he called 'having his pudding' – and a pudding that didn't cost anything! She in turn struggled playfully to escape, wriggling her waist and bust in vain.

'Stop being so silly, for heaven's sake . . . And with Estelle sitting there looking at us! Wait till I turn her round!'

When he had got off her, Maheu simply pulled on some dry trousers. Once he was clean and had had his bit of fun with his wife, he liked to leave his chest bare like this for a while. On his skin, which was as white as that of an anaemic girl, the cuts and scratches made by the coal had left what looked like tattoos – 'graft marks' the miners call them – and he seemed proud of them as he displayed his broad torso and thick arms, which gleamed like blue-veined marble. In summer all the miners sat out on their doorsteps like this. Even now, despite the damp weather, he went out for a moment and shouted some ribald remark to a similarly bare-chested comrade on the other side of the gardens. Other men came out also. And the children playing on the pavements looked up and laughed with them, joining in the general joy as all this tired workmen's flesh was given its airing.

While he drank his coffee, having still not put on his shirt, Maheu told his wife how angry the engineer had been about the timbering. He felt relaxed now, all tension gone, and he listened with approving nods to the wise advice being given by La Maheude, who always showed great good sense in matters of this kind. She was forever repeating that there was nothing to be gained by confronting the Company head on. Then she told him about Mme Hennebeau's visit. Though they said nothing, it made them both feel proud.

'Is it all right to come down?' Catherine asked from the top of the stairs.

'Yes, yes, your father's drying off now.'

The girl was dressed in her Sunday best, an old, dark-blue poplin dress that was faded and worn at the pleats. She was wearing a bonnet of simple black tulle.

'Goodness! You're all dressed up . . . Where are you off to?'

'I'm going into Montsou to buy a ribbon for my bonnet . . . I took the old one out, it was filthy.'

'Have you got some money?'

'No, but La Mouquette's promised to lend me ten sous.'

Her mother let her go. But when she reached the door, she called to her.

'By the way, don't buy your ribbon at Maigrat's ... He'll only rip you off, and anyway he'll think we've got money to burn.'

Her father, who had squatted down in front of the fire to dry his neck and armpits more quickly, merely added:

'And don't be still wandering the streets after dark.'

That afternoon Maheu worked in his garden. He had already sown his potatoes, beans and peas; and he began to put in some cabbage and lettuce plants that he had heeled in the day before. This little patch of garden provided them with all the vegetables they needed, except for potatoes, of which there were never enough. He was good at gardening as it happened and even managed to grow artichokes, which his neighbours regarded as showing off. While he was preparing his bed, Levaque had chosen that moment to come and smoke his pipe in his own patch, and he was now inspecting the romaine lettuce which Bouteloup had planted that morning; for if it hadn't been for the lodger's determination with the spade, there would have been nothing but nettles growing there. And so they began to chat across the trellis fence. Refreshed and invigorated after beating his wife, Levaque tried unsuccessfully to drag Maheu off to Rasseneur's. Come on, one pint wouldn't do him any harm, would it? They could have a game of skittles, wander round with the comrades for a bit, and then come home for their dinner. This was what people generally did after work, and no doubt there wasn't any harm in it, but Maheu stubbornly refused: if he didn't get his lettuce plants in, they'd have withered by the next day. In fact he was being good: he didn't want to ask his wife for a single sou out of what she had left of the hundred she'd borrowed.

The clock was striking five when La Pierronne came to see if it was Jeanlin that her Lydie had gone off with. Levaque told her that something of the sort must have happened for Bébert, too, had vanished: those little rascals were always up to no good together. Once Maheu had told them about the dandelion salad and set their minds at rest, he and his comrade began to chaff La Pierronne with crude joviality. She was cross but made no effort to leave, secretly aroused by their dirty talk, which had her clutching her stomach and screaming back at them. Help arrived in the form of a skinny-looking woman whose angry splutterings made her sound like a clucking hen. Other women, standing in their doorways at a safe distance, made a show of being scandalized. School was out now and there were small children everywhere, swarms of little creatures screaming and fighting and rolling on the ground; while their fathers, at least those who were not off drinking, gathered in groups of three or four, squatting on their heels as though they were still down the mine, and smoking their pipes in the shelter of a wall as they exchanged a desultory word. La Pierronne departed in high dudgeon when Levaque asked to see if her thighs were nice and firm, and he decided to go to Rasseneur's on his own while Maheu got on with his planting.

It was rapidly getting dark and La Maheude lit the lamp, annoyed that neither her daughter nor the boys were back yet. She could have bet on it: they never did manage all to be there for the one meal when they could have sat down and eaten together. On top of which she was still waiting for the dandelions. What could that little rascal possibly be picking at this hour when it was pitch dark! A salad would go so well with the vegetable stew she had simmering on the stove, a mixture of potatoes, leeks and sorrel chopped up and then cooked with fried onion! The whole house reeked of this fried onion, which is a pleasant smell at first but soon turns rancid. Its foul odour penetrates the brickwork of the miners' houses to such an extent that the strong stench of this pauper cuisine announces their existence from far off in the countryside.

Once it was dark, Maheu came in from the garden and immediately slumped down on to a chair with his head against the wall. As soon as he sat down like this each evening, he fell asleep. The cuckoo clock was striking seven. Henri and Lénore had just broken a plate, having insisted on giving Alzire a hand setting the table, when old Bonnemort arrived back first, in a hurry to have his dinner before returning to the pit. So La Maheude woke Maheu:

'Oh well, let's eat anyway . . . They're old enough to find their own way home. But it's a shame about the salad!'

V

At Rasseneur's Étienne had eaten some soup and then gone up to the tiny room he was to occupy in the attic, overlooking Le Voreux, where he fell exhausted on to the bed still fully dressed. In two days he had had less than four hours' sleep. When he woke up at dusk, he was momentarily at a loss, unable to remember where he was; and he felt so groggy and ill that he struggled to his feet with the intention of getting some fresh air before having dinner and going to bed for the night.

Outside the weather was becoming much milder: the sooty sky was turning copper and threatening one of the long, steady downpours that are so common in this part of northern France and which can always be predicted from the warm moisture in the air. Night was falling, and great swathes of murk were enveloping the remoter reaches of the plain. The lowering sky seemed to be dissolving into black dust over this immense sea of reddish earth, and not a single breath of wind stirred the darkness at this hour. It was like the scene of some drab and sorry burial.

Étienne simply walked, at random and with no other aim than to clear his head. When he passed Le Voreux, already sunk in darkness at the bottom of its hollow and as yet unlit by a single lantern, he paused a moment to watch the day shift coming out. It was presumably six o'clock because stonemen, onsetters and stablemen were heading off in small groups and mingling with the blurred shapes of the women from the screening-shed, who were laughing in the gloom.

First came La Brûlé and her son-in-law Pierron. She was having a row with him because he hadn't stood up for her during an argument with a supervisor over her tally of stones.

'Bloody wimp! God! Call yourself a man, do you, crawling to those bastards like that? They'll have us all for breakfast, they will.'

Pierron was calmly following her, making no reply. Eventually he said:

'So I should have jumped the boss, should I? Thanks. A great way to get myself into trouble.'

'Show him your backside, then!' she shouted. 'Christ Almighty! If only that daughter of mine had listened to me! . . . As if it wasn't enough that they killed her father for me, now you want me to thank them too. Well, not me. I'll have their guts for bloody garters.'

Their voices died away. Étienne watched her depart, with her hooked nose and her straggling white hair and her long, skinny arms that were gesticulating furiously. But behind him the sound of two young voices caught his ear. He had recognized Zacharie, who had been waiting there and had now been joined by his friend Mouquet.

'Are you coming?' asked the latter. 'We're just going to get something to eat and then head for the Volcano.'

'Maybe later. I'm busy.'

'How do you mean?'

Mouquet turned and saw Philomène coming out of the screening-shed. He thought he understood.

'Oh, I see, that's it . . . Well, I'm off then.'

'Yes, all right. I'll catch up with you later.'

As he departed, Mouquet ran into his father, old Mouque, who was also coming out of Le Voreux; and the two men exchanged a simple 'hallo' before the son took the main road and the father made off along the canal.

Zacharie was already pushing a reluctant Philomène towards the same deserted towpath. No, she was in a hurry, some other time; and they quarrelled, as though they'd been married for years. It wasn't much fun only ever seeing each other out of doors like this, especially in the winter when the ground's wet and there's no corn to lie on.

'No, it's not a case of that,' he muttered impatiently. 'I've got something to tell you.'

He put his arm round her waist and led her gently forward. When they had reached the shadow of the spoil-heap, he asked if she had any money on her.

'What for?' she demanded.

Then he started mumbling something about owing two francs and how upset his family was going to be.

'Stop right there! ... I saw Mouquet. You're off to the Volcano again, and those filthy women that sing there.'

He protested his innocence, hand on heart, word of honour. When she merely shrugged, he said abruptly:

'Why not come with us, if you like ... It wouldn't worry me. What would I be doing with any singers anyway? ... How about it?'

'And the little one?' she replied. 'How can I go anywhere with a kid screaming all the time? ... It's time I went home. I expect they can't hear themselves think by now.'

But he stopped her, begged her. Please, he'd promised Mouquet and he'd only look a fool if he didn't go. A man can't just go home every evening like some roosting hen. Admitting defeat, she lifted the flap of her jacket, broke a thread with her nail and took some fifty-centimes coins from a corner of the hem. She was afraid of being robbed by her mother, and so this was where she hid the money she earned by doing overtime at the pit.

'Look, I've got five,' she said. 'You can have three if you want ... Only you've got to promise me that you'll try and persuade your mother to let us get married. I've had enough of this outdoor life! And what's more, Mum keeps blaming me for having so many mouths to feed ... So come on, promise me first. Promise.'

She spoke in the listless voice of a gangling, sickly girl who felt no passion and was simply weary of living. He for his part promised faithfully, loudly giving her his word as God was his witness. Once he had the three coins in his hand, he kissed her and tickled her and made her laugh, and he would have gone the whole way, here in this little corner of the spoil-heap which served as the winter bedroom of their domestic bliss, but she said no, it would give her no pleasure. And she returned to the village alone while he took a short cut across the fields to rejoin his comrade.

Étienne had followed them absent-mindedly at a distance, not realizing at first and thinking that this was an innocent meeting. They grew up quickly, these mining girls; and he remembered the ones back in Lille and how he used to wait for them behind the factories, whole gangs of them, already corrupted at the age of fourteen by living in the kind of destitution that makes people simply let themselves go.

But another encounter surprised him even more, and he stopped in his tracks. There at the bottom of the spoil-heap, in a space between some large rocks that had rolled down, was little Jeanlin giving a furious telling-off to Lydie and Bébert seated either side of him.

'What have you got to say for yourselves, eh? . . . You can each have your share of this fist if you think you can start demanding things . . . Whose idea was it in the first place, eh?'

It had indeed been Jeanlin's idea. After spending an hour roaming about the fields beside the canal picking dandelions with the two others, it had occurred to him as he gazed at the amount they had collected that they would never eat all that at home; and instead of going back to the village he'd gone to Montsou, taking Bébert along to keep watch and making Lydie ring the doorbells of the bourgeois and offer to sell them some dandelion salad. Already versed in the ways of the world, he said that girls could sell whatever they had a mind to. In the heat of the commercial moment they'd sold the whole lot, but Lydie had made eleven sous. And now, bereft of salad, the three of them were sharing out the proceeds.

'It's not fair!' Bébert protested. 'You should divide by three . . . If you keep seven, that'll only leave us two each.'

'What do you mean "not fair"?' Jeanlin retorted furiously. 'I picked more of them than you did, for a start.'

Bébert usually conceded out of timorous respect, forever the gullible victim. Though older and stronger he even allowed himself to be punched. But this time the prospect of so much money stirred him to resistance.

'He's diddling us, isn't he, Lydie? . . . If he doesn't share properly, we'll tell his mother on him.'

At once Jeanlin stuck a fist under his nose.

'You just say that once more and I'll go and tell yours how you sold my mum's salad . . . Anyway, you bloody idiot, how am I supposed to divide eleven by three? You try it if you're so clever . . . So there's two sous for each of you. Quick, take 'em or I'll stick 'em back in my pocket.'

Bébert had no answer and accepted the two sous. Lydie, who was trembling, had said nothing for, like the child equivalent of a battered wife, she felt afraid of Jeanlin and yet loved him too. As he offered her the two sous, she reached out her hand with a submissive smile. But he suddenly changed his mind.

'No, wait. What bloody use is two sous to you? . . . Your mother'll only pinch 'em off you. Bound to, unless you hide them. I'd better look after them. Whenever you need money, you can just ask me.'

And the nine sous vanished. To keep her quiet, he grabbed her and rolled her over on the spoil-heap. She was his little woman, and together in dark corners they would experiment at the love they heard and saw going on at home behind partition walls or through cracks in the door. They knew all about it but had scarcely the means; as yet too young, they spent hours groping each other and pretending to do it like two naughty young puppies. He called it 'playing mums and dads', and whenever he took her off somewhere, she eagerly followed. She trembled with the delicious instinctive thrill of it as she allowed herself to be taken; and though he often did things that made her cross, she always yielded in the hope of something which never came.

Since Bébert was not allowed to participate in these particular games and got thumped each time he tried to touch Lydie, he felt angry and put out and didn't know where to look when the pair of them messed about like this together, which they did quite happily in his presence. Hence his one idea was to scare them and to interrupt them by shouting that someone was looking.

'It's no good. There's a man watching.'

In this case it was true, for Étienne had decided to continue his walk. The children leaped up and ran away as he came past the corner of the spoil-heap and continued along the edge of the canal, amused to see the rascals get such a fright. No doubt it was too soon for them to be up to this kind of thing at their age; but, well, they saw such goings-on and heard such filthy stories, you'd have to have tied them up if you wanted to stop them. Nevertheless, deep down, he found it depressing.

A hundred paces further on he encountered more couples. He had reached Réquillart, and here at the old, ruined mine every girl in Montsou was to be found loitering with her man. It was where everybody met, a remote, deserted spot where the putters came and conceived their first babies when they didn't want to risk it on the shed roof back at home. The broken fences meant that everyone could get into the old pit-yard, which was now a wasteland littered with the remains of two collapsed sheds and the still-standing supports of the overhead railway. Disused tubs lay strewn about, and half-rotten timbering stood stacked in piles, while lush vegetation was vigorously reclaiming the place in the form of thick grass and some young trees, which had sprouted and were already sturdy. Each girl felt at home here: there were secret places for all, and their lovers could have their wicked way with them on top of the beams, behind the woodpiles or inside the tubs. They made themselves as comfortable as they could, cheek by jowl and yet oblivious to their neighbours. And it was as though, all around the defunct headgear and this shaft that was weary of disgorging its coal, creation itself were taking its revenge, as though unfettered love, lashed by instinct, were busy planting babies in the wombs of these girls who were hardly yet women.

All the same a caretaker still lived there, old Mouque. The Company had let him have two rooms situated almost directly beneath the derelict headgear, whose last remaining beams threatened daily to come crashing down on top of them. He had even had to prop up part of his roof. But he and his family were comfortable living there, with himself and Mouquet in one room and La Mouquette in the other. As there wasn't a single pane of glass left in the windows, they had decided to board them up: this made it dark indoors, but at least it was warm. In fact the caretaker had nothing to take care of; he simply went off to look after his horses at Le Voreux and never bothered about the ruins of Réquillart, where all that was kept under repair was the mine-shaft itself so that it could serve as a flue for the engine which ventilated the neighbouring pit.

And this was how old Mouque came to be living out his days surrounded by young love. From the age of ten La Mouquette had been having sex in every corner of the ruins, not, like Lydie, as a timid and unripe little urchin-child, but as a girl who had filled out and was ready for boys with beards. There was nothing her father could say or do about it, for she always showed him proper respect and never asked any of her boyfriends into the house. Anyway, he was used to such things. Whether he was on his way out to Le Voreux or coming home again, the moment he ventured out of his lair he was always tripping over some couple hidden in the grass. Even worse, whenever he wanted to fetch some wood to cook his soup or pick some burdock for his rabbit over on the far side of the mine, there all the girls of Montsou would be, popping their pretty little noses up out of the grass, and he had to be careful where he trod so as not to step on any of the legs stretched out across the path. But gradually such encounters had ceased to trouble either party, neither himself, who simply tried to make sure that he didn't trip over, nor the girls themselves, whom he left to get on with the business in hand as he tiptoed discreetly away like a good fellow who has no quarrel with the workings of nature. Except that just as they had now got to know him, so too he had come to recognize them, the way one recognizes amorous magpies disporting in the pear trees in the garden. Oh, these youngsters! They were always at it, they simply never stopped! Sometimes he shook his head in silent regret as he turned away from the noisy trollops panting loudly in the dark. Only one thing actually annoyed him: a particular pair of lovers had acquired the unfortunate habit of embracing against the outside wall of his room. Not that it kept him awake at night or anything of that sort; it was just that they pushed so hard that they were gradually damaging the wall.

Every evening old Mouque was visited by his friend Bonnemort, who would regularly take the same walk before dinner. The two old codgers barely spoke and rarely exchanged more

than a dozen words during the half-hour they spent in each
other's company. But it cheered them up to be together like this,
to reflect on past times and turn things over in their minds
without ever feeling the need to talk about them. At Réquillart
they would sit on a beam, side by side, utter a word or two, and
then off they went, nose to the ground, thinking old thoughts
and dreaming old dreams. No doubt it made them feel young
again. All around them the lads were lifting young lasses' skirts,
there was kissing and whispering and laughing, and the warm
aroma of girls rose in the air, mingling with the cool scent of
crushed grass. It was behind this pit, forty-three years ago, that
old Bonnemort had first had his wife, such a skinny little putter
that he had been able to pick her up and sit her on a tub so as
to kiss her more easily. Ah, those were the days! And the two
old men would shake their heads and finally take their leave,
often without even saying goodbye.

That particular evening, however, as Étienne arrived, Bonnemort was just getting up from the beam to return to the village
and saying to Mouque:

'Good-night, my old friend . . . Incidentally, did you ever
know that girl they called La Roussie?'

Mouque was silent for a moment, then shrugged; and as he
went back into his house, he simply said:

'Good-night, my old friend, good-night.'

Étienne came and sat on the beam. He felt even sadder now,
without knowing quite why. The sight of the old fellow disappearing into the distance reminded him of his arrival that
morning and how the nagging insistence of the wind had made
this otherwise taciturn man so voluble. All this hardship! And
all these girls, shattered with exhaustion but stupid enough
come the evening to make babies for themselves, yet more flesh
fit only for toil and suffering! There would be no end to it if
they just went on producing more hungry mouths to feed. Would
they not have done better to stop up their wombs and cross
their legs in recognition of the impending disaster? But perhaps
he was only mulling over such gloomy thoughts because he was
fed up at finding himself alone while everyone else was pairing
off to take their pleasure. He felt suffocated in the muggy

atmosphere, and a few spots of rain were beginning to fall on his feverish hands. Yes, they all went the same way, and reason was powerless to alter the fact.

Just then, as Étienne sat motionless in the dark, a couple coming down from Montsou happened to brush past without seeing him as they made their way into the overgrown yard. The girl, obviously a virgin, was struggling to break free, resisting and pleading with the man in soft, urgent whispers while he silently pushed her nevertheless towards the dark recesses of a piece of shed that was still standing, under which lay a pile of old, mouldering rope. It was Catherine, accompanied by the tall figure of Chaval. But Étienne had not recognized them as they went past, and his eyes followed them, watching to see how things would turn out and overtaken by a quickening of sensual interest, which quite altered the course of his reflections. After all, why interfere? If girls say no, it's only because they like a spot of rough treatment first.

On leaving Village Two Hundred and Forty, Catherine had walked to Montsou along the main road. Since the age of ten, when she had begun to earn her living at the pit, she had been used to going about the countryside on her own like this with the complete freedom that was customary among mining families; and if, at the age of fifteen, no man had yet laid a hand on her, it was because she was a late developer and still awaiting the onset of puberty. When she reached the Company yards, she crossed the street and went into a laundry-woman's house where she knew she would find La Mouquette; for the latter virtually lived there, in the company of women who treated each other to endless cups of coffee from morning to night. But she was disappointed to discover that La Mouquette had just bought her round of coffees and so could not lend her the ten sous she'd promised. By way of consolation they offered Catherine a glass of steaming hot coffee, but she would not hear of La Mouquette borrowing the money off another woman on her behalf. She had a sudden urge to economize, a kind of superstitious fear amounting almost to certainty that if she bought the ribbon now it would bring her bad luck.

She hurriedly set off back to Montsou, and she was just

reaching the first houses when a man hailed her from the door of Piquette's bar.

'Hey, Catherine, where are you off to in such a hurry?'

It was Chaval. She was vexed, not because she didn't like him but because she was in no mood for a laugh.

'Come in and have a drink . . . A small glass of sweet wine or something?'

She refused politely: it was getting dark, and they were expecting her back home. Chaval, meanwhile, had stepped forward and was now quietly pleading with her in the middle of the street. He had been trying for some time to persuade her to come up to his room on the first floor of Piquette's, a lovely room with a nice double bed in it. Why did she keep saying no? Was she afraid of him, then? She laughed good-naturedly and said she'd come up the day people stopped having babies. Then the conversation led on from one thing to another and, without knowing how, she started talking about the blue ribbon she hadn't been able to buy.

'But I'll buy you one, then!' he exclaimed.

She blushed, thinking that it would be best to refuse again but all the while longing to have her piece of ribbon. The idea of a loan occurred to her once more, and so she eventually accepted on condition that she would pay back the money he spent on her. They made a joke of it: it was agreed that if she never did sleep with him, she would repay him the money. But there was a further difficulty when he talked of going to Maigrat's.

'No, not Maigrat's. Mum told me not to go there.'

'That doesn't matter. You don't need to say where you got it! . . . He sells the prettiest ribbons in Montsou!'

When Maigrat saw Chaval and Catherine walk into his shop like a pair of lovers buying themselves a wedding present, he went red in the face and showed them the blue ribbons he had with the fury of a man who knows he's being mocked. After the young couple had made their purchase he stood at the door and watched them disappear into the twilight; and when his wife came and timidly asked him about something, he rounded on her, insulting her and shouting that one day he'd make the dirty beggars show some gratitude, he'd have them flat on their faces grovelling at his feet.

Chaval accompanied Catherine along the road. He walked close beside her, arms by his side but pushing her with his hip, guiding her while all the time pretending not to. Suddenly she realized that he had made her leave the road and that they were now on the narrow path that led to Réquillart. But she had no time to get cross; already his arm was round her waist and he was turning her head with his smooth patter. Silly girl, being afraid like that! How could anyone want to harm a pretty little thing like her? She was as soft and gentle as silk, so tender he could almost eat her. As Catherine felt his warm breath behind her ear and on her neck, her whole body began to quiver. She could hardly breathe and found no reply. He really did seem to love her. The previous Saturday night, when she had blown out the candle, she had lain there in bed wondering what would happen if he were to make his move like this; and when she fell asleep she had dreamed that she stopped saying no, that the prospect of pleasure had weakened her resolve. So why now did the same prospect fill her with revulsion and even somehow with a sense of regret? As he stroked the back of her neck with his moustache, so gently that she began to close her eyes, the shadow of another man, of the person she had glimpsed so briefly that morning, passed across the darkness of her unseeing pupils.

Catherine suddenly looked about her. Chaval had led her to the ruins of Réquillart, and she recoiled with a shudder at the sight of the dark, dilapidated shed.

'Oh no, oh no,' she muttered. 'Please, let me go.'

She was beginning to panic out of some instinctive fear of the male, the kind of fear that makes muscles tauten in self-defence even when girls are perfectly willing but sense that nothing will halt the man's all-conquering advance. Though not ignorant of life she felt threatened in her virginity as though by a terrifying blow, by a wound whose pain, as yet unknown, she feared.

'No, no, I don't want to! I've told you, I'm too young . . . Really I am! Later on, maybe, when I'm ready for it at least.'

'That just means it's safe, you idiot!' he growled in a low voice. 'Anyway, what difference does it make?'

But he said no more. He grabbed her firmly and shoved her under what remained of the shed. She fell back on to the coils of old rope and ceased to resist, submitting herself to the male even though she was not yet ready for him and doing so out of that inborn passivity which, from childhood onwards, soon had mining girls like her flat on their backs in the open air. Her terrified protestations died away, and all that could be heard was the man, panting hotly.

Étienne, meanwhile, had stayed where he was and listened. One more girl taking the plunge! Having now witnessed the whole performance, he stood up to leave, feeling a disturbing mixture of jealous excitement and mounting anger. He stopped trying to be tactful and stepped smartly over the beams: that particular couple would be far too busy by now to worry about him. So he was surprised, having gone a hundred paces along the road, when he turned round and saw that they were already on their feet and apparently on their way back to the village like him. The man had his arm round the girl's waist once more, holding her to him with an air of gratitude and continually whispering in her ear, whereas she was the one who seemed to be annoyed by the delay and in a hurry to get home.

Étienne was then seized with a sudden, overriding desire: to see their faces. It was silly, and he quickened his step in order to stop himself. But his feet slowed despite himself and, eventually, at the first street-lamp, he hid in the shadows. He was thoroughly astonished to recognize Chaval and Catherine as they went past. At first he wasn't sure: was this girl in a dark-blue dress and a bonnet really her? Was this the young scamp he'd seen wearing trousers, with a cotton cap pulled down over her ears? That's why she'd been able to walk right past him at Réquillart without his realizing who she was. But now he was in no doubt, for he had just seen those limpid green eyes again, like deep, clear springs. What a slut! And for no reason at all he suddenly felt a terrible urge to get his own back on her by despising her. Girl's clothes didn't suit her either, what's more: she looked dreadful!

Slowly Catherine and Chaval had gone past, quite unaware

of being watched like this. He was busy trying to make her stop so that he could kiss her behind the ear, while she had begun to linger under his caresses, which were making her laugh. Étienne, now behind them and obliged to follow, was irritated to find them blocking his path and to be forced to witness this exasperating spectacle. So it was true what she'd promised him that morning, that she hadn't yet been with a man; and to think that he hadn't believed her, that he'd held back so as not to be like the other fellow! And now he'd let her be taken from under his very nose! He'd even been stupid enough to sit there enjoying the thrill of watching them at it! It was infuriating, and he clenched his fists; he could readily have killed that man in one of those terrible moments of his when he saw red and felt the desperate urge to slaughter.

They continued on for another half-hour. When Chaval and Catherine came to Le Voreux, they slowed down even more, stopping twice by the canal and three times beside the spoilheap, for by now they were both in high spirits and absorbed in their amorous little games. Étienne had to stop too when they did, in case they saw him. He tried to persuade himself that he had but one, cynical, regret: that this would teach him to be polite and easy on the girls! Once they were past Le Voreux and he could have gone back to have dinner at Rasseneur's, he continued instead to follow them. He accompanied them all the way back to the village and stood there waiting in the shadows for a quarter of an hour before Chaval finally let Catherine go home. Now that he had made sure they were no longer together, he went on walking, far along the road to Marchiennes, simply trudging along with his mind a blank, too miserable and upset to go and shut himself away in a room.

It was not until one hour later, towards nine, that Étienne made his way back through the village, having told himself that he really ought to have something to eat and go to bed if he was to be up at four the next morning. The village was already asleep, plunged in darkness beneath the blackness of the night. Not a single gleam of light filtered through the closed shutters, and row after row of houses lay deep in slumber like so many barracks filled with snoring soldiers. A solitary cat made off across the deserted gardens. It was day's end, the final stupor of workers who had slumped from their tables into bed, stunned by food and sheer exhaustion.

Back at Rasseneur's a light was still burning in the bar, where a mechanic and two other miners from the day shift were drinking their beer. But before going in Étienne paused and took one last look out into the darkness. He found the same black immensity that he had seen that morning when he had arrived in the middle of a gale. In front of him Le Voreux squatted like some evil beast, barely visible, dotted here and there with a few pinpricks of light from the lanterns. The three braziers up on the spoil-heap blazed away in mid-air like bloodshot moons, and from time to time the shadows of old Bonnemort and his yellow horse could be seen passing across them in enormous silhouette. Out on the bare and empty plain beyond, everything lay submerged in darkness: Montsou, Marchiennes, the forest of Vandame and the vast sea of beetfields and cornfields where, like distant lighthouses, the blast-furnaces with their flames of blue and the coke-ovens with their flames of red alone provided the last vestiges of light. Little by little the night crept in like a black flood. Rain had begun to fall now, slow, steady rain that blotted out the yawning darkness with its relentless streaming; and only one voice could still be heard, the long, slow gasps of the drainage-pump, panting, panting, night and day.

PART III

The next day, and on the days that followed, Étienne returned to work at the pit. He gradually became accustomed to it, and his life began to shape itself round this new form of labour and the novel routines which he had found so hard at the beginning. Only one episode of note interrupted the monotony of the first fortnight, a brief fever that kept him in bed for forty-eight hours with aching limbs and a throbbing head, during which time he kept having semi-delirious visions of pushing his tub along a road that was too narrow for his body to pass through. But this was simply the debilitating result of his apprenticeship, an excess of fatigue from which he soon recovered.

Days followed days; weeks and months went by. Now, like his comrades, he would get up at three in the morning, drink his coffee, and set off with the bread-and-butter sandwich that Mme Rasseneur had prepared the night before. As he walked to the pit he would regularly bump into old Bonnemort on his way home to bed, and in the afternoon he would pass Bouteloup coming in the opposite direction to begin his shift. Étienne had acquired his own cap, trousers and cotton jacket, and he too would shiver and warm his back at the roaring fire in the changing-room. Then there was the wait, barefoot, at the pit-head, with its howling draughts. He no longer noticed the winding-engine or its thick, brass-studded limbs of steel gleaming above him in the shadows, nor the cables that flitted up and down with the silent, black swoop of some nocturnal bird, nor the cages that rose and vanished in ceaseless succession amid the din of clanking signals, barked commands and tubs rumbling across the iron floor. His lamp wasn't burning properly, the damned lamp-man must have forgotten to clean it; and he began to thaw only once Mouquet had got them all into the cages with a few laddish whacks on the bottom for the girls. The cage left its keeps and fell like a stone into a well without his so much as raising his head to catch a last glimpse of the light above. The thought of a possible crash never occurred to him now, and he felt at home as he descended into the darkness with the water raining down on top of him. After Pierron had unloaded them all at the bottom with his usual canting servility, the daily tramp of the herd began as each team of miners wearily headed off to its own coal-face. He could now find his way round the mine's roads better than he could the streets of Montsou, and he knew where to turn, where to duck, where to step over a puddle. He was so familiar with these two kilometres underground that he could have walked them without a lamp and with his hands in his pockets. And each time there were the same encounters: a deputy shining his lamp in their faces, old Mouque fetching a horse, Bébert leading a snorting Battle, Jeanlin running along behind the train to shut the ventilation doors, a plump Mouquette or a skinny Lydie pushing their tubs.

In due course Étienne also began to suffer less from the humidity and airlessness at the coal-face. The chimney now seemed an ideal way up, as though he himself had somehow become molten and could pass through chinks in the rock where once he wouldn't even have ventured his hand. He could breathe in the coal-dust without discomfort, he could see perfectly well in the dark, and he sweated normally, having got used to feeling wet clothes against his skin all day long. Moreover, he no longer squandered his energy in clumsy movements, and his comrades were amazed at the speed and skill with which he now did things. After three weeks he was spoken of as one of the best putters in the pit: no one rolled his tub up the slope more smartly than he did, nor then dispatched it more neatly. His slim figure allowed him to squeeze past everything, and for all that his arms were as white and slender as a woman's, there seemed to be iron beneath that delicate skin so stoutly did they do their work. He never complained, as a matter of pride no doubt, not even when he was gasping with exhaustion. His only failing was that he couldn't take a joke, and he would flare up the moment anyone criticized him. Otherwise he was accepted and looked on as a real miner even as the crushing mould of daily routine gradually reduced him to the level of a machine.

Maheu in particular took a liking to Étienne, because he always respected good workmanship. Moreover, like the rest of them, he could sense that Étienne was better educated: he saw him reading, writing, sketching little plans, and he heard him talking about things that he, Maheu, had never even heard of. That didn't surprise him: colliers are a tough bunch with thicker skulls than mechanics. But he was surprised by the young fellow's courage, by the way he'd put a brave face on things and just got on with it, knowing that otherwise he'd starve. He was the first casual labourer to have adapted so quickly. And so whenever they were under pressure to produce coal and he couldn't spare one of his hewers, he'd ask Étienne to do the timbering, knowing he'd make a good solid job of it. The bosses were continuing to badger him about this damnable business of the timbering, and he went in constant fear of Négrel, the engineer, turning up with Dansaert and shouting and arguing and making them do it all over again. But he had noticed that Étienne's timbering seemed more likely to pass muster with these particular gentlemen, despite the fact that they never looked happy and kept saying that one day the Company would have to sort the matter out once and for all. The issue was still dragging on, and sullen resentment was brewing in the pit. Even Maheu, normally so peaceable, seemed to be spoiling for a fight.

At the beginning there had been some rivalry between Zacharie and Étienne, and one evening they had almost come to blows. But Zacharie was a good-natured lad who didn't give a damn about anything other than his own pleasures, and so he was quickly pacified by the friendly offer of a beer. Soon he was obliged to recognize the newcomer's superiority. Levaque, too, was now well disposed to Étienne and talked politics with this putter who, he said, had some interesting ideas. And so among the men in the team the only mute hostility that Étienne now encountered came from Chaval. Not that there was apparently any coldness between them; on the contrary, they seemed to be on friendly terms. It was just that when they laughed and joked together their eyes betrayed a mutual animosity. Now caught between them, Catherine carried on as before, the weary, submissive young girl forever arching her back and putting her shoulder to her tub. She was always kind towards her fellow-putter, who in his turn did what he could to assist her; but otherwise she was subject to the wishes of her lover, whose

caresses she now publicly submitted to. It was an accepted
situation, an acknowledged relationship to which her family
turned a blind eye, so that each evening Chaval took Catherine
off behind the spoil-heap and then brought her back to her
parents' front door, where they gave each other one last kiss
in full view of the village. Étienne, who thought he'd come to
terms with the situation, often teased her about these walks of
hers, talking dirty with her for a laugh the way the lads and girls
did down the mine; while she would give as good as she got and
brag about what her lover had done to her. And yet when
their eyes met, she would turn pale and feel uncomfortable.
Then they would both look away again, and sometimes they
went an hour without exchanging a word, as though they
hated each other for some deep-seated reason that they never
talked about.

    Spring had arrived. Coming up out of the mine-shaft one day
Étienne had caught the full blast of a warm April breeze on his
face, a lovely smell of fresh earth, tender green shoots and pure,
clean air; and now, every time he came up, spring felt even
warmer and smelled still sweeter after ten hours spent working
in the eternal winter down below, where no summer sunshine
ever penetrated to banish the darkness and the damp. The days
were drawing out and by May he was going down at sunrise,
when Le Voreux would be bathed in the vermilion light of a
powdery dawn and the white steam from the drainage-pump
would turn pink as it rose into the sky. No one shivered now.
Warm air wafted in from across the distant plain, while way up
in the sky the larks would sing. Later, at three o'clock, he would
be blinded by the dazzling hot sun, which seemed to have set
the horizon ablaze and turned the grimy, coal-stained brickwork
red. By June the corn was already high, a bluish green against
the blacker green of the beet. It was like a boundless sea that
seemed to swell and stretch with every day that passed, rippling
in the faintest breeze, and in the evening it surprised him sometimes as if he could distinguish the new growth it had achieved
even since morning. Along the canal the poplars sprouted leaves
like plumes. Weeds overran the spoil-heap, and flowers carpeted
the meadows. As he toiled away beneath the earth, groaning with

effort and exhaustion, here were the seeds of life germinating and springing up out of the soil.

These days, whenever Étienne went for a stroll in the evening, it was no longer behind the spoil-heap that he came upon young couples. Now he would follow their tracks through the fields, and he could tell where the lovebirds were nesting from the movement of the ripening ears of corn or the tall red poppies. Zacharie and Philomène went back there out of habit, like an old married couple; La Brûlé, in her endless chasing after Lydie, was constantly running her to ground there with Jeanlin, the pair of them so deeply dug in that she had practically to step on them before they would take flight; and as for La Mouquette, she seemed to have lairs all over the place. It was impossible to cross a field without seeing her head ducking down and then just her legs sticking up as she lay pinned to the ground. As far as Étienne was concerned, they could all do as they pleased, except on the evenings when he came across Catherine and Chaval. Twice he saw them drop down in the middle of a field when they spotted him coming, and not a stalk moved afterwards. On another occasion, when he was walking along a narrow path, he saw Catherine's crystal-clear eyes appear just above the corn and then sink from view. After that the whole vast plain seemed much too small a place, and he preferred to spend his evenings at Rasseneur's bar, the Advantage.

'A beer, please, Madame Rasseneur . . . No, I shan't be going out this evening. I'm exhausted.'

And then he would turn towards a comrade who was sitting in his usual place at the far table, his head resting against the wall.

'How about you, Souvarine?'

'No, nothing, thanks.'

Étienne had got to know Souvarine by virtue of living there in close proximity with him. He worked as a mechanic at Le Voreux, and he rented the furnished room next to his in the attic. He must have been thirty or so, slim, blond, with delicate features framed by thick hair and a light beard. His white, pointed teeth, his small mouth and thin nose, and his rosy complexion all gave him the appearance of a determinedly sweet girl, while the steely glint in his eye gave periodic glimpses of a more savage side. His room, which was otherwise like that of any impoverished workman, contained just a single chest full of books and papers. He was Russian, but he never talked about himself and was content to let various tales circulate on his account. The miners, being deeply suspicious of foreigners and sensing from the sight of his small, bourgeois hands that he belonged to a different class, had originally imagined some story about his being a murderer on the run. But he had then behaved in such a friendly way with them, not at all proud and distributing every coin in his pocket among the village children, that they now accepted him, reassured by the tag of 'political refugee' that was bandied about, a rather vague term, which they interpreted as a kind of excuse, even for crime, and which made him seem like their comrade in adversity.

During the first few weeks Étienne had found him fiercely reserved, and so it was only later that he heard the full story. Souvarine was the youngest child of a noble family in the province of Tula. While studying medicine in St Petersburg, he had been swept up in the great wave of socialist fervour just like every other young person in Russia and decided to learn a manual skill instead. Thus he became a mechanic, so that he could mix with the common people and get to know them and help them as one of their own. And this was how he now earned his living, having fled after a failed assassination attempt on the Tsar:[1] for a month he had lived in a greengrocer's cellar while he dug a tunnel under the street and primed his bombs at constant risk of blowing the house up and himself with it. Disowned by his family, penniless, and blacklisted as a foreigner in French workshops where he was suspected of being a spy, he had been dying of hunger when the Montsou Mining Company had eventually taken him on during a labour shortage. For a year now he had shown himself to be a good worker, sober, quiet, doing the day shift one week and the night shift the next, and always so reliable that the bosses cited him as a model.

'Aren't you ever thirsty?' asked Étienne with a laugh.

And he replied in his gentle voice, with barely the trace of an accent:

'I only drink at mealtimes.'

Étienne also used to tease him on the subject of girls; he could swear he'd seen him in the cornfields one day with a putter over by the First Estate. But Souvarine would simply shrug his shoulders with calm indifference. A putter? What would he be doing with one of them? As far as he was concerned, women were workmates, comrades, assuming they showed the same courage and sense of solidarity as men. And anyway, why risk developing a soft spot which might one day prove to be a weakness? No girls, no friends: he wanted no ties. He was free, free of his own flesh and blood, and free of everyone else's.

Each evening towards nine, when the bar emptied, Étienne would remain there talking with Souvarine. He would sip his beer slowly while the mechanic chain-smoked, a habit which had eventually turned his slender fingers a ruddy brown. His eyes had the blank expression of a mystic, and they would follow the smoke upwards as he pursued his dream. He used to search restlessly with his left hand for something to occupy it and often ended up by installing on his knee a large female rabbit that enjoyed the run of the house and was always pregnant. This pet rabbit, whom he had named Poland,[2] now adored him: she would come and sniff his trousers, stand on her hind legs and then scratch him until he picked her up, as though she were a small child. As she snuggled down in his lap with her ears flattened along her back, she would close her eyes; and he would stroke her automatically, tirelessly running his hand through the grey silk of her fur and evidently soothed by this warm, living softness.

'Incidentally,' Étienne said one evening, 'I've had a letter from Pluchart.'

They were alone except for Rasseneur. The last customer had returned to the village, where it was time for bed.

'Ah, Pluchart!' exclaimed Rasseneur, next to the table where his two lodgers were sitting. 'What's he doing now?'

For the previous two months Étienne had been in regular correspondence with Pluchart, the mechanic he'd known in Lille. He had thought he would write and tell him about finding a job in Montsou, and Pluchart was now indoctrinating him, realizing how useful Étienne could be for spreading propaganda among the miners.

'He's doing fine, the Association's going very well. People are joining all over the place, it seems.'

'What do you think about this organization of theirs?' Rasseneur asked Souvarine.

Souvarine, who was gently scratching Poland's head, blew out a plume of smoke and murmured gently:

'More nonsense.'

But Étienne had the bit between his teeth. Fundamentally rebellious by nature and in the first flush of his ignorant illusions, he was immediately attracted by the idea of labour's struggle against capital. They were talking about the International Association of Workers, the famous International that had just been founded in London.[3] Wasn't it just wonderful, a plan of action that would at last bring justice to all? No more national frontiers, the workers of the world uniting and rising up to ensure that they each received their due wage. And how simple and yet grand the organization was. At the lowest level you had the section, which represented the district; then you had the federation, which brought together all the sections in one province; then came the nation, and finally, above that, humanity itself, embodied in a General Council on which each nation was represented by a corresponding secretary. Before six months were up, they would have conquered the world and be laying down the law to the bosses if they tried to be difficult.

'It's all nonsense!' Souvarine repeated. 'That Karl Marx of yours is still at the stage where he thinks he can just let nature take its course. No politics, no conspiracies, isn't that the way of it? Everything out in the open, and all with the sole aim of getting better wages . . . And as for his idea of gradual evolution, don't make me laugh! No. Put every town and city to the torch, mow people down, raze everything to the ground, and when there's absolutely nothing left of this rotten, stinking world, then maybe, just maybe, a better one will grow up in its place.'

Étienne started laughing. He didn't always understand what his comrade said, and this theory about destroying everything seemed something of a pose. As for Rasseneur, who was even more pragmatically minded and preferred the sensible approach of the man with a position in life, he didn't even bother to be irritated. But he did want to be quite clear about the matter.

'So, then. Are you going to try and start a section here in Montsou?'

This was what Pluchart wanted as secretary of the Federation of the Département du Nord, and he laid particular stress on the various ways the Association could help the miners if ever they were to come out on strike. Étienne did in fact think that a strike was imminent: the business over the timbering would turn out badly, and it only needed the Company to make one more demand and every single pit would be up in arms.

'But the subscriptions are a problem, though,' Rasseneur said in a measured tone. 'Fifty centimes a year for the general fund and two francs for the section. It may not seem much, but I bet a lot of them will refuse to pay.'

'Especially,' Étienne added, 'as we ought to start by setting up a miners' provident fund, which could if necessary be used as a fighting fund . . . At any rate, it's time we thought about these things. I'm game if the others are.'

There was a silence. The paraffin lamp was smoking away on the counter. Through the door, which was wide open, they could distinctly hear a stoker down at Le Voreux shovelling coal into one of the boilers that powered the drainage-pump.

'And everything's so expensive now!' continued Mme Rasseneur, who had just come in and was listening with a sombre expression. The black dress she always wore made her look taller than she really was. 'I tell you, those eggs I bought cost me twenty-two sous! Really, things can't go on like this.'

This time the three men were in agreement. One after another they spoke in despairing tones, and theirs was a long tale of woe. The working man wouldn't be able to survive; the Revolution had only made things worse for him; the bourgeois had been living off the fat of the land since 1789, greedily taking everything for themselves and leaving not so much as the scraps off their plates. How could anyone say that the workers had had their fair share of the extraordinary increase in wealth and living standards that had taken place over the previous hundred years? People had simply told them they were free and then washed their hands of them. Free? Yes, free to die of starvation. There was no shortage in that department. But you didn't get bread on your table by voting for splendid fellows who then promptly went off and led the life of Riley and spared no more of a thought for the poor than they did for an old pair of boots. No, one way or another it was time to put a stop to things, whether they did it all nice and friendly by agreeing new laws between them, or else like savages, torching the place and fighting each other down to the last man. It would happen in their children's time if not in their own, because there would have to be another revolution before the century was through. A workers' revolution this time, a right bust-up that would sort society out from top to bottom and rebuild it on a just and proper basis.

'Things can't go on like this!' Mme Rasseneur repeated insistently.

'Quite right!' the three of them cried. 'Things can't go on like this!'

Souvarine was now stroking Poland's ears, and she wrinkled her nose with pleasure. Staring into space, he said softly and as though to himself:

'But how can they put the wages up? Wage levels are fixed by the iron law of the irreducible minimum,[4] the amount which is just sufficient for the workers to be able to eat stale bread and make babies ... If the amount falls too low, the workers die and the demand for new men pushes it up again. If it goes up too high, the surplus supply of labour pushes it down again ... The point of equilibrium is the empty stomach, life imprisonment in the house of hunger.'

Whenever he let go like this and touched on socialist theories in the way of an educated man, Étienne and Rasseneur became anxious. It unsettled them to hear these grim assertions, and they did not quite know how to respond.

'Can't you see!' he went on in his usual calm way, looking at them now. 'We've got to bring the whole lot down, or the hunger will simply start all over again. Yes, anarchy! All gone, a world washed clean by blood, purified by fire! ... And then we'll see.'

'The gentleman's quite right,' declared Mme Rasseneur, who was always most polite in the expression of her extreme revolutionary views.

Étienne, in despair at his own ignorance, had had enough of this discussion. Getting to his feet, he said:

'Time for bed. That's all well and good, but I've still got to get up at three o'clock tomorrow morning.'

Souvarine had put out the remains of a cigarette that continued to cling to his lips and was already lifting Poland gently under the belly to set her down on the floor. Rasseneur began to lock up. Then they all went their separate ways in silence, their ears buzzing and their heads filled to bursting with the weighty matters they had just been debating.

And every evening, here in this bare room, they had further conversations of this kind, gathered round the single beer that it took Étienne an hour to drink. A whole store of half-conscious thoughts that had lain dormant in Étienne's mind now began to stir and develop. Though preoccupied above all by a need for greater knowledge, he had nevertheless hesitated for a long time before asking his fellow-lodger if he could borrow some of his books, most of which unfortunately were in either German or Russian. Eventually he had borrowed a French book about co-operative societies[5] (more nonsense, Souvarine said); and he also regularly read a news-sheet which Souvarine subscribed to, *Le Combat*, an anarchist paper published in Geneva. Otherwise, despite their daily contact, he continued to find Souvarine as uncommunicative as ever, like someone who was merely camping out in life without interests or feelings or belongings of any sort.

It was towards the beginning of July that Étienne's situation took a turn for the better. A chance occurrence had interrupted the endless, monotonous routine of life down the mine: the teams working the Guillaume seam had come across a so-called jumbling, a disturbance in the rock stratum, which meant that they were certainly nearing a fault; and, sure enough, they soon discovered the fault itself, which the engineers had had no inkling of despite their extensive knowledge of the terrain. The life of the mine was turned upside down, and people talked about nothing else but how the seam had vanished, with the section beyond the fault having no doubt settled lower in the earth. The old hands were already beginning to sniff the air like clever dogs at the prospect of a hunt for new coal. But the mining teams couldn't just stand around doing nothing while they waited for it to be found, and already notices had gone up announcing that the Company would be auctioning off new contracts.[6]

One day, at the end of the shift, Maheu walked along with Étienne and offered him a place in his team as a hewer, to replace Levaque, who was joining another team. It had all been agreed with the engineer and the overman, who had said they were very pleased with the young man's work. For Étienne it was simply a matter of accepting this rapid promotion, and he was gratified by Maheu's growing respect for him.

That evening they both went back to the pit to study the notices. The contracts being put up for auction were in the Filonnière seam, off Le Voreux's north roadway. They did not seem very attractive propositions, and Maheu shook his head as Étienne read out the conditions of sale to him. When they were below ground the next day, Maheu duly took him to the seam to show him how far it was from pit-bottom and to point out the crumbling rock, the thinness of the seam, and the hardness of the coal. Still, if you wanted to eat, you had to work. So on the following Sunday they attended the auction, which took place in the changing-room and, in the absence of the divisional engineer, was presided over by the pit engineer and the overman. Five or six hundred colliers were there, facing the small platform that had been set up in one corner; and the contracts were sold off at such a speed that all they could hear was a dull roar of people talking and of bids being shouted and drowned out by further bids.

For a moment Maheu was afraid he wouldn't get any of the forty contracts being offered by the Company. All his rivals were bidding lower and lower rates of pay for themselves: they were rattled by the rumours of an impending crisis and panicking at the prospect of being out of a job. The engineer, Négrel, took his time in the face of this fierce bidding in order to allow the offers to fall as low as possible, while Dansaert tried to hurry things along by lying to everyone about what excellent deals they had just made. In order to secure fifty metres of seam, Maheu was obliged to compete with a comrade who was every bit as determined as he was. One after the other each of them reduced his bid by one centime per tub; and if Maheu eventually emerged the victor, it was only by reducing his men's pay to such a level that Richomme, the deputy, who was standing behind him muttering angrily under his breath, nudged him with his elbow and complained crossly that at that price he'd never be able to make ends meet.

As they left, Étienne was swearing and cursing. He exploded when he saw Chaval on his way back from the cornfields with Catherine, calmly sauntering along and happy to leave it to Catherine's father to deal with the serious matters.

'Christ Almighty!' Étienne exclaimed. 'It's a complete bloody massacre. Now they're setting the workers at each other's throats!'

Chaval lost his temper. Never! He'd never have lowered his price like that! And when Zacharie wandered up to see what was going on, he said it was disgusting. But Étienne shut them up with a gesture of sullen violence:

'It's got to stop. One day we *will* be the masters!'

Maheu, who had been silent since the auction, seemed to rouse himself, and he repeated after Étienne:

'The masters! . . . Yes, and about bloody time, too!'

II

It was the last Sunday in July, the day of the *ducasse*[1] at Montsou. On the previous evening, throughout the village, all good house-wives had given their parlour a thorough clean, sluicing their walls and flagstone floors with bucket after bucket of water; and their floors were still wet despite the white sand they had strewn on it, an expensive luxury on a pauper's budget. Meanwhile the day looked as though it was going to be swelteringly hot. The atmosphere was heavy with a gathering storm, and an oppressive, airless heat smothered the bare, flat expanses of the seemingly boundless countryside of the Département du Nord.

Sunday always disrupted the early-morning routine in the Maheu household. While it infuriated Maheu to have to stay in bed any later than five, when he preferred to get up and dress as usual, the children would have a long lie-in till nine o'clock. That particular day Maheu went into the garden to smoke a pipe before eventually returning indoors to eat a slice of bread and butter on his own, as he waited for everyone else to get up. He spent the rest of the morning pottering about in a similar manner: he mended a leak in the bath-tub, and beneath the cuckoo clock he put up a picture of the Prince Imperial,[2] which someone had given to the little ones. In due course, one by one, the others came downstairs. Old Bonnemort had taken a chair outside to sit in the sunshine; La Maheude and Alzire had immediately set to with the cooking. Then Catherine appeared, ushering Lénore and Henri ahead of her, having just dressed them; and by the time Zacharie and Jeanlin came down last of all, bleary-eyed and still yawning, it was eleven o'clock and the house was already filled with the smell of rabbit and potatoes.

The whole village was in a state of great excitement, relishing the prospect of the fair and eager to have their dinner and be off to Montsou one and all. Gaggles of children were rushing all over the place, while men in shirtsleeves sauntered about aimlessly with that easy slouch which comes with days off. The fine weather meant that every door and window had been flung open, revealing parlour after parlour all crammed to bursting with the teeming life of vociferous, gesticulating families. And from one end of a row to the other the rich smell of rabbit vied that day with the persistent reek of fried onion.

The Maheus dined at twelve noon precisely. They made very little noise compared with the constant chatter and bustle going on outside as women hailed or answered their neighbours from doorstep to doorstep, lending things, chasing their kids outside or ordering them back indoors with a smack. In any case the Maheus had not been on speaking terms with their own neighbours, the Levaques, for the past three weeks on account of

Zacharie and Philomène getting married. The men were still talking, but the women pretended not to know each other any more. The quarrel had brought each household closer to La Pierronne. But she had gone off early that morning, leaving her mother to look after Pierron and Lydie, and was spending the day with a cousin in Marchiennes; and everybody joked about how they knew this cousin, and how she had a moustache and was an overman at Le Voreux. La Maheude declared that it was just not right abandoning one's family like that on the Sunday of the *ducasse*.

As well as the rabbit and potatoes (they had been fattening the rabbit in the shed for the past month), the Maheus had broth and some beef. The fortnightly pay-day had fallen the day before. They could not remember when they had last had such a spread. Even on St Barbe's Day, when the miners are allowed a three-day holiday, the rabbit had been neither as plump nor as tender. Accordingly ten sets of jaws, from little Estelle, who was just getting her first teeth, to old Bonnemort, who was in the process of losing his, were all chomping away so merrily that not even the bones were left. It was good having meat like this, but indigestible too because they ate it so rarely. They consumed the lot, and only a small quantity of boiled beef was left for the evening, when they could have some bread and butter as well if they were still hungry.

Jeanlin was the first to slip off. Bébert was waiting for him behind the school. They had to prowl about for a long time before they could entice Lydie away with them, because La Brûlé had decided not to go out and wanted to keep her at home. When she discovered that the child had gone, she screamed and waved her skinny arms about, while Pierron, irritated by the racket, quietly took himself off for a stroll with the air of a husband unabashedly having his own little bit of fun in the full knowledge that his wife is having hers.

Old Bonnemort was the next to leave, and Maheu decided that he, too, would get a breath of air, having first asked La Maheude if she would join him later at the fair. No, how could she, it was such a problem with the little ones; but, well, maybe she would all the same, she'd think about it, they'd always find

each other anyway. Once outside he hesitated, then went into
his neighbours' to see if Levaque was ready to go. But instead
he found Zacharie waiting for Philomène, and La Levaque, who
had just raised the eternal topic of their marriage, shouting her
head off about how no one gave a damn about her in all this
and how she was going to have the whole thing out, once and
for all, with La Maheude. What sort of a life was it, eh, looking
after her daughter's fatherless children while the daughter herself was always off somewhere rolling in the hay with her man?
Philomène having calmly put on her bonnet, Zacharie escorted
her out of the door, saying that as far he was concerned he had
no objection if his mother agreed. In fact Levaque had already
made himself scarce, so Maheu sent La Levaque round to see
his wife and beat a hasty retreat. Bouteloup, who was sitting
with his elbows on the table finishing off a piece of cheese,
stubbornly refused Maheu's friendly offer of a beer. He intended
to stay at home, as though he were the devoted husband.

Meanwhile the village was gradually emptying; the men were
all setting out now, one group after another, while the girls
watched them from their doorsteps and then made off in the
opposite direction, each on the arm of her sweetheart. As her
father turned the corner by the church, Catherine caught sight
of Chaval and hurried to join him for the walk along the road
to Montsou. La Maheude, left alone amid the chaos of her
children, and without the strength to get up from her chair,
poured herself a second glass of scalding coffee, which she
proceeded to sip. Throughout the village only the women were
left, and they invited each other in to sit round tables that were
still warm and greasy from their dinner and to finish off the
contents of their coffee-pots.

Maheu had an idea that Levaque would be at the Advantage,
and he walked slowly down to Rasseneur's. Sure enough, there
in the narrow, hedge-lined garden behind the house was Levaque
playing a game of skittles with some comrades. Standing beside
them, though not actually playing, Grandpa Bonnemort and
old Mouque were watching the progress of the game so closely
that they quite forgot to nudge each other in their usual way.
The blazing sun was beating straight down and there was only

one thin strip of shade, running the length of the building; and this was where Étienne was sitting at a table, drinking his beer, rather put out that Souvarine had gone up to his room and left him on his own. Almost every Sunday he shut himself away like this to write or read.

'Fancy a game?' Levaque asked Maheu.

But the latter refused. It was too hot, he was already dying of thirst.

'Rasseneur!' shouted Étienne. 'Bring us another beer.'

And turning towards Maheu he said:

'On me, you understand.'

They all knew each other well by now. Rasseneur seemed to be in no hurry, and they had to call him three times. Eventually it was Mme Rasseneur who brought them some warm beer. Étienne dropped his voice as he began to complain about the place; nice enough people no doubt, and they had the right ideas about things; but the beer wasn't worth drinking, and the soup they served was revolting. Ten times or more he'd have changed lodgings by now if Montsou hadn't been quite so far away. One of these days he'd look for digs with one of the families in the village.

'Quite right, quite right,' Maheu said slowly. 'You'd be better off with a family.'

Just then a shout went up, Levaque had knocked over all the skittles with one shot. Amid the uproar Mouque and Bonnemort stood staring at the ground, deep in appreciative silence. The general delight at the shot gave rise to various jokes, especially when the participants caught sight of La Mouquette's beaming face looking over the hedge. Having been wandering about outside for the past hour, she had finally plucked up the courage to approach when she heard the laughter.

'What, all on your own?' shouted Levaque. 'Where have all your boyfriends gone, then?'

'I've chucked them all,' she replied with brazen cheerfulness. 'And I'm looking for a new one.'

Everyone volunteered and chatted her up with improper suggestions. She shook her head and laughed even louder, pretending coyly to resist. In any case her father was present throughout this exchange of banter, even if he was still gazing at the fallen skittles.

'Go on with you!' Levaque persisted, glancing at Étienne, 'We all know who you're after, my girl! . . . But you'll have to take him by force.'

Étienne now joined in the fun. It was indeed him that the putter had her eye on. But he said no; she was good fun, all right, but he didn't fancy her in the slightest. For a few minutes longer she stood there by the hedge, staring at him with her big eyes; then slowly she departed, with a serious expression on her face all of a sudden as though she were finding the hot sunshine too much to bear.

Étienne had now resumed his conversation with Maheu, lowering his voice and explaining to him at length about how the Montsou colliers needed to set up a provident fund.

'The Company says it wouldn't stop us,' he insisted, 'so what is there to be afraid of? All we've got is the pension they give us, and since we don't contribute to it, they can dish them out just as they feel like it. Well, their grace and favour's all very fine, but it would be sensible to back it up it with a mutual aid association which we could at least count on in cases of urgent need.'

He went into the details and explained how it would be organized, promising to do all the hard work himself.

'Well, all right, I'm in favour,' Maheu said at length, now persuaded. 'But it's the others . . . You'll have to convince the others.'

Levaque had won, and they abandoned the skittles to down their beer. But Maheu refused a second: later maybe, the day was still young. He had just remembered Pierron. Where could he be? At Lenfant's bar in all likelihood. Having persuaded Étienne and Levaque to join him, the three of them set off for Montsou just as a new group of people came and took over the skittle-alley at the Advantage.

As they made their way along the road, they had to call in at Casimir's bar first and then at the Progress. Comrades hailed them through the open doors: how could they say no! Each stop meant having a beer, two if they returned the round. They would stay for ten minutes, exchange a few words, and then begin again further on, always perfectly well behaved, knowing just how much beer they could take and only sorry that they had to piss it out as fast they took it in, as clear as the water from a spring. At Lenfant's they ran straight into Pierron, who was just finishing his second beer and who then drank a third rather than refuse to have one with them. Naturally they had one themselves. There were four of them now, and they set off to see if Zacharie might perhaps be at Tison's. The place was empty, so they ordered a beer and waited to see if he would turn up. Next they thought of the Saint-Éloi, where Richomme the deputy bought them a round, and then they drifted on from bar to bar with no particular aim in view other than to have a bit of a wander.

'Let's go to the Volcano!' Levaque said suddenly, now thoroughly well oiled.

The others laughed, unsure whether to agree, but then followed their comrade through the growing crowds who had come for the *ducasse*. In the long, narrow room at the Volcano, on a platform of wooden planks that had been erected at the far end, five singers – the worst that the prostitute population of Lille could provide – were busy parading themselves, monstrously grotesque in their gestures and their *décolletage*; and the customers paid ten sous whenever they fancied having one of them behind the platform. They were mostly putter lads and banksmen, but there were pit-boys of fourteen too; in short the entire youth of the pits, and all of them drinking more gin than beer. A few older miners tried their luck also, these being the local womanizers whose home life was not quite what it might be.

Once their party was seated round a small table, Étienne buttonholed Levaque to explain his idea about the provident fund. He had all the proselytizing zeal of the newly converted who believe they are on a mission.

'Each member could easily afford to contribute twenty sous a month,' he repeated. 'Once all those twenty sous had mounted up over four or five years, we'd have a sizeable sum; and when you've got money, you can do anything, can't you? Whatever the circumstances . . . Eh? What do you say?'

'Well, I've nothing against the idea,' Levaque replied absently. 'We must talk about it again some time.'

He had his eyes on an enormous blonde girl, and when Maheu and Pierron finished their beers and suggested they leave rather than wait for the next song, he insisted on remaining behind.

Étienne followed them outside, where he found La Mouquette; she appeared to be following them. She was always there watching him with her big, staring eyes and laughing in her good-natured way as though to say: 'Do you want to?' Étienne made a joke of it and shrugged, whereupon she gestured angrily and disappeared into the crowd.

'Where's Chaval?' asked Pierron.

'That's a point,' Maheu replied. 'He's sure to be at Piquette's . . . Let's go and see.'

But as the three of them arrived at Piquette's, there was a fight going on at the door and they stopped. Zacharie was brandishing his fist at a stocky, placid-looking fellow, a Walloon[3] nailer, while Chaval stood watching with his hands in his pockets.

'Look, there's Chaval,' Maheu said. 'He's with Catherine.'

For five long hours Maheu's daughter and her lover had been strolling about the fair. All the way into Montsou, along the broad street that winds its way down between low, brightly painted houses, there had been a constant flow of people, streaming along in the sunshine like a colony of ants, tiny specks in the vastness of the bare and empty plain. The ubiquitous black mud had dried, and a cloud of black dust rose into the air where it was blown along like a storm-cloud. On each side of the road the bars were crammed with people, and the tables spilled out on to the pavement where there was a double row of stalls, a kind of open-air bazaar selling scarves and mirrors for the girls, knives and caps for the lads, as well as various sweet things such as biscuits and sugared almonds. Archery was going on in front of the church, and people were playing bowls opposite the Company yards. At the corner of the road to Joiselle, beside the Board of Directors' office, a piece of ground had been fenced off with planks, and people were crowding round watching a cockfight between two large, red cockerels with iron spurs on their legs and bloody gashes in their necks. Further on, at Maigrat's, there was billiards, with aprons and trousers for prizes. And everywhere there were long silences as the throng quietly drank and guzzled in a mute orgy of indigestion. Quantity upon quantity of beer and chips was gradually consumed in the sweltering heat, itself made hotter still by all the frying-pans sizzling in the open air.

Chaval bought Catherine a mirror for nineteen sous and a scarf for three francs. As they went up and down the rows they kept bumping into Mouque and Bonnemort, who had come to see the fair and were slowly trudging through it, side by side, deep in thought. But another chance encounter made them cross, as they caught sight of Jeanlin inciting Bébert and Lydie to steal some bottles of gin from a temporary bar which had been set up on the edge of some waste ground. All Catherine could do was give her brother a clout, for Lydie had already fled clutching a bottle. Those little devils would end up in prison one day.

Then they came to the Severed Head, and Chaval thought he would take Catherine in to watch a songbird competition which had been advertised on the door for the past week. Fifteen nailers had turned up from the nail-works at Marchiennes, each with a dozen cages; and these little cages, each one covered so that the sightless bird inside remained quite still, were already in place, hanging from a fence in the yard. The object was to see which bird would repeat its song the greatest number of times in one hour. Each nailer would stand next to his own cages, recording the tally on a slate and keeping an eye on his neighbours just as they kept an eye on him. And then the birds began: the *chichouïeux* with their deeper note, the *batisecouics* with their high-pitched trill, all of them hesitant at first, venturing only a few snatches of song, then gradually getting each other going, increasing the tempo, and eventually becoming so carried away by the spirit of competition that some of them actually fell off their perch and died. The nailers would urge them on roughly, shouting at them in Walloon to keep singing, more, more, just one last little burst of song; while the spectators, a hundred or more of them, stood there in silence, riveted, surrounded by this infernal music of a hundred and eighty

finches all repeating the same song at different intervals. A
batisecouic won first prize, which was a metal coffee-pot.

Catherine and Chaval were still there when Zacharie and
Philomène arrived. They shook hands and stood around together. But suddenly Zacharie flew into a rage when he caught
a nailer, who had come along with his comrades out of curiosity,
pinching his sister in the thigh. Catherine went bright red and
told him to be quiet, terrified at the prospect of a punch-up and
all these nailers rounding on Chaval if he were to make an issue
of them pinching her. She had felt the man's hand all right but
thought it better not to say anything. But her lover simply
sneered at him, and the four of them left; the matter seemed to
be forgotten. Hardly had they arrived at Piquette's for another
drink, however, than the nailer showed up again, quite unconcerned, laughing in their faces with an air of provocation.
Zacharie, his family honour at stake, had promptly set upon the
insolent man.

'That's my sister, you bastard! . . . You wait and see if I don't
bloody teach you some respect!'

People rushed to separate the two men, while Chaval, who
had remained very calm, reacted as before:

'Leave him be. This is my business. And as far as I'm concerned, he can go to hell!'

Maheu arrived with his group, and he tried to comfort
Catherine and Philomène, who were already in tears. By now
people were laughing, and the nailer had gone. Piquette's was
Chaval's local, and so to help everyone forget about the incident
he ordered a round. Étienne found himself clinking glasses with
Catherine, and they all drank together, the father, the daughter
and her lover, the son and his mistress, all politely saying:
'Cheers everyone!' Then Pierron insisted on buying his round,
and everyone seemed to be on the best of terms when Zacharie
flew into a rage again on catching sight of his friend Mouquet.
He shouted to him to come and help him sort that nailer out, as
he put it.

'I've got to get the bastard! . . . Here, Chaval, you and
Catherine look after Philomène for me, will you? I'll be back.'

Now it was Maheu's turn to buy a round. After all, it wasn't such a bad thing if the lad wanted to stick up for his sister. But Philomène, who had calmed down when she saw Mouquet arrive, just shook her head. You could be sure the buggers had gone off to the Volcano together.

Come the evening on *ducasse* days, everyone would end up at the Jolly Fellow. This dance-hall was run by Widow Desire, a stout matron of fifty who was as round as a barrel but still so full of energy that she had six lovers, one for each day of the week, she used to say, and all six at once on Sundays. She referred to the miners as her children in fond remembrance of the river of beer she had poured down them over the past thirty years; and she also liked to boast that no putter ever got pregnant without having first had a spot of slap and tickle at the Jolly Fellow. The place consisted of two rooms: the bar itself, where the counter and tables were, and then, on the same level but through a broad archway, the dance-hall. This was a huge room, with an area of wooden floor-boards in the middle surrounded by brick. The only decoration was provided by garlands of paper flowers strung from opposite corners of the ceiling and joined together in the middle by a wreath of matching flowers. Round the walls ran a line of gilt shields bearing the names of saints, like St Éloi, the patron saint of ironworkers, St Crispin, the patron saint of cobblers, St Barbe, the patron saint of miners, in fact the whole calendar of saints celebrated by tradesmen's guilds. The ceiling was so low that the three musicians sitting on the stage, itself no bigger than a pulpit, banged their heads on it. To light the room in the evenings four paraffin lamps were hung, one in each corner.

That Sunday there was dancing from five o'clock onwards, when daylight was still streaming through the windows. But it was nearer seven by the time the rooms filled up with people. Outside a storm was gathering: the wind had got up and was stirring large clouds of black dust, which got into everybody's eyes and sizzled in the frying-pans. Maheu, Étienne and Pierron had come to the Jolly Fellow in search of somewhere to sit and found Chaval dancing with Catherine while Philomène stood watching on her own. Neither Levaque nor Zacharie had re-appeared. Since there were no benches round the dance-floor,

Catherine came and sat at her father's table between dances.
They called Philomène over, but she said she preferred to stand.
The light was fading, the musicians were in full swing, and all
that could be seen was a flurry of hips and busts and a general
flailing of arms. There was a roar when the four lamps arrived,
and suddenly everything was lit up, the red faces, the tumbling
hair clinging to wet skin, the swirling skirts fanning the air with
the pungent smell of sweating couples. Maheu drew Étienne's
attention to La Mouquette, round and plump like a bladder of
lard, who was gyrating wildly in the arms of a tall, thin banksman. She must have decided to make do with someone else.

It was eight o'clock by the time La Maheude finally arrived
with Estelle at her breast and her brood of Alzire, Henri and
Lénore trailing behind her. She had come straight to the Jolly
Fellow, knowing that that was where she would find Maheu.
Supper could wait; no one was hungry, their stomachs were
either full of coffee or bloated with beer. Other women arrived,
and people began to whisper when they saw La Levaque walk
in behind La Maheude and accompanied by Bouteloup, who
was leading Philomène's children, Achille and Désirée, by the
hand. The two neighbours seemed to be on perfectly friendly
terms as the one turned and chatted with the other. On their
way over the women had had things out once and for all. La
Maheude was now resigned to Zacharie's marriage, and while
she was wretched at the thought of losing her eldest child's
earnings, she had finally been won over by the realization that
she couldn't in all fairness hang on to him any longer. So she
had tried to put a brave face on the matter, despite the anxiety
she felt as a housewife wondering how on earth she was going
to make ends meet now that such an important source of her
housekeeping was leaving.

'Sit yourself down, love,' she said, pointing to a table near
where Maheu was having a drink with Étienne and Pierron.

'Isn't my husband with you?' asked La Levaque.

His comrades told her he'd be back soon. Everyone squeezed
in, Bouteloup, the little ones, all so tightly packed amid the
pressing throng of drinkers that the two tables merged into
one. They ordered some beer. Seeing her mother and children,

Philomène had finally decided to come and join them. She accepted the offer of a seat and seemed happy at the news that she was at last to be married. When they asked where Zacharie was, she replied in her usual flat tone:

'I'm expecting him any moment. He's not far away.'

Maheu had exchanged a look with his wife. So she had agreed, then? He became pensive and smoked in silence. He, too, was thinking anxiously about what tomorrow would bring, and about the ingratitude of these children who, one by one, were going to get married and leave their parents destitute.

People continued to dance, and the final steps of a quadrille filled the hall with a reddish dust. The place was bursting at the seams now, and a cornet was sounding a series of high-pitched whistles, like a locomotive in distress. When the dancers came to a stop, they were steaming like horses.

'Do you remember,' La Levaque asked, leaning towards La Maheude's ear, 'how you said you'd strangle Catherine if she did anything silly!'

Chaval had escorted Catherine back to the family table, and the two of them were now standing behind Maheu finishing their beer.

'Oh, well,' La Maheude answered softly in a resigned tone. 'One says these things but . . . Anyway, my one consolation is that she can't have children yet. I know that for a fact! . . . Just imagine if she were to have one, too, and I had to find her a husband. What would we live on then?'

The whistling cornet was now playing a polka; and as the deafening noise began again, Maheu whispered to his wife what he had in mind. Why didn't they take a lodger? Étienne, for example. He was looking to board somewhere. With Zacharie leaving they'd have enough room, and they could make back some of the money they were losing. La Maheude's face lit up: of course, what a good idea, they must do it. It seemed to her as though she had been saved from starvation once again, and her good humour returned so promptly that she proceeded to order another round of beer.

Étienne, meanwhile, was trying to indoctrinate Pierron and explaining his plans for a provident fund. He had already persuaded him to join when he made the mistake of revealing his real purpose.

'And if we came out on strike, you can see how useful the fund would be. We could tell the Company to go to hell because we'd have the beginnings of a fighting fund . . . So it's a deal then? You'll join?'

Pierron had lowered his eyes and turned pale.

'I'll think about it,' he stammered. 'Good behaviour, though, that's the best provident fund.'

Maheu interrupted Étienne and offered there and then, in his blunt, friendly way, to take him in as a lodger. The young man accepted in the same spirit, keen as he was to live in the miners' village and share more in the life of his comrades. The matter was quickly settled, though La Maheude said they'd have to wait till the two children were married.

At that very moment Zacharie finally turned up, with Mouquet and Levaque. The three of them reeked of the Volcano, of gin and the sharp, musky scent of loose women. They were very drunk and looked extremely pleased with themselves, nudging each other and sniggering. When he learned they were finally marrying him off, Zacharie began to laugh so loudly he nearly choked. Unfazed, Philomène declared that she'd rather see him laugh than cry. Since there were no more chairs, Bouteloup had squeezed along to let Levaque share half of his; whereupon the latter, suddenly overcome at seeing everyone together like this in one big happy family, ordered yet another round of beer.

'God! This is the life, eh?' he roared.

They sat on till ten o'clock. Women were still arriving, trailing hordes of children and having come to collect their menfolk and take them home. The mothers among them, past caring, pulled out long, pale breasts like so many sacks of oats and splattered chubby babies with milk, while toddlers full of beer crawled on all fours beneath the tables and relieved themselves unconcernedly. And all around them rose a tide of beer from Widow Desire's emptying barrels, turning bellies round and taut, flowing out of every orifice, from noses, eyes and elsewhere. There was such a general swelling among this mass of people that by now each of them had an elbow or a knee digging into their neighbour, and everyone beamed away merrily at being packed in so tight. In the continuous laughter mouths gaped fixedly, like cracks running from ear to ear. It was baking hot, and as they took their ease and bared their flesh, they all gently cooked, golden brown amid the thick pall of pipe smoke. The only disturbance came when they had to let someone past, for every so often a girl got up, went out to the place by the pump at the far end of the hall, hitched her skirts and then returned. Beneath the paper garlands the dancers were sweating so much they couldn't see each other, which encouraged the pit-boys to try knocking the putters flying with a casual collision of backsides. But whenever a girl fell over with a man on top of her, the cornet's furious tooting covered the sound of their fall, and they would be buried under a whirl of feet as though the whole dance-hall had rolled over them like a landslide.

Someone alerted Pierron as they passed that his daughter Lydie was asleep at the door and lying across the pavement. Having had her share of the stolen bottle, she was drunk, and he had to sling her over his shoulder and carry her home, while Jeanlin and Bébert, who could take their drink better, followed him at a distance, finding the whole thing very funny. This was the cue that it was time to go home. Families began to leave the Jolly Fellow, and the Maheus and the Levaques eventually decided to return to the village. At the same moment Bonnemort and old Mouque were also leaving Montsou, still walking as though in their sleep and stubbornly absorbed in the silence of their memories. And they all went home together, taking one last walk through the fair, past the frying-pans and their congealing fat, past all the bars where the last beers were streaming out to the tables in the middle of the road. The storm was still brewing, and the sound of laughter rang in the air as they left the lights of Montsou behind and vanished into the blackness of the countryside. From the fields of ripe corn rose warm, urgent breath: many a child must have been fathered that night. They straggled limply into the village. Neither the Levaques nor the Maheus had much of an appetite for their supper, and the latter fell asleep as they tried to finish their leftover beef.

Étienne had taken Chaval off for another drink at Rasseneur's.

'Count me in!' Chaval had said when his comrade explained to him about the provident fund. 'Shake on it. Ah, you're a good'un all right.'

Étienne's shining eyes were beginning to show the effects of his drinking, and he cried:

'Yes, let's shake on it . . . I could go without everything, you know, the beer, the women, all of it, if we could just have justice. It's the only thing I really care about, the thought that one day we'll get rid of these bourgeois once and for all.'

III

Towards the middle of August Étienne moved in with the Maheus, once Zacharie had married and was able to obtain a vacant house in the village for Philomène and her two children; and at first the young man felt awkward in Catherine's presence.

They lived in ceaseless and intimate proximity, for he was taking the elder brother's place in all things and shared a bed with Jeanlin, just beside his big sister's. In the mornings, and at night, he had to dress and undress next to her, and he could see her too as she removed her clothes or put them on again. When the last underskirt fell to the floor, there she would be in all her pale whiteness, with that snowy transparency of skin character-istic of the fair-haired anaemic; and he never failed to be shocked at seeing her so white (when her hands and face were already stained), as if she had been dipped in milk from her heels right up to her neck, where the hauling-rope had left its mark like an amber necklace. He pretended to look away, but gradually he came to know her: first the feet, visible to his lowered gaze; then a knee, glimpsed as she slid beneath the blanket; and later her firm little breasts as she bent over the wash-basin in the mornings. While she seemed to pay him no heed, she would nevertheless undress as quickly as possible and in no time was lying next to Alzire, having slithered into bed so fast, like a snake, that he had hardly got his shoes off before she was vanishing from view, with her back towards him and only her thick bun now to be seen.

Moreover, she never had call to complain. Though a kind of obsession drove him, in spite of himself, to watch out for the moment when she got into bed, he never made smutty remarks, and he kept his hands to himself. Her parents were near by, and anyway the mixture of friendship and resentment he felt on her account prevented him from treating her as a girl to be desired, surrounded as they were by the unreserve of their newly shared existence, washing and eating and working side by side, with nothing left to hide, not even their most intimate personal needs. The last bastion of the family's modesty was the daily bath, which Catherine now took alone upstairs while the men bathed in turn down below.

And so by the end of the first month it was as though Étienne and Catherine had ceased to notice each other, as they wandered about at bedtime in a state of undress before putting out the candle. She no longer hurried as she took off her clothes, and she had resumed her old practice of sitting on the edge of the bed while she put her hair up, causing her nightdress to ride up her thighs as she stretched her arms above her head; and sometimes, even with no trousers on, he would help her look for lost hairpins. Habit overcame the shame of their nakedness; it felt quite natural to them, for after all they meant no harm by it, and it wasn't their fault if there was only one room for so many people. Yet there were moments when they would suddenly find it disturbing, and this when they were not even thinking improper thoughts. Having taken no notice of her pale skin for several nights, he would suddenly see her again in all her whiteness, that whiteness which made him tremble and turn away, for fear he might yield to his desire to take her. On other occasions, and for no apparent reason, she would suddenly feel coy and start avoiding him, sliding quickly under the sheets as if she had felt the young man's hands take hold of her. Then, when the candle was out, they would know that neither of them was able to sleep and that they were thinking of each other, despite their exhaustion. And that left them feeling irritable and out of sorts the next day, because they much preferred the quiet evenings when they could relax together and be just good friends.

Étienne's only cause for complaint was Jeanlin, who slept curled up like a gun dog. Alzire breathed gently as she slept, while in the mornings Lénore and Henri would still be lying in each other's arms exactly as they had been put to bed the night before. Amid the darkness the only other sound in the house was of Maheu and La Maheude snoring, rumbling at regular intervals like bellows in a forge. All in all Étienne was more comfortable here than he had been at Rasseneur's; the bed wasn't bad, and they changed the sheets once a month. The soup was better, too, and his only regret was the lack of meat for dinner. But everyone was in the same straits, and he could hardly expect rabbit at every meal when he was paying forty-five francs for his board and lodging. Those forty-five francs helped the family to make ends meet more or less, while leaving various small debts to accumulate. And the Maheus showed their gratitude towards their lodger; his laundry was washed and mended, his buttons were sewn back on and his things tidied. In short, he could feel the benefits of a woman's touch.

This was the point at which Étienne acquired a firmer grasp of the ideas that had been floating around in his head for some time. Until then he had experienced only an instinctive sense of resistance amid the silent, festering resentment of his comrades. All sorts of confusing issues puzzled him. Why were some men poor and other men rich? Why were some men under the heel of other men, and with no hope of ever taking their place? And the first forward step was the realization of his own ignorance. But then a deep sense of shame, a secret sorrow, began to gnaw away at him: he knew nothing, and he didn't dare discuss with others these things he cared so passionately about, like equality among men, or the fairness and justice which demanded that the fruits of the earth be shared among all. So he acquired a taste for study, but of the unmethodical kind characteristic of people taken with a craze for knowledge. He was now in regular correspondence with Pluchart, who was better educated and already very involved in the socialist movement. He had books sent to him, whose poorly digested contents finally turned his head: especially a book on medicine, *The Hygiene of Miners*,[1] in which a Belgian doctor had summarized the various illnesses that people working in the coal industry were dying of; not to mention a number of arid and impenetrably technical treatises on political economy, some anarchist pamphlets, which made his head spin, and old newspaper articles, which he kept for use as irrefutable ammunition in any future discussion. On top of which, Souvarine also lent him books, and the one about co-operative societies had set him dreaming for a whole month about a universal exchange system which abolished money and based the whole of social life on the value of labour. The shame he felt at his own ignorance receded, to be replaced by a new sense of pride now that he was aware of himself starting to think.

During these first few months Étienne remained at the level of the enthusiastic beginner, his heart bursting with generous indignation against the oppressor and eagerly espousing the prospect of imminent triumph for the oppressed. He had not yet put together a system of his own from all his sundry reading. The practical measures demanded by Rasseneur were all mixed up in his mind with the violence and destruction advocated by Souvarine; and when he came out of the Advantage, where the three of them spent time almost every day ranting and railing against the Company, he would walk along in a kind of dream in which he was witness to the radical regeneration of all the peoples of the world with not a window broken or a drop of blood shed. Admittedly the means to this end remained obscure, and he preferred simply to believe that everything would turn out fine, for he soon got lost when he tried to formulate a specific programme of reform. Indeed he was full of moderation and illogicality, insisting from time to time that politics had to be kept out of the 'social question',[2] an opinion he had read somewhere and which seemed like the right thing to say among the apathetic colliers he worked with.

In the Maheu household they had taken to sitting up half an hour longer every evening before going to bed, and Étienne kept returning to the same subject. Now that he was becoming more refined, he was increasingly offended by the cheek-by-jowl nature of life in the village. Were they animals to be herded together like this in the middle of the fields, and all penned in so tightly, one on top of the other, that you couldn't so much as change your clothes

without showing your backside to the neighbours! It was so good
for your health, of course! And no wonder girls and boys went to
the bad, being thrown together like that!

'Obviously,' Maheu would reply, 'if we had a bit more money,
things would be easier . . . All the same, you're quite right, it
doesn't do anybody any good living on top of each other like
this. And it's always the same old story in the end: the men get
drunk and the girls have a baby.'

This started everyone off, and each member of the family said
their piece, as the fumes from the paraffin lamp mingled with
the reek of fried onion and turned the air fouler still. No,
certainly, life was hardly a bed of roses. You worked like an
animal doing what used to be done by convicts as a punishment,
more often than not it killed you, and still you didn't have meat
on the table come dinner-time. All right, so you did get your
daily plate of mash, you did eat, but so little, just enough so you
could suffer without actually dying, up to your eyes in debt and
chased after as though you'd stolen the bread you ate. Come
Sunday you just slept from the exhaustion of it all. The only
pleasures were getting drunk or giving your wife a baby, and
even then, the beer gave you a paunch, and the child wouldn't
give a damn about you when it was older. No, it was not what
you'd call a bed of roses.

Then La Maheude would join in:

'The worst of it, you know, is when you start telling yourself
that things can never change . . . When you're young, you think
happiness is just round the corner, you hope for things; but then
the poverty grinds on and on, and you find you can never escape
it . . . Me, I don't wish harm to anyone, but there are times when
the injustice of it all just sickens me.'

There would be a silence, and everyone would draw breath
for a moment, full of vague unease at the prospect of this closed
horizon. Only old Bonnemort, if he was there, would stare in
surprise, for in his day they didn't use to torment themselves
like this: you were a miner, you worked your seam, and you
didn't ask for more; whereas nowadays a new wind was
blowing, and the miners were getting some fancy ideas.

'You should take what you're given,' he muttered. 'A glass of beer is a glass of beer . . . Yeah, the bosses are often bastards all right, but there will always be bosses, won't there? So there's no point worrying about it.'

At once Étienne was roused. What! A worker shouldn't think for himself! Ah, but that's precisely why things were soon going to change, because now the worker *had* started thinking! In the old man's day the miner lived down the pit like an animal, like a machine for extracting coal, always underground, his eyes and ears closed to what was going on outside. Which meant that the rich and powerful could suit themselves, buying and selling the miner as they pleased, living off his flesh while he himself didn't even realize what was going on. But now, deep in the earth, the miner was waking from his slumber and germinating in the soil like a real seed; and one fine day people would see what was growing in the middle of these fields: yes, men, a whole army of men, would spring up from the earth, and justice would be restored. Were all citizens not equal since the Revolution? Why should the worker remain the slave of the boss who paid him when both of them now voted? The big companies with all their machines crushed everything in their path, and people didn't even have the safeguards to protect them like they used to in the old days when men of the same trade banded together and knew how to defend themselves. And that was the reason, God help us! among many others, why everything would blow up in their faces one day, and all thanks to education. You only had to look around you: the grandfathers couldn't even have signed their own names but the fathers could, and the sons were able to read and write as well as any teacher. Oh yes, they were growing and growing, one big harvest of men ripening in the sun! Now that they weren't all stuck in one particular job for life and you could look to take the place of the next man, why wouldn't you use your fists and show who's strongest?

This had its effect on Maheu, though he remained very sceptical:

'As soon as you try anything, they hand you your cards,'[3] he said. 'The old man's right. It'll always be the miner's lot to suffer, and without even the prospect of a nice joint of meat once in a while to keep him going.'

Having been silent for some time, La Maheude spoke as though in a dream:

'If only it were true what the priests tell you, about the poor in this world being rich in the next!'

She was interrupted by howls of laughter, and even the children gestured in disbelief. For the harsh wind of reality had left them all unbelievers, secretly fearful of the ghosts in the pit but full of mockery at the emptiness of heaven.

'Oh, don't give me priests!' Maheu exclaimed. 'If they really believed it, they'd eat less and work harder, so they could book a nice spot for themselves up above . . . No, when you're dead, you're dead.'

La Maheude sighed deeply.

'Dear God, dear God.'

Then, with her hands on her knees and an expression of profound weariness, she said:

'Well, that's it, we're done for, the lot of us.'

They all looked at each other. Old Bonnemort spat into his handkerchief. Maheu's pipe had gone out, but he just sat there with it in his mouth. Alzire listened, flanked by Lénore and Henri, who had both fallen asleep at the table. But Catherine in particular, her chin in her hands, stared intently at Étienne with her big, bright eyes as he disagreed and began to proclaim his faith, opening up the prospect of a magical future and expounding his dream of a new social order. Around them the village was retiring to bed, and all that could be heard were the distant wailings of a child or the angry reception of a drunk returning home late. Inside the room the cuckoo clock ticked away slowly, and a cool dampness rose from the sanded flag-stones, despite the stuffiness.

'And there's another load of nonsense!' said the young man. 'Why do you need a God and a paradise to be happy? Can't you make your own happiness in this world?'

And he would begin to talk, urgently, on and on. All of a sudden the closed horizon had burst asunder, and a shaft of light was breaking through into the grim lives of these poverty-stricken people. The endless round of deprivation, the brutish labour, living like animals to be shorn and slaughtered, all this wretchedness vanished, as though swept away by a great blaze of sunshine; and justice, as if by some dazzling enchantment, came down from above. Now that God was dead, justice would be the means of human happiness, ushering in the age of equality and the brotherhood of man. A new society would emerge in a single day, as in a dream, a great city shining like a vision, in which each citizen would be paid the rate for the job and have his share of the common joy. The old world, already rotten, had crumbled to dust; and humankind, newly young and purged of its crimes, would be one nation of workers, with the motto: 'To each according to his deserts, and to his deserts according to his works.' And the dream would grow ever grander and more wonderful, and the higher it reached towards the impossible, the more beguiling it became.

At first La Maheude would refuse to listen, seized with silent apprehension. No, no, it was too wonderful, it didn't do to go having ideas like that, it just made life awful afterwards when you felt as though you couldn't care who or what you destroyed just so long as you could be happy. When she saw the troubled look in Maheu's eyes replaced by a gleam of conviction, she became anxious and interrupted Étienne loudly:

'Don't you listen to him, my love! You know it's all pie in the sky . . . Do you think the bourgeois will ever agree to work the way we do?'

But gradually she, too, fell under the spell. Her imagination had been caught, and with a smile on her face she entered the fairyland of hope. How good it was to be able to forget their grim reality for a time! When you live like an animal, with your nose to the ground, you need a little corner somewhere, a place of make-believe where you can go and play at imagining delights that will never be yours. And what really excited her, what made her of one mind with this young man, was the idea of justice.

'You're right there!' she would cry. 'If the cause is just, they can cut off my right arm if they want . . . And it would be a just cause, I can tell you, if it was our turn to enjoy life for once.'

Then Maheu risked a show of enthusiasm:

'God Almighty! I may not be rich but I'd give a fair bit to be able to see all that before I die . . . Then we'd see the fur fly! Eh?

How long will it take, do you think? And how are we to go about it?'

Étienne would begin talking again. The old society was falling apart, it couldn't last more than a few months now, he roundly declared. As to how they were to go about it, he was less specific and quoted various things he had read, undaunted by these ignorant people and launching himself into explanations before losing the thread himself. He drew on every political system there was, each one sweetened by the certainty of easy victory and the prospect of a universal embrace that would put an end to class division – apart from a few awkward types among the factory-owners and the bourgeois, who might have to be brought to their senses. The Maheus listened with the air of people who understood, nodding their approval and accepting these miraculous solutions with the blind faith of new converts, like members of the early Christian Church calmly awaiting the emergence of the perfect society from the dunghill of the ancient world. Little Alzire caught a word here and there and pictured happiness as a lovely warm house where children played and ate as much as they liked. Catherine, her head propped on her hand, just sat staring at Étienne, and when he stopped, she shivered slightly and looked pale, as though she had suddenly caught a chill.

But then La Maheude would catch sight of the clock:

'It's gone nine. Really to goodness! We'll never get up in the morning.'

And the Maheus left the table, feeling sick at heart, despairing. It was as though they had momentarily been rich and had now suddenly fallen once more into the mire. Old Bonnemort, leaving for the pit, would mutter crossly that such talk never made a man's soup taste any better; while the rest of them went up to bed, one by one, now noticing the damp walls and the foul, stale air. Upstairs Catherine was the last to get into bed, and after she had blown out the candle, with the rest of the village in silent slumber, Étienne could hear her tossing and turning before she finally fell asleep.

Often neighbours would join them during these talking sessions – Levaque, who got excited at the thought of sharing wealth, or Pierron, whom caution sent home again the moment they started attacking the Company. Occasionally Zacharie would drop by for a while; but politics bored him, and he preferred to go down to the Advantage for a beer. As for Chaval, he would up the stakes and start baying for blood. He spent an hour at the Maheus' almost every evening, and his keen attendance bespoke a secret jealousy, the fear of losing Catherine. Though he was already tiring of her, the girl had become dear to him ever since there had been a man sleeping next to her each night, a man who could have her.

Étienne's influence was growing, and he was gradually revolutionizing the village. His was a propaganda by stealth, which became more and more effective as he slowly rose in people's esteem. La Maheude, though filled with the scepticism of a prudent housewife, nevertheless treated him with a certain deference as a young man who paid his rent on time, neither drank nor gambled, and always had his nose in a book; and among the women in the neighbourhood she created a reputation for him as an educated lad, a reputation which they took advantage of by asking him to write their letters for them. He became a sort of business agent, charged with their correspondence and consulted by households over ticklish matters. And so by September he had finally managed to set up his famous provident fund, as yet a very precarious enterprise with only the inhabitants of the village for members; but he hoped soon to secure the membership of the miners in all the pits, especially if the Company, which had so far done nothing, continued not to bother him. He had been made secretary of the fund, and even drew a small salary, to cover his clerical expenses. He was almost a rich man. While a married miner has trouble making ends meet, a steady bachelor without dependants can begin to save.

From then on Étienne underwent a gradual transformation. An instinctive fastidiousness about his personal appearance and a taste for comfortable living, both hitherto dormant beneath his destitution, now declared themselves, and led to the purchase of some good-quality clothes. He treated himself to a fine pair of boots, and at once he was a leader; the village began to rally to him. There now came moments of delicious gratification for his self-esteem, as he drank deep of these first, heady draughts of popularity: to lead like this, to command, when he was still so young, indeed until recently a mere labourer, it all filled him with pride and fed his dream of an imminent revolution in which he would have his role to play. His facial expression changed, he grew solemn and began to enjoy the sound of his own voice; and burgeoning ambition added fiery urgency to his theorizing and prompted thoughts of combat.

Meanwhile autumn was drawing on, and the October chill had turned the little village gardens the colour of rust. Behind the scraggy lilac bushes pit-boys had ceased to pin putters to the shed roof; all that was to be seen were a few winter plants, cabbages covered in pearly beads of frost, leeks and winter greens. Once again the rain beat down on the red roof tiles and gushed into the water-butts beneath the gutters with the roar of a torrent. In every house the iron stove stayed permanently lit, repeatedly stoked with coal and poisoning the close atmosphere of the parlour. Another season of grinding poverty had begun.

On one of the first of these frosty October nights Étienne was feeling so excited after all the talk downstairs that he could not get to sleep. He had watched Catherine slip into bed and blow out the candle. She, too, seemed restless, a prey to one of her occasional fits of modesty when she still undressed in such clumsy haste that she uncovered herself even more. She lay in the darkness with the stillness of a corpse; but he knew she could not sleep any more than he could; and he could sense her thinking of him, just as he was thinking of her. Never had this silent exchange of their being unsettled them so. Minutes went by, and neither stirred; only their breathing betrayed them, coming in awkward snatches as they strove to control it. Twice he was on the point of going over and taking her. It was daft to want each other so much and never do anything about it. Why be so set against their own desire? The children were asleep, she wanted it, here and now, he knew for certain that she was breathless with the expectation of it, that she would wrap him in her arms, silently, with her mouth tight shut. Nearly an hour went by. He did not go over and take her, and she did not turn towards him, for fear of summoning him. And the longer they lived in each other's pocket, the more a barrier grew up between them, feelings of embarrassment and distaste, a sense of the proprieties of friendship, none of which they could have explained even to themselves.

IV

'Look,' said La Maheude, 'since you're going to Montsou to collect your wages, can you bring me back a pound of coffee and a kilo of sugar?'

Maheu was in the middle of stitching up one of his shoes, to save on the repair.

'All right,' he muttered, without pausing in his task.

'And maybe you'd drop in at the butcher's, too? . . . And get us a bit of veal, eh? It's so long since we had any.'

This time he looked up.

'It's not thousands I'm collecting, you know . . . A fortnight's pay just doesn't stretch these days, what with them bloody making us stop work all the time.'

They both fell silent. It was after lunch, one Saturday towards the end of October. Once again the Company had cited the disruption caused by pay-day as an excuse for halting production throughout its pits. Panicked by the worsening industrial crisis, and not wanting to add to its already considerable stockpiles, it was using the slightest pretext to deprive its ten thousand employees of work.

'You know Étienne's going to be waiting for you at Rasseneur's,' La Maheude continued. 'Why not take him with you? He'll be better at sorting things out if they don't pay you your full number of hours.'

Maheu nodded.

'And ask them about that business with your father. The doctor's in cahoots with management over it . . . Isn't that right, Grandpa? The doctor's got it all wrong. You're still fit to work, aren't you?'

For the past ten days old Bonnemort had not moved from his chair; his pegs had gone to sleep, as he put it. She had to ask him again.

'Of course I can work,' he growled. 'No one's done for just cos their legs is playing up. It's all stuff and nonsense, so they don't have to pay me that hundred and eighty francs for my pension.'

La Maheude thought of the forty sous that the old man might never earn again, and she gave an anxious cry:

'My God! We'll all be dead soon if things go on like this.'

'At least when you're dead,' said Maheu, 'you don't feel hungry any more.'

He knocked a few more nails into his shoes and eventually left.

Those who lived in Village Two Hundred and Forty would not be paid until four o'clock or thereabouts. So the men were in no hurry, lingering at home before setting off one by one, and then pursued by entreaties from their wives to make sure and come straight home again. Many were given errands to run, so they wouldn't end up in the bars drowning their sorrows.

At Rasseneur's Étienne had come in search of news. Worrying rumours were circulating, and the Company was said to be getting more and more dissatisfied with the standard of timbering. The miners were being fined heavily now, there was bound to be a stand-off. Anyway, that wasn't the real problem. There was far more to it than that, there were deeper issues at stake.

In fact, just as Étienne arrived, a workmate who had come in for a beer on his way back from Montsou was busy telling everybody about how there was a notice up in the cashier's office; but he didn't rightly know what it said. Another man appeared, then a third; and each one had a different story. What was clear, however, was that the Company had come to some sort of a decision.

'What do you think?' Étienne asked, as he sat down beside Souvarine at a table where the only visible refreshment was a packet of tobacco.

Souvarine took his time to finish rolling a cigarette.

'I think it's been obvious all along. They want to force you to the brink.'

He was the only one with sufficient intelligence to analyse the situation accurately, and he explained it with his usual calm. Faced with the crisis, the Company had been forced to reduce its costs in order to avoid going under; and naturally the workers were the ones who were going to have to tighten their belts. The Company would gradually whittle their wages down, using whatever pretext came to hand. Coal had been piling up at the pit-heads for two months now, since all the factories were idle. But the Company didn't dare lay off its own workers because it would be ruinous not to maintain the plant, and so it was looking for some middle way, perhaps a strike, which would bring its workforce to heel and leave it less well paid than before. Last but not least, it was worried about the provident fund: this could prove to be a threat one day, whereas a strike now would eliminate it by depleting the fund while it was still small.

Rasseneur had sat down next to Étienne, and the two of them listened in consternation. They could talk freely since there was only Mme Rasseneur left, sitting at the counter.

'What a thought!' Rasseneur muttered. 'But why? It's not in the Company's interest to have a strike, nor in the workers'. It would be better to come to some agreement.'

This was the sensible way forward. He was always the one for making reasonable demands. In fact, since the sudden popularity of his former lodger, he had been rather overdoing his line about politics and the art of the possible, and how people who wanted 'everything, and now!' got nothing. He was a jovial man, the typical beer-drinker with a fat belly, but deep down he felt a growing jealousy, which was not helped by the fall in his trade: the workers from Le Voreux were coming into his bar less and less to have a drink and listen to him, which meant that sometimes he even found himself defending the Company and forgetting his resentment at having been sacked when he was a miner.

'So you're against a strike?' Mme Rasseneur shouted over from the counter.

And when he energetically said 'yes', she cut him short.

'Pah! You've no guts. You should listen to these two gentlemen.'

Deep in thought, Étienne was gazing down at the beer she had brought him. Eventually he looked up:

'Everything our friend here says is perfectly possible, and we simply will have to strike if they force us to it . . . As it happens, Pluchart's recently sent me some sound advice on the subject. He's against a strike, too, because the workers suffer as much as the bosses but end up with nothing to show for it. Except that he sees the strike as a great opportunity to get our men involved in his grand plan . . . Here's his letter, in fact.'

Sure enough, Pluchart, despairing of the Montsou miners' sceptical attitude towards the International, was hoping to see them join *en masse* if a dispute were to set them at odds with the Company. Despite all his efforts, Étienne had failed to get a single person to join, though he had mainly been using his influence in the cause of his own provident fund, which had been much better received. But the fund was still so small that it would, as Souvarine said, be quickly exhausted; and then, inevitably, the strikers would rush to join the Workers' Association, in the hope that their brothers throughout the world would come to their aid.

'How much have you got in the fund?' asked Rasseneur.

'Barely three thousand francs,' Étienne replied. 'And, you know, management asked to see me the day before yesterday. Oh, they were all nice and polite, and kept saying they wouldn't prevent their workers from setting up a contingency fund. But I could see they wanted to run it themselves . . . Whatever happens, we're in for a fight over it.'

Rasseneur had begun to pace up and down, and gave a whistle of contempt. Three thousand francs! What good was that, for heaven's sake? It wouldn't even provide six days' worth of bread, and if they were going to count on foreigners, people who lived in England, well, they might as well roll over now and hold their tongues. No, really, this talk of a strike was just daft.

And so, for the first time, bitter words were exchanged between the two men who were normally of one mind in their hatred of capital.

'So, what do you think?' Étienne asked again, turning towards Souvarine.

The latter replied with his usual pithy scorn.

'Strikes? More nonsense.'

Then, breaking the angry silence that had now fallen, he added gently:

'Mind you, I don't say you shouldn't, if you fancy it. A strike ruins some and kills others, which at least makes for a few less in the world . . . Only at that rate it would take a thousand years to renew the world. Why not start by blowing up Death Row for me!'

With his slender hand he gestured towards the buildings at Le Voreux, which could be seen through the open door. Then he was interrupted by unforeseen drama: Poland, his plump pet rabbit, had ventured outside but come bounding back in to avoid the stones being hurled by a gang of pit-boys; and in her terror she was cowering against his legs, ears back, tail tucked in, scratching and begging to be picked up. He laid her on his lap, under the shelter of his hands, and then fell into a kind of trance, as he did each time he stroked her soft, warm fur.

Almost at once Maheu walked in. He didn't want a drink, despite some polite insistence from Mme Rasseneur, who sold her beer as if she were making a present of it. Étienne had already stood up, and the two men left for Montsou.

On pay-days at the Company yards Montsou wore an air of celebration, as though it were a fine Sunday on the day of the *ducasse*. A horde of miners converged from the surrounding villages. Since the cashier's office was very small, they preferred to wait outside, standing about in groups on the road and causing an obstruction with their continuous queue. Hawkers made the most of the opportunity, setting up their mobile stalls and displaying everything from crockery to cooked meats. But it was the taverns and bars that did a particularly brisk trade, since the miners would go and stand at the counter to pass the time till they were paid, and then return there to celebrate once the money was in their pockets. And they were always very well behaved about it, presuming they didn't go and blow the lot at the Volcano.

As Maheu and Étienne moved along in the queue, they could sense the underlying mood of discontent. This wasn't the usual carefree atmosphere of men collecting their pay and then leaving half of it on the counter of some bar. Fists were clenched, and fighting words were exchanged.

'So it's true, then?' Maheu asked Chaval when he met him outside Piquette's. 'They've gone and done the dirty on us?'

But Chaval merely snarled in fury and threw a sideways glance at Étienne. When the concessions were renewed, he had signed on with a different team, increasingly consumed with envy of his comrade, this Johnny-come-lately who'd set himself up as a leader, and whose boots, he said, the whole village now seemed ready to lick. Nor were the lovers' tiffs helping: each time he took Catherine to Réquillart or behind the spoil-heap, he would accuse her in the foulest terms of sleeping with her mother's lodger, after which, in a frenzy of renewed desire, he would almost kill her with his love-making.

Maheu inquired again:

'Is it Le Voreux's turn yet?'

And when Chaval nodded and turned away, Maheu and Étienne decided it was time to enter the yard.

The cashier's office was a small rectangular room, divided in two by a grille. Five or six miners were waiting on the benches along the wall, while the cashier, assisted by a clerk, was paying another miner, who was standing, cap in hand, at his window. Above the bench on the left a yellow notice had recently been posted, fresh and clean against the grey, smoke-stained plaster; and all day long the men had been filing past it. They would arrive in their twos and threes, stand looking at it for a while, and then silently leave with a sudden sag of the shoulders, as though this was the final straw.

At that moment two colliers were standing in front of the notice, one of them young with a square, brutish head, and the other old and very thin, with a face rendered expressionless by age. Neither could read; the younger man's lips were spelling out the words while the older was content to stare blankly. Many of them came in like this, wanting to have a look but unable to understand.

'Tell us what it says,' Maheu asked Étienne, reading not being his strong suit either.

So Étienne began to read the notice. It was an announcement from the Company addressed to all miners in its pits and informing them that, in view of the continuing negligence in the matter of timbering, and having wearied of imposing fines which had no effect, it had resolved to introduce a new method of payment for the extraction of coal. Henceforth timbering would be paid for separately, by the cubic metre of wood taken below and used, having due regard to the amount appropriate for a satisfactory performance of the task. The price payable per tub of extracted coal would naturally be reduced from fifty to forty centimes, depending on the type and location of the seam. There followed a rather opaque calculation designed to show that this reduction of ten centimes would be exactly offset by the rate payable for timbering. The Company noted in addition that, in its wish to allow each miner sufficient time to be persuaded of the advantages of this new method of payment, it intended to defer its introduction until Monday, 1 December.

'Must you read so loud?' the cashier shouted across. 'We can't hear ourselves think.'

Étienne ignored the remark and went on reading. His voice was shaking, and when he had finished they all continued to stare at the notice. The old miner and his younger companion both seemed to be waiting for something, but then they left, with the air of broken men.

'God Almighty!' Maheu muttered.

He and Étienne had sat down. Gazing at the floor, deep in thought, they did the sums in their heads, as people continued to file past the yellow notice. What did the Company take them for? The timbering would never allow them to recoup the ten centimes lost on each tub. They'd make eight at most, so the Company was robbing them of two centimes, not to mention the time it would take them to make a proper job of the timbering. So that's what they were up to, a disguised reduction in pay. The Company was saving money by taking it from the miners' pockets.

'God Al-bloody-mighty!' Maheu repeated, looking up again. 'We'd be bloody daft to accept!'

But by now the cashier's window was free, so he stepped up to get his pay. Only the team leaders collected pay, which they then distributed among their team, to save time.

'Maheu and associates,' said the clerk, 'the Filonnière seam, coal-face number seven.'

He checked his lists, which were compiled from the notebooks in which the deputies recorded the number of tubs per team per day. Then he said again:

'Maheu and associates, the Filonnière seam, coal-face number seven . . . One hundred and thirty-five francs.'

The cashier paid him.

'Excuse me, sir,' Maheu stammered in disbelief. 'Are you sure there hasn't been some mistake?'

He looked at the paltry sum where it lay, and his blood ran cold. Yes, he had expected his pay to be low, but it couldn't be that low, or else he hadn't counted right. Once Zacharie, Étienne and Chaval's replacement had each had their share, he'd be left with no more than fifty francs for himself, his father, Catherine and Jeanlin.

'No, no, there's no mistake,' the official replied. 'Two Sundays and four days' lay-off have to be deducted, which leaves you nine days' work.'

Maheu made the calculation, totting up the figures under his breath: nine days meant roughly thirty francs for himself, eighteen for Catherine and nine for Jeanlin. Old Bonnemort was due pay for only three days. Even so, if you added on the ninety francs for Zacharie and the other two, it surely all came to more.

'And don't forget the fines,' the clerk concluded. 'Twenty francs off for defective timbering.'

Maheu gestured in despair. Twenty francs' worth of fines, and four days laid off! So it was right. To think that he'd once collected up to a hundred and fifty for a fortnight's work, when old Bonnemort was still working and before Zacharie had left home.

'Do you want it or not?' the clerk shouted impatiently. 'You can see there are people waiting . . . If you don't want it, you've only got to say.'

As Maheu's large, trembling hand reached out for the money, the official stopped him.

'Wait, your name's down here. Toussaint Maheu, isn't it? . . . The Company Secretary wants to see you. You can go in now, he's free.'

Bewildered, Maheu found himself in an office full of old mahogany furniture and drapes of faded green cord. For five minutes he listened to the Company Secretary, a tall, pale man, who remained seated and spoke to him over the piles of papers on his desk. But the pounding in Maheu's ears prevented him from hearing properly. He vaguely grasped that it was about his father, whose retirement pension of a hundred and fifty francs – due to anyone over fifty with forty years' service – was coming up for assessment. Then the Company Secretary's voice seemed to harden. He was being reprimanded, accused of meddling in politics, and there were references to his lodger and the provident fund; in short, he was being advised not to get mixed up in all this foolishness, especially as he was one of the best workers in the pit. He wanted to protest but he couldn't get the words out, and he stood there nervously twisting his cap in his hands before mumbling on his way out:

'Certainly, sir . . . I can assure the Company Secretary that . . .'

Outside, where Étienne was waiting for him, Maheu exploded.

'I'm a bloody hopeless fool, I should have answered him back! . . . Not even enough to buy bread, and then I have to listen to all that nonsense! But you're right, it's you he's got it in for. He says people's minds have been poisoned. But what the hell can we do? He's quite right. Knuckle down and be grateful, it's the only sensible thing.'

Maheu fell silent, torn between anger and apprehension. Étienne brooded darkly. Once again they found themselves among the groups of men blocking the roadway, and the discontent was growing, a muttering of otherwise peaceable men, without violence of gesture but rumbling like a terrible, gathering storm over the dense throng. The few who could count had done the sums, and word was spreading about the two centimes the Company would gain on the timbering, causing even the most level-headed among them to warm with outrage. But more than anything it was a feeling of fury at the disastrously low pay, the fury of hungry people rebelling against lay-offs and fines. Already they lacked enough to eat, so what was to become of them if their pay was cut even further? In the bars people voiced their anger openly, which left their throats so dry that what little money they had received remained where it lay on the counter.

Neither Étienne nor Maheu said a word on the way home from Montsou. When her husband walked in, La Maheude, alone with the children, could see at once that he was empty-handed.

'Well, that's nice!' she said. 'What about my coffee and the sugar and the meat? A piece of veal wouldn't have broken the bank, would it?'

He remained silent, desperately trying to choke back his feelings. Then the heavy features of a man toughened by years of working down the mines began to swell with despair, and large tears sprang from his eyes, falling like warm rain. He slumped on a chair, crying like a child, and threw the fifty francs on to the table.

'There,' he stammered, 'see what I've brought you ... And that's for the work all of us did.'

La Maheude looked at Étienne and noted his silent air of defeat. Then she, too, wept. How was she to feed nine people for a fortnight on fifty francs? Her eldest had left home, the old man could scarcely move his legs any more: soon they'd all be dead. Alzire threw her arms round her mother's neck, appalled by her tears. Estelle was wailing, Lénore and Henri sobbed.

And soon, from all over the village, the same cry of anguish went up. The men were back now, and every household was grieving over the catastrophe of their depleted pay. Doors opened, women appeared, screaming into the open air as though their laments could not be contained beneath the ceilings of their cramped homes. A fine drizzle was falling, but they didn't feel it as they called out to each other from the pavements and held out the palms of their hands to show how little money they had received.

'Look what they've given him. It's a bloody joke, isn't it?'

'What about me? I've not even got enough to buy the fort-night's bread.'

'And me! You can count it if you like. I'm just going to have to sell my blouses again.'

La Maheude had gone outside like the others. A group formed round La Levaque, who was shouting the loudest; for her drunkard of a husband hadn't even come home yet, and she could guess that whether the pay was large or small, it would simply melt away at the Volcano. Philomène was keeping an eye out for Maheu, so Zacharie wouldn't get his hands on the money first. La Pierronne was the only one who seemed fairly calm, since that mealy-mouthed informer Pierron had managed as always, God knows how, to have more hours recorded in the deputy's notebook than his fellow-miners. But La Brûlé thought her son-in-law a gutless coward for it, and she was among the women raising hell, standing there in the middle of the group, thin and erect, brandishing her fist in the direction of Montsou.

'To think,' she said loudly, without mentioning the Hennebeaus by name, 'that I saw their maid go past this morning in a carriage! ... Yes, the cook in a carriage and pair. Off to Marchiennes to buy some fish, I shouldn't wonder!'

There was uproar at this, and renewed abuse. They were indignant at the thought of that maid in her white apron being driven to market in the neighbouring town in her master's carriage. The workers might be dying of hunger, but of course they still had to have their fish, didn't they? Well, they just might not be eating fish for much longer: one day it would be the turn of the poor. The ideas that Étienne had sown were beginning to take root and grow, burgeoning in this cry of revolt. People were impatient for the promised land, in a hurry for their share of happiness and to reach beyond the horizon of poverty that enclosed them like a tomb. The injustice of it all was becoming too great, and if the bread was now to be snatched from their mouths, they would finally demand their rights. The women especially would like to have launched an immediate assault upon the city on a hill, upon that terminus of Progress where people were poor no longer. Though night had almost fallen and the rain was coming down hard, they continued to fill the village with their tears, surrounded by the shrieking of their unruly children.

That evening, in the Advantage, the decision was taken to strike. Rasseneur had ceased to oppose it, and Souvarine accepted it as a first step. Étienne summed the matter up: if it was a strike the Company wanted, then a strike they could have.

V

A week passed, and work continued in an atmosphere of sullen wariness as people awaited the coming battle.

In the Maheu household the fortnight in prospect promised to be even more difficult than the last, which made La Maheude increasingly sour despite her good sense and even temper. And then hadn't Catherine taken it into her head to spend the night away from home! She'd come back the next morning so exhausted and ill after this escapade that she hadn't been able to go to the pit; she cried and said it wasn't her fault, that Chaval had prevented her from coming home by threatening to beat her up if she tried to run away from him. He was becoming violently jealous now and wanted to stop her returning to Étienne's bed, which, he said, he knew full well her family made her share. La Maheude was furious and, having forbidden her daughter to see such a brute again, she threatened to go to Montsou and slap his face for him. None of which stopped it being one day's pay less. As for Catherine, now that she had got herself a man she preferred not to swap him.

Two days later there was another drama. On Monday and Tuesday Jeanlin did a bunk, and all the time everyone thought he was quietly working away at Le Voreux he was actually out on the loose with Bébert and Lydie, roaming the marshes and the Vandame forest. He was the ringleader, and nobody ever discovered quite what manner of precocious and larcenous games the three of them got up to. He himself received a heavy punishment, a thrashing from his mother, which she conducted out in the street and in front of the terrified child population of the village. Had anyone ever seen the like? A child of hers! Who'd cost her money since the day it was born, who should

now be earning its keep! And her outrage carried the memory
of her own harsh childhood, the heritage of destitution which
made her see every child in the brood as a future breadwinner.

That morning, when Catherine and the men left for the pit,
La Maheude raised herself up in bed and shouted to Jeanlin:

'And if you try it again, you little brat, I'll thrash the living
daylights out of you.'

It was hard going at Maheu's new coal-face. The Filonnière
seam narrowed so much at this point that the hewers were
wedged between the face itself and the ceiling and kept grazing
their elbows as they extracted the coal. Also it was becoming
very wet, and with every hour that passed they became more
and more anxious about being flooded by one of those sudden
torrents that can burst through the rock and sweep a man away.
The previous day, when Étienne was pulling his pick out of the
rock, having driven it in hard, water suddenly spurted out from
a spring and hit him in the face; but this was no more than an
early warning, and it simply left the coal-face wetter and muckier
than before. Anyway he hardly ever thought about the possibility of an accident now and simply worked away down there
with his comrades, oblivious to the danger. They lived in firedamp, not even noticing how it weighed on their eyelids
and veiled their eyelashes like a cobweb. Sometimes, when the
flame in their lamps turned paler and bluer, they did think
about it, and one of the miners would put his ear to the seam
and listen to the faint hiss of the gas, which sounded as though
air bubbles were fizzing from each crack in the rock. But rock-
falls were the one real and constant threat since, apart from the
fact that the timbering was botched from being done in a hurry,
the earth itself was unstable on account of the water running
through it.

Three times that day Maheu had been forced to make them
strengthen the timbering. It was half past two, and it would
soon be time to return to the surface. Étienne, lying on his side,
was just finishing cutting out a block of coal when a distant
rumble of thunder shook the entire mine.

'What the hell's that?' he shouted, dropping his pick to listen.

He thought the whole road was caving in behind him.

But already Maheu was slithering down the slope of the coal-face and shouting:

'It's a fall! Quick! Hurry!'

They all slid down as fast as they could, in a rush of anxious concern for their fellow-miners. A terrible silence had fallen, and the lamps bobbed up and down in their hands as they raced along the roads in single file, bending so low that it was almost as if they were galloping on all fours. Without slackening speed they exchanged rapid question and answer: whereabouts? Up here by the coal-faces? No, it came from lower down! Near the haulage roadway more like! When they reached the chimney, they plunged down it one on top of the other, heedless of the bruises.

Jeanlin, his bottom still red from the previous day's thrashing, had not tried to escape his work that day. He was busy trotting along barefoot behind his train, shutting the ventilation doors one by one. Sometimes, when he thought there were no deputies around, he would climb up on to the last tub, which he'd been told not to do in case he fell asleep on it. But his main source of amusement was, each time the train pulled in to let another one pass, to set off and find Bébert, who was up at the front holding the reins. He would sneak up on him, without his lamp, and pinch him hard, or else he would play tricks on him, looking like some evil monkey with his yellow hair and big ears and his thin, pointed face with its little green eyes that glowed in the dark. Unnaturally precocious for his years, he seemed to have the instinctual intelligence and quick dexterity of some freakish human runt which had reverted to its original animal state.

That afternoon Mouque brought Battle along to do his stint with the pit-boys; and while the horse was taking a breather in a siding, Jeanlin crept up behind Bébert and asked:

'What's wrong with the old nag, stopping dead like that? . . . He'll make me break a leg one day.'

Bébert could not answer; he was having to restrain Battle, who was becoming excited at the approach of the other train. The horse had caught the scent in the distance of his comrade, Trumpet, for whom he had developed a deep affection ever since the day he had seen him arrive at pit-bottom. His was the warm compassion of an elderly philosopher wanting to comfort a young friend by imbuing him with his own patience and resignation; for Trumpet had not been able to adapt, and he hauled his tubs with reluctance, head down, blinded by the dark, and in constant longing for the sunshine. So each time Battle met him, he would stretch out his head, snort and give him an encouraging lick.

'Christ Almighty!' swore Bébert. 'There they go again, slobbering all over each other.'

Once Trumpet had passed, he replied to Jeanlin's question about Battle:

'The old fellow's got the wind up, that's why. When he stops like that, it's because he senses something's wrong, like a rock in the way or a hole. He takes care of himself, he does, wants to make sure he comes to no harm. Today there must be something up beyond that door. He keeps pushing it and then not moving an inch . . . Have you noticed anything?'

'No,' said Jeanlin. 'There's a lot of water, though. I'm up to my knees in it.'

The train set off again. And on the next trip Battle once again pushed the ventilation door open with his head and just stood there, whinnying and trembling. All at once he made up his mind and went through.

Jeanlin had hung back to close the door. He stooped to peer at the pool of water he was wading through; then he raised his lamp and saw that the timbers were sagging under the weight of a spring seeping down. At that moment a hewer, whose name was Berloque but whom everyone called Chicot, was on his way back from his coal-face, anxious to be with his wife, who was in labour. He, too, stopped to look at the timbering. And suddenly, just as Jeanlin was about to rush off after his train, there had been an almighty crack, and man and boy were buried beneath the rock-fall.

There was a long silence. The draught created by the fall was pushing thick clouds of dust along the roads. Blinded and choking for air, the miners were on their way down from every part of the mine, even from the most distant workings. Their lamps bobbed about but barely illuminated these black men

racing along like moles in a run. When the first of them reached
the rock-fall, they shouted out loudly to summon their comrades. A second group had come from the coal-faces beyond
and found themselves on the other side of the mass of earth
blocking the roadway. It was immediately obvious that at most
ten metres of roof had caved in. The damage was not serious.
But their blood ran cold when they heard the sound of groaning
coming from beneath the rubble.

Bébert had abandoned his train and was running towards
them, shouting:

'Jeanlin's under there! Jeanlin's under there!'

At that precise moment Maheu came tumbling down the
chimney with Zacharie and Étienne. He was beside himself with
despair and helplessness, and could only keep swearing:

'Christ! Christ! Christ!'

Catherine, Lydie and La Mouquette had also rushed up and
now stood there sobbing, screaming with terror in the midst of
this appalling mayhem, which the darkness made only more
terrible. People tried to quieten them, but they were panicking
and screamed louder with each groan they heard.

Richomme, the deputy, had arrived at the double, dismayed
to find that neither Négrel the engineer nor Dansaert was down
in the pit. He put his ear to the rocks to listen and eventually
declared that the groans were not the groans of a child. It must
be a man under there, no question about it. Twenty times
already Maheu had called for Jeanlin. Not a whisper. The lad
must have been crushed to death.

And on the groaning went, unvarying. People spoke to the
dying man and asked his name. A groan was the only reply.

'Come on, quick,' urged Richomme, having already organized
the rescue operation. 'There'll be time for talking later.'

The miners attacked the rock-fall from both sides with pick
and shovel. Chaval worked in silence alongside Maheu and
Étienne, while Zacharie saw to the removal of the rubble. The
end of the shift had come and gone, and no one had eaten; but
you didn't go home to your soup when there were comrades in
danger. However, it occurred to them that they would be
worried in the village if no one came home, and it was suggested

that the women should go back. But neither Catherine nor La
Mouquette nor even Lydie would budge from the spot, so desperate were they to know the worst and busy helping to clear
away the earth. Hence Levaque accepted the job of telling people
about the rock-fall and how there had been just a small amount
of damage that needed repairing. It was nearly four o'clock, and
in less than an hour the miners had done the equivalent of a
day's work: half the earth would already have been cleared if
further pieces of rock had not fallen from the roof of the road.
Maheu worked away in such a frenzy of stubborn determination
that he angrily waved another man away when he offered to
relieve him for a moment.

'Gently does it!' said Richomme eventually. 'We're nearly
there . . . We don't want to finish them off.'

It was true: the groaning was becoming more and more audible. Indeed it was this continuous groaning that was guiding
the men, and now it seemed to be coming from directly beneath
their picks. Suddenly it stopped.

Everyone looked at each other in silence, shivering as the chill
of death passed over them in the darkness. They kept digging,
bathed in sweat, with every sinew in their bodies stretched to
breaking-point. They came on a foot and then started removing
the rubble with their bare hands, uncovering the limbs one by
one. The head was unscathed. Lamps were lowered, and the
name of Chicot began to circulate. He was still warm, his spine
broken by a rock.

'Wrap him in a blanket and put him in a tub,' Richomme
ordered. 'Now for the young lad. Quickly!'

Maheu gave one last blow with his pick, and a gap opened
up; they were through to the men digging from the other side.
They called out: they'd just found Jeanlin, unconscious, with
both legs broken but still breathing. His father took him in his
arms; and even now all he could think to mutter through
clenched teeth, by way of expressing his pain, was 'Christ!
Christ! Christ!' Catherine and the rest of the women had begun
to wail again.

They quickly formed themselves into a procession. Bébert had
fetched Battle, who was harnessed to the two tubs: in the first

lay the body of Chicot, with Étienne watching over it; in the second was Maheu, seated, with Jeanlin lying unconscious across his knees, covered with a piece of woollen cloth ripped from a ventilation door. And off they set, at the walk. Over each tub a lamp shone like a red star. Then behind came the long line of miners, some fifty shadowy figures in single file. By now completely exhausted, they were dragging their feet and slipping on the mud, like some grim herd of animals struck down by a fatal disease. It took nearly half an hour to reach pit-bottom as this seemingly endless subterranean cortège made its way through the thick darkness along the roadways, which forked and twisted and unravelled before them.

At pit-bottom Richomme, who had gone on ahead, had given orders for a cage to be kept empty. Pierron loaded the two tubs immediately. In the one, Maheu sat with his injured child on his knees, while in the other Étienne had to cradle Chicot's body in his arms so as to hold it steady. Once the other miners had piled into its other levels, the cage began its ascent. This took two minutes. The water falling from the lining of the shaft felt very cold, and the men gazed upwards, impatient for daylight.

Fortunately a pit-boy who had been sent to fetch Dr Vanderhaghen had found him and was bringing him to the pit. Jeanlin and the dead man were taken into the deputies' room where there was always a roaring fire burning from one year's end to the next. The buckets of hot water lined up ready for the men to wash their feet were moved to one side; and having spread two mattresses on the flagstone floor, they laid the man and the boy down on them. Only Maheu and Étienne were allowed in. Outside, various putters, hewers and young lads who'd come to see stood around in a group talking quietly.

The doctor took one look at Chicot and muttered:

'He's had it! . . . You can wash him now.'

Two supervisors undressed him and then sponged down his body, which was black with coal-dust and still covered in the sweat of his day's work.

'The head's all right,' the doctor continued, kneeling on Jeanlin's mattress. 'So's his chest . . . Ah! it's the legs that took the brunt of it.'

As deftly as a nurse he undressed the child himself, loosening his cap, removing his jacket and pulling his trousers and shirt off. And his poor little body emerged, as thin as an insect's, filthy with black dust and yellowish earth and mottled with patches of blood. He couldn't be examined properly in this state, and so they had to wash him too. The sponging then seemed to make him even thinner, and his flesh was so pallid and transparent that one could see his bones. He was a pitiable sight, the last, degenerate offspring of a destitute breed, a suffering scrap of a thing half crushed to death by rock. Once he was clean, they could see the bruises on his thighs, two red blotches against the whiteness of his skin.

Jeanlin recovered consciousness and groaned. At the foot of the mattress, arms dangling by his side, Maheu stood gazing at him; and huge tears rolled down his cheeks.

'So you're his father?' asked the doctor, looking up. 'There's no call for tears. You can see he's not dead . . . Here, give me a hand instead.'

He diagnosed two simple fractures. But he was worried about the right leg; it would probably have to be amputated.

At that point Négrel and Dansaert, having eventually been notified, arrived with Richomme. Négrel listened to the deputy's report with growing exasperation. He exploded: it was always the damned timbering! If he'd said it once, he'd said it a hundred times: men would die! And now the brutes were talking about going on strike if anyone forced them to timber properly! The worst of it was that this time the Company would have to pay for the damage itself. Monsieur Hennebeau *would* be pleased!

'Who is it?' he asked Dansaert, who was standing silently by the body as it was being wrapped in a sheet.

'Chicot, one of our best,' the overman replied. 'He's got three children . . . Poor bugger!'

Dr Vanderhaghen asked for Jeanlin to be transported immediately to his parents' house. It was six o'clock and already getting dark, so it would be best to move the body as well; and the engineer gave orders for the horses to be harnessed to a wagon and for a stretcher to be fetched. The injured boy was placed on the stretcher, and the dead man was loaded into the wagon on his mattress.

Putters were still standing outside the door, chatting with some miners who had remained behind to see what was happening. When the door of the deputies' room opened again, the group fell silent. A new funeral cortège formed up, with the wagon in front, then the stretcher, and finally the line of people following. They moved out of the pit-yard and slowly climbed the road towards the village. The first frosts of November had stripped the vast plain bare, and night was slowly burying it in a shroud of livid white as though a pall had detached itself from the paling sky.

Then Étienne whispered to Maheu that he should send Catherine on ahead to warn La Maheude and soften the blow. Her father, looking dazed as he followed the stretcher, nodded his agreement; and the girl ran on, since they were nearly there now. But the familiar dark outline of the box-shaped wagon had already been spotted. Women were careering out on to the pavements, and three or four were tearing along in a panic, not a bonnet on their heads. Soon there were thirty, fifty of them, all gripped by the same terror. Had someone been killed? Who was it? Levaque's story had earlier set their minds at rest, but now the tale assumed the dimensions of a nightmare: it wasn't just one man who had perished but ten, and the funeral-wagon was going to bring each one of them back like this, body by body.

Catherine had found her mother in a lather of foreboding; and before she could blurt out a few words, La Maheude screamed:

'It's your father!'

The girl tried in vain to say it wasn't and to tell her about Jeanlin. But La Maheude wasn't listening, she had already rushed out of the house. When she saw the wagon emerge opposite the church, she faltered and turned deathly pale. From every doorway women stared in silent shock, craning their necks to see, while others followed, fearful to discover which house the procession would stop at.

The wagon went past; and behind it La Maheude caught sight of her husband accompanying the stretcher. When they had set it down at her door and she saw that Jeanlin was alive and that his legs were broken, she felt such sudden relief that instead of crying she began to choke and splutter with anger:

'Now we've seen everything! Now they're going to cripple our children for us! Both legs, for God's sake. And just what am I supposed to do with him?'

'Be quiet!' said Dr Vanderhaghen, who had come to bandage Jeanlin. 'Would you rather he were still lying at the bottom of the pit?'

Alzire, Lénore and Henri were all in tears, but La Maheude was growing more and more angry. As she helped them take the injured child upstairs and supplied the doctor with what he needed, she kept cursing fate and asking where in God's name she was supposed to find the money to feed the sick. Wasn't it enough for the old man to lose the use of his legs? No, now it was the lad's turn! And on she went, while all the time other, heart-rending screams of lament could be heard coming from a nearby house: Chicot's wife and children were grieving over his dead body. It was pitch dark now, and the exhausted miners were finally able to have their soup. And a grim silence fell upon the village, punctuated only by these cries of anguish.

Three weeks went by. Amputation had been avoided; Jeanlin would keep both his legs, but he would always have a limp. Following an inquiry the Company had resigned itself to making the family a grant of fifty francs. It also undertook to find the young cripple a surface job as soon as he had recovered. Nevertheless it all meant that they had even less money now, especially as Maheu had experienced such a shock that he fell ill with a high temperature.

He had been back at work since Thursday, and it was now Sunday. That evening Étienne mentioned the imminence of 1 December and wondered anxiously whether the Company would carry out its threat. They stayed up till ten waiting for Catherine, who must have been with Chaval. But she did not return. La Maheude was furious and without a word locked the door. Disturbed by her empty bed – for Alzire hardly took up any room at all – Étienne found it hard to get to sleep.

Next day, still no Catherine; and it was only in the afternoon, at the end of the shift, that the Maheus learned that Chaval was going to keep Catherine. He made such awful scenes all the time that she had decided to live with him. To avoid the inevitable recriminations he had immediately quit Le Voreux and signed on at Jean-Bart, M. Deneulin's pit, where Catherine followed him as a putter. The new couple continued none the less to live in Montsou, at Piquette's.

At first Maheu talked about going off to punch the fellow and to fetch his daughter home if he had to kick her up the backside all the way. Then he gestured resignedly: what was the use? It always turned out this way, you couldn't stop girls pairing up with someone when they took a notion to it. Better to wait patiently for them to marry. But La Maheude was not for taking the matter so calmly.

'Now tell me. Did I ever hit her when she took up with this Chaval?' she shouted at Étienne, who looked vey pale and listened to her in silence. 'Come on, answer me, you're a reason-able man . . . We left her to her own devices, didn't we? Because, God help us, they all do it in the end. Like me, for example. I was expecting when Father married me. But I didn't run away from home, did I? I wasn't the sort to play a dirty trick like that and go handing my pay over to a man who didn't need it, *and* before I was even of age . . . It just sickens you, really it does! . . . I mean in the end people will simply stop having children.'

And as Étienne would still only nod by way of reply, she persisted.

'A girl who could go out every night of the week, wherever she wanted. What on earth's got into her? She couldn't even help us out of our trouble and *then* let me find her a husband, I suppose! Eh? I mean daughters are supposed to work, it's what's normal . . . But no, we were just too good to her, we simply shouldn't have let her go out with a man like that. Give them an inch and they take a mile.'

Alzire was nodding. Lénore and Henri, terrified by this raging, cried softly as their mother proceeded to list their various misfor-tunes: first, there was having to let Zacharie get married; then there was old Bonnemort, stuck on his chair with his gammy legs; and then there was Jeanlin, who'd be in bed for another

ten days yet, with his bones that didn't stick together right; and
finally the last straw was this trollop Catherine going off with
some man! The whole family was falling apart. There was only
Father left now at the pit. How on earth were the seven of them,
not counting Estelle, supposed to live on the three francs Father
earned? They might as well all throw themselves in the canal
and be done with it.

'Moaning never helped anyone,' Maheu said in a hollow
voice. 'And anyway, we might not have seen the end of it yet.'

Étienne, who was staring at the floor, looked up; and, with
his eyes fixed on a vision of the future, he murmured quietly:

'The time has come! The time has come!'

PART IV

That Monday the Hennebeaus were having the Grégoires and
their daughter Cécile to lunch. And quite an occasion it was to
be. When they had eaten, Paul Négrel was to show the ladies
round a mine, the Saint-Thomas mine, which was in the process
of being lavishly refitted. But this was by way of being a delightful pretext: the visit was Mme Hennebeau's device for hastening
the marriage between Cécile and Paul.

And then out of the blue, that very Monday, at four o'clock
in the morning, the strike had started. When the Company had
begun to operate its new wages system on 1 December, the
miners had remained calm. Come pay-day a fortnight later, not
one of them had raised any objection. The whole staff, from the
manager down to the most junior supervisor, thought that the
new rates had been accepted; and so since early morning there
had been widespread surprise at this declaration of war, and at
the tactics and concerted action which seemed to point to strong
leadership.

At five o'clock Dansaert woke M. Hennebeau with the news
that not a single man had gone down the pit at Le Voreux. He
had just come through Village Two Hundred and Forty and
found all the windows and doors shut and everyone fast asleep.
And from the moment the manager leaped bleary-eyed out of
bed, he was swamped: messengers had been rushing in every
quarter of an hour, and his desk had disappeared beneath a hail
of telegrams. At first he hoped that the unrest was confined to
Le Voreux; but the news grew worse with every minute that
passed. Next it was Mirou, and then Crèvecœur, and Madeleine,
where only the stablemen had turned up; then it was La Victoire
and Feutry-Cantel, the two pits with the tightest discipline, yet
where only a third of the men had reported for work. Saint-
Thomas alone had its full complement and seemed unaffected by
the action. It took him till nine o'clock dictating telegrams to be
sent in all directions, to the Prefect[1] in Lille, to the Company's
directors, warning the authorities and asking for instructions. He

had sent Négrel off on a tour of the neighbouring pits to gather accurate information.

Suddenly M. Hennebeau remembered the lunch; and he was about to send the coachman to let the Grégoires know that the party had been postponed when he had a moment's hesitation and his resolve faltered – he who had just prepared for battle in a few brief, military sentences. He went upstairs to speak to Mme Hennebeau in her dressing-room, where the maid was just finishing attending to her hair.

'So they're on strike,' she said calmly, after he had asked her what they should do. 'Well, what's that to us? . . . We've still got to eat, haven't we?'

She would not yield. Try as he might to tell her that the lunch was likely to be interrupted and that the visit to Saint-Thomas could not go ahead, she had an answer for everything. Why forgo a lunch that was already half prepared? And as for visiting the mine, they could cancel that later if it really did seem unwise.

'What's more,' she continued when her maid had left the room, 'you know perfectly well why I am so anxious to have these people to lunch. And you ought to care more about this marriage yourself than about all this nonsense with your workmen . . . So there we are. I want them to come, and I shall not have you stand in my way.'

He looked at her, trembling slightly, and the hard, closed face of this man of discipline registered the secret pain of a heart that was used to being bruised. She had continued to sit there with her shoulders bare, a woman already past her prime and yet still dazzling and desirable, and with the bust of an earth goddess turned golden brown by autumn. For a moment, no doubt, he felt the animal urge to take her, to roll his head from side to side between those two breasts thus presented for display, here in this warm room with its luxurious, intimate aura of female sensuality and its provocative scent of musk; but he drew back. For ten years now they had slept apart.

'Very well,' he said as he left her. 'We'll leave things as they are.'

M. Hennebeau was a native of the Ardennes. He came from a poor background and had been abandoned as an orphan on

the streets of Paris. After several years of arduous study at the
École des Mines[2] he had left at the age of twenty-four for La
Grand 'Combe,[3] where he had been appointed engineer at the
Sainte-Barbe pit. Three years later he became divisional engineer
at the Marles collieries in the Pas-de-Calais; and there, by one
of those strokes of good fortune which seem to be the rule for
graduates of the École des Mines, he married the daughter of a
rich spinning-mill owner from Arras. For fifteen years the couple
lived in the same small provincial town, and not a single note-
worthy event broke the monotony of their lives, not even the
birth of a child. A growing irritation began to distance Mme
Hennebeau from her husband, for she had been brought up to
respect money and she looked down on this man who worked
hard to earn a paltry salary and who had brought her none of
the vain gratifications she had dreamed of as a schoolgirl. He, a
man of strict integrity, never took financial risks and merely did
his job, sticking to his post like a soldier. The gulf between them
had quite simply grown wider and wider, exacerbated by one
of those curious instances of physical incompatibility that can
cool even the warmest ardour: he adored his wife, and she had
the sensuality of the voluptuous blonde, and yet already they
had ceased to share a bed, both of them ill at ease with the other
and quick to take offence. Unbeknownst to him, she then took
a lover. Eventually he left the Pas-de-Calais for a desk job in
Paris, hoping that this would make her grateful to him. But Paris
drove them apart completely, for this was the Paris she had
dreamed of ever since she had played with her first doll and
where she now sloughed off her provincial existence in the space
of a single week, becoming all at once the woman of fashion in
pursuit of every latest foolish luxury. The ten years she spent
there were filled by one great passion, a public liaison with a
man whose abandonment of her nearly destroyed her. This time
her husband had been unable to remain in ignorance of the
facts, and after many terrible scenes he resigned himself to the
situation, powerless in the face of the total lack of remorse
shown by this woman who took her pleasure where she found
it. It was following the end of this affair, when he saw how ill
her unhappiness was making her, that he had accepted the job

as manager of the Montsou mines, hoping that up there in that black wilderness he might yet manage to make her mend her ways.

Since their arrival in Montsou the Hennebeaus had relapsed into the state of irritable boredom that had characterized the earlier days of their marriage. At first Mme Hennebeau seemed to derive comfort from the immense tranquillity of the place, finding peace in the featureless monotony of its vast plain; and she buried herself away, as one whose life is over, affecting to be dead to all affection, and so detached from the world that she no longer cared about putting on weight. Then, amid this listless indifference, one last bout of fever declared itself, an urge to go on living, which she assuaged by spending six months rearranging and refurbishing the manager's small residence to suit her taste. She said it was hideous and filled it with tapestries and ornaments and all manner of expensive art, news of which spread as far as Lille. Now the whole region exasperated her, with its stupid fields stretching away as far as the eye could see, and the interminable black roads with never a tree, and this crawling mass of ghastly people who disgusted and alarmed her. And so began the laments of exile, as she accused her husband of having sacrificed her happiness for a salary of forty thousand francs, a pittance on which it was barely possible to run a household. Ought he not to have done as others did, demand a partnership, or acquire shares in the company, any-thing, but at least make something of himself? She warmed to her theme with the cruelty of the heiress who has brought her own fortune to the marriage. He always remained civil, hiding his feelings behind the mask of the cool administrator while all the time eaten up with desire for this creature – and a desire of that violent kind which develops later in life and continues to grow with the years. He had never possessed her as a lover, and he was continually haunted by the thought of having her for himself, just once, the way another man would have had her. Each morning he would dream that by evening he would have won her; but then, when she looked at him with her cold eyes and he could feel how her whole body rejected him, he would avoid even the merest touch of her hand. His was a sickness

without cure, disguised by his stiff manner, the sickness of a
tender nature in secret agony at failing to find happiness in
marriage. After six months, when the refurbishment was complete and no longer required her attention, Mme Hennebeau
reverted to a state of languorous boredom, the self-proclaimed
victim of an exile that would kill her but of which she would be
glad to die.

At this precise moment Paul Négrel turned up in Montsou.
His mother, the widow of a Provençal captain, lived on a meagre
income in Avignon and had gone without in order to get him
into the École Polytechnique.[4] He had graduated with a low
rank, and M. Hennebeau, his uncle, had recently told him to
resign and offered him a job as engineer at Le Voreux. Since
then he had been treated as one of the family; he had his own
room, and he ate and lived there, which enabled him to send his
mother half his salary of three thousand francs. In order to
disguise this largesse, M. Hennebeau talked about how difficult
life was for a young man who had to set up house in one of the
little wooden houses reserved for the mine's engineers. Mme
Hennebeau had immediately adopted the role of kindly aunt,
calling him by his first name and making sure he had everything
he wanted. During the first few months especially she was full
of motherly advice about the merest trifle. But she was still a
woman, and she began to share more intimate confidences with
him. She found the boy amusing, so youthful and pragmatic,
with an intelligence unfettered by scruple and a penchant for
professing philosophical theories about love; and she liked the
urgency of his pessimism, which seemed to make his thin face
and pointed nose look more angular still. One evening, naturally, he ended up in her arms; and she seemed to yield out of
kindness, telling him that she was dead to love and simply
wanted to be his friend. And indeed she was not possessive: she
teased him about the putters he claimed to find repellent, and
almost sulked when he had no young man's escapades to tell
her about. Then she became obsessed with the idea of seeing
him married, and dreamed of being the trusty go-between who
would herself unite him with some wealthy girl. They continued
to have relations, by way of amusing recreation, and she lavished

on these the residual affectionateness of an idle and superannuated woman.

Two years had elapsed. One night M. Hennebeau heard
someone brush past his door, evidently barefoot, and he began
to have suspicions. But the thought of this new romance disgusted him: here, in his own home, when they were virtually
mother and son! However, the very next day his wife told him
that she had chosen Cécile Grégoire as a suitable match for their
nephew, and she had since been devoting herself to the prospect
of this marriage with such zeal that he blushed to have imagined
such a monstrous thing. Now he was simply grateful to the
young man that since his arrival the house had become less
gloomy.

On coming down from his wife's dressing-room, M. Hennebeau met Paul, who had just returned. He seemed to find the
whole business of a strike hugely entertaining.

'Well?' his uncle inquired.

'Well, I've been round the villages, and they all seem to be on
their best behaviour . . . Only I think they're sending a deputation to see you.'

But at that moment Mme Hennebeau could be heard calling
from the landing.

'Is that you, Paul? . . . Come up and tell me the news! What
silly people they are, being naughty like this when they're all
perfectly happy really!'

Since his wife had now stolen his messenger, the manager was
obliged to abandon hope of obtaining further information. He
returned to his study and sat down at a desk piled high with a
fresh batch of telegrams.

When the Grégoires arrived at eleven, they were astonished
to find the Hennebeaus' servant, Hippolyte, mounting guard
and glancing anxiously up and down the road before he bundled
them inside. The drawing-room curtains were drawn and they
were ushered directly into the study, where M. Hennebeau
apologized for receiving them like this; but the drawing-room
gave on to the road, and there was no point in appearing to
provoke people.

'What? Haven't you heard?' he continued, on seeing their surprise.

When M. Grégoire learned that the strike had finally begun, he gave a placid shrug. Pah! It wouldn't come to much, those miners were decent people. Mme Grégoire nodded approvingly at her husband's confidence in the colliers' traditional quiescence; while Cécile, who was in high spirits that day and looking a picture of health in her nasturtium-coloured dress, smiled at the mention of a strike, which brought back memories of visiting the villages and distributing alms.

But then Mme Hennebeau appeared in the doorway, dressed entirely in black silk, and followed by Négrel.

'It really is very tiresome, isn't it?' she said loudly. 'I mean, they could at least have waited! . . . And now Paul is refusing to take us to see Saint-Thomas.'

'Then we shall stay here,' M. Grégoire said obligingly. 'I'm sure everything will be just as delightful.'

Paul had merely bowed to Cécile and her mother. Put out by his lack of enthusiasm, his aunt at once dispatched him to the girl's side with a look; and when subsequently she heard them laughing together, she wrapped them in a maternal gaze.

Meanwhile M. Hennebeau finished reading his telegrams and drafted some replies. The conversation continued around him as his wife explained how she had not concerned herself with redecorating the study: it retained the same faded red wallpaper as before, as well as its heavy mahogany furniture and its cardboard filing-boxes that were scuffed with use. Three quarters of an hour went by, and they were just about to sit down to lunch when Hippolyte announced M. Deneulin, who came in looking very agitated and bowed to Mme Hennebeau.

'Oh goodness, it's you,' he said, catching sight of the Grégoires.

And he turned animatedly towards M. Hennebeau:

'So it's begun, then? My engineer's just told me . . . My men all went down as normal this morning. But the strike may spread . . . I'm worried . . . How are things with you?'

He had just ridden over, and his anxiety was evident in his

loud voice and brusque gestures, which gave him the air of a retired cavalry officer.

M. Hennebeau was in the middle of bringing him up to date when Hippolyte opened the dining-room door. So he broke off and said:

'Why not have lunch with us? Then I can tell you the rest over dessert.'

'Yes, if you like,' Deneulin replied, so preoccupied that he forgot his manners.

He realized his discourtesy, however, and turned to apologize to Mme Hennebeau. She, of course, was charming. Once she had ordered a seventh place to be laid, she seated her guests: Mme Grégoire and Cécile on either side of her husband, then M. Grégoire and Deneulin beside herself, which left Paul to sit between Cécile and her father. As they began the hors-d'œuvre, she resumed conversation with a smile:

'Do forgive me, I had wanted to serve you oysters . . . On Mondays, as you know, Marchiennes has a delivery of Ostends, and I had intended to send cook in the carriage . . . But she was worried that people might throw stones at her –'

Everyone burst out laughing. They found this idea most amusing.

'Shh!' said M. Hennebeau rather crossly, looking towards the windows from where they could see out on to the road. 'The whole world doesn't need to know we're having guests today.'

'Well, here's one slice of sausage they're not going to get their hands on!' declared M. Grégoire.

They started laughing again, but more discreetly. The guests began to feel at ease in the room, with its Flemish tapestries and old oak cabinets. Silverware gleamed from glass-fronted sideboards, while above them hung a large brass chandelier with rounded sides that reflected the greenery of a palm tree and an aspidistra, which were growing in majolica pots. Outside it was a bitterly cold December day, with a keen north-east wind blowing. But not a draught was to be felt indoors; it was as warm as a greenhouse, and this brought out the delicate scent of the cut pineapple that was sitting in a crystal bowl.

'Should we not close the curtains?' suggested Négrel, who was enjoying the idea of terrifying the Grégoires.

Mme Hennebeau's maid, who was helping Hippolyte, took this as an order and went to draw one of the curtains. This was the cue for endless jokes as everyone affected extravagant care in setting down their glass or fork, and they all greeted each course as though it had been rescued from looters in a newly conquered city. But beneath the forced merriment lay an unspoken fear, evident from all the involuntary glances towards the road, as if a band of starving ne'er-do-wells were out there spying on their table.

After the scrambled egg with truffles came the river trout. The conversation had now switched to the industrial crisis, which had been worsening for the past eighteen months.

'It was inevitable,' Deneulin said. 'There's been too much prosperity recently, so it was bound to come ... Just think of the enormous capital sums that have been tied up in the railways and the docks and the canals, and all the money that's been sunk into the most speculative schemes. Even round here they've built so many sugar-refineries you'd think the region was producing three beet harvests a year ... And now money's scarce, of course, and people have got to wait for a return on all the millions they've spent. Which is why there is this fatal gridlock in the system and why businesses are just not growing.'

M. Hennebeau disputed this interpretation of events, but he did concede that the good years had spoiled the workers.

'When I think,' he cried, 'that these fellows used to be able to make as much as six francs a day in our pits, double what they're getting now. And they lived well on it, too, and started developing expensive tastes ... Well, of course, today they find it hard to go back to their frugal ways.'

'Please, Monsieur Grégoire,' Mme Hennebeau cut in, 'won't you have a little more trout ... Such a lovely, delicate flavour, don't you think?'

The manager continued:

'But it's not really our fault, is it? We've been just as badly hit as they have ... Ever since factories started closing down one after another, we've had the devil of a time disposing of our stock. And with demand falling we've just had to cut our production costs ... That's what the workers refuse to understand.'

There was silence. Hippolyte was serving roast partridge, while the maid began to pour some red burgundy for the guests.

'There's been a famine in India,' Deneulin went on in a low voice, as though he were talking to himself. 'America has stopped ordering iron and cast-iron from us, which has been a major setback for our blast-furnaces. Everything's connected, one distant tremor can eventually shake the whole world . . . And to think how proud the Empire was of the white heat of its industry!'

He attacked the wing of his partridge. Then, speaking more loudly:

'The worst of it is that if you want to reduce your production costs, then logically you should try and increase the amount you produce. Otherwise the reduction has to come from wage costs, and then the worker's quite right to say that he's the one who ends up paying the piper.'

This unexpectedly frank admission started an argument. The ladies were not amused. But everyone's principal concern was the plate in front of them, which they addressed with an appetite as yet unblunted. When Hippolyte returned, he seemed to have something to say but hesitated:

'What is it?' asked M. Hennebeau. 'If it's more messages, leave them with me . . . I'm expecting some replies.'

'No, sir, it's Monsieur Dansaert, he's waiting in the hall . . . But he doesn't want to disturb you, sir.'

M. Hennebeau apologized to the company and had the over-man shown in. The latter came and stood a few feet away from the table, as everyone turned to look at this large man who was breathless with the news he brought. Things were still quiet in the villages, but there was no question now, they were sending a deputation. It might even arrive in the next few minutes.

'That will be all, thank you,' said M. Hennebeau. 'And I want a report twice a day. Understood?'

And as soon as Dansaert had gone, the joking began again, and they fell upon the Russian salad declaring that they had not a moment to lose if they hoped to finish it. But the hilarity reached fever pitch when the maid, having been asked by Négrel for some bread, said 'yes, sir' in such a low, terrified voice that there could have been a whole gang of men behind her bent on rape and pillage.

'You may speak up,' said Mme Hennebeau obligingly. 'They're not here yet.'

M. Hennebeau was brought a pile of letters and telegrams and wanted to read one of the letters out. It was from Pierron, who wrote respectfully to inform him that he found himself under the obligation to come out on strike with his comrades, for fear he might be roughly treated; and he added that he had been similarly forced to be part of the deputation, much as he deplored this particular initiative.

'So much for workers' freedom!' cried M. Hennebeau.

So everyone started talking about the strike again, and they asked him for his opinion on the matter.

'Yes,' he replied, 'we've had strikes before ... It means a week's idleness, two weeks' at the most, like last time. They'll do the rounds of the bars, and then when they get too hungry, they'll go back to the pits.'

Deneulin shook his head.

'I'm not so sure ... They seem better organized this time. In fact, they've got a provident fund, I believe?'

'Yes, but there's barely three thousand francs in it. How far's that going to get them? ... I suspect that a chap called Étienne Lantier is their leader. He's a good worker, and I'd be sorry to have to sack him, like I had to with the famous Rasseneur, who's still poisoning Le Voreux with his thoughts and his beer ... Never mind, half of them will be back down the pit inside a week, and the whole ten thousand before the fortnight's out.'

He was in no doubt. His only concern was about the possible disgrace to himself if the Board of Directors held him responsible for the strike. For some time now he had been sensing that he was out of favour. And so he abandoned the helping of Russian salad he had just served himself and reread the telegrams from Paris, trying to plumb the significance of each word in the replies. His behaviour was forgiven, for the lunch had now become something of a military event, taken on the field of battle before the action began.

Then the ladies joined in the conversation. Mme Grégoire felt sorry for these poor people who were going to be left with nothing to eat, and already Cécile was making plans to distribute bread and meat coupons. But Mme Hennebeau was astonished to hear anyone talk about the miners of Montsou as being poor. Were they not perfectly fortunate? Men and women who were provided with housing, heating and medical care all at the Company's expense! Given her indifference to the common herd, all she knew about them was what she had been told to tell others, and this was the version she used to pass on to her Parisian visitors, who were duly impressed. In the end she had come to believe it herself and so felt indignant at the people's ingratitude.

Meanwhile Négrel was continuing to frighten M. Grégoire. He found Cécile not unattractive and he was prepared to marry her, if only to please his aunt; but he brought no amorous zest to the idea, for, as he said, he was a seasoned bachelor who had long since grown out of such infatuations. *And* he was a republican, so he claimed, though this did not prevent him from treating his workers with harsh discipline nor from making witty jokes about them in front of the ladies.

'I do not share my uncle's optimism either,' he declared. 'I fear there may be serious disturbances ... And so, Monsieur Grégoire, I would advise you to barricade yourself in at La Piolaine. You may find yourself being looted.'

Just then, his face beaming with its usual kindly smile, M. Grégoire had been vying with his wife in expressions of paternal solicitude for the miners.

'Loot me!' he cried in amazement. 'Why on earth would they loot me?'

'Are you not a Montsou shareholder? You don't do anything, you just live off the work of others. So that makes you a dirty capitalist in their book ... You may be certain that if the revolution succeeds, you will be forced to hand back your fortune as if you had stolen it.'

In an instant M. Grégoire lost his innocent trust in the ways of the world and woke from the serene unawareness in which he had hitherto lived.

'Stolen it?' he gasped. 'My fortune? Did my great-great-grandfather not earn the money he invested all those years ago, and earn it the hard way, too? Were we not the ones who took all the risks in setting the company up? And do I make improper use of the income I receive from it now?'

Mme Hennebeau was alarmed to see mother and daughter both white with terror, and she hastened to intervene:

'My dear Monsieur Grégoire, Paul's only joking.'

But M. Grégoire was beside himself. When Hippolyte came round with a platter of crayfish, he absent-mindedly grabbed three and started crushing the claws with his teeth.

'Of course, I'm not saying there aren't shareholders who abuse their position. I mean, for example, I've heard stories of government ministers receiving shares in Montsou as a *douceur* for services rendered to the Company. And there's that nobleman who shall remain nameless, a duke, who's our largest shareholder and lives a life of scandalous extravagance, throwing away millions on women and parties and useless luxuries . . . But what about the rest of us who lead quiet lives like the good, decent people we are, who don't speculate, who live soberly and make do with what we've got and give our fair share to the poor! . . . Go on with you! The workers would need to be proper thieves to steal so much as a pin from us!'

Négrel had to calm M. Grégoire himself, for all that he found his anger highly entertaining. The crayfish were still doing the rounds, and the sound of cracking shells was to be heard as the conversation turned to politics. In spite of everything, and still shaking, M. Grégoire declared himself to be a liberal and longed for the days of Louis-Philippe.[5] Deneulin, for his part, was in favour of strong government and maintained that the Emperor was on a slippery slope with his concessions.[6]

'Just remember '89,'[7] he said. 'It was the nobility who made the Revolution possible by their complicity and their taste for the latest intellectual fashions . . . Well, it's the same today with the bourgeoisie. They're playing the same foolish game with this passion for liberalism and this crazy desire to destroy how things were, and all this sucking up to the people . . . Yes, you're just sharpening the monster's teeth so it can devour us faster. And devour us it will, make no mistake!'

The ladies bid him be quiet and tried to change the subject by asking him for news of his daughters. Lucie was at Marchiennes, singing with a friend; Jeanne was painting the portrait of an old beggar. He told them all this with a distracted air, his eyes fixed on M. Hennebeau, who was engrossed in his telegrams and oblivious of his guests. Beyond those thin sheets of paper he sensed Paris and the Board of Directors. Their orders would determine the outcome of the strike, and so he could not help coming back to the subject that preoccupied him.

'Well, what will you do?' he asked abruptly.

M. Hennebeau gave a start and then passed the matter off with a non-committal reply:

'We shall see.'

'No doubt you will,' said Deneulin, as he began to think aloud. 'You're strong enough, you can afford to wait. But it'll be the ruin of me if the strike spreads to Vandame. It was all very well my modernizing Jean-Bart, but I can't survive on only one pit unless I can keep the production going uninterrupted ... At any rate, I can't see myself making a fortune, that's for sure.'

This involuntary admission seemed to strike a chord in M. Hennebeau. As he listened, a plan was forming in his mind: if the strike should get worse, why not use the situation and let things get so bad that his neighbour was eventually ruined, and then he could buy back the concession at a knock-down price. That was the one sure way to get back into favour with the Board of Directors, who had been dreaming for years of one day getting their hands on Vandame.

'If Jean-Bart's such a weight round your neck,' he laughed, 'why not let us have it?'

But already Deneulin regretted what he had said.

'Not on your life!' he cried.

Everyone was amused by this vehemence, and they had forgotten about the strike by the time the dessert appeared. An apple charlotte topped with meringue received wide acclaim. Then the ladies started discussing a recipe, on account of the pineapple, which which was judged to be equally delicious. A dish of fruit – grapes and pears – added a final touch to that sense of happy surrender which comes at the end of copious meals. Everyone had become rather emotional, and they were all talking at once as Hippolyte went round pouring them some hock, rather than champagne, which was considered common.

And the marriage between Paul and Cécile came a step nearer thanks to the warm sympathies fostered during this dessert. Paul's aunt had been looking at Négrel so imploringly that he became his charming self once more, and with his winning ways he soon renewed his conquest of a Grégoire family still crushed by his talk of looting. For a moment, seeing this close understanding between his wife and nephew, M. Hennebeau again had a horrible suspicion, as if he had witnessed not an exchange of glances but a squeeze of the hand. But once more he was reassured by the spectacle of this marriage being planned here in front of his very eyes.

Hippolyte was serving the coffee, when the maid rushed in looking terrified:

'Sir! Sir! They're here!'

It was the deputation. Doors banged, and the panic could be heard passing from room to room.

'Show them into the drawing-room,' said M. Hennbeau.

Round the table the guests had exchanged uneasy looks. There was silence. Then they tried to make light of it again, pretending to put the remainder of the sugar in their pockets and talking about hiding the cutlery. But when M. Hennebeau continued to look serious, the laughter ceased, and their voices dropped to a whisper as they listened to the heavy tread of the deputation entering the drawing-room next door and tramping across the carpet.

Mme Hennebeau said softly to her husband:

'I trust you have time for your coffee.'

'No doubt. They can wait.'

He was tense, apparently preoccupied by his coffee-cup but with his ear cocked for any sound he could make out.

Paul and Cécile had just got up from the table, and he dared her to peep through the keyhole. They were trying not to laugh and busily whispering to each other:

'Can you see them?'

'Yes . . . There's a big one, and two other little ones behind.'

'And pretty horrible they look, too, I expect?'

'No, not at all, they look perfectly sweet.'

Abruptly M. Hennebeau left the table, saying his coffee was too hot and that he would drink it afterwards. As he left the room, he placed a finger to his lips urging them to caution. Everyone had sat down again at the table, and there they remained without a word, not daring to move but straining to hear, unnerved by the loud voices of these men.

II

The day before, during a meeting held at Rasseneur's, Étienne and some of his comrades had together chosen the members of the deputation who were to meet management the following day. When La Maheude discovered that evening that Maheu was one of them, her heart sank, and she asked him if he really wanted them all turned out on to the street. Maheu himself had not accepted without a certain reluctance. Now that the moment to act had come, and despite the injustice of their poverty, they both lapsed back into their habitual state of inbred acquiescence, fearful of the morrow and still preferring to toe the line. Usually Maheu let his wife make all the key decisions in the running of their lives, for she had good judgement. This time, however, he ended up losing his temper, largely because he secretly shared her fears.

'Leave me bloody well be,' he said as he got into bed and rolled over on to his side. 'A fine thing it would be to let my comrades down! . . . I'm doing what I have to do.'

She in turn got into bed. Neither of them spoke. Then, after a long silence, she said:

'Very well, you win. The only trouble is, my poor love, we're done for already.'

It was midday when they sat down to eat, because they were due to meet at the Advantage at one o'clock prior to going on from there to M. Hennebeau's. The meal was one of potatoes.

As there was only a tiny portion of butter left, nobody touched it. They would save it and have it on bread come the evening.

'We're counting on you to do the talking, you know,' Étienne said suddenly to Maheu.

Maheu was taken aback, unable to speak in the emotion of the moment.

'No, that does it!' cried La Maheude. 'He can go if he wants to, but I'm not having him be the leader . . . And why him, anyway? Why not somebody else?'

Then Étienne explained, with his usual vehemence. Maheu was the best worker in the pit, the most popular and the most respected, the person everyone cited as a model of good sense. Which meant that the miners' demands would carry more weight coming from him. Originally Étienne was going to do it; but he had been at Montsou for only such a short time. They would listen more to a local. In short, the men were entrusting their interests to the worthiest man among them: he simply couldn't refuse, he'd be a coward if he did.

La Maheude gestured despairingly.

'Off you go, my love, go and get yourself killed for everybody else's sake. Go on, be my guest.'

'But I c-couldn't,' Maheu stuttered. 'I'd say something daft.'

Étienne patted him on the shoulder, delighted to have convinced him.

'You'll say what you feel, and that'll be just fine.'

Old Bonnemort, whose swollen legs were getting better, listened with his mouth full, shaking his head. There was silence. Whenever they had potatoes, the children tucked in and were very well behaved. When the old man had swallowed his mouthful, he said slowly:

'You can say whatever comes into your head, but it'll make no difference . . . Oh, I've been here before, I can tell you! Forty years ago they threw us out of the manager's office, and at sabre-point what's more! These days they might agree to see you, but they won't listen to you any more than this wall'll listen to you . . . What do you expect? They've got the money, so what the hell do they care?'

There was another silence: Maheu and Étienne got up and

left the family sitting gloomily in front of their empty plates. On their way out they collected Pierron and Levaque, and then the four of them headed for Rasseneur's, where the delegates from the surrounding villages were arriving in small groups. When the twenty members of the deputation had gathered there, they agreed on the conditions they were going to state to the Company; and off they set for Montsou. The bitter north-east wind was sweeping across the road. Two o'clock struck as they arrived.

At first Hippolyte told them to wait, and then shut the door in their faces. When he returned, he showed them into the drawing-room and opened the outer curtains. Soft daylight filtered through the lace behind. Having been left alone in the room, the miners were afraid to sit down, and waited awkwardly, all clean and scrubbed, with their yellow hair and moustaches, for they had shaved that morning and put on their best clothes. As they stood nervously fingering their caps, they threw sideways glances at the furniture. Many different styles were represented, with that eclecticism which the taste for antiques has made fashionable: Henri II armchairs, some Louis XV occasional chairs, a seventeenth-century Italian cabinet, a fifteenth-century *contador*,[1] an altar-front, which hung as a valance from the mantelpiece, and embroidered panels taken from old chasubles and stitched on to the door-curtains. All this ecclesiastical finery of antique gold and old fawn-coloured silks had filled them with uneasy respect, and the thick wool pile of the Oriental carpets seemed to wind itself round their feet. But what felt most overwhelming of all was the heat, this extraordinary enveloping heat provided by the central-heating system, which brought a glow to cheeks still frozen from the icy wind along the road. Five minutes went by. And their awkwardness grew, amid the sumptuous ease of a room so comfortably insulated from the world.

Finally M. Hennebeau came in, with his frock-coat buttoned up in the military manner, and wearing the trim little rosette of his decoration in his lapel. He spoke first:

'So here you are! . . . And up in arms, it appears.'

And he broke off to add, with stiff courtesy:

'Be seated. I like nothing better than to talk.'

The miners looked round for somewhere to sit. Some ventured to occupy a chair, but the rest were put off by the embroidered silk and preferred to stand.

There was a further silence. M. Hennebeau had rolled his armchair across in front of the fireplace and now quickly took stock, trying to recall their faces. He had just recognized Pierron hiding in the back row; and now his eyes came to rest on Étienne, sitting opposite him.

'So,' he began, 'and what have you come to tell me?'

He was expecting the young man to speak and was so surprised to see Maheu step forward that he could not help adding:

'What! You? Such a good worker, and always so reasonable, one of Montsou's old guard, whose family's been working down the mine since the first coal was cut! . . . Oh, this is not good, not good at all. I don't like seeing you here at the head of these troublemakers!'

Maheu listened, his eyes on the floor. Then he began, quiet and hesitant at first:

'Sir, that's exactly why the men have chosen me, because I'm a peaceful man and I've never done anyone any harm. Surely that must prove to you this isn't just a matter of a few hotheads wanting a fight, or people with the wrong ideas trying to stir up trouble. We only want what's fair. We've had enough of starving to death, and it seems to us high time that we came to some arrangement, so that at least we can have enough bread to live on each day.'

His voice grew firmer. He looked up and continued, with his eyes fixed on M. Hennebeau:

'You know very well we can't accept your new system . . . They say we're not doing the timbering right. And it's true. We don't give it the time we should. But if we did, our day's pay would be even less, and since we don't earn enough to live on as it is, that would be the final straw, you might as well say goodbye to the lot of us. But pay us more and we'll do better timbering. We'll put in the proper time it should take, instead of trying to hew as much coal as we can just because that's the only work that earns money. No other system's possible. If you want the job doing, you've got to pay for it . . . But no, what do you come up with instead? Really, it just beggars belief! You lower the rate per tub and then pretend to make up the reduction by paying for the timbering separately. If that was actually true, you'd still be robbing us because timbering always takes longer. But what really makes us angry is that it isn't even true. The Company's not compensating us at all, it's simply pocketing two centimes for every tub of coal. It's as simple as that!'

'Yes, that's right, that's right,' the other delegates muttered when they saw M. Hennebeau about to interrupt with a curt wave of the hand.

But in any case Maheu was not about to stop. Now that he was launched, the words came automatically. Occasionally he would listen to himself in astonishment, as though he were a stranger talking. These were things that had been building up inside him, things he didn't even know were there, and that now came pouring out of him, straight from the heart. He described their poverty, the hard work, the animal existence, the wife and children at home crying out with hunger. He referred to the recent disastrous pay-days and the derisory pay that was eaten into by fines and temporary lay-offs. How were they supposed to take that home to a family in tears? Had the Company decided to finish them off once and for all?

'Because we came to tell you, sir,' he said finally, 'that if it's a question of dying, we'd rather die doing nothing. That way, at least, we spare ourselves the exhaustion . . . We've left the pits, and we'll only go down again if the Company accepts our conditions. It wants to reduce the rate per tub and pay for the timbering separately. Well, we want the system we had before, and on top of that we want five centimes more per tub . . . And now it's up to you to decide whether you believe in justice and the value of work.'

Some of the miners could be heard saying:

'That's it . . . That's what we all think . . . We only want what's right.'

Others nodded silently in agreement. The sumptuous room had melted away, with its gilt and its embroidered silks and its mysterious assembly of old things; and they weren't even conscious of the carpet any more, crushed beneath their heavy shoes.

'Will you listen to me or not!' shouted M. Hennebeau finally, beginning to get angry. 'First of all, it's not true that the Company is making two centimes on each tub . . . Let's look at the figures.'

A chaotic discussion followed. In an effort to sow division, M. Hennbeau appealed to Pierron, who muttered something non-committal. Levaque, on the other hand, led the more aggressive contingent, but he got things mixed up and kept making assertions without knowing the facts. The loud hubbub of voices seemed to be absorbed by the heavy curtains and the hothouse atmosphere.

'If you're all going to talk at once,' said M. Hennebeau, 'we shall never reach agreement.'

He had regained his composure, together with the brusque but not unfriendly courtesy of a manager who has been given a job to do and intends to see it carried out. Since the very beginning of the discussion he had been watching Étienne, trying to find some way of making him break the silence that he seemed intent on maintaining. Accordingly, in a sudden change of tack, he stopped talking about the two centimes and began to broaden the discussion.

'No, come on now, admit the truth. It's all this recent agitation that's got you in a froth. Really, it's as though some plague had come among working men, and even the best ones catch it . . . Oh, you don't need to tell me, I can see somebody's been at you. You used to be so peaceable before. That's it, isn't it? Somebody's been saying you can have jam today, that it's your turn to be the masters . . . And now they've made you sign up to this International everyone's talking about, a horde of thieves and robbers whose one ambition is to destroy society –'

Now Étienne did interrupt:

'You're mistaken, sir. Not one collier in Montsou has joined yet. But if they're pushed any further, every man in every pit will join. It all depends on the Company.'

From then on the battle lay between M. Hennebeau and Étienne, as though the other miners were no longer present.

'The Company provides for these men, you're wrong to threaten it. This year alone it has spent three hundred thousand francs building villages for the miners, and it gets a return of less than two per cent on that. Not to mention the pensions it pays out, and the free coal, and the medicines it distributes. You seem an intelligent enough young man, and in just a few months you've become one of our most skilful workers. Wouldn't you do better to tell people things that are true rather than ruining your future by mixing with the wrong sort? Yes, I do mean Rasseneur. We had to part company, he and us, if we were going to save our pits from all that socialist rot ... You're always round at his place, and I'm sure he gave you the idea of setting up this provident fund, which incidentally we would be happy to tolerate if it were only for savings, except that we think it's a weapon to be used against us, an emergency fund to pay for the costs of war. And while we're on the subject, I may as well tell you that the Company intends to exercise control over that fund.'

Étienne let him go on, gazing steadily at him with a nervous quivering of the lips. The last sentence made him smile, and he replied simply:

'So I take it, sir, that you are laying down a new condition, since up till now there has been no demand to exercise control ... Our wish, I regret to say, is that the Company should take less of a part in our lives, not more, and that instead of playing the role of bountiful provider, it should simply do what's fair and pay us what is our due – meaning pay us the money *we* make but which *it* takes a share of. Is it right every time there's a crisis to let workers die of starvation so you don't have to cut the shareholders' dividend? ... You can say what you will, sir, but the new system is a disguised pay-cut, and that's what sickens us, because if the Company needs to make economies, it is very wrong of it to do so exclusively on the backs of the workers.'

'Ah, now we come to it!' cried M. Hennebeau. 'I was wondering when you'd start accusing us of starving the people and living off the sweat of their toil! How can you talk such rubbish, when you must know perfectly well the enormous risks entailed in investing capital in industry, and particularly in an industry like mining? A fully-equipped pit costs today in the region of one and a half to two million francs, and then there's all the hard work before you begin to see even a modest return on such a huge investment! Almost half the mining companies in France have gone bankrupt . . . Anyway, it's stupid accusing the successful ones of being cruel. While their workers are feeling the pain, so are they. Do you not think that the Company has got just as much to lose in the present crisis as you have? It can't decide the level of pay all on its own, it has to compete or go under. So blame the facts, not the Company . . . But you don't want to listen, do you? You don't want to understand!'

'Oh yes, we do,' Étienne replied. 'We understand perfectly well that there can be no improvement for us as long as things continue the way they are, and that's exactly why sooner or later the workers will make sure things happen differently.'

This statement, so temperately couched, was made almost in a whisper, but with such tremulous menace and conviction that there was a long silence. A wave of embarrassment and apprehension disturbed the quiet repose of the drawing-room. The other members of the deputation did not quite follow, but they sensed none the less that here, surrounded by this leisured ease, their comrade had just laid claim to their rightful share; and once again they began to cast sideways glances at the warm curtains and the comfortable seats, and at all this expense, when the price of the smallest ornament would have kept them in soup for a month.

Eventually a pensive M. Hennebeau rose to his feet, preparing to send them away. Everyone else stood up also. Étienne gently nudged Maheu in the elbow, and he began to speak, awkward and tongue-tied once more:

'Well, if that's all you have to say in reply, sir . . . We shall tell the others that you reject our terms.'

'But, my dear fellow,' exclaimed M. Hennebeau, 'I have rejected nothing! . . . I am just a paid employee, like you. I have no more say in what is decided than the youngest pit-boy. I receive my instructions, and my sole function is to see that they are properly carried out. I have said to you what I thought it my duty to say to you, but I should certainly refrain from deciding the matter . . . You have brought me your demands, I shall pass them on to the Board of Directors, and I shall let you know how it responds.'

He spoke with the correctness of the senior administrator taking care not to become involved in the issues and deploying the soulless courtesy of a simple instrument of authority. And now the miners looked at him with suspicion, wondering what his game was, what it might pay him to lie, what ways he might have of lining his own pocket, positioned as he was like this between them and the true masters. A devious sort, perhaps, since he was paid like a worker and yet he lived so well!

Étienne risked a further intervention:

'But you must see how regrettable it is, sir, that we cannot plead our case in person. There are many things we could explain and reasons we could give that inevitably you wouldn't know about yourself . . . If only we knew who to talk to!'

M. Hennebeau was not angry. In fact he smiled:

'Ah well now, if you're not going to have confidence in me, that complicates matters . . . It would mean you having to try elsewhere.'

The men's eyes followed as he gestured vaguely in the direction of one of the drawing-room windows. Where was 'elsewhere'? Paris probably. But they didn't quite know, and wherever it was, it seemed like a distant, forbidding place, some remote and sacred region where that unknown deity squatted on its throne deep in the inner recesses of its temple. They would never ever set eyes on this god, they just sensed it, as a force weighing from afar on the ten thousand colliers of Montsou. And when the manager spoke, this force was behind him, concealed and speaking in oracles.

They felt defeated. Even Étienne shrugged as though to say they would do better to leave. M. Hennebeau gave Maheu a friendly tap on the arm and asked him news of Jeanlin.

'That was a harsh lesson all right, and to think you're the one who defends the bad timbering! . . . Think it over, my friends, and you'll soon see that a strike would be a disaster for everyone concerned. Within a week you'll all be starving to death. How are you going to manage? ... Anyway, I'm counting on your good sense, and I'm sure you'll be going back down by next Monday at the latest.'

They all took their leave, tramping out of the room like a herd of animals, with their heads bowed and offering not a word of response to this prospect of surrender. As he saw them out, the manager had perforce to summarize their meeting: on one side the Company and its new rates, on the other the workers with their demand for an increase of five centimes per tub. And, so that they should be under no illusion, he felt obliged to warn them that the Board of Directors would certainly reject their terms.

'And think twice before you do anything silly,' he said again, uneasy at their silence.

Out in the hall Pierron made a very low bow while Levaque made a point of putting his cap back on. Maheu was searching for something more to say, but once again Étienne gave him a nudge. And off they went, accompanied by this ominous silence. The only sound was of the door banging shut behind them.

When M. Hennebeau came back into the dining-room, he found his guests sitting silent and motionless in front of their liqueurs. He quickly briefed Deneulin, whose expression grew even more sombre. Then, as he drank his cold coffee, everyone tried to talk about something else. But the Grégoires themselves returned to the subject of the strike and expressed their astonishment that there were no laws preventing the workers from leaving their work. Paul tried to reassure Cécile, saying that the gendarmes were on their way.

Finally Mme Hennebeau summoned her servant:

'Hippolyte, would you open the windows before we go into the drawing-room and let some fresh air in?'

III

A fortnight had elapsed, and on the Monday of the third week the attendance lists sent to management indicated a further reduction in the number of men working underground. They had been counting on a general return to work that morning, but because of the Board's intransigence the miners' resistance was hardening. Le Voreux, Crèvecœur, Mirou and Madeleine were no longer the only pits out on strike; at La Victoire and Feutry-Cantel barely a quarter of the colliers were going down; and even Saint-Thomas was now affected. Gradually the strike was spreading.

At Le Voreux a heavy silence hung over the pit-yard with that hushed vacancy of a deserted workplace where labour has ceased and life departed. Along the overhead railway, etched against the grey December sky, three or four abandoned tubs sat with the mute dejection of mere things. Underneath, between the trestle-supports, the dwindling coal-piles had left the ground bare and black; and the stock of timbering stood rotting in the rain. At the canal jetty a half-laden barge lay abandoned, as though dozing on the murky water; while up on the deserted spoil-heap, where decomposing sulphide continued to smoke despite the wet, the shafts of a solitary cart rose forlornly into the air. But it was the buildings especially that seemed to be sinking into torpor: the screening-shed with its closed shutters, the headgear that had ceased to echo with the rumble of the pit-head beneath, and the boiler-house where the fire-grates had cooled and whose huge chimney now seemed excessively wide for the occasional wisp of smoke. The winding-engine was fired up only in the mornings. The stablemen delivered fodder to the horses down the pit, where the sole people working were the deputies, miners once more as they endeavoured to prevent the damage to the roads that inevitably occurs when these are no longer properly maintained. From nine o'clock onwards any further maintenance work had to be carried out by using the ladders for access. And over these lifeless buildings, wrapped in their black shroud of coal-dust, hung the steam from the drainage-pump as it continued its slow, heavy panting, the last vestiges of life in a pit, which would be destroyed by flooding if this panting should ever stop.

Opposite, on its plateau, Village Two Hundred and Forty seemed dead also. The Prefect had hastened from Lille to visit the scene, and gendarmes had patrolled the roads; but with the strikers remaining perfectly calm, Prefect and gendarmes alike had decided to return home. Never had the village set a better example throughout the vast plain. The men would sleep all day to avoid going drinking; the women rationed their consumption of coffee and became more reasonable, less obsessed with gossip and feuding; and even the gangs of children seemed to understand, so well behaved that they ran about barefoot and scrapped without making a noise. The watchword, repeated and passed on from person to person, was simple: there was to be no trouble.

Nevertheless the Maheus' house was constantly full of people coming and going. It was here that Étienne, as secretary, had shared out the three thousand francs in the provident fund among the most needy families. After that a few hundred francs more had come in from various sources, some as fund contributions and some from collections, but their resources were running out now. The miners had no money left to carry on the strike, and hunger was staring them in the face. Maigrat had promised everyone a fortnight's credit but then suddenly changed his mind after the first week and cut off supplies. Generally he did what the Company told him, so perhaps they were trying to force the issue by making everyone starve. On top of which he acted like some capricious tyrant, providing or withholding bread depending on the looks of the girl the parents had sent for their food; and he was never open for La Maheude, since he bore her a deep grudge and wanted to punish her for the fact that he had not yet had Catherine. To make matters even worse the weather was bitterly cold, and the women watched their supply of coal dwindling with the anxious thought that it would not be replenished as long as the men refused to go down the pits. As if it were not enough that they were going to die of hunger, they were now going to freeze to death as well.

The Maheus were already running short of everything. The Levaques could still eat, thanks to a twenty-franc piece lent by Bouteloup. As for the Pierrons, they still had money; but in order to appear as destitute as everyone else – in case anyone should ask them for a loan – they bought on credit at Maigrat's, who would have let La Pieronne have his entire shop if she'd only lift her skirt for him. Since Saturday many families had gone to bed without supper. But, as they faced up to the terrible days ahead, not one complaint was heard, and everyone heeded the watchword with steadfast courage. Despite everything they had absolute confidence in the outcome, a kind of religious faith, like some nation of zealots blindly offering up the gift of their own selves. They had been promised the new dawn of justice, and so they were ready to suffer in the pursuit of universal happiness. Hunger turned their heads, and closed horizons had never opened on to broader vistas for these men and women who were drunk on their own deprivation. They beheld before them, as their eyes grew dim with fatigue, the ideal city of their dreams, a city now close at hand and almost real, where the golden age had come to pass, where all men were brothers, living and working in the common cause. Nothing could shake their absolute conviction that now at last they were entering its gates. The provident fund was exhausted, the Company would not yield, the situation would worsen with each day, and yet still they hoped and still they scoffed at life's realities. Even if the earth should open up beneath their feet, a miracle would surely save them. Such faith took the place of bread and warmed their bellies. When the Maheus, like the others, had downed their thin and watery soup, only too soon digested, they would become elated at this dizzying prospect and their minds would fill with ecstatic visions of a better life such as had once caused the early martyrs to be thrown to the lions.

From this point on Étienne was the undisputed leader. During their evening conversations he was the oracle, and his studies continued to sharpen his judgement and give him firm opinions on all issues. He would read all night long, and received more and more letters. He had even begun to subscribe to *The Avenger*, a socialist paper published in Belgium, and the arrival

of this journal, the first ever seen in the village, had caused him
to be held in exceptional regard among his comrades. With each
day that passed he became more and more intoxicated with his
growing popularity. To be corresponding like this with a wide
range of people, to be debating the workers' future up and down
the region, to be giving individual advice to the miners of Le
Voreux, and – most especially – to have become the centre of
things and to feel the world revolving round him, it all served
constantly to feed his vanity. Him! The ex-mechanic, the coal-
worker with the filthy black hands! He was going up in the
world, he was becoming one of the detested bourgeois and,
without admitting as much to himself, he was beginning to enjoy
the pleasures of the intellect and the comforts of easy living.
Only one thing still gave him pause, the awareness of his lack
of a formal education, which made him embarrassed and timid
the moment he found himself in the presence of anyone in a
frock-coat. Though he continued to teach himself and read
everything he could, his want of method made the process of
assimilation very slow, leading eventually to a state of confusion
in which he knew things but had not understood them. Indeed
in some of his more rational moments he had doubts about his
mission and feared that he might not after all be the man the
world was waiting for. Perhaps it needed a lawyer, a man of
learning capable of speaking and acting without endangering
his comrades' cause? But he soon rejected the idea and recovered
his poise. No, no, they didn't want lawyers! Crooks, the lot of
them, using their knowledge to get fat at the people's expense!
It would all turn out as it might, but the workers were better off
fending for themselves. And once again he would nurse his fond
dream of becoming the people's leader: Montsou at his feet,
Paris in the misty distance and, who knows, election to the
Chamber of Deputies, addressing the Assembly[1] in its opulent
setting? He could just see himself there fulminating against an
astonished bourgeoisie in the first parliamentary speech ever
made by a working man.

For the past few days Étienne had been in a quandary. Pluchart kept writing letter after letter offering to come to Montsou
to raise the strikers' morale. The idea was to arrange a private

meeting, which Étienne would chair, but behind this lay the intention of using the strike to recruit the miners to the International, which they had so far regarded with suspicion. Étienne was worried that there might be trouble, but he would nevertheless have allowed Pluchart to come if Rasseneur had not been so strongly against his intervening. Despite his power and influence Étienne had to reckon with Rasseneur, who had served the cause for longer and still had a number of supporters among his customers. And so he was still hesitating, not knowing how to reply.

That particular Monday, at about four in the afternoon, yet another letter arrived from Lille, just as Étienne was sitting with La Maheude in the downstairs room. Maheu, irritable on account of the enforced idleness, had gone fishing: if he was lucky enough to catch a nice fish, below the canal lock, they would sell it and buy bread. Bonnemort and young Jeanlin had recently gone for a walk, to try out their new legs, while the little ones had left with Alzire, who spent hours on the spoil-heap scavenging for half-burned cinders. Next to the paltry fire, which nobody dared keep going now, La Maheude sat with her blouse undone feeding Estelle from a breast which hung down to her stomach.

When Étienne folded up the letter, she inquired:

'Good news? Are they going to send us some money?'

He shook his head, and she went on:

'I just don't know how we're going to manage this week . . . Still, we'll get through somehow, I expect. It gives you heart, doesn't it, when you've got right on your side? You know you'll win out in the end.'

By now she was in favour of the strike, but in a reasonable way. It would have been better to force the Company to deal with them fairly without stopping work. But stopped they had, and they should not return until justice was theirs. On that point she was implacable. She'd rather die than appear to have been in the wrong, especially when they actually were in the right!

'Oh,' Étienne burst out, 'if only we could have a nice cholera epidemic that would wipe out all those Company people who are busy exploiting us!'

'No, no,' she retorted, 'you mustn't wish anyone dead. Anyway, it wouldn't get us very far, others would come along and take their place . . . All I ask is that the people we do have to deal with start seeing sense. And I expect they will, because there are always some decent people around . . . You know I don't hold with all your politics.'

And it was true. She was given to blaming him for the vehemence of his language, and she accused him of being aggressive. If people wanted to get paid a fair wage, all well and good; but why bother with all these other things, all this stuff about the bourgeoisie and the government? Why get involved in other people's business when it would only end in tears? And yet she continued to respect him for the fact that he never got drunk and that he continued to pay her regularly his forty-five francs for board and lodging. When a man was honest in his dealings, you could forgive him the rest.

Étienne then talked about the Republic and how it would provide bread for all. But La Maheude shook her head, for she could remember 1848[2] and what a miserable year that had been, when she and Maheu had been left without a penny to their name in the first days of their marriage. In a sad, absent voice she began to reminisce about all the problems they had had, her eyes gazing into space and her breast still exposed as her daughter Estelle fell asleep in her lap without letting go. Similarly engrossed, Étienne stared at this enormous breast and its soft whiteness that was so different from the ravaged, yellowing skin of her face.

'Not a penny,' she whispered. 'Not a crumb to eat, and every pit out on strike. The old, old story, in fact, of the poor starving to death. Just like now!'

But at that moment the door opened, and they stared in speechless astonishment as Catherine walked in. She had not been seen in the village since the day she ran off with Chaval. She was in such a state that she just stood there, mute and trembling, leaving the door open behind her. She had been counting on finding her mother alone, and the sight of Étienne robbed her of the speech she had been mentally preparing on the way over.

'What the hell are you doing here?' La Maheude shouted from where she sat. 'I don't want anything more to do with you. Just go away.'

Catherine struggled for her lines:

'I've brought some coffee and sugar, Mum . . . I have, for the children . . . I've been working extra hours, and I thought they . . .'

From her pockets she produced a pound of coffee and a pound of sugar, which she ventured to place on the table. She had been tormented by the thought of everyone being on strike at Le Voreux while she continued to work at Jean-Bart, and this was all she had been able to think of as a way of helping her parents out, on the pretext of being concerned for the children. But her kindness failed to disarm her mother, who retorted:

'You'd have done better to stay and earn something here, instead of bringing us treats.'

She now poured out all her pent-up abuse, throwing in Catherine's face all the things that she had been saying about her for the past month. Getting involved with a man and her only sixteen, and running off like that when her family hadn't a penny! You'd have to be the most unnatural of daughters to do such a thing. One could forgive a stupid mistake, but no mother could ever forget a dirty trick like that. And it wasn't as if they'd kept her on a tight leash either! No, not at all, she'd been as free as the air to come and go as she pleased. All they'd asked was that she came home at night.

'Eh? What's got into you? At your age?'

Catherine stood motionless beside the table, hanging her head and listening. Her thin, girlish body quivered from head to toe, and she tried to blurt out a reply:

'Oh, if the decision was left to me . . . As if I enjoyed any of it . . . It's him. What he wants I have to want too, don't I? Because he's stronger than me. It's as simple as that . . . Who knows why things turn out like they do? Anyway, what's done is done, there's no going back. As soon him as another now. He'll just have to marry me.'

She was defending herself but in an unrebellious sort of way, with the meek resignation of the young girl who has to submit to the male from an early age. Wasn't that the way of things? She'd never imagined anything else: raped behind the spoil-heap, a mother at sixteen, and then a life of wretched poverty together – if her lover married her, that was. And if she blushed with shame and trembled in this way, it was only because she was so upset at being treated like a whore in front of this young man whose presence overwhelmed her and made her feel such despair.

Étienne, meanwhile, had got up and pretended to see to the fire, so as to keep out of the row. But their eyes met, and he found her pale and exhausted-looking, though pretty all the same, with those bright eyes of hers surrounded by a face that was gradually turning brown; and a strange feeling came over him, a sense that his resentment had all gone and that he simply wanted her to be happy with this man she had preferred to him. He still felt the need to look after her, and he wanted to go to Montsou and force the man to treat her properly. But she saw only pity in this continuing tenderness and took his staring as a sign of disdain. And she felt such a constriction in her heart that she choked on her words and could stammer out no further excuses.

'Yes, that's right. You'd much better hold your tongue,' La Maheude continued mercilessly. 'If you're here to stay, then come in. If not, clear off, and you can count yourself lucky that I've got my hands full at the minute, otherwise by now you'd have got a good kick you know where.'

Almost as if this threat had suddenly been carried out, Catherine received a violent kick full in the buttocks, which left her reeling with pain and shock. It was Chaval, who had burst in through the open door and lashed out at her with his foot like some crazed beast. He had been watching her from outside for the last minute or so.

'You whore!' he screamed. 'I followed you. I knew bloody well you came here for a good fuck! And so you pay him, do you? Treating him to the coffee you've bought with *my* money!'

La Maheude and Étienne were so astonished that they did not move as Chaval waved his arms about like a madman and tried to chase Catherine towards the door.

'Get the bloody hell out of here!'

As she cowered in a corner of the room, he turned on her mother:

'And a fine job you do, keeping watch for her while your slut of a daughter is lying upstairs with her legs in the air.'

Eventually, having grabbed Catherine by the wrist, he started shaking her and trying to drag her outside. In the doorway he turned once more towards La Maheude, who was still unable to move from her chair. She had quite forgotten to cover her breast. Estelle had fallen asleep with her face buried in her mother's woollen skirt; and the enormous, naked breast just hung there, like the udder of some particularly productive cow.

'And when the daughter's away, it's the mother that gets screwed!' screamed Chaval. 'That's right! Go on! Show that bastard of a lodger what you've got. Any old piece of meat will do him!'

At that, Étienne was ready to hit Chaval. He had been afraid that a fight might destroy the atmosphere of calm in the village, and this had kept him from snatching Catherine out of the man's hands. But now it was his turn to be furious, and the two men stood face to face, with blood in their eyes. Theirs was an ancient hatred, a long, unspoken, jealous rivalry, and it burst into the open. This time one of them would have to pay.

'Watch yourself!' Étienne spluttered through clenched teeth. 'I'll soon sort you out.'

'Just you try!' answered Chaval.

They stared at each other for a few seconds longer, standing so close that each could feel the other's hot breath burning into his face. Then Catherine took hold of her lover's hand and pleaded with him to leave. And she dragged him away from the village, running by his side without a backward glance.

'What an animal!' Étienne muttered under his breath, slamming the door. He was shaking with anger so much that he had to sit down again.

Opposite him, La Maheude had still not moved. She waved her hand dismissively, and an awkward silence followed, heavy with their unspoken thoughts. Étienne could not keep his eyes off her breast, and its lava-flow of white flesh disturbed him with its dazzling brightness. Yes, she was forty and her figure had gone – every bit the trusty female who has had too many children – but many a man still desired her broad, solid frame and the long, full face that had once been beautiful. Slowly and calmly she had grasped her breast with both hands and replaced it under her blouse. A corner of pink flesh refused to disappear, so she pressed it back with her finger and buttoned herself up. And she became once more the frump in her old, loose-fitting jacket, dressed in black from head to foot.

'He's a pig,' she said finally. 'Only a filthy pig could think such disgusting things . . . Not that I bloody care! It wasn't worth wasting my breath on him.'

Then she looked Étienne in the eye and said frankly:

'I have my faults all right, but that's not one of them . . . Only two men have ever laid a finger on me, a putter long ago, when I was fifteen, and then Maheu. If he'd left me like the first one, God knows what might have happened to me. Not that I'm boasting about being faithful either. If people behave themselves, it's often because they haven't had a chance not to . . . But I'm just saying how it is, and there are some women round here who couldn't say the same, could they?'

'That's true enough,' replied Étienne, getting to his feet.

And off he went, while La Maheude decided to relight the fire and pulled two chairs together to set the sleeping Estelle down on them. If Maheu had managed to catch a fish and sell it, they might have some soup after all.

Outside night was already falling, and Étienne walked along in the freezing cold, his bowed head full of black thoughts. He no longer felt anger against Chaval nor pity for the poor girl he was treating so badly. The brutal scene was gradually fading to a blur as his mind was recalled to the prospect of everyone else's suffering and the terrible reality of their poverty. What he saw was a village without bread, a village of women and children who would go to bed hungry that night, a whole community straining to keep up the struggle on an empty stomach. And the doubt that sometimes overcame him now returned amid the awful melancholy of the dusk and tortured him with misgivings that were stronger than any he had known. What a terrifying responsibility he was taking on! Was he going to drive them still further, make them pursue their stubborn resistance despite the fact that the money and credit were all gone? And how would it all end if no help came, if hunger were to get the better of their courage? Suddenly he could see how it would be, the full calamity: children dying, mothers sobbing, while the men, starved and gaunt, went back down the pits. And on he walked, stumbling over the stones in his path, consumed with unbearable anguish at the thought that the Company would win and that he would have brought disaster upon his comrades.

When he looked up, he found himself outside Le Voreux. The dark, hulking mass of its buildings seemed to be settling lower in the gathering darkness. In the middle of the deserted yard, large, motionless shadows crowded the space, lending it the air of an abandoned fortress. When the winding-engine stopped, the place seemed to give up its soul. At this hour of the night there was not a sign of life anywhere, no lantern shining, not even a voice; and within the vast nothingness that the pit had become, even the sound of the drainage-pump seemed to issue from some mysterious, far-away place, like the gasps of a dying man.

As Étienne gazed at the scene, his pulse began to quicken. The workers might be starving, but the Company was eating into its millions. Why should it necessarily prove the stronger in this war between labour and money? Whatever happened, victory would cost it dear. They would see afterwards who counted the greater number of casualties. Once more he felt a lust for battle, a fierce desire to put an end to their wretched poverty once and for all, even at the price of death. The whole village might just as well perish straight away if the only alternative was to die one by one of famine and injustice. He recalled things from his ill-digested reading, instances of people setting fire to their own town in order to halt the enemy and vague stories about mothers saving their children from slavery by smashing their skulls on the ground, and men starving themselves to death rather than eat the bread of tyrants. His spirits soared and his black thoughts began to glow with the warm cheer of optimism, banishing all doubt and making him ashamed of his momentary cowardice.

And as his confidence returned, so did his swelling pride, bearing him up on a wave of joy at being the leader, at seeing men and women ready to sacrifice themselves in the execution of his orders, and he was consumed with his ever-evolving dream of the power he would enjoy on the night of victory. He could see it all now, the moment of simple grandeur as he refused to take the reins of power and, as their master, handed authority back to the people.

But he was roused with a start by the voice of Maheu, who told him of his good fortune in catching a superb trout and selling it for three francs. They would have their soup. Étienne told Maheu to return to the village on his own, that he would be along later. Then he went and sat at a table in the Advantage, waiting for a customer to leave before telling Rasseneur firmly that he intended to write and tell Pluchart to come at once. He had made up his mind: he was going to organize a private meeting, for victory seemed assured if the colliers of Montsou would join the International *en masse*.

IV

The meeting was fixed for the following Thursday at two o'clock in the Jolly Fellow, the bar run by Widow Desire. She was outraged by the suffering being inflicted on her children and was in permanent high dudgeon about the situation, especially since people had stopped coming to her bar. She had never known less thirst during a strike, the heavy drinkers having shut themselves away at home for fear of disobeying the order to stay out of trouble. The result was that the main street of Montsou, once seething with people during the *ducasse*, now lay gloomily silent, a place of desolation. With no more beer running off the counters or out of people's bladders, the gutters were dry. The only thing to be seen along the road outside Casimir's bar and the Progress was the pale faces of the land-ladies anxiously looking out for approaching customers; while in Montsou itself the whole row of bars and taverns was deserted, from Lenfant's at one end past Piquette's and the Severed Head to Tison's at the other. Only the Saint-Éloi, where the deputies went, was still serving the occasional beer. Even the Volcano was empty, and its ladies unemployed, bereft of takers, even though they would have cut their price from ten sous to five, since times were hard. It was as though someone had died and broken everyone's heart.

'God damn it!' Widow Desire had exclaimed, slapping both hands on her thighs. 'It's all the fault of the men in blue. I don't care if they do put me in bloody prison. I'll soon show 'em!'

For her all representatives of authority, like all bosses, were 'the men in blue', a term of general abuse in which she included all enemies of the people. Therefore she had accepted Étienne's request with delight: her entire establishment was at the miners' disposal, they could use the dance-hall at no charge, and she would send out the invitations herself if that was what the law required. Anyway, so much the better if the law wasn't happy! She'd like to see a long face on it! The next day Étienne brought her fifty letters to sign, which he had got copied by neighbours in the village who were able to write; and then they sent the letters off to all the mines, to the men who had been part of the deputation and to others they were sure of. The ostensible agenda was to discuss whether or not to continue the strike; but in reality they would be coming to hear Pluchart, and they were relying on him to give a speech that would lead to people joining the International *en masse*.

On Thursday morning Étienne was getting worried because his old foreman had still not arrived, having sent a message promising to be there by Wednesday evening. What could have happened? He was disappointed that he wouldn't be able to have a word with him in private before the meeting to discuss how they were going to proceed. By nine o'clock Étienne was already in Montsou, thinking that perhaps Pluchart had gone straight there without stopping at Le Voreux.

'No, I haven't seen your friend yet,' said Widow Desire. 'But everything's ready. Come and see.'

She led him into the dance-hall. The decorations were still the same: on the ceiling the streamers holding up a wreath of paper flowers, and along the walls the line of gold cardboard shields bearing the names of saints. But the stage for the musicians had been replaced by a table and three chairs set in one corner, and benches had been arranged in diagonal rows across the rest of the room.

'Perfect,' declared Étienne.

'And just make yourself at home, you understand,' Widow Desire went on. 'Make as much noise as you please . . . And if the men in blue try to come in, it'll be over my dead body!'

Despite his anxiety he could not help smiling at the sight of her. How could one embrace such a vast woman, when one of her breasts alone was more than enough for any man; which was why people said that she had started having her six weekday lovers two at a time, so they could help each other with the task.

To Étienne's surprise Rasseneur and Souvarine walked in; and as Widow Desire departed and left the three of them alone in the large empty hall, he exclaimed:

'You're early, aren't you?'

Souvarine had worked the night shift at Le Voreux – the mechanics were not on strike – and had come out of simple curiosity. As for Rasseneur, he had been looking ill at ease for the past two days, and his big round face had lost its ready smile.

'Pluchart's not here yet,' Étienne went on. 'I'm extremely worried.'

Rasseneur looked away and mumbled:

'I'm not surprised. I don't think he'll be coming.'

'What do you mean?'

Then Rasseneur made up his mind and, looking Étienne in the eye, announced defiantly:

'Because I, too, wrote him a letter, if you must know, and asked him not to come . . . That's right. It seems to me we ought to handle these things on our own and not go bringing strangers into it.'

Étienne was beside himself, trembling with rage as he stared at his comrade and stammered:

'You didn't! You can't have!'

'I certainly can – and I did. And as you know, it's not that I don't trust Pluchart either! He's a clever one all right, and solid with it, someone you can count on . . . But the point is I don't give a damn about all these fancy ideas of yours! All this stuff about politics and the government, I just don't give a tuppenny damn. What I want is better treatment for the miners. I worked down the mine for twenty years, and I promised myself – after all that sweat and toil just to end up poor and exhausted the whole time – that I'd try and make things better, somehow, for the poor buggers that are still down there. And all I can say is, you'll get nowhere with all this bloody nonsense of yours, all you'll succeed in doing is making the worker's lot even more bloody miserable than it already is . . . When he's finally so hungry that he's forced to go back, they'll just make things worse for him. That'll be his reward. The Company'll kick him while he's down, and kick him hard, like a dog being put back in its kennel after it's got out . . . And *that*'s what I want to prevent! Understood?'

As he stood there foursquare on his stout legs, belly out, he began to raise his voice. Here was the patient man of reason speaking his mind in plain language, and the words just poured out of him without his even having to think about them. Didn't they realize it was just plain daft to think you could change the world overnight, to think the workers could take the place of the bosses and share out the cash as if it were an apple or something. It would take an eternity before that ever happened, and even then! If it was miracles they were after, forget it! The only sensible thing to do if they didn't want to end up with a bloody nose was to keep their eye on the real issue, to take every opportunity that presented itself to demand reforms that were possible, things that would actually improve the worker's lot. If it was left to him, he had no doubt he could get the Company to bring in better working conditions; whereas with everyone digging their heels in like this, they were all going to bloody die, thank you very much!

Speechless with indignation, Étienne had let him go on. But now he shouted:

'Christ Almighty! Have you got no feelings at all?'

For a moment he was on the verge of hitting him; but to stop himself he walked off, taking his fury out on the benches as he cleared a path through the hall.

'You might at least shut the door, you two,' observed Souvarine. 'We don't need everyone to hear.'

After going to shut it himself, he came back and sat down quietly on one of the chairs by the table. He had rolled a cigarette and now sat watching the two men with the usual gentle, intelligent look in his eyes and a thin, pursed smile on his lips.

'You can get as cross as you like,' Rasseneur continued evenly, 'but it won't get us anywhere. I used to think you were sensible. That was a good idea of yours to get the comrades to keep out of trouble, making them stay at home like that, using your influence to maintain law and order. But now you're all set to land them in it!'

After each trip across the hall Étienne would return to where Rasseneur was standing, grab him by the shoulders and shake him, screaming in his face with each reply:

'Bloody hell! I do want us to keep out of trouble. Yes, I did impose discipline on them! And yes, I am still telling them to stay calm. But only just as long as people don't walk all over us . . . Good for you if you can stay all calm and collected. There are times when I feel as though my head's going to blow off.'

Now it was his turn to speak his mind. He laughed at his earlier idealism, his schoolboy vision of a brave new world in which justice would reign and men would be brothers. But the one way to make sure that men were at each other's throats until the end of time was to sit back and wait for things to happen. No! You had to get involved, otherwise injustice would never end and the rich would forever be sucking the blood of the poor. Which was why he couldn't forgive himself for having once been stupid enough to advocate keeping politics out of the 'social question'. He knew nothing then, whereas he had since read things, studied things. His ideas had matured now, and he liked to think that he had a system which would work. Nevertheless he explained it badly, in a muddle of statements which bore the trace of all the theories he had encountered and abandoned along the way. At the centre was still the idea put forward by Karl Marx: capital was the result of theft, and labour had the duty and the right to recover this stolen wealth. As to putting this into practice, Étienne had at first been seduced, like Proudhon, by the attractions of mutual credit, of one vast clearing bank that would cut out all the middlemen; then it had been Lassalle's idea of co-operative societies,[1] funded by the State, which would gradually transform the earth into one great big industrial city, and he had been wildly in favour of this until the day he was finally put off by the problem of controls; and recently he had been coming round to collectivism, which called for the means of production to be returned into the ownership of the collective. But this was all still somewhat vague, and he couldn't quite see how to achieve this new goal, prevented as he was by scruples of humanity and common sense from enjoying the fanatic's ability to advance ideas with uncompromising conviction. For the moment his line was simply that what they had to do first was take power. Afterwards they'd see.

'But what on earth's got into you? Why have you gone over to the bourgeois?' Étienne continued angrily, as he returned once more to confront Rasseneur. 'You used to say it yourself: things can't go on like this!'

Rasseneur flushed slightly.

'Yes, that's what I used to say. And if things do get rough, you'll soon see that I'm no more of a coward than the next man . . . Only I refuse to support people who are busy making matters worse so they can exploit the situation.'

It was Étienne's turn to colour. The two men had stopped shouting, and there was now bitterness and ill-will in their cold hostility. Antagonism breeds extremism, and it was turning one into the zealous revolutionary and the other into an excessive advocate of caution, taking them beyond what they really thought and forcing them to adopt positions of which they then became prisoners. And the expression on Souvarine's fair, girlish face as he listened to them was one of silent disdain, the crushing contempt of one who is ready to sacrifice his own life, anonymously, without even the glory of being a martyr.

'That's aimed at me, I suppose?' Étienne inquired. 'Jealous, are you?'

'Jealous of what?' Rasseneur retorted. 'I'm not claiming to be anyone special. I'm not the one trying to create a branch of the International at Montsou just so he can be secretary of it.'

Étienne was about to interrupt, but Rasseneur forestalled him:

'Admit it! You don't give a damn about the International. You just want to be our leader and play the educated gentleman who corresponds with the wonderful Federal Council for the Département du Nord.'

There was silence. Étienne quivered:

'Very well, then . . . I thought I'd been careful not to act out of turn. I've always consulted you, because I knew you'd been involved in the struggle here long before I came. But no, since you obviously can't stand to work with anyone else, I shall now act alone . . . And I can tell you for a start that this meeting's going to go ahead, with or without Pluchart, and that the comrades will join whether you like it or not.'

'Oh, will they?' Rasseneur muttered under his breath. 'We'll soon see about that . . . You'll have to persuade them to pay their subscription first.'

'Not at all. The International lets men on strike defer their subscription. We can pay later. But it will come to our aid immediately.'

With this Rasseneur lost his temper:

'Fine. We'll see, then . . . I'm coming to this meeting of yours, and I'm going to speak. These are my friends, and I'm not going to let you turn their heads. I'll show them where their real interests lie. And then we'll see who they intend to listen to. Me, who they've known this past thirty years, or you, who's made a bloody mess of everything in less than one . . . No, that's enough. Not another bloody word. This time it's to the death.'

And out he went, slamming the door behind him. The paper streamers shook beneath the ceiling, and the gold-coloured shields bounced against the walls. Then a heavy silence fell in the large hall.

Souvarine was still sitting at the table, quietly smoking. Étienne paced up and down for a moment in silence, and then out it poured. Was it his fault if the men were deserting that fat, lazy bastard and siding with him now? He hadn't set out to be popular, he didn't really even know how it had come about, why everyone in the village looked on him as a friend, why the miners trusted him, why he had such power over them at present. He was indignant at the accusation that he was making matters worse so as to further his ambitions, and he thumped his chest by way of protesting solidarity with his brothers.

Suddenly he stopped in front of Souvarine and said loudly:

'You know, if I thought a friend of mine was going to lose so much as a single drop of blood over this, I'd emigrate to America this very minute.'

Souvarine shrugged, and his lips parted once more in a thin smile:

'Oh, blood,' he said softly. 'What does that matter? It's good for the soil.'

Étienne began to calm down and went and sat opposite Souvarine, propping his elbows on the table. He was unnerved by his fair complexion and those dreamy eyes that would occasionally turn red and assume a look of wild savagery. In some curious way they seemed to sap his will. Without his comrade even needing to speak, indeed overpowered by his very silence, Étienne felt as though he were gradually being absorbed by him.

'Look here,' he said, 'what would you do if you were in my position? Aren't I right to want to make things happen? . . . And joining the International is the best thing for us, isn't it?'

Souvarine slowly exhaled a cloud of cigarette smoke and then replied with his favourite word:

'Nonsense. All nonsense. But for the moment it's better than nothing. What's more, that International of theirs will soon be on the move. *He*'s taking a hand in it now.'

He had spoken the word in a hushed voice and with an expression of religious fervour on his face as he glanced towards the east. He was talking about the Master, about Bakunin, the exterminator.[2]

'He's the only one who can deliver the real hammer-blow,' Souvarine continued, 'whereas these intellectuals of yours with all their talk of gradual change are just cowards . . . Under his leadership the International will have crushed the old order within three years.'

Étienne was listening with rapt attention. He was longing to learn more, to understand this cult of destruction that Souvarine only rarely and darkly referred to, as though he wanted to keep its mysteries for himself.

'So, come on then . . . What exactly is your objective?'

'To destroy everything . . . No more nations, no more governments, no more property, no more God or religion.'

'I see. But where does that lead?'

'To community in its basic, unstructured form, to a new world order, to a new beginning in everything.'

'And how is it to be done? How are you planning to go about it?'

'By fire, sword and poison. The criminal is the real hero, the avenger of the people, the revolutionary in action, and not just someone who trots out phrases he's learned from books. What we need is a whole succession of horrific attacks that will terrify those in power and rouse the people from their slumber.'

While he spoke, Souvarine presented an awesome sight. As though in the grip of an ecstatic vision, he almost levitated from his chair; a mystic flame shone from his pale eyes, and his delicate hands clenched the edge of the table as though they would crush it. Étienne watched him, afraid, remembering some of the things Souvarine had semi-confided in him about the Tsar's palaces being mined, and police chiefs being hunted to their deaths like wild boar, and how a mistress of his, the only woman he had ever loved, had been hanged one rainy morning in Moscow while he stood in the crowd and kissed her goodbye with his eyes.

'No, no,' said Étienne under his breath, waving his hand as though to banish these appalling scenes. 'We aren't that desperate here yet. Murder? Arson? Never. It's monstrous and unjust. The comrades would soon get their hands on whoever did it and strangle them!'

In any case he still didn't understand. There was something in his blood that made him reject this dark prospect of global destruction, of a world where everything was scythed down like a field of rye. What would happen afterwards? How would the peoples of the earth rise again? He wanted to know.

'Explain to me what you have in mind. The rest of us want to know where we're headed.'

Then, with that dreamy, distant look in his eye again, Souvarine quietly concluded:

'Any rational analysis of the future is criminal, because it prevents things from being simply destroyed. It impedes the Revolution.'

That made Étienne laugh, despite the fact that it also sent shivers down his spine. For the rest he readily acknowledged the good sense in some of these ideas, which attracted him by their terrifying simplicity. But it would hand the advantage to Rasseneur if they were to tell the comrades this sort of thing. They had to be practical.

Widow Desire came in to offer them some lunch. They accepted and went through to the bar area, which was closed off from the hall during the week by a sliding partition.

When they had finished their omelette and cheese, Souvarine wanted to leave; and when Étienne tried to make him stay, he said:

'What's the point? To listen to you all talking nonsense? . . . I've heard enough for one day, thanks!'

He departed with his customary air of quiet determination, a cigarette between his lips.

Étienne was becoming increasingly worried. It was now one o'clock: clearly Pluchart was going to let him down. By half past one the delegates began to appear, and he had to receive them because he wanted to vet them as they entered in case the Company had sent its usual spies along. He examined each letter of invitation and scrutinized each man carefully as he came past, although in fact many were able to get in without the letter since if he knew them already they were automatically allowed in. At the stroke of two he saw Rasseneur arrive and go to the bar, where he took his time finishing his pipe and talking to people. This impudent show of unflappability succeeded in irritating him, especially as one or two humorists had turned up just for the laugh, such as Zacharie, Mouquet and some others. This bunch didn't care a jot about the strike and just found it hilarious to have nothing to do; and as they sat at their tables spending their last few coins on a glass of beer, they sneered and made fun of the comrades who were seriously committed to the strike, and who walked away, determined to hold their tongues despite their annoyance.

Another quarter of an hour went by. The men in the hall were growing restive. Eventually, having given up hope, Étienne braced himself for action. And he was just about to enter the hall when Widow Desire shouted from the front entrance where she had been keeping a lookout:

'Wait, your gentleman's here!'

It was indeed Pluchart. He arrived in a carriage drawn by a broken-down nag. At once he jumped down on to the road, a thin, foppish-looking man with a disproportionately large, square head, and wearing the Sunday best of a well-to-do artisan beneath his black woollen coat. It was five years since he had last touched a metalworker's file, and he took great care of his appearance, his hair especially, as well as great pride in his skills as an orator; but manual labour had left him stiff in the joints, and the nails on his large hands had not grown back after all the metalwork. As someone who liked to keep busy, he served his ambitions by criss-crossing the region in the relentless diffusion of his political ideas.

'Now don't be angry!' he said, forestalling any question or reproach. 'Yesterday I had a lecture at Preuilly in the morning and a meeting at Valençay in the evening. Today it was lunch in Marchiennes, with Sauvagnat . . . And then I finally managed to get a cab. I'm exhausted, just listen to my voice. But never mind, I shall speak just the same.'

He had reached the door of the Jolly Fellow when he suddenly remembered something.

'Heavens! I nearly forgot the membership cards! Right fools we'd look!'

He returned to the cab, which the coachman was now backing into a shed, removed a small black wooden chest from the baggage compartment and tucked it under his arm before walking back.

A beaming Étienne followed after him while Rasseneur, at a loss, didn't even venture to hold out his hand. But already

Pluchart had grasped it and was making passing reference to his letter. What a funny thing to suggest! Not hold the meeting? You should always hold a meeting if you could. Widow Desire asked if she could get him anything, but he declined. No need! He could speak without having a drink first. But time was pressing, he wanted to make it to Joiselle that evening and sort things out with Legoujeux. And so the whole group entered the hall together. Maheu and Levaque, arriving late, followed them in. The door was locked so that they could 'make themselves at home', which had the laughter-merchants guffawing even louder when Zacharie asked Mouquet at the top of his voice if this meant they were *all* going to get a screw.

A hundred or so miners were waiting on the benches in the stuffy hall, where the warm odours remaining from the most recent dance rose from the wooden floor. People were whispering and turning round in their seats as the new arrivals came and occupied the empty places. They eyed the gentleman from Lille, whose frock-coat surprised and unsettled them.

But immediately Étienne moved that a committee be appointed. He proposed some names, and others raised their hands in approval. Pluchart was elected chairman, and as his assistants they chose Maheu and Étienne himself. Chairs were moved around, and the committee took up position. They lost the chairman for a moment, but he had only disappeared under the table to stow the wooden chest that he had been hanging on to until then. When he resurfaced, he banged his fist gently on the table to call the meeting to order; and then, in a hoarse voice, he began:

'Citizens . . .'

A small side-door opened, and he had to pause. It was Widow Desire, who had gone round by the kitchen and brought back six glasses of beer on a tray.

'Don't mind me,' she whispered. 'Talking makes a man thirsty.'

Maheu took the tray and Pluchart was able to continue. He said how touched he was to receive such a warm welcome from the workers of Montsou, and he apologized for being late, telling them about his sore throat and how tired he was. Then he gave way to Citizen Rasseneur, who had asked for the floor.

Rasseneur had already taken up position beside the table, next to the beers. He had turned a chair round to use it as a rostrum. He seemed very emotional, and cleared his throat before launching forth in a loud voice:

'Comrades . . .'

The reason for his influence over the colliers lay in the ease with which he spoke and the genial way he could go on talking to them for hours on end and never flagged. He didn't attempt any hand gestures but just plodded smilingly on, drowning them in his words until they were all so dazed that to a man they would shout: 'Yes, yes, it's true, you're right!' Yet that day, from the moment he opened his mouth, he had sensed an unspoken hostility. And so he proceeded cautiously, confining himself to saying how they must continue the strike, waiting for the applause before he attacked the International. Yes, indeed, honour meant that they could not yield to the Company's demands; and yet what suffering, what suffering, what terrible times lay ahead if they had to hold out much longer! And without explicitly calling for an end to the strike, he set about weakening their resolve, painting a picture of starving villages and asking where the supporters of the strike were hoping to find the resources with which to continue. Three or four friends tried to show their support, but this only accentuated the cold silence of the remainder and the growing irritation and dis-approval with which his speech was being received. Then, despairing of winning them over, he lost his temper and started predicting disaster if they allowed their heads to be turned by strangers who had come to agitate. By now two thirds of the men were on their feet, angrily trying to shut him up if all he was going to do was insult them and treat them like naughty children. But on he went despite the uproar, taking repeated swigs of beer and shouting that no man alive could stop him doing his duty!

Pluchart had stood up. Having no bell, he banged loudly on the table and repeated in a strangled voice:

'Citizens! Citizens!'

Eventually he managed to restore some order and put the

matter to the meeting, which voted to withdraw Rasseneur's right to speak. Those delegates who had represented the different pits during the talks with M. Hennebeau gave the lead, and the rest of the men, their heads full of all the new ideas and goaded to a frenzy by hunger, followed. The result of the vote was a foregone conclusion.

'It's all right for you, you bastard. You've got food!' screamed Levaque, shaking his fist at Rasseneur.

Étienne had leaned over behind Pluchart to calm Maheu, who had gone very red in the face in his fury at the hypocrisy of Rasseneur's speech.

'Citizens,' said Pluchart. 'Allow me to say something.'

There was complete silence. He spoke. His voice sounded hoarse and strained, but with his busy schedule he was used to it: laryngitis was all part of the programme. Gradually he began to increase the volume, and some touching sounds he made. With arms spread wide and shoulders dipping to the rhythm of his phrasing, he displayed a preacher's eloquence, dropping his voice at the end of each sentence to a kind of religious hush and gradually convincing his listeners by the insistence of his rolling cadence.

He delivered his set speech on how marvellous the International was and the benefits it could provide, for this was how he usually chose to present it at venues where he was speaking for the first time. He explained how its aim was the emancipation of the workers, and he described its grandiose structure, with the commune at the bottom, then the province, above that the nation, and lastly, at the very summit, humanity in general. His arms moved slowly through the air, piling level upon level and constructing the vast cathedral of the future. Then he spoke about how the organization was run: he read out its statutes, talked about the congresses, drew attention to the way the scope of its activities was growing, how its agenda had moved beyond the debate about pay and was now focused on dissolving social distinctions and abolishing the very notion of a wage-earning class. No more nationalities! The workers of the world united in the common pursuit of justice, sweeping away the dead wood of the bourgeoisie and finally creating the free society in which he who works not, reaps not! He was now bellowing, and his breath set the streamers fluttering beneath the smoke-stained ceiling, itself so low that it magnified the sound of his voice.

Heads began to nod in waves of unison. One or two men called out:

'That's the way! . . . We're with you!'

Pluchart went on. Within three years they would have conquered the world. And he listed the countries that had been conquered already. People everywhere were rushing to join. No new religion had ever made so many converts so quickly. Later, once they were the masters, it would be their turn to lay down the law, and then the bosses could have a taste of their own medicine for once.

'Yes! Yes! . . . The bosses can go down the pits!'

He motioned to them to be silent. Now he was coming to the question of strikes. In principle he was against them: they took too long to have an effect and in fact just made life worse for the workers. Things would be better arranged in future, but for the moment – and when there was just no other way – you had to accept them, because at least they had the merit of disrupting capitalism. And in that kind of situation, as he pointed out, the International could be a godsend for strikers. He gave examples: one from Paris, when the bronze-founders went on strike and the bosses had met all their demands immediately because they were terrified at the news that the International was sending aid; another from the London branch, which had saved the miners at one colliery by paying for the repatriation of a team of Belgian pitmen brought over by the mine-owner. You had only to join and the companies started running scared, and that way the workers became part of labour's great army, ready to die for one another rather than remain the slaves of capitalist society.

He was interrupted by applause. He mopped his forehead with his handkerchief, refusing the glass of beer that Maheu wanted to pass him. When he tried to continue, he was prevented by further applause.

'That should do it!' he said quickly to Étienne. 'They've heard enough . . . Quick! The cards!'

He had dived under the table and soon re-emerged with the little black chest.

'Citizens!' he shouted above the noise, 'here are the membership cards. If your delegates will come forward, I will give them some to hand round . . . We can settle up later.'

Rasseneur rushed forward and started protesting again. Étienne for his part was getting worried because he, too, had a speech to make. There was complete chaos. Levaque was punching the air, ready for a fight. Maheu was on his feet saying something that nobody could hear a word of. And as the uproar increased, dust rose from the floor, the dust of dances past, fouling the air with the reek of pit-boys and putters.

Suddenly the side-door opened, and Widow Desire stood there, her stomach and bust filling the doorway as she boomed:

'Quiet, for God's sake! . . . The men in blue are here.'

The local superintendent had turned up, rather belatedly, with the intention of breaking up the meeting and reporting the matter to his superiors. He was accompanied by four gendarmes. For the previous five minutes Widow Desire had been trying to delay them on her doorstep, telling them that it was her house and she had a perfect right to invite what friends she pleased. But then they had pushed their way in, so she had hurried to come and warn her brood.

'You'd better come this way,' she continued. 'There's a bloody gendarme watching the yard. But don't worry, you can get out into the alley through my woodshed . . . Get a move on, for heaven's sake!'

Already the superintendent was banging his fist on the main door to the hall; and since no one was opening it, he was threatening to break it down. He must have had inside information because he was shouting that the meeting was illegal on account of the fact that a large number of miners present had no letter of invitation.

Inside the hall confusion mounted. They couldn't leave just like that, they hadn't even voted yet, neither about joining the International nor about continuing the strike. Everybody was trying to speak at once. Eventually the chairman hit on the idea of voting by acclamation. Hands shot up, and the delegates hastily declared that they were joining on behalf of their absent comrades. Thus did the ten thousand miners of Montsou become members of the International.

Meanwhile the rout had begun. To cover their retreat Widow Desire had gone over to stand with her back to the main door, and she could feel the police slamming their rifle-butts into it behind her. The miners were clambering over the benches and streaming out through the kitchen and woodshed one after another. Rasseneur was one of the first to disappear, followed by Levaque, who had completely forgotten how he had insulted him earlier and was now hoping to cadge a beer, just to steady his nerves. Étienne, having grabbed the little chest, was waiting behind with Pluchart and Maheu, for whom it was a point of honour to be the last out. Just as they were leaving, the lock finally gave, and the superintendent found himself in the presence of Widow Desire and the further obstacle of her stomach and bust.

'A lot of good that's done you, smashing the place up like this,' she said. 'You can see perfectly well there's nobody here!'

The superintendent was of the ponderous sort: he disliked fuss and simply warned her that if she weren't careful, he'd lock her up. And off he went to make his report, taking the four gendarmes with him, while Zacharie and Mouquet jeered at them, so impressed by their comrades' clever escape that they were not afraid to mock the arm of the law.

Outside in the alleyway Étienne broke into a run, despite the encumbrance of the wooden chest, and the others followed. He suddenly remembered Pierron and asked why they hadn't seen him. Maheu, running beside him, replied that he'd been ill: a convenient illness, too, otherwise known as the fear of being implicated. They tried to persuade Pluchart to stay for a while but, without breaking step, he told them that he must be off at once to Joiselle, where Legoujeux was waiting for instructions. So they shouted goodbye as they continued to race through Montsou as fast as their legs could carry them. They talked in snatches between gasping for breath. Étienne and Maheu were laughing happily, certain now of victory: once the International had sent them aid, the Company would be begging them to go back to work. And in this surge of hope, amid the sound of these stampeding boots clattering over the cobbled streets, there was something else, something dark and savage, like a wind of violence that would soon be whipping every village in every corner of the coal-field into a storm of frenzy.

V

Another fortnight went by. It was now early January, and cold mists numbed the vast plain. Things were worse than they had ever been: with food increasingly scarce, each hour that passed was bringing the villages closer to death. Four thousand francs from the International in London had barely provided bread for three days. Since then, nothing. The failure of their one great hope was undermining everyone's courage. Who could they count on now if even their brothers were going to abandon them to their fate? They felt completely lost, all alone in the world and surrounded by the deep midwinter.

By Tuesday Village Two Hundred and Forty had run out of everything. Étienne had been working round the clock with the delegates: they undertook collections, they organized public meetings, they tried to recruit new members in the neighbouring towns, even as far away as Paris. Their efforts had little effect. At the beginning they had succeeded in arousing public concern, but now, as the strike dragged quietly on without dramatic incident, people were gradually losing interest. Such meagre donations as they did raise were scarcely enough to support the most destitute families. Others survived by pawning their clothes or selling off their household effects one by one. Everything was disappearing in the direction of the second-hand dealers, whether it was the wool stuffing out of their mattresses, or kitchen utensils, or even furniture. For a brief moment they thought they were saved when the small shopkeepers in Montsou started offering credit as a way of taking back customers from Maigrat, who had been gradually putting them out of business; and for one week Verdonck the grocer and Carouble and Smelten the two bakers had virtually held open house; but the credit they gave didn't go very far, and the three of them then stopped giving it. The bailiffs were pleased, but the net result for the miners was a burden of debt that was to weigh on them for a long time to come. With no more credit available anywhere and not even an old saucepan left to sell, they might as well lie down and die in a corner like so many mangy dogs.

Étienne would have sold his flesh. He had stopped taking his secretarial salary and pawned his smart woollen coat and trousers in Marchiennes, happy to be able to keep the Maheus' pot on the boil. All he had left were his boots, which he had kept, he said, so that his kicks would hurt. His major regret was that the strike had come too soon, before his provident fund had had time to accumulate. For him that was the only explanation for why they were in the present disastrous situation: come the day when they had saved enough money to fund their struggle, the workers would surely triumph over the bosses. And he remembered how Souvarine had accused the Company of provoking the strike so as to destroy the fund while it was still small.

The sight of the village and all these wretched people without food or coal upset him deeply, and he preferred to absent himself on long, tiring walks. One evening, as he was passing Réquillart on his way home, he came on an old woman who had collapsed by the side of the road and was presumably suffering from starvation. When he had lifted her into a sitting position, he called out to a girl he had seen on the other side of the fence.

'Oh, it's you,' he said, recognizing La Mouquette. 'Give me a hand, will you? We need to give her something to drink.'

Tears welled in La Mouquette's eyes, and she ran into her house, the rickety shack that her father had constructed amid the ruins. She was back in a trice with some gin and a loaf of bread. The gin revived the old woman, who gnawed greedily at the loaf without saying a word. She was the mother of one of the miners and lived in a village over towards Cougny; she had collapsed here on her way back from Joiselle, where she had gone in vain to try and borrow ten sous from a sister of hers. After she had eaten, she tottered off in a daze.

Étienne remained behind in the waste ground of Réquillart, with its tumbledown sheds that were gradually disappearing beneath the brambles.

'Won't you come in and have a drink?' La Mouquette asked him cheerfully.

And when he hesitated:

'So you're still afraid of me, are you?'

Won over by her laughter, he followed her in. He was touched by how readily she had given the old woman her bread. She didn't want to receive him in her father's room and so she led him into her own, where she immediately poured out two small glasses of gin. Her room was very clean and tidy, and he compli-mented her on it. In fact the family seemed well provided for: her father was still working as a stableman at Le Voreux; and she herself, not being the sort to stand idly by, had started taking in laundry, which earned her thirty sous a day. Just because you enjoy a laugh with the lads doesn't mean you're lazy.

'What is it?' she said softly, as she came and put her arms round his waist. 'Don't you like me, then?'

She had said this so appealingly that he, too, couldn't help laughing.

'But I do like you,' he replied.

'No, you don't, not the way I mean . . . You know how much I want to. Please? It would make me so happy!'

She meant it all right; she'd been asking him for the past six months. He gazed at her as she clung to him tightly with trem-bling arms, her face raised towards him in such amorous entreaty that he was deeply affected. There was nothing pretty about her big round face, with its yellowish, coal-stained complexion; but a flame glowed in her eyes, and a magical quivering of desire turned her skin as pink as a child's. And so, being presented with such a humble, eager offer of her person, he simply could not refuse any longer.

'Yes! You *do* want to!' she stammered in delight, 'You really do!'

And she gave herself clumsily, in a kind of virginal swoon, as though this were her first time and she had never known any other man. Later, when he was leaving, she was the one who was full of gratitude, and she kept thanking him and kissing his hands.

Étienne was a little ashamed of this piece of good fortune. Men did not brag about having La Mouquette. As he made his way home he promised himself that there would be no repeat. And yet he remembered her fondly, she was a fine girl.

In any case, when he reached the village, news of a serious kind soon drove all thought of the episode from his head. It was rumoured that the Company would perhaps agree to a further concession if the members of the deputation would make a new approach to the manager. At least this was the word from the deputies. The truth was that the mines were suffering even more than the miners as a result of the stand-off. The stubbornness of both parties was wreaking increasing damage: while labour was dying of hunger, capital was bleeding to death. Each day's stoppage meant the loss of hundreds of thousands of francs. The machine that lies idle is a machine that is dying. The plant and equipment were deteriorating, and the money invested in them was draining away like water into the sand. Since the meagre stockpiles of coal had started disappearing from the pit-yards, customers had been talking of obtaining their supplies from Belgium; and that posed a threat for the future. But what worried the Company most, and what it was most careful to conceal, was the growing damage to the roadways and coal-faces. There weren't enough deputies to keep up with the repairs; timbering was giving way all over the place, and there were rock-falls almost by the hour. The damage was soon so extensive that it would require long months of repair work before they could start hewing coal again. Stories were already going round: at Crèvecœur three hundred metres of road had subsided in one piece, blocking access to the Cinq-Paumes seam; at Madeleine, the Maugrétout seam was breaking up and filling with water. Management was refusing to confirm the stories when two disasters happened in quick succession which forced them to come clean. One morning, near La Piolaine, they found that a crevasse had opened above Mirou's northern roadway, where there had been a rock-fall the day before. The next day part of Le Voreux subsided and sent such a tremor under one whole corner of the neighbourhood that two houses had nearly vanished completely.

Étienne and the delegates were reluctant to make a move without knowing the intentions of the Board of Directors. When they tried to find out from Dansaert, he ducked their questions: certainly the Board deplored the misunderstandings that had arisen, and it would do everything in its power to resolve the issues: but he would not be more specific. Eventually the men decided that they would go and see M. Hennebeau so as not to find themselves in the wrong later on and be accused of having refused to allow the Company a chance to admit the error of its ways. But they promised themselves that they would make no concessions and that they would still continue to insist on the conditions they had set, which were the only fair ones.

The meeting took place on Tuesday morning, the day when the village finally found itself staring into the abyss. The encounter was less cordial than the first. Once more it was Maheu who spoke, explaining that his comrades had sent them to inquire if the gentlemen had anything new to say to them. At first M. Hennebeau pretended to be surprised: he had not received any new instructions, and there could be no change in the position as long as the miners persisted in this detestable protest of theirs. This unbending and authoritarian attitude had the worst possible effect, to the extent that even if the delegates had come to the meeting in the most conciliatory frame of mind the manner of their reception would have been enough to stiffen their resistance. Then the manager indicated his willingness to explore a possible basis for compromise: for example, the workers might accept to be paid separately for the timbering and the Company would increase payment by the two centimes which they were alleged to be gaining from the new system. Of course this offer was being made on his own initiative, nothing had been decided, though he flattered himself that he would succeed in getting Paris to agree to this concession. But the delegates refused and restated their terms: the old system to remain, and an increase of five centimes per tub. Then M. Hennebeau admitted that he did have the power to negotiate directly, and he urged them to accept for the sake of their starving wives and children. But the

men stared resolutely at the floor and said no, still no, fiercely
shaking their heads. The meeting ended abruptly. M. Hennebeau slammed the doors, while Étienne, Maheu and the others
made their way home, their heavy boots thudding over the
cobbles with the silent rage of defeated men who have been
pushed as far as they will go.

About two o'clock it was the women's turn to try one last
approach to Maigrat. Their only remaining hope was to talk the
man round and extract another week's credit from him. The
idea came from La Maheude, who tended to rely too often on
people's goodness. She persuaded La Brûlé and La Levaque to
go with her; La Pierronne excused herself on the grounds that
she had to stay and look after Pierron, who was still not well.
Other women joined the group, which numbered about twenty.
When the bourgeois of Montsou saw them arriving, a line of
sombre, wretched-looking women taking up the whole width
of the road, they shook their heads with misgiving. Doors were
shut, and one lady hid her silver. It was the first time they had
been seen like this, and it was a very grave sign indeed: things
usually went from bad to worse once the women took to the
highways. There was a terrible scene at Maigrat's. At first he
had ushered them in with with a sneering laugh, affecting to
believe that they had come to pay their debts; how kind of them
to have arranged to come all together like this, and just so they
could return all his money at once! Then, when La Maheude
began to speak, he pretended to fly into a rage. What kind of a
joke was this? More credit? Did they want him to end up sleeping
in the gutter? No, not a single potato, not so much as a single
crumb of bread! He suggested they try Verdonck the grocer or
Carouble and Smelten the bakers, for wasn't that where they took
their custom now? The women listened to him with an air of
frightened humility, apologizing to him and watching his eyes
for any sign that he might relent. Instead he started on his usual
banter, offering La Brûlé his whole shop if she would have him.
They were all so cowed that they laughed; and La Levaque went
one better by declaring that she personally was ready and willing.
But he became rough with them again and herded them towards
the door. When they went on begging him, he shoved one of them

aside. Outside in the street the other women were accusing him of being a Company stooge, and La Maheude raised her arms to the sky in vengeful outrage, calling death down upon him and screaming that such a man did not deserve to eat.

The journey back to the village was a sorry affair. When the women returned home empty-handed, the men looked at them and then lowered their eyes. That was that: the day would end without so much as a spoonful of soup, and thereafter the days stretched into icy darkness without a single glimmer of hope. They had chosen this path themselves, and no one spoke of surrender. Such an extreme of poverty simply hardened their resistance, like cornered animals silently resolved to die at the bottom of their lairs rather than come out. Who would have dared be the first to talk of giving in? They had all promised their comrades to stick together, and stick together they would, just like they did down the pit when somebody was trapped under a rock-fall. It was what you did, and there was nowhere better than the pit for learning how to put up with things: you could manage without food for a week if you'd been swallowing fire and water since the age of twelve. And in this way their commitment to each other was accompanied by a sense of military pride, the self-respect of men who were proud of their job and who vied for the honour of self-sacrifice in their daily struggle to stay alive.

In the Maheu household that evening was a terrible one. They sat in silence round the dying fire, a smoking heap of their last remaining cinders. Having emptied the mattresses handful by handful, they had finally decided two days ago to sell the cuckoo clock for three francs; and the room seemed bare and dead without its familiar ticking. The only superfluous item left was the pink cardboard box in the middle of the dresser, a present from Maheu which La Maheude treasured as though it were a jewel. The two good chairs had already gone, and old Bonnemort and the children squeezed together on a mouldy old bench which they had brought in from the garden. The pale twilight seemed to add to the cold.

'What's to be done?' La Maheude kept saying, squatting beside the stove.

Étienne, standing, was looking at the pictures of the Emperor and Empress stuck to the wall. He would have torn them down long ago if the family had not wanted to keep them for decoration. And so he muttered between clenched teeth:

'It's odd to think that we wouldn't get a penny out of those two useless individuals, but here they are watching us as we die.'

'Why don't I pawn the box?' La Maheude continued after some hesitation, looking pale as she said it.

Maheu, perched on the edge of the table, legs dangling and head bowed, immediately sat up:

'No, I won't have it.'

La Maheude struggled to her feet and began to walk round the room. How in God's name had it come to this? Not a crumb of bread in the dresser, nothing left to sell, and not the semblance of a notion how they could lay their hands on a loaf of bread! And a fire that was about to go out! She vented her anger on Alzire, whom she had that morning sent to look for cinders on the spoil-heap and who had returned empty-handed, saying that the Company had forbidden any further scavenging. What the hell did they care what the Company said? As if it were robbing anyone if they picked up tiny, forgotten pieces of coal. The little girl tearfully explained that a man had threatened to hit her, and then she promised to go back the next day even if she did get beaten.

'And what about that brat Jeanlin?' cried his mother. 'Where the hell is he, I'd like to know? He was supposed to be bringing us back some leaves. At least we could have grazed like the rest of the animals! You wait, I bet he doesn't come home. He didn't last night either. I don't know what he's up to, but that little devil always seems to be well enough fed.'

'Perhaps he collects money on the road.'

She at once started shaking her fists, beside herself with rage.

'If I thought that! ... My children begging! I'd rather kill them, and myself afterwards.'

Maheu had resumed his slumped posture on the edge of the table. Lénore and Henri, astonished that they weren't eating, began to moan; while old Bonnemort sat in silence, resignedly rolling his tongue round his mouth trying to stave off the pangs

of hunger. Nobody spoke now, numbed by this further deterio-
ration in their fortunes, with Grandpa coughing up black
phlegm and troubled once more by his old rheumatic pains,
which were turning into dropsy; with Father asthmatic, and his
knees swollen with fluid retention; and with Mother and the
little ones afflicted by congenital scrofula and anaemia. No
doubt it *was* the fault of their jobs, and they only complained
about it when lack of food actually started killing people (and
they were beginning to drop like flies in the village). But they
really did have to find something for supper. The question was:
how? and, God help them, where?

Then, as the room filled with the gathering gloom of twilight,
Étienne reluctantly made up his mind and said with a heavy
heart:

'Wait here. There's somewhere I can try.'

And out he went. He had remembered La Mouquette. She
was sure to have a spare loaf, and she would be only too glad
to give it to him. It annoyed him to have go back to Réquillart:
she would start kissing his hands again, like some lovesick
servant-girl. But a man didn't leave his friends in the lurch, he'd
be nice to her again if he had to be.

'Me too, I'm going to see what I can find,' said La Maheude
in turn. 'This is just ridiculous!'

She opened the door again after Étienne had left and then
slammed it behind her, leaving the rest of them sitting silent and
motionless in the meagre light of a candle-end which Alzire had
just lit. Outside La Maheude paused to consider for a moment
and then went into the Levaques' house.

'You know that loaf I lent you the other day. How about
letting me have it back?'

But she stopped, for the sight that met her eyes was not
encouraging; and the house reeked of poverty even more than
her own did.

La Levaque was staring at her fire, which had gone out, and
Levaque was slumped across the table, having gone to sleep
there on an empty stomach after some nailers had got him
drunk. Bouteloup was leaning against the wall, absent-mindedly
rubbing his shoulders against it and with the bewildered look

of a decent fellow who has let other people squander his savings and now finds himself having to tighten his belt.

'A loaf of bread? Oh, my dear,' La Levaque replied. 'And there was I about to ask you if I could borrow another one!'

At that moment her husband groaned with pain in his sleep, and she crushed his face into the table.

'Quiet, you pig! Serves you right if it rots your guts! ... Couldn't you have asked a friend for twenty sous instead of getting everyone to buy you a drink?'

And on she went, swearing and cursing and getting things off her chest, surrounded by a filthy home which had been let go for so long that an unbearable stench now rose from its floor. What did she care if the whole world was going to rack and ruin! That vagabond of a son, Bébert, had been gone since morning, and good riddance it would be too, she shouted, if he never came back. Then she said that she was going to bed. At least she'd be warm there. She gave Bouteloup a shove.

'Come on, look sharp! We're going upstairs! ... The fire's gone out, and there's no point lighting the candle just to stare at empty plates ... Did you hear me, Louis? I said we're going to bed. We can cuddle up close, which'll be a relief from this cold at any rate ... And that drunken bastard can catch his death all on his own down here!'

Once more outside, La Maheude took a short cut directly across the gardens to go and see the Pierrons. The sound of laughter could be heard coming from inside. She knocked on the door, and everything went suddenly quiet. It was at least a minute before anyone came.

'Oh, it's you!' exclaimed La Pierronne, pretending to be very surprised. 'I thought it was the doctor.'

Without letting La Maheude get a word in, she motioned towards Pierron, who was sitting in front of a big coal fire, and added:

'He's not well, I'm afraid, still not well. He looks all right in the face, but it's his stomach that's plaguing him. He has to keep warm, so we're burning everything we've got.'

Pierron did indeed seem to be in fine form; he had a good colour, and there was plenty of flesh on him. He pretended

without success to wheeze like a sick man. In any case La
Maheude had noticed a strong smell of rabbit as she came in:
but of course they had cleared everything away! There were still
crumbs on the table, and right in the middle stood a bottle of
wine they had forgotten to remove.

'Mother has gone to Montsou to try and find some bread,'
La Pierronne continued. 'There's nothing we can do but wait
for her to come home.'

But her voice died away as her eyes followed La Maheude's
and lit on the bottle. She recovered herself at once and proceeded
to tell the story: yes, the people at La Piolaine had brought the
wine for her husband, because the doctor had recommended
that he drink claret. And she went on about how grateful she
was, and what fine people they were, especially the young mistress, who wasn't a bit proud, coming into working folks' homes
and distributing her charity in person!

'Yes,' said La Maheude, 'I know them.'

It depressed her to think that unto those that have shall be
given. It was always the same, and those people from La Piolaine
would have given bread to a baker. How had she missed them
in the village? Perhaps she might have got something out of
them all the same?

'I just called,' La Maheude admitted finally, 'to see if your
cupboards were as bare as ours ... You wouldn't have any
vermicelli, would you? I'd let you have it back.'

La Pierronne voiced loud despair.

'Not a thing, my dear. Not even a grain of semolina ... And
Mother's not back yet, so that must mean she's had no luck.
We'll be going to bed hungry tonight.'

At that moment a sound of crying could be heard coming
from the cellar, and La Pierronne banged on the door angrily
with her fist. It was Lydie. The little trollop had been gallivanting
about the place all day, and she'd locked her up to punish her
for not coming home till five. There was nothing to be done
with her now, she was always disappearing off like that.

Meanwhile La Maheude just stood there, unable to tear herself away. The penetrating warmth of the fire felt so good that
it almost hurt, and the thought that people had been eating here

made her stomach feel even more empty. Obviously they had sent the old woman off and then locked up the girl so that the pair of them could feast on the rabbit. Ah, indeed, there was no denying: when a woman strayed, it brought good fortune on her home!

'Good-night,' she said abruptly.

Night had fallen outside, and the cloud-decked moon shed a strange light over the earth. Instead of going back across the gardens, La Maheude went the long way round, sick at heart and unable to face going home. But there was no sign of life coming from the line of houses, and every door spoke of famine and empty stomachs. What was the use of knocking? This was the village of Misery For All. After weeks of starvation even the reek of onion had disappeared, that pungent aroma which meant that one could smell the village from far away in the countryside. Now there was just a smell of old cellars, of dank holes where nothing lives. Vague sounds died away, stifled sobs and curses that faded on the air; and in the deepening silence one could sense the approach of famine's rest, the slumber of exhausted bodies sprawled on their beds and racked by the nightmare visions that feed on empty stomachs.

As she was passing the church, she saw a shadowy figure hurrying away. In a moment of hope she quickened her step, for she had recognized Father Joire, the parish priest in Montsou, who came each Sunday to say Mass in the village chapel: he must have had something to see to in the vestry. He scurried past, head bowed, with that air of a plump and kindly man whose only wish is to live in peace with everyone about him. No doubt he had run his errand at night for fear of compromising himself among the miners. Not that it mattered. It was said that he had just been promoted, and even that he had already shown his successor round, a thin man with eyes like burning embers.

'Father, Father,' La Maheude gasped.

But he did not stop.

'Good-night, my dear, good-night.'

She found herself standing outside her own house. Her legs would carry her no further, and so she went in.

Nobody had moved. Maheu was still sitting slumped forward on the edge of the table. Old Bonnemort and the children were huddled together on the bench, trying to keep each other warm. Not a word had been exchanged, and the candle had burned so low that soon there would be no more light. As they heard the door open, the children looked round; but when they saw that their mother had brought nothing back with her, they stared at the floor once more, choking back a strong desire to cry in case they got scolded. La Maheude sank down into her former place beside the non-existent fire. No one asked her how she had got on, and the silence continued. Everyone had understood, and they saw no point in tiring themselves with talk. So now they waited in complete dejection, drained of courage, waiting on the one last chance that Étienne might have found something, somewhere. The minutes went by, and eventually they gave up hoping even for that.

When Étienne did reappear, he was carrying a dozen cold potatoes wrapped up in a cloth.

'This is all I could find,' he said.

At La Mouquette's they were short of bread too: this was her dinner, and she had insisted on wrapping it in a cloth for him, kissing him passionately as she did so.

'No, thanks,' he said to La Maheude, when she offered him his share. 'I had something earlier.'

He was lying, and he watched despondently as the children attacked the food. Maheu and La Maheude held back also, to leave more for them; but the old man greedily devoured all he could. They even had to retrieve a potato for Alzire.

Then Étienne announced that he had news. Goaded by the strikers' obstinacy, the Company was talking of firing the miners responsible. Clearly it wanted war. And there was a still more serious rumour going round about the Company claiming to have persuaded a large number of workers to go back to work: tomorrow La Victoire and Feutry-Cantel would be at full strength, and there was even talk of a third of the men going back at Madeleine and Mirou. The Maheus were beside themselves.

'God Almighty!' Maheu exclaimed. 'If there are traitors, then we must deal with them!'

Now standing, he gave vent to his pain and fury:

'Tomorrow night, in the forest! . . . Since we're not allowed to meet in the Jolly Fellow, we'll use the forest as our local.'

His cry had roused old Bonnemort, who was sleepy after all his eating. It was the old rallying cry, and the forest was where the miners of old used to plot their resistance to the King's soldiers.

'Yes, yes, Vandame! If that's where you're going, you can count me in!'

La Maheude gestured vehemently.

'We'll all go. There has to be an end to this injustice and treachery.'

Étienne decided that notice would be given in all the mining villages of a meeting to be held the following night. But by now the fire had gone out, as it had earlier at the Levaques', and the candle suddenly guttered into darkness. There was no more coal and no more paraffin, and so they had to feel their way up to bed in the biting cold. The little ones were crying.

VI

Jeanlin was better now and able to walk again, but his bones had been so badly set that he limped with both legs. He made quite a sight waddling along like a duck, though he still had the agility of a predatory vermin and could run just as fast as before.

That evening at dusk, Jeanlin, accompanied by his trusty followers Bébert and Lydie, was out on the Réquillart road keeping watch. He had chosen their hiding-place behind a fence on a piece of waste ground, opposite a seedy grocer's shop, which stood at an angle on the corner of a side-path. It was run by an old woman who was almost blind, and her display consisted of a few sacks of lentils and haricot beans, each one covered in black dust. Jeanlin's narrow eyes were fixed on an ancient, fly-blown dried cod hanging in the dorrway. Twice already he had dispatched Bébert to go and unhook it, but both times somebody had chanced to come round the corner. How was a fellow supposed to get on with his business with all these people in his way!

A man on horseback emerged from the side-path, and the children threw themselves flat on the ground by the fence: they had recognized M. Hennebeau. Since the beginning of the strike, he was often to be seen out on the roads like this, riding alone through the hostile villages and displaying quiet courage in coming to ascertain in person how things stood. No stone had ever whistled past his ears; the men he passed were simply silent and slow to return his greeting, while more often than not it was lovers he came across. They didn't give a damn about politics and took their fill of pleasure where they could. He would trot past on his mare, eyes front so as not to embarrass anyone, while his heart would pound with unfulfilled desires in the presence of a sexual freedom so greedily enjoyed. He could see the three children perfectly, two young lads in a heap on top of the girl. God, even the kids were at it now, forgetting their poverty as they happily rubbed against each other! There were tears in his eyes as he rode on, ramrod straight in the saddle, his coat buttoned up like a uniform.

'Just our bloody luck!' said Jeanlin. 'It never stops . . . Go on, Bébert, grab it by the tail.'

But once again two men were coming, and Jeanlin suppressed a further oath when he heard the voice of his brother Zacharie, who was busy telling Mouquet how he'd found a two-franc piece sewn into one of his wife's skirts. The pair were laughing cheerfully and clapping each other on the back. Mouquet suggested a full-scale game of *crosse* the next day: they would set out from the Advantage at two and head for Montoire, near Marchiennes. Zacharie agreed. What did they want to be bothered with this strike for, anyway? May as well have fun since there was nothing else to do! And they were just turning the corner when Étienne appeared from the direction of the canal and stopped to talk to them.

'Are they going to stay all night?' Jeanlin groaned again in exasperation. 'It's getting dark, the old woman's taking her sacks in.'

Another miner came past on his way to Réquillart. Étienne

joined him, and as they were passing the fence Jeanlin heard them talking about the forest: they'd had to postpone the meeting till the following day for fear of not being able to alert all the villages within twenty-four hours.

'Hey,' he whispered to his two comrades, 'the big do's on for tomorrow. We should go, eh? We'll leave in the afternoon.'

Now that the road was completely clear, he dispatched Bébert.

'Go on. And mind you grab it by the tail! . . . And watch out, the old woman's got her brush.'

Fortunately it was getting very dark. In a split second Bébert had leaped at the cod and started pulling on it. The string broke, and away he raced, trailing it like a kite, while the other two dashed after him. The old woman emerged bewildered from her shop, not understanding what had happened and unable to make out the gang disappearing into the darkness.

These young scamps had become the scourge of the region, gradually overrunning it like some alien horde. At first they had stuck to the pit-yard at Le Voreux, scrapping on the coal-stacks from which they emerged looking like negroes, or playing hide-and-seek among the wood stores, where they could lose themselves as in a virgin forest. Then they had stormed the spoil-heap, sliding down the smooth parts on their bottoms while it continued to smoulder away underneath; or else they would disappear among the brambles that grew in the older parts of the mine, vanishing from sight for the entire day and occupying themselves with quiet little games like mischievous mice. And gradually they extended their empire. They fought till they bled among the piles of bricks, they roamed the fields and ate all kinds of lush grasses, just as they came, without bread, or they grubbed along the banks of the canal where they caught fish in the mud and swallowed them raw. Then they ventured even further afield, whole kilometres away, as far as the woods at Vandame, where they feasted on strawberries in the spring, in summer on hazelnuts and bilberries. Little by little they had made the vast plain their own.

But if they were now to be found prowling round the paths between Montsou and Marchiennes with the look of young wolves in their eyes, it was because of their growing compulsion to plunder. Jeanlin was always the leader of these expeditions, ordering his troops into battle against all manner of target, laying waste onion fields, pillaging orchards, swooping on shop displays. People round about accused the striking miners, and there was talk of a huge, organized gang. One day he had even forced Lydie to rob her mother, making her bring him two dozen sticks of barley sugar that La Pierronne kept in a jar on a shelf in one of her windows; and though she was beaten for it, the little girl had not betrayed him, so much did she fear his authority. The worst of it was that he kept the lion's share of everything for himself. Bébert, too, had to hand all booty over to him, happy just not to be hit and that Jeanlin didn't keep the lot.

For a while now Jeanlin had been overstepping the mark. He would beat Lydie as if she were a regular wife, and he exploited Bébert's gullibility in order to involve him in various unpleasant escapades. It amused him greatly to lead this big lad by the nose when he was much stronger than he was and could have laid him out with a single blow. He despised them both, treating them like slaves and telling them that he had a princess for a mistress and that they were not worthy to appear before her. And indeed for the past week he had taken to leaving them suddenly at the end of a street or a turning in the road, wherever he happened to be, having ordered them with a terrifying air to return at once to the village. First, though, he would pocket their plunder.

And this was what happened on this particular evening also.

'Give it here,' he said, grabbing the cod out of his comrade's hands when the three of them stopped at a bend in the road just outside Réquillart.

Bébert protested.

'I want some, too, you know. It was me that took it.'

'What do you mean?' Jeanlin shouted. 'You'll get some if I say so, but not now, that's for sure. Tomorrow, if there's any left.'

He punched Lydie and lined the pair of them up like soldiers at attention. Then he went behind them:

'Now you're both going to stand like that for the next five

minutes, and you're not to turn round . . . And, by God, if you
do turn round, wild beasts will come and eat you . . . After that
you're to go straight home. And if you, Bébert, so much as lay
a finger on Lydie on the way, I shall know all about it, and I'll
thump the pair of you.'

Then he slipped away into the darkness, so quietly that they
didn't even hear the sound of his bare feet as he left. The two
children stood quite still for the whole five minutes, not daring
to look behind them in case they received a clout from the blue.
A deep affection had slowly grown up between them, born of
their common terror. Bébert, for his part, thought constantly
about taking Lydie and holding her very tightly in his arms, the
way he had seen others do; and she would have liked him to,
for it would have made a nice change to receive a kind caress.
But neither would have dared to disobey. When they set off for
home they didn't even embrace, despite the fact that it was pitch
dark, but simply walked along side by side in loving misery,
certain that if they were to touch each other, their leader would
come and clout them from behind.

At the same moment Étienne had reached Réquillart. The
previous evening La Mouquette had begged him to come back
and see her again, which he was now rather ashamedly doing,
for though he refused to admit it to himself, he had taken a
fancy to this girl who worshipped him like the Lord and Saviour.
Anyway he was coming to break things off. He would see her
and explain that she was to stop chasing after him, because of
the comrades. Times were hard, and it didn't do to indulge
oneself when people were dying of hunger. But not finding her
at home, he had decided to wait, and now he was keeping a
watchful eye over every passing shadow.

Beneath the ruined headgear yawned the entrance to the old
mine, which was half blocked up. A beam stuck up into the air
with a piece of roof attached to it, looking like a gibbet suspended over the black hole; and two trees were growing out of
the crumbling masonry that encircled the lip of the shaft, a plane
and a rowan, which looked as if they had sprung from the very
depths of the earth. Nature had been allowed to run wild here,
with thick tangles of grass surrounding the entrance to the

chasm, which was full of old timbers and overgrown with sloe and hawthorn where warblers nested in the spring. Reluctant to incur heavy expenditure on its upkeep, the Company had been planning for the past ten years to fill in the disused mine; but it was waiting until it had installed a ventilator at Le Voreux, because the furnace that drove the ventilation system for the two interconnecting pits was located at the bottom of Réquillart, where what was formerly a ventilation shaft now served as a flue. In the meantime they had simply reinforced the shaft's lining by installing cross-stays, which prevented coal from being extracted; they had abandoned the upper roadways and now maintained only the bottom one where the hellish furnace blazed, an enormous brazier of coal, which created such a powerful draught that the air blew like a tempest from one end of the neighbouring mine to the other. As a precaution there had been an order to maintain the ladders in the escape shaft so that people could still go up and down, but nobody had bothered; the ladders were rotting, and some of the staging platforms had already collapsed. At the top an enormous bramble blocked the entrance to the shaft; and because the first ladder had lost some of its rungs, in order to reach it you had to dangle from a root of the rowan tree and let yourself down into the blackness below, hoping for the best.

Étienne was waiting patiently behind a bush when he heard a prolonged slithering through the branches. He thought he might have disturbed an adder. But the sudden flaring of a match startled him, and he was astonished to see Jeanlin lighting a candle and disappearing below ground. Full of curiosity he approached the hole: the child had vanished, but a faint gleam of light could be seen coming from the second platform down. After a moment's hesitation Étienne grabbed some roots and lowered himself, wondering if he would fall the full five hundred and twenty-four metres of the shaft's depth, but eventually feeling a rung beneath his foot. And then gently he descended. Jeanlin could not have heard him because the light continued to recede beneath him, and the huge menacing shadow cast by the small boy flickered on the walls of the shaft as his hips swayed wildly on account of his damaged legs. He was swinging downwards like a monkey, using hands or feet or chin to hold on whenever rungs were missing. Ladder followed ladder, each seven metres long, some still solid, others loose or cracking and ready to break; and platform followed narrow platform, each one rotting and green with mould, which made it like stepping on moss; and as they descended, the heat became suffocating, because of the fumes coming up the shaft from the furnace. Fortunately it had barely been fired since the strike began, because under normal working conditions, when the furnace consumed five thousand kilograms of coal per day, no one could ever have risked such a descent unless he was ready to be roasted alive.

'Bloody little toad!' Étienne swore as he gasped for breath. 'Where the hell's he going?'

Twice he had nearly fallen. His feet kept slipping on the damp wood. If only he'd had a candle like Jeanlin; but as it was, he kept banging into things, and his only guide was the faint glimmer of light vanishing beneath him. He was already on his twentieth ladder, and still they were going down. Then he began to count them one by one: twenty-one, twenty-two, twenty-three, down he went, down and down. His head was nearly exploding in the boiling heat, it was like sinking into an oven. At last he reached a loading-bay, where he caught sight of the candle disappearing at the far end of a roadway. Thirty ladders: that meant about two hundred and ten metres.

'How long's this going to go on?' Étienne wondered to himself. 'I bet he holes up in the stable.'

But the road that led away on the left towards the stable was blocked by a rock-fall. They were off again, and this time the terrain was even more difficult and dangerous. Startled bats flitted about and clung to the roof of the loading-bay. He had to hurry so as not to lose sight of the light, and rushed into a roadway after it; but where the child was able to wriggle through easily with the suppleness of a snake, he could only squeeze past, bruising his arms and legs as he went. Like all old mine workings, this particular roadway had narrowed and was continuing to get narrower by the day from the constant pressure of the earth; and in places it was no bigger than a tube, which would eventually disappear of its own accord. As a result of this gradual strangulation the timbering had split and its jagged edges presented a real danger, threatening to saw through his flesh or to impale him on the points of its sword-like splinters as he went by. He had to exercise the greatest care as he edged forward on his knees or stomach, groping in the darkness ahead of him. Suddenly a swarm of rats ran over the top of him, dashing the length of his body in terrified flight.

'Christ Almighty! Are we nearly there yet?' he groaned crossly, gasping for breath, every bone in his body aching.

They were there. After a kilometre the passage widened, and they reached a part of the road that was still remarkably well preserved. It was the terminus of the old haulage road, which had been hollowed out against the grain of the rock and looked like a natural grotto. Étienne had to stop, for he could see Jeanlin up ahead setting his candle down between two rocks and generally making himself comfortable with the calm, relieved air of a man who is glad to be home. The place had been thoroughly fitted out and turned into a cosy dwelling. In one corner a pile of hay provided a soft bed; some old timbers had been stacked to make a table, and on it there was everything, from bread and apples to half-empty bottles of gin. It was a real robber's den, full of plunder amassed over many weeks, and useless plunder too, like the soap and polish that had been stolen for the sheer hell of it. And all alone in the middle of his spoils sat little, selfish Jeanlin, gloating like some pirate king.

'You don't give a bloody damn, do you?' Étienne shouted, having caught his breath. 'You just come down here and stuff your face while the rest of us up there are busy starving to death, is that it?'

Jeanlin, dumbstruck, was trembling. But when he recognized Étienne, he quickly recovered his equanimity.

'Would you like to join me?' he said eventually. 'A nice piece of grilled cod, perhaps? . . . Look.'

He was still clutching his dried cod and had begun to scrape the fly dirt off it with a shiny new knife, one of those small, bone-handled sheath-knives that have mottoes on them. This one simply said: 'Love'.

'That's a good-looking knife you've got there,' Étienne commented.

'It's a present from Lydie,' replied Jeanlin, omitting to mention that Lydie had stolen it on his orders from a street-seller in Montsou, outside the Severed Head.

Then, as he carried on scraping, he added proudly:

'It's nice, my place, isn't it? . . . A bit warmer than it is up there, and it smells a damn sight better, too!'

Étienne had sat down, curious to make the boy talk. His anger had gone, and he was intrigued by this little scoundrel who could show such courage and industry in the pursuit of his vicious ways. And indeed it did feel nice and cosy down here in this hole: it was not too hot, and the temperature remained constant whatever the season, like a warm bath, while the harsh December weather chapped the skin of the poor wretches up above. As time passed, the disused roads lost their noxious gases; the firedamp had gone, and the only smell left was of musty old timbers, a subtle aroma of ether with a sharp hint of clove. Moreover, the wood itself took on a fascinating appearance, like pale-yellow marble fringed with whitish lace and draped in fluffy growths like braids of silk and pearls. Others were covered in fungus. And white moths flew about, and snow-white flies and spiders, a whole population of colourless insects that had never known the sun.

'Aren't you ever scared?' asked Étienne.

Jeanlin looked at him in astonishment.

'Scared of what? There's only me here.'

By now the cod had finally been scraped clean. Jeanlin lit a small fire, spread the embers, and began to grill it. Then he cut a loaf into two. It all made for an extremely salty feast, but delicious all the same for hardened stomachs.

Étienne had accepted his portion.

'Now I see why you've been getting fat while the rest of us have been getting thin. But it's not right, you know, pigging out on your own like this . . . Don't you ever think about other people?'

'Why on earth! It's not my fault if they're stupid!'

'Mind you, you're right to hide. If your father found out you were stealing, he'd soon sort you out.'

'And I suppose the bourgeois don't steal from us! You're the one who's always saying they do. When I pinched this bread from Maigrat's, it was only what he owed us anyway.'

Nonplussed, Étienne fell silent and continued to eat. He looked at Jeanlin and his thin snout-like face, his green eyes and big ears, a degenerate throwback possessed of intuitive intelligence and native cunning who was gradually reverting to his former animal state. The mine had created him and now it had destroyed him by breaking his legs.

'What about Lydie?' Étienne began again. 'Do you bring her down here sometimes?'

Jeanlin laughed scornfully.

'Her? Not on your life! . . . Women just talk all the time!'

And he went on laughing, full of enormous contempt for both Lydie and Bébert. Did you ever see such fools! It tickled him hugely to think how easily they swallowed all his nonsense and went home empty-handed while he was down here eating cod in the warm. Then he declared with all the seriousness of a little philosopher:

'You're much better off on your own. That way you never fall out with anyone!'

Étienne had finished his bread. He downed a mouthful of gin. For a moment he wondered ungratefully if he was going to repay Jeanlin's hospitality by hauling him up to the daylight by his ear and telling him never to steal again or else his father would hear about it. But as he surveyed this underground hideaway, he began to have an idea: who knows if one day he might not need it for himself or his comrades, if things started going badly wrong up there above ground? He made the boy swear not to stay out all night again, as he had been doing recently whenever he dropped off to sleep on his hay. Then Étienne took a stump of candle and left first, leaving Jeanlin to tidy his home in peace.

Despite the severe cold, La Mouquette had been waiting anxiously for him, seated on an old beam. When she caught sight of him, she threw her arms round his neck; and it was as though he had plunged a knife into her heart when he told her that he did not want to see her any more. My God! Why not? Surely she loved him enough? Afraid that he might succumb to

his desire to go inside with her, he walked her towards the road
and explained as gently as he could that she was compromising
him in the eyes of his comrades, that she was endangering the
political cause. She was amazed: what on earth had it got to do
with politics? Eventually she decided that he must be ashamed
of her – not that she was offended, it was perfectly natural – and
so she offered to let him slap her in public so as to give the
impression that they had broken up. But he would still see her
from time to time, just for a little while. She pleaded madly with
him, promising to keep out of sight and that she wouldn't
keep him more than five minutes. Étienne was very torn, but
continued to refuse. He had to. Then, by way of goodbye, he
made to kiss her. Imperceptibly they had reached the first houses
in Montsou, and they were standing there with their arms round
each other under a broad full moon when a female figure passed
them and gave a sudden start as if she had tripped on a stone.

'Who is it?' Étienne asked anxiously.

'It's Catherine,' La Mouquette replied. 'She's on her way back
from Jean-Bart.'

The female figure was now disappearing into the distance,
head bowed and dragging her feet as though she were very tired.
Étienne watched her go, wretched at the thought of having been
seen by her, and his heart heavy with groundless remorse. She
had someone of her own, didn't she? Had she not made him
suffer just like this when she had given herself to that man here
on this very same Réquillart road? But it made him miserable
all the same to think that he had now done the same to her in
return.

'Shall I tell you something?' La Mouquette murmured tearfully as she left him. 'The reason you don't want me is because
you've got your eye on somebody else.'

Next day the weather was glorious, with a bright frosty sky,
one of those fine winter days when the hard earth rings like iron
underfoot. By one o'clock Jeanlin had already vanished from
the house; but he had to wait for Bébert behind the church, and
they very nearly left without Lydie, who had again been locked
in the cellar by her mother. She had just been let out and handed
a basket with instructions to fill it with dandelion leaves before

she came home or else she'd be locked up for the whole night with the rats for company. Terrified, therefore, she wanted to go and pick the salad at once; but Jeanlin talked her out of it. They would see about that later. For a long time now Rasseneur's large rabbit Poland had been preying on his mind, and just as he was passing the Advantage, the rabbit happened to come out on to the road. In an instant he grabbed it by the ears and stuffed it into Lydie's basket; and off the three of them dashed. What fun they were going to have making it run like a dog all the way to the forest.

But they stopped to watch Zacharie and Mouquet who, after a beer with two comrades, were just starting their big game of *crosse*. They were playing for a brand-new cap and a red silk neckerchief, which had been deposited at Rasseneur's. The four players, playing in pairs, were bidding for the first leg, from Le Voreux to Paillot Farm, a distance of nearly three kilometres; and Zacharie won with a bid of seven strokes against Mouquet's eight. The *cholette*, a small boxwood egg, had been placed on the cobbled road sharp end up. Each player had his *crosse*, a mallet with a slanting iron head and a long handle tightly bound with string. They began at two o'clock precisely. In his first go, a series of three successive strokes, Zacharie hit the *cholette* a masterly four hundred metres across fields of beet, it being forbidden to play the game in the villages or along the roads on account of the fatal accidents that had occurred. Mouquet, a strong player also, was able to hit the *cholette* so hard that with a single stroke he drove it a hundred and fifty metres back in the opposite direction. And so the game continued, with one side driving forward and the other back, all at great speed, which left their feet severely bruised by the frozen ridges between the ploughed furrows.

At first Jeanlin, Bébert and Lydie had run along behind the players, excited by the spectacle of these mighty drives. Then they remembered that Poland was in the basket they were jolting about, and so, abandoning the game in the middle of the countryside, they released the rabbit to see how fast she could run. And off she went, with the three of them in hot pursuit; and they chased her hard for an hour, twisting and turning, yelling their heads off to scare her in one direction or another, throwing their arms wide to catch her only to end up clutching at thin air. If she hadn't been in the early stages of pregnancy, they would never have caught her.

As they were catching their breath, the sound of cursing made them look round. They had ended up back in the middle of the game of *crosse*, and Zacharie had just nearly split his brother's skull open. The players were on their fourth leg: from Paillot Farm they had headed towards Quatre-Chemins, from Quatre-Chemins towards Montoire, and now they were trying to get from Montoire to Pré-des-Vaches in six strokes. That meant they had covered two and a half leagues in one hour, not to mention stopping for a few beers at Vincent's bar and then at the Three Wise Men. Mouquet had won the bidding this time. He had two strokes left and was certain of victory, when Zacharie, gleefully exploiting the rules, drove back so accurately that the *cholette* rolled into a deep ditch. Mouquet's playing partner could not get it out, and all was lost. The four of them were shouting their heads off and getting more and more worked up, for the scores were level. They would have to start a new leg. From Pré-des-Vaches it was only two kilometres to the tip of Les Herbes-Rousses, a matter of five strokes. And there they could have a drink at Lerenard's.

But Jeanlin had other ideas. He let the players go on ahead and then took a piece of string from his pocket and tied it to Poland's left hind paw. And what fun that was, with the rabbit running along in front of the three young rascals, hoisting its thigh and limping in such a pathetic fashion that they had never laughed so much in their lives. Then they tied the string round her neck so that she could run properly; and when she became tired, they dragged her along on her stomach or her back as if she were a toy on wheels. This lasted more than an hour, and the rabbit was almost gasping her last when they shoved her quickly back in the basket having heard the players near Cruchot wood. Once again they had strayed into the path of their game.

By this stage Zacharie, Mouquet and the other two men were covering enormous distances, pausing only to have a beer in every bar they fixed on as their goal. From Les Herbes-Rousses they had made for Buchy, then La Croix-de-Pierre, then Chamblay. The earth rang out beneath their feet as they raced along in relentless pursuit of the *cholette*, which kept bouncing off the ice. The weather was perfect: there was no mud to get stuck in, and the only risk was a broken leg. In the dry air the *cholette* exploded off their mallets like gunfire. Their muscular hands gripped the twine-bound handles, and with their whole bodies they launched themselves into the drive as though an ox were to be slain; and so they continued, for hour upon hour, from one end of the plain to the other, over ditches and hedges, over road embankments and low boundary walls. You needed stout bellows in your chest and iron hinges in your knees. For the hewers it was a wonderful way of stretching their legs after all the time spent underground. There were some fanatics of twenty-five who could cover ten leagues in a game. But by the age of forty you stopped; you were just too heavy.

Five o'clock struck, and dusk was already falling. Just one more leg, as far as the forest of Vandame, a decider to see who would get the cap and scarf; and Zacharie, with his satirical indifference to politics, thought it would be a great joke if they suddenly just dropped in on their comrades like this. As for Jeanlin, though he might have given the appearance of simply wanting to roam about the countryside, the forest had been his one goal since leaving the village. When Lydie, full of anxious remorse, started talking about returning to Le Voreux to gather dandelion leaves, Jeanlin was indignant and started threatening her. Were they to miss the meeting? He personally intended to hear what the grown-ups had to say. He chivvied Bébert to keep going and, as a way of entertaining the two of them over the short distance to the trees, he suggested letting Poland go and throwing stones at her as she tried to escape. His real intention was to kill her, for he now longed to take her down to his den at Réquillart and eat her. The rabbit ran off again, nose twitching, ears back; one stone grazed her back, another cut her tail; and despite the gathering darkness she would have died there and then if the youngsters had not spotted Étienne and Maheu standing in the middle of a clearing. They pounced on her frantically and put her back in the basket. Almost at the same moment Zacharie, Mouquet and the two other men, now on their final stroke, drove the *cholette* and saw it roll to within a few metres of the clearing. They had arrived bang in the middle of the meeting.

Since dusk, people throughout the region had been slowly making their way towards the purple thickets of the forest, silent shadows streaming across the empty plain along every highway and byway, some walking alone, others in groups. Every village was emptying, and even the women and children were leaving, as though setting off for a stroll beneath the clear open sky. By now the roads were sunk in darkness and the advancing throng could no longer be seen, but as it stole towards its common destination its presence could be felt, a myriad of steps with one single purpose. Along the hedgerows, between the bushes, all that could be heard was a quiet shuffling and a faint murmuring of voices in the night.

M. Hennebeau was riding home just then, and he listened to these far-away sounds. He had passed many couples this fine winter's evening, a whole procession of them out for a stroll. Still more lovers off to take their pleasure behind some wall or other, mouth against mouth! Was not this what he usually encountered, girls flat on their backs in some ditch and good-for-nothing lads busy enjoying the only pleasure that didn't cost money! And to think that these fools complained about life, when they could have love, the one and only happiness, and as much as they jolly well pleased! He would gladly starve like them if he could start life over again with a woman who would give herself to him on the bare ground, unreservedly, body and soul. In his own unhappiness he was not to be consoled, and he envied these poor wretched people. Head bowed, he rode slowly home, deep in despair at all these noises he could hear far away in the countryside and which for him could only be the sounds of love.

VII

The clearing was at Le Plan-des-Dames, where a vast open space had been created by some recent tree-felling. It sloped gently and was ringed by tall forest, magnificent beeches whose straight, regular trunks provided a colonnade of white pillars stained green with lichen. Some still lay like fallen giants among the grass, while over to the left a pile of sawn logs stood in a tidy cube. The cold had sharpened with the dusk, and the frozen moss crackled underfoot. At ground level it was pitch black, but the topmost branches of the trees were etched against the pale sky, where a full moon was rising on the horizon and beginning to snuff out the stars.

Almost three thousand miners had come to the meeting, a swarming mass of men, women and children that gradually filled the clearing and overflowed under the trees. As the latecomers continued to arrive, a sea of faces stretched away in the darkness into the further reaches of the forest. And amid the icy stillness a deep murmur of voices could be heard, like a stormy moan of wind.

At the front, facing down the slope, stood Étienne with Rasseneur and Maheu. A row was going on, and raised voices could be heard in snatches. Close by, other men were listening to them: Levaque with his fists clenched, Pierron with his back towards them, very worried now that he could no longer plead reasons of health for staying away; and Bonnemort and Mouque were there too, sitting side by side on a tree-stump deep in thought. Behind them were the jokesters, Zacharie, Mouquet and others, who had come for the laugh; whereas many of the women, on the contrary, were standing about in respectful groups and wearing an earnest expression as though they were at church. La Maheude nodded in silent agreement as La Levaque muttered her imprecations. Philomène was coughing, her bronchitis having returned with the winter months. Only La Mouquette was laughing, hugely amused by the way La Brûlé was tearing into her daughter and saying how it was just not natural, sending her own mother off like that so that she could stay and stuff herself on rabbit: a whore she was, who'd grown fat on her husband's cowardly collaborations. Meanwhile Jeanlin had installed himself on top of the pile of logs, pulling Lydie up beside him and ordering Bébert to follow, so that now the three of them were sitting way up high above the entire crowd.

The row had been started by Rasseneur, who wanted to elect a committee in the proper fashion. He was still smarting after his defeat at the Jolly Fellow; and he had sworn to have his revenge, fondly believing that he would be able to regain his authority once they were in front of the whole community of miners and not just the delegates. Étienne was outraged by the idea of a committee, which he considered ridiculous out here in the forest. They had to act like revolutionaries, like wild men, since it was as wolves and wild animals that they were being hunted down.

Seeing no end to this argument, he took control of the crowd at once by climbing on to a tree-trunk and shouting:

'Comrades! Comrades!'

The hubbub of the crowd died away like a long sigh, as Maheu silenced Rasseneur's protests. Étienne continued in a rousing tone:

'Comrades, we are having to meet here because they have forbidden us to talk to each other and because they have sent the gendarmes after us as if we were common criminals. Here we shall be free, here we shall be on home ground, and nobody will be able to come and tell us to shut up, any more than they can tell the birds and the animals to shut up!'

This brought a thunderous response of cries and exclamations.

'Yes, yes, this is our forest! It's our right to speak! . . . Give us a speech!'

Étienne stood still for a moment on his log. The moon was still too low in the sky and shone only on the uppermost branches of the trees, so that the crowd remained plunged in darkness as it gradually settled and fell silent. Above them, at the top of the slope, the equally dark figure of Étienne stood out like a stripe of shadow.

Slowly he raised one arm and began; but the voice of righteous indignation had gone, and he now spoke in the cold, dispassionate tone of a simple envoy of the people delivering his report. At last he was able to give the speech that the police superintendent had interrupted at the Jolly Fellow; and he began with a brief history of the strike, presenting it in the style of a fluent and informed analysis: facts, nothing but the facts. First he said how he didn't like strikes: the miners hadn't wanted one, it was management who had driven them to it with its new timbering rate. Then he recalled the first meeting the deputation had sought with the manager and how the Board of Directors had acted in bad faith, and then the delegates' second approach and the manager's belated concession, with the Company being prepared to restore the two centimes it had earlier tried to steal from them. That was how matters presently stood. He provided figures showing that the provident fund was exhausted, described how the financial help they had received had been used, and said a few words by way of excusing the International, Pluchart and the others, for not having been able to do more for them, preoccupied as they were with their plans to conquer the world. In a word, things were getting worse by the day: the Company was sacking people and threatening to recruit workers from Belgium. Not only that, it was intimidating potential blacklegs and had already persuaded a certain number of miners to return to work. Étienne said all this in the same, even tones as though to insist on the gravity of the bad news; hunger had beaten them, he said, all hope was lost, and they were now in the death throes of their courageous struggle. Then abruptly he ended, as matter-of-fact as when he had begun:

'That is the situation, comrades, and tonight you must decide. Do you want to continue the strike? And, if so, how do you intend to defeat the Company?'

A deep silence fell from the starry sky. The invisible crowd made no reply from out of the darkness, sick at heart after what they had just heard; and the only sound among the trees was its long sigh of despair.

But then Étienne continued, in a different voice. This was no longer the local secretary of the International speaking, but the leader of men, the apostle of truth. Were they going to be cowards and go back on their word? What? Had they suffered to no purpose this past month? Were they going to return to work with their tails between their legs, return to the same endless poverty? Would they not do better to die here and now in the attempt to destroy the tyranny of capital that reduced the worker to a state of permanent starvation? Were they forever going to play the same stupid game of submitting to hunger and poverty only then to rise up when the hunger and poverty became too great to bear? That game could not go on. And he showed the miners how they were exploited, how they alone had to bear the consequences of industrial crises and were brought to the point of starvation the moment the demands of competition led to a reduction in prices. No, the new timbering rate was unacceptable, it was nothing but a concealed pay-cut, they were trying to rob every man of an hour of his daily work. This time they had gone too far, and the day was now approaching when the poor would take no more, when they would demand justice, when they would obtain justice.

He stood there with his arms raised. At the word 'justice' a long shudder ran through the crowd, and a burst of applause rippled away into the distance like rustling leaves.

Voices cried out:

'Justice! . . . The time has come! Justice!'

Gradually Étienne warmed to his theme. He did not have the smooth articulacy of Rasseneur's effortless delivery. He was frequently at a loss for a word, and he would get tied up in his sentences and struggle to finish them, reinforcing his point as he did so with a forward jerk of his shoulder. But in the course of these repeated hesitations he would chance on ways of saying things that struck home with immediate force and gripped the attention of his audience; while his gestures also had an extraordinary effect on the comrades, the gestures of a man at work, elbows back one minute and then released the next, as he brandished his fists and stuck out his chin as though he were ready to bite someone. Everyone said the same: he wasn't a great speaker, but he made you listen.

'The wage-system is a new form of slavery,' he continued in even more rousing tones. 'The mine should belong to the miner as the sea belongs to the fisherman or the land belongs to the peasant ... Do you understand what I'm saying? The mine belongs to you, to every one of you. You've paid for it with your blood and suffering these past hundred years!'

Unabashed, he launched into discussion of various recondite legal questions, the whole panoply of laws that applied specifically to mining, but he soon lost the thread. What was beneath the land belonged to the nation just as much as the land itself; but, following the granting of a vile privilege, the companies now had sole rights to it. The situation in Montsou was even less acceptable because the alleged legality of the concessions was compromised by earlier agreements made with the owners of what had once been fiefdoms, in accordance with ancient Hainaut[1] custom. For the miners, therefore, it was simply a matter of taking back what belonged to them; and with outstretched hands he gestured beyond the forest to the country at large. Just then the moon, which had risen in the sky and was gleaming through the highest branches, shone on him. When the crowd, who were still standing in darkness, saw him like this, bathed in white light and bestowing riches with his open palms, they burst once more into prolonged applause.

'Yes, yes, he's right. Bravo!'

Then Étienne turned to his favourite subject, the collectivization of the means of production, a barbarous mouthful of a phrase, which he loved to trot out when he could. His own political education was now complete. Having begun with the neophyte's sentimental taste for solidarity and a belief in the need to reform the wage system, he had come to the view that it should be abolished as a matter of policy. At the time of the meeting in the Jolly Fellow his idea of collectivism had been essentially humanitarian and unsystematic, but it had now evolved into a rigid and complex programme, each article of which he was knowledgeably ready and able to discuss. First, he took it as axiomatic that freedom could not be achieved other than by the destruction of the State. Second, once the people had taken power, the reforms would begin: namely, the return to an earlier form of community life in which a family structure based on oppression and the moral code would be replaced by a family whose members were free and had equal rights; absolute civil, political and economic equality for all; guaranteed independence for the individual, based on the ownership of, and the right to enjoy all the fruits of, the means of production; and finally, free vocational training paid for by the collective. All this required a complete overhaul of a society that was old and rotten to the core; and he duly attacked marriage and the rights of inheritance, talked about regulating the amount of money each person could have, and grandly abolished all manner of entrenched and time-honoured iniquity with a single sweep of his arm, like a reaper scything ripe corn to the ground. Then, with his other hand, he would set about the process of rebuilding, constructing the humanity of the future, the great edifice of truth and justice that would rise with the dawn of the twentieth century. In the course of his mental journey the claims of reason faltered and gave way to sectarian obsession. Any scruples prompted by common sense or normal feelings were swept aside: nothing could be simpler than the realization of this brave new world. He had it all planned, and he talked about it all as if this were simply some machine he could assemble in a matter of hours come what may.

'Our day has dawned,' he proclaimed in a final flourish. 'It is our turn to have all the power and the wealth!'

The roar of acclamation rolled towards him from the depths of the forest. The whole clearing was now bathed in the pale light of the moon, and the sea of faces resolved itself into sharply delineated rows that stretched away beyond the tall grey tree-trunks into the darker recesses of the forest. Here in the freezing cold there swirled a tide of angry expressions, of shining eyes and bared teeth, a pack of starving humanity, of men, women and children unleashed upon the rightful pillage of ancient property that others had taken from them. They no longer felt the cold, for this fiery oratory had warmed them to the cockles of their hearts. They were borne up on a wave of religious exaltation, filled with the feverish expectancy of the early Christians living in hope of the new age of justice. Many obscure phrases had passed them by, and they understood little of all the more technical and abstract arguments; but the very obscurity and abstraction of the speech simply enhanced the vista of a promised land and dazzled them into agreement. What a vision! To be the masters! To know an end to suffering! To live and enjoy life at last!

'That's the way, by God! Our day has come! . . . Death to the oppressors!'

The women were hysterical. La Maheude was no longer her usual calm self, for hunger had made her light-headed; La Levaque was yelling; La Brûlé was quite beside herself and waving her arms about like a witch; Philomène was coughing her lungs up, and La Mouquette was so carried away that she started shouting endearments at the speaker. As to the men, Maheu was now persuaded and shouted his anger, flanked by Pierron who was trembling and Levaque who kept talking too much. Meanwhile the jokesters, Zacharie and Mouquet, tried to make fun of everything but were put off their stroke by their comrade's astonishing capacity to say so much at once without having a drink. But up on the log-pile Jeanlin was making even more of a racket, egging Bébert and Lydie on to action and brandishing the basket that had Poland in it.

The crowd was in uproar, and Étienne savoured the heady joy of his popularity. It was as if his power had here assumed human form, since one word from him now sufficed to set the pulse racing in three thousand hearts. If Souvarine had deigned to come, he would have applauded his ideas – once he had made out what Étienne was saying – and he would have noted happily his pupil's progress towards anarchism and agreed with his programme, except for the article about vocational training, a piece of sentimental foolishness, for the sacred and salutary ignorance of the people was to provide the very waters for their cleansing and renewal. As for Rasseneur, he was shrugging his shoulders with angry contempt.

'Will you finally let me speak!' he shouted at Étienne.

The latter jumped down from his tree-trunk.

'Speak, then, and let's see if they listen to you.'

Already Rasseneur had taken his place and was appealing for silence. But the noise continued unabated as his name was passed from those at the front who had recognized him to those at the back beneath the beech trees; and they all refused to listen to him. He was like a fallen idol, and the very sight of him was enough to make his former followers angry. His gift of the gab and his easy, good-natured manner had charmed them for so long, but what he had to say now seemed rather tepid stuff, suitable merely for reassuring the faint-hearted. He tried in vain to speak through the noise, intending to deliver his usual message of moderation about how you couldn't change the world just by passing a lot of laws, how you had to give society time to evolve: but they just laughed and hissed and shouted him down. It was the defeat at the Jolly Fellow all over again, only this time much worse – and definitive. Eventually they started throwing lumps of frozen moss at him, and a woman shouted in a shrill voice:

'He's a scab!'

He explained why the mine could not belong to the miner in the same way that the craft of weaving belonged to the weaver, and he stated his preference for profit-sharing, with the worker having a stake in the company, like one of the family.

'He's a scab!' a thousand voices repeated, as stones began to whistle through the air.

Rasseneur turned pale, and his eyes filled with tears of despair. For him this meant the end of everything, the fruits of twenty years of power-seeking comradeship swept away by the ingratitude of the crowd. Cut to the quick and without the strength to go on, he climbed down from the tree-trunk.

'You think it's funny, don't you!' he stammered to a triumphant Étienne. 'Very well. But I just hope it happens to you one day . . . And it will happen. Just you wait!'

And as if to disclaim all responsibility for the disasters that he could see about to happen, he gestured the end of his involvement and departed alone across the white and silent countryside.

There was a sound of jeering, and everyone looked round in surprise to see old Bonnemort standing on a tree-trunk and trying to speak above the noise. Until then Mouque and he had appeared preoccupied, with that air they always had of thinking back to the old days. No doubt he had been taken with one of his periodic fits of garrulousness in which his memories were so

strongly stirred that they welled up inside him and poured out
of his mouth for hours on end. A deep silence fell and people
listened to the old man, who looked as white as a ghost standing
there in the moonlight; and as he talked of things that had no
immediate bearing on the recent debate, long tales that no one
could quite follow, so their amazement grew. He was talking
about his youth and about his two uncles who had been buried
alive in Le Voreux, and then he moved on to the pneumonia
that had carried off his wife. But he kept to his point all the
same: things had never been good, and they never would be.
They, too, had met like this in the forest, five hundred of them,
because the King had refused to reduce the number of working
hours; but then he stopped and began to talk about another
strike. He had seen so many! It always ended up with them
meeting here under the trees at Le Plan-des-Dames, or over at
La Charbonnerie, or even as far away as Le Saut-du-Loup.
Sometimes it was freezing cold, sometimes it was hot. One
evening it had rained so hard that they had had to go home
again without a word being said. And always the King's soldiers
would come, and always it would end in a shooting match.

'We raised our hands like this, and we took an oath not to go
back down. And I took that oath! Yes I did, I took that oath!'

The crowd listened open-mouthed, and it was beginning to
have misgivings when Étienne, who had been attending keenly,
leaped on to the fallen tree-trunk and stood beside the old man.
He had just recognized Chaval among the people he knew in
the front row. The thought that Catherine must be there had
put new fire in his belly and a strong desire to be acclaimed in
front of her.

'Comrades, you've just heard what he said. Here is one of our
oldest miners, and this is what he has suffered and what our
children will suffer, too, if we don't have done with these thieves
and murderers once and for all!'

He was awesome: he had never spoken with such vehemence
before. With one arm he held on to old Bonnemort, displaying
him like an emblem of misery and grief and baying for vengeance
as he did so. Speaking very quickly, he went back in time to the
first of the Maheus and described how since then the whole

family had been worn out by the mine and exploited by the Company and now found itself, after a hundred years of toil, even hungrier than it had ever been before; and then he compared them with the fat-bellied directors, men who oozed money from every pore, and with all those shareholders who had spent the past century living like kept women with nothing to do but delight in the pleasures of the flesh. Wasn't it terrible? A whole lineage of human beings working themselves to death down the mine from father to son so that government ministers could have their kickbacks and generations of noble lords and gentlemen could give grand parties or sit and grow fat by their firesides! He had studied the occupational diseases of miners, and he regaled them with the full panoply in gruesome detail: anaemia, scrofula, the bronchitis that made them spit black coal, the asthma that choked them, the rheumatisms that stopped them walking. The miserable devils were no better than machine-fodder, they were penned in villages like livestock, and the big companies were gradually absorbing them all, regulating their slavery and threatening to enlist every worker in the country, millions upon millions of hands, in order to make the fortunes of a thousand idle men. But the miner was no longer the ignorant brute who could be crushed underfoot in the bowels of the earth. An army was taking root in the depths of the mines, a crop of citizens whose seed was slowly germinating under the surface of the earth and who would, one fine sunny day, finally break through to the light. And then they'd learn whether anyone would still dare to offer a pension of a hundred and fifty francs to a sixty-year-old miner after forty years' service, a man who was coughing up coal-dust and whose legs were swollen with the water from the coal-faces he had worked. Yes, labour was going to call capital to account and confront this anonymous god that the worker never met, the god that squatted somewhere in its mysterious inner sanctuary and sucked the blood of the poor devils that kept it alive! They would go there themselves and they would finally see its face by the light of the coming conflagration; and then they would drown the filthy swine in its own blood, they would destroy this monstrous idol that had gorged on human flesh!

He fell silent, but his other arm was still outstretched, pointing at the enemy in the distance, over there, wherever, somewhere on this earth. This time the cheering of the crowd was so loud that the bourgeois heard it in Montsou and cast anxious glances in the direction of Vandame, thinking that there had been some terrible collapse in the mine. Birds of the night flew up out of the forest into the vast, clear sky.

Étienne decided to bring things to a head:

'Comrades, what is your decision? . . . Do you vote to continue the strike?'

'Yes, yes!' they screamed.

'And what action do you propose to take? . . . We are certain to be defeated if those cowards go back down tomorrow.'

'Death to the cowards!' came the reply, like the blast of a storm.

'So you are resolved to remind them of their duty, of their sworn oath . . . Then this is what I propose. We shall go to the pits ourselves, and just by being there we'll shame the traitors into stopping work. And that way we'll show the Company that we're all of one mind, that we are ready to die rather than surrender.'

'Yes, yes! To the pits.'

Since he had started speaking again, Étienne had been trying to catch sight of Catherine among the pale, seething mass of faces beneath him. There was absolutely no sign of her. But he could still see Chaval, who was shrugging his shoulders and pretending to sneer at the whole thing; he was consumed with envy and would have sold himself to the highest bidder if he could have obtained but one small part of this popularity.

'And if there are any informers among us here, comrades,' Étienne continued, 'they'd better watch their step. Because we know who they are . . . Yes, I can see some Vandame miners here who haven't left their pit . . .'

'I suppose that's meant for me, is it?' Chaval asked cockily.

'You or anyone else . . . But since it's you that's spoken, you might as well understand that people that can eat shouldn't meddle in the affairs of those that can't. You're working at Jean-Bart . . .'

They were interrupted by a taunting voice:

'Him? Working? . . . More like he has a woman who does the working for him.'

Chaval flushed and swore:

'Christ! Aren't we allowed to work, then?'

'No!' shouted Étienne. 'At a time when your comrades are going through hell for the good of all, you're not allowed to be a selfish hypocrite and side with the bosses. If the strike had been general, we'd have been the masters long ago . . . Should any Vandame miner have gone down when Montsou was out on strike? The great thing would be if the whole area stopped work, at Monsieur Deneulin's as well as here. Don't you see? The people working the coal-faces at Jean-Bart are scabs. You're all scabs!'

The crowd around Chaval was beginning to look menacing; fists were raised, and people began to shout: 'Kill them! Kill them!' He had turned very pale. But in his furious desire to outdo Étienne, he suddenly had an idea.

'Listen to me! Come to Jean-Bart tomorrow, and then you'll see if I'm working or not! . . . We're with you, they sent me here to tell you so. And we must shut down the furnaces and get the mechanics to join the strike too. So much the better if the pumps stop! The water will destroy the pits, and then the whole bloody lot will be ruined!'

He in turn was furiously applauded, and from then on even Étienne was overrun. Speaker after speaker came to the tree-trunk, gesticulating above the noise and making wild proposals. It was faith gone mad, the impatience of a religious sect that has tired of waiting for the expected miracle and has decided to bring one about by itself. Minds emptied of all thought by hunger now saw red and dreamed of burning and killing, of a glorious apotheosis that would usher in the dawn of universal happiness. Meanwhile the quiet moon bathed the heaving mass of people in its light, and the thick forest cast a deep ring of silence around their murderous cries. The only other sound was the continued crunch of frozen moss as it was trampled underfoot; and the beech trees simply stood there, strong and tall, the delicate tracery of their branches etched in black against the pallor of the sky, and they neither saw nor heard the commotion of these wretched beings at their feet.

People started shoving and pushing, and La Maheude found herself next to Maheu; and now, after months of growing frustration and having lost all sense of proportion, they both supported Levaque when he went one further than everybody else and called for the death of the engineers. Pierron had disappeared. Bonnemort and Mouque were both talking at once and saying vague and terrible things that no one quite understood. As a joke Zacharie called on them to demolish the churches, while Mouquet, who was still holding his *crosse*, banged it on the ground just to add to the racket. The women were in a frenzy: La Levaque, hands on hips, was ready for a fight with Philomène, whom she accused of laughing; La Mouquette said she would soon sort the gendarmes out with a good kick up the you-know-where; La Brûlé had just slapped Lydie, having come across her without basket or salad leaves, and was continuing to beat the air in an imaginary assault on all the bosses she would dearly have laid her hands on. Jeanlin had panicked for a moment when Bébert heard from a pit-boy that Mme Rasseneur had seen them take Poland; but once he had decided he would take the rabbit back to the Advantage and quietly release it outside the door, he began to yell louder; and he got out his new knife and brandished the blade, proudly making it gleam.

'Comrades! Comrades!' an exhausted Étienne kept repeating in a hoarse voice, as he tried to obtain a moment's silence and conclude the meeting.

Eventually they paid attention.

'Comrades! Are we agreed? Tomorrow morning at Jean-Bart!'

'Yes! Yes! Jean-Bart! Death to the scabs!'

And a tempest of three thousand voices filled the sky and died away in the pure light of the moon.

PART V

At four o'clock the moon had set, and it was pitch dark. Everyone was still asleep in the Deneulin household; and the old brick house stood dark and silent, with its doors and windows shut, at the end of the large, untidy garden that lay between it and the Jean-Bart mine. Along the other side of the house ran the now deserted road to Vandame, a small town about three kilometres away and hidden from view by the forest.

Deneulin, tired from having spent part of the previous day down the pit, was snoring with his face to the wall when he dreamed that someone was calling him. When he eventually woke up, he heard a real voice and rushed to open the window. It was one of his deputies, standing in the garden below.

'What is it?' he asked.

'It's mutiny, sir. Half the men are refusing to work, and they won't let the others go down.'

Deneulin did not understand at first. His head felt dizzy and heavy with sleep, and the cold air struck him with the force of an icy shower.

'Then damn well make them go down!' he spluttered.

'It's been going on for an hour now,' the deputy continued, 'so we thought we'd better come and fetch you. You're the only one who can maybe make them see sense.'

'All right, I'm coming.'

He quickly got dressed: his mind had cleared, and he was very worried. They could easily have looted the house, for neither the cook nor the manservant had stirred. But from across the landing he could hear the sound of anxious voices; and when he came out, he saw the door to his daughters' bedroom open and the two girls appear, having hurriedly thrown on their white dressing-gowns.

'What's happening, Father?'

Lucie, the elder, was already twenty-two, tall, dark, with a regal air; while Jeanne, the younger one and just nineteen, was short, with golden hair and an easy grace.

'Nothing serious,' he replied in order to reassure them. 'Some troublemakers kicking up a fuss over at the mine, apparently. I'm off to see what's going on.'

But they would not hear of it and insisted that he must have something to warm his stomach before he left. He would only come back ill otherwise, with his digestion ruined as usual. He endeavoured to say no and that as God was his witness he simply did not have the time.

'Now look,' said Jeanne eventually, wrapping herself round his neck. 'You'll just have a little glass of rum and a biscuit or two. Or else I'll hang on to you like this and you'll have to take me with you.'

He had to give in, declaring that he would surely choke on the biscuits. Already they were on their way downstairs ahead of him, each with her own candlestick. Below, in the dining-room, they hurried to wait on him, one pouring the rum, the other running to the pantry for a packet of biscuits. Having lost their mother when they were very young, they had brought themselves up, rather badly it must be said, since their father spoiled them. The elder girl dreamed constantly of singing on the stage, while the younger one was mad about painting, with a boldness of taste which set her apart. But when serious business difficulties had obliged them to cut back on their style of living, these two apparently extravagant girls had suddenly blossomed into thoroughly sensible and resourceful housekeepers who could spot the merest discrepant centime in the household accounts. And now, for all that they lived the part of bohemian spinsters, they managed the domestic budget, watched every last penny, haggled with the tradesmen, endlessly refurbished their wardrobes, and ultimately managed to lend an air of decent respectability to the worsening financial straits in which they lived.

'Eat, Papa,' Lucie insisted.

Then, noticing how quickly he seemed preoccupied again as he sat there with a silent and gloomy expression, she became alarmed once more.

'Is it serious, then? Judging by your face, it must be . . . Why don't we stay here with you? They can manage without us at that lunch today.'

She was referring to an outing which had been planned for the coming morning. Mme Hennebeau was to fetch Cécile from the Grégoires' in her carriage; after that she would come and collect Lucie and Jeanne, and then they were all going to Marchiennes to have lunch at Les Forges as guests of the manager's wife. It would be a chance to visit the workshops and to see the blast-furnaces and the coke-ovens.

'Of course we'll stay,' declared Jeanne in her turn.

But he became cross.

'What sort of an idea is that! I tell you there's nothing to worry about . . . Kindly do me the pleasure of tucking yourselves up in bed again. And then you will dress and be ready at nine o'clock as planned.'

He kissed them and hurried away. The sound of his boots on the frozen ground could be heard disappearing across the garden.

Jeanne carefully replaced the cork in the bottle of rum, while Lucie locked the biscuits away. The dining-room had the clean and tidy look of a place where the fare is frugal. And they both took advantage of this early-morning visit to check that nothing had been left lying around from the night before. A napkin had been forgotten, so the servant would be scolded. Finally they went back upstairs to bed.

As he took a short cut along the narrow paths of his kitchen-garden, Deneulin was thinking about the danger to his fortune, his Montsou denier, the million francs he had realized and dreamed of increasing tenfold, and which was now in such grave peril. It had been one long tale of bad luck: the unforeseen and enormously expensive repair programme, the ruinous running costs, and now this disastrous industrial crisis just when he was beginning to make a profit. If the strike went ahead, he would be finished. He pushed open a small gate: in the pitch darkness the colliery buildings could be identified by their even blacker shadows and a sprinkling of lanterns.

Jean-Bart was not as big as Le Voreux, but in the opinion of the engineers the new plant and machinery had made it a fine pit. Not only had the shaft been widened by a metre and a half and taken down to a depth of seven hundred and eight metres, it had been completely re-equipped with a new winding-engine, new cages and new fittings, and all to the very latest specifications. Moreover, there was even a hint of conscious elegance in the way things had been designed: the screening-shed had a carved frieze, the headgear had been adorned with a clock, the pit-head and the engine-house had the rounded contours of a Renaissance chapel, and the chimney above them was spiral-shaped and constructed from a mosaic of black and red brick. The pump had been located in the other mine-shaft belonging to the concession, the disused Gaston-Marie pit, which was now used solely for drainage. Jean-Bart had only two subsidiary shafts, to the right and left of the winding-shaft, one for the steam-driven ventilator and the other for the emergency ladders.

That morning Chaval had arrived first, as early as three o'clock, and had gone round sowing the seed of dissent among his comrades and trying to persuade them that they ought to imitate the Montsou miners and demand an increase of five centimes per tub. Soon the four hundred underground workers had left the changing-room and streamed into the pit-head hall amid much shouting and gesticulating. Those who wanted to work were standing there in their bare feet holding their lamps and clutching a pick or a shovel under their other arm; while the remainder, still in their clogs and with a coat over their shoulders on account of the bitter cold, were barring the way to the pit-shaft. The deputies were shouting themselves hoarse in their attempts to restore order, begging the miners to be reasonable and not to prevent those who had the good sense and decency to want to work from duly doing so.

But Chaval lost his temper when he saw Catherine in her jacket and trousers, with her hair tucked into her blue cap. When he had got up earlier, he had ordered her roughly to stay in bed. She was dismayed at the thought of a stoppage and had followed him nevertheless, for he never passed on any money to her and she often had to support both of them; and what would become of her if she was no longer earning? One thing in particular terrified her, the prospect of ending up in the brothel at Marchiennes, which is what happened to putters who had no money and nowhere to sleep.

'What the bloody hell are you doing here?' Chaval screamed.

She answered haltingly that she had no other source of income and that she wanted to work.

'So you're going to cross me, are you, you bitch? . . . You can go home this minute, or I'll bloody come and kick your backside for you all the way there!'

She backed nervously away but did not leave, determined to see how things would turn out.

Deneulin was now coming down the stairs from the screening-shed. Despite the poor light cast by the lanterns he took in the scene at a glance, the shadowy mass of people whose every face he knew, the hewers, the onsetters, the banksmen, the putters, down to the youngest pit-boy. In the great hall, which was still clean and pristine, normal activity was in a state of suspended animation: the winding-engine, fully primed, was letting off little whistles of steam; the cages hung from motionless cables; and the tubs, abandoned in mid-journey, were cluttering up the cast-iron floor. Only about eighty lamps had been claimed, the others were still burning in the lamp-room. But no doubt a single word from him would suffice, and the regular routine would resume once more.

'So what's this all about then, boys?' he asked in a loud voice. 'What's the problem? Tell me, I'm sure we can sort it out.'

As a rule he adopted a paternal air when dealing with his men, even though he made them work hard. Authoritarian and brusque in his manner, he would begin by trying to win them over with a rather obvious mateyness; and often he succeeded, for the workers respected the courage of a man who was constantly down at the coal-face with them and who was always the first on the scene whenever anything terrible happened in the pit. Twice now, after firedamp explosions, when even the bravest miners had balked, they had lowered him down on a rope tied under his armpits.

'Look here,' he continued, 'I hope you're not going to make me regret having trusted you. You know I refused to have a police guard here . . . Take your time, I'm listening.'

Everybody was silent and embarrassed and began to edge away. At length Chaval spoke up:

'It's like this, Monsieur Deneulin. We just can't go on. We must have five centimes more per tub.'

He was taken aback.

'What? Five centimes! What's brought this on? I'm not complaining about your timbering, I'm not trying to impose a new rate like they are at Montsou.'

'Maybe not, but the Montsou comrades are right all the same. They're rejecting the timbering rate and demanding an increase of five centimes because it's just not possible to do the job properly under the present terms ... We want an increase of five centimes. Isn't that right, comrades?'

Various voices expressed their support, and the noise level rose again, accompanied by violent gestures. Gradually everyone gathered round in a tight semicircle.

Deneulin's eyes blazed, and this man who had a taste for firm government had to clench his fists for fear that he might yield to temptation and grab somebody by the scruff of the neck. He preferred to discuss things, to talk things through sensibly.

'You want five centimes more, and I agree with you that the job is worth it. But I can't give it to you. If I were to pay you that, I would simply be ruined ... You've got to understand that for you to make a living I've got to make a living first. And I've reached my limit. The slightest increase in operating costs would bankrupt me ... Two years ago, if you remember, at the time of the last strike, I conceded. I could still afford to then. But that increase has been ruinous for me all the same, and I've been struggling ever since ... Today I would rather give the whole thing up at once than not know from one month to the next where I was going to find the money to pay you.'

Faced with this master who was ready to give them such a frank account of his business affairs, Chaval gave an ugly laugh. The others looked at the floor in disbelief, stubbornly refusing to get it into their heads that a boss didn't automatically make millions off the back of his workers.

Deneulin persisted. He told them about his ongoing battle with Montsou, who were always on the lookout for some way to gobble him up if he should ever fall on hard times. The competition with them was fierce, forcing him to make savings

wherever he could, and all the more so because the considerable
depth of Jean-Bart added to the cost of extraction, a disadvan-
tage only barely offset by the greater thickness of its seams. He
would never have increased their pay at the time of the last
strike if it hadn't been for the need to match Montsou, so as
not to lose his workforce. Then he threatened them with the
consequences: what a fine outcome it would be for them if they
forced him to sell and they ended up under the heel of Montsou!
He didn't rule them like some god in a far-away temple, he
wasn't one of those invisible shareholders who pays managers
to fleece the miners for them; he was their employer, and it
wasn't just his own money he was risking, it was his peace of
mind, his health, his whole life. Any stoppage would mean the
end of him, it was as simple as that, for he had no stock in
reserve and yet he had to meet his orders. At the same time he
couldn't let the money invested in equipment stand idle. How
was he to meet his commitments? Who was going to pay the
interest on the money his friends had entrusted to him? It would
mean bankruptcy.

'So there you have it, my friends!' he concluded. 'I wish I
could convince you . . . You really can't ask a man to sign his
own death warrant, can you? And whether I give you the five
centimes or I let you go ahead and strike, either way I'll be
slitting my own throat.'

He stopped. People started muttering. Some of the miners
seemed to be having second thoughts, and several moved back
towards the shaft.

'At least let everyone decide for themselves,' said one deputy.
'Which of you wants to work?'

Catherine was one of the first to step forward. But Chaval
was furious and shoved her back, shouting:

'We're all of one mind here. Only lousy bastards leave their
comrades in the lurch!'

Thereafter all hope of compromise seemed out of the question.
People started shouting again, and men were shouldered away
from the shaft and nearly crushed against the wall. For a moment
Deneulin tried desperately to fight the battle single-handedly
and to bring the mob smartly to heel; but it was pointless folly,

and he was forced to withdraw. So he went and sat for a few minutes at the far end of the checkweighman's office. The stuffing had been knocked out of him, and he was so dazed by his powerlessness that he could not think what to do next. At length he calmed down and told a supervisor to go and fetch Chaval. Then, when the latter had agreed to the meeting, he dismissed everyone else with a wave of his hand.

– Leave us.

Deneulin's intention was to get the measure of this character. The moment he spoke, he could sense his vanity and the desperate envy that drove him. So he tried flattery and pretended to be surprised that a worker of his calibre should jeopardize his future in this way. From the way he talked he made it sound as though he had for some time now been marking him out for rapid promotion, and eventually he ended by offering there and then to make him a deputy, when circumstances allowed. Chaval listened to him in silence and gradually unclenched his fists. He was thinking hard: if he persisted with the strike, he would always be playing second fiddle to Étienne, whereas he now began to harbour a different ambition, that of becoming one of the bosses. His face flushed with pride, and his excitement grew. Anyway, the group of strikers he'd been waiting for since early morning would not come now; they must have been held up, by the gendarmes perhaps. So it was time to yield. But this did not stop him from shaking his head and indignantly beating his breast, every inch the unbiddable man of integrity. Eventually, while omitting to mention the meeting he had arranged with the Montsou miners, he undertook to calm his comrades and persuade them to go back to work.

Deneulin kept away, and even the deputies stayed in the background. For the next hour they listened to Chaval holding forth and arguing with the miners from the top of a coal-tub. One section of men booed him, and a hundred and twenty left in disgust, determined to stick to the decision he had made them take in the first place. It had already gone seven, and the dawn was breaking on a bright and cheerful frosty day. Suddenly the pit jolted back into action, and work resumed its course. First there was the plunging of the crank-rod as it began to wind the cables on and off the drums. Then, amid a clanking of signals, came the first descent, with cages filling and vanishing and reappearing as the shaft swallowed its portion of pit-boys, hewers and putters. Meanwhile the banksmen wheeled the tubs across the iron floor with a great rumble of thunder.

'What the bloody hell are you doing standing there?' Chaval shouted at Catherine, who was waiting her turn. 'Stop hanging about and get yourself down below!'

At nine o'clock, when Mme Hennebeau arrived in her carriage with Cécile, she found Lucie and Jeanne dressed and ready, a picture of elegance despite the fact that their clothes had been mended twenty times over. But Deneulin was surprised to see Négrel accompanying the carriage on horseback. Was this to be a mixed party? So Mme Hennebeau explained in her motherly way that people had been frightening her with tales about the roads being full of villainous creatures and that she had preferred to bring along a protector. Négrel laughed and sought to reassure them: there was nothing to be worried about, just the usual threats from the loudmouths, but not one of them would dare throw a stone through a window. Still full of his success, Deneulin told them about how he had crushed the revolt at Jean-Bart. Things would be fine now, he said. And as the young ladies climbed into the carriage on the Vandame road, everyone was in high spirits because of the fine weather, little realizing that far off in the countryside there was a stirring and that it was slowly gathering pace. The people were on the march; and if they had placed their ears to the ground, they would have heard the sound coming towards them.

'So that's agreed, then,' Mme Hennebeau said once more. 'You'll come and fetch these young ladies this evening, and you'll stay and have dinner with us . . . Madame Grégoire has promised to collect Cécile also.'

'You may count on me,' replied Deneulin.

The carriage set off towards Vandame. Jeanne and Lucie had leaned out of the carriage to wave a cheerful goodbye to their father standing by the roadside, while the gallant Négrel trotted along behind the whirring wheels.

They drove through the forest and at Vandame took the road

to Marchiennes. As they were approaching Le Tartaret, Jeanne asked Mme Hennebeau if she knew of La Côte Verte, and she admitted that, despite having lived there for five years, she had never been this way before. So they made a detour. Situated at the edge of the wood, Le Tartaret was a stretch of barren, volcanic moorland, beneath which a coal-seam had been burning permanently for centuries past. The origins of the place were lost in the mists of time, and the local miners told a story about how the fire of heaven had fallen upon this underground Sodom where putters defiled themselves in all manner of abomination; and it had struck so suddenly that they had not even had time to return to the surface and continued to roast in its hell-fires to this very day. The rock had burned to a dark red and was covered in a leprous bloom of potash. Sulphur grew along the fissures like yellow flowers. After dark those brave enough to put an eye to these cracks in the earth swore that they could see flames and the souls of the damned frying in the hot coals beneath. Gleams of light flickered along the ground, and hot vapours rose continually, like a foul and poisonous stench from the devil's kitchen. And in the middle of this accursed moor of Le Tartaret, La Côte Verte rose as though miraculously blessed by an eternal spring, with grass that was forever green, beech trees that were continually producing new leaves, and fields that yielded as many as three crops a year. It was a natural hothouse, warmed by the combustion taking place in the deep strata beneath. Snow never settled there. And on this December day its enormous bouquet of greenery rose beside the bare trees of the forest, and the frost had not even blackened the edges of the leaves.

Soon the carriage sped off across the plain. Négrel made fun of the legend and explained how a fire like that at the bottom of a mine was generally caused by coal-dust fermenting. Once it got out of control, it burned for ever; and he quoted the example of a pit in Belgium which they had flooded by diverting a river into its shaft. But then he stopped talking, for they had begun to meet group after group of miners coming the other way. The miners went past in silence, casting hard sideways glances at all this luxury that was forcing them off the road.

Their number kept increasing, and on the little bridge over La Scarpe the horses had to slow to a walk. What was bringing all these people out on to the roads? The young ladies were becoming anxious, and Négrel could sense trouble brewing in the countryside. And so it was with some relief that they finally arrived at Marchiennes. In the sunlight, which seemed to dim their fires, the batteries of coke-ovens and the tall chimneys of the blast-furnaces stood belching forth clouds of smoke, which fell through the air in an endless rain of soot.

II

At Jean-Bart Catherine had already been rolling tubs for an hour, delivering them as far as the relay-point; and she was drenched in such a lather of sweat that she stopped for a moment to wipe her face.

From the depths of the seam where he was digging out coal with the rest of his group, Chaval was surprised not to hear the usual rumble of wheels. The lamps were not burning well, and the dust made it impossible to see.

'What's up?' he shouted.

When she replied that she thought she was surely going to melt and that her heart was fit to burst, he called back angrily:

'Bloody fool! Why don't you take off your shirt like the rest of us?'

They were at a depth of seven hundred and eight metres, in the first road of the Désirée seam, about three kilometres away from pit-bottom. Whenever this part of the mine was mentioned, the local miners would turn pale and lower their voices, as if they were talking about hell itself; and more often than not they merely shook their heads in the way of people who didn't want to discuss this deep, remote place where the coal burned red and fierce. As they extended northwards, the roadways drew closer to Le Tartaret and entered the area of the underground fire that had turned the rock overhead a dark red. At the point to which they had now dug, the average temperature at the coal-face was some forty-five degrees. They were right in the middle of the accursed city of the plain and in among those flames that passers-by up on the surface could see through the cracks, spitting out sulphur and foul-smelling gases.

Catherine, who had already taken off her jacket, hesitated for a moment and then removed her trousers also; and with her arms and legs bare, and her shirt tied round her hips like a smock with a piece of string, she began once more to roll her tubs.

'I'll be fine,' she shouted.

If the heat stifled her, it also made her dimly afraid. For the past five days since they had started working there, she had been remembering the stories she had heard in her childhood about the putters of the past who were still being roasted alive under Le Tartaret as a punishment for unmentionable deeds. Of course she was too old now to believe such nonsense; but what would she have done nevertheless if she'd seen a girl come through the wall looking as red as a hot stove and with eyes like burning coals? The very idea of it made her sweat even more.

At the relay-point another putter would come and take the tub and roll it a further eighty metres along the track to the edge of the incline, where the seizer would dispatch it along with all the others that were coming down from the roads above.

'Blimey! Make yourself at home, why not?' said the woman, a thin-looking widow of thirty, when she saw Catherine dressed only in her shirt. 'I can't do that. The lads on my stretch never give me a minute's peace with all their dirty nonsense.'

'Oh, to hell with the men!' replied Catherine. 'It's this heat I can't stand.'

And off she went, pushing her empty tub. The worst of it was that down in this remote part of the mine the proximity of Le Tartaret was not the only cause of the unbearable heat. The road ran parallel with some old workings, deep in Gaston-Marie, next to an abandoned roadway where a firedamp explosion ten years earlier had set fire to the seam; and the fire was still raging behind the break, a wall of clay which had been built alongside it and which was kept in constant repair in order to contain the disaster. Starved of oxygen the fire ought to have gone out; but draughts from unknown sources must have continued to feed it, and so it was still burning ten years later, warming the clay in the break like the bricks in a kiln, with the result that the heat could be felt through it along the whole length of the wall. And it was beside this break, over a distance of a hundred metres, that the tubs had to be rolled, in a temperature of sixty degrees.

After two more trips Catherine was again overcome with the heat. Fortunately the road was broad and easy to move around in, the Désirée vein being one of the thickest in the region. The band of coal was one metre ninety high, which meant that the miners could work standing up. But they would have preferred cramped conditions if it meant they could have had some cooler air.

'God help us! Are you asleep?' Chaval shouted angrily again as soon as he heard Catherine stop. 'How did I get stuck with such a bloody hopeless bitch, would you tell me? Will you for God's sake fill your tub and take it away!'

She was standing at the foot of the coal-face, leaning on her shovel; and she began to feel faint, staring at everyone with a blank expression and ignoring Chaval's order. She could barely see them in the reddish glow from the lamps; and though they were stark naked, like animals, they were so black with the grime of sweat and coal-dust that their nakedness did not trouble her. They seemed bent upon some indeterminate labour, an array of monkeys' backs straining with effort, an infernal vision of ruddy limbs caught up in a great thudding and grunting. But they must have been able to see her better because the picks stopped tapping and the men started teasing her about having taken off her trousers.

'Mind you don't catch cold now!'

'What a pair of legs! Hey, Chaval, how about one each?'

'Give us a peep, then! Come on, lift your shirt! Higher! Higher!'

Not at all put out by this ribaldry, Chaval laid into her again:

'For Christ's sake, get a move on! . . . Oh, she doesn't mind that kind of talk. She'd stand there listening to it till the cows come home.'

With great effort Catherine had made herself fill the tub, and now she began to push it. The roadway was too wide for her to be able to gain purchase by arching her back against the timbering on either side, and she kept twisting her ankles as she tried to get a grip on the rails with her bare feet; and so progress was slow as she strained forward with her arms stretched out taut in front of her and her body bent in half. As soon as she reached the break, the torture by fire began again, and enormous beads of sweat started falling from every part of her body like heavy raindrops in a storm. By the time she was scarcely a third of the way along, it was pouring off her, and she could see nothing. She, too, was covered in black grime. Her tight shirt looked as though it had been soaked in ink; and as it clung to her skin, the movement of her thighs made it ride up over her hips, restricting her movements so painfully that once more she was forced to stop.

What was wrong with her today? Never before had her legs felt so much as though they were made of jelly. It must be the bad air. The ventilation did not reach the end of this remote road, and the atmosphere was full of all manner of gases which gently fizzed from the coal with the sound of spring-water, and sometimes in such quantity that the lamps refused to burn; to say nothing of the firedamp, which everyone had ceased to care about since the seam blew so much of the stuff into the miners' faces from one week's end to the next. She knew all about this bad air – 'dead air'[1] the miners called it – which consisted of a lower layer of heavy gases that caused asphyxiation and an upper layer of light gases that spontaneously combusted and could blow up every coal-face in a pit, killing hundreds of men in one single thunderous blast. She had breathed in so much of it since she was a child that she was surprised not to be able to tolerate it better, but her ears were buzzing and her throat was on fire.

Unable to bear the heat any longer, she felt a desperate need to remove her shirt. The cloth was torturing her, and the merest crease seemed to cut into her and burn her flesh. She resisted the urge and made another attempt to push the tub, but she had to straighten up again. Then, all of a sudden, telling herself that she would cover up at the relay-point, she stripped completely, untying the string and removing her shirt in such feverish haste that she would have torn her skin off, too, had she been able. Now completely naked and pitifully reduced to the level of an animal padding along a muddy path in search of food, she went about her work, her buttocks splattered in soot and her front covered in grime up to her belly, like a filth-covered mare between the shafts of a hansom cab. She was pushing the tub on all fours.

But she began to despair: being naked brought no relief. What else could she remove? The buzzing in her ears was deafening, and she felt as though her temples were caught in a vice. She slumped to her knees. She had the impression that her lamp, wedged into the coal on the tub, was about to go out; and in her confused mind she clung to the thought that she must turn up the wick. Twice she tried to examine the lamp, and twice, as she set it on the ground in front of her, it dimmed as if it, too, were wanting for oxygen. Suddenly the lamp went out. Then everything began to spin in the darkness, a millstone was whirring round in her head, and her heart slowed and stopped, numbed by the immense torpor that had overtaken her limbs. She had fallen backwards and lay dying on the ground in the asphyxiating air.

'Damn me if she's not bloodly dawdling again!' grumbled Chaval.

He listened from the top of the coal-face but heard no sound of wheels.

'Catherine! I know you, you sly bitch!'

The sound of his voice vanished down the dark roadway, and not a breath could be heard in response.

'Have I got to come and chase after you?'

Nothing stirred, and there was still the same deathly silence. Furious, he climbed down and began to run along the road, holding up his lamp but going so fast that he nearly tripped over Catherine's body, which was blocking the way. He stared at it open-mouthed. What was the matter with her? She wasn't pretending, was she, just so she could have a quick nap? But when he lowered his lamp to shine it in her face, it threatened to go out. He raised it and lowered it again, and finally he realized: the air must be bad. His rage had subsided, and the miner's instinctive devotion to a comrade in danger took over. Already he had shouted for someone to bring his shirt, and now he seized the girl's naked, lifeless body and lifted it as high as he possibly could. Once they had thrown his and Catherine's clothes over his shoulders, he set off at the run, holding his burden up with one hand and carrying their two lamps with the other. The long roadways unwound as he raced ahead, taking a right here, a left there, searching for the cold, life-giving air of the plain coming from the ventilator. At length the sound of a spring brought him to a halt: some water was streaming through a crack in the rock. He found himself at a crossroads in the main haulage roadway which had once served Gaston-Marie. Here the ventilator was blowing up a storm, and the air was so cold that he even shivered after setting Catherine down on the ground, propped against some timbers. Her eyes were shut, and she was still unconscious.

'Come on, Catherine. For God's sake, a joke's a joke ... Here, don't you move while I go and dip this in a bit of water.'

It frightened him to see her so limp. Nevertheless he was able to wet his shirt in the stream and bathe her face. She seemed for all the world to be dead, as though this slight, girlish body on which puberty was hesitating to place its mark were down here because it had already been buried. Then a shudder ran through her, through her undeveloped breasts and her belly down to the slender thighs of this poor, wretched girl who had been deflowered before her time. She opened her eyes and muttered:

'I'm cold.'

'Ah, that's better! That's more like it!' Chaval exclaimed with relief.

He dressed her, passing the shirt easily over her head but cursing as he struggled to get her trousers on, for she could do little to help herself. Still dazed, she did not understand where she was nor why she had been naked. When she remembered, she was filled with shame. How on earth had she dared take everything off! She questioned Chaval: had anyone seen her like that, without so much as a neckerchief round her waist to cover her? Being fond of a laugh and given to making up stories, he told her how their comrades had all stood in a line as he brought her past. And what had possessed her to take him seriously when he'd told her to take her clothes off! Then he gave her his word that he had carried her there so fast that his comrades could not even have known whether her bum was round or square!

'Blimey but it's cold,' he said, as he too got dressed again.

She had never known him be so nice. Usually for every kind word he spoke to her, she got two insults as well. How good it would have been to live in harmony together! In her state of exhausted lassitude she felt a warm fondness for him. She smiled and said softly:

'Give me a kiss.'

He kissed her and lay down beside her to wait until she was ready to walk.

'You know,' she said, 'you were wrong to shout at me back there, because I just couldn't go on any more. Even at the face it's cooler. But if you knew how baking hot it is along at the other end of the road!'

'I know,' he replied. 'We'd be better off under the trees . . . But you, poor girl, it's difficult for you working this section. I can see that.'

She was so touched to hear him agree that she put on a show of bravery.

'Oh, I just had a weak turn. Anyway the air's bad today . . . But you'll soon see if I'm a sly one or not. If you've got to work, you've got to work. Isn't that right? I'd rather die than not do my fair share.'

There was silence. He had his arm round her waist, holding her to his chest so that no harm should come to her. And while she already felt strong enough to return to the coal-face, she preferred to revel in the moment.

'Only I wish,' she went on very quietly, 'that you could be kinder to me . . . If people can just love each other a little bit, they can be so happy.'

And she began to cry softly.

'But I do love you,' he protested, 'or I wouldn't have taken
you to live with me.'

She simply nodded. Often men took women just so that they
could have them for themselves, not caring a button whether
they were happy or not. Her tears were flowing more hotly now
as she thought with despair of the good life she could have had
if she had ended up with someone else, someone who would
always have had his arm round her waist like this. Someone
else? And dimly she could perceive this person in the midst of
her distress. But that was finished and done with now, and all
she wanted was to be able to spend her life with the man she
was with, just as long as he didn't always treat her so roughly.

'Well then,' she said, 'just try sometimes to be like you are now.'

Her sobbing stopped her from saying more, and he kissed
her again.

'You silly thing! . . . Look, I promise to be nice to you.
Anyway, it's not as if I'm any worse than the next man.'

She looked at him and began to smile again through her tears.
Perhaps he was right: you didn't come across many happy
women. Then, although she only half believed his promise, she
gave herself up to the joy of seeing him be nice to her. My God,
if only it could have lasted! They were now in each other's arms
again; and while they were still holding each other in one long
embrace, the sound of approaching footsteps brought them
quickly to their feet. Three comrades who had seen them go
past were coming to see if they were all right.

They all set off together. It was nearly ten o'clock, and they
chose a cool spot to eat their lunch before going back to the
sweltering heat at the coal-face. But just as they were finishing
their sandwiches and about to take a swig of coffee from their
flasks, they were alarmed by the sound of voices coming from
far off in the mine. What could it be? Had there been another
accident? They got to their feet and ran to find out. Hewers,
putters and pit-boys were streaming past in the opposite direction, but nobody knew anything; everyone was shouting, it must
be some terrible disaster. Panic was gradually beginning to
spread throughout the mine, and shadowy figures emerged
terrified from the roadways, their lamps bobbing into view

before disappearing again into the darkness. Where was it? Why wouldn't anyone say?

Suddenly a deputy rushed past shouting:

'They're cutting the cables! They're cutting the cables!'

Then the panic took hold, and people were rushing madly along the dark roads. Everyone was completely bewildered. Why would anyone cut the cables? And who was cutting them, when there were workers still below? It seemed monstrous.

But the voice of another deputy rang out before it, too, vanished.

'The Montsou crowd are cutting the cables! Everybody out!'

When he had grasped what was happening, Chaval stopped Catherine dead. His legs had gone quite weak at the thought that they might encounter the Montsou men if they went up. So they had come after all then, and there was he thinking they'd been stopped by the gendarmes! For a moment he thought of retracing their steps and going back up via Gaston-Marie; but that shaft was no longer in working order. He cursed, not knowing what to do, and trying to hide his fear, and he kept saying that there was no point running so fast. People were hardly going to leave them down here.

The deputy's voice could be heard again, getting closer.

'Everybody out. Use the ladders! Use the ladders!'

And so Chaval was swept along by his comrades. He started bullying Catherine, accusing her of not running fast enough. Did she want them to be left behind in the mine so that they could starve to death? Because those Montsou bastards were quite capable of smashing the ladders before everyone had got out. The voicing of this terrible possibility proved to be the last straw, and everyone around them began to career wildly along the roadways in a mad race to see who could get to the ladders first and go up before the others. Men were shouting that the ladders had already been smashed and that nobody would get out. And when groups of terrified people started pouring into pit-bottom there was a wholesale rush for the ladders, with everyone trying to squeeze through the narrow door to the emergency shaft all at the same time. Meanwhile an old stable-man who had wisely just led the horses back to their stall looked on with the contemptuous indifference of one who was used to spending his nights down the pit and was quite certain that some way would always be found to get him out.

'For Christ's sake, would you go in front of me!' Chaval shouted at Catherine. 'At least that way I can catch you if you fall.'

Dazed and completely out of breath after this three-kilometre dash, which had once more soaked her in sweat, Catherine allowed herself to be swept along by the crowd, oblivious to what was happening. Then Chaval tugged her arm so hard he nearly broke it, and she let out a cry of pain and began to cry. He had forgotten his promise already, she would never be happy.

'You must go first!' he screamed at her.

But she was too frightened of him. If she went first, he would keep pushing and shoving her all the time. So she resisted, and their comrades pushed them aside in their mad rush. The water that seeped into the shaft was falling in large drops, and the floor of pit-bottom, suspended above the *bougnou*, a muddy pit some ten metres deep, was vibrating under the weight of all these trampling feet. And it was indeed at Jean-Bart that there had been a terrible accident two years previously when a cable had snapped and sent a cage hurtling down into the sump, drowning two men. Everybody remembered and was thinking that they might all end up down there if too many people crowded on to the floor at once.

'Bugger it, then!' Chaval shouted. 'Die if you want to. And good riddance!'

He began climbing, and she followed.

From bottom to top there were one hundred and two ladders, each approximately seven metres long and standing on a narrow platform that filled the width of the shaft. A square hole in each landing was just wide enough to let a man's shoulders through. It was like a squashed chimney some seven hundred metres high, between the outer wall of the main shaft and the lining of the winding-shaft, a damp, dark, endless tube in which the ladders stood almost vertically one above the other at regular intervals. It took a strong man twenty-five minutes to climb this giant column, though in fact it was used only in emergencies.

At first Catherine climbed cheerfully enough. Her bare feet were used to the sharpness of the coal along the roadway floors, and so the protective iron edging on the square rungs did not bother her. Her hands, hardened by pushing tubs, grasped the uprights easily enough even though they were too thick for her grip. Indeed this unexpected climb helped to occupy her mind and to take her out of her misery, as she became one of a long, snaking line of people coiling and hoisting its way upwards, three to a ladder, so long a line indeed that the head of the snake would emerge at the top while the tail was still dragging over the sump at the bottom. But they were not there yet, and the people at the top could scarcely have reached a third of the way up. Nobody was talking now, and the only sound was the dull rumble and thud of feet; and the lamps spaced out at regular intervals looked like an unravelling string of wandering stars.

Behind her Catherine heard a pit-boy counting the ladders, which made her want to count them too. They had already climbed fifteen, and they were coming to a loading-bay. But just at that moment she bumped into Chaval's legs. He swore and told her to be more careful. One by one, the whole column of people slowed to a halt. What now? What had happened? Everyone found their voices again and started asking frightened questions. Their anxiety had been increasing ever since they had left the bottom, and the closer they drew to the daylight the more they were gripped by fear about what would happen to them once they reached the surface. Someone said they had to go back down, the ladders were broken. This was what everyone had been afraid of, that they might find themselves marooned in the void. Another explanation was passed down from mouth to mouth: a hewer had slipped and fallen from a ladder. Nobody knew what to believe, and the shouting prevented them from hearing properly. Were they all going to spend the night there? Eventually, without them being any the wiser, they began to climb again, in the same slow, laborious way as before, amid the rumble of feet and the bobbing of lamps. No doubt the broken ladders were further up!

By the thirty-second ladder, as they were passing a third loading-bay, Catherine felt her arms and legs grow stiff. At first she had sensed a slight prickling of the skin. Now she could no longer feel the wood and metal beneath her hands and feet. Her muscles ached, and the pain, slight at first, was gradually becoming more acute. In her dazed state she remembered Grandpa Bonnemort's stories about the days when there was no proper ladder shaft and girls of ten would carry the coal up on their shoulders by means of ladders that were completely unprotected and simply placed against the wall of the shaft; so that when one of them slipped or even a piece of coal just fell out of a basket, three or four children would be sent flying, head first. The cramp was becoming unbearable, she would never make it to the top.

Further delays allowed her some respite. But these repeated waves of panic passing down the ladders eventually made her dizzy. Above and below her she could hear that people were having increasing difficulty in breathing: the interminable ascent was beginning to make them giddy, and like everyone else she wanted to be sick. Fighting for air, she felt almost drunk on the darkness, and the walls of the shaft seemed to press maddeningly against her flesh. The wet conditions made her shiver, as large drops of water fell on her sweat-drenched body. They were nearing the water table, and the water was raining down so heavily that it threatened to put out the lamps.

Twice Chaval asked Catherine a question but received no reply. What was she up to down there? Had she lost her tongue? She could at least tell him if she was all right. They had been climbing for half an hour now, but so laboriously that they had reached only the fifty-ninth ladder. Forty-three to go. Catherine eventually gasped that she was just about managing. He would have called her a lazy bitch again if she had told him how exhausted she was. The iron on the rungs must be biting into her feet, because she felt as though they were being sawn through to the bone. Each time she moved her hands up the ladder she expected to see them lose their grip and come away so raw and stiff that she could no longer clench her fingers; and she felt as though she were falling backwards, as though her arms and hips had been wrenched from their sockets by the constant effort. What she found most difficult was the lack of angle on the ladders, the fact that they were almost vertical and that she had to pull herself up by her wrists with her stomach pressed hard against the wood. The sound of people gasping for breath now drowned out the tramping of feet; and a vast wheezing, made ten times louder by the partitioning of the shaft, rose from the bottom and died away at the top. There was a groan of pain, then word came down that a pit-boy had cracked his head underneath one of the platform landings.

And up Catherine went. They passed the water-table. The deluge had ceased, and now the cellar-like air was thick with mist and the musty stench of old iron and rotting wood. She persisted in counting quietly and mechanically to herself under her breath: eighty-one, eighty-two, eighty-three, nineteen to go. Only the steady rhythm of the repeated numbers kept her going, for she had ceased to be conscious of her movements. When she looked up, the lamps spiralled into the distance. Her blood was draining away, and she felt as though she were dying, as though the merest draught would send her flying. The worst of it was that people were now pushing and shoving their way up from below, and the whole column was on the stampede, yielding in its exhaustion to growing anger and a desperate need to see daylight again. The first comrades were out of the shaft, so no ladders had been smashed; but the thought that they still could be – to prevent the remainder from getting out while others were already up there breathing the fresh air – was enough to drive them into a frenzy. And when there was a further hold-up, people started cursing and continued to climb anyway, elbowing others aside or clambering over them in a general free-for-all.

Then Catherine fell. She had shouted out Chaval's name in one last desperate appeal. He didn't hear her, he was too busy fighting and kicking a comrade's ribs with his heels to make sure he stayed ahead of him. She was trodden underfoot. In her unconscious state she dreamed that she was one of the young putters from long ago and that a piece of coal had dropped out of a basket above her and pitched her into the shaft like a sparrow felled by a stone. Only five ladders remained to be climbed, and so far it had taken them nearly an hour. She had no memory of how she reached the surface, borne aloft on people's shoulders and prevented from falling only by the narrowness of the shaft. Suddenly she found herself in the blinding sunlight surrounded by a noisy crowd of people who were all jeering at her.

III

That morning, since before daybreak, there had been a stirring in the villages, a stirring which was now growing and spreading along the highways and byways of the entire region. But the miners had not been able to set out as planned because it was rumoured that the plain was being patrolled by dragoons and gendarmes. It was said that they had arrived from Douai during the night, and some accused Rasseneur of having betrayed the comrades by warning M. Hennebeau; one putter even swore blind that she had seen his servant taking the message to the telegraph office. The miners clenched their fists and watched out for the soldiers behind their shutters in the pale light of dawn.

At about seven-thirty, as the sun was rising, another rumour circulated, which reassured the impatient. It had been a false alarm, simply a military exercise of the kind that the general had occasionally ordered during the strike at the request of the Prefect in Lille. The strikers hated this particular official, whom they accused of having double-crossed them by promising to act as a go-between, when in fact all he had done was to parade troops through Montsou every week to keep the miners in their place. So when the dragoons and gendarmes quietly departed in the direction of Marchiennes, having been content to deafen every village with the noise of their horses trotting past on the hard ground, the miners scoffed at this naïve Prefect whose troops took to their heels the moment things looked like hotting up. Until nine o'clock they stood around in front of their houses, as cheerful and peaceful as can be, watching until the back of the last harmless gendarme disappeared down the road. Meanwhile the bourgeois of Montsou remained safely tucked up in their warm beds. At the manager's house Mme Hennebeau had just been seen leaving in her carriage, presumably having left M. Hennebeau at work, for the place was all shut up and silent, seemingly deserted. Not a single pit was under armed guard, which demonstrated a fatal lack of foresight at this perilous moment and just the sort of natural stupidity that occurs at times of impending disaster, the very thing a government fails to think of when it needs to be paying attention to the practicalities of the situation. And nine o'clock was striking when the colliers finally set out along the Vandame road for the meeting-place that had been agreed on the previous evening in the forest.

In any case Étienne realized at once that he was not going to get the three thousand comrades at Jean-Bart he had been counting on. Many people thought that the demonstration had been postponed, but the worst of it was that two or three groups of men were already on their way and would compromise the cause if, like it or not, he wasn't there to lead them. Nearly a hundred had left before daybreak and had presumably taken shelter in the forest under the beech trees while they waited for everyone else. Étienne went up to consult Souvarine, who merely shrugged: ten good strong men and true could achieve more than a mob; and he went back to reading his book, having declined to take any part in the proceedings. There would be more sentimental nonsense no doubt, whereas all that was needed was to set fire to Montsou, which was a perfectly straightforward matter. As Étienne left the house by the front path, he saw a pale Rasseneur sitting by the stove while his wife, looking taller than she was because of her perennial black dress, was firmly and politely giving him a piece of her mind.

Maheu thought that they ought to keep their word. An appointed meeting of this sort was sacrosanct. Nevertheless a night's sleep had calmed everyone down; he himself was afraid that something bad might happen, and he argued that it was their duty to turn up and make sure that the comrades remained within the law. La Maheude nodded in agreement. Étienne kept complacently insisting that they must act in a revolutionary manner but without threatening anyone's life. Before leaving he refused his share in a loaf of bread he had been given the night before, along with a bottle of gin; but he did drink three quick tots, just to keep out the cold, and even took a full flask of it with him. Alzire would look after the little ones. Old Bonnemort's invalid legs were feeling the effects of last night's exertions, and he had remained in bed.

They thought it wiser not to leave together. Jeanlin was long gone. Maheu and La Maheude went in one direction, heading for Montsou by an indirect route, while Étienne made for the forest, where he expected to join his comrades. On the way he caught up with a party of women, among whom he recognized La Brûlé and La Levaque: as they walked along, they were eating some chestnuts which La Mouquette had brought them, and swallowing the husks so that they stayed down better. But Étienne found no one in the forest, the comrades were already at Jean-Bart. So he started running and reached the pit just as Levaque and a hundred others entered the yard. Miners were straggling in from every direction, the Maheus by the main road, the women from across the fields, all of them unarmed and leaderless, gravitating there naturally like a stream overflowing down a slope. Étienne spotted Jeanlin perched up on a gangway as though he were waiting for the show to begin. He quickened his pace and entered the yard with the leading group. There were barely three hundred of them altogether.

The men faltered when Deneulin appeared at the top of the steps leading to the pit-head.

'What do you want?' he asked loudly.

Having seen the carriage depart with his daughters gaily bidding him farewell, he had returned to the pit, filled with renewed unease. Yet everything seemed to be in order: the workers had gone down, the extraction of coal was proceeding, and he was beginning to take heart once more as he chatted with the overman when someone told him about the approaching strikers. He had at once taken up a position by the window in the screening-shed; and as the swelling crowd poured into the yard, he was immediately aware of his powerlessness. How could he defend these buildings that were open on all sides to anyone who cared to enter? He could barely have mustered twenty workers to protect him. He was lost.

'What do you want?' he asked again, pale with suppressed anger and trying hard to put a brave face on his defeat.

There was jostling and muttering among the crowd. Eventually Étienne stepped forward and said:

'We mean you no harm, sir. But all work must stop.'

Deneulin replied to him as if he were quite clearly an idiot.

'What good do you think you'll do by stopping work here? You might as well shoot me in the back, point blank . . . Yes, my men are below, and they're not coming up unless you kill me first.'

This plain speaking caused an uproar. Maheu had to restrain Levaque, who lunged forward with a menacing air, while Étienne continued to parley, trying to convince Deneulin of the legitimacy of their revolutionary action. But the latter's response was that everyone had the right to work. And anyway he wasn't about to discuss such nonsense, he intended to be the master on his own premises. His only regret was that he didn't have four gendarmes there to rid him of this riff-raff.

'Of course, I can see it's my own fault. I deserve what I get. Force is the only way with fellows like you. It's the same with the government. It thinks it can buy you off with concessions, but you'll simply shoot it dead the moment it gives you the arms.'

Étienne was shaking but still managing to restrain himself. He lowered his voice:

'I would ask you, sir, to order your men up. I cannot answer for what my comrades may do. You have it in your power to avoid a disaster.'

'No. You can go to hell! Anyway, who are you? You're not one of my men, you've no business with me . . . And the whole lot of you are no better than thieves and bandits, rampaging round the countryside like this robbing people of their property.'

His voice was now drowned by shouting, and the women in particular hurled insults at him. But he continued to hold firm, and it was a relief to be able to speak his authoritarian mind so frankly. Since he was ruined whatever happened, he considered it cowardly to engage in useless platitudes. But the numbers were continually growing, there were now nearly five hundred

miners advancing towards the door, and he was just about to
be set upon when his overman dragged him back.

'For pity's sake, sir! . . . There'll be a wholesale massacre.
There's no point getting men killed for nothing.'

Deneulin refused to give in, and he flung one last protest at
the crowd.

'You're just a bunch of common criminals. But you'll see. Just
you wait till we've got the upper hand again!'

He was led away: the crowd had surged forward, pressing the
people at the front against the stairway and bending the hand-
rail. It was the women pushing from behind, goading the men
with their shrill cries. The door, which had no lock and was
simply fastened with a latch, gave way immediately. But the
stairway was too narrow, and in the crush people would have
taken for ever to get in if the rest of the assailants had not
decided to seek out other means of entrance. And in they poured,
through the changing-room, through the screening-shed,
through the boiler-house. In less than five minutes the entire pit
was theirs, and they ran about the place on all three floors
shouting and gesticulating, completely carried away by this
victory over a boss who had tried to stand in their way.

Maheu, horrified, had rushed off with the first group, calling
to Étienne:

'They mustn't kill him.'

Étienne was already running, too; but when he realized that
Deneulin had barricaded himself in the deputies' room, he
shouted back:

'So what if they do? It would hardly be our fault! The man's
off his head!'

Nevertheless he was very worried and as yet too self-possessed
to yield to such mass violence. Also his pride as a leader had
been hurt by the way the mob had escaped his control and were
running wild like this rather than coolly carrying out the will of
the people in the manner he had expected. He called in vain for
calm, shouting that they mustn't put their enemies in the right
by engaging in senseless destruction.

'The boilers!' La Brûlé was screaming. 'Let's put out the fires.'

Levaque had found an iron-file, which he was brandishing like a dagger, and his terrible cry rang out over the tumult:

'Cut the cables! Cut the cables!'

Soon everybody was repeating this; only Étienne and Maheu continued to protest, trying desperately to make themselves heard above the racket but quite unable to obtain silence. Finally Étienne managed to say:

'But, comrades, there are men down there!'

The racket grew even louder, and voices could be heard coming from all directions:

'Too bad! They shouldn't have gone down in the first place! . . . Serves the scabs right! . . . Let them stay there! . . . Anyway, they've always got the ladders!'

When they remembered the ladders, everyone became even more determined, and Étienne realized that he would have to give way. Fearing an even worse disaster, he rushed towards the engine-house in the hope of at least being able to bring the cages up, so that if the cables were severed above the shaft, they wouldn't smash the cages to pieces with their enormous weight when they fell on top of them. The mechanic in charge of it had disappeared along with the few other surface workers, and so Étienne grabbed the starting lever and pulled it while Levaque and two other men clambered up the iron framework that supported the pulleys. The cages had scarcely been locked into their keeps before the rasping sound of the file could be heard as it bit through the steel. There was total silence, and the sound seemed to fill the entire pit; everyone looked up in tense anticipation to watch and listen. Standing in the front row Maheu felt a surge of wild joy run through him, as though the blade of the file would deliver them all from evil by eating through the cable: this would be one miserable hole in the ground they would never have to go down again.

But La Brûlé had disappeared down the steps into the changing-room, still screaming at the top of her voice:

'Let's put out the fires! To the boilers! To the boilers!'

Other women followed her. La Maheude hurried to stop them wrecking everything, just as her husband had tried to reason

with the comrades. She was the calmest person present: they
could demand their rights without destroying people's property.
When she entered the boiler-room, the women were already
chasing the two stokers out, and La Brûlé, armed with a large
shovel, was squatting in front of one of the boilers and emptying
it as fast as she could, throwing the red-hot coal on to the brick
floor, where it continued to smoulder. There were ten fire-grates
for five boilers. Soon all the women had set to, La Levaque with
both hands on her shovel, La Mouquette hoisting her skirts so
that she didn't catch fire, all of them dishevelled and covered in
sweat, and all bathed in the blood-red glow coming from the
fires of this witches' sabbath. As the burning embers were piled
higher and higher, the fierce heat began to crack the ceiling of
the vast room.

'Stop!' cried La Maheude. 'The storeroom's on fire.'

'So much the better!' answered La Brûlé. 'That'll save us the
bother . . . By God, I always said I'd make them pay for my old
man's death!'

At that moment they heard the high-pitched voice of Jeanlin.

'Watch out! I'll soon see to those fires! Here goes!'

Having been one of the first in, he had been darting about in
the crowd, delighted by the free-for-all and looking for mischief.
That was when he had the idea of opening the steam-cocks and
releasing all the steam. Jets escaped like gunshot, and the five
boilers blew themselves out like hurricanes, their thunderous
hissing loud enough to burst an eardrum. Everything had disappeared in a cloud of steam, the burning coal paled, and the
women were like ghosts gesturing wearily through the haze.
Only Jeanlin was visible, up in the gallery behind the billowing
clouds of white mist, a look of sheer delight on his face, his
mouth gaping with joy at having unleashed this tempest.

All this lasted nearly a quarter of an hour. People had thrown
buckets of water on to the heaps of coal, finally putting them
out; all danger of the building catching fire had been averted.
But the anger of the crowd had not abated, on the contrary it
had been whipped to a new frenzy. Men were descending into
the mine with hammers in their hands, even the women armed
themselves with iron bars; and there was talk of puncturing

the boilers and smashing the machines, of demolishing the whole mine.

When Étienne was told this, he hurried to the scene with Maheu. Even he was in a state of high excitement, carried away by this feverish thirst for revenge. Nevertheless he did what he could to persuade everyone to calm down, now that the cables had been cut and the fires put out and the boilers emptied of steam, making all further work impossible. But still they refused to listen, and he was about to be overridden once again when booing could be heard outside, coming from beside a small, low door which was the entrance to the emergency ladder shaft.

'Down with scabs! . . . Look at the filthy cowards! . . . Down with scabs!'

Those who had been working underground were beginning to emerge. The first ones stood there blinking, blinded by the daylight. Then they walked past, one by one, hoping to reach the road and make a run for it.

'Down with scabs! Down with false friends!'

The whole crowd of strikers had come running. In less than three minutes there wasn't a soul left inside, and the five hundred men from Montsou lined up in two rows opposite each other, forcing the Vandame miners who had betrayed them by working to run the gauntlet between them. And as each new miner appeared at the door of the shaft, his clothes in tatters and covered in the black mud of his labour, he was met by renewed booing and savage ribaldry. Here, look at him, the short-arse runt! And him! The tarts at the Volcano must have done for his nose. And just look at the wax coming out of that man's ears! You could light a cathedral with that lot! And that tall one with no bum on him and a face as long as Lent! A putter rolled out of the door, so fat that her breasts, her stomach and her backside all merged into one, and she was met by a storm of laughter. Could they have a feel? Then the jokes turned nasty, cruel even, and fists were about to fly. Meanwhile the rest of the poor devils continued to file past, shivering and silent amid all the insults, throwing anxious sideways glances in case they were about to be hit, and relieved when they were finally able to run away from the pit.

'Just look at them! How many of them are there in there?' asked Étienne.

He was surprised to see people still coming out, and it irritated him to think that it wasn't just a case of a few workers who had been driven to it by hunger or by sheer terror of the deputies. So had they lied to him in the forest? Almost the whole of Jean-Bart had gone down. But he gave an involuntary cry and rushed forward when he caught sight of Chaval standing in the doorway.

'In God's name, is this what you call meeting up?'

People started cursing, and some wanted to jump on the traitor. What was going on? He had taken a solemn oath with them the night before, and here he was going down the mine with everyone else! Was this some sort of bloody joke?

'Take him away. Throw him down the pit.'

Chaval, white with fear, was desperately trying to stammer out an explanation. But Étienne cut him short, beside himself with anger, and quite taken up by the general fury.

'You wanted to join us, and join us you bloody well will . . . Come on, you bastard. Off we go, left, right, left, right.'

His voice was drowned by a fresh clamour. Catherine herself had just appeared, dazzled by the bright sunshine and terrified to find herself surrounded by these savages. As she stood there trying to catch her breath, her hands bleeding and her legs about to give way beneath her after climbing those hundred and two ladders, La Maheude saw her and ran forward with her arm raised.

'You too, you little bitch? . . . Your own mother is dying of hunger, and you go and betray her for that pimp of yours!'

Maheu caught her arm and prevented the blow. But he started shaking his daughter and, like his wife, reproaching her furiously for how she had behaved. They had both lost control and were screaming wildly above the noise of their comrades.

The sight of Catherine had been the final straw for Étienne.

'Come on!' he kept insisting. 'Let's go to the other pits! And as for you, you filthy bastard, you're coming with us!'

Chaval scarcely had time to fetch his clogs from the changing-room and to throw his jersey round his freezing shoulders. They dragged him away with them, forcing him to run along in their midst. Distraught, Catherine also put her clogs back on and buttoned up the old jacket, a man's one, which she had been wearing since the weather turned cold; and she hurried along behind her man, not wanting to let him out of her sight, for they were surely going to slaughter him.

Jean-Bart emptied in two minutes. Jeanlin had found a horn and was blowing it raucously as though he were rounding up cattle. The women, La Brûlé, La Levaque, La Mouquette, all gathered up their skirts in order to run better, while Levaque twirled an axe about as though it were a drum-major's baton. Other comrades were still arriving, and there was nearly a thousand of them now, a disorderly rabble that flowed out on to the road like a river in spate. The exit was too narrow, and fences were smashed.

'To the pits! Let's get the scabs! No more work!'

And suddenly Jean-Bart fell completely silent. Not a worker to be seen, not a breath to be heard. Deneulin came out of the deputies' room and, all alone, gesturing that no one should follow, he went round inspecting the pit. He was pale and very calm. First he stopped at the shaft and looked up at the severed cables: the steel strands dangled uselessly in the air, and he could see where the file had left its wound, a gleaming sore surrounded by black grease. Then he went up to the winding-gear and stared at the motionless crank-rod, which looked like the joint of some colossal limb that had been suddenly paralysed; he felt the metal, which had already cooled, and its cold touch made him shiver as though he had laid his hand on a corpse. Then he went down to the boilers, where he walked slowly along the line of extinguished fire-grates, now wide open and flooded, and he tapped his foot against the boilers, which sounded hollow. Well, this was it. His ruin was complete. Even if he mended the cables and relit the fires, where would he find the men? Another two weeks of the strike and he was bankrupt. And in the certain prospect of this disaster he no longer felt hatred towards these bandits from Montsou but rather a kind of complicity, as though together they were all expiating the one same everlasting and universal sin. Animals no doubt they were, but animals who could not read and who were starving to death.

IV

And so, out on the open plain that lay white with frost beneath the pale winter sun, the mob departed along the road, spilling out on both sides into the fields of beet.

By the time they had reached La Fourche-aux-Bœufs, Étienne had taken charge. Without interrupting their advance, he shouted out commands and organized the march. Jeanlin raced along in front, playing barbarous tunes on his horn. Then came the women, in rows, some armed with sticks: La Maheude had a wild look in her eye, as though she were straining to catch a distant glimpse of the promised land of justice, while La Brûlé, La Levaque and La Mouquette strode out in their tattered skirts like soldiers marching off to war. If they ran into any opposition, they'd soon see if the gendarmes would dare to hit a woman. The men followed, a disorderly herd that spread wider and wider as it stretched away into the distance: and among the forest of crowbars Levaque's solitary axe stood out, its blade glinting in the sunlight. Étienne, in the middle, was keeping an eye on Chaval, whom he made walk in front of him; while behind him Maheu looked thunderous and kept casting dirty looks at Catherine, who was the only woman back here among the men and who had insisted on running along beside her lover to prevent any harm coming to him. Some were without caps, their hair tousled by the breeze; and apart from the wild blasts of Jeanlin's horn all that could be heard was the clatter of clogs, which sounded like cattle stampeding.

But all at once a new cry rang out.

'We want bread! We want bread!'[1]

It was midday: the hunger consequent on six weeks of strike was gnawing at empty bellies, and appetites had been whetted by all this rushing about the countryside. The odd crust eaten that morning and the few chestnuts brought by La Mouquette were already a distant memory; stomachs were crying out to be fed, and the pain of it added to their fury against the traitors.

'To the pits! Everybody out! We want bread!'

Étienne, who had earlier refused his share of food in the village, felt an unbearable wrenching sensation in his chest. He said nothing, but every so often he would automatically raise his flask to his lips and take a mouthful of gin: he felt so shaky that he had convinced himself he needed it if he were to carry on. His cheeks were burning, and a fire shone in his eyes. Nevertheless he continued to keep his head, and he was still determined to try and prevent pointless destruction.

When they reached the Joiselle road, a hewer from Vandame who had joined the mob to get his own back on his boss screamed to the comrades to turn right:

'Let's go to Gaston-Marie! We'll stop the pump and flood Jean-Bart!'

The crowd, easily led, was already turning, even though Étienne protested and begged them not to stop the drainage. What was the point of destroying the roadways? Despite all his grievances it offended the workman in him. Maheu, too, thought it not right to vent anger on a machine. But the hewer continued to call for vengeance, and Étienne had to shout even louder:

'Let's go to Mirou. There are still scabs down there . . . Mirou! Mirou!'

With a sweep of his arm he had steered the mob on to the road that led off to the left, while Jeanlin resumed his position at the head and blew even harder on his horn. There was a great commotion and, for the time being, Gaston-Marie was saved.

They covered the four kilometres to Mirou in half an hour, proceeding almost at the double over the boundless plain. On this side the canal cut across it like a long ribbon of ice; and only the bare trees along its banks, looking like giant candelabras in the frost, interrupted the flat monotony of the landscape as it stretched away into the distance and eventually merged with the sky like a sea. A slight undulation in the terrain hid Montsou and Marchiennes from view, leaving nothing but a vast featureless space.

As they reached the pit, they saw a deputy take up position on the overhead railway next to the screening-shed, waiting for them. Everybody recognized Quandieu, who was the senior deputy in Montsou, an old man getting on for seventy, whose hair and skin were white and who was still in quite miraculously good health for a miner.

'What the bloody hell do you lot want,' he shouted, 'wandering about the countryside like this?'

The mob came to a halt. They were no longer dealing with a boss but a comrade, and their respect for the old worker gave them pause.

'There are men below,' Étienne said. 'Tell them to come up.'

'Yes, there are! A good six dozen,' Quandieu replied. 'Everyone else is too scared of you, you buggers! . . . But I can tell you here and now, not one of them is coming up, or you'll have me to answer to!'

People started shouting; the men jostled, and the women stepped forward. The deputy quickly came down from the railway and blocked their path to the door.

Maheu tried to intervene.

'Come on, mate, we're within our rights. How are we going to have a general strike if we can't force the comrades to join us?'

The old man was silent for a moment. Plainly his ignorance of the procedures of joint action was as great as Maheu's. Finally he replied:

'Within your rights? That's as may be. But I have my orders, and there's only me here. The men are down there till three, and till three they'll stay.'

His last few words were lost amid the booing. Fists were raised, and already the women were screaming at him, so that he could feel their hot breath on his face. But he stood his ground, his head held high, with his snow-white hair and little pointed beard; and courage lent such power to his voice that he could be heard quite clearly above the din.

'As God is my witness, you shall not pass! . . . As sure as night follows day, I'd rather die than have you lay a finger on those cables . . . So stop your pushing and shoving, or I'll throw myself down the shaft here and now!'

This caused a great stir, and the crowd drew back in shocked amazement. He continued:

'And which bastard among you doesn't understand that? . . . I'm just a worker, the same as the rest of you. I've been told to guard the place, and guard it I will.'

And this was the limit of Quandieu's logic as, with a soldier's sense of duty, he refused to yield, standing there with his narrow head and his eyes that had been dimmed by the gloomy darkness of half a century spent working underground. The comrades gazed at him, moved by what he said, for somewhere within them this soldierly obedience, this sense of brotherhood and resigned acceptance in the face of danger, had struck a chord. Thinking them not yet persuaded, he insisted:

'I will! I'll throw myself down the shaft here and now!'

The mob reacted as one: everybody wheeled round and made off down the road to the right, racing away across the country-side and into the distance. Once more the cries went up:

'To Madeleine! And Crèvecœur! Everybody out! We want bread! We want bread!'

But in the middle of this onward rush a scuffle had broken out. Chaval had evidently tried to take advantage of the situation and escape, for Étienne had just grabbed him by the arm and was threatening to beat the daylights out of him if he so much as tried anything. Chaval, meanwhile, was struggling to get free and protesting furiously:

'What the hell is this? It's a free country, isn't it? I've been freezing to death for the last hour, and I need a wash. Let go of me!'

It was true that sweat had glued the coal-dust to his skin, which was becoming quite painful, and his jersey afforded little protection against the elements.

'Keep moving, or you'll soon see what sort of a wash you get,' Étienne replied. 'This'll teach you to go round stirring things.'

On they raced, and eventually Étienne looked round to find Catherine, who was still keeping up. It pained him to sense her close by and to know that she was in a wretched state, shivering from the cold in her scruffy man's jacket and her muddy trousers. She must have been fit to drop, and yet still she kept on running.

'It's all right. You can go,' he said finally.

Catherine appeared not to hear. But her eyes met Étienne's and shot him a brief look of reproach. And on she ran. Why did he want her to abandon her man? True, Chaval had hardly been very kind to her; in fact sometimes he beat her. But he was her man, the one who had had her first; and it made her furious to see them all ganging up on him like this, a thousand against one. She would have defended him if she'd had to, not from love but as a matter of pride.

'Clear off!' Maheu insisted vehemently.

This order from her father slowed her for a moment. She was trembling, and tears welled in her eyes. But despite her fear she caught up again and continued to run with them. After that they let her be.

The mob crossed the Joiselle road and then briefly made for Cron before heading up towards Cougny. Here factory chimneys stood like stripes across the flat horizon, and the road was lined with wooden sheds and brick-built workshops with wide, dusty windows. They raced through Villages One Hundred and Eighty and Seventy-Six one after the other, in quick succession, past the tiny houses; and in both villages the noise of their shouting and the clarion calls of the horn brought whole families out to see, men, women and children, who started running also, joining on behind their comrades. By the time they reached Madeleine there were at least fifteen hundred of them. The road sloped gently downwards, and the roaring torrent of strikers had to flow round the spoil-heap before streaming out across the pit-yard.

It had barely gone two o'clock. But the deputy had been alerted and had brought forward the end of the shift, so that when the mob arrived only about twenty men were left at the bottom. When they surfaced and emerged from the cage, they fled while people ran after them and threw stones at them. Two men were beaten up, and another got away only by forfeiting the sleeve of his jacket. This pursuit of human quarry saved the plant, not a cable or boiler was touched; and already the torrent was departing, rolling on towards the neighbouring pit.

This was Crèvecœur, a mere five hundred metres from Madeleine. There, too, the mob arrived just as the men were coming up. One putter was seized by the women, who ripped her trousers open and started flogging her bare buttocks in full view of the men, to their great amusement. The pit-boys got a clip round the ear, while some of the hewers escaped only after receiving bruised ribs or a bloody nose. As the ferocity of the encounter intensified, fuelled by the demented fury of this immemorial thirst for revenge which had turned everybody's heads, cries rang out or died in the throat, the roar of empty bellies demanding death to the scabs and an end to low wages. They began to cut the cables, but the file was blunt. Anyway it would take too long, for they were in a frenzy now, desperate to be on the move, on, on. A tap was smashed in the boiler-room and buckets of water were thrown on to the fires, causing the cast-iron grates to crack.

Outside there was talk of marching on Saint-Thomas. As the pit with the most docile workforce, it had been unaffected by the strike, and nearly seven hundred men must be underground, which infuriated them. They would wait for them with cudgels, in battle formation, and then they'd see who left the field victorious! But word went round that there were gendarmes at Saint-Thomas, the very gendarmes they'd made fun of that morning. Yet how did anyone actually know that? It was impossible to say. No matter! They lost their nerve and opted for Feutry-Cantel instead. The thrill of the chase took hold of them once more as they found themselves rushing along the road to the sound of their clattering clogs: To Feutry-Cantel! To Feutry-Cantel! There were a good four hundred spineless bastards there, what a laugh! Situated some three kilometres away, the mine was hidden in a dip near La Scarpe. They were already climbing the hillside at Les Plâtrières, beyond the road to Beaugnies, when somebody or other – they never discovered who – started a rumour that maybe the dragoons were at Feutry-Cantel. This was then repeated from from one end of the column to the other: the dragoons were there. They faltered and slowed their pace; and, after all these hours spent careering round a countryside that seemed to have fallen asleep from the torpor of having so many people out of work, there was a wave of panic. Why hadn't they come across any soldiers? It worried them that they had got away with it so far, for they could sense the repression to come.

Though no one had any idea where it started, a new rallying cry sent them all rushing off to another pit.

'La Victoire! La Victoire!'

Were there no gendarmes or dragoons at La Victoire, then? Nobody could say, but everyone seemed reassured. And so they turned on their heels and raced down the Beaumont hill, cutting across the fields to rejoin the Joiselle road. The railway line stood in their path, but they knocked down the fences and passed over it. They were now getting close to Montsou, the gently undulating terrain was flattening out, and the sea of beetfields was beginning to stretch away towards the dark buildings of Marchiennes in the distance.

This time there were at least five kilometres to be covered, but such was the exhilaration that their momentum carried them forward, and they felt neither their terrible exhaustion nor their bruised and aching feet. The stream of people kept getting longer and longer as they picked up comrades in the villages along the way. By the time they had crossed the canal by the Magache bridge and arrived in front of La Victoire, their number had grown to two thousand. But it was after three o'clock, the shift had already ended and there wasn't a man left underground. They vented their frustration in empty threats, but all that was left to them was to throw broken bricks at the stonemen arriving for their shift. A rout ensued, and the deserted pit was theirs. In their fury at not having a blackleg to hit, they set about inanimate objects. It was as though an ulcer of resentment had been growing within them, a poisonous abscess, which had finally burst. Year after year of hunger had made them ravenous for a feast of massacre and destruction.

Behind one of the sheds Étienne spotted loaders busy filling a cart with coal.

'Clear off, you bastards!' he shouted. 'Not one lump of coal is going out of here.'

At his command a hundred or so strikers came running up, and the loaders only just had time to get away. Men unhitched the horses, who took fright and ran off, having been pricked in the flanks; while others turned the cart upside down and, in so doing, broke its shafts.

Levaque had set about the trestles with great blows of his axe, hoping to bring down the overhead railway. They refused to give, and so it occurred to him instead to start ripping up the track, so as to sever the connection between one end of the yard and the other. Soon the entire mob was doing the same. Maheu prized up the cast-iron fixings for them, using his crowbar as a lever. Meanwhile La Brûlé led the women off to invade the lamp-room, where a flurry of sticks soon covered the floor with the remains of smashed lamps. La Maheude, beside herself with rage, hit them every bit as hard as La Levaque. Everyone got covered in paraffin-oil, and La Mouquette was busy wiping her hands on her skirt, laughing delightedly at getting so dirty. For a joke Jeanlin had just emptied a lamp down the back of her blouse.

But such vengeance did not feed hungry mouths. Their stomachs cried out even louder. And the great lament could again be heard above the din:

'We want bread! We want bread!'

As it happened, a retired deputy ran a canteen at La Victoire. Doubtless he had taken fright, because his booth was deserted. When the women returned from the lamp-room and the men had finished tearing up the railway, they all attacked the canteen, and its shutters soon gave way. There was no bread there, only two pieces of raw meat and a sack of potatoes. But in the course of their looting they came across fifty bottles of gin, which vanished like water into sand.

Étienne, having emptied his flask, was able to refill it. He was gradually succumbing to that ugly form of drunkenness that comes from drinking on an empty stomach, and it was turning his eyes bloodshot and causing him to bare his teeth, like a wolf's, between his pale lips. Suddenly he realized that in the general commotion Chaval had escaped. He cursed, and men ran off and seized the fugitive where he was hiding with Catherine behind the woodpile.

'You fucking bastard!' Étienne screamed. 'You're afraid of getting into trouble, aren't you? Back there in the forest you were the one who wanted to call out the mechanics and shut down the pumps, and here you are now trying to land us all in the shit . . . Well, by God, we're going to go back to Gaston-Marie, and you're going to smash that pump. Yes you are, you can bloody well smash it!'

He really was drunk now, for here he was dispatching his men against the very pump he had saved from destruction some hours earlier.

'Gaston-Marie! Gaston-Marie!'

Everyone cheered and began to rush off. Some men grabbed Chaval by the shoulders, hustling him forward roughly while he continued to demand a wash.

'Clear off, I tell you!' Maheu shouted at Catherine, who had also begun to run with them again.

This time she did not even falter, but raised her burning eyes to her father's and continued to run.

Once more the mob cut a swathe across the open plain. It was now retracing its steps, along the long straight highways and across fields that had grown bigger and bigger over the years. It was four o'clock: the sun was setting on the horizon, and the shadows cast by the horde and its wild gesticulations fell across the frozen ground.

They avoided Montsou by joining the Joiselle road higher up, and in order to save having to go round by La Fourche-aux-Bœufs they came past the walls of La Piolaine. By chance the Grégoires had just left, meaning to visit a notary before going on to dine at the Hennebeaus', where they were to collect Cécile. The place seemed sunk in slumber, with its deserted avenue of limes, and its orchard and kitchen-garden both stripped bare by winter. Nothing stirred in the house, and the closed windows were steamed up with the warmth inside: the deep silence exuded a sense of well-being and good cheer, a patriarchal aura of comfortable beds and good food, all bespeaking the well-regulated happiness in which its owners lived out their lives.

Without breaking step the mob cast sullen glances through the iron railings and along the perimeter walls topped with broken bottles. Again the cry went up:

'We want bread! We want bread!'

Only the dogs replied, a pair of Great Danes with tawny coats, who barked ferociously and stood on their hind legs baring their teeth. And behind a closed shutter there were just the two maids – Mélanie the cook and Honorine the housemaid – who had been drawn there by the noise of the chanting and now stood sweating with fear, deathly pale at the sight of these savages marching past. They fell to their knees and thought their last hour had come when they heard a single stone breaking a pane of glass in a nearby window. This was one of Jeanlin's little jokes: he had made a sling out of a piece of rope, and it was his way of leaving his calling card at the Grégoires'. Already he had started blowing his horn again, and as the mob receded into the distance its cry grew fainter and fainter:

'We want bread! We want bread!'

They arrived at Gaston-Marie in even bigger numbers than before, more than two and a half thousand maniacs bent on destruction and sweeping everything before them with the accumulated energy of a torrent in spate. Gendarmes had been there an hour earlier and then departed in the direction of Saint-Thomas; some farm labourers had given them false information, and they had left in such a hurry that they hadn't even taken the precaution of leaving a squad of men to guard the pit. In less than a quarter of an hour, the fire-grates were emptied, the boilers drained and the buildings invaded and ransacked. But it was the pump they were really after. It wasn't enough for it to give out a last gasp of steam and stop working, they had to throw themselves at it as though it were a living person they wanted to kill.

'Right, you go first!' Étienne insisted, as he thrust a hammer into Chaval's hand. 'Come on, you took the oath like the rest of us!'

Chaval was shaking and backing away. In the general scrimmage the hammer fell to the ground, and the comrades, who could wait no longer, began to smash the pump with their crowbars or bricks or whatever came to hand. Some of them even broke their sticks over it. The screws worked loose, and the steel and brass plating began to come apart, as though the pump were being torn limb from limb. One mighty blow with a pickaxe shattered the cast-iron casing, the water spurted out, and the chamber emptied out completely, giving one last gurgle like a death rattle.

That was that. The mob found itself outside once again, still in a state of demented fury, and pushing and shoving behind Étienne, who was refusing to let go of Chaval.

'Death to the scab! Throw him down the shaft!'

The wretched man was white in the face and, with the obsessive stubbornness of an imbecile, kept repeating absently that he needed a wash.

'Well if that's your problem,' said La Levaque, 'here's your sink!'

There was a pool where water had previously leaked from the pump. It was white with a thick coat of ice; and having pushed him towards it, they broke the ice and forced him to plunge his head into the extremely cold water.

'In you go!' La Brûlé urged. 'God damn it! If you won't do it yourself, we'll soon bloody make you ... And now you can have a drink too. Yes, that's right, just like the animals! With your snout in the trough!'

He was forced to drink, crouching on all fours. Everybody joined in the cruel laughter. One woman pulled his ears, while another threw a pile of dung in his face, having gathered it fresh from the road. His old jersey hung off him in shreds. And with a wild look in his eye he kept jerking forward, trying to break loose and run away.

Maheu had helped to push him forward, and La Maheude was among the women attacking him, both of them eager to satisfy their long-standing sense of grievance against him; and La Mouquette herself, who usually remained on good terms with her former lovers, was furious with this one, shouting at him that he was a useless bastard and threatening to remove his trousers to see if he could still call himself a man.

Étienne told her to be quiet.

'Enough! There's no need for everyone to join in ... Come on, you. What do you say we sort this out once and for all?'

His fists were clenched, and his eyes blazed with murderous fury as his drunkenness turned into an urge to kill.

'Are you ready? One of us has got to die. Give him a knife someone. I've got mine here.'

Catherine, on the point of collapse, stared at him in horror. She remembered what he had told her about wanting to kill someone whenever he drank, and how the third glass was enough to make him turn nasty, thanks to all the poison his drunkard parents had already deposited in his system. At once she leaped forward and slapped him with both her girlish hands, choking with indignation and screaming in his face:

'Coward! Coward! Coward! . . . Haven't you done enough? First you treat him in this revolting way and now you're going to kill him when he can't even stand up!'

She turned to her father and mother and to everyone else standing there.

'You're all cowards! Cowards! . . . Go on, you can kill me too! I'll scratch your eyes out if you try and lay a finger on him. You cowards!'

She had taken up position in front of her man, ready to defend him, forgetting how he hit her, forgetting their life of misery together, mindful only that since he had taken her she belonged to him and that it brought shame on her that he should be abused like this.

Étienne had turned white when the girl slapped him. At first he had almost struck her back. Then, running a hand over his face with the gesture of somebody sobering up, he broke the deep silence and said to Chaval:

'She's right, that's enough . . . Bugger off!'

At once Chaval took to his heels, and Catherine raced off after him. The crowd stood rooted to the spot and stared as they disappeared round a bend in the road. But La Maheude muttered:

'That was a mistake. You should have kept him with us. He's bound to do the dirty on us somehow.'

But the mob had set off again. It was nearly five o'clock, and at the edge of the horizon the sun, like red-hot embers, was setting the immense plain ablaze. A passing pedlar told them that the dragoons were on their way and were now in the vicinity of Crèvecœur. So they turned back, and a new rallying cry went up:

'To Montsou! Let's get the manager! . . . We want bread! We want bread!'

V

M. Hennebeau had gone to the study window to see his wife depart in the carriage for lunch at Marchiennes. For a moment he had watched Négrel riding at the trot beside the carriage door, and then he had quietly gone back to his desk and sat down. The house seemed empty when neither his wife nor his nephew filled it with the sound of their existence. Indeed on this particular day, with the coachman away driving Madame and with Rose the new maid having the day off until five, the only ones left were the manservant, Hippolyte, who was drifting about from room to room in his slippers, and the cook, who had been busy since dawn doing battle with her saucepans, completely preoccupied by the dinner party that her master and mistress were giving that evening. M. Hennebeau was thus looking forward to a day's uninterrupted work in the peace and quiet of the deserted house.

At about nine, although he had received orders to admit no one, Hippolyte took the liberty of announcing Dansaert, who had news. Only then did M. Hennebeau learn of the meeting that had taken place on the previous evening in the forest; and the details were so precise that, as he listened, his thoughts turned to La Pierronne and her amours, which were such common knowledge that two or three anonymous letters would arrive each week denouncing the overman's excesses. Clearly the husband had talked, for the intelligence being imparted carried the whiff of pillow talk. M. Hennebeau even took advantage of this opportunity to convey that he was fully in the picture, going no further than to recommend caution, for fear of a scandal. Nonplussed at being ticked off in the middle of his report, Dansaert spluttered denials and excuses as meanwhile his large nose confessed his guilt by turning immediately scarlet. But he did not protest too vigorously, for actually he was pleased to have got off so lightly; normally the manager was sternly implacable on this subject, quite the man of rectitude when it came to an employee having fun with a pretty girl from the mine. They continued to discuss the strike: this meeting in the forest was no more than another piece of bravado, they were under no serious threat. In any case things were bound to be quiet in the villages for the next few days, given that the appearance of the military that morning would duly have instilled some fear and respect.

Nevertheless, once he found himself alone again, M. Hennebeau was on the point of sending a message to the Prefect. Only a reluctance to reveal his anxiety unnecessarily caused him to hold back. He was already cross with himself for his lack of judgement in telling all who cared to listen, including even writing to the Board, that the strike would last a fortnight at most. It had now been dragging on for nearly two months, much to his surprise; and he despaired. With each day that passed he felt diminished, compromised by it, and he needed to think of some great coup if he were ever to return to favour among the members of the Board. He had in fact asked them for instructions in the event that fighting broke out. He had not yet had a reply and was expecting one by the afternoon post. So he kept telling himself that there would be time enough then to send off telegrams requesting the military to occupy the pits, if such proved to be the gentlemen's decision. In his view it would mean outright war, with bloodshed and people getting killed, and despite his customary decisiveness such a responsibility weighed on him.

He worked quietly until eleven, to the accompaniment of no other sound in the deserted house than that of Hippolyte's polishing stick in a distant first-floor room. Then he received two telegrams in quick succession, one informing him that Jean-Bart had been invaded by the Montsou mob, and the second telling him about the severed cables, the emptied furnaces and all the rest of the damage. He did not understand. What were the strikers doing attacking Deneulin instead of one of the Company's mines? In any case they could wreck Vandame all they liked, it simply helped him in his plan to take it over. So at midday he had lunch, alone in the vast dining-room and served in silence by Hippolyte, oblivious even to the shuffle of his slippers. The solitude only added to the gloominess of his thoughts, and his blood ran cold when a deputy, having run all the way, was shown in and told him about the mob's march on Mirou. Almost immediately, as he was finishing his coffee, a telegram informed him that Madeleine and Crèvecœur were now threatened in their turn. He was thoroughly unsure how to proceed. He was expecting the post at two o'clock. Should he ask for troops at once? Or was it better to do nothing and wait until he had received the Board's instructions? He went back to his study, intending to read through a note to the Prefect he had asked Négrel to draft the day before. But he could not put his hand on it and thought that perhaps the young man had left it in his bedroom, where he often did his writing at night. Still undecided and wholly preoccupied by the thought of this note, he hurried upstairs to look for it.

On entering the bedroom, M. Hennebeau was taken aback: the room had not been attended to, presumably because Hippolyte had either forgotten or been too lazy to do so. The room seemed warm and clammy, stuffy from having been shut up all night, especially as the door of the stove had been left open; and his nostrils were assailed by a strong, suffocating smell of perfume that he thought must be coming from the wash-basin, which had not been emptied. The room was extremely untidy: clothes lay scattered about, wet towels had been tossed over the backs of chairs, the bed was unmade, and one sheet had been pulled half off on to the floor. But at first he barely took all this in, as he made for the table covered in papers and searched for the missing note. He went through them twice, examining each one, but it was plainly not there. What the devil had that scatterbrain Paul done with it?

As M. Hennebeau returned to the middle of the room, casting an eye over each piece of furniture, his attention was caught by a speck of brightness in the middle of the unmade bed, something glowing like a spark. Without thinking he went over, and his hand reached out. There, between two creases in the sheet, was a small gold scent-bottle. In an instant he had recognized it as one of Mme Hennebeau's, the phial of ether which she always carried with her. But he could not explain how this object came to be here: what was it doing in Paul's bed? Suddenly he turned deathly pale. His wife had slept here.

'Excuse me,' came Hippolyte's low voice through the doorway, 'I saw Monsieur come up and . . .'

The servant had come in and was filled with consternation at the state of the room.

'Heavens! Of course! The room's not been cleaned. It's that Rose going out and leaving me to do everything!'

M. Hennebeau had hidden the bottle in his hand, and he was clutching it so tightly that he might have broken it.

'What do you want?'

'Monsieur, there's another man downstairs . . . He's come from Crèvecœur, with a letter.'

'Very well, you may go. Kindly tell him to wait.'

His wife had slept here! Once he had bolted the door, he unclenched his fist and looked at the bottle, which had left a red mark on his skin. Suddenly he understood, he saw it all, this abominable thing that had been going on under his roof for months past. He recalled his former suspicion, the sound of clothes brushing past the door, of bare feet padding through the silent house in the middle of the night. It had indeed been his wife, on her way to sleep up here.

Slumped on a chair and staring at the bed opposite, he remained for several minutes as though poleaxed. A noise roused him, somebody was knocking at the door and trying to open it. He recognized the servant's voice.

'Monsieur . . . Ah, Monsieur has locked the door . . .'

'What is it now?'

'Apparently it's urgent, the workers are smashing everything. There are two more men downstairs. And some telegrams have arrived.'

'Leave me be! I'll be down in a moment.'

The terrible thought had just occurred to him that Hippolyte would have found the bottle himself if he had cleaned the room that morning. In fact the servant probably knew already, there must have been dozens of times when he had found the bed still warm from their adultery, with Madame's hairs on the pillow and unmentionable stains on the bed-linen. If he insisted on disturbing him like this, it was no doubt with malicious intent. Perhaps he had even listened at the door and been aroused by the sound of debauchery coming from his mistress and young master.

M. Hennebeau sat on. He continued to stare, his eyes never leaving the bed. The long years of unhappiness passed before him, his marriage to this woman, their instant incompatibility of body and heart, the lovers she had had without his knowing who they were, and the one he had tolerated for ten years the way one tolerates some unwholesome craving in a person who is ill. Then there had been the move to Montsou and his foolish hope that he might cure her, by the months spent languishing in this sleepy exile and by the advancing years that would finally bring her back to him. Then their nephew turns up, this Paul to whom she had started playing mother, and to whom she had spoken about her heart being dead to passion, a cinder beneath the ashes. And there was he, the idiot husband who failed to see it coming, adoring this woman who was rightfully his, whom other men had possessed and whom only he was not allowed to have! He adored her with a shameful passion, to the extent that he would have fallen on his knees before her if she had deigned to give him what was left over after all the others! But what was left over was now being given to this child.

At that moment the distant sound of a bell made him start. He recognized it as the signal he had ordered to be given when the postman arrived. He stood up and exclaimed aloud, as in his pain a stream of foul language poured unbidden from his lips:

'They can go to hell! They can go to fucking hell with their telegrams and their letters!'

He was now filled with rage and felt as though he had need of a cesspit into which he could have trodden all this filth under the heel of his boot. The woman was a slut, and he searched for other crude words with which to defile her image. Suddenly remembering the marriage that she was seeking, so sweetly and calmly, to engineer between Cécile and Paul, he quite lost patience. Wasn't there even any passion, any jealousy, in this perennial lust of hers? It had become no more than a depraved form of play, the mere habit of having a man, a pastime engaged in with the regularity of pudding at the end of a meal. He laid all the blame on her and in the process almost exonerated the young man to whom she had thus attached herself in this reawakening of her appetites, like someone reaching out to plunder the first unripe fruit encountered on a country walk. Whom would she consume next, how much lower would she stoop, when she could no longer call on obliging nephews sufficiently pragmatic to accept this household regime of free board, free lodging and a free wife?

There was a timid scratching at the door, and the sound of Hippolyte's voice could be heard as he ventured to whisper through the keyhole:

'Monsieur, the post . . . And Monsieur Dansaert has come back, he says people are killing each other . . .'

'I'm coming, God damn it!'

What was he going to do to them? Throw them out of the house the moment they returned from Marchiennes, as though they were smelly animals he no longer wanted under his roof? Grab a large stick and scream at them to take their filthy coupling elsewhere? It was their mingled breath and their pleasured sighs that had made the air so heavy in this warm, clammy room; the pungent odour that had taken his breath away was the scent of musk from his wife's skin, this bodily need for very strong perfume being yet another of her perverse tastes; and for him it was the warm smell of fornication, of real flesh-and-blood adultery, which rose from the scattered chamberpots and the unemptied basins, from the unmade bed and the untidy furniture, from every inch of this room that reeked of vice. In his impotent fury he threw himself on the bed and pounded it with his fists, savaging it, pummelling the places where he could identify the imprint of their bodies, and driven wilder still when the discarded blankets and the crumpled sheets remained soft and unresponsive beneath his fists, as though they too were exhausted after a night of passion.

But suddenly he thought he heard Hippolyte coming back

upstairs again. Ashamed of himself, he stopped. He remained motionless for a moment, panting and mopping his forehead as he waited for his pulse to slow. Having stood to look at himself in the mirror, he gazed at his face, its features so distorted that he no longer recognized it. He observed them slowly resume an air of calm and then, by a supreme act of will, he went downstairs.

Below, five messengers were standing waiting, in addition to M. Dansaert. Each brought increasingly worrying news about the strikers' march through the pits; and the overman gave him a long account of the events at Mirou, which had been saved by the stout action of old Quandieu. He listened, nodded, but took nothing in; his thoughts were still on the bedroom upstairs. Eventually he bid them good day, saying that he would take the appropriate measures. When he was alone again, seated at his desk, he seemed to doze off, with his head buried in his hands and his eyes covered. His post was lying there, and he roused himself to look for the expected letter of reply from the Board. But the words swam before his eyes. At length, however, he grasped that these gentlemen were hoping for violent incidents: not that they were instructing him to aggravate the situation, of course, but they did imply that disturbances would hasten the end of the strike by provoking firm action to contain them. With that he ceased to hesitate and sent telegrams off in all directions, to the Prefect in Lille, to the garrison at Douai, to the gendarmerie at Marchiennes. It was a great relief, and now all he had to do was lie low, indeed he let it be thought that he was suffering from an attack of gout. And throughout the afternoon he hid himself away in his study, refusing to see anyone and content merely to read the telegrams and letters that continued to arrive by the dozen. In this manner he followed the mob at a distance as they proceeded from Madeleine to Crèvecœur, from Crèvecœur to La Victoire, and from La Victoire to Gaston-Marie. At the same time he received news of the disarray of the gendarmes and the dragoons as they were misled by false information and kept finding themselves heading in the opposite direction from the pits that were being attacked. But they could all kill each other and destroy what they pleased, for he had put his head back in his hands, his fingers over his eyes, and now lost himself in the great silence of the empty house, hearing only the occasional clatter of a saucepan as the cook busied herself mightily for the dinner party ahead.

It was five o'clock and dusk was already filling the room when a loud noise made M. Hennebeau jump, and he sat there dazed and motionless, his elbows on his papers. He thought that the wretched pair must have returned. But the commotion grew louder, and a terrible shout went up just as he approached the window:

'We want bread! We want bread!'

It was the strikers invading Montsou, just as the gendarmes, thinking they were headed for Le Voreux, were racing off in the opposite direction to occupy it.

At that very moment, some two kilometres beyond the first houses in Montsou and just before the crossroads where the road to Vandame met the main highway, Mme Hennebeau and the two young ladies had been watching the mob file past. Their day out in Marchiennes had been a jolly one: they had had a pleasant lunch at the house of the manager of Les Forges, followed by an interesting tour of the workshops and a visit to a neighbouring glass factory, which had taken care of the afternoon; and then, as they were making their way home through the clear twilight of this bright winter's day, Cécile had noticed a small farmstead at the side of the road and taken a fancy to a cup of milk. The women had all stepped down from the carriage, and Négrel had gallantly dismounted to accompany them. Meanwhile the farmer's wife, flustered at being visited by gentry, rushed about and declared that she must put a cloth on the table before she could serve them. But Lucie and Jeanne wanted to see the cow being milked, and so they had all gone to the cowshed with their cups; it was almost like going on a picnic, and they laughed with delight as their feet sank into the straw.

Mme Hennebeau was rather warily sipping her milk with the air of an indulgent mother when she became alarmed by a strange roaring noise outside.

'What's that?'

The barn stood right at the edge of the road and had large double doors, for it also served for storing hay. Already the girls had poked their heads out and, on looking left, were astonished to see a screaming horde of people pouring out of the Vandame road like a black river.

'Oh God!' muttered Négrel, who had also gone out to look. 'Don't say our troublesome miners are turning nasty.'

'It must be the folk from the mines,' said the farmer's wife. 'They've been past twice already. It seems things aren't too good at the minute, and they mean to show who's boss.'

She spoke each word cautiously, watching for the reaction on their faces; and when she saw how alarmed everyone was and how deeply anxious the encounter had made them, she hastily concluded:

'Ruffians, the lot of them. Ruffians.'

Négrel, seeing that it was too late to get back to the carriage and drive into Montsou, ordered the coachman to hurry and bring it into the farmyard, where they hid it still harnessed behind a shed. He took his own horse, which a young lad had been holding, and tethered it inside the shed. When he returned, he found his aunt and the young ladies quite distraught and ready to accept the suggestion from the farmer's wife that they take refuge in her house. But Négrel thought that they would be safer where they were, since no one would ever think to come looking for them among the hay. The barn doors did not shut properly, however, and there were also such large gaps in its rotten wood that the road was perfectly visible.

'Come now, we must have courage. We shall sell our lives dearly!'

This joke made everyone even more afraid. The noise was growing louder, but there was still nothing to be seen; and out on the empty road it was as though a great gust of wind was blowing, like the sudden squalls that precede great storms.

'No, no, I don't want to look,' said Cécile, as she went to hide in the hay.

Mme Hennebeau, who now looked very pale, was angry that people should spoil her fun like this, and she stood well back, her gaze averted with an air of distaste; while Lucie and Jeanne, though they were trembling, each had one eye glued to a chink in the door, anxious not to miss the show.

The rumble of thunder drew nearer, the ground shook, and Jeanlin appeared first, racing along in front and busily blowing his horn.

'Scent-bottles at the ready, ladies. The sweaty masses are nigh!' whispered Négrel, who, despite his republican leanings, liked to mock the common man when he was in the company of the ladies.

But his jibe was lost amid the tempest of the shouting, gesticulating mob. The women had now come into view, almost a thousand of them, with their straggling hair that had come loose during all the rushing about, and with their ragged clothes revealing patches of bare flesh, the nakedness of female bodies weary of giving birth to tomorrow's starving children. Some carried a baby in their arms, which they would wave about in the air as though it were an emblem of grief and vengeance. Others, young and full-breasted, like warriors going off to war, were brandishing sticks; and the old frights were screaming so loudly that the sinews in their scraggy necks seemed as though they might snap. Then the men came spilling out on to the road, two thousand of them in a solid raging mass, pit-boys, hewers and banksmen moving along as one, and so tightly bunched together that their faded trousers and ragged jerseys all merged into a single mud-brown blur. Their eyes were blazing, and their mouths were no more than black empty holes as they sang 'La Marseillaise',[1] the words of which were audible only as an indistinct bellowing accompanied by the sound of clogs clattering over the hard ground. Above the men's heads, carried upright amid the bristling array of crowbars, an axe went past; and against the clear sky this single axe, as though it were the mob's banner, stood out sharply like the blade of the guillotine.

'What terrible faces!' Mme Hennebeau stammered.

'I'm damned if I recognize a single one of them!' Négrel said under his breath. 'Where on earth have all these blackguards come from?'

It was indeed true that anger and starvation had combined,

after the past two months of suffering, and this wild stampede from pit to pit, to turn the placid features of the Montsou miners into the ravenous jaws of wild beasts. At that moment the sun was setting, and its last rays of dark-crimson light were turning the plain blood red. The road seemed to flow with blood as the men and women raced past, and they too appeared to drip with blood, like butchers in the midst of slaughter.

'What a wonderful sight!' said Lucie and Jeanne softly, as the artist in each of them was moved by the horrible beauty of the scene.

They were frightened all the same, and they retreated towards Mme Hennebeau, who was leaning against a trough for support. She was gripped with cold fear at the thought that they might be killed if anyone so much as caught a glimpse of them between the planks of these rickety doors. Négrel, too, felt the colour drain from his face, this man who was usually so brave but who was now seized by a terror which he was powerless to overcome, a terror laced with the threat of the unknown. In the hay Cécile remained perfectly still. As for the others, though they tried to look away, they could not help watching.

And what they saw was a vision in red, a vision of the revolution that would come and sweep them all away, without fail, one murderous night before the century was out. Yes, one night the masses would slip their leash and seethe through the highways and byways just like this, unchecked; bourgeois blood would flow, their severed heads would be paraded for all to see, their coffers would be emptied, and their gold scattered far and wide. The women would howl, and the men would have the jaws of wolves, gaping wide and ready to bite. Yes, it would be just like this, the same tatters and rags, the same thunderous clatter of clogs, the same terrible rabble with its foul breath and dirt-stained skin, overrunning the place like a barbarian horde and sweeping the old order away. There would be conflagration, and in every town and city not one stone would be left standing upon another; and when the great feasting and the orgies were done, and when the poor had emptied the rich man's cellars and flayed his womenfolk alive, they would all go back to living in the woods like savages. There would be nothing left, not a penny

of their fortunes would remain, not a single deed of property
nor bill of contract, until such day perhaps as a new order might
come to take the place of the old. Yes, this was what was passing
along the road at this very minute, like a force of nature, and
they felt it hit them in the face like a violent blast of wind.

A loud cry went up, drowning out 'La Marseillaise':

'We want bread! We want bread!'

Lucie and Jeanne clung to Mme Hennebeau, who had nearly
passed out, while Négrel stood in front of them as though to
protect them with his body. Was this the night when the old
order would finally crumble? What they saw next rendered them
quite speechless. The main body of the mob was moving away,
leaving only some stragglers, when La Mouquette emerged on
to the road. She had been taking her time, watching out for any
bourgeois at a window or a garden gate; and when she spotted
one, being unable to spit in their face, she would treat them to
what was for her the supreme expression of her contempt. Now,
having presumably just seen one, she suddenly lifted her skirts
and showed them her buttocks, proffering her enormous naked
bottom in the dying rays of the sun. And there was nothing
at all obscene about this bottom nor anything comic in its
uncompromising display.

Everyone vanished, and the mob flowed on towards Montsou,
following each bend in the road and passing between the squat,
gaily-coloured houses. The carriage was brought out of the yard,
but the coachman refused to take responsibility for conveying
Madame and the young ladies safely home as long as the strikers
were blocking the road. The worst of it was that there was no
other way back.

'But we simply must get home. Dinner will be waiting for us,'
said Mme Hennebeau, quite beside herself and maddened by
fear. 'On top of everything these beastly workers have chosen
the very day that I am entertaining guests. Really! And then they
expect to be treated better!'

Lucie and Jeanne were busy trying to drag Cécile from the
hay but she kept refusing to move, believing that the wild
savages were still going past and insisting that she had no desire
to watch. But eventually they all resumed their seats in the

carriage, and it now occurred to Négrel, who had remounted, that they could go round by the back lanes of Réquillart.

'Go carefully,' he told the coachman, 'the road is atrocious. If there are gangs preventing you rejoining the main highway afterwards, then stop behind the old pit. We'll walk home from there – we can use the side-gate – and then you can go and find somewhere to put the carriage and horses, an inn with a coach-shed perhaps.'

Off they set. In the distance the mob was now streaming through Montsou. Having twice seen gendarmes and dragoons go by, the local inhabitants were in a terrible panic. Appalling stories were going the rounds, and there was talk of handwritten posters telling the bourgeois that they were about to get a knife in their bellies; nobody had seen them, but this did not stop anyone from quoting them verbatim. At the notary's house the panic was at its height, for he had just received an anonymous letter through the post warning him that a barrel of gunpowder had been hidden in his cellar ready to blow him up if he did not immediately declare himself on the side of the people.

The Grégoires, whose visit had been prolonged by the arrival of this letter, were just in the middle of discussing it and deciding that it must be a practical joke when the arrival of the invading mob finally reduced the household to a state of blind terror. They themselves, however, remained smiling. Lifting a corner of the curtain they looked outside, but they refused to concede that there was any danger, certain as they were that everything would end amicably. Five o'clock struck, there was still time for them to wait for the coast to clear before proceeding across the road to have dinner at the Hennebeaus', where Cécile would no doubt already be waiting for them following her safe return. But nobody else in Montsou seemed to share their confidence: people were running about madly, doors and windows were being slammed shut. On the opposite side of the road they caught sight of Maigrat busy barricading his shop with a great array of iron bars, and he was so pale and shaken that his slip of a wife had to tighten the nuts herself.

The mob had come to a halt outside the manager's house, and the cry went up once more:

'We want bread! We want bread!'

M. Hennebeau was standing at the window when Hippolyte came in to close the shutters, in case any windows were broken by stones. He closed all the others on the ground floor to the same end and then went up to the first floor, from where a squeaking of handles could be heard and the sound of shutters being banged to one by one. Unfortunately the bay window in the basement kitchen could not be similarly protected, which was a cause for some concern given the glowing red coals burning beneath the saucepans and the spit.

Wanting to observe what was going on, M. Hennebeau made his way up to the second floor and, without thinking, into Paul's bedroom: being on the left-hand side of the house, it was the best place because it afforded a clear view down the road as far as the Company yards. And there he stood, behind the shutters, overlooking the crowd. But once again his attention was caught by the state of the room: the wash-stand had been tidied and cleaned, and the bed was now cold, its crisp sheets neatly tucked in. All the rage he had felt that afternoon and the furious row he had conducted in total silence inside his own head had now given way to an immense fatigue. His whole being was like this room, cooler, swept clean of the morning's filth, and restored to its usual state of propriety. Why cause a scandal? Had anything changed between them? His wife had simply taken one more lover, and it barely made matters worse that she should have chosen him from among the family; indeed perhaps it was even better that she had, for it preserved appearances. How pathetic he had been, he thought, remembering his wild fit of jealousy. How ridiculous he had been, pounding the bed with his fists like that! He had already put up with one man, so why not this one too! It would mean only that he despised her that little bit more. It all left a bitter taste in his mouth, the terrible pointlessness of everything, the endless pain and suffering of living, the shame at himself for still adoring and wanting the woman in the midst of this filth, which he was doing nothing to prevent.

Beneath the window, the shouting rang out with renewed violence.

'We want bread! We want bread!'

'Fools!' M. Hennebeau muttered between clenched teeth.

He could hear them shouting abuse about his fat salary and his fat belly, calling him a dirty pig who never did a day's work and who ate himself sick on fine food while the workers were being starved to death. The women had seen the kitchen, and a storm of curses was unleashed by the sight of pheasants roasting and by the rich aroma of sauces that tormented their empty stomachs. Oh, those bourgeois scum! One day they'd stuff 'em with champagne and truffles till their guts burst!

'We want bread! We want bread!'

'You fools!' M. Hennebeau said again. 'I suppose you think I'm happy!'

He was filled with anger at these people who did not understand. He would gladly have swapped his fat salary just to have their thick skin and their unproblematic sex. If only he could sit them down at his table and let them gorge themselves on pheasant while he went off to fornicate behind the hedges, screwing girls and not giving a damn who had screwed them before him. He would have given everything, his education, his security, his life of luxury, his managerial powers, if he could just, for one single day, have been the lowliest among his own employees, master of his own flesh and enough of a boor to beat his wife and pleasure himself with the woman next door. And he wished, too, that he was starving to death, that his own belly was empty and writhed with the kind of cramp that makes your head spin: perhaps that way he could have put an end to his own interminable misery. Oh to live like an animal, to have no possessions, to roam the cornfields with the ugliest, dirtiest putter, and to wish for nothing else!

'We want bread! We want bread!'

Then he lost his temper and burst out furiously above the din:

'Bread! Do you think that's all that matters, you fools?'

He had all the bread he could eat, but that didn't stop him groaning with pain. His household was in ruins, his whole life a source of grief. The very thought of it choked him, and he gave what sounded like the gasp of a dying man. Things didn't go right just because you had bread. Who was idiot enough to think that happiness in this world comes from having a share of its wealth? These starry-eyed revolutionaries could destroy society and build another one if they liked, but it wouldn't add one jot to the sum total of human joy. They could hand out a slice of bread to every man, woman and child, but not one of them would be the slightest bit less miserable. Indeed they would be spreading yet more unhappiness across the face of the earth, for the fact was that one day even the dogs would howl in despair when they had finally stirred everyone from the tranquillity of sated instinct and raised them to the higher suffering of unfulfilled desire. No, the only good in life lay in not being – or, if one had to be, then in being a tree, a stone, or even less than that, the grain of sand that cannot bleed beneath the grinding heel of a passer-by.

And in his frustration and torment tears filled M. Hennebeau's eyes and began to course in burning drops down the length of his cheeks. The road was fading from view in the gathering dusk when the first stones began to rain against the front wall of the house. No longer angry at these starving people, maddened only by the running sore of his heart, he continued to mutter through his tears:

'You fools! You fools!'

But the cry of empty stomachs was louder, and the howling rose like a raging tempest, sweeping all before it:

'We want bread! We want bread!'

VI

Being slapped by Catherine had sobered Étienne up, and he had continued to lead the comrades. But as he urged them on towards Montsou in his hoarse voice, he could hear another voice within him, the voice of reason, asking in astonishment what the point of it all was. He had not meant for any of this to happen, so how had it come about that, having set off for Jean-Bart with the intention of keeping a cool head and preventing disaster, he now found himself ending a day of mounting violence by laying siege to the manager's house?

And indeed it was Étienne who had just cried 'Halt!' But he had done so to protect the Company yards, which people had begun to talk of ransacking. Now that the stones were already bouncing off the front wall of the house, he was trying desperately to think of some legitimate prey upon which to unleash the mob and so prevent even more serious disasters. As he stood helpless and alone in the middle of the road, someone called to him. It was a man standing in the door of Tison's bar, where the landlady had hastily put up the shutters and left only the doorway clear.

'Yes, it's me . . . Listen for a second.'

It was Rasseneur. Some thirty men and women, almost all from Village Two Hundred and Forty, had come to find out what was going on, having spent the earlier part of the day at home; and they had rushed into the bar when they saw the strikers approaching. Zacharie was sitting at one table with his wife Philomène, while further in sat Pierron and La Pierronne, their backs turned and their faces hidden. Not that anyone was actually drinking, they had simply taken refuge there.

Étienne recognized Rasseneur and was beginning to move away when Rasseneur added:

'Rather not see me here, eh? . . . Well, I warned you. And now the trouble's starting. You can demand all the bread you want, but bullets are all you'll get.'

Étienne then walked back and gave his answer:

'What I don't want to see are cowards standing about twiddling their thumbs while the rest of us are busy risking our necks.'

'What are you going to do? Loot the manager's house?'

'What I'm going to do is to stick by my friends, even if we do all get killed.'

A despairing Étienne then rejoined the crowd, ready to die. Three children were standing in the road throwing stones: he gave them a mighty kick and told them loudly, for the benefit of the comrades, that smashing windows wouldn't get anyone anywhere.

Bébert and Lydie had just caught up with Jeanlin, who was teaching them how to use a sling. They took it in turns to aim a stone, and the game was to see who could cause the greatest amount of damage. Lydie had just bungled her go and cut a woman's head open in the crowd, leaving the two boys clutching their sides with mirth. On a bench behind them, Bonnemort and Mouque sat watching. Bonnemort's swollen legs made it so hard for him to get about that he had had great difficulty in dragging himself this far, and no one quite knew what it was that he had come to see, for he had that ashen look on his face which he wore on days when it was impossible to get a word out of him.

In any case nobody was heeding Étienne now. Despite his orders the stones continued to rain down, and he gazed in astonishment and growing horror at these brutes he had unmuzzled, so slow to anger and yet, once roused, so fearsome in the stubborn ferocity of their wrath. Here was old Flemish blood at work, thick, placid blood that took months to warm to a task but then sallied forth with unspeakable savagery, deaf to all entreaty until the beast had drunk its fill of terrible deeds. Down south, where he came from, crowds would flare up more quickly but they did less damage in the end. He had to fight Levaque to part him from his axe, and as to the Maheus, who were now throwing stones with both hands, he had no idea how to restrain them. It was the women especially who scared him, La Levaque, La Mouquette and the others, every one of them in the grip of a murderous frenzy, baring tooth and claw and snarling like dogs, all the while urged on by La Brûlé, who held sway over them with her tall, skinny frame.

But there was a sudden lull, as momentary surprise produced some of the calm that all Étienne's pleading had been unable to obtain. It was only the Grégoires, who had resolved to take leave of their notary and were now proceeding across the road to the manager's house; and they looked so peaceable, seemed so clearly to believe that this was all just some joke on the part of these worthy colliers whose submissiveness they had lived off for the past century, that the astonished miners stopped throwing stones for fear of hitting this elderly couple who had appeared from nowhere. They allowed them to enter the garden,

climb the steps and ring the bell at the barricaded door, which
no one hurried to open. At that moment Rose, the maid, had
just returned from her day out and was laughing gaily in the
face of the furious workers for, being from Montsou, she knew
them all. And it was she who banged her fists on the door and
managed to get Hippolyte to open it a few inches. Just in time,
for, as the Grégoires disappeared inside, the stones began to
rain down once more. Having recovered from its astonishment,
the crowd was now clamouring louder than ever:

'Death to the bourgeois! Long live socialism!'

Rose continued to laugh merrily in the hallway, as though she
found the whole episode highly entertaining, and she kept saying
to a terrified Hippolyte:

'They mean no harm. I know them!'

M. Grégoire, in his tidy way, hung up his hat. Then, when he
had helped Mme Grégoire to remove her thick woollen cape, he
said in turn:

'I'm sure that underneath it all they don't mean any real harm.
Once they've had a good shout, they'll all go home with a better
appetite for supper.'

At that moment M. Hennebeau was on his way down from
the second floor. He had seen what happened, and he was
coming to receive his guests, with his usual cool politeness. But
the pallor of his face bore witness to the tears that had left him
shaken. The man in him, the man of flesh and blood, had
given up the struggle, leaving only the efficient administrator
determined to carry out his duty.

'You do know,' he said, 'that the ladies are not back yet.'

For the first time the Grégoires became concerned. Cécile not
back! How could she return if the miners carried on with this
silly nonsense of theirs?

'I did think of having them moved away from the house,' M.
Hennebeau added. 'The trouble is that I'm alone here, and in
any case I don't know where to send my servant to fetch four
men and a corporal who could get rid of this rabble for me.'

Rose was still standing there, and she ventured to mutter once
more:

'Oh, sir! They mean no harm.'

As M. Hennebeau shook his head, the uproar outside grew louder still, and they could hear the dull thud of stones hitting the front of the house.

'I've nothing against them. Indeed I can excuse them, because you would need to be as stupid as they are to believe that our sole purpose is to do them harm. But it is my responsibility to keep the peace . . . To think that the roads are swarming with gendarmes – at least so everyone keeps telling me – and that I haven't been able to get hold of a single one all day!'

He broke off and gestured to Mme Grégoire to walk ahead:

'Please, Madame, let us not remain here. Do come into the drawing-room.'

But they were detained in the hall a few minutes longer by the cook, who had come up from the basement having quite lost her patience. She declared that she could no longer answer for the dinner: she was still waiting for the vol-au-vent cases, which she had ordered to be delivered from the pastry shop in Marchiennes at four o'clock. Obviously the pastryman must have got lost on the way, no doubt scared by these ruffians. Perhaps his baskets had even been looted. She could see it all, the hold-up behind a bush, the vol-au-vent cases surrounded on all sides and then disappearing into the bellies of these three thousand wretches screaming for bread. Whatever happened, Monsieur had better be warned, she would rather put the whole dinner on the fire if it was going to be ruined on account of this here revolution of theirs.

'Patience, patience,' said M. Hennebeau. 'All is not lost. The pastryman may still come.'

As he turned round towards Mme Grégoire and opened the drawing-room door for her himself, he was very surprised to catch sight of someone he had not previously noticed sitting on the hall bench in the gathering darkness.

'Goodness, it's you, Maigrat. What are you doing here?'

Maigrat had risen to his feet, and his fat, pallid face could now be seen, blank with terror. Gone was the bluff demeanour of old as he meekly explained how he had slipped across to Monsieur's house to ask for his help and protection if these criminals should attack his shop.

'You can see perfectly well that I'm in danger myself, and I've got no one to help me,' M. Hennebeau replied. 'You'd have done better to remain where you were and guard your stock.'

'Oh, I've put the iron bars up, and my wife's looking after things.'

M. Hennebeau grew impatient and could not hide his contempt. Some guard she would be, that puny creature Maigrat'd beaten so often she was no more than skin and bones!

'Well, there's nothing I can do. Defend yourself as best you can. And I advise you to go back at once, because they're still out there demanding bread . . . Listen to them.'

The clamour was growing louder again, and Maigrat thought he could hear his name being called amid the shouting. It simply wasn't possible for him to go back, he'd be lynched. At the same time he was distraught at the thought of being ruined. He stood with his face glued to the glass panel in the front door, sweating and trembling, on watch as disaster loomed. The Grégoires, meanwhile, finally consented to go into the drawing-room.

M. Hennebeau calmly went through the motions of doing the honours of the house. But he was unable to get his guests to sit down, for, in this airless, barricaded room, which required two lamps even though dusk had not yet fallen, the atmosphere of terror grew with each new round of shouting outside. Muffled by the curtains the crowd's anger became a dull roar, which made it sound all the more alarming and conveyed a sense of some terrible, indeterminate menace. There was conversation none the less, although they could not keep off the subject of this extraordinary revolt. M. Hennebeau, for his part, was surprised not to have seen it coming: and so poorly informed was he that he grew particularly incensed with Rasseneur, whose despicable hand he claimed to recognize in all this. Of course the gendarmes would arrive soon, they were hardly going to abandon him. As for the Grégoires, they had thoughts only for their daughter: the poor darling did take fright so! Perhaps, in view of the danger, the carriage had returned to Marchiennes. The waiting continued for another quarter of an hour, and nerves were stretched by the racket out in the road and the sound of stones hitting the shutters from time to time and making them reverberate like drums. The situation was becoming intolerable, and M. Hennebeau was talking of going outside to chase the braggarts away himself and to meet the carriage, when Hippolyte appeared, shouting:

'Monsieur, Monsieur! Madame's arrived. They're killing Madame!'

When the carriage had been unable to get beyond the Réquillart lane because of the threatening groups of people, Négrel had kept to his plan to walk the last hundred yards to the house and then knock on the little gate leading into the garden, next to the outbuildings: the gardener would hear them, there was bound to be someone there who would let them in. Things had gone well at first, and Mme Hennebeau and the young ladies were already knocking on the gate when some women who had been tipped off came rushing into the lane. Then everything went wrong. No one would open the gate, and Négrel had then vainly tried to force it open with his shoulder. The oncoming crowd of women was growing and he was afraid of being swept away in their path, so in desperation he ushered Mme Hennebeau and the girls forward in front of him, through the besieging mob, all the way to the front steps. But this manœuvre led to further commotion: they were still being pursued by a screaming horde of women, and meanwhile the crowd around them was swirling this way and that, not yet having realized what was going on and merely astonished to see these well-dressed ladies wandering about in the midst of battle. Such was the confusion at this point that there occurred one of those inexplicable things that can happen at moments of blind panic. Lucie and Jeanne, having reached the steps, had slipped in through the front door, which the maid was holding ajar: Mme Hennebeau had managed to follow them in; and finally Négrel entered the house and bolted the door, convinced that he had seen Cécile go in first before any of them. She was not there, she had vanished on the way: she had been so frightened that she had walked off in the opposite direction and straight into danger.

At once the cry went up:

'Long live socialism! Death to the bourgeois!'

At a distance, and because of the veil covering her face, some

people took her for Mme Hennebeau. Others said she was a
friend of Mme Hennebeau's, the young wife of a neighbouring
factory-owner who was hated by his workers. Not that it mattered, for what infuriated them was the silk dress, the fur coat,
everything about her down to the white feather in her hat. She
smelled of scent, she wore a watch, and she had the delicate skin
of an idle creature who had never had to handle coal.

'Just you wait!' shouted La Brûlé. 'We'll soon wipe your arse
for you with all that lace.'

'Those bitches would steal the clothes off your back,' La
Levaque added. 'Wrapping themselves in furs while the rest of
us all freeze to death . . . Come on, undress her. Let's show her
what life's really like!'

Suddenly La Mouquette rushed forward:

'Yes, yes, let's whip her.'

Spurred on by this savage rivalry the women piled in, rag-
covered arms outstretched as each of them tried to grab a piece
of this little rich girl. No reason why her bum should be prettier
than anyone else's! In fact plenty of those bourgeois women
were just plain filthy beneath all that finery of theirs. No, this
injustice had gone on long enough: they'd soon make them dress
like working women, these trollops that spent fifty sous on
having their petticoats laundered!

Surrounded by these furies Cécile stood there quaking, her
legs paralysed with fear, and she kept mumbling the same thing
over and over again:

'Ladies, please, ladies, please don't hurt me!'

But then she gave a hoarse cry: cold hands had closed round
her throat. It was Bonnemort. The crowd had pushed her up
against him, and he had then seized hold of her. He appeared
giddy with hunger and somehow dazed and bewildered after all
his long years of poverty. It was as if he had now suddenly
awoken from half a century's submissiveness, although it was
impossible to tell what particular upsurge of rancour had
brought this about. Having in the course of his life saved some
dozen comrades from death, risking his own skin amid the
firedamp and the rock-falls, he was now responding to inner
promptings which he could not have described, to the simple

need to do what he was doing, to his fascination with this young girl's white neck. And since this was one of the days when he had temporarily lost his power of speech, he tightened his grip like some old, sick animal and seemed to ruminate his memories.

'No! No!' the women screamed. 'Her knickers! Take her knickers off!'

Inside the house, as soon as they realized what was happening, Négrel and M. Hennebeau had bravely opened the front door to rush to Cécile's aid. But the crowd was now pressing up against the garden railing, and it was no longer easy to get out. There was a struggle, and the Grégoires appeared at the top of the steps with a look of horror on their faces.

'Leave her alone, Grandpa! It's the girl from La Piolaine!' La Maheude shouted, having recognized Cécile when another woman tore her veil.

Étienne for his part was shocked to see them taking out their thirst for vengeance on a mere child, and he did everything he could to get the mob to back off. In a moment of inspiration he started brandishing the axe that he had torn from Levaque's hands.

'Come on, for God's sake, let's get Maigrat! ... He's got bread. Let's smash his shop!'

Whereupon he hit the door of the shop with a random swing of his axe. Some comrades followed his lead, Levaque, Maheu and a few others. But the women were not to be denied. Cécile had escaped the clutches of Bonnemort only to fall into the hands of La Brûlé. Led by Jeanlin, Lydie and Bébert were down on all fours crawling between the skirts to get a glimpse of the young lady's bottom. Cécile was being tugged this way and that and already her clothes were beginning to split when a man on horseback appeared, urging his mount on and using his whip on anyone who was slow to get out of his way.

'So, you dirty rabble. Now you want to whip our daughters, do you?'

It was Deneulin, arriving for his dinner engagement. In an instant he had jumped down on to the road and grabbed Cécile by the waist. With his other hand he manœuvred his horse with exceptional skill and strength and used it as a living wedge to drive a path through the crowd, which recoiled from its flying hooves. At the railings the battle was still going on. Nevertheless he managed to get past, crushing various limbs as he did so. Amid the oaths and the fisticuffs this unexpected assistance brought deliverance to Négrel and M. Hennebeau, who had been in considerable danger. And as the young man finally took the unconscious Cécile inside, Deneulin, who was shielding the manager with his large body, was hit by a stone as he reached the top of the steps, and the force of it nearly dislocated his shoulder.

'That's right!' he cried. 'You've wrecked my machinery, so why not break my bones while you're at it!'

He promptly shut the door. A volley of stones rained against the wood.

'They've gone mad!' he continued. 'Another couple of seconds and they'd have split my skull open, like cracking a nut . . . There's really no talking to them now. They've lost their senses, the only thing for it is brute force.'

In the drawing-room the Grégoires were in tears as they watched Cécile recover from her faint. She was unharmed, not even a scratch: only her little veil had been lost. But their dismay increased when they found their cook Mélanie standing in front of them recounting how the mob had demolished La Piolaine. Terrified, she had rushed over to inform her master and mistress at once. At the height of the commotion she, too, had managed to get in through the half-opened front door, unnoticed; and in the course of her rambling narrative the single stone thrown by Jeanlin, which had broken one window-pane, became a veritable broadside of cannon fire rending the walls of the house asunder. M. Grégoire was completely bemused. Here they were strangling his child and razing his house to the ground. Was it then true? Was it actually possible that the miners bore him a grudge for living a sober, decent life off the fruits of their labour?

The maid, who had brought a towel and some eau de Cologne, insisted:

'But it's strange all the same. They're not bad people.'

Mme Hennebeau sat looking very pale, unable to get over

the shock; and she managed a smile only when Négrel was congratulated. Cécile's parents were particularly grateful to the young man: the marriage was settled. M. Hennebeau looked on silently, his gaze passing from his wife to this lover he had that morning sworn to kill, and then to this young girl who would no doubt soon take him off his hands. He was in no hurry: his only remaining fear was that his wife might stoop lower still, with a servant perhaps.

'And how about you, my dear little ones?' Deneulin asked his daughters. 'No bones broken?'

Lucie and Jeanne had had a considerable fright, but they were glad to have seen it all and were now laughing about it.

'My goodness, what a day we've had!' their father continued. 'If you want a dowry, you'll have to earn it yourselves now, I'm afraid. And what's more you can expect to have me to feed as well!'

He was joking, but his voice was shaking. His eyes filled with tears as his two daughters flung themselves into his arms.

M. Hennebeau had heard this confession of ruin. A sudden thought lit up his face. Yes, Vandame would become part of Montsou. Here was the compensation he'd hoped for, the stroke of luck that would restore him to favour in the eyes of the Board. Each time he had met with catastrophe during his life he had habitually fallen back on the resort of carrying out his orders to the letter, and from this personal version of military discipline he derived the one small share of happiness he enjoyed.

But everyone was now beginning to relax, and an atmosphere of weary calm fell on the room, thanks to the soft, steady light from the two lamps and the cosy warmth created by the door-curtains. But what was happening outside? The shouting had died away, and stones had ceased to rain against the front wall of the house. All that could be heard was a dull thudding, like the sound of an axe far off in the wood. Everybody wanted to know what was going on, so they returned to the hall and ventured to look through the glass panel in the front door. Even the ladies went upstairs to peep through the shutters on the first floor.

'Just look at that scoundrel Rasseneur standing in the entrance to that bar over there?' M. Hennebeau said to Deneulin. 'I knew it. I knew he had to be involved.'

Yet it was not Rasseneur but Étienne who was attacking Maigrat's shop with an axe. He kept on calling to the comrades: didn't everything in the shop belong to the miners? Wasn't it their right to take back what was theirs from this thief who had been exploiting them for so long and who reduced them all to starvation the minute the Company told him to do so? Gradually everyone abandoned the manager's house and rushed across to start looting the nearby shop. Once more the cry went up: 'We want bread! We want bread!' And bread they would find, beyond this door. They were seized by a frenzy of hunger as if all of a sudden they could wait no longer, as though otherwise they would die right here on this road. And they pressed so hard towards the door that Étienne was afraid of injuring someone each time he swung the axe.

Meanwhile Maigrat had left the hall and taken refuge in the kitchen; but he could hear nothing from there and kept picturing the most terrible assaults taking place against his shop. So he had just come back upstairs again and gone to hide behind the pump outside when he distinctly heard his own front door cracking and people calling his name as they prepared to loot the shop. So it wasn't all simply a bad dream: while he couldn't see, he could now hear what was going on, and his ears rang as he followed the progress of the attack. Each blow of the axe struck at his heart. A hinge must have given way, in another five minutes the shop would be theirs. He could see the whole thing in his mind's eye, real, terrifying images, the plunderers rushing in, breaking open the drawers, emptying the sacks, eating and drinking everything in sight, stripping their living quarters bare and leaving him nothing, not even a stick to go begging with in the neighbouring village. No, he would not let them ruin him completely. Over his dead body! As he stood there, he had been observing a side-window of the house where he could make out the pale, blurred form of his wife in puny silhouette through the glass: no doubt she was watching the attack on the shop with her usual blank expression, like the poor, battered creature she was. Beneath the window was a lean-to shed which was so positioned that it was possible to climb on to it from the manager's garden by means of the trellis attached to the boundary wall; and from there it was a simple matter to crawl up the tiles as far as the window. He was now obsessed by the thought of returning home in this way, for he bitterly regretted ever having left. Perhaps he would still have time to barricade the shop with furniture; indeed he was busy imagining other forms of heroic defence, like pouring boiling oil or burning paraffin down from above. A desperate struggle was taking place between his fear and his devotion to his stock, and he was panting with the effort of battling against his cowardice. Suddenly, as he heard the axe sink deeper into the door, he made up his mind. Avarice won the day: he and his wife would protect the sacks with their own bodies rather than give up one single loaf of bread.

The jeering started almost at once.

'Look! Up there! It's the tomcat himself! After him! After him!'

The mob had just caught sight of Maigrat up on the shed roof. In his desperation he had managed to shin up the trellis with ease, despite his weight, quite oblivious to the sound of breaking wood; and now he was stretched out flat over the tiles, trying to reach the window. But the pitch of the roof was very steep, his stomach impeded his progress, and his nails were breaking off. Nevertheless he would have made it to the top if he had not begun to tremble at the thought of being stoned; for down below the crowd, whom he could no longer see, was still shouting:

'Catch the cat! Catch the cat! . . . Let's thrash him!'

Suddenly both hands lost their grip, and he rolled down the roof like a ball, bounced off the guttering and landed so awkwardly on the boundary wall that he rebounded on to the road beneath and split his skull on the corner of a milestone. Brains spurted out. He was dead. And the pale blur of his wife continued to gaze down from above.

At first there was a stunned silence. Étienne had stopped, and the axe fell from his hands. Maheu, Levaque and the others forgot about the shop, and all eyes turned to look at a slow trickle of blood running down the wall. The shouting had ceased, and a deep hush fell amid the gathering gloom. All at once the jeering started up again. It was the women, now rushing forward and thirsting for blood.

'So there is a God after all! That's the end of you, you pig!'

They all stood round the still-warm corpse and shouted insults and laughed at it, calling the shattered skull a dirty gob and flinging all the accumulated resentment of their long starvation in the face of death itself.

'I owed you sixty francs, you thief! And there's your payment!' said La Maheude, in as much of a rage as anyone. 'You won't refuse me credit any more, that's for sure ... Wait a minute, though. Let me just fatten you up a bit more.'

And, scratching at the ground with her fingers, she scooped up two handfuls of dirt and rammed them into his mouth.

'There! Eat that! ... Go on, stuff yourself, like you used to stuff us!'

The abuse intensified as the dead man lay there motionless on his back, staring with his big wide eyes at the vast sky where darkness was falling. This earth stuffed into his mouth was the bread he had refused to let them have. And it was the only sort of bread he'd be eating from now on. Much good it had done him, starving the poor to death like that.

But the women had further scores to settle. They prowled round him, nostrils flaring, sizing him up like she-wolves. Each of them was trying to think of some terrible deed, some savage act of vengeance, which might relieve their pent-up fury.

The sour voice of La Brûlé was heard.

'If he's a tomcat, let's cut him!'

'Yes, yes. Cut him, cut him. The bastard's used it once too often!'

Already La Mouquette was busy pulling his trousers off as La Levaque lifted his legs. And then, with her old, wizened hands, La Brûlé parted his naked thighs and seized hold of his now defunct manhood. She grabbed the whole thing in one hand and pulled, her bony spine tense with the effort, her long arms cracking. When the flabby skin refused to give, she had to pull even harder, but finally it came away in her hand, a lump of hairy, bleeding flesh which she proceeded to brandish in triumph:

'I've got it! I've got it!'

Shrill voices acclaimed the terrible trophy with their imprecations.

'That's the last time you shove that up our daughters, you dirty sod!'

'Yeah, no more of your payments in kind. No more spreading our legs just so we can each have a loaf of bread!'

'That reminds me, I still owe you six francs. Would you like something on account? I'm game . . . if you feel up to it!'

This joke had them in fits of terrible laughter. They all pointed at the bloody lump of flesh as though it were some nasty animal that had harmed them and they had just crushed it to death and could gaze at its lifeless form, now wholly in their power. They spat on it and from jutting jaws poured out their furious contempt:

'He can't get it up! He can't get it up! . . . Some man they'll be burying! . . . You can rot in hell, you're no good for anything now!'

La Brûlé then stuck the whole thing on the end of her stick, raised it aloft, and set off down the road carrying it like a flag, followed by the screaming horde of women. Blood dripped everywhere, and the miserable lump of flesh hung down like a piece of meat being displayed on a butcher's stall. Up at the window Mme Maigrat had still not moved; but, caught in the last rays of the sun, the flaws in the glass distorted her pale features, and she seemed to be grinning. Having been beaten by a man who was unfaithful to her at every turn, and having spent her days bent double over a ledger from dawn till dusk, perhaps she was indeed laughing as the band of women rushed past with the remains of the evil beast stuck on the end of a stick.

This dreadful act of mutilation had been witnessed with frozen horror. Neither Étienne nor Maheu nor any of the others had had time to intervene: and now they remained where they were as the furies raced off into the distance. Faces began to appear at the doorway of Tison's bar, Rasseneur, ashen with revulsion, and Zacharie and Philomène, both dumbstruck at what they had seen. The two old men, Bonnemort and Mouque, looked very grave and shook their heads. The only one sniggering was Jeanlin, who was elbowing Bébert in the ribs and trying to make Lydie look up. But the gaggle of women was already returning, doubling back on itself and now passing beneath the windows of the manager's house. And there, behind the shutters, the fine ladies craned their necks to see. They had not been able to observe what had happened, which had been hidden from their view by the wall, and now that it was completely dark they could not make things out properly.

'Whatever have they got on the end of that stick?' asked Cécile, who had plucked up the courage to watch.

Lucie and Jeanne declared that it must be a rabbit skin.

'No, I don't think so,' Mme Hennebeau said quietly. 'They must have looted the meat counter. It looks more like a scrag-end of pork.'

Then she gave a start and fell silent. Mme Grégoire had nudged her with her knee. The pair of them stood there openmouthed. The young ladies, who had gone very pale, ceased their questions and watched with wide eyes as this crimson apparition vanished into the depths of the night.

Étienne raised his axe again. But the general sense of uneasiness persisted, and the corpse lying across the road now served to protect the shop. Many people had drawn back. It was as though they had all suddenly had their fill. Maheu was standing with a very grim expression on his face when he heard a voice whispering in his ear and telling him to make a run for it. He turned and saw Catherine, still in her man's coat, grime-stained and out of breath. He waved her away. He would not listen and made as if to hit her. Gesturing in despair, she hesitated for a moment and then ran towards Étienne:

'Quick, run for it, the gendarmes are coming!'

He, too, told her to go away and shouted abuse; and as he did so, he could feel his cheeks still stinging from the slaps she had given him. But she would not be put off. She forced him to drop the axe, and with both arms began to drag him away. He could not match her strength.

'I promise you, the gendarmes are coming! You've got to listen to me . . . Chaval went to fetch them, if you must know. He shouldn't have done it, so I came to warn you . . . You must get away. I don't want them to catch you.'

And Catherine led him away just as they began to hear the heavy clatter of hooves in the distance, approaching along the cobbled road. At once the cry went up: 'The gendarmes! The gendarmes!' There was chaos as everyone made a run for it, such a wild flight that within a couple of minutes the road was clear, absolutely empty, as though it had been swept by a hurricane. All that was left was the dark patch of shadow made by Maigrat's corpse where it lay on the white ground. Outside Tison's only Rasseneur remained, with a look of open relief on his face, applauding the easy victory of the men with sabres; and as Montsou lay silent and deserted, with not a light to be seen, the bourgeois sweated behind closed shutters, not daring to look out, teeth chattering. The plain had now merged with the pitch darkness, and all that could be seen were the blast-furnaces and the coke-ovens, blazing away against the backdrop of a doom-laden sky. The sound of thundering hooves drew closer, and suddenly the gendarmes were there in the street, visible only as one dark, solid mass. Following behind, under their protection, the pastryman's cart arrived from Marchiennes at last: and a delivery-boy jumped down and calmly proceeded to unload the vol-au-vent cases.

PART VI

The first fortnight in February came and went, and a bitter cold spell prolonged the hard winter, offering no mercy to the poor, wretched people. The authorities had once again come to carry out their investigations: the Prefect from Lille, a public prosecutor and a general. The gendarmes had not sufficed, and troops had arrived to occupy Montsou, a whole regiment of them, camped out from Beugnies to Marchiennes. Armed guards were posted at the pit-shafts, and soldiers stood watch over the machinery. The manager's house, the Company yards and even the houses of some of the bourgeois all bristled with bayonets. The only sound to be heard along the cobbled highway was the slow tramp of army patrols. On top of the spoil-heap at Le Voreux, in the icy wind that blew there constantly, a sentry was permanently positioned, like a lookout standing watch over the entire plain; and every two hours, as though this were enemy territory, the calls of the changing guard would ring out:

'Who goes there? . . . Step forward! Password!'

There had been no resumption of work anywhere. On the contrary, the strike had spread: Crèvecœur, Mirou and Madeleine had ceased production, like Le Voreux; Feutry-Cantel and La Victoire were losing more workers with every day that passed; and at Saint-Thomas, which had previously remained unaffected, there were absentees. Faced with this show of military might, which offended their pride, the miners' mood was now one of mute obstinacy. Amid the beetfields the villages lay seemingly deserted. Not a worker stirred from his house, and if the occasional person was to be seen, he would be walking alone, his eyes averted and his head lowered as he passed the men in uniform. And beneath this bleak tranquillity, this passive refusal to register the presence of all these rifles, there lay a deceptive docility, the patient, enforced obedience of wild animals in a cage, never taking their eyes off the trainer and just waiting to sink their teeth into his neck the moment he turns his back. For the Company the halt in production was ruinous, and it was talking of taking on miners from Le Borinage, on the

Belgian border. But it did not dare do so, which meant that the confrontation had now reached an impasse, with the miners staying at home while the troops guarded idle pits.

This period of calm had set in, all of a sudden, on the morning following those terrible events, and it concealed a sense of panic so great that as little as possible was said about the damage and atrocities which had been committed. The public inquest established that Maigrat had died as the result of his fall, and the circumstances surrounding the dreadful mutilation of his body, already the subject of legend, were left vague. For its part the Company did not publicly acknowledge the damage that had been incurred, no more than the Grégoires were eager to expose their daughter to the scandal of a lawsuit in which she would have had to give evidence. Nevertheless a number of arrests had been made, mere bystanders as usual, witless, gawping folk who had no idea what was going on. Pierron had been taken to Marchiennes in handcuffs by mistake, which was still a source of great amusement to the comrades. Rasseneur, too, had almost been marched off by two gendarmes. Management was content to draw up lists of those to be dismissed, and whole batches of people were being handed their cards: Maheu had been given his, and Levaque also, along with thirty-four of their comrades from Village Two Hundred and Forty alone. And the harshest penalties were in store for Étienne, who had vanished without trace since the evening of the riot. Chaval in his hatred had denounced him, though he refused to name the others, having been implored not to by Catherine, who wanted to protect her parents. As the days went by, there was a sense of unfinished business, and people waited tensely to see how things would turn out.

In Montsou thenceforth the bourgeois woke up every night with a start, their ears ringing with the sound of imaginary alarm bells and their nostrils filled with the smell of gunpowder. But the final straw was a sermon given by their new priest, Father Ranvier, the scrawny cleric with the blazing red eyes who had taken over from Father Joire. What a change from the diplomatic smiles of that plump and inoffensive man whose sole aim in life had been to get on with everyone! Had not Father

Ranvier had the effrontery to defend these frightful criminals who were bringing dishonour on the region? He had made excuses for the strikers' villainies and launched a violent attack on the bourgeoisie, whom he held entirely responsible. It was the bourgeois themselves who, in robbing the Church of its age-old rights and freedoms only then to abuse them, had turned the world into an accursed place of suffering and injustice; it was they who stood in the way of the strike being settled, and it was they who would precipitate a terrible catastrophe by their godlessness and their refusal to return to the beliefs and brotherly traditions of the early Christians. And Ranvier had even dared to threaten the rich, warning them that if they continued not to listen to the voice of God, God would surely side with the poor: He would take back the fortunes of these self-indulgent heathens and distribute them among the humble of this earth for His greater glory. Pious ladies trembled, while the notary declared that this was the worst kind of socialism, and everyone pictured their priest at the head of a mob, brandishing a crucifix and with mighty blows smashing the bourgeois society born of 1789.

M. Hennebeau, an experienced observer of such things, merely shrugged and said:

'If he proves to be too much of a nuisance, the bishop will soon get rid of him for us.'

And all the while such panic raged from one end of the plain to the other, Étienne was living underground, in the depths of Réquillart, in Jeanlin's lair. For this was where he had taken refuge, and no one suspected that he was so close: the brazen cheek of his hiding in the mine itself, in this disused road down in the old pit, had defeated all attempts to find him. Above him the entrance was blocked by the sloe bushes and hawthorns that had grown up through the collapsed timbers of the headgear; nobody ventured down there now, and you had to know the routine of hanging from the roots of the rowan tree and then keeping your nerve and letting yourself drop till you reached the ladder rungs that were still solid. And there were other obstacles to protect him too: the suffocating heat in the shaft, a perilous descent of a hundred and twenty metres, then the painful slide on your front down a quarter of a league, between the narrow walls of the roadway, before you came to the robber's den and its hoard of plunder. Here Étienne lived surrounded by plenty: he had found some gin, the remains of the dried cod and further provisions of every kind. The large bed of hay was excellent, there were no draughts, and the temperature was constant, like a warm bath. The only imminent shortage was light. Jeanlin had taken on the job of supplying Étienne, which he carried out with all the careful secretiveness of a young rascal who delights in outsmarting the police; and he brought him everything, even hair-oil, but he simply could not lay his hands on a packet of candles.

By the fifth day Étienne lit a candle only when he needed to eat. The food simply wouldn't go down if he tried to swallow it in the dark. This interminable total darkness with its unchanging blackness was proving to be his greatest hardship. It was all very well being able to sleep in safety and to have all the bread and warmth he needed, but the fact remained that he had never before felt so oppressed by the dark. It seemed to be crushing the very thoughts out of him. So here he was, living off stolen goods! Despite his communist theories, the old scruples instilled in him by his upbringing continued to trouble him, and he made do with dry bread, eking it out. But what else could he do? He still had to live, his task was not yet accomplished. And something else weighed on him, too: remorse for the drunken savagery that had resulted from his drinking gin on an empty stomach in the bitter cold and which had made him attack Chaval with a knife. The episode had brought him into contact with an uncharted region of terror within himself, his hereditary disease, the long lineage of drunkenness which meant that he couldn't touch a drop of alcohol without lapsing into homicidal rage. Would he end up killing someone? When he had finally reached this shelter, in the deep calm of the earth, sated with violence, he had slept for two whole days like an animal in a stupor of repletion; and the disgust persisted. His body ached all over, there was a bitter taste in his mouth, and his head hurt, as though he had been attending some wild party. A week went by, but the Maheus, who knew where he was, were unable to send him a candle: and so he had to renounce all hope of being able to see, even to eat by.

Now Étienne would spend hours lying on his bed of hay, turning over vague ideas which he didn't even know he had. He felt a sense of superiority that set him apart from the rest of the comrades, as though in the process of educating himself he had acceded to some higher plane. He had never reflected so much before, and he wondered why he had felt such disgust the day after that furious rampage from pit to pit; but he was loath to answer his own question, feeling repugnance as he thought back to certain things, to the base nature of people's desires, to the crudeness of their instincts, to the reek of all that poverty borne on the wind. Despite the tormenting darkness he eventually began to dread the moment when he would return to the village. How revolting it was, all those wretched people living on top of each other and washing in each other's dirty water! And not one of them could he talk to seriously about politics. They might as well be animals, and always that same foul air which stank of onions and left you choking for breath! He wanted to broaden their horizons, to show them the way to the life of comfort and good manners led by the bourgeoisie, to make them the masters. But how long it was all going to take! And he no longer felt he had the courage to wait for victory, here in this prison-house of hunger. Gradually his vanity at being their leader and his constant concern to do their thinking for them were slowly setting him apart and lending him the soul of one of those bourgeois he so despised.

One evening Jeanlin brought him the remains of a candle, which he had stolen from a wagoner's lantern; and for Étienne this was a great relief. When the darkness began to get to him and his thoughts started weighing on him as though he might soon go mad, he would light it for a moment; and then, when he had chased away the gremlins, he would extinguish it, determined to economize on this bright light that was as necessary to his survival as bread itself. The silence made his ears hum, and all he ever heard was the scuttling of rats, the creaking of the old timbering, or the tiny sound of a spider weaving its web. And as he stared into the warm void, his mind kept returning to the same old question: what were his comrades doing up there? To abandon them would have seemed to him the worst possible act of cowardice. If he was hiding down here like this, it was so that he could remain free, ready to advise and act. His long periods of reflection had shown him where his true ambition lay: pending something better he wanted to be like Pluchart, to stop work and devote himself entirely to politics, but alone, in a nice clean room somewhere, on the grounds that brain work is a full-time job and requires much peace and quiet.

At the beginning of the second week, Jeanlin having told him that the gendarmes believed him to have crossed into Belgium, Étienne ventured out of his hole after nightfall. He wanted to assess the situation, to see if it was still worth resisting. For his own part he thought that their chances of success had been compromised. Before the strike he had had his doubts about the possibility of victory but had simply gone along with things; now, having experienced the heady excitement of rebellion, he had reverted to his original doubts and despaired of ever getting the Company to concede. But he did not yet admit as much to himself, and he was tortured with anguish at the thought of the miseries that defeat would bring, of all the heavy responsibility which he would have to bear for people's suffering. Would not an end to the strike also mean an end to his own role in the matter, the collapse of his ambitions, a return to his brutish existence in the mine and the revoltingness of life in the village? And he tried in all honesty, without base or false calculations, to recover his sense of commitment, to convince himself that resistance was still feasible, that capital would destroy itself when faced with the heroic suicide of labour.

And indeed news of ruin after ruin was now reverberating across the whole region. At night, as he roamed the dark countryside like a wolf that has left the shelter of its wood, he could almost hear the companies collapsing from one end of the plain to the other. Along the roadsides he was continually passing empty, lifeless factories whose buildings stood rotting beneath a pale, ghostly sky. The sugar-refineries had suffered particularly; Hoton and Fauvelle, having both reduced their workforces, had just gone bust one after the other. At the

Dutilleul flour-mills the last grindstone had stopped turning on the second Saturday of the month, and the Bleuze rope-works, which made cables for the pits, had been been brought down once and for all by the halt in production. Around Marchiennes the situation was daily getting worse: not one furnace operating at the Gagebois glass factory, continual lay-offs at the Sonneville construction works, only one of the three blast-furnaces at Les Forges still functioning, and not a single battery of coke-ovens was to be seen burning on the horizon. The strike by the Montsou miners, itself the result of the industrial crisis which had been worsening for the past two years, had in turn exacerbated that crisis by precipitating this widespread bankruptcy. To the several causes of this painful predicament – the lack of orders from America, the fact that so much capital was tied up in excess production capacity – was now added an unforeseen lack of coal to fuel the few boilers that were still functioning; and this was the final agony, machines deprived of their sustenance because the pits themselves were no longer supplying it. Alarmed by the poor economic outlook, the Company had reduced output and starved its workers, with the inevitable result that since the end of December it had not had a single lump of coal in any of its pit-yards. It was a case of chain reaction: the problems began far away, one collapse led to another, industries knocked each other over as they fell, and all in such a rapid series of disasters that the effects could be felt as close as the neighbouring towns and cities of Lille, Douai and Valenciennes, where whole families were being ruined by bankers calling in their loans.

Often, at a bend in the road, Étienne would stop in the freezing night air and listen to the sound of structures giving way. He would take deep lungfuls of the darkness, filled with euphoria at the prospect of this black void and with the hope that the new day would dawn on the extermination of the old world, with not a single fortune still intact and everything levelled to the ground by the scythe of equality. But amid this general destruction it was the Company's pits which interested him the most. He would set off again, blinded by the darkness, and visit each of them one by one, delighted every time he learned of some further damage. New rock-falls were occurring constantly,

and with increasing seriousness the longer the roadways
remained out of use. Above the northern roadway at Mirou the
subsidence was so great now that a whole hundred-metre stretch
of the Joiselle road had fallen in as though there had been an
earthquake; and the Company would compensate landowners
at once when their fields disappeared, not even bothering to
haggle over the price, so anxious were they not to let the news
of such accidents spread. Crèvecœur and Madeleine, where the
rock was particularly unstable, were suffering more and more
blockages. There was talk of two deputies being buried alive
at La Victoire; there had been flooding at Feutry-Cantel; one
kilometre of roadway at Saint-Thomas would have to be bricked
where the timbering had been poorly maintained and was splitting all along its length. Huge repair bills were thus mounting
by the hour, making severe inroads into shareholders' dividends,
and in the long run the rapid destruction of the pits would end
up consuming those famous Montsou deniers that had increased
in value one hundredfold over the course of a century.

    And so, presented with the news of this series of disasters,
Étienne began once more to hope, and he came to believe that
a third month of resistance would finish the monster off, that
weary, sated beast squatting like an idol in its far-away temple.
He knew that the trouble at Montsou had caused much excitement in the Paris press: a furious debate was raging between the
newspapers sympathetic to the government and those which
supported the opposition, and terrifying stories were circulating
and being used in particular against the International, which
the Emperor and his government had at first encouraged but
which it now viewed with increasing apprehension. Moreover,
since the Company's Board of Directors could no longer continue to turn a deaf ear to what was going on, two of its members
had deigned to come and hold an inquiry, but with such a
reluctant air and with such apparent lack of concern for how
things would turn out, so thoroughly uninterested, in fact, that
they had left three days later saying that everything was perfectly
fine. But Étienne had learned from other sources that during
their visit these gentlemen had been in permanent session, working at fever pitch and investigating all manner of things which

no one in their entourage was prepared to divulge. Whistling in the dark was how Étienne saw it, and he even managed to interpret their hurried departure as sheer panic. Now he was certain of victory, for those fearsome gentlemen had clearly thrown in the towel.

But by the following night Étienne was once more in despair. The Company was just too solid to be so easily broken: it could lose millions but it would soon retrieve them at the workers' expense by trimming their wages. That night, having gone as far as Jean-Bart, he realized the truth when a supervisor mentioned to him that there was talk of letting Montsou take over Vandame. It was said that the Deneulins were in a pitiful state, suffering the misery of the rich who have fallen on hard times: the financial worries had aged Deneulin, and he was ill from the sheer frustration of being unable to do anything, while his daughters fought with their creditors and tried to save what clothes they could. There was less suffering in the starving villages than there was in this well-to-do household where they had to drink water in secret for fear anyone should see them do it. Work had not resumed at Jean-Bart, and the pump had had to be replaced at Gaston-Marie, in addition to which, even though they had acted with all speed, there had been some initial flood damage and the repairs were going to be costly. Deneulin had finally plucked up courage to ask the Grégoires for a loan of a hundred thousand francs, and their refusal, which he had in any case expected, had been the final straw. If they refused, they said, it was out of kindness, to spare him an impossible struggle; and they advised him to sell. He still refused, vehemently. It infuriated him that the cost of the strike should fall on him, and he hoped he would die of a rush of blood to the head, choked by apoplexy. But what was to be done? He had listened to the various offers. People tried to beat him down, to minimize the value of this splendid prize, this pit that had been completely renovated and refitted, where only a lack of ready cash was preventing production. He would be jolly lucky to recoup a sufficient sum to pay off his creditors. For two whole days he had wrangled with the two Board directors who had descended on Montsou, infuriated by the calm manner in which they were taking advantage of his difficulties: 'Never!' he would shout at them in his thunderous voice. And there the matter rested, for they returned to Paris to wait patiently for him to give up the ghost. Étienne saw only too well how one man's misfortune became another man's gain, and once more it discouraged him deeply to think of the invincible power wielded by the sheer weight of capital, so strong in adversity that it grew fat on the defeat of others, gobbling up the small fry who fell by the wayside.

Fortunately, on the following day, Jeanlin brought him a piece of good news. At Le Voreux the lining of the main pit-shaft was threatening to give way, water was seeping in through every joint, and a team of joiners had had to be sent in to repair the damage as a matter of urgency.

Until then Étienne had avoided Le Voreux, unnerved by the ever-present black silhouette of the sentry up on the spoil-heap, overlooking the plain. You couldn't miss him, planted there against the sky like the regiment's flag and dominating the landscape. Towards three o'clock in the morning the sky grew very dark, and Étienne went over to the pit, where some comrades briefed him on the poor state of the shaft lining: indeed in their view the whole thing needed to be replaced immediately, which would have meant halting production for three months. He wandered around for a long time, listening to the tap-tap of the joiners' mallets down in the shaft. It cheered him to think of the mine being injured and that they were having to bind the wound.

At dawn, on his way back, he found the sentry still standing on the spoil-heap. This time he would surely be spotted. As he walked along, he thought of these soldiers, of these men of the people who had been armed against the people. How easily the revolution would have triumphed had the army suddenly come over to their side! All it needed was for the working man or the peasant in his barracks to remember his origins. This was the supreme danger, the doomsday vision which set bourgeois teeth chattering when they thought about the possibility of the troops defecting. In two short hours they would be swept away, wiped out, along with all the pleasures and abominations of their iniquitous lives. Already it was said that whole regiments had become infected with socialism. Was it true? Would the age of justice dawn thanks to the very cartridges issued by the bourgeois themselves? And as his mind raced with new hope, the young man imagined the regiment deployed to guard the mines deciding instead to support the strike, turning their guns on the Company's directors, and at last delivering the mine into the hands of the miners themselves.

He suddenly found himself climbing the spoil-heap, his head spinning with these thoughts. Why not have a chat with the soldier? That way he'd learn how the fellow saw things. Casually he drew nearer, pretending to scavenge for old wood among the rubbish. Still the sentry did not move.

'Hallo, comrade. Bloody awful weather!' Étienne said finally. 'It looks like snow.'

The soldier was short, with very fair hair and a pale, gentle face covered in freckles. Wrapped in his cape he looked ill at ease, every inch the raw recruit.

'Yes, it does, doesn't it?' he muttered.

And his blue eyes gazed at the wan sky and a grey misty dawn in which coal-dust seemed to hang like lead over the distant plain.

'Damned stupid of them to stick you up here like this so you can freeze to death!' Étienne went on. 'It's not as if we're expecting the Cossacks,[1] is it? ... And there's always such a terrible wind up here, too!'

The little soldier shivered uncomplainingly. In fact there was the dry-stone hut in which old Bonnemort used to shelter on the nights when it was blowing a gale; but the soldier's orders were not to move from the summit of the spoil-heap, and so he stayed where he was, his hands so stiff from the cold that he could no longer feel his rifle. He belonged to a detachment of sixty men whose job it was to guard Le Voreux; and as this cruel watch fell to him frequently, he had more than once nearly breathed his last up here, all feeling gone from his feet. But it was what the job required; passive obedience had finally numbed his brain, and he replied to questions with the garbled mumblings of a child who is half asleep.

For a quarter of an hour Étienne tried in vain to get him to talk politics. He answered yes and no but without appearing to understand; some comrades said the captain was republican; as for himself, he didn't really know, it was all the same to him. If they ordered him to shoot, he'd shoot, so as not to be punished. As Étienne, the working man, listened to him, he was filled with the people's instinctive hatred of the army, of these brothers whose allegiance changed the minute they pulled on a pair of red trousers.

'So what's your name?'

'Jules.'

'And where are you from?'

'From Plogoff, over yonder.'

He gestured randomly with his arm. It was in Brittany, that was all he knew. His small, pale face lit up, and he began to laugh with renewed cheer and warmth.

'I have a mother and sister back there. They can't wait for me to come home, of course. Though it'll be some time yet ... When I left, they came with me as far as Pont-l'Abbé. We borrowed the horse from the Lepalmecs, and he nearly broke his legs on the journey down from Audierne. My cousin Charles met us with some sausages, but the women were crying so much we just couldn't enjoy them ... Oh God, oh God, how far away home seems now!'

Tears sprang to his eyes although he continued to laugh. He had a vision of the bleak Plogoff moorland and the wild, storm-wracked Pointe du Raz all bathed in dazzling sunshine, in the season of pink heather.

'Tell me,' he said, 'if I behave myself, do you think I might get a month's leave in two years' time?'

Then Étienne talked about Provence, which he had left when he was very small. It was getting lighter now, and snowflakes were beginning to flutter down from a grubby sky. But eventually he became anxious when he saw Jeanlin prowling about among the brambles, amazed to see him up there. The boy was beckoning to him. Why dream of fraternizing with the military? It would take years and years, and his futile attempt depressed him, as though he had expected to succeed. But suddenly he understood what Jeanlin's gesture meant: the sentry was about to be relieved. And so Étienne left to return to Réquillart, running to earth with a heavy heart once more at the certain prospect of defeat; and Jeanlin raced along beside him, accusing that dirty bastard of a soldier of calling out to the guard to shoot at them.

Up on the spoil-heap Jules had not moved, and he went on gazing out into the falling snow. The sergeant was approaching with his men, and the regulation calls were exchanged.

'Who goes there? . . . Step forward! Password!'

Then heavy footsteps could be heard receding into the distance, like the ringing gait of a conqueror. Though it was now light, nothing stirred in the villages; and the miners continued to rage in silence beneath the jackboot.

II

Snow had been falling for two days. That morning it had stopped, and had now frozen hard in one vast sheet: the entire region, which had once been black, with its inky roads and its walls and trees covered in coal-dust, was now one single expanse of uniform whiteness stretching to infinity. Buried beneath the snow, Village Two Hundred and Forty seemed to have disappeared. Not a wisp of smoke was to be seen coming from its roof-tops. Without fires the houses were as cold as the stones in the road, and there was nothing to melt the thick layer of snow covering the tiles. The place looked like a quarry of white slabstones set in the midst of the white plain, like some vision of a dead village draped in a shroud. Along the streets only the passing patrols had trampled the snow into a muddy mess.

At the Maheus' the last shovelful of gleanings from the spoil-heap had been burned the evening before; and in this terrible weather it was out of the question to think of fetching some more when even the sparrows were unable to find a blade of glass. Alzire, whose poor little hands had stubbornly scrabbled through the snow, was dying. La Maheude had had to wrap her in a scrap of blanket as she waited for Dr Vanderhaghen, whom she had been to see twice already without finding him in. The maid, however, had just promised her that the doctor would visit her in the village before dark, and so La Maheude was standing by the window watching out for him while the sick girl, who had insisted on coming downstairs, sat shivering on a chair in the fond belief that she was warmer there next to the cold stove. Opposite her sat old Bonnemort, his legs bad again, apparently asleep. Neither Lénore nor Henri was home yet, still out tramping the highways and byways with Jeanlin, asking people if they had any spare change. Only Maheu moved about, lumbering up and down the other side of the bare room and bumping into the wall each time with the dazed look of an animal that can no longer see the bars of its cage. The paraffin-oil, too, was finished; but the reflection from the snow outside was still so bright that it dimly lit the room even though night had fallen.

There was a sound of clogs, and La Levaque burst in like a gale, beside herself with fury and shouting at La Maheude from the open doorway:

'So it was you that told everyone I made my lodger give me twenty sous each time he slept with me!'

La Maheude shrugged.

'Leave me be. I never said such a thing . . . Anyway, who told you I did?'

'Somebody told me, never mind who . . . And you said you could hear our dirty goings-on through the wall, and that my place was filthy because I was always flat on my back . . . Just try telling me again you never said it!'

Quarrels like this broke out every day as a result of the women's constant gossiping, and, particularly between families who lived next door to each other, it was one daily round of rows and reconciliation. But never before had they gone for each other with such bitter ill-will. Since the start of the strike hunger had sharpened everyone's grudges, and there was a general desire to come to blows: an argument between two women would end in a fight to the death between two men.

Indeed at that very moment Levaque himself arrived, dragging Bouteloup with him by force:

'Here he is. Let's hear him say whether he gave my wife twenty sous to sleep with her!'

Their meek lodger was shocked and started mumbling a protest into his beard:

'What an idea. No, of course not. Never.'

At once Levaque turned nasty and shoved a fist under Maheu's nose.

'I'm not having it, you hear? When a man's got a wife like that, he should beat some sense into her ... Or maybe you actually believe what she's been saying?'

'What *is* all this, for Christ's sake?' Maheu exclaimed, furious at being roused from his gloom. 'Who are you trying to stir up with all this "he said" and "she said"? Haven't we got enough problems already? Bugger off, or you'll get this in your face! And anyway, who told you my wife said such a thing?'

'Who told me? . . . I'll tell you who told me! La Pierronne!'

La Maheude gave a shrill laugh and turned towards La Levaque:

'So La Pierronne told you, did she? . . . Well, just let me tell you what she told me! Oh yes! She said you were sleeping with the two men at once, one beneath and one on top!'

After that any reconciliation was out of the question. Everybody was angry, and the Levaques retorted that La Pierronne had told them all sorts about the Maheus, like how they'd sold Catherine off, and how Étienne had caught a dose at the Volcano, and now the whole filthy lot of them had it, even the children.

'She said that! She said that!' Maheu screamed. 'Right. I'm off. And if she admits to my face she said it, I'll knock her bloody block off.'

Already he had rushed outside, pursued by the Levaques, who wanted to see this, while Bouteloup, who hated scenes, sloped off home. Incensed by the row, La Maheude, too, was about to leave when a moan from Alzire detained her. She pulled the ends of the blanket over the little girl's shivering body and resumed her position by the window, where she gazed blankly into the distance. Still the doctor didn't come!

Outside the Pierrons' door Maheu and the Levaques ran into Lydie, who was pacing up and down in the snow. The house was shut up, but a chink of light could be seen through one of the shutters; and the child replied to their questions with some embarrassment: no, her father wasn't in, he had gone to meet La Brûlé at the wash-house so as to carry the washing home. Then she became flustered and refused to say what her mother was doing. Eventually she revealed all, with a vindictive snigger: her mother had thrown her out because M. Dansaert was there and they couldn't talk if she was around. Dansaert had been touring the village since morning in the company of two gendarmes in an attempt to recruit some workers, putting pressure on the weak and announcing to all and sundry that if they didn't go back to work at Le Voreux next Monday the Company had decided to take on men from Belgium. And at dusk, finding La Pierronne alone, he had sent the gendarmes away and stayed to drink a glass of gin with her in front of her warm fire.

'Shh! Be quiet, this we must see!' Levaque whispered, giving a dirty laugh. 'The other business can wait . . . And you can hop it, you little hussy!'

Lydie stepped back a few paces, while he put his eye to the crack in the shutter. He gave short muffled cries of exclamation as his back rose and shuddered. Then it was La Levaque's turn to look; but she announced, as though she were about to vomit, that the whole thing was disgusting. Wanting to have a look, too, Maheu pushed her out of the way, and then declared that you certainly got value for money! And they repeated the process, each taking a turn to look, just like in a peep-show. The sitting-room, which was sparklingly clean, looked bright and cheerful with its roaring fire; there were cakes on the table, as well as a bottle and some glasses – quite a party, in fact. So much so that the sight of it all was enough to infuriate the two men, they who in other circumstances would have laughed at the episode for a good six months. The fact that she was lying there with her skirts in the air getting screwed for all she was worth was funny all right. But God Almighty if it wasn't a rotten trick to be doing it in front of such a huge fire and after getting her strength up with all those biscuits when the comrades hadn't a crumb of bread or a lump of coal to their name!

'Here's Father!' cried Lydie as she made her escape.

Pierron was returning from the wash-house, minding his own business, with the bundle of washing over one shoulder. Maheu bearded him at once:

'Here you! I've been told that your wife said I sold Catherine and that everyone in our house has got a dose of the clap . . . So, tell me, what's he paying you for her, eh? You know who I mean, the fellow that's screwing her stupid right at this very minute.'

Taken by surprise, Pierron was completely nonplussed when La Pierronne, alarmed by the sound of all these voices, forgot herself and opened the door a little to see what was going on. There she stood, all red, her bodice unbuttoned, her skirt still hitched up and tucked into her belt, while in the background Dansaert was desperately pulling on his trousers. The overman made his escape and disappeared from view, terrified that a story of this kind would soon reach the ears of the manager. Then all hell broke loose as people laughed and jeered and flung insults at each other.

'And you're the one who's always saying how filthy everyone else is!' La Levaque shouted at La Pierronne. 'No wonder you're so clean if you're getting the bosses to scrub the floor for you!'

'Oh, she's a fine one to talk, she is!' said Levaque, taking up the theme. 'That's the bitch who said my wife sleeps with me and the lodger together, one beneath and one on top! . . . Oh, yes, that's what they told me you said.'

But La Pierronne had recovered her composure, and she listened unbowed to the insults and the crude remarks, thoroughly disdainful in the certainty that she was richer and prettier than any of them.

'I said what I said, so now clear off . . . Do you hear me? What business is it of yours what I get up to? You're all just jealous and resent us because we've got money to put in the bank! Oh, yes, you can say what you like, but my husband knows perfectly well why Monsieur Dansaert was in our house.'

And indeed by now Pierron was angrily defending his wife. So they rounded on him instead, calling him a lackey, a grass, the Company's poodle, accusing him of locking himself in at home so that he could stuff himself on the choice morsels with which the bosses paid him for his treachery. He retaliated, claiming that Maheu had been slipping threatening notes under his door, one with a dagger and crossbones on it. And of course it all ended with the men fighting, just like all the other rows the women had started ever since hunger had turned even the mildest among them into a fury. Maheu and Levaque laid into Pierron with their fists, and they had to be dragged off him.

The blood was pouring from her son-in-law's nose when La Brûlé in turn arrived from the wash-house. Once they had told her what was going on, all she said was:

'That pig's a disgrace to me.'

The street was once again deserted, with not a shadow to blot the bare whiteness of the snow; and the village, having relapsed into its state of mortal inactivity, continued to starve to death surrounded by the intense cold.

'Any sign of the doctor?' Maheu asked, closing the door after him.

'He's not been,' replied La Maheude, who was still standing by the window.

'Are the little ones back?'

'No, not yet.'

Maheu resumed his heavy pacing, from one wall to the other, like some dazed ox. Old Bonnemort, sitting stiffly on his chair, had not even raised his head. Alzire, too, was silent and tried not to shiver, so as not to upset them; but despite her courage in the midst of her suffering she sometimes shook so violently that one could hear her thin, ailing young body almost rattling under the blanket. Meanwhile her big, wide eyes stared up at the ceiling where the pale reflection from the white gardens outside filled the room as though with moonlight.

They had reached their final hour: the house had been completely emptied, stripped terminally bare. The mattress covers had followed the wool stuffing to the second-hand shop; then the sheets had followed, and their linen, anything that could be sold. One evening they had got two sous for one of Grandpa's handkerchiefs. Tears were shed over each object that the penniless household found it had to part with, and La Maheude still rued the day she had taken along the little pink box, an old present from Maheu, wrapped in her skirt, as though she were taking an infant off to abandon it on someone's doorstep. They were destitute, and all they had left to sell was the skin on their bodies, which in any case was so damaged and used that no one would have paid a penny for it. So now they didn't even bother to search for something to sell, they knew there wasn't anything, that the end had come, that there was no hope of their ever again having a candle or a piece of coal or a potato; and as they waited to die, their only grievance was on behalf of the children, for they were outraged by the pointless cruelty of the little girl being afflicted with illness before she then starved to death anyway.

'At last. Here he comes!' said La Maheude.

A dark shape passed the window. The door opened. But it was not Dr Vanderhaghen. Instead they recognized the new priest, Father Ranvier, who did not appear in the least surprised to find the house dead, without light or fire or bread. He had just come from three other neighbouring households, doing the rounds of the families in an effort to recruit men of goodwill to his cause, just as Dansaert had done earlier in the company of the gendarmes. At once he explained his purpose in the feverish voice of the fanatic:

'Why did you not come to Mass last Sunday, my children? You are wrong, only the Church can save you . . . Now then, promise me you'll come next Sunday.'

Maheu had paused to see who it was and then resumed his heavy pacing, without a word. It was La Maheude who replied:

'To Mass, Father? Whatever for? When the good Lord couldn't care less about us? . . . Look! What harm did my little girl ever do Him? Yet now she's got the fever. We weren't suffering enough, I suppose, so He had to make her ill just when I haven't even got a warm drink to give her.'

The priest stood there and held forth at great length. He was using the strike – the terrible poverty, the sense of grievance sharpened by hunger – with the ardour of a missionary preaching to savages for the greater glory of his religion. He said that the Church was on the side of the poor and that one day it would cause justice to triumph by calling down the wrath of God upon the iniquities of the rich. And that day would soon dawn, for the rich had usurped God's place and were even now governing without God, having wickedly stolen His power. But if the workers were seeking the fair distribution of the fruits of the earth, then they should begin by placing their faith in the priests of the Church, just as the humble and the meek had gathered round the apostles upon the death of Jesus. What power the Pope would have then, what an army the clergy would be able to call upon if it could command the workers in their countless hosts! Within a week they would cleanse the world of the evildoers, they would dispatch the unworthy masters, and the true kingdom of God would be at hand, where each man would be rewarded according to his just desserts and the laws of the workplace would ensure the happiness of all.

As she listened, La Maheude thought she could hear Étienne, back on those autumn evenings when he told them that their troubles would soon be over. The only difference was that she had always been suspicious of men of the cloth.

'That's all very fine, Father,' she said. 'But you're only saying that because you've fallen out with the bourgeois ... All our other priests used to dine with the manager, and then they'd threaten us with hell-fire the moment we asked for bread.'

He continued, turning now to the deplorable rift that had occurred between the Church and the people. And in veiled terms he began to attack the urban priesthood, the bishops, the higher clergy, all of them sated on self-indulgence, bloated with power, and in their foolish blindness living hand in glove with the liberal bourgeoisie, not seeing that it was the bourgeoisie which was robbing them of their dominion over the world. Deliverance would come at the hands of the country priests, who would rise up as one to restore the kingdom of Christ, with the aid of the poor. And it was as though he were already at their head as he drew himself up to the full height of his bony frame, a leader of men, a Gospel revolutionary, his eyes filled with such a blazing light that they lit up the dark room. His fervent preaching so bore him up on the language of mysticism that for some time now the poor Maheus had not understood a thing he said.

'We don't need all your words,' Maheu interrupted crossly. 'You'd have done better to start by bringing us a loaf of bread.'

'Come to Mass on Sunday,' cried the priest. 'God will provide!'

And away he went, off to catechize the Levaques next, so uplifted by his dream of the Church's final victory and so disdainful of the realities of life that he continued empty-handed on his rounds of the villages, bringing no alms among this mass of people who were dying of hunger, a poor devil himself who regarded suffering as the very catalyst of salvation.

Maheu was still pacing up and down, and all that could be heard in the room was the regular thud of his feet as the flagstones shook beneath him. Then there was the sound of a rusty pulley turning as old Bonnemort spat into the fireplace. After which the rhythmic pacing began again. Alzire, drowsy with fever, had begun to mutter deliriously and to laugh, thinking that it was warm and that she was playing in the sunshine.

'God in heaven!' La Maheude murmured, having felt her cheeks. 'She's on fire . . . I'm not waiting for that bastard any more. Those criminals must have told him not to come.'

She was referring to the Company doctor. She gave a cry of joy none the less when she saw the door open once again. But she lowered her raised arms and stood there, ramrod straight, with a scowl on her face.

'Evening,' Étienne said softly, having carefully shut the door after him.

He would often call in like this when it was completely dark. From the second day the Maheus had known about his hiding-place, but they kept the secret, and no one in the village knew exactly what had become of the young man. As a result he was now a figure of legend. People continued to believe in him, and mysterious rumours circulated, like how one day he would return at the head of an army with coffers full of gold; and it was still as though everyone was waiting religiously for a miracle, for their hour to come, for the sudden entry into the city of justice that he had promised them. Some said they'd seen him in a smart carriage, with three other gentlemen, heading for Marchiennes; others maintained that he would be remaining in England for another couple of days. Eventually, however, they began to doubt him, and some jokers accused him of hiding in a cellar with La Mouquette to keep him warm; for his affair with her was public knowledge and had done him harm. His widespread popularity was slowly beginning to give way to disillusion as more and more of the faithful began to despair. Their number would grow.

'What filthy weather!' he added. 'How about you? Any news? Things still getting worse? . . . I heard that young Négrel had gone off to Belgium to fetch men from the Borinage coal-field. Christ, we're done for if it's true!'

He had given an involuntary shudder on entering this dark, icy-cold room, where he had to wait for his eyes to get used to the gloom before he could make out these poor, wretched people inside, and whom even then he discerned only as a thickening of shadow. He felt the repugnance and unease of the working man who has been lifted out of his class by the refinement of study and the thrust of ambition. The poverty and the smell and all these people living on top of one another! And the desperate pity of it all that was bringing a lump to his throat! Their last hour had come, and he found the spectacle so upsetting that he searched for some way to advise them to give up the struggle.

But suddenly there was Maheu standing foursquare in front of him and shouting:

'Belgians! They wouldn't dare, the useless bastards! . . . Well, just let them send their Belgians down, and then watch us destroy their pits for them!'

Looking embarrassed, Étienne explained that it was impossible to move an inch round the place: the soldiers guarding the pits would protect the Belgian workers as they went down. And Maheu clenched his fists, infuriated above all at having a bayonet in his back, as he put it. So the miners were no longer masters in their own backyard? Were they to be treated like galley-slaves and forced to work at rifle-point? He loved his pit, and it had hurt him greatly not to go down it for the last two months. So he saw red at the thought of being insulted like this, by these foreigners they were talking of bringing in. Then he remembered that he had been sacked, and it broke his heart.

'I don't know why I'm getting worked up about it,' he muttered. 'I don't belong in the bloody place any more . . . And once they've kicked me out of this house, I may as well go and die along the road somewhere.'

'Enough!' said Étienne. 'They'd take you back tomorrow if you wanted. Nobody sacks good workers.'

He broke off in astonishment on hearing Alzire, who was still laughing away quietly in the delirium of her fever. So far he had been able to identify only the stiff outline of old Bonnemort, and this gaiety on the part of a sick child disturbed him. This time things had gone too far, if the children were now starting to die. In a trembling voice, he took the plunge:

'Look here, this can't go on. We're done for . . . We'll have to give in.'

La Maheude, who had remained motionless and silent until then, now let fly, screaming in his face as though he were one of her own, swearing like a man:

'What did you say? *You?* Of all bloody people!'

He tried to explain, but she wouldn't let him speak.

'Don't you bloody well dare say that again, or God help me! I may be a woman but you'll soon feel the back of my hand across your face . . . We'd have spent the last two months dying of starvation, I'd have sold every object I possess, and my children would have been ill, but all for no purpose, all to keep on with the same old injustice . . . Oh, I tell you, the very thought of it makes my blood boil. No! No! I'd sooner set fire to the whole bloody lot and kill every single one of them rather than give up now.'

She gestured towards Maheu through the darkness with a grand, menacing wave of her hand:

'I tell you here and now. If that man returns to work, I'll be there waiting for him on the road, and I'll spit in his face and tell him he's one filthy coward!'

Étienne could not see her, but he could feel the heat coming from her, like the breath of a barking dog; and he recoiled in shock at this furious outburst of which he had been the cause. He found her so changed that he no longer recognized the woman who had once been full of good sense and used to reproach him for his violence. She used to say that one should never wish anyone dead, and yet here she was refusing to listen to reason and talking of killing everyone in sight. Now it was her not him who was taking the political line, wanting to get rid of the bourgeoisie in one fell swoop, demanding a republic and calling for the return of the guillotine to rid the world of the thieving rich who had grown fat on the toil of the starving poor.

'Yes indeed, I'd skin them alive with my own bare hands . . . No, we've had quite enough, thank you very much! Our time has come, you said so yourself . . . When I think that our fathers and grandfathers and grandfathers' fathers and everyone before them have all suffered as we're suffering now, and that our sons and their sons will all suffer the same, it makes me absolutely wild. Just give me the knife . . . We didn't do the half of what we should have done the other day. We should have demolished the whole of Montsou, down to the last sodding brick! And do you know what? My one big regret is that I didn't let Grandpa choke the life out of that girl from La Piolaine . . . After all, they're happy enough to choke the life out of my kids, aren't they?'

Her words cut through the darkness like the blows of an axe. The closed horizon had refused to open and, deep inside her head, riven by suffering, the unattainable ideal was now turning to poison.

'You've misunderstood me,' Étienne managed to say finally, beating a retreat. 'I meant we ought to try and reach an agreement with the Company. I know for a fact that the pits are deteriorating badly, and it would most likely consent to some form of compromise.'

'No, not one inch!' she screamed.

At that moment Lénore and Henri came home, empty-handed. A gentleman had given them two sous right enough, but as Lénore was always kicking her little brother, the money had fallen into the snow. Jeanlin had helped them look, but they had not been able to find the coins.

'Where is Jeanlin, then?'

'He went off somewhere, Mum. He said there were things he had to do.'

Étienne listened, sick at heart. Previously she used to threaten to kill them if they went begging. Now she sent them out on to the roads herself, and she even talked of them all going, all ten thousand miners from Montsou, each with stick and bundle like the paupers of old, roaming the region and terrifying its inhabitants.

The anguish in that dark room grew deeper still. The children had come home, hungry and wanting food, and now they wondered why no one was eating; they grumbled and mooched about, eventually treading on the feet of their dying sister, who uttered a groan. Furious, La Maheude tried to slap them and lashed out at random in the dark. When they started howling and demanding bread, she burst out crying and slumped down on to the floor, hugging the pair of them as well as the sick Alzire in one single embrace; and the tears poured out of her, copiously, in a form of nervous reaction which left her feeling completely limp and exhausted, as she repeated the same phrase over and over, calling on death to come: 'Dear God, why will You not take us all now? For pity's sake, take us and be done with it!' The grandfather continued to sit motionless like a gnarled old tree battered by the wind and the rain, while the father paced up and down from fireplace to dresser, his eyes firmly fixed in front of him.

But then the door opened, and this time it was Dr Vanderhaghen.

'What the devil!' he exclaimed. 'A candle won't harm your eyesight, you know . . . Come on, quick, I'm in a hurry.'

As usual he kept on grumbling, worn out by work. Fortunately he had some matches, and Maheu had to light six of these, one after the other, and hold them up so that the doctor could examine the sick girl. Stripped of her blanket, she lay shivering in the flickering light, like a thin, starving bird in the snow, so puny now that all one could see was her hump. And yet she was smiling, with that absent smile of the dying, wide-eyed, while her poor little fists lay clenched on her hollow chest.

And when La Maheude asked, choking back the tears, whether it was right that this child – the only one who helped her round the house, who was so intelligent and so sweet-natured – should be taken before her, the doctor lost his temper.

'There. She's gone now . . . The damned child's died of starvation. And she's not the only one either. I've just seen another, down the street . . . You all call me out, but there's nothing I can do. Meat's what you all need. That'll cure you.'

Maheu, his fingers burned, had dropped the match; and darkness fell once more on the little corpse that was still warm. The doctor had rushed away. And in the blackness of the room all Étienne could hear was La Maheude sobbing and crying out again and again, in ceaseless funereal lament, for death to come:

'Oh God, it's my turn now, take me! . . . Dear God, take my husband, take the others, for pity's sake. Please, no more!'

III

By eight o'clock that Sunday evening Souvarine was already the only one left in the saloon at the Advantage, sitting in his usual seat with his head against the wall. There wasn't a miner now who could lay his hands on the two sous needed for a pint, and the bars had never had so few customers. So Mme Rasseneur, with nothing to do but sit at the counter, maintained a tetchy silence, while Rasseneur stood by the cast-iron stove with a pensive air, seemingly preoccupied with the russet smoke rising from the coal.

Suddenly the stuffy tranquillity characteristic of overheated rooms was broken by the sound of three sharp taps on a window-pane, and Souvarine looked round. He got to his feet, having identified the signal that Étienne had already used several times before as a way of attracting his attention whenever he saw him sitting at an empty table smoking his cigarette. But before Souvarine could reach the door, Rasseneur had opened it; and, having recognized the man standing there, thanks to the bright light from the window, he said:

'What's up? Are you afraid I'm going to inform on you? . . .
Come on, you'll be much more comfortable talking in here than
out in the road.'

Étienne walked in. Mme Rasseneur politely offered him a beer,
but he refused with a wave of his hand. Rasseneur went on:

'I guessed long ago where you've been hiding. If I were a
grass, like your friends say, I'd have had the gendarmes after
you days ago.'

'It's all right, you don't need to defend yourself,' Étienne
replied. 'I know telling tales isn't your style . . . People can have
different ideas about things and still respect each other.'

Silence fell once more. Souvarine had returned to his seat,
with his back to the wall, gazing absently at the smoke from his
cigarette; but his restless fingers were fidgeting anxiously and he
kept running them over his knees, searching for the warm fur of
Poland, who was absent that evening. His uneasiness was quite
unconscious, a sense of something missing even though he could
not rightly say what it was.

Sitting on the other side of the table, Étienne said finally:

'Le Voreux's starting up again tomorrow morning. The Belgians have arrived with young Négrel.'

'Yes, they brought them in after dark,' murmured Rasseneur,
who had remained standing. 'Just as long as there's no more
bloodshed!'

Then, in a louder voice:

'Look, I don't want to start having an argument with you
again, but things really are going to turn nasty if you all carry
on being stubborn . . . It's just the same with that International
of yours, you know. I met Pluchart the day before yesterday in
Lille . . . I had business to attend to there. That whole set-up of
his is falling apart, it seems.'

He gave details. Having won over the workers of the world
with a propaganda campaign that still had the bourgeoisie
quaking in their shoes, the International was now being consumed by internal rivalries born of vanity and ambition, and
day by day these were gradually destroying it. Ever since the
anarchists had taken control, forcing out the gradualists who
had founded it in the first place, everything had been going

wrong; the original goal, the reform of the wage-system, had been lost sight of amid all the infighting, and the intellectuals were in disarray because they hated being regimented. The writing was already on the wall for this mass movement,[1] which for one brief moment had threatened to sweep away the old, rotten structures of society at a stroke.

'Pluchart's very frustrated about it all,' Rasseneur went on. 'And what's more he's lost his voice completely now. But he keeps making speeches, he's thinking of going to give one in Paris . . . And he told me three times that our strike had failed.'

Staring at the ground, Étienne let him have his say. The previous evening he had talked to some of the comrades, and he had felt the first waves of resentment and suspicion being directed at him, the first stirrings of the unpopularity that presages ultimate defeat. And he sat there gloomily, not wanting to admit his own sense of helplessness in front of a man who had predicted that one day the crowd would jeer at him too when the moment came for it to wreak vengeance for its own miscalculation.

'No doubt the strike has failed,' he replied. 'I know that as well as Pluchart. But we foresaw it would. We only went on strike against our better judgement, and we never thought it would mean the end of the Company . . . But people get carried away, they start hoping for all sorts of things, and then, when it all goes wrong, they forget that it was only to be expected, and they start wailing and arguing with each other as though the whole disaster were a bolt from the blue.'

'Well, then,' asked Rasseneur, 'if you think the game's up, why don't you get the comrades to see sense?'

Étienne glared at him:

'Look here, enough's enough . . . You have your ideas and I have mine. I came in because I wanted to show you that I respect you all the same. But I still think that even if we die in the attempt, our starved corpses will do more for the people's cause than any amount of your sensible approach . . . Ah, if only one of those bloody soldiers would put a bullet through my chest! It would be the perfect end!'

His eyes had begun to fill as he gave vent to his feelings,

betraying the secret desire of the vanquished for a place of eternal refuge in which all torment shall cease.

'Well said!' declared Mme Rasseneur, who shot a disdainful look at her husband in which the radical nature of her own opinions was plain to see.

Souvarine, gazing dreamily into the distance and still fidgeting nervously with his fingers, seemed not to have heard. His mystic reverie, full of sundry bloodthirsty visions, lent an air of savagery to his pale girlish face, with its thin nose and tiny pointed teeth. And now he had begun to think aloud, responding to something Rasseneur had said earlier about the International:

'They're all cowards. Only one man could have turned their organization into a truly fearsome instrument of destruction.[2] But you have to want to do it, and nobody does, and that's why yet again the revolution is going to fail.'

He proceeded, in a tone of disgust, to lament the general stupidity of men, while Rasseneur and Étienne listened uneasily as this sleepwalker shared his innermost thoughts with the realms of darkness. In Russia nothing was going right, and he despaired at the news he had been getting. His former comrades were all turning into politicians; the notorious nihilists[3] before whom the whole of Europe had trembled, the sons of the petit bourgeois, of priests and shopkeepers, could think no further than liberating their own country and seemed to believe they would have delivered the whole world once they had killed their own particular despot. And the moment he talked to them of razing the old society to the ground like a ripe harvest, or even used that meaningless word 'republic', he could see they didn't understand him, regarding him instead as a loose cannon and writing him off as a man who had stepped outside his class only to become one of the failed princes of international revolution. But he was still a patriot at heart, and it was with painful bitterness that he kept repeating his favourite phrase:

'It's all nonsense ... They'll never get anywhere with that nonsense.'

Then, lowering his voice, he began to speak bitterly about his old dream of brotherhood. He had given up his rank and fortune and thrown in his lot with the workers in the sole hope of seeing

a new society founded on the communality of labour. Every
penny he possessed had long since ended up in the pockets of
the village children, and he had always treated the miners with
brotherly affection, amused by their distrust of him and eventually winning them round by his quiet manner and the fact that
he took pride in his work and kept himself to himself. But quite
plainly he was never going to fit in completely, because in their
eyes he would always remain a foreigner, a stranger in their
midst, what with his scorn for all human ties and his determination to remain true to the cause, uncompromised by the
pursuit of pleasure or spurious honour. And since that morning
he had been feeling particularly exasperated by an item that was
in all the newspapers.

His voice changed and his eyes lost their dreamy air, as he
fixed Étienne with a stare and addressed him directly:

'Can you believe it? Those hat-makers in Marseilles who've
won the first prize of a hundred thousand francs in the lottery
and then immediately announce they're going to invest it and
live off the dividend and never work again! . . . That's it, you
see, that's all you French workers ever think about. Find hidden
treasure somewhere and keep it all to yourself, like everyone
else who's selfish and lazy. It's all very well your complaining
about the rich, but when good fortune brings you money, you
simply don't have the courage of your convictions to give it
back to the poor . . . You will never deserve to be happy while
you still have things you call your own or while your hatred of
the bourgeoisie is still no more than a desperate desire to be
bourgeois yourselves.'

Rasseneur burst out laughing; the idea that the two Marseilles
workers should hand back their first prize struck him as idiotic.
But Souvarine's face went white and his features contorted into
a terrifying expression, moved by the kind of religious wrath
that can exterminate entire races.

'You will all be cut down and tossed aside, cast on to the
rubbish-heap of history!' he cried. 'One day there shall come a
man who will rid the world of all you faint-hearts and pleasure-
seekers! Look at these hands! If they were strong enough, I'd

pick the whole world up just like this and shake it into little pieces, and you'd all be dead and buried beneath the ruins!'

'Well said!' Mme Rasseneur declared again, with her usual air of polite conviction.

There was another silence. Then Étienne returned to the subject of the Belgian workers. He asked Souvarine what arrangements had been made at Le Voreux. But the mechanic was once more deep in his own thoughts, and he barely answered; all he knew was that cartridges were to be issued to the soldiers guarding the pit. The nervous fidgeting of his fingers across his knees now reached such a pitch that he finally realized what it was that he was missing, the soft, soothing fur of his pet rabbit.

'Where's Poland?' he asked.

Rasseneur started laughing again and glanced across at his wife. After an embarrassed pause he plucked up courage:

'Poland? She's keeping warm.'

Ever since her escapade with Jeanlin, when she must have been injured, every litter the plump rabbit had produced had been stillborn; and so as not to have an unproductive mouth to feed, they had reluctantly decided that very day to serve her up with the potatoes.

'That's right. You had one of her legs this evening . . . Remember? You even licked your fingers!'

Souvarine did not understand at first. Then he turned very pale, his chin twitched as though he were going to be sick, and, despite his cultivation of a stoical indifference, two large tears began to well up in his eyes.

But no one had the time to notice this display of emotion because the door had suddenly been flung open and Chaval had appeared, pushing Catherine forward in front of him. Having got drunk on beer and brave talk in every bar in Montsou, it had suddenly occurred to him to visit the Advantage and show his former friends that he wasn't afraid of anybody. As he entered, he was saying to Catherine:

'By Christ, I tell you you're coming in here and you're going to have a beer, and I'll smash anyone's face in that so much as looks at me!'

Seeing Étienne there, Catherine was taken aback, and the colour drained from her face. When Chaval spotted him also, he gave a nasty snigger.

'Two beers, please, Madame Rasseneur! We're celebrating the return to work!'

Without saying a word, she poured the beer with the air of one who will always serve a customer. Everyone had fallen silent, and neither Rasseneur nor the other two men had moved from their places.

'I know some as have accused me of informing,' Chaval continued with a swagger, 'and I'm waiting for them to say it to my face so we can have the matter out once and for all.'

No one answered him, and the men turned away to gaze absently at the walls.

'There are bastards as works and some as don't,' he went on, raising his voice. 'Me, I've got nothing to hide. I've quit Deneulin's rotten outfit and tomorrow I'm going down Le Voreux with twelve Belgians. People think well of me there, so they've put me in charge of them. And if anyone doesn't like it, he can say so, and then we'll see.'

When his attempts at provocation met with the same contemptuous silence, he rounded on Catherine:

'Drink, for God's sake! . . . Come on, let's drink to the death of all them bastards that refuse to work!'

She joined him in the toast, but her hand was trembling so much that there was a noisy clink as the glasses met. Chaval had now taken a fistful of shiny coins from his pocket, which he proceeded to display with drunken ostentation, saying that it took the sweat of a man's brow to earn that sort of money and challenging idle layabouts to produce even ten sous. His comrades' response infuriated him, so he resorted to direct insults.

'Moles come out at night, it seems? The gendarmes must be asleep if the robbers are about!'

Étienne had now risen to his feet with calm resolve.

'Look, you're getting on my nerves . . . Yes, you are an informer, and your money must mean you've betrayed us again. And the very thought of even touching your toady skin turns my stomach. But no matter! I'm your man. It's high time one of us sorted the other out.'

Chaval clenched his fists.

'Christ, it doesn't half take a lot to get you going, you cowardly bugger! ... Just you, then? Fine. Well, I can tell you, you're going to pay for all those filthy things they did to me!'

Stretching her arms out imploringly, Catherine stepped between them, but they had no difficulty in moving her aside, for she could sense the inevitability of this fight, and slowly she backed away of her own accord. She stood silently against the wall, so paralysed with anxiety that she did not even tremble, and stared wide-eyed at these two men who were going to kill each other on account of her.

Mme Rasseneur calmly removed the glasses from the counter in case they got broken. Then she sat down again on her bench, demonstrating a discreet lack of interest in the proceedings. But it was Rasseneur's view that two former comrades simply could not be allowed to beat the life out of each other like this, and he persistently attempted to intervene. Souvarine had to grab him by the shoulder and lead him back to the table, saying:

'It's none of your business ... Even two's a crowd for them, so let the fittest survive.'

Without waiting to be attacked, Chaval was already punching the air. He was the taller of the two, an ungainly figure, and using both arms he made furious slashing movements in the direction of Étienne's face, as if he were wielding a pair of sabres. And he kept on talking, playing to the gallery and working himself up even further by unleashing a stream of insults:

'Right, you little pimp, let's see if we can shove that nose of yours somewhere where the sun don't shine! ... Mmm, and I think we'll just rearrange that tarty little pretty-boy mouth of yours, too! Then we'll see if the bitches still come running after you!'

But Étienne, clenching his teeth and drawing himself up to his full, diminutive height, was fighting like a boxer, using his fists to protect his face and chest; and he waited for his openings, jabbing away fiercely as though his arms were tightly coiled springs.

At first they did each other little harm. The violent windmill action of the one and the cool waiting game of the other both served to prolong the encounter. A chair was knocked over, and their heavy shoes crunched on the white sand strewn over the flagstone floor. But eventually the two men were winded and could be heard gasping for breath, while their red faces began to swell as though there were braziers inside and the flames could be seen through the bright holes that were their eyes.

'Take that!' screamed Chaval. 'Bull's eye!'

And, indeed, like a flail launched at an angle, his fist had caught his opponent's shoulder. Étienne stifled a groan of pain, and the only sound was a dull thud as his muscles absorbed the bruising blow. And he responded with a straight punch to the chest, which would have floored the other man if he hadn't been leaping about like a goat. All the same the punch caught him on his left side, and so hard that he staggered and had to catch his breath. When he felt his arms grow limp with the pain, he flew into a rage and started lashing out with his feet like an animal, trying to rip Étienne's stomach open with his heel.

'And that one's for your guts!' he spluttered in a choking voice. 'It's time your innards were pulled.'

Étienne dodged the kick and was so outraged by this infringement of the rules of fair combat that he broke his silence:

'Shut your mouth, you brute! And no kicking, for Christ's sake, or I'll get a chair and knock your brains out!'

The fight now grew fiercer. Rasseneur was sickened and would again have tried to intervene if his wife had not dissuaded him with a stern look: surely two customers were entitled to settle their differences here? So he had merely placed himself in front of the fireplace, for fear they might topple in. With his usual calm air Souvarine had rolled himself a cigarette, but he omitted to light it. Catherine was still standing motionless against the wall: only her hands had moved, rising unbidden to her waist, where they had writhed and begun to tear at her dress in recurrent spasms of nervous anxiety. It took her all her strength not to cry out, not to be the death of one man by proclaiming her preference for the other, though in fact she was so distraught that she no longer knew which one that might be.

Chaval soon grew weary, and he was now drenched in sweat and hitting out at random. Despite his anger Étienne kept up his guard and parried most of the punches, although some did get through. His ear was split, and Chaval's nail had gouged out a piece of his neck, which smarted so much that he, too, started cursing and swearing as he tried to land one of his direct blows to the chest. Once again Chaval leaped out of the way; but he had bent forward in the process, and Étienne's fist hit him in the face, flattening his nose and closing an eye. Blood spurted from his nostrils at once, and the eye swelled up and turned blue. Blinded by this red stream and dazed by the blow to his skull, the wretched man was wildly beating the air when another punch straight to the chest finished him off. There was a cracking sound, and he fell backwards on to the floor with a heavy thud like a sack of plaster dumped off a cart.

Étienne waited.

'Get up. We can start again if you want.'

Chaval made no reply, but after lying there dazed for a few seconds he began to stir and to stretch his limbs. He struggled painfully to his knees, where he paused bent double for a moment while his hand rummaged in his pocket on some invisible errand. Then, as he got to his feet, he lunged forward again, and a wild cry burst from his bulging throat.

But Catherine had seen: and in spite of herself she screamed, from the heart, surprising even herself as though she had just admitted a preference she didn't even know she had.

'Watch out! He's got his knife!'

Étienne had only just had time to ward off the first thrust with his arm. His woollen jersey was cut by the thick blade, one of those blades that are attached to a boxwood handle by a copper ferrule. Already he had grabbed hold of Chaval's wrist, and a fierce struggle ensued, with Étienne thinking that he would be lost if he let go, and his opponent jerking his arm away repeatedly in order to break free and strike again. Slowly the weapon was coming lower and lower, their straining limbs were beginning to give out, and twice Étienne felt the cold touch of steel against his skin; but with one last, supreme effort he squeezed Chaval's wrist so hard that the knife fell from his open hand.

Both men flung themselves to the ground at once, and it was
Étienne who reached it first and now brandished it in his turn.
He had Chaval pinned to the floor beneath his knee, and he was
threatening to slit his throat.

'Right, you cheating bastard, you've had it this time!'

Within him he sensed a terrible prompting, blotting out all
else. It surged up from his entrails and pounded inside his skull,
a sudden, crazed desire to kill, a desperate thirst for blood.
Never before had he had such a strong attack as this. And yet
he wasn't drunk. And as he struggled to resist this hereditary
evil, he shook violently like some maniacal lover trembling on
the brink of rape. At length he managed to control himself and
tossed the knife behind him, spluttering in a hoarse voice:

'Get up. And bugger off.'

This time Rasseneur had rushed forward, but without trying
too hard to come between them in case he should get hit by
mistake. He didn't want anyone getting killed on his premises,
and he became so angry that his wife, standing at the counter,
told him that he always did get roused too quick. Souvarine,
who had almost got the knife in his legs, was now finally getting
round to lighting his cigarette. Was that it? Catherine continued
to stare in stupefaction at the two men, both of them still alive.

'Bugger off!' Étienne said again. 'Go on, or I really will finish
you off!'

Chaval rose to his feet and with the back of his hand wiped
away the blood that was still pouring from his nose; and then,
his chin spattered with blood, his eye blackened, he sloped off
in sullen fury at his defeat. Automatically Catherine made to
follow him. Then he drew himself up, and his hatred poured
out in a torrent of obscene abuse.

'Oh no you don't. Oh no! If it's him you want, then fucking
sleep with him, you filthy slut! And don't you set foot in my
house again either, if you want to live!'

He slammed the door after him. A heavy silence fell in the
warm room, where the only sound was the gentle puttering of
the coal. On the floor all that remained were the upturned chair
and a spattering of blood, which was gradually soaking into the
sand.

IV

After they left Rasseneur's, Étienne and Catherine walked along
in silence. It was beginning to thaw, a slow, chilly thaw that
dirtied the snow without really melting it. In the ghostly
pale sky the full moon could be glimpsed behind large clouds
that were being swept along by a gale, high above them, like
black rags; down below there was not a breath of wind, and
all that could be heard was the water dripping from the roofs
and the gentle thud as another lump of whiteness slid to the
ground.

Étienne felt awkward with this female companion he had
suddenly acquired, and in his embarrassment he could think of
nothing to say. The idea of taking her into hiding with him at
Réquillart seemed ridiculous. He had wanted to escort her home
to her parents in the village; but she had refused with a look of
absolute terror: no, no, anything rather than become a burden
to them, especially after abandoning them in such a despicable
way! Since then neither of them had spoken, and they trudged
along at random down paths that were becoming rivers of mud.
At first they had headed towards Le Voreux; then they turned
right and passed between the spoil-heap and the canal.

'But you've got to sleep somewhere,' Étienne said eventually.
'I mean, if I had a room of my own, I'd gladly take you with
me . . .'

But in a moment of curious shyness he stopped short. He
remembered their previous passionate desire for each other, and
their hesitations and the sense of embarrassment that had got
in the way. Did this mean he still wanted her, then, that he
should feel awkward like this and sense his heart warming
with renewed attraction? The memory of her slapping him at
Gaston-Marie now excited him instead of making him resentful.
And to his surprise it suddenly seemed perfectly natural and
feasible that he should take her with him to Réquillart.

'Come on, you decide. Where do you want me to take you?
Do you really still hate me so much that you won't go with me?'

She was slowly following him, but her clogs kept slipping on the ruts and she found it difficult to keep up. Without looking up, she muttered:

'I've got enough troubles as it is, for God's sake, I don't need any more. Where would be the good if I did what you're asking? I've got a man, and you've got someone too.'

She meant La Mouquette. She thought he was going with her because that had been the rumour for the past fortnight; and when he swore to Catherine that he wasn't, she just shook her head, recalling the evening she'd seen them kissing each other on the mouth.

'It's a shame, isn't it, all this stupid nonsense?' he said softly, stopping for a moment. 'We could have got on so well together!'

She gave a little shiver and answered him:

'Oh, there's nothing to be sorry about. You're not missing much. If you only knew what a useless specimen I am. I hardly weigh more than a tuppenny tub of butter, and I think the way I'm made I'll never be a proper woman!'

And she continued to speak freely, accusing herself for the long delay in the onset of her puberty as though it were her own fault. Even though she had had a man it diminished her, it meant she was still no more than a girl. At least there's some excuse when you can actually have a baby.

'My poor little thing,' Étienne said softly, suddenly feeling great pity for her.

They were standing at the bottom of the spoil-heap, hidden in the shadow cast by the enormous mound. An ink-black cloud was just then passing in front of the moon; they couldn't even see their faces any more, but their breath mingled and their mouths sought each other out for the kiss they had so tormentedly longed for all these months past. But suddenly the moon appeared again, and above them, on top of the rocks that were white with moonlight, they saw the outline of the sentry standing stiffly to attention. And so, still without ever having kissed, they drew back, parted by their modesty of old, which was a mixture of angry resentment, physical reserve and a great deal of friendship. Slowly they resumed their walking, up to their ankles in slush.

'So your mind's made up? You don't want to?' asked Étienne.

'No,' she said. 'You after Chaval? Then somebody else after you? ... No, the whole thing disgusts me. Anyway, I get no pleasure out of it, so what's the point?'

They fell silent and walked on a hundred paces without exchanging a further word.

'Do you at least know where you're going?' he continued. 'I can't just leave you out here alone on a night like this.'

She replied simply:

'I'm going home. Chaval is my man, and it's the only place I have to sleep.'

'But he'll beat the daylights out of you!'

There was silence again. She had merely shrugged in resignation. He would beat her, and when he had tired of beating her, then he would stop. But wasn't that better than roaming the streets like a beggar? Besides, she was getting used to the beatings, and she told herself by way of consolation that eight out of ten girls ended up no better off than she was. And if he married her some day, well, that would actually be quite decent of him.

Étienne and Catherine had automatically headed in the direction of Montsou, and as they drew nearer, their silences grew longer and longer. Already it was as if they had never been together. Étienne could think of nothing that might make her change her mind, even though it pained him deeply to see her go back to Chaval. His heart was breaking, but he had little better to offer her himself: a life of poverty, a life on the run, perhaps even no future at all if a soldier's bullet should blow his brains out. Perhaps it was wiser after all to endure the suffering one was used to rather than swap it for another kind. And so, with his eyes fixed on the ground, he escorted her home to her man; and he offered no protest when she stopped on the main road at the corner by the Company yards, twenty metres short of Piquette's bar, and said:

'Don't come any further. If he sees you, it'll just mean another row.'

The church clock was striking eleven. The bar was closed, but light could be seen through chinks in the shutters.

'Goodbye,' she murmured.

She had given him her hand but he refused to let go of it, and it was only by slow, determined effort that she managed to retrieve it and depart. Without a backward glance she unlatched the little side-door and let herself in. He did not leave, however, but continued to stand there, on the very same spot, staring at the house and anxiously wondering what was happening inside. He listened intently, dreading that he might hear the howling screams of a woman being beaten. But the house remained dark and silent, and all he saw was a light appearing at a first-floor window; and when this window opened and he recognized the slender shadow leaning out into the road, he stepped forward.

Then Catherine whispered very softly:

'He's not back yet. I'm going to bed ... Please go away, please.'

Étienne left. The thaw was gathering pace: water was stream- ing from the roofs, and a damp sweat seemed to be running off every wall and fence throughout the jumble of industrial buildings that stretched away into the darkness on this side of the town. His first thought was to make for Réquillart; ill with exhaustion and sick at heart, he wanted nothing more than to disappear into the void below ground. But then he remembered Le Voreux and thought about the Belgian workers who were about to go down, and the comrades in the village who were fed up with the continual presence of the soldiers and determined not to have outsiders working in their pit. And so once more he walked along the canal, through the puddles of melted snow.

As he reached the spoil-heap, the moon was riding high. He looked up at the sky and saw the clouds scudding past, whipped along by the great wind that was blowing up there; but now they were whiter, unravelling in thin streaks and passing over the face of the moon with the blurred transparency of troubled water; and they followed so fast one upon the other that the moon was veiled only for a moment and kept reappearing again in all its clarity.

His eyes filled with this brilliance, Étienne was just lowering his gaze when he caught sight of something on top of the spoil-heap. The sentry, frozen stiff by the cold, was now walking up and down, twenty-five paces towards Marchiennes and then back in the direction of Montsou. The white flash of the bayonet could be seen above his dark silhouette, itself sharply etched against the pallor of the sky. But what had attracted Étienne's attention, over behind the hut where Bonnemort used to shelter on stormy nights, was a moving shadow, an animal crawling stealthily forward, which he at once recognized as Jeanlin, with his long, supple back like a ferret's. Unable to be seen by the sentry, the little devil was no doubt about to play some trick on him, for he was always going on about the soldiers and asking when they would ever be rid of these murderers who had been sent here to shoot the people.

For a moment Étienne wondered if he should call out to him, to stop him doing anything silly. Just as the moon went behind a cloud, he had seen him getting ready to pounce; but then the moon came out again, and the child was still crouching there. On each occasion the sentry would come as far as the hut, then turn on his heels and walk away. Suddenly, just as another cloud cast everything into darkness, Jeanlin sprang on to the sentry's shoulders in one enormous bound, like a wild cat, clung on by his nails, and plunged his opened knife into the man's throat from behind. The soldier's horse-hair collar obstructed the blade, and Jeanlin had to press the handle in with both hands and pull it towards him using the full weight of his body. He was used to slitting chicken's throats, having caught them unawares behind some farm building. It was all over so quickly that the only sound in the darkness was a muffled cry, followed by the clatter of the gun as it fell to the ground. The moon was already gleaming a brilliant white once more.

Rooted to the spot in astonishment, Étienne continued to watch. His intended shout vanished back into his chest. Above him the spoil-heap was deserted, and no shadowy figure was now to be seen outlined against the stampeding clouds. He ran up as fast as he could and found Jeanlin crouching beside the body, which lay flat on its back with arms outstretched. In the bright moonlight the red trousers and grey overcoat stood out starkly against the snow. Not a drop of blood had fallen: the knife was still lodged in the man's throat up to the hilt.

In a fit of unthinking rage he knocked the boy over with his fist beside the corpse.

'Why on earth did you do that?' he stammered in disbelief.

Jeanlin struggled to his knees and crawled away on all fours, arching his bony spine like a cat. His large ears and jutting jaw were quivering, and his eyes blazed with the excitement of his dirty deed.

'In God's name, why did you do that?'

'Dunno. Just felt like it.'

It was the only reply he could manage. For three days now he had felt like it. The idea had been tormenting him, and he had thought about it so much that it had made his head hurt, right there, behind the eyes. And anyway why should he give a damn about these bloody soldiers who'd only come to make a nuisance of themselves in the miners' backyard? Having heard all the rousing speeches in the forest and the calls to death and destruction throughout the pits, he had retained five or six key words, which he repeated to himself like a child playing at revolutions. And that was all he knew, nobody had put him up to it, he had thought of it all by himself, just like he sometimes fancied stealing onions from a field.

Étienne was appalled at the idea of these criminal urges quietly seething inside the child's head, and he gave him a kick to send him packing, as though he were a dumb animal. He was afraid that they might have heard the sentry's muffled cry from the guardroom at Le Voreux, and each time the moon came out from behind a cloud he would glance over towards the pit. But nothing had stirred, so he bent over and touched the man's hands, which were gradually turning to ice; and he listened in vain to the silent heart beneath the greatcoat. All that could be seen of the knife was the bone handle, on which a romantic motto was carved in black letters: the simple word 'Love'.

His eyes travelled up from the throat to the face. All of a sudden he recognized the young soldier: it was Jules, the raw recruit he had spoken to one morning. And he felt an enormous wave of pity at the sight of this fair, gentle face all covered in freckles. The blue eyes were wide open, gazing at the sky with that fixed stare Étienne had seen before as he scanned the horizon searching for his native soil. Where was this Plogoff that had appeared to him as in a sun-drenched vision? Somewhere over yonder. Far away the sea would be roaring on this stormy night. Perhaps this gale that was passing so high above them had already swept across his moorland. Two women would be standing there, the mother and the sister, holding on to their bonnets in the wind and gazing into the distance as if they, too, might see far enough and discover what the boy was doing all those miles away. Now they would wait for ever. What a truly dreadful thing it was that poor devils should kill each other like this and all on account of the rich!

But they would have to get rid of the body, and at first Étienne considered throwing it into the canal. But he was deterred by the thought that it would certainly be found. He then became extremely worried; time was ticking by, what should he do? He had a sudden inspiration: if he could carry it as far as Réquillart, he could bury it there for all eternity.

'Come over here,' he ordered Jeanlin.

The child was wary.

'No, you'll only hit me again. Anyway, I've got something to do. Bye.'

He had indeed arranged to meet Bébert and Lydie, at a secret hiding-place they'd made for themselves under the timber-stack at Le Voreux. It was all to be a big adventure, sleeping away from home so as to be part of the action if people started stoning the living daylights out of the Belgians when they tried to go down the pit.

'Do as I say,' Étienne insisted. 'Come over here, or I'll call the soldiers and they'll cut your head off.'

As Jeanlin was making up his mind, Étienne rolled up his handkerchief and wrapped it tightly round the soldier's neck, leaving the knife in place because it was stopping the blood from pouring out. The snow was melting, and the ground bore no traces of blood nor signs of a struggle.

'Take his legs.'

Jeanlin grabbed the legs, while Étienne slung the rifle over his shoulder and took hold of the body under the arms. Slowly the pair of them made their way down the spoil-heap, trying hard

not to dislodge any rocks. Fortunately the moon had gone in.
But as they were going along the side of the canal, it came out
again and shone brightly; it was a miracle the guards at Le
Voreux didn't see them. They hurried on in silence, but the
swaying of the corpse made progress difficult, and they were
forced to set it down every hundred metres. At the corner of the
lane leading to Réquillart a sudden noise struck terror into their
hearts, and they only just had time to hide behind a wall before
a patrol came past. Further on they bumped into a man, but he
was drunk and went on his way cursing and swearing at them.
But finally they reached the old mine, drenched in sweat and in
such a state that their teeth were chattering.

Étienne had realized already that it would not be easy to
manhandle the body down the shaft. It was a nasty job. First,
Jeanlin had to lower the body from above while he hung from
the bushes and guided it down past the first two ladders, where
some of the rungs were broken. Then with each new ladder he
had to repeat the same manœuvre, climbing down ahead and
then taking it in his arms; and there were thirty ladders in all,
two hundred and ten metres in which to feel the body continually
falling into his arms. The rifle was rubbing on his spine, and he
had stopped the lad from fetching his one bit of candle, which
he was jealously preserving. What would have been the point?
The light would only have been a further encumbrance in the
confined space. All the same, when they finally reached the
loading-bay, completely out of breath, he did send the boy off
to get it. He sat down and waited in the darkness, next to the
corpse, his heart pounding.

As soon as Jeanlin came back with the candle, Étienne asked
his advice, for the child had explored every inch of these old
workings, down to the narrow clefts, which were impossible for
a grown man to pass through. They set off again, dragging the
dead man behind them for nearly a kilometre through a maze
of ruined roadways. Eventually the roof began to sink lower,
and they found themselves on their knees beneath some crumbling rock that was held up only by some half-broken timbering.
The space had the dimensions of a long box, and they laid the
young soldier down in it as though it were a coffin, placing the

rifle alongside him; then they gave the props a few hefty kicks with the backs of their heels to break them completely, even though they themselves risked being buried alive. The rock gave way at once, and they barely had time to crawl free on their hands and knees. Unable to resist a last look, Étienne saw the roof gradually collapse and slowly crush the corpse beneath its enormous weight. And then that was all that was left, just the earth's solid mass.

Jeanlin, now back home in his robber's den, flung himself down on the hay and muttered in a weary voice:

'Phew! Lydie and Bébert will just have to wait for me. I've got to have an hour's kip.'

Étienne had blown out the candle, of which only a tiny stub remained. He, too, was completely exhausted, but he did not feel sleepy since painful nightmarish thoughts were hammering away inside his head. Soon only one remained, a single tormenting question that nagged away at him but which he could not answer: why had he not stabbed Chaval when he had held him at knife-point? And why had this child just slit a soldier's throat without even knowing his name? It all undermined his revolutionary notions about being prepared to kill, about having the right to kill. Did this mean he was a coward? Over in the hay the child had begun to snore, like a drunk, as though he had binged on slaughter. And Étienne felt disgust and irritation at knowing the boy was there and at having to listen to him. Suddenly he gave a shudder, he had just felt the breath of fear on his face. It was as though a faint ripple of air, like a sob, had issued from the depths of the earth. The picture of the young soldier lying there beneath the rocks with his rifle by his side sent shivers down his spine and made his hair stand on end. It was ridiculous, but the whole mine seemed to fill with the sound of voices, and he had to relight the candle; he only regained his composure once he could see the empty roadways in its pale glow.

For a further quarter of an hour he pondered things, still wrestling with the same question, his eyes fixed on the burning wick. Then there was a sizzling sound, the wick drowned in wax, and everything was once more plunged into darkness. His shudders returned, and he felt like hitting Jeanlin to stop him snoring so loudly. The proximity of the boy became so intolerable that he fled, filled with a desperate need for fresh air, and rushed through the roadways and up the shaft as though he could hear a ghost panting at his heels.

Back on the surface, amid the ruins of Réquillart, Étienne could at last breathe freely. Since he hadn't dared to kill, he would have to die himself, and the prospect of his own death, which had already vaguely occurred to him, now loomed once more and lodged firmly in his mind, like one last hope. If he died a valiant death, if he died for the revolution, that would be the end of it, that would resolve things one way or another, for good or ill, it would mean he didn't have to think about the matter any further. If the comrades were going to attack the Belgians, he would make sure he was in the front line, and with a bit of luck he might get shot. And so it was with a resolute step that he returned to Le Voreux to see what was going on. Two o'clock struck, and the sound of voices could be heard coming noisily from the deputies' room, which had been taken over by the military guards. The sentry's disappearance had caused a considerable stir; they had gone to wake the captain, and in the end, after a careful inspection of the scene, it was decided that the soldier must have deserted. As Étienne listened from the shadows, he remembered the republican captain the young soldier had told him about. Supposing he could be persuaded to come over to the people's side? The troops would carry their guns reversed, and that could prove to be a general signal for the wholesale slaughter of the bourgeois. A new dream took hold of him. He forgot all about dying and continued to stand there in the mud, for hour after hour; and as the drizzle from the thaw settled on his shoulders, he was filled with the feverish hope that victory might yet be possible.

He kept an eye out for the Belgians until five o'clock. Then he realized that the Company had cunningly arranged for them to spend the night at Le Voreux itself. The men were already beginning to go down, and the handful of strikers from Village Two Hundred and Forty who had been posted as lookouts were unsure whether to inform the comrades or not. It was Étienne who told them about the clever ploy, and they ran off, while he waited on the towpath behind the spoil-heap. Six o'clock struck, and the murky sky was beginning to turn pale in the light from a russet dawn when Father Ranvier emerged from a path, his cassock hoisted over his spindly legs. Every Monday he went to say early-morning Mass at a convent chapel on the other side of the pit.

'Good-morning, my friend,' he called loudly, having given Étienne a long hard stare with his blazing eyes.

But Étienne made no reply. In the distance he had caught sight of a woman passing between the supports of the overhead railway at Le Voreux, and he had rushed off anxiously, thinking it was Catherine.

Since midnight Catherine had been wandering the streets in the slush. When Chaval had returned home to find her in bed, he had soon got her up again with a slap in the face. He had screamed at her to leave at once, by the door if she didn't want to leave by the window; and so, in tears, with barely any clothes on, and badly bruised where he had kicked her in the legs, she had been forced downstairs and then dispatched into the street with one last blow. Dazed and bewildered by this brutal separation, she had sat down on a milestone, watching the house and waiting for him to call her back. For he was bound to; he would be waiting to see what she did, and when he saw her shivering in the cold like this, abandoned, with nobody in the world to put a roof over her head, he would surely call her back upstairs.

Two hours later, having sat there motionless like a dog turned out into the street, and now freezing to death, she made up her mind and left Montsou. But back she came, though she still didn't dare to call up from the pavement or knock at the door. In the end she departed down the long straight road out of Montsou, meaning to return to her parents' house in the village. But when she got there, she suddenly felt so ashamed that she began to run the length of the gardens, afraid she might be recognized despite the fact that behind all the closed shutters everyone was fast asleep. After that she just wandered about. The slightest sound made her jump, and she was terrified of being picked up as a vagrant and marched off to the brothel at

Marchiennes, a prospect that had been giving her nightmares for several months. Twice she ended up at Le Voreux, took fright at the loud voices coming from the guardroom, and scurried away in breathless panic, glancing behind her to make sure that no one was following her. Réquillart was always full of drunks, but she went back there nevertheless in the vague hope of meeting the man she had rejected a few hours earlier.

Chaval was due to go down that morning, and knowledge of the fact drew Catherine to the pit even though she realized the futility of trying to speak to him: it was all over between them. Work had now stopped completely at Jean-Bart, and he had threatened to throttle her if she went back to her old job at Le Voreux, where he was afraid her presence might make things awkward for him. But what could she do? Go somewhere else, die of starvation, yield to every passing man who beat her up? She struggled on, stumbling over the ruts in the road, her legs almost giving way beneath her, and covered up to the waist in dirt. The thaw had turned the roads into rivers of mud, but she floundered on, not even daring to find a stone to sit on.

Daylight came. Catherine had just recognized Chaval's back as he cautiously turned the corner of the spoil-heap, and then she caught sight of Lydie and Bébert peeping out of their den beneath the timber-stack. They had been keeping watch there all night, refusing to give in and go home on account of Jeanlin's order to wait for him; and while the latter was sleeping off his murderous excesses at Réquillart, the two children had been holding each other tight to keep warm. The wind whistled through the props of oak and chestnut, and they snuggled together as though they were in some abandoned woodman's hut. Lydie no more dared to talk openly about all she had suffered as the child version of a battered wife than Bébert could find the courage to complain of the slaps in the face he got from their leader and which made his cheeks swell up. But really, Jeanlin had gone too far, making them risk their necks in all these mad escapades and then refusing to share the spoils; their hearts rebelled, and eventually they kissed, despite his having forbidden it and despite the risk of getting a clip round the ear from out of the blue, as he had threatened. The clip round the ear did not materialize, and they continued to exchange soft kisses, having no thought to any other form of contact and putting into their embrace all the pent-up passion of their forbidden feelings, every moment of affection and painful martyrdom they had ever known. They had kept each other warm like this the whole night through, so happy in their remote hideaway that they could not remember ever having felt happier, even on St Barbe's Day when everyone had fritters and wine.

A sudden bugle-call made Catherine jump. She craned her neck and saw the guards at Le Voreux taking up their weapons. Étienne was running towards her, Bébert and Lydie had leaped out of their hiding-place. And in the distance, in the growing daylight, a band of men and women could be seen coming down from the village, angrily waving their arms.

V

All the entrances to Le Voreux had just been closed; and the sixty soldiers of the guard, with their rifles at their sides, were barring the way to the only door still left open, the one that led up to the pit-head via a narrow flight of steps and past the doors to the deputies' office and the changing-room. The captain had lined the men up in two ranks with their backs to the brick wall so that they could not be attacked from behind.

At first the band of miners from the village kept its distance. There were thirty of them at most, and they were busy arguing loudly about the best course of action to take.

La Maheude had been the first to reach the pit, with her dishevelled hair bundled hastily under a black scarf and carrying a sleeping Estelle on her arm; and she kept repeating with feverish urgency:

'No one goes in and no one comes out! We're going to corner the lot of them!'

Maheu was nodding in agreement when old Mouque arrived from Réquillart. They tried to stop him getting through. But he would have none of it; his horses, he said, still had to have their oats and they didn't give a tinker's cuss about any revolution. Besides, one of the horses was dead, and they were waiting for him to arrive before bringing it out. Étienne cleared a path for the old stableman, and the soldiers let him climb the steps into the mine. A quarter of an hour later, as the swelling band of strikers was becoming more threatening, a large door opened at ground level and some men appeared, hauling the dead animal, a sorry bundle still wrapped in its rope net, which they then abandoned among the puddles of melted snow. Everybody was so shocked that no one tried to prevent them going back inside and barricading the door again after them. They had all recognized the horse by its head, which was bent back stiffly against its side. People whispered to each other:

'That's Trumpet, isn't it? I'm sure it is.'

And indeed it was. He had never been able to accustom himself to life underground. He had always looked miserable and never wanted to work, as though tormented by longing for the daylight he had lost. Battle, the doyen of the pit horses, had tried in vain to pass on some of his ten years' accumulated compliance by rubbing up against him in a friendly way and nibbling at his neck. Such caresses had only made Trumpet more miserable, and his coat would quiver as he received these confidences from his elderly comrade who had grown old in the darkness. Each time they met and exchanged a snort, they both seemed to be uttering a lament, the older horse because he could no longer remember, the younger because he could not yet forget. In the stables they shared a manger and spent their time together hanging their heads and blowing into each other's nostrils, sharing their constant dream of daylight, their visions of green grass and white roads and yellow brightness stretching into infinity. Then, as Trumpet lay dying in the straw, bathed in sweat, Battle had begun to nuzzle him, in despair, with short snuffles that sounded like sobs. He could feel him getting cold: the mine was taking away his one last joy in life, this friend who had come down from above all full of lovely smells that recalled the days of his own youth up in the fresh air. And when he had seen that the other horse was no longer moving, he had broken his tether and whinnied with fear.

In fact Mouque had been warning the overman for the past week. But what did they care about a sick horse at a time like this! These gentlemen were not keen on moving horses. But now they really would have to do something about getting him out. The previous day the stableman and two other men had spent an hour trying ropes round Trumpet, and then Battle was harnessed to haul him as far as the shaft. Slowly the old horse pulled his dead comrade along, dragging him through a tunnel which was so narrow that he had to jerk him forward from time to time, at the risk of skinning him. It was heavy going, and the horse kept shaking his head as he listened to this mass of flesh scraping against the rock on its way to the knacker's yard. When they unharnessed him at pit-bottom, he gazed with a doleful eye at the preparations for Trumpet's ascent, watching as they pushed him on to cross-beams placed over the sump and roped him to the bottom of a cage. Eventually the onsetters signalled that the 'meat' was on its way, and he raised his head to watch him leave, gently at first, then suddenly being whisked away into the darkness, lost for ever up the black hole. And as he stood there craning his neck, the animal could perhaps dimly remember the things of this earth. But it was all over, his comrade would never see anything ever again, and one day he too would be tied into a miserable parcel like this and make his way to the surface. His legs started trembling, and he began to choke on the fresh air coming down from those distant landscapes; and as he plodded slowly back to his stable, it was as though he were drunk.

In the pit-yard the mood was sombre as the miners stood round Trumpet's corpse. One woman said softly:

'At least a person can decide if they want to go down there or not.'

But a new wave of people was arriving from the village, and Levaque, marching at their head followed by La Levaque and Bouteloup, was shouting:

'Death to the Belgians! No foreigners in our pit! Death to the Belgians.'

They all surged forward, and Étienne had to check them. He walked up to the captain, a tall, thin young man in his late twenties, who looked grim but determined, and he explained the situation to him, trying to win him over, watching carefully to see what effect his words would have. Why risk a pointless massacre? Wasn't justice on the side of the miners? They were all brothers, they ought to be able to come to some agreement. At the mention of a republic, the captain gestured nervously, but he maintained his stiff military bearing and said abruptly:

'Stand back. Don't force me to do my duty!'

Three times Étienne tried again. Behind him the comrades were becoming restive. A rumour was going round that M. Hennebeau was at the pit, and somebody suggested letting him down the shaft by his neck to see if he would dig out the coal himself. But the rumour was false; only Négrel and Dansaert were there, and they appeared briefly at a pit-head window. The overman remained in the background, unwilling to show his face since his episode with La Pierronne, but the engineer boldly surveyed the crowd with his sharp little eyes, smiling with the cheerful contempt that he habitually bestowed on all men and all things. People started hissing and booing, and the two men vanished from sight. And in the place where they had been standing, only the fair, pale face of Souvarine could now be seen. It happened to be his shift. Since the beginning of the strike he had never left his machinery even for a single day, but he had become more and more taciturn and more and more preoccupied by some obsession or other, which seemed to gleam like a bolt of steel in the depths of his pale eyes.

'Stand back!' the captain repeated very loudly. 'I'm not here to negotiate. My orders are to guard the pit, and guard it I shall . . . And stop pushing into my men, or I'll soon give you a reason to stand back.'

Despite the firmness of his voice he was turning paler and paler, his anxiety growing at the sight of the steadily rising tide of miners. He was due to be relieved at noon but, fearing that he might not be able to hold out till then, he had just sent a pit-boy off to Montsou to summon reinforcements.

He was answered by a storm of yelling:

'Death to the foreigners! Death to the Belgians! . . . We work here, and what we say goes!'

Étienne stepped back in dismay. It had come to this, and now all that remained was to fight and die. He gave up trying to restrain the comrades, and the mob gradually rolled forward towards the small detachment of soldiers. The miners numbered nearly four hundred now, and people were still emptying out of the surrounding villages and rushing to the scene. They were all sending up the same cry, as Maheu and Levaque shouted furiously at the soldiers:

'Just go! Leave us! We've no quarrel with you!'

'This has got nothing to do with you,' La Maheude continued. 'Leave us to sort out our own business.'

Behind her La Levaque added even more vehemently:

'Have we got to kill you to get past? Come on, just kindly bugger off!'

And even Lydie's little, high-pitched voice could be heard coming from the densest part of the crowd where she and Bébert had endeavoured to get out of sight:

'Look at those silly soldiers all in rows!'

Catherine was standing a few paces away, watching and listening in bewilderment as she surveyed this further scene of violence in which it was her bad luck to have been caught up. Hadn't she been through enough already? What had she done wrong for fate to hound her like this? Even as recently as the day before she had still not been able to understand why people were getting so worked up about this strike. Then it had seemed to her that if you were already in trouble, you didn't go looking for more. But now her heart was bursting with the need to hate; she remembered all the things Étienne had said on those long evenings and she tried to hear what he was saying to the soldiers. He was treating them like comrades, reminding them that they, too, were men of the people and telling them that they ought to be siding with the people against those who exploited the people's poverty.

But then there was a disturbance in the crowd, and an old woman was suddenly ejected at the front. It was La Brûlé, looking terrifyingly thin, her arms and neck bare, who had arrived in such great haste that her grey hair was tumbling down over her eyes:

'Thank God for that. I made it!' she stammered, gasping for breath. 'That damned toady Pierron locked me in the cellar!'

And without further ado she rounded on the troops, spewing abuse from her blackened mouth:

'You lousy bunch of sods! Always licking your masters' boots, aren't you, but never afraid to attack the poor. Oh no!'

Then everyone else joined in, and the insults flew thick and fast. Some still shouted: 'Long live the squaddies! Throw the officer down the shaft!' But soon there was only one cry: 'Down with the army!' These men who had listened impassively, without a flicker of expression, to the appeals to brotherly solidarity and the friendly attempts to make them change sides remained no less passive and unflinching under the barrage of bad language. Behind them the captain had drawn his sword; and as the crowd pressed closer and closer, threatening to crush them against the wall, he ordered his men to present bayonets. They obeyed, and a double row of steel points descended in front of the strikers' chests.

'You filthy bastards!' screamed La Brûlé as she retreated.

But already everybody was returning to the charge, drunk on their heedlessness of death. Women rushed forward, and La Maheude and La Levaque screamed:

'Kill us, then! Come on, kill us! But we want our rights!'

At the risk of getting cut to shreds, Levaque had grabbed a bunch of three bayonets with his bare hands and was pulling them towards him in an attempt to pull them off; in his anger he became ten times as strong and managed to twist them. Bouteloup, meanwhile, standing to one side and annoyed at having come with his friend, calmly looked on.

'Come on, you buggers,' Maheu kept saying. 'Come on, let's see what you're made of.'

He unbuttoned his jacket and opened his shirt, exposing his naked, hairy chest with its tattoos of coal-stains. He pressed himself against the points of the bayonets, forcing the soldiers to recoil and presenting an awesome spectacle of insolent bravado. One point had pricked him near the nipple, and it seemed to madden him so much that he kept trying to make it go deeper in, till he could hear his ribs crack.

'Admit it! You'd never dare . . . There are ten thousand more on their way. You can kill us if you like, but you'll have ten thousand more to kill after that.'

The soldiers' position was becoming critical, for they had received strict orders not to use their weapons except as a last resort. How were they supposed to stop these crazy people skewering themselves to death? Moreover they had less and less room to move, and they were now backed up against the wall without any means of retreating further. Nevertheless this small squad of soldiers, a handful of men against the rising tide of miners, was still holding firm and coolly obeying their captain's brief commands. As he stood there nervously, tight-lipped, his eyes shining, his one fear was that his men would be provoked by all this abuse. Already a young sergeant, a tall, thin chap, was blinking in an alarming manner, and his apology of a moustache was bristling. Near by a seasoned veteran with a skin tanned by umpteen campaigns had turned pale on seeing his bayonet twisted like a straw. Another man, a recent recruit no doubt, who still smelled of the ploughfield, flushed crimson every time he heard himself called a sod or a bastard. And there was no let-up in the violence of the intimidation, of the clenched fists and the foul language, of all the threats and accusations that were thrown in their faces by the shovelful. It took every ounce of military discipline to keep the men standing there like this in gloomy, disdainful silence as they carried out their orders without the shadow of an expression on their faces.

A showdown was seeming inevitable when suddenly Richomme, the deputy, appeared behind the soldiers with his white hair, looking like a friendly policeman. He was deeply shaken, and said loudly:

'In God's name, this is idiocy! We really must stop this nonsense!'

And he thrust himself between the bayonets and the miners.

'Comrades, listen to me . . . You know that I used to be one of the workers, that I've always been one of you. Well, by God, I promise you that if you don't get fairly treated, I'll speak to the bosses myself and tell them loud and clear . . . But this is all getting out of hand. It doesn't do any good at all screaming bad language at these fine men and trying to get a hole in your belly.'

They listened, and they hesitated. But just then, unfortunately, the sharp features of young Négrel appeared up at the window. He was no doubt afraid that he might be accused of sending a deputy instead of daring to go down himself, and he tried to make himself heard. But the sound of his voice was lost amid such a terrible uproar that he had to back away from the window at once, shrugging as he did so. From then on Richomme could try as he might to appeal to them on his own behalf and to insist that the only way to settle the matter was by talking it through man to man, but still they rejected him, for he was now suspect. Nevertheless he persevered and stood his ground:

'God help me, they can smash my head in if they like, but if you're going to carry on with this madness, I'm not going to desert you.'

Étienne, whose assistance he had sought as he tried to make them see reason, gestured helplessly. It was too late, there were more than five hundred of them now, and not just the hardliners who had raced to the mine determined to get rid of the Belgians. Some people had simply come for the show, while the laddish contingent thought the confrontation was a great lark. In the middle of one group, some way off, Zacharie and Philomène were watching as though it were a display, and so unconcerned that they had even brought the two children, Achille and Désirée, along to watch. A new wave of people was arriving from Réquillart, including Mouquet and La Mouquette; Mouquet immediately went over and clapped his mate Zacharie on the shoulder with a laugh, while his sister, who was very worked up, rushed forward to join the troublemakers in the front row.

Meanwhile, with each minute that passed, the captain kept looking towards the Montsou road. The reinforcements he had requested had not yet arrived, and his sixty men could not hold out much longer. Eventually it occurred to him to stage a show of strength, and he ordered his men to load their rifles in full view of the crowd. The soldiers duly obeyed, but the crowd continued to grow restive, and there was much brave talk and mockery.

'Oh, look. It's time for target-practice. They *will* be tired!' sneered the women, La Brûlé, La Levaque and the others.

La Maheude was still carrying Estelle, who had woken up and now started crying; and as she clutched the child's tiny frame to her chest, she walked up so close to the sergeant that he asked her what she thought she was doing bringing a poor little thing like that along with her.

'What do you bloody care?' she replied. 'Shoot her, if you dare.'

The men shook their heads in contempt. Nobody believed that anyone would fire on them.

'They've only got blanks anyway,' said Levaque.

'You'd think we were bloody Cossacks!' shouted Maheu. 'You're not going to shoot your own countrymen, for God's sake!'

Others kept saying they'd served in the Crimea[1] and that a bit of lead had never frightened anyone, and they all continued to push forward towards the rifles. If the soldiers had fired at that moment, the mob would have been mown down.

Now in the front row, La Mouquette was almost speechless with indignation at the thought that the soldiers might want to put a bullet through a woman's skin. She had spat out her full repertoire of foul language at them and still could think of no obscenity that was sufficiently demeaning, when suddenly, having only this one last deadly insult to fling in the squad's face, she decided to display her bottom. She hoisted her skirts with both hands, bent forward and exposed a huge, round expanse of flesh.

'Here, take a look at this! Even this is too good for you, you dirty bastards!'

She bent over double and swivelled from side to side so that each should have his share, and with each thrust of her bottom she said:

'One for the officer! And one for the sergeant! And one for the squaddies!'

There were gales of laughter; Bébert and Lydie were in fits, and even Étienne, despite his grim forebodings, applauded this offensive exhibition of naked flesh. Everyone, the hardliners as

well as the jokers, was now jeering at the soldiers as though
they had actually been spattered with filth; and only Catherine,
standing over to one side on a pile of old timbering, remained
silent as she sensed the gall rising to her throat and the warm
fire of hate gradually spreading through her body.

But then a scuffle broke out. In order to calm his men's nerves
the captain had decided to take some prisoners. La Mouquette
jumped up in an instant and darted away between the comrades'
legs. Three miners, including Levaque, were seized from among
the worst troublemakers and placed under guard in the deputies'
office.

From up above Négrel and Dansaert were shouting at the
captain to come in and take refuge with them. He refused, aware
that the doors had no locks and that when the buildings were
stormed he would suffer the ignominy of being disarmed.
Already his small detachment of men was beginning to mutter
crossly about not running away from a miserable rabble in clogs.
Once again the sixty men stood with their backs to the wall,
rifles loaded, and faced the mob.

At first people pulled back a little, and there was complete
silence. The show of force had taken the strikers by surprise
and left them nonplussed. Then a cry went up, demanding the
immediate release of the prisoners: some even claimed they were
being murdered. And then, quite unprompted but acting as one
in their common need for vengeance, they all rushed over to the
nearby stacks of bricks, which were made on the premises out
of the local marly clay. Children carried them one by one,
women filled their skirts with them, and soon everyone had a
pile of ammunition at their feet. The stoning began.

La Brûlé was the first to take up position. She broke each
brick across her bony knee and then, with both hands, hurled
the two pieces at once. La Lévaque was nearly wrenching her
arm out of its socket, so fat and flabby that she had to go right
up close in order to hit the target, despite the entreaties of
Bouteloup, who kept pulling her back, hoping to take her home
now that her husband was out of the way. All the women were
getting very excited. La Mouquette had got tired of cutting
herself trying to break the bricks across her thighs, which were

too fleshy, and decided to throw them whole instead. Even some of the children joined the line, and Bébert was showing Lydie how to chuck them underarm. It was like a hailstorm, with enormous hailstones thudding to the ground. Suddenly Catherine appeared in the midst of these furies, brandishing broken bricks and throwing them as hard as she could with her small arms. She could not have said why, but she felt an absolute, desperate need to slaughter. Was this filthy bloody existence of theirs never going to end? She had had enough, enough of being slapped and thrown out by her man, enough of tramping along muddy roads like a lost dog, not even able to ask her father for a bowl of soup when he was starving to death just like her. Things never got better, ever since she could remember they had only got worse; and she broke the bricks and just threw them, wanting to destroy everything and anything, her eyes so blinded by rage that she couldn't even see whose jaws she was smashing.

Étienne, who was still standing in front of the soldiers, nearly had his head split open. His ear began to swell up, and he turned round and was shocked to realize that the brick had come from the frenzied hands of Catherine; and, even though he could get killed, he just stood there watching her. Many people were standing like that, with their arms by their sides, absorbed in the spectacle of the battle. Mouquet was assessing the throws as though he were at a cork-tossing contest: good shot! bad luck! He was laughing away and nudging Zacharie, who was having an argument with Philomène because he had smacked Achille and Désirée and refused to lift them on to his shoulders so that they could see better. In the background the road was lined with crowds of onlookers. At the top of the hill, at the entrance to the village, old Bonnemort had just appeared: he had hobbled there on his stick but was now standing still, silhouetted against the rust-coloured sky.

As soon as the bricks started flying, Richomme had again intervened between the soldiers and the miners, entreating one side and rallying the other, heedless of the danger and so distraught that huge tears were running down his cheeks. Nobody could hear what he was saying amid the uproar, they just saw the quivering of his grey moustache.

But the hail of bricks was getting thicker, for the men were now following the women's example.

Just then La Maheude noticed Maheu, who was hanging back with a grim look on his face.

'What's up with you?' she shouted to him. 'Are you scared? You're not going to let your comrades be taken to prison, are you? . . . Oh, if it weren't for this kid, I'd soon show you how to do it!'

Estelle was hanging on to her neck and screaming, preventing her from joining La Brûlé and the others. When Maheu seemed not to hear, she kicked some bricks over towards his feet.

'For God's sake, take some. Have I got to spit in your face to give you the courage?'

The blood rushed to his cheeks, and he broke some bricks and threw them. She whipped him on so hard that it made his head spin, baying at him from behind and urging him to the kill, all the while nearly suffocating the child across her chest with her tensed arms; and he kept moving forward until eventually he stood directly in front of the rifles.

The small squad of men could barely be seen through the hail of brick. Fortunately the bricks were carrying too far, pitting the wall behind them. What should they do? The captain's pale face flushed momentarily at the thought of going inside and turning their backs, but even that wasn't possible any more, they'd be torn to pieces the instant they moved. A brick had just broken the peak on his cap, and blood was dripping from his forehead. Several of his men were injured; he could sense their fury and realized that they were now in the grip of the instinct for survival that makes men cease to obey their superiors. The sergeant had cursed aloud as his left shoulder was almost dis-located by a brick thumping into his flesh, bruising it like a laundry-woman's paddle thudding into a pile of washing. Hav-ing been hit twice already, the young recruit had a broken thumb and could feel a burning sensation in his right knee: how much longer were they going to put up with this nonsense? A piece of brick had ricocheted and hit the veteran in the groin; he had turned green, and his rifle shook as his thin arms held it raised in front of him. Three times the captain was on the point of ordering them to fire. He was paralysed by anguish, and for a few seconds, which seemed like an eternity, he debated between duty and his own mind, between his beliefs as a soldier and his beliefs as a man. The bricks rained down even more fiercely, and just as he was opening his mouth, about to give the order 'Fire!', the rifles went off of their own accord, three shots at first, then five, then a general volley, and finally – in the midst of a great silence – one single shot, long after the others.

There was general stupefaction. They had actually fired, and the crowd stood there open-mouthed, motionless, unable to believe it. But then there were piercing shrieks, and a bugle sounded the cease-fire. Wild panic followed, a mad flight through the mud like a stampede of wounded cattle.

Bébert and Lydie had collapsed on top of each other after the first three shots; the girl had been hit in the face, while the young boy had a hole through his chest beneath his left shoulder. Lydie lay motionless, as though struck by a thunderbolt. But Bébert was still moving, and in the convulsions of his death throes he grabbed her, as though he wanted to hold her close again as he had held her in the dark hiding-place where they had spent their last night together. And at that moment Jeanlin, who had finally arrived from Réquillart, came skipping bleary-eyed through the smoke just in time to see Bébert embrace his little woman, and die.

The next five shots had brought down La Brûlé and Richomme. Hit in the back just as he was begging the comrades to stop, he had fallen to his knees; and having slumped over on to his side, he now lay gasping for breath, his eyes filled with the tears he had shed. The old woman, her bosom ripped apart, had keeled straight over, landing with a crack like a bundle of dry firewood as she stammered a final curse through a gargle of blood.

But after that the general volley of gunfire had cleared the terrain, mowing down the groups of onlookers who were standing about laughing a hundred paces away. One bullet entered Mouquet's mouth, shattering his skull and knocking him flat at the feet of Zacharie and Philomène, whose two children were spattered in blood. At the same instant La Mouquette was hit twice in the belly. She had seen the troops take aim and instinctively, with her characteristic generosity of spirit, she had thrown herself in front of Catherine, shouting at her to mind out. With a scream she tumbled backwards under the force of the shots. Étienne rushed across to lift her up and carry her away, but she gestured that it was too late. Then she gave a last gasp, still smiling at the two of them as though she were happy to see them together now that she was taking her leave.

That was it, or so it seemed; the storm of bullets had passed, and the echo was fading away as it reached the houses in the village when the last shot went off, one single, solitary shot, after the others.

It went through Maheu's heart: he spun round and fell with his face in a puddle of coal-black water.

Stunned, La Maheude bent down.

'Come on, love! Up you get. Just a little scratch, eh?'

Because of Estelle she did not have her hands free, and she had to tuck her under one arm in order to be able to turn Maheu's head.

'Say something! Where does it hurt?'

His eyes were blank, and his mouth was foaming with blood. She understood. He was dead. And she sat down in the mud, holding her daughter under her arm like a parcel, and stared at her husband in utter disbelief.

The pit had been cleared. The captain had nervously removed his damaged cap and then replaced it on his head, but even as he palely surveyed the greatest disaster of his life he maintained his stiff, military bearing. Meanwhile, expressionless, his men reloaded their rifles. The horrified faces of Négrel and Dansaert could be seen at the window of the loading area. Souvarine was standing behind them, a deep furrow etched across his brow as though the steel bolt of his obsession had ominously planted itself there. Over in the other direction, on the crest of the hill, Bonnemort had not moved, still propped on his stick with one hand and shading his eyes with the other so that he could get a better view of the slaughter of his kin below. The wounded were screaming, and the dead were growing rigid in various twisted postures; all were splashed with the liquid mud left by the thaw, and here and there some were sinking into the inky patches of coal that were now re-emerging from under the tatters of dirty snow. And in the midst of these tiny, wretched human corpses, all shrivelled by hunger, lay the carcass of Trumpet, a pitiful, monstrous heap of dead flesh.

Étienne had not been killed. Standing beside Catherine, who had collapsed with exhaustion and shock, he was still awaiting the arrival of death when the ringing tones of a man's voice startled him. It was Father Ranvier on his way back from saying Mass, and there he stood with his arms in the air like some crazed prophet, calling down the wrath of God on the murderers. He was proclaiming the dawn of a new age of justice and the imminent extermination of the bourgeoisie by the fires of heaven on account of this, the latest and most heinous of their crimes, for it was they who had brought about the massacre of the workers and caused the poor and outcast of this world to be slain.

PART VII

The shots fired at Montsou had reverberated as far away as Paris, where the echo was considerable. For the past four days every opposition newspaper had been voicing its outrage and filling its front page with horrifying tales: twenty-five people wounded and fourteen dead, including two children and three women; and then there were the prisoners, with Levaque now something of a hero, credited with having displayed a grandeur worthy of the Ancients in his replies to the examining magistrate. The Empire had received a direct hit from these few bullets, but it was putting on a show of calm omnipotence, oblivious to the gravity of the wound it had sustained. There had simply been an unfortunate encounter, a remote incident somewhere or other in the coal-mining region, very far removed from the streets of Paris where public opinion was formed. People would soon forget, and the Company had been unofficially instructed to hush the matter up and put an end to this strike, which was dragging on in such a tiresome manner and beginning to pose a threat to society.

And so it was that on the following Wednesday morning three members of the Board were to be seen arriving in Montsou. The little town, hitherto shocked and not daring to rejoice in the massacre, now breathed again and tasted the joy of being saved at last. As it happened, there had been a marked improvement in the weather, and there was now bright sunshine, the sunshine of early February whose warmth begins to tinge the lilac shoots with green. The shutters of the Board's offices had been thrown open, and the huge building seemed to have sprung back to life; the most reassuring rumours began to issue forth, how the gentlemen had been deeply affected by the disaster and how they had hastened to the scene to open their paternal arms and embrace the wayward miners. Now that the blow had been delivered, admittedly rather more violently than they would have wished, they were falling over themselves in their desire to rescue the situation, and they took a number of welcome if overdue measures. First, they dismissed the Belgian workers and

made a great fuss about what an enormous concession this was
to their workforce. Next, they ended the military occupation of
the pits, which were no longer under threat from the crushed
miners. By their efforts also a line was drawn under the affair
of the vanished sentry at Le Voreux. The whole area had been
searched and neither the rifle nor the corpse had been found,
and so it was decided to post him as a deserter even though a
crime was still suspected. In all matters they endeavoured in this
way to take the heat out of the situation, fearful of what the
morrow might bring and considering it dangerous to acknowledge their powerlessness in the face of a savage mob let loose
on the creaking timbers of the old order. At the same time these
attempts at conciliation did not prevent them from getting on
with their own administrative affairs, for Deneulin had been
seen returning to the Board's offices, where he had meetings
with M. Hennebeau. Negotiations were in hand for the purchase
of Vandame, and it was confidently expected that Deneulin
would soon accept the gentlemen's terms.

But what caused a particular stir throughout the district were
the large yellow notices that the directors had had posted in
great numbers on the walls. They carried these few lines, in very
large print: 'Workers of Montsou, we do not wish the misguided
behaviour whose sorry consequences you have witnessed in
recent days to deprive workers of good sense and goodwill of
their livelihood. We shall therefore reopen all pits on Monday
morning, and when work has resumed, we shall investigate with
due care and consideration all areas where it may be possible to
make some improvement. We shall do everything that is just
and within our power.' In one morning the ten thousand colliers
filed past these notices. Not one of them said anything; many
just shook their heads, while others simply sloped off without
any trace of a reaction on their impassive faces.

Until then Village Two Hundred and Forty had persisted in
its fierce resistance. It was as though the comrades' blood that
had turned the mud at the pit red now barred the way for the
others. Barely a dozen had gone back down, Pierron and a few
toadies of his sort, and people merely watched them grimly as

they departed and returned, without a gesture or threat of any kind. Accordingly the notice posted on the wall of the church was greeted with sullen suspicion. There was no mention of the men who had been sacked: did that mean that the Company was refusing to take them back? The fear of reprisals, together with the thought of protesting as comrades against the dismissal of those who had been most directly involved, hardened their stubborn resolve. It was all a bit fishy, the whole thing needed looking into, they would return to work as and when these gentlemen were kind enough to state plainly what they meant. Silence hung heavily over the squat houses; even hunger was no longer of relevance, for now that the shadow of violent death had passed over their roofs it was evident that they might all be going to die whatever happened.

But one house among all the others, that of the Maheus, remained especially dark and silent, plunged in overwhelming grief. Since she had accompanied her husband's body to the cemetery, La Maheude had not said a word to anyone. After the shooting she had let Étienne bring Catherine home with them, half dead and covered in mud; and as she was undressing her in front of the young man before putting her to bed, she had imagined for a moment that she, too, had returned with a bullet in her stomach, for there were large blood stains on her shirt. But she soon realized why; the flow of puberty had finally broken through under the shock of this terrible day. Ah, what a marvellous stroke of good fortune this menstruation was! A fine blessing indeed to be able to make babies for gendarmes to slaughter in their turn! But she did not speak to Catherine, any more than she spoke to Étienne for that matter. He was now sharing a bed with Jeanlin, at the risk of being arrested, having been seized with such dread at the idea of returning to the dark depths of Réquillart that he preferred prison: the prospect of that horrific blackness after all these deaths made him shudder, and he was secretly afraid of the young soldier at rest down there beneath the rocks. Indeed, amid the torment of his defeat, he dreamed of prison as a place of refuge; but nobody even gave him a thought, and time dragged as he endeavoured in vain to find

ways of tiring himself out. Occasionally, however, La Maheude
would look at them both with an air of resentment, as though
she were asking them what they were doing in her house.

Once more they all found themselves sleeping on top of each
other. Old Bonnemort had the bed the two little ones used to
sleep in, and they slept with Catherine now that poor Alzire was
no longer there to stick her hump into her big sister's ribs. It
was when they went to bed that La Maheude most sensed the
emptiness of the house, in the cold of her own bed that was now
too large. Vainly she clutched Estelle to her, to fill the gap, but
she was no substitute for her husband; and she wept silently for
hours at a time. Then the days began to pass as before: still no
bread, and yet no opportunity either to die once and for all; just
scraps picked up here and there which did the poor the disservice
of keeping them alive. Nothing about their lives had changed,
it was simply that her husband wasn't there any more.

On the afternoon of the fifth day, Étienne, thoroughly
depressed by the spectacle of this silent woman, left the parlour
and walked slowly down the cobbled street through the village.
The inactivity was difficult to bear and had prompted him to
take endless walks, with his arms by his side, head down, always
tormented by the one single thought. He had been trudging
along like this for half an hour when he became aware, from an
increase in his own sense of discomfort, that the comrades were
coming out on to their doorsteps to watch him. What little
popularity he still enjoyed had vanished with the first rifle shot,
and now wherever he went he was met with blazing eyes that
burned into his back as he passed. Each time he looked up, he
saw men standing with a menacing air, or women peering from
behind their curtains; and, confronted by their as yet unvoiced
accusations and the suppressed anger evident in these staring
eyes that were widened still further by hunger and tears, he
became so ill at ease that he could scarcely walk. And behind
him the mute reproach continued to intensify. He was so afraid
that the entire village might appear on their doorsteps and
scream their wretchedness at him that he returned home
shaking.

But at the Maheus' he was greeted by a scene which shocked

him even more. Old Bonnemort was sitting near the empty fireplace, rooted to his chair ever since the day of the slaughter, when two neighbours had found him slumped on the ground beside his broken stick, felled like an old tree that has been struck by lightning. Lénore and Henri, by way of cheating their hunger, were making a deafening racket scraping an old saucepan in which cabbage had been boiled the night before; and La Maheude, having set Estelle down on the table, was standing there brandishing her fist at Catherine:

'You what? In God's name, what did you just say?'

Catherine had declared her intention of returning to work at Le Voreux. The thought of not earning her living, of being tolerated like this at her mother's as though she were some useless animal that was only in the way, was becoming more and more unbearable with each day that passed; and if she hadn't been afraid of further trouble from Chaval, she would already have gone back on Tuesday. She continued haltingly:

'What else is there? We can't just do nothing and expect to live. At least we'll have something to eat.'

La Maheude broke in:

'You just listen to me. I'll strangle the first one of you that goes back to work. No, really, it's too much. So they can kill the father and then go on exploiting the children just like before? I'm not having it, I tell you. I'd rather see you all carried out in a box, same as him that's already gone.'

And her long silence was rent by a furious torrent of words. Some improvement that would be, the paltry sum that Catherine would bring in! Thirty sous at most, plus a further twenty if the bosses would be so kind as to find a job for that little thief Jeanlin. Fifty sous, and seven mouths to feed! And of course all the little ones ever did was eat. And as for Grandpa, he must have damaged his brain when he fell, for he seemed to have lost his wits; or else it was the shock of seeing the soldiers firing on the comrades.

'Isn't that right, Grandpa? They've finished you off, eh? You might still have strength in your arms, but you're done for.'

Bonnemort gazed uncomprehendingly at her from expressionless eyes. He would sit for hours like this just staring ahead of him, capable only of spitting into a dish filled with ash which they placed beside him, for cleanliness' sake.

'They still haven't sorted out his pension yet,' she went on, 'and I know they're going to refuse it, because of our views . . . No, it's too much. I've had it with the whole bloody lot of them!'

'But,' ventured Catherine, 'on the notice they promise –'

'To hell with the notice! . . . Just more tricks to trap us and eat us for breakfast. They can afford to be all sweetness and light now they've put their bullets through us.'

'But then where shall we go, Mum? They won't let us stay in the village, that's for sure.'

La Maheude gestured in a wild, indeterminate way. Where would they go? She had no idea and tried not to think about it, for it made her head spin. They would go somewhere else, anywhere. And as the noise of the saucepan finally became unbearable, she rounded on Lénore and Henri and smacked them. Estelle, who had been crawling around on the table, fell off and added to the din. By way of comforting her, La Maheude gave her a good whack and told her she'd have done better to have killed herself outright. She started talking about Alzire and about how she wished the rest of them might be as fortunate. Then suddenly she began to sob and pressed her head against the wall.

Still standing there, Étienne had not dared to intervene. He counted for nothing in the household now, even the children backed away from him in distrust. But the tears of this unhappy woman were breaking his heart, and he said softly:

'Come now, steady. We'll pull through somehow.'

She appeared not to hear him and poured out her sorrow in a low, continuous lament.

'Heaven help us, how is it possible? We used to manage all right, before these terrible things. The bread was stale, but at least we were all together . . . But how did it happen, for God's sake? What did we do to deserve this grief, with some of us in our graves and the rest of us dearly wishing that we were too? . . . And yet it's true, they used to treat us like workhorses, and it just wasn't right that we should be whipped for our pains while we were busy swelling the coffers of the rich, and with no chance of ever tasting the good things in life for ourselves. The pleasure goes out of living when there's nothing to hope for any more. No indeed, things couldn't go on like that any longer, we deserved some respite . . . But if only we'd known! How is it possible to have made ourselves so wretched when all we wanted was justice!'

Her chest rose with each sigh, and her voice was strangulated by an immense sadness.

'And then there are always the people who know better, promising you that everything can be sorted out if you'll just make that little bit of effort . . . And you get carried away, you're suffering so much because of what does exist that you start wanting what doesn't. And there was I dreaming away like a fool, imagining a life where everyone was friends with everyone else. Floating on air I was, no question about it, with my head in the clouds. And then you fall flat on your face again, and you hurt all over . . . It wasn't true, all those things you thought you could see were just not there. What was really there was simply more misery, oh yes, as much misery as you could possibly want, and then getting shot into the bargain!'

As Étienne listened to this lamentation, he felt a pang of remorse with each tear that fell. He didn't know what to say to comfort La Maheude, who was utterly bruised by her terrible fall from the summit of the ideal. She had returned into the middle of the room, where she now stood looking at him; and in a final surge of rage she addressed him without ceremony:

'And what about you? Are you planning to go back to the pit, now that you've landed us all in the shit? . . . Not that I blame you, of course. Only if it was me, I'd have died of shame long ago for having brought so much harm on my friends.'

He was going to reply, but instead he just shrugged in despair: why bother to offer explanations which in her grief she would not understand? It was all too much to bear, and so he departed once more on one of his sorry walks.

Again it was as though the village was waiting for him, the men on their doorsteps, the women at their windows. As soon as he appeared, the muttering started and a crowd began to gather. A storm of whispering had been brewing for the past four days, and now it broke in universal condemnation. Fists were raised in his direction, mothers pointed him out to their sons with gestures of reproach, and old men spat when they saw him. Here was the sudden reversal in sentiment that follows on the heels of a defeat, the inevitable other side of popularity, a hatred fuelled by all the suffering endured to no purpose. He was being made to pay for the hunger and the deaths.

Zacharie, arriving with Philomène, bumped into Étienne as he was leaving and sneered:

'Blimey, he's getting fatter! Must be cos he feeds off the rest of us.'

Already La Levaque had stepped out on to her doorstep, with Bouteloup. Mindful of Bébert, her boy who had been killed by a bullet, she shouted:

'Yeah, there are some cowards about the place who like to get the children slaughtered instead. If he wants to give me mine back, he'd better go and dig him out of the ground.'

She had forgotten all about her imprisoned husband, and her household was no longer on strike since Bouteloup was working. Nevertheless the thought of Levaque did now suddenly occur to her, and she continued in a shrill voice:

'Shame on you! It's only the villains that walk about as they like when the good men are locked up inside!'

In trying to avoid her Étienne had run into La Pierronne, who was arriving in a hurry across the gardens. She had welcomed her mother's death as a blessed relief, for her violent behaviour had threatened to get them all hanged. Nor did she grieve over the loss of Pierron's daughter, that little minx Lydie. Good riddance! But she now sided with her neighbours, hoping to patch things up with them:

'And what about my mother? And the little girl? Everybody saw you hiding behind them when they stopped all those bullets that were meant for you!'

What should he do? Throttle La Pierronne and the other women, take on the whole village? For a moment Étienne felt like doing just that. The blood was throbbing in his head, and he now considered the comrades little better than dumb animals. He was irritated by their primitiveness and the lack of intelligence that had led them to blame him for the logic of events. How stupid could you get! In his inability to influence them any more he felt disgust for them; and he simply quickened his step, as if deaf to their abuse. But soon he was in headlong flight, with each household booing him as he passed, and people chasing after him, a whole crowd cursing him in a thunderous crescendo as their hatred spilled over. He was the one, the one who had exploited them, the one who had murdered them, the unique cause of all their wretchedness. Pale and frightened, Étienne ran from the village with the screaming horde at his heels. Eventually, once they were out on the open road, many stopped chasing; but a few were still after him when, at the bottom of the hill, outside the Advantage, he met another group coming out of Le Voreux.

Old Mouque and Chaval were among them. Since the death of La Mouquette, his daughter, and of his son, Mouquet, the old man had continued to work on as a stableman without a word of regret or complaint. But suddenly, on catching sight of Étienne, he was seized with fury; tears streamed from his eyes, and a torrent of bad language came pouring out of his mouth, which was black and bleeding from chewing tobacco:

'You bastard! You shit! You sodding, fucking bastard! . . . Just you wait! You're damn well going to pay me back for my poor bloody children! It's your turn now.'

He picked up a brick, broke it in two, and threw both pieces at Étienne.

'Yeah, come on, let's get rid of the scum!' sneered Chaval loudly, overjoyed at this opportunity for revenge and in a lather of excitement. 'We'll take it in turns . . . There, how does that feel to have your back to the wall, you filthy piece of shit!'

And he too attacked Étienne, with stones. A wild clamour broke out, and everybody picked up bricks and started breaking them and throwing them. They wanted to slaughter him, as though it was the soldiers themselves they were slaughtering. Dazed and bewildered, Étienne ceased his attempts at escape and turned to face them, trying to placate them with his words. His old speeches, which had previously been so warmly acclaimed, sprang once more to his lips. He repeated the phrases with which he had turned the heads of his loyal followers in the days when they had listened to him with rapt attention; but his power had gone, and the only response was brickbats. He had just been hit on the left arm and was backing away, in some considerable danger, when he found himself pinned against the front wall of the Advantage.

Rasseneur had recently appeared on his doorstep.

'Come in,' he said simply.

Étienne hesitated. It galled him to take refuge there.

'Come in, for goodness' sake. I'll speak to them.'

Étienne accepted reluctantly and hid at the far end of the saloon while Rasseneur blocked the doorway with his broad shoulders.

'Now then, my friends, easy does it . . . You know that I at least have never let you down. I've always been one for the softly softly approach, and if you'd listened to me, there is no doubt that you would not be in the position you're all in now.'

Shoulders back and belly out, he spoke at length, letting his undemanding eloquence pour forth with the soothing gentleness of warm water. And once more he succeeded as of old, effortlessly regaining his former popularity, quite naturally, as though only one month ago the comrades had never booed him or called him a coward. Voices shouted their approval. Hear, hear! You can count on us! That's the stuff! There was a thunderous burst of applause.

Standing in the background, Étienne felt sickened, and his heart was filled with bitterness. He remembered Rasseneur's prediction in the forest when he had warned him about the ingratitude of the crowd. What mindless brutality! How appalling it was, the way they had forgotten everything he had done for them! They were like a blind force constantly feeding on itself. But beneath his anger at seeing these brutes wrecking their own cause there lay despair at his own collapse, at the tragic end of his own ambitions. So that was it? It was all over? He remembered the occasion, under the beech trees, when he had listened to three thousand hearts beating in time with his own. That day he had been in control of his popularity, these people had belonged to him, he had felt himself to be their master.

Then he had been drunk on wild dreams: Montsou at his feet, Paris beckoning, perhaps election to the Chamber of Deputies, lambasting the bourgeois with his oratory, the first parliamentary speech ever made by a working man. And now it was all over! Now he had awoken from the dream, wretched and hated, and his people had just thrown bricks at him and banished him from their midst.

Rasseneur's voice grew louder.

'Violence has never succeeded. You can't remake the world in a single day. Those who promised you they could change things at a stroke were either fools or rogues.'

'Hear, hear!' cried the crowd.

So who *was* to blame? For Étienne this question, which he had never ceased to ask himself, was the last straw. Was it really his fault, all this suffering – which affected him too after all – this poverty, the shooting, these emaciated women and children who had no bread to eat? He had once had a dire vision of this kind, one evening before everything began to go wrong. But at that stage he had already felt buoyed up by some external force, which had carried him away with the rest of the comrades. Besides, it had never been a case of his telling them what to do; rather it was they who had led him, forcing him to do things that he would never have done on his own without the pressure of the mob urging him on from behind. With each new act of violence he had been left stunned by the outcome, which he had neither sought nor foreseen. How could he have ever predicted, for example, that one day his loyal flock from the village would actually stone him? These madmen were lying when they accused him of having promised them a life of leisure and plenty to eat. Yet behind his attempts at self-justification, behind all the arguments with which he tried to combat his remorse, lay the unspoken fear that he had not been equal to his task and the niggling doubt of the semi-educated man who realizes that he doesn't know the half of it. But he had run out of courage, and he no longer felt the same bond with the comrades, indeed he was afraid of them, of the huge, blind, irresistible mass that is the people, passing like a force of nature and sweeping away everything in its path, beyond the compass of rule or theory. He had begun to view them with distaste and had gradually grown apart from them, as his more refined tastes made him feel ill at ease in their company, and as his whole nature slowly began to aspire towards membership of a higher class.

At that moment Rasseneur's voice was drowned by enthusiastic shouting.

'Three cheers for Rasseneur! He's the man for us! Hip, hip!'

Rasseneur shut the door as the mob dispersed; and the two men looked at each other in silence. They both shrugged. Then they had a drink together.

That same day there was a grand dinner at La Piolaine, where they were celebrating the engagement of Négrel and Cécile. The previous twenty-four hours had seen much dusting and polishing in the Grégoires' dining-room and drawing-room. Mélanie reigned supreme in the kitchen, supervising the roasts and stirring the sauces, the smell of which wafted all the way up through the house as far as the attic. It had been decided that Francis the coachman would help Honorine to wait at table. The gardener's wife was to wash up, while the gardener himself was to open the front gates for the guests. Never before had such a festive occasion turned this grand and well-appointed house so thoroughly upside down.

Everything went perfectly. Mme Hennebeau behaved charmingly towards Cécile, and she gave Négrel a smile when the notary from Montsou gallantly proposed a toast to the future happiness of the couple. M. Hennebeau, too, was most affable. His cheerful air was noted by the guests, and it was rumoured that, being once more in favour with the Board, he was soon to be appointed Officer in the Legion of Honour, in recognition of his firm action in dealing with the strike. They tried not to talk about the recent events, but there was an element of triumph in the general rejoicing, and the dinner turned into something of an official celebration of victory. They had been delivered at last, and they could begin once more to eat and sleep in peace! Discreet allusion was made to the dead, whose blood still lay fresh in the mud of Le Voreux: they had had to be taught a lesson, and everybody said how sorry they were, with the Grégoires adding that it was now everyone's duty to visit the villages and to try and bind the wounds. The Grégoires were their old placid, benevolent selves again: they made excuses for their good miners and already they could picture them down the pits providing a fine example of their traditional willingness to knuckle under. The grandees of Montsou, now that they had stopped feeling so nervous, all agreed that the question of pay needed to be looked at carefully. Victory was complete when, during the main course, M. Hennebeau read out a letter from the bishop announcing that Father Ranvier was to be transferred to another parish. The assembled bourgeois of the district thereupon exchanged heated comment on the subject of this priest who considered that the soldiers had been murderers. Finally, with the appearance of dessert, the notary valiantly presented his free-thinking views.

Deneulin was there with his two daughters. Amid all this merriment he tried to conceal his sadness at his own ruin. That very morning he had signed the papers conveying his concession at Vandame into the ownership of the Montsou Mining Company. Cornered and wounded, he had given in to the Board's demands, finally relinquishing this prize that they had had their eyes on for so long and barely extracting enough money to pay his creditors. When they had made him a last-minute offer to stay on at the level of divisional engineer, he had accepted it as a stroke of good fortune, resigned to being a mere employee whose job was to oversee the pit that had swallowed up his fortune. This action sounded the death-knell for the small, private company and presaged the imminent disappearance of individual mine-owners, who were being gobbled up one by one by the insatiable ogre of capital and drowned in the rising tide of corporations. The costs of the strike had thus fallen on his shoulders alone, and for him it was as though everyone was drinking to his misfortune as they toasted M. Hennebeau's new honour. His only slight consolation was the wonderfully brave face being put on by Lucie and Jeanne, who both looked charming in their patched-up dresses, pretty young single girls laughing in the teeth of disaster and thoroughly disdainful of bank accounts.

When they moved into the drawing-room for coffee, M.

Grégoire took his cousin aside and congratulated him on the courage of his decision.

'You see? Your one mistake was to risk the million you got from your share in Montsou by investing it in Vandame. You went to all that effort, and now it's disappeared along with all your devilish hard work, whereas my share hasn't moved from its drawer, and it still supports me nicely and allows me a life of leisure, just as it will support my grandchildren and my grandchildren's children.'

II

On Sunday Étienne fled from the village at nightfall. An extremely clear sky, dotted with stars, cast a blue, crepuscular light across the land. He went down to the canal and walked slowly along the bank in the direction of Marchiennes. It was his favourite walk, a grassy path two leagues long running dead straight beside this geometrically precise strip of water, which stretched into the distance like an unending bar of molten silver.

He never met anyone there. But that day he was very put out to see a man coming towards him. And in the pale starlight the two solitary walkers did not recognize each other until they came face to face.

'Oh, it's you,' muttered Étienne.

Souvarine nodded silently. For a moment they just stood there; then, side by side, they set off together towards Marchiennes. Each man seemed to be continuing with his own train of thought, as if they were separated by a large distance.

'Did you read in the paper about Pluchart's success in Paris?' Étienne asked eventually. 'After that meeting at Belleville people waited on the pavement and gave him a great ovation . . . Oh, he's a coming man all right, whether he's lost his voice or not. He'll go far now.'

Souvarine shrugged. He despised the silver-tongued type, the sort that enters politics the way some people are called to the Bar, just to earn a lot of money with smooth talk.

Étienne had now got as far as Darwin.[1] He had read this and that, as summarized for a popular audience in a volume costing five sous; and on the basis of his patchy understanding he had come to see revolution in terms of the struggle for survival, with the have-nots eating the haves, a strong people devouring a worn-out bourgeoisie. But Souvarine became angry and started in on the stupidity of socialists who accepted Darwin, that scientific apostle of inequality whose great notion of natural selection might as well be the philosophy of an aristocrat. But Étienne refused to be persuaded and wanted to argue the point, illustrating his reservations with a hypothesis. Say the old society no longer existed and that every last trace of it had been swept away. Wasn't there a risk that the new order which grew up in its place would slowly be corrupted by the same injustices, that there would again be the weak and the strong, that some people would be more skilful or intelligent than others and live off the fat of the land, while the stupid or lazy once more became their slaves? At this prospect of everlasting poverty Souvarine exclaimed fiercely that if justice could not be achieved with man, it would have to be achieved without him. For as long as there were rotten societies, there would have to be wholesale slaughters, until the last human being had been exterminated. The two men fell silent again.

For a long time, with his head bowed, Souvarine walked on over the soft new grass, so deep in thought that he kept to the extreme edge of the water with all the tranquil certainty of a sleep-walker walking beside a gutter. Then, for no apparent reason, he gave a start, as though he had bumped into a shadow. He looked up, and his face was very pale. He said softly to his companion:

'Did I ever tell you how she died?'

'Who?'

'My girl, back in Russia.'

Étienne gestured vaguely, astonished at the catch in Souvarine's voice, at this sudden need to confide on the part of someone who was usually so impassive and who lived in such stoic detachment from people, including from himself. All he knew was that the girl in question had been his mistress and that she had been hanged in Moscow.

'It all went wrong,' Souvarine explained, his misty eyes now fixed on the white strip of canal as it vanished into the distance between the bluish colonnades of tall trees. 'We had spent fourteen days down a hole, in order to mine the railway line; but instead of the Imperial train, it was an ordinary passenger train that went up . . . Then they arrested Annouchka.[2] She used to bring us food each evening, disguised as a peasant. And it was she who had lit the fuse, too, because a man might have attracted attention . . . I followed the trial, hidden in the crowd, for six long days . . .'

His voice faltered, and he started coughing as though he were choking.

'Twice I wanted to shout out, to leap over all those people and be near her. But where was the use? One man less is one man less fighting for the cause; and each time she looked over at me with those big, wide eyes of hers, I could see she was telling me not to.'

He coughed again.

'That last day, in the square, I was there . . . It was raining, and the clumsy idiots started panicking because it was raining so hard. It had taken them twenty minutes to hang four others: the rope broke, and they couldn't manage to finish the fourth off . . . Annouchka was standing there, waiting. She couldn't see me and kept trying to find me in the crowd. I climbed up on to a milestone, and then she saw me. Our eyes never left each other. After she was dead, she still looked at me . . . I waved my hat and left.'

Again there was silence. The white avenue of the canal seemed to unfurl without end, and the two men walked on with the same muffled tread, as though each had returned to his own private world. At the horizon the pale water seemed to pierce the sky with a thin wedge of light.

'That was our punishment,' Souvarine continued in a hard voice. 'We were guilty of loving each other . . . Yes, it's a good thing she's dead. Heroes will be born out of the blood she shed, and there is no weakness left in my heart . . . Ah yes, nothing, no parents, no girl, no friend, nothing to make my hand hesitate come the day when I shall have either to take other people's lives or else lay down my own!'

Étienne had stopped, shivering in the cold night air. He made no comment but simply said:

'We've come quite far. Shall we go back?'

Slowly they began to make their way back towards Le Voreux, and after a few metres Étienne added:

'Have you seen the new notices?'

He was referring to some more large yellow posters that the Company had had pasted up that morning. Their message was plainer and more conciliatory, promising to re-employ all dismissed miners who returned to work the next day. Everything would be forgotten, and the pardon extended even to those who had been mostly closely involved.

'Yes, I've seen them,' Souvarine replied.

'Well? What do you think?'

'I think it's all over . . . The herd will go back. You're all too cowardly.'

Étienne roundly defended the comrades; one man alone can be brave, but a starving crowd is powerless. Little by little they had returned to Le Voreux; and as they reached the black hulk of the pit, he carried on talking, swearing that he himself would never go down the mine again, although he forgave those who would. Then, since there had been a rumour that the joiners had not had time to repair the tubbing in the pit-shaft, he wanted to find out about it. Was it true? Had the pressure of the earth on the wooden casing round the shaft made it bulge so much that one of the extraction cages actually rubbed against it over a distance of more than five metres? Souvarine, who had gone quiet again, replied briefly. He had just been working there the day before, and the cage did indeed catch the side, so much so that the operators had even had to make it go twice as fast just to get it past that spot. But when this was pointed out to the bosses, they all made the same irritated reply: it was coal that was needed, they could do the shoring later.

'Imagine if it gave way!' Étienne murmured. 'Some fun we'd have then!'

Staring through the shadows at the vague outline of the pit, Souvarine quietly concluded:

'Well, the comrades will soon know about it if it does give way, seeing as you're advising them to go back down.'

The church clock at Montsou was just striking nine; and when Étienne said that he was going home to bed, Souvarine added, without even holding out his hand:

'Well then, goodbye. I'm leaving.'

'Leaving? What do you mean?'

'Yes, I've asked for my cards. I'm off.'

Astonished and hurt, Étienne stared at him. Two whole hours walking together, and now he tells him! And all so cool and calm, when the mere announcement of this sudden separation had made his own heart miss a beat. They had got to know each other, they had been through difficult times together; and the idea of never seeing someone again is always grounds for sadness.

'So you're off, then. Where to?'

'Oh, somewhere. I don't know.'

'But we'll meet again?'

'No, I don't expect so.'

They fell silent, and remained standing in front of each other without finding anything else to say.

'Well, goodbye then.'

'Goodbye.'

As Étienne climbed towards the village, Souvarine turned round and went back to the bank of the canal; and there, alone now, he walked and walked, with his head down, so much a part of the darkness that he was little more than a moving shadow of the night. Occasionally he would stop and count the hours chiming in the distance. When midnight struck, he left the towpath and headed towards Le Voreux.

At that hour the pit was empty, and he met only a bleary-eyed deputy. They wouldn't be firing up till two, ready for the return to work. First, he went up to fetch a jacket, which he pretended he'd left in a cupboard. Rolled up inside the jacket were tools, a brace and bit, a small but very sharp saw, and a hammer and chisel. Then he left. But instead of going out through the changing-room he slipped into the narrow corridor that led to the escape shaft. And with his jacket tucked under his arm he climbed gently down, without a lamp, measuring the depth by counting the ladders. He knew that the cage was catching at the three-hundred-and-seventy-four metre point, against the fifth section of the lower tubbing. When he had counted fifty-four ladders, he felt about with his hand and came on the bulge in the timbering. This was the spot.

With the skill and cool deliberateness of a good worker who has given much thought to the task in hand, he set to work. He immediately began by cutting a panel out of the shaft partition with his saw, so as to gain access to the main winding-shaft. Then, with the aid of matches, which flared and quickly went out, he was able to assess the state of the tubbing and the extent of the recent repairs.

In the area between Calais and Valenciennes the sinking of a pit-shaft was an exceptionally difficult business as they had to pass through the water tables, immense sheets of water that lay at the level of the lowest valleys. Only by installing tubbing, in the form of pieces of wood joined together like the staves of a barrel, was it possible to contain the springs that fed them and to insulate the shafts in the middle of these deep, dark lakes whose waters lapped against their outer walls. When they sank the shaft at Le Voreux, they had had to put in two sections of tubbing: an upper one, through the shifting sands and white clay that are found in the vicinity of cretaceous rock, which is itself riddled with cracks and swollen with water like a sponge; and then a lower one, directly above the coal itself, passing through a yellow, flour-like sand of almost liquid consistency; and this was where the Torrent was, the subterranean sea that terrified the pitmen of that region, a real sea with its own storms and wrecks, a forgotten, unfathomable sea of rolling black waves more than three hundred metres below the sunlight. Generally the tubbing held firm, despite the enormous pressure, and the only real problem came from the settling of the surrounding earth, which had been destabilized by the constant movement of abandoned workings gradually caving in. When the rock sank like this, large cracks sometimes appeared and spread as far as the tubbing, causing it to buckle; and this was where the main danger lay, the threat of major subsidence and the flooding that followed, when the pit would be filled with an avalanche of earth and a deluge of underground springs.

Sitting astride the opening he had made between the two shafts, Souvarine saw that the fifth section of the tubbing had been very badly warped. The wooden staves were bellying out beyond the framework that held them in place, and indeed several had come loose. Numerous little jets of water, *pichoux* as the miners called them, were spurting from the joints, despite the tow and pitch with which they were lagged. And because they had been in such a hurry, the joiners had simply fitted iron brackets at the corners of the shaft without bothering to insert all the screws. It was clear that considerable movement was taking place in the sands of the Torrent that lay behind.

Then, using his brace, he loosened the screws in the brackets so that one last push would tear them all out. This was an extremely risky job, and twenty times or more he nearly lost his balance and plunged down the hundred and eighty metres to the bottom. He had had to grab hold of the oak guides along which the cages travelled up and down, and then, suspended above the void, he moved back and forth along the crossbeams by which these vertical rails were connected at intervals; he would slide along or sit or lean over backwards, with only an elbow or a knee for support, coolly contemptuous of death. The merest draught of air could have sent him flying, and three times he caught himself just in time, unfazed. First he would feel about with his hand, then he would set to, lighting a match only when he had lost his bearings among the greasy beams. Having loosened the screws he set about the tubbing itself; and the danger grew. He had sought out the one key piece of timbering that jammed the others in place, and he attacked it, drilling holes in it, sawing at it, and gradually making it thinner so as to lessen its resistance. And all the time the water continued to spurt in thin jets from every crack and chink, blinding him and soaking him in an icy rain. Two matches failed to light properly. They were all wet now, and it was pitch dark, a bottomless chasm of blackness.

From this point on he was seized with fury. He was exhilarated to feel the breath of the invisible on his skin, and the black horror of this rainswept abyss drove him to a frenzy of destruction. He attacked the tubbing at random, striking where he could, with his brace, with his saw, suddenly determined to rip it open and bring everything crashing down on his head. And he did so with the ferocity of a man plunging a knife into the living flesh of a person he loathed. He would kill it in the end, this foul beast that was Le Voreux, with its ever-gaping maw that had devoured so much human fodder. The sound of his tools rang out, biting into the wood; he stretched, he crawled, he climbed up, he climbed down, always managing by some miracle or other to hang on, ceaseless in his movement like a bird of the night flitting among the rafters of a bell-tower.

But gradually he grew calmer, and then he was cross with himself. Was he incapable of proceeding with due deliberation? Calmly he paused to recover his breath and then returned to the escape shaft, where he blocked the hole by replacing the panel he had sawn out. Enough was enough, he didn't want to give the game away by creating too much damage, which they would only have tried to repair at once. The beast had been wounded in its belly, and it remained to be seen whether it would survive the day. Moreover, he had left his signature: a horrified world would know that this was no death from natural causes. He took his time wrapping his tools carefully in his jacket, and slowly he climbed back up the ladders. Once he had left the pit without being seen, it didn't even occur to him to go and change his clothes. Three o'clock struck. He just stood in the road and waited.

At that same hour Étienne, who had been unable to sleep, was disturbed by a slight noise in the thick darkness of the room. He could hear the gentle breathing of the children and the snores of Bonnemort and La Maheude, while next to him Jeanlin was making a long-drawn-out whistling sound, like a flute. He must have dreamed it, and he was just resuming his attempts to go to sleep when he heard the noise again. It was the sound of a mattress creaking, as though someone were trying to get out of bed without being heard. He supposed that Catherine must be feeling unwell.

'Is that you? What's the matter?' he whispered.

There was no reply, only the snoring could still be heard. For the next five minutes nothing stirred, but then there was another creaking sound. Certain this time that he had not been mistaken, he crossed the room, holding his hands out in front of him to feel for the bed opposite. He was extremely surprised to find Catherine sitting there, holding her breath, awake and on her guard.

'Why didn't you answer? What are you up to?'

Eventually she said:

'I'm getting up.'

'At this hour of the night?'

'Yes, I'm going back to work at the pit.'

Étienne was shocked, and he had to sit down on the edge of the bed while Catherine explained her reasons to him. She could not bear to live like this, not working and always feeling that she was being reproached for it; she would rather run the risk of some rough treatment from Chaval down the mine; and if her mother wouldn't take the money she brought in, well, she was old enough to fend for herself and make her own soup.

'Off you go. I've got to dress. And please, not a word about this to anyone.'

But he remained beside her, having now put his arm round her waist in a gesture of sorrowful compassion. As they sat close together in their nightshirts, here on the edge of a bed that was not yet cold after being slept in, they could each feel the warmth of the other's bare skin. At first she had tried to pull away; then she had begun to cry softly and put her arms round his neck to hold him against her, in a desperate embrace. And there they sat, with no other desires, mindful of their past unhappy love, which they had never been able to satisfy. Was it over between them for ever? Though now the way was open, would the day never come when they would dare to love each other? It would have taken only a brief taste of happiness to dispel the shame and embarrassment that was keeping them apart, the sundry notions they had got into their heads and which even they did not fully understand.

'Go back to bed,' she murmured. 'I don't want to light the

candle, it would wake Mum ... Off you go. It's time I was leaving.'

He wasn't listening but continued to hold her tight as an immense sadness filled his heart. He was overwhelmed by a desire for peace, by an irresistible need to be happy; and he saw himself married and living in a nice little house, with no other ambition than to live and die there, just the two of them together. A piece of bread would be all they'd need; and even if there were only enough for one, then she could have it. Why ask for anything more? Was there anything else worth having in life?

Meanwhile she unwrapped her bare arms from round his neck.

'Please, let me go.'

Then, on a sudden, heartfelt impulse, he whispered in her ear: 'Wait. I'll come with you.'

And he was astonished at himself for saying such a thing. He had sworn never to go back down the mine again, so where had this sudden decision come from, springing from his lips like that without his ever having dreamed of such a thing, without his ever having thought the possibility over in his mind? He now felt such calm, such a complete release from all his doubts, that he held stubbornly to his decision, like a man saved by accident, who has found the only possible way out of his torment. Thus he refused to listen to her when she, believing that he was doing this just for her and fearful of the nasty comments with which he would be greeted at the pit, expressed some alarm. He could not have cared less: the notices promised a pardon, and that was all that mattered.

'I want to work. It's my decision ... Come on, let's get dressed. We must be quiet.'

They got dressed in the dark, taking every possible precaution not to wake anyone. Catherine had secretly got her miner's clothes ready the night before, and Étienne fetched a jacket and trousers out of the cupboard; they did not wash, for fear of making a noise with the basin. Everyone was asleep, but they still had to pass along the narrow corridor where La Maheude's bed was. On their way out, as ill luck would have it, they knocked into a chair. She woke up and called out sleepily:

'What is it? Who's there?'

Catherine, trembling, had stopped at once and clutched Étienne's hand very tightly.

'It's only me,' he said. 'Don't worry. I'm just going out for a breath of air. It's too stuffy in here.'

'Oh! All right.'

And La Maheude went back to sleep. For a time Catherine dared not move. Eventually she went downstairs to the parlour, where she took the slice of bread she had kept from a loaf given them by a lady from Montsou and cut it in half. Then they quietly shut the front door and departed.

Souvarine had remained standing at the corner of the road, near the Advantage. For the past half-hour he had been watching the miners return to work, a jumble of vague shapes in the darkness, tramping past like a herd. He was counting them, as a butcher might count his animals as they enter the abattoir; and he was surprised by how many there were, for, pessimistic though he was, he had not foreseen that there would be quite so many cowards. The queue showed no sign of coming to an end; and as he stood there in the bitter cold, his teeth clenched and his eyes shining, his body stiffened.

But he gave a start. Among the men filing past, whose faces he could not make out, he had nevertheless just recognized one by the way he walked. He stepped forward and stopped him.

'Where do you think you're going?'

Étienne was so startled that instead of answering him he stammered out:

'Goodness! I thought you'd left!'

Then he admitted that he was returning to the mine. Yes, all right, he had sworn not to; but what sort of life was it to be standing about with your hands in your pockets waiting for things that might take another hundred years to come about. Besides, he had personal reasons.

Souvarine was shaking as he listened to him. Then he grabbed him by the shoulder and shoved him in the direction of the village.

'Go home! I insist. Do you hear me?'

But just then Catherine stepped forward, and he recognized her too. Étienne was busy protesting that it was nobody's place but his own to judge his conduct. Souvarine looked from the girl to the comrade, and then stepped back and gestured in sudden resignation. Once a woman had got under a man's skin, he was done for, he might as well die. Perhaps Souvarine had a sudden memory of his mistress, back there in Moscow, the mistress who had been hanged, severing the last tie that bound his flesh and setting him free to dispose of the lives of others and of his own. He said simply:

'On you go.'

Embarrassed, Étienne lingered, searching for a friendly word in order not to part on this note.

'So are you still planning to leave?'

'Yes.'

'Well then, give me your hand, mate. Good luck, and no hard feelings.'

Souvarine held out an ice-cold hand. No friend, no girl.

'This time it is goodbye.'

'Yes, goodbye.'

And, standing there motionless in the darkness, Souvarine watched as Étienne and Catherine entered Le Voreux.

III

At four o'clock they began to go down. Dansaert in person had installed himself in the clerk's office in the lamp-room, where he wrote down the name of each miner who stepped forward and then handed him a lamp. He accepted everybody back without comment, just as the notices had promised. Nevertheless, when he saw Étienne and Catherine standing at the window, he gave a start and went red in the face. He opened his mouth, on the point of refusing to take them on again, but was then content to gloat mockingly: aha! and how are the mighty fallen! So the Company must be doing something right if the scourge of Montsou was back wanting to earn his daily bread? Silently Étienne took his lamp and climbed the stairs to the pit-shaft with Catherine.

But it was here, at the pit-head, that Catherine feared there would be abuse from the comrades. Sure enough, the moment they walked in she spotted Chaval in the middle of twenty or so miners waiting for an empty cage. He started walking towards her with a furious look on his face but caught sight of Étienne and stopped. Then he affected to sneer and started shrugging his shoulders in a theatrical manner. Oh, fine, fine! What did he bloody care anyway! Étienne was welcome to her, he'd warmed her up nicely for him! Good riddance! It was no skin off his nose if the gentleman preferred other people's cast-offs! But underneath this show of contempt he was quivering with jealous rage, and his eyes blazed. In fact nobody else reacted at all, and the comrades just stood there in silence, their eyes on the ground. They merely glanced over at the new arrivals, and then, demoralized and without anger, went back to staring fixedly at the entrance to the pit-shaft, clutching their lamps and shivering in their thin cotton jackets thanks to the perpetual draughts that blew in the large hall.

Eventually the cage settled on its keeps, and they were told to get in. Catherine and Étienne squeezed into a tub which already contained Pierron and two hewers. Next to them, in the other tub, Chaval was busy telling old Mouque at the top of his voice how wrong management was not to use the opportunity to rid the pits of a rotten apple or two; but the old stableman, who had reverted to his usual state of weary resignation at the dog's life he led, no longer felt angry about the death of his children and simply replied with a conciliatory gesture.

The cage was released, and they dropped quickly into the darkness. No one spoke. Suddenly, about two thirds of the way down, there was a terrible scraping noise. The ironwork creaked, and everyone was thrown on top of each other.

'Christ Almighty!' Étienne muttered crossly. 'Do they want to crush us to death? What with this bloody tubbing of theirs we'll never see daylight again. And they say they've fixed it!'

Nevertheless the cage had got past the obstacle. It was now

descending beneath such a heavy shower of water that the miners listened with some concern to the sound of it streaming down. Had the caulking sprung many new leaks?

They asked Pierron, who had been back at work for some days, but he didn't want to let on that he was afraid in case it was interpreted as criticism of the management; and so he replied:

'Oh, there's no danger! It's always like this. They probably just haven't had time to caulk the *pichoux*.'

The torrential deluge roared down on top of them, and by the time they reached pit-bottom it was like being in the middle of a waterspout. Not one deputy thought of climbing up the ladders to take a look. The pump would do the trick, and the caulkers could inspect the joints the following night. As it was, they were having enough problems reorganizing the work in the roadways. Before letting the hewers return to their individual coal-faces, the engineer had decided that for the first five days everyone would carry out urgent shoring work. Rock-falls were threatening all over the place, and the main roads had suffered so badly that the timber supports needed replacing over stretches of several hundred metres. So at pit-bottom they were forming ten-man teams, each under the direction of a deputy, and then setting them to work at the worst-affected spots. Once everyone was down, there were three hundred and twenty-two of them, about half of the total workforce when the pit was in full production.

Chaval had just become the tenth member of the team that included Étienne and Catherine. It was no accident; he had hidden behind his comrades and then given the deputy no other option. This particular team set off to clear the far end of the northern roadway, nearly three kilometres away, where a rock-fall was blocking access to the Eighteen-Inch seam. They set to with their picks and shovels to remove the rubble. Étienne, Chaval and five others did the digging while Catherine and two pit-boys pushed the tubs full of spoil up to the incline. Nobody said much, as the deputy never left their side. Meanwhile Catherine's two lovers were on the point of coming to blows. Though busy muttering that he had no more use for the whore, Chaval refused to leave her alone and kept knocking into her on the sly, with the result that Étienne had threatened to give him what for if he didn't leave her in peace. They glared ferociously at each other and had to be separated.

At about eight o'clock Dansaert came round to see how the work was progressing. He seemed to be in a foul mood, and he tore into the deputy: it was all wrong, the props needed to be replaced as you went along, the whole thing was a mess! And off he went, announcing he'd be back with the engineer. He had been expecting Négrel since the early morning and could not understand why he was so late.

Another hour went by. The deputy had stopped the men clearing the rubble and set everyone to the task of strengthening the roof. Even Catherine and the two pit-boys had stopped pushing their tubs and instead were getting the props ready and bringing them along. Here at the end of the roadway the team was like a remote outpost at the furthest point of the mine, and it was now completely cut off from the other workings. On three or four occasions they heard strange noises, like the sound of people running, and they looked up from their work. What was happening? It was as if all the roads were emptying, as if the comrades were already returning to the surface, and as fast as they possibly could. But the sounds faded away in the deep silence, and they resumed their task of ramming timber props under the ceiling, dazed by the deafening blows of the sledge-hammer. Eventually they returned to clearing away the rocks, and the tubs began moving again.

Catherine returned from her first trip looking very frightened and saying that there was nobody left at the incline.

'I called out, but there was no reply. Everybody's cleared off.'

Everyone was so shocked that they downed tools and ran. They were horrified at the thought of being left behind all alone in the pit like this so far from the shaft. They had kept only their lamps and ran along in single file, the men, the boys and Catherine. Even the deputy was panicking and shouting for help, more and more terrified by the silence and the endless series of deserted roadways. What was going on? Why wasn't there a soul to be seen? What could have happened to make everyone vanish like this? Their terror increased with the uncertainty of the danger facing them, of the threat that they could sense but could not understand.

At length, as they were approaching pit-bottom, they were met by a stream of water blocking their path. At once they found themselves up to their knees; they could no longer run but instead had to wade through the water, all the while thinking that a minute's delay might cost them their lives.

'God Almighty! The tubbing's burst!' cried Étienne. 'I told you we'd never see daylight again!'

Ever since the miners had come down, Pierron had been extremely concerned as he watched the water pouring from the shaft in ever-greater quantities. As he helped two other men load tubs into the cages, he kept looking up: his face was splashed with large drops of water, and his ears rang with the roar of the tempest above him. But he became particularly anxious when he noticed that the *bougnou*, the ten-metre sump, was filling up beneath him; already the water was seeping up through the wooden planks and spilling out on to the cast-iron floor, proof that the pump could no longer keep up with the leaks. He could hear it panting away in exhausted gasps. He then warned Dansaert, who swore angrily and said they would have to wait for the engineer. Twice he mentioned it again, but all he got by way of reply was an exasperated shrug of the shoulders. So the water was rising. What was he supposed to do about it?

Mouque appeared with Battle, leading him to work; and he had to hold on to him with both hands, for the usually sleepy old horse had suddenly reared up, straining his neck towards the shaft and whinnying at the prospect of death.

'What's up, my philosopher friend? What's the matter? ... The rain, is it? Come on now, it's no concern of yours.'

But the animal was quivering all over, and Mouque had to drag him off towards the haulage road.

Almost at the same instant as Mouque and Battle were disappearing down a roadway, there was a loud crack up above, followed by the prolonged clatter of something falling. A piece of tubbing had come away and was bouncing off the walls of the shaft as it fell the hundred and eighty metres to the bottom. Pierron and the other onsetters were able to get clear in time so that the oak plank crushed only an empty tub. At the same time a great sheet of water came hurtling down, as though a dyke had burst. Dansaert wanted to climb up and take a look; but even as he spoke, a second piece came tumbling down. Terrified, and with disaster staring him in the face, he hesitated no longer but gave the order to return to the surface and dispatched the deputies to raise the alarm throughout the mine.

There followed a terrible stampede. Miners came streaming out of every roadway, pushing and shoving as they made for the cages, crushing each other and ready to kill the next man if they could just get taken up at once. Some had tried to go up by the escape shaft, but they came back down again shouting that it was already blocked. With each cage that departed the nightmare began for those who remained: that one had got past all right, but who could say if the next one would, what with all the debris now blocking the shaft? Up above them the tubbing must have been continuing to disintegrate because, amid the continuous and growing roar of cascading water, they heard a series of muffled explosions, which was the timbers splitting and bursting. One cage was soon out of action: it had been severely dented and would no longer run smoothly on the guides, which in any case had probably been broken. The other was catching so badly that the cable was bound to snap soon. And there were still a hundred men to be got out, all of them screaming their heads off and struggling to get nearest to a cage, each one covered in blood and soaked to the skin. Two men were killed by falling planks. A third, who had grabbed hold of the cage from below, had fallen fifty metres and disappeared into the sump.

Dansaert, meanwhile, was trying to restore order. Armed with a pick, he was threatening to smash the skull of the first man who disobeyed him; and he endeavoured to get everyone to form a queue, shouting out that the onsetters would be the last to leave once they had seen their comrades safely away. Nobody was listening to him, indeed he had just stopped a pale and frightened Pierron from being one of the first to make his escape. Each time the cage left he had to strike him to make him stand back. But his own teeth were chattering; a minute longer, and they'd all be buried alive: everything was giving way up there, it was as though a river had burst its banks, and bits of tubbing were raining down murderously on those below. A few miners were still left when, crazed with fear, he jumped into a tub and let Pierron jump in behind him. The cage rose.

At that very moment Étienne and Chaval's team reached pit-bottom. They saw the cage disappear and rushed forward; but they were driven back as the tubbing finally gave way altogether. The shaft was blocked, the cage would not be coming down again. Catherine was sobbing, and Chaval swore till he choked. There were twenty of them left: were those bloody bosses just going to abandon them here like this? Old Mouque, having led Battle slowly back, was still standing there holding him by the bridle; and the pair of them, the old man and the horse, gazed in astonishment at the speed with which the floodwater was rising. Already it had reached thigh level. Étienne said nothing but gritted his teeth and picked Catherine up in his arms. And the twenty of them were screaming, their faces upturned, twenty people stubbornly gazing like imbeciles at a shaft that was now a collapsed hole in the ground spewing forth a river and from which there could be no further hope of rescue.

On emerging into the daylight Dansaert saw Négrel hurrying towards him. As luck would have it, Mme Hennebeau had kept him at home since first thing that morning because she wanted to look through some catalogues with a view to choosing some wedding presents for Cécile. It was now ten o'clock.

'So what's happening?' he shouted while still some way off.

'The pit's done for,' replied the overman.

He blurted out the story of the disaster, while the engineer listened in disbelief and gave a shrug. Who'd ever heard of tubbing coming apart of its own accord like that? They must be exaggerating, he would have to take a look.

'Presumably there's nobody still down there?'

Dansaert looked shifty. No, nobody. At least he hoped not. Still, some miners might have got delayed.

'But in God's name why did you come up, then? You don't just leave your men like that!'

He immediately gave orders for the lamps to be counted. Three hundred and twenty-two had been issued that morning, and only two hundred and fifty-five had been handed in. However, several miners admitted that they had left theirs behind after dropping them in the general panic. They tried to have a roll-call, but it was impossible to establish precise figures: some miners had already rushed away, others did not hear their names. Nobody could agree on who was missing. Twenty of them perhaps, or forty. But for Négrel one thing was clear: there were still men below. If you leaned over the edge of the shaft, you could make out their screams coming up through the debris from the collapsed tubbing, despite the noise of the falling water.

Négrel's first thoughts were to send for M. Hennebeau and to shut the pit. But it was too late: miners had already raced off to Village Two Hundred and Forty as though they were being pursued by the collapsing mine itself and had spread alarm through every household. Groups of women and an assortment of old men and children were all rushing down the hill towards them, sobbing and screaming. They had to be driven back, and a cordon of supervisors was detailed to hold them off so as to prevent them from hampering operations. Many of the workers who had come up from the mine were still standing there in a daze, oblivious to the fact that they might change their clothes, and frozen with fear as they contemplated this terrifying hole in which they had nearly lost their lives. Distraught women milled round them, quoting names and besieging them with questions. Had so-and-so been down there? And this person? And that person? They had no idea and simply mumbled, shivering violently and making wild gestures as though to ward off some ghastly vision that haunted them. The crowd was growing rapidly, and the sound of wailing filled the surrounding roads. Up on the spoil-heap, in Bonnemort's shelter, a man was sitting on the ground: it was Souvarine, who had stayed to watch.

'Names! Just tell us the names!' cried the women, their voices choked with tears.

Négrel appeared briefly and said:

'As soon as we have the names, we'll let you know. But all is not lost. Everyone will be rescued . . . I'm on my way down.'

Then, in silent anguish, the crowd waited. And, indeed, with quiet bravery, the engineer was preparing to go down. He had had the cage unhitched and ordered a small tub to be attached to the end of the cable instead; and, suspecting that his lamp would be extinguished by the water, he instructed the men to hang another one underneath, where it would be protected.

Some deputies were helping with these preparations, shaking all over, their faces white and drained.

'You're coming down with me, Dansaert,' Négrel said curtly.

But when he saw that none of them had the courage and watched the overman swaying on his feet, faint with terror, he brushed him aside with contempt.

'On second thoughts, you'll only get in my way . . . I'd rather go alone.'

Already he had climbed into the narrow bucket dangling on the end of the cable; and, holding his lamp in one hand and the communication rope in the other, he called out to the operator himself:

'Gently now!'

The engine started the pulleys turning, and Négrel disappeared down into the chasm, where the wretched souls could still be heard screaming.

At the top nothing had shifted, and he noted that the upper tubbing was in good condition. As he hung in the middle of the shaft, he swivelled this way and that, shining his light on the sides: so few of the joints were leaking that his lamp was unaffected. But when he reached the lower tubbing, at a depth of three hundred metres, it went out just as he had foreseen: a spurt of water had landed in the tub. From then on he could see only by the light of the lamp underneath, which preceded him into the darkness. Despite his cool nerve he shivered and turned pale at the sight of the full horror of the disaster. Only a few timber staves in the tubbing remained; the others had disappeared along with their frames. Behind them yawned huge cavities from which the yellow sand, as fine as flour, was pouring out in considerable quantities, while the waters of the Torrent, that forgotten, underground sea with its own storms and wrecks, were gushing forth as though from an open sluice. He went lower, lost in the midst of these empty spaces that were now growing ever wider. The water spouting from the underground springs battered his tub and spun him round, and he was so poorly served by the red star of his lamp as it sped downwards that it was like seeing the streets and crossroads of some distant, ruined city when he gazed into the huge, dancing shadows. It would never be possible for human beings to work down here again, and he had but one hope left, that of rescuing the miners whose lives were in danger. The further he descended, the louder grew the screaming, but then he had to stop, for an impassable obstacle was blocking the shaft: a pile of tubbing staves, the broken beams of the cage-rails, and the shattered remains of the escape shaft partitions all lay in a tangled mass together with the splintered cable-guides that had once led to the pump. As he stared steadily down at the scene, his heart sinking, the scream-ing suddenly stopped. No doubt, faced with the rapidly rising flood, the poor people had fled into the roadways – if the water had not already filled their lungs.

Négrel was obliged to admit defeat and pulled on the rope in order to be returned to the surface. But then he signalled for another stop. He was still amazed by how suddenly the disaster had occurred, and he did not understand why. He wanted to find out, and started examining the pieces of tubbing that were still intact. From a distance he had been surprised by the scratches and dents in the wood. His lamp had almost gone out because of the wet, and so he felt around with his fingers and was able to make out very easily the saw marks and the drill holes, the whole, ghastly process of destruction. Quite clearly someone had wanted this disaster to happen. As he stared open-mouthed, these last pieces gave way and plunged down the shaft, frames and all, in a final moment of disintegration that nearly took him with it. His courage had vanished, and the thought of the man who had done this made his hair stand on end, chilling the blood in his veins with the awestruck dread of evil, as if the man were still there, like some monstrous presence in all this darkness, a witness to his own inordinate crime. He screamed and pulled frantically on the rope. And it was high time he did so, for he noticed that a hundred metres above him the upper tubbing was starting to show signs of movement: the joints were opening up and the caulking beginning to give way, releasing streams of water. It was now only a matter of hours before the mine-shaft would lose its entire tubbing and cave in completely.

On the surface M. Hennebeau was anxiously waiting for Négrel.

'Well? How does it look?' he asked.

But the engineer could not get the words out. He was on the point of collapse.

'It's just not possible. Really, it's quite unheard of . . . Did you have a good look?'

Yes, Négrel nodded, glancing round warily. He did not want to explain further while some of the deputies were listening, and he led his uncle some ten metres away and then, having judged the distance insufficient, further away still. Speaking very softly in his ear, he told him about the sabotage, how the planks had been sawn and drilled, how the pit had had its throat slit and was now breathing its last. M. Hennebeau turned very pale and also lowered his voice, instinctively respecting the silence that attends the monstrousness of great crimes or wanton acts of immorality. There was no point in appearing to be frightened in front of Montsou's ten thousand miners: they would reflect on the consequences later. And the two men continued to whisper together, appalled by the thought that any man could have found the courage to go down the shaft, hang there in the void, and risk his life twenty times over in order to carry out this dreadful deed. They could not begin to grasp this mad bravery in the cause of destruction, and they refused to believe it, despite the evidence, just as people refuse to believe the stories of famous escapes and prisoners who must have sprouted wings and flown from windows that are thirty metres up.

When M. Hennebeau walked back over to the deputies, his face was twitching nervously. With a gesture of helplessness he gave the order for the pit to be evacuated at once. Everyone departed mournfully as though they were at a funeral, silently abandoning the place while glancing back from time to time at the large, empty buildings, still standing there but now beyond salvation.

The manager and the engineer were the last to leave the pit-head, and the crowd greeted them with its noisy chant:

'Give us the names! Give us the names!'

La Maheude had now arrived to join the other women. She remembered the noise in the night: her daughter and the lodger must have left together, and they were down there for certain. Having initially screamed that it was a good job and that the heartless cowards deserved to stay there, she had then rushed to the scene and was now standing in the front row, shivering with apprehension. In any case, she no longer dared to doubt the fact, as she realized from listening to the discussion going on around her about the identity of those still down there. Yes, yes, Catherine was one of them, and Étienne too; a comrade had seen them. But opinion was still divided as to the others. No, no, not him, more likely that other chap, or perhaps Chaval, even though one of the pit-boys swore blind he'd come up with him. La Levaque and La Pierronne had nobody in danger but shouted and wailed as loudly as the rest of the women. Zacharie had been one of the first up and, despite his usual air of cynicism, had embraced his wife and mother in tears. Having remained by La Maheude's side, he was sharing in her trembling anxiety and displaying unexpected depths of affection for his sister, refusing to believe that she was down there until management officially confirmed the fact.

'Give us the names! For God's sake, tell us the names!'

Négrel shouted crossly at the supervisors in a loud voice:

'Make them be quiet, for God's sake. Things are bad enough as they are. We don't know the damned names yet.'

Two hours had already gone by. In the initial panic nobody had thought of the other shaft, the old one at Réquillart. M. Hennebeau was just announcing that they were going to try and mount a rescue attempt from that direction when the word went round that five men had just escaped the flooding by climbing up the rickety ladders in the disused escape shaft. The name of Mouque was mentioned, which caused some surprise since

nobody had thought he was down there. But the story told by
the five who had escaped brought further tears; fifteen comrades
had been unable to follow them, having lost their way after
being blocked by rock-falls. It would be impossible to rescue
them now, for Réquillart was flooded to a depth of ten metres.
They knew the names of all of them, and the air was filled
with anguished lament as though an entire people had been
slaughtered.

'For God's sake, tell them to be quiet!' Négrel repeated furiously. 'And make them stand back. Yes, yes, a hundred metres
back. It's dangerous here. Push them back, push them back!'

The poor people had to be driven back by force. They in turn
imagined fresh horrors and thought that this was an attempt to
conceal further deaths from them; the deputies had to explain
that the shaft was about to swallow up the entire mine. This
prospect shocked them into silence, and eventually they began
to inch backwards; but the number of guards had to be doubled
in order to contain them, for despite themselves they kept
coming forward again, as though irresistibly drawn to the scene.
A thousand people were milling about in the road, and people
were still flocking from the villages, and even from Montsou
itself. Meanwhile the man up above on the spoil-heap, the
fair-skinned man with the girlish face, smoked cigarette after
cigarette to pass the time, and his pale eyes never left the pit.

Then the waiting began. It was midday: nobody had eaten,
yet nobody left. Rust-coloured clouds passed slowly overhead
in the dirty grey, overcast sky. Behind Rasseneur's hedge a large
dog was barking fiercely, without respite, unsettled by this
living, breathing crowd. The crowd itself had gradually spread
out over the surrounding land and formed a circle around the
pit at a distance of a hundred metres. At the centre of this empty
space stood Le Voreux. Not a soul was left, not a sound was to
be heard: it was deserted. The windows and doors had been left
open, and through them one could see the abandoned interiors.
A ginger cat, which had been left behind, sensing the danger in
this solitude, leaped down from a stairway and fled. The boiler
fires must have barely died down because small puffs of smoke
continued to rise from the tall, brick chimney towards the dark

clouds above; and the weathercock on the headgear squeaked in the wind with a small, shrill cry, a sad, lonely voice amid all these vast buildings that were about to perish.

Two o'clock, and still no movement. M. Hennebeau, Négrel and other engineers who had hurried to the pit stood around in front of the crowd in a huddle of frock-coats and black hats. They, too, could not tear themselves away, though their legs were weary and they felt ill, sick at heart to be the helpless witnesses of such a disaster, and exchanging only the occasional whisper, as though they were standing by the bed of a dying man. The upper tubbing must have been in the last stages of disintegration now because they could hear sudden bangs followed by the clatter of something falling a long way and then a long silence: the gaping wound was getting wider, and the process of collapse that had begun further down was now steadily rising to the surface. Négrel was gripped with nervous impatience and kept wanting to take a look; and he was beginning to walk forward alone into that terrifying, empty space when they all grabbed him by the shoulders. What was the point? There was nothing he could do. Meanwhile a miner, one of the old hands, had got past the guards and raced across to the changing-room. But he calmly reappeared, having merely gone to fetch his clogs.

Three o'clock came. Still nothing. A shower of rain had soaked the crowd, but it had not retreated one step. Rasseneur's dog had started barking again. And it was not until about twenty past three that the earth was shaken with the first tremor. Le Voreux shook slightly, but it was stoutly built and held firm. But a second shock followed at once, and from the open mouths of the crowd came a long scream: the screening-shed with its pitch roof tottered twice and then came tumbling down with a terrible cracking sound. Under the enormous pressure the beams split and rubbed together so violently that they gave off showers of sparks. From then on the earth never ceased to shake, and there was tremor after tremor each time the ground shifted beneath the surface, like the rumblings of an erupting volcano. In the distance the dog had stopped barking and was now howling pitifully, as though heralding the shocks which it knew to be coming; and the women and children, indeed everybody who was watching, could not refrain from a cry of distress each time they felt the earth move beneath them. In less than ten minutes the slate roof of the headgear fell in, the pit-head and the engine-house were split asunder, and a huge gap appeared in the wall. Then the noises stopped, the collapse halted, and once again there was a long silence.

For an hour Le Voreux remained like this, breached, as though it had been bombarded by some barbarian horde. The screaming had stopped, and the growing circle of onlookers simply watched. Beneath the pile of beams that had once been the screening-shed, they could see the shattered tipplers and the smashed and twisted hoppers. But the worst damage was at the pit-head, where bricks had come raining down and whole sections of wall had crumbled. The framework of iron girders that supported the winding-pulleys had given way, and half of it was now hanging down the shaft; one cage was suspended in mid-air, and a piece of severed cable was dangling loose; tubs, ladders, sheets of cast-iron flooring all lay in a jumbled heap. By some chance the lamp-room had remained intact, and one could see its bright rows of little lamps over to the left. And there at the far end of its demolished housing was the winding-engine, sitting foursquare on its plinth of masonry, its brasses gleaming, its thick steel rods looking like indestructible tendons, and its huge crank sticking up at an angle like the mighty knee of some recumbent giant reposing in the sure knowledge of his own strength.

Following this hour of respite, M. Hennebeau began to entertain some hope. The earth must have stopped shifting, they would be able to save the winding-engine and the remainder of the buildings. But he still forbade people to go near and wanted to give it another half-hour. The waiting was becoming unbearable, and the raised hopes made the anxiety worse; every heart was beating wildly. A dark cloud looming over the horizon was hastening the onset of dusk, and a sinister twilight began to fall on the wreckage left by the earth's tumult. They had all been standing there for seven hours now, not moving, not eating.

And suddenly, just as the engineers were starting to edge

forward, one last convulsion of the earth put them to flight.
There was a whole series of underground explosions, as though
some monstrous artillery were firing cannon in the void. On the
surface the remaining buildings toppled over and crumpled to
the ground. The ruins of the screening-shed and the pit-head
were swallowed up in a kind of whirlpool. Then the boiler-house
burst apart and vanished. Next it was the turn of the square
tower where the drainage-pump used to pant away at its work;
the tower fell flat on its face like a man hit by a bullet. And
then came the terrifying spectacle of the winding-engine, now
wrenched from its moorings, fighting for its life on spread-eagled
limbs. It was on the move, stretching its crank – its giant's knee
– as though it were trying to struggle to its feet; but then it fell
back dead, crushed, and was swallowed up by the earth. Now
only the tall, thirty-metre chimney remained standing, shaking
like a mast in a hurricane. It looked as though it might shatter
into tiny pieces and be blown away like powder when suddenly
it sank in one piece, absorbed into the ground, melted away like
some colossal candle; and nothing visible remained, not even
the tip of the lightning-conductor. It was all over: the vile beast
squatting in its hollow in the ground, gorged on human flesh,
had drawn the last of its long, slow, gasping breaths. Le Voreux
had now vanished in its entirety down into the abyss.

The crowd fled, screaming. Women covered their eyes as they
ran, and the men were swept along like a swirl of dead leaves
by the sheer horror of the scene. They tried not to scream, but
scream they did, with their arms in the air and their lungs
bursting, at the sight of the vast hole that had opened up. Like
the crater of some extinct volcano it stretched from the road as
far as the canal, fifteen metres deep and at least forty metres
wide. The whole pit-yard had gone the way of the buildings, the
gigantic trestles, the overhead railway and all its track, an entire
train of tubs, as well as three railway wagons, not to mention
the store of pit-props, a forest of newly cut poles that had been
swallowed up like so many straws. At the bottom of the crater
all that could be seen was a tangled mass of wooden beams,
bricks, ironwork and plaster, a dreadful array of wreckage that
had been pounded, mangled and splattered with mud by the

raging storm of catastrophe. And the hole was spreading: fissures ran from the edge of it far off into the surrounding fields. One stretched as far as Rasseneur's public house, where there was a crack in the front wall. Was the whole village going to be engulfed as well? How far did they have to run to find safe ground, in this fearsome twilight and under a leaden sky that looked as though it, too, were bent on destroying the world?

But Négrel gave a cry of despair. M. Hennebeau, who had moved back, began to weep. The catastrophe was not over yet. The canal bank gave way, and a sheet of water started gushing out into one of the cracks in the ground. There it vanished, cascading like a waterfall into a deep valley. The mine drank the river down: its roads would be flooded for years to come. Soon the crater began to fill; and where once Le Voreux had been, there now lay an expanse of muddy water, like one of those lakes in which doomed cities lie submerged. A terrified silence had fallen, and all that could be heard was the sound of the water pouring down and rumbling through the bowels of the earth.

At that moment, up on the shaken spoil-heap, Souvarine rose to his feet. He had recognized La Maheude and Zacharie sobbing together at the spectacle of this collapse, the weight of which would be piling down on to the heads of those wretched people still fighting for their lives below. He threw away his last cigarette and, without a backward glance, walked off into the darkness which had now fallen. In the distance his shadowy figure faded from view and melted into the blackness of the night. He was headed somewhere, anywhere, off into the unknown. In his usual calm way he was bound upon extermination, bound for wherever there was dynamite to blow cities and people to smithereens. And in all probability, when the bourgeoisie's final hour arrives and every cobble is exploding in the road beneath its feet, there he will be.

IV

That very night, following the collapse of Le Voreux, M. Hennebeau had left for Paris, wanting to inform the Board in person
before the newspapers had had a chance to report even the bare
details of the event. And when he returned the next day, people
found him very calm, quite the manager in charge. He had
evidently succeeded in absolving himself of all responsibility
and seemed to be no less in favour than before; indeed the decree
appointing him Officer in the Legion of Honour was signed
twenty-four hours later.

But while the manager's position was safe, the Company itself
was reeling from this terrible blow. It was not so much the loss
of money that mattered as the injury to its corporate body and
the nagging, unspoken fear, in the light of this attack on one of
its pits, of what the morrow might bring. Once again the shock
was so great that it felt the need for silence. Why cause a stir
over this abominable act? Even if they were to identify the
criminal responsible, why make a martyr of him? His appalling
heroism would serve only to give others the wrong idea and
breed a long line of incendiaries and assassins. In any case it did
not suspect the real culprit and eventually laid the blame on an
army of accomplices, as it could not believe that one man alone
could have had the courage and daring to carry out such a deed.
And that precisely was what worried the Company most: the
thought that its pits might now be under a growing threat. The
manager had been instructed to set up an extensive network
of informants and then quietly, one by one, to dismiss the
troublemakers who were suspected of having had a hand in the
crime. A purge of this kind, being the wisest political course to
take, would suffice.

Only one person was dismissed immediately, namely Dansaert, the overman. Since the scandal with La Pierronne he had
become quite impossible, but the pretext was his response in the
face of danger, his cowardice as a leader in abandoning his men.
At the same time his dismissal was intended as something of an
overture to the miners, who detested the man.

Meanwhile rumours had spread among the general public, and the management had had to write to one newspaper correcting its version of events and denying that the strikers had exploded a barrel of gunpowder. After a rapid inquiry the report by the government-appointed engineer had already concluded that the tubbing in the pit-shaft had given way of its own accord following some subsidence in the surrounding earth; and the Company had preferred to keep quiet and accept the blame for inadequate maintenance supervision. By the third day the disaster had become one of the topical news items in the Parisian press: people talked of nothing else but the workers still fighting for their lives at the bottom of the mine, and each morning everyone avidly scanned the latest reports. In Montsou itself the bourgeois turned pale and seemed to lose the power of speech as soon as Le Voreux was mentioned, and a legend was beginning to form which even the bravest were afraid to whisper in each other's ear. The whole region was full of pity for the victims, and people organized excursions to the demolished pit, with entire families rushing to the scene to treat themselves to the horror of its ruins and the heavy mass of debris hanging over the heads of the wretched people incarcerated below.

Deneulin, as newly appointed divisional engineer, found himself in the thick of dealing with the aftermath of the catastrophe; and his first priority was to stop the flooding from the canal, which was steadily aggravating the damage to the pit with each hour that passed. Substantial work was required, and he put a hundred workers on the job of building a dyke. Twice the sheer weight of water had swept away the initial dams. Now they were installing pumps, and it was a long, hard struggle as they fought inch by inch to reclaim the land that had been submerged.

But the rescue of the trapped miners was causing even more excitement. Négrel's orders were still to make one last attempt, and he did not lack for volunteers as all the miners rushed to offer their services in an upsurge of fraternal solidarity. Now that comrades' lives were in danger they had forgotten all about the strike, and their rate of pay was no longer an issue; as far as they were concerned it wouldn't matter if they weren't paid at all, just as long as they could be allowed to risk their own lives to save them. They were all there, tools at the ready and raring to go, just waiting to be told where to dig first. Many had not recovered from the shock of the accident and still had constant nightmares about it. But though they had the shakes and kept breaking out in cold sweats, they dragged themselves from their beds none the less and were among the most determined to engage in combat with the earth, as if they wanted revenge. Unfortunately the one difficult question was precisely that of how best to proceed: what should they do? How could they get down? Which side should they attack the rocks from?

In Négrel's view none of the poor wretches would have survived; all fifteen would certainly have perished, whether by drowning or from lack of oxygen. But in mining disasters the rule is always to assume that the people trapped are still alive, and so he reasoned accordingly. The first problem was to work out where they might have tried to seek refuge. When he consulted the deputies and the old hands among the miners, everyone was agreed: faced with the rising floodwater, the comrades would definitely have made their way upwards from roadway to roadway, until they reached the coal-faces nearest the surface, which meant that they were probably trapped at the end of one of the higher roads. Moreover, this tallied with the information given by old Mouque, whose garbled account even suggested that in the general panic as they tried to escape the miners might have split up into smaller groups, with people disappearing off in all directions and ending up on separate levels within the mine. But when it came to deciding what they could do to rescue them, opinion among the deputies was divided. Since even the roads nearest to the surface were a hundred and fifty metres down, sinking a new shaft was out of the question. This left Réquillart, which was the only way in and the only way of getting near them. But the worst of it was that the old mine, which had itself been flooded, no longer connected with Le Voreux, and that the only free means of access, above the flood-level, were a few short roadways running out from the first loading-bay. Draining the mine was going to take years, so the best plan would be to inspect these areas to see if they might not be close to the flooded roads at the far end of which they suspected the trapped miners to be. Before reaching this logical conclusion there had been considerable discussion, and a whole host of other, impracticable suggestions had been rejected.

At this point Négrel went through the files and found the original plans for the two pits, which he studied carefully, identifying the places where they ought to search. Little by little, this hunt for the trapped miners had begun to excite him, and he, too, now felt passionately committed to finding them, despite his customary ironic nonchalance towards the affairs of men and the things of this world. There were initial difficulties in getting into Réquillart: they had to clear the entrance to the shaft by removing the rowan tree and cutting back the sloe and hawthorn bushes, and then there were the ladders to be repaired as well. After that the preliminary search began. Négrel went down with ten men and had them tap their iron tools against certain parts of the seam which he indicated; and then in complete silence each man pressed his ear to the coal and listened for answering taps in the distance. They tried every roadway they could reach, but in vain; there was no answer. Now they were in even more of a quandary: where should they start cutting through the coal? In which direction should they go, since there was nobody there to guide them forward? But they kept at it, searching and searching, and the tension rose as they became increasingly concerned.

From the very first day La Maheude had come to Réquillart each morning. She would sit down on an old beam opposite the entrance and stay there till the evening. Whenever a man came out, she stood up and gave him a questioning look. Anything yet? No, nothing. And then she would sit down again and continue to wait, without a word, her face set hard and closed. Jeanlin, too, on seeing that his den was being invaded, had been prowling around with the frightened look of an animal whose burrow full of plundered prey is about to be uncovered. He was also thinking about the young soldier whose body lay under the rock, worried that the men might be about to disturb his peaceful resting-place; but that part of the mine had been flooded, and in any case the search was being carried out further over to the left, in the west part. At first Philomène had come along also, to accompany Zacharie, who was part of the rescue team; but she had got fed up getting cold for no good reason and with nothing to show for it. And so she remained behind in the village and spent her days mooching about, unconcerned, coughing from morning till night. Zacharie, on the other hand, had no thought for his own life and would have eaten the earth beneath him if it meant finding his sister. He cried out in his sleep: he saw her, he heard her, shrivelled by starvation, her throat worn out from shouting for help. Twice he had been about to start digging of his own accord, without authorization, saying this was the spot, he could feel it in his bones. Négrel wouldn't let him go down any more, but he refused to leave the mine even though it was out of bounds; he couldn't even sit down and wait beside his mother, but instead kept walking round and round, desperate with the need to do something.

It was the third day. Négrel despaired, and was resolved to abandon the search that evening. At noon, after lunch, when he came back with his men to make one last attempt, he was surprised to see Zacharie coming out of the shaft, all red in the face, waving frantically and shouting:

'She's there! She answered me! Come on, quickly!'

He had sneaked down the ladders unseen by the guard, and he swore that he'd heard tapping over in the first road in the Guillaume seam.

'We've checked there twice already,' Négrel objected in disbelief. 'But, all right, let's go and see.'

La Maheude had risen to her feet and had to be prevented from going down with them. She stood waiting at the edge of the shaft, staring into the dark hole.

Down below Négrel tapped three times himself, leaving a reasonable space between each tap, and then pressed his ear to the coal, bidding the men be as quiet as possible. Not a sound came, and he shook his head; the poor lad had plainly been imagining it. Zacharie tapped frantically himself, and again he did hear something; his eyes shone, and he was shaking all over with joy. Then the other men repeated the exercise, one after another; and they all became excited as they distinctly made out a response coming from far away. Négrel was astonished, and when he listened again he eventually heard the faintest of sounds, like the waft of a breeze, a barely audible rhythmic drumming that followed the familiar pattern used by miners when they tap out the signal to evacuate at times of danger. For coal can transmit crystal-clear sound over a great distance.

A deputy who was there estimated the thickness of the intervening mass of coal at not less than fifty metres. But for everyone present it was as though they could shake hands with them already, and they were elated. Négrel duly gave orders at once to dig towards them.

When Zacharie saw his mother again back above ground, they hugged each other.

'I shouldn't get carried away,' La Pierronne was cruel enough to say, having come out for a walk to see what was going on. 'If Catherine's not there, it'll only make it worse for you.'

It was true, Catherine might be somewhere else.

'Mind your own bloody business!' Zacharie said savagely. 'She's there all right. I know she is!'

La Maheude had resumed her seat, silent and expressionless, and once more she settled down to wait.

As soon as word reached Montsou, people again arrived in their droves. There was nothing to see, but they stayed all the same, and the more curious among them had to be kept back. Below ground, work continued round the clock. In case they met anything that completely blocked their way, Négrel had ordered three sloping shafts to be cut through the seam, which would all converge down at the point where the miners were thought to be trapped. In the cramped space at the end of each shaft there was room for only one miner at a time to cut the coal, and he was replaced every two hours; the coal itself was loaded into baskets, which were passed back along a human chain which grew longer with the shaft. They made rapid progress at first: six metres in one day.

Zacharie had managed to get himself included among those selected for the task of cutting the coal. It was a position of honour and much sought after. He would get cross when they tried to relieve him after his regulation two-hour stint, and he would pinch the comrades' turns and refuse to relinquish his pick. His shaft was soon ahead of the others, and he attacked the coal with such ferocity that the panting and grunting coming up from below sounded like the noise of bellows in an underground forge. When he emerged, covered in black dirt and giddy with exhaustion, he would collapse on the ground and have to be covered with a blanket. Then back he would go, still staggering with exhaustion, and battle recommenced to the sound of thudding pick and muffled groan as he slew the coal in furious triumph. The worst of it was that the coal was becoming hard, and twice he broke his tool on it in his rage at not being able to go as fast as before. He was also suffering from the heat, which was increasing with every metre, and it was quite unbearable at the bottom of the tiny shaft where the air had no room to circulate. A hand-operated ventilator was working well enough, but it was difficult to get a draught going, and three times they had to pull a man free after he passed out for lack of air.

Négrel lived underground with his men. Meals were sent down to him, and occasionally he snatched a couple of hours' sleep, wrapped in his coat on top of a bale of straw. What kept everyone going was the desperate pleading of the poor wretches below, who could be heard tapping out the signal more and more distinctly and urging them to come quickly. This tapping was now clearly audible, like a tune being played on the keys of a harmonica. It helped to guide them, and they advanced to its music like soldiers marching to the sound of cannon on a battlefield. Each time a hewer was relieved, Négrel would go down himself, tap and listen; and each time, so far, the response had come, swiftly and urgently. He no longer had any doubt, they were heading in the right direction. But how dangerously slow it all was! They would never get there in time. Over the first two days they had cut their way through no less than thirteen metres; but on the the third day this had fallen to five, and on the fourth to three. The coal was becoming so much denser and harder that now they could barely manage two metres in a day. By the ninth day, thanks to their superhuman efforts, they had covered a distance of thirty-two metres, and they calculated that another twenty remained in front of them. For the trapped miners it was their twelfth day that was starting, twelve times twenty-four hours without food or warmth in that icy darkness! This horrific thought brought tears to the eyes of the men and stiffened their sinews to the task in hand. It seemed impossible that any God-fearing soul could survive much longer; the distant tapping had been growing fainter since the previous day, and they were extremely concerned that it might cease at any minute.

La Maheude still came regularly to sit at the entrance to the pit. She would bring Estelle along in her arms, since she could not be left on her own all day. For hour after hour she followed the progress of the rescue work, sharing in the hopes and the disappointments. The tension among the groups of people waiting around, and even in Montsou, was at fever pitch, and nobody talked of anything else. Every heart in the district was beating in time with those beneath the ground.

On the ninth day, at lunch-time, Zacharie failed to answer when they called to him that it was time for he be replaced. It was as though he had gone mad, and with much cursing and swearing he refused to stop. Négrel, who had left the mine for a moment, was not there to make him obey; and in fact the only people present were a deputy and three miners. Unable to see properly and frustrated by the delay caused by the dim, flickering light from his lamp, Zacharie must have been foolish enough to turn it up. Strict orders had been given not to do so: firedamp had been detected, and huge pockets of gas had been building up in the narrow, unventilated shafts. Suddenly there was a thunderous explosion, and a jet of flame shot out of the shaft like the flash from a gun loaded with grapeshot. Everything ignited, and from one end to the other each shaft caught fire like a trail of gunpowder. The sudden torrent of flame engulfed the deputy and the three miners, travelled up the main pit-shaft, and erupted into the open air, spewing out rock and broken timber. The onlookers fled, and La Maheude leaped to her feet, clutching a terrified Estelle to her chest.

When Négrel and the other men returned, they were filled with unspeakable rage. They stamped their feet on the earth as if it were some wicked stepmother who had gratuitously slaughtered her children in an act of cruel, mindless whimsy.

You did what you could as best you could, you rushed to the rescue of your comrades, and then you lost even more men! After three long, exhausting and dangerous hours they finally managed to reach the rescue shafts, and then they had the gruesome task of bringing the victims up to the surface. Neither the deputy nor the three men were dead, but they were covered in terrible burns and giving off a smell of roast meat; having inhaled the burning air, they had suffered further burns all the way down their throats. They kept screaming and begging to be put out of their misery. One of the three miners was the man who, during the strike, had demolished the pump at Gaston-Marie with that final blow of his pick; the other two still had the scars on their hands where their fingers had been cut or rubbed raw from throwing bricks at the soldiers. As they were carried past, the crowd of onlookers, each of them white-faced and trembling with shock, bared their heads.

La Maheude stood waiting. Eventually Zacharie's body appeared. His clothes had been burned away and the body reduced to an unrecognizable, charred lump. The head was missing, blown to bits by the explosion. After his ghastly remains had been placed on a stretcher, La Maheude followed them mechanically, her eyes blazing, without a tear. Holding the sleeping Estelle in her arms, she cut a tragic figure as she left the scene, with her loose hair blowing in the wind. Back in the village Philomène received the news in stunned silence but soon found relief in floods of tears. La Maheude, on the other hand, had immediately turned round and gone back to Réquillart: the mother had brought home her son and was now returning to wait for her daughter.

Another three days went by. The rescue work had resumed, despite the appallingly difficult conditions. Fortunately the new shafts had not collapsed in the firedamp explosion, but they were thick with hot, foul air and more ventilators had to be installed. The hewers relieved each other every twenty minutes. And on they went, with only two metres remaining between them and their comrades. But now they worked with a heavy heart, and if they struck hard into the coal, it was only by way of revenge; for the tapping had stopped, and its bright little tune was no longer to be heard. This was the twelfth day of the rescue work and the fifteenth since the disaster; and that morning a deathly silence had fallen.

This latest accident had revived the interest of people in Montsou, and so many bourgeois were enthusiastically arranging excursions to the mine that the Grégoires decided to follow the fashion. They wanted to make a party of it, and so it was agreed that they would drive to Le Voreux in their carriage while Mme Hennebeau would bring Lucie and Jeanne along in hers. Deneulin would show them how his repair work was progressing, and then they would come back via Réquillart, where Négrel would be able to tell them how far the rescue shafts had got and whether he thought there was still hope. And then they would all have dinner together that evening.

At three o'clock, when the Grégoires and their daughter Cécile stepped down from their carriage at the ruined pit, they found Mme Hennebeau already there, dressed in navy blue and carrying a parasol to protect herself from the pale February sun. The sky was perfectly clear, and there was a spring-like warmth in the air. M. Hennebeau happened to be there also, with Deneulin; and she was listening with a rather absent air as the latter told her about everything that had been done to mend the breach in the canal. Jeanne, who always had her sketchbook with her, had begun to draw, captivated by the violent beauty of the scene; while Lucie, sitting beside her on a wrecked railway wagon, was in similar ecstasies and finding it all 'thrilling'. The dyke, as yet unfinished, was still leaking in many places, and foaming water was tumbling into the enormous cavity of the flooded mine. Nevertheless the crater was gradually emptying, and as the water-level dropped, so it uncovered the terrible mess beneath. On this beautiful day, under the soft blue of the sky, it looked like a cesspit, the remains of a ruined city that had sunk into the mire.

'So much fuss just to see this?' exclaimed a disappointed M. Grégoire.

Cécile, quite pink with health and enjoying the pure fresh air, was laughing and joking, but Mme Hennebeau grimaced with distaste and muttered:

'It's not a very pretty sight, I must say.'

The two engineers began to laugh. They tried to make it interesting for the visitors by taking them round everywhere and explaining how the pumps operated and how the pile-driver did its work. But the ladies were starting to fret. It gave them goose-pimples when they learned that the pumps would need to keep going for years, perhaps six or seven, before the pit-shaft was rebuilt and all the water had been drained from the mine. No, they would rather think about something else, an upsetting scene like this only gave you bad dreams.

'Let's go,' said Mme Hennebeau, making for her carriage.

Jeanne and Lucie protested. What! So soon! The drawing wasn't finished yet! They wanted to stay, their father could bring them on for dinner that evening. And so only M. Hennebeau climbed into the carriage beside his wife, for he too wished to talk to Négrel.

'Very well, you go on ahead,' said M. Grégoire. 'We'll catch you up. We have a little visit to make in the village. No more than five minutes . . . Off you go. We'll reach Réquillart by the time you do.'

He climbed in after Mme Grégoire and Cécile; and while the other carriage sped off along the canal, theirs slowly made its way up the hill.

Their excursion was to include an act of charity. Zacharie's death had filled them with pity for the tragic Maheu family, whom everyone was talking about. They didn't feel sorrow for the father, that scoundrel of a man who killed soldiers and who had had to be shot dead like a wolf. But they were touched by the mother, that poor woman who'd lost her son when she'd only just lost her husband, and when her daughter might even now be lying dead beneath the ground. Moreover there was some talk of an ailing grandfather, and a boy crippled in a rock-fall, and a little girl who had died of hunger during the strike. So, while this family had partly deserved its misfortunes, because of its hateful attitude, the Grégoires had nevertheless decided to demonstrate the broad-mindedness of their charity and their wish to forgive and forget by bringing alms to them in person. Two carefully wrapped parcels were stowed under a seat in the carriage.

An old woman directed the coachman to the Maheus' house, number sixteen in the second block. But when the Grégoires alighted with their parcels and knocked, there was no answer. They eventually resorted to banging on the door with their fists, but still there was no response. The house echoed mournfully, like some cold, dark place that has been emptied by death and then abandoned for a long time.

'There's nobody there,' Cécile said disappointedly. 'How tiresome! What are we going to do with all these things?'

Suddenly the door of the adjoining house opened, and La Levaque appeared.

'Oh, Monsieur! Madame! I do beg your pardon! Please forgive me, Mademoiselle! . . . It must be my neighbour you want. She's not in. She's at Réquillart . . .'

She poured out the whole story and kept saying how people had to help each other and how she was looking after Lénore and Henri so that their mother could go and wait down at the mine. She had spotted the parcels and began to talk about her poor daughter who'd been widowed, expatiating on her own poverty with a covetous gleam in her eye. Then she mumbled hesitantly:

'I've got the key. If Monsieur and Madame really want . . . The grandfather's in.'

The Grégoires looked at her in astonishment. The grandfather was in! But nobody was answering. Was he asleep, then? But when La Levaque finally opened the door, the spectacle which greeted their eyes brought them up short.

There was Bonnemort, alone, sitting on a chair in front of the empty grate and staring into space. Around him the room looked bigger now, devoid of the cheering presence of the cuckoo clock and the varnished pine furniture; all that remained, hanging against the crude green walls, were the portraits of the Emperor and Empress, their pink lips smiling down with an official air of benevolence. The old man did not move, nor did his eyelids blink at the sudden light from the doorway; rather he sat with an imbecilic air as if he had not even seen all these people come in. At his feet lay his plate of ash, like a litter-tray set down for a cat.

'You mustn't mind his manners,' La Levaque said obligingly. 'Appears he's a bit cracked in the head. He's not said a word for the past fortnight.'

But Bonnemort began to shake as a rasping sound seemed to rise up from the depths of his stomach, and he spat a thick, black gob of phlegm into the plate. The ash was saturated, a black sludge where he had heaved up all the coal-dust that had ever passed down his throat. Again he was still. He never moved now, except every once in a while like this to spit.

Unnerved and physically disgusted, the Grégoires attempted nevertheless to find a few friendly and encouraging words to say.

'So, my good man,' said Papa. 'Got a bit of a cold, have you?'

Bonnemort continued to stare straight ahead of him at the wall, and again there was a heavy silence.

'They ought to make you a cup of tea,' said Mamma.

He just sat there not saying a word.

'But wait, Papa,' Cécile said softly. 'People did say he was ill. We ought to have realized . . .'

She stopped, thoroughly embarrassed. Having set a dish of stew and two bottles of wine down on the table, she was untying the second parcel and lifting out an enormous pair of shoes. This was the gift they had intended for the grandfather; and, holding a shoe in each hand, she stared in dismay at the swollen feet of this man who would never walk again.

'A bit late, eh, old chap?' M. Grégoire went on, trying to ease the situation. 'Not to worry. They'll always come in useful somehow.'

Bonnemort heard nothing and said nothing, and his face wore a terrifying expression of cold, hard stone.

Cécile then gingerly put the shoes down beside the wall. But despite her best efforts the hobnails clattered on the floor; and the enormous shoes sat there looking completely out of place in the room

'Oh, don't wait for him to say "thank you"!' cried La Levaque, who had shot a glance of deepest envy at the shoes. 'You might as well give a pair of spectacles to a duck. Begging your pardon!'

And on she went, trying to lure the Grégoires into her own house in the hope of touching their hearts with its prospect. Eventually she thought of a pretext and began to sing the praises of Henri and Lénore, saying what nice, sweet children they were, and how intelligent too, and how they replied like little angels whenever anyone asked them a question. They would be able to tell Monsieur and Madame anything they wished to know.

'Do you want to come next door for a moment, my dear?' M. Grégoire asked Cécile, glad of the chance to leave.

'Yes, I'll be along presently.'

Cécile remained alone with Bonnemort. She had stayed behind out of trembling fascination because she thought she recognized the old man. But where had she seen this pale, square, coal-stained face before? Suddenly she remembered. She saw herself once more surrounded by a screaming crowd of people and felt the cold hands closing round her neck. Yes, it was him, it was the same man, and she looked down at the hands resting on his knees, the hands of someone who had spent his entire working life squatting on his knees and whose whole strength was in his wrists, wrists that were still firm and strong despite his age. Bonnemort had been showing gradual signs of coming back to life, and he now noticed Cécile and began to examine her with his usual gaping expression. His cheeks flushed, and a nervous tic began to pull at his mouth, from which dribbled a thin trickle of black saliva. They faced each other, as though irresistibly drawn together, she in her bloom, plump and fresh-cheeked from the long hours of idleness and the sated well-being of her sort, he swollen with liquid and as pitifully hideous as some broken-down animal, just one in a long line of men destroyed by a hundred years of hunger and toil.

Ten minutes later, the Grégoires, surprised not to see Cécile, went back to the Maheus' house, where they let out a terrible scream. Their daughter was lying on the floor, blue in the face, having been strangled. On her neck were red marks that looked as though they had been left by some giant's fist. Bonnemort,

having staggered forward on his paralysed legs, had collapsed
beside her, unable to get up again. His fingers were still bent,
and he was staring up at them with bulging, imbecilic eyes. He
had broken his dish when he fell, spilling the ash, and the black
sludge of his phlegm had splashed across the room. But the huge
pair of shoes was still sitting there lined up against the wall,
untouched.

It never proved possible to establish exactly what had happened. Why had Cécile gone so close to him? How had Bonnemort, riveted to his chair, been able to grab her by the throat?
Clearly, once he had got hold of her, he must have gripped her
tight for all he was worth and not let go, toppling over on to the
ground with her and stifling her screams until she breathed her
last. For not a single sound or cry had been heard through the
thin partition separating the two houses. He must have had a
sudden fit of madness, an inexplicable urge to murder at the sight
of this young girl's white neck. Such savagery was astonishing on
the part of this sick old man who had always been very much
the stout fellow following orders like some obedient animal,
and never one for the new ideas. What deep sense of grievance,
unknown to himself, had slowly festered inside him and risen
thus from his gut to his skull? The horror of it was such that
people decided he must have acted unconsciously, that it was
the crime of an idiot.

Meanwhile the Grégoires were down on their knees, sobbing
and choking with grief. Their beloved little girl, this daughter
they had wanted for so long and then showered with all their
riches, whose bedroom they would creep into to make sure she
was asleep, who could never be well enough fed, who was never
plump enough! Their life was in ruins, for what was the point
of living now that they would have to live without her?

La Levaque was screaming wildly:

'Oh God, what's the old bugger gone and done? Who would
ever have thought such a thing? . . . And La Maheude won't be
back till evening. Perhaps I should run and fetch her.'

Overwhelmed by their suffering, the Grégoires made no reply.

'It would be best, wouldn't it? . . . I'll go now.'

But as she was leaving she caught sight of the shoes. The

whole village was in uproar, and a crowd was already forming
outside. Somebody might steal them. And anyway there were
no men left in the Maheu household to wear them. She quietly
removed them. They must be just Bouteloup's size.

At Réquillart the Hennebeaus waited a long time for the
Grégoires, talking to Négrel. He had come up from the mine
and was giving them details: they hoped to break through to the
trapped miners that evening, but they'd only be bringing out
bodies, it was still as silent as the grave down there. La Maheude
was sitting behind the engineer on the beam, listening ashen-
faced, when La Levaque arrived to tell her about the old man's
remarkable exploit. Her only reaction was a gesture of impatient
annoyance. Nevertheless she followed her.

Mme Hennebeau was on the verge of fainting. How perfectly
dreadful! That poor little Cécile, who had been so cheerful all
day and so full of life but one hour earlier. Hennebeau had to
usher her into old Mouque's shack for a moment. There, with
fumbling hands, he loosened her stays, and his head spun with
the scent of musk that rose from her open corset. And while she
tearfully embraced Négrel, himself appalled by this death which
had put an end to his marriage plans, her husband watched
them grieving together and felt relieved. This tragedy solved
everything, for he would rather keep his nephew than fear that
the coachman might be next.

V

At the bottom of the pit-shaft the wretched people who had
been left behind were screaming with terror. The water had now
risen to waist-level. The noise of the torrent was deafening, and
with the final collapse of the tubbing it seemed as though the
end of the world had come; but the greatest horror was the
whinnying of the horses shut up in the stable, the terrible,
unforgettable death-cry of animals being slaughtered.

Mouque had let go of Battle. The old horse stood there
trembling, staring wide-eyed at the rising flood. The pit-bottom

was filling up rapidly, and they could see the greenish water spreading wider and wider in the red glow cast by the three lamps still burning up near the ceiling. Suddenly, as he began to feel the icy water through his coat, Battle took off at a furious gallop and disappeared down one of the haulage roads.

A rout ensued, as everyone tried to follow the horse.

'We've bloody had it here!' shouted Mouque. 'We'll have to try Réquillart.'

Now they were all swept along by the one idea that they might be able to get out through the adjoining disused mine if they reached it before being cut off. The twenty of them scurried along in single file, holding their lamps up high so that the water wouldn't put them out. Fortunately the roadway sloped imperceptibly uphill, and they continued forward for two hundred metres against the flow of the current without the water-level gaining on them. Dormant superstitions sprang newly to life in their frightened souls, and they called upon the earth for mercy, this earth that was taking its revenge by spouting blood because somebody had severed one of its arteries. One old man was muttering long-forgotten prayers and crossing his fingers to calm the evil spirits of the mine.

But at the first crossroads an argument broke out. The stable-man wanted to go left, while others swore that they would save time if they went right. A minute was lost.

'You can all bloody die here if you want!' Chaval shouted savagely. 'I'm going this way.'

He headed off right, and two comrades followed him. The others continued to run after old Mouque, who had grown up in the Réquillart mine. But he, too, was unsure and didn't know which direction to take. They were all losing their heads and even the older ones could no longer recognize the roads, which seemed to have twisted themselves into an inextricable knot before their very eyes. At each fork they came to, further uncertainty stopped them in their tracks, and yet they had to choose one way or the other.

Étienne was running along at the back, slowed down by Catherine, who was paralysed with fear and exhaustion. He would have gone right, with Chaval, because he thought that

that was the proper direction; but he had let him go, even if it meant never getting out of the mine. In any case the rout had continued, and other comrades had gone their own way, so that now there were only seven of them behind old Mouque.

'Put your arms round my neck and I'll carry you,' Étienne told Catherine, seeing her falter.

'No, leave me be,' she muttered. 'I can't go on. I'd rather die here and now.'

They had fallen fifty metres behind, and he was just picking her up, despite her resistance, when they suddenly found the way ahead blocked: an enormous slab of rock had collapsed in front of them and cut them off from the others. The floodwater was already seeping through the earth, causing subsidence everywhere. They had to retrace their steps, and soon they lost all sense of direction. This was it, there was no chance now of getting out through Réquillart. Their only hope was to reach the upper coal-faces, where somebody might come and rescue them if the floodwater fell.

Eventually Étienne recognized the Guillaume seam.

'Right,' he said. 'I know where we are. Christ Almighty, we were on the right track before! But that's no bloody good to us now! ... Look, let's go straight on, and then we'll climb up through the chimney.'

The water was lapping against their chests, and progress was very slow. As long as they had light, they would still have hope; and so they put out one of the lamps, to save on oil, intending to pour it into the other lamp later. They had just reached the chimney when a noise behind them made them turn round. Was it other comrades who had been forced back this way after being blocked like them? There was a kind of snorting sound in the distance and, inexplicably, a storm seemed to be approaching and churning the water into foam. Then they screamed when a massive white shape loomed out of the darkness. It was trying to reach them, but the roof props were too close together and it was jammed.

It was Battle. After leaving the loading area he had been galloping along the dark roadways in a state of panic. He seemed to know his way round this underground city which had been his home for the past eleven years; and he could see perfectly clearly in the never-ending blackness that had been his life. On and on he galloped, ducking his head and picking up his feet, racing along the earth's narrow entrails and filling them with his own large body. Turning after turning came and went, paths would fork, but he never once hesitated. Where was he heading? Towards some yonder horizon perhaps, towards his vision of younger days, the mill where he was born on the banks of the Scarpe, and a distant memory of the sun burning up above like a lamp. He wanted to live, and his animal memories were stirring; he longed to breathe the air of the plains once more, and it drove him on, on towards the hole in the ground that would lead out into the light beneath a warm sky. And all his old docility was swept away by a new spirit of rebellion against a pit that had first taken away his sight and now sought to kill him. The water was pursuing him, whipping his flanks and nagging at his quarters. But the further he went the narrower the roadways became, as the roof became lower and the sides began to bulge inwards. But he galloped on none the less, grazing against the walls and leaving tatters of flesh on the timber props. It was as though the mine were pressing in on him from every side, trying to capture him and crush the life out of him.

As he came nearer, Étienne and Catherine watched the rocks seize him in a stranglehold. The horse stumbled, breaking both forelegs. With one last effort he dragged himself forward for a few metres, but his haunches were wedged and he could not get through; he was trapped, caught in a noose by the earth itself. Blood was pouring from his head as he stretched out his neck and searched with wide, glazed eyes for some other way through the rock. The water was rapidly covering him, and he began to whinny with the same long, agonized cry that the other horses had given when they died in the stable. It was an appalling death as the old animal lay there in the depths of the earth, wedged tight, his bones broken, fighting for his life far from the light of day. His cry of distress went on and on, and even when the water washed over his mane it continued, only more rasping as he stretched his mouth wide, up into the air. There was one last, muffled snort, like the gurgle from a filling barrel. Then a deep silence fell.

'Oh, my God! Take me away!' sobbed Catherine. 'Oh, my God! I'm so frightened, I don't want to die . . . Take me away! Take me away!'

She had seen death. The collapse of the shaft, the flooding of the mine, none of it had had the immediate horror of Battle's dying screams. And she could still hear them: her ears rang, her whole body shook with them.

'Take me away! Take me away!'

Étienne had grabbed her and was dragging her away. It was high time in any case: as they began to climb the chimney, the water was already up to their shoulders. He had to help her, for she no longer had the strength to hold on to the timbering. Three times he thought he'd lost her and that she was about to fall back into the deep sea of water whose rising tide was still growling at their heels. However, they were able to rest for a few minutes when they reached the first level, which was still clear. But the water soon appeared again, and they had to hoist themselves up once more. And they went on climbing for hours as the floodwater pursued them from one level to the next and forced them ever upwards. At the sixth level there was a moment's respite of hope and elation when it seemed as though the water had stopped rising. But then it rose again even more quickly than before, and they had to climb up to the seventh level, and then the eighth. There was only one more left, and when they reached it, they anxiously watched each centimetre of the water's progress. What if it didn't stop? Were they going to die like the old horse, crushed against the roof with their lungs full of water?

Rock-falls could be heard all the time. The whole mine had been profoundly disturbed, and its frail intestines were bursting under the pressure of the enormous quantity of water it had imbibed. The air was being pushed back to the end of each roadway, where it accumulated in compressed pockets and then exploded with tremendous force, splitting the rock and convulsing its formations. It was the terrifying noise of subterranean cataclysm, a reminder of the ancient battles between earth and water when great floods turned the land inside out and buried mountains beneath the plains.

Catherine, shaken and dazed by this continual collapse, pressed her hands together and kept burbling the same words over and over again:

'I don't want to die . . . I don't want to die . . .'

To reassure her, Étienne swore that the water was no longer rising. They had been running away from it for six hours now, somebody was bound to come and rescue them. Six hours was a pure guess, for neither of them had any real idea what time it was. In fact a whole day had passed while they were clambering up through the Guillaume seam.

Soaked to the skin, their teeth chattering, they tried to make themselves comfortable. Catherine took off her clothes, without embarrassment, in order to wring the water out of them; then she put her trousers and jacket back on, and they dried on her body. She was barefoot, and Étienne made her put on his clogs. They could settle down to wait now, and they lowered the wick on the lamp till it gave off no more than the faint gleam of a night-light. But their stomachs were racked by cramps, and they both realized that they were dying of hunger. Until that moment they had been quite oblivious to how they felt. When disaster had struck, they had not yet eaten their lunch, and now they had just found their sandwiches, soaking wet and turned to sops. Catherine had to get cross with Étienne before he would take his share. As soon as she had eaten, she fell asleep with exhaustion on the cold ground. Étienne, tormentedly unable to sleep, sat watching over her, his head in his hands, staring into space.

How many hours went by like this? He could not have said. But what he did know was that there in front of him, at the mouth of the chimney, he could see the black water moving, like a beast arching its back higher and higher to reach them. At first, it was just a thin trickle, like a writhing snake straightening out; then it grew into the swarming, crawling spine of an animal; and then it caught up with them, wetting Catherine's feet as she slept. He was anxious not to wake her. It would

surely be cruel to rouse her from her rest and from her blissful
unawareness, perhaps even from pleasant dreams of fresh air
and life in the sunshine. And anyway, where could they go now?
He thought for a while, and then he remembered that the top of
the incline serving this part of the seam connected with the foot
of the incline serving the level above. It was a way out. He let
her sleep on for as long as possible, watching the water rise and
waiting till it chased them on. Eventually he lifted her gently,
and she gave a great shudder:

'Oh, my God! So it's true! . . . It hasn't stopped. Oh, my God!'

She had remembered where she was, and she screamed to find
death so close.

'No, no, it's all right,' he said softly. 'There's a way through.
I promise you.'

In order to reach the incline they had to walk bent over double
and so once more found themselves up to their shoulders in
water. Another climb began, a more dangerous one this time,
up through a cavity a hundred metres long entirely lined with
timber. They began by trying to pull on the cable so as to lodge
one tub securely at the bottom, because if the other were to
come down as they were climbing up, it would crush them to
death. But nothing would move, something must be in the way
and preventing the mechanism from working properly. They
decided to risk it. Not daring to hold on to the cable, which was
in their way, they scrabbled up the smooth wood, tearing their
nails as they went. Étienne followed behind Catherine, stopping
her with his head when she slid back, her hands bleeding.
Suddenly they found themselves up against some fractured
beams which were blocking the incline. The earth had shifted,
and the rubble was preventing them from going any higher.
Fortunately there was a doorway there, which led out into a
road.

Ahead of them they were astonished to see the glow of a lamp.
A man was angrily shouting at them:

'More bloody fools with the same bright idea as me!'

They recognized Chaval, who had found himself cut off by
the same rock-fall that had filled the incline with rubble; the
two comrades who had gone with him had been killed on the

way, their skulls smashed open by the rock. Though he had injured his elbow, Chaval had had the courage to crawl back to them to retrieve their lamps and to search them for their sandwiches, to which he helped himself. As he was making his escape, one last collapse behind him had blocked off the roadway.

His first thought was to promise himself that he wasn't going to share his provisions with these people who had suddenly appeared from nowhere. He would sooner kill them! Then he in his turn realized who it was, and as his anger subsided, he began to laugh with malicious glee:

'Ah, it's you, Catherine! It's all ended in tears, and now you want to come back to your old man! Good! Good! Well, we'll have ourselves a little party then.'

He pretended not to notice Étienne. The latter, shocked by this chance encounter, had immediately put a protective arm round Catherine as she huddled closer to him. Nevertheless there was no way round the situation, and so, as if he and his comrade had parted on the friendliest terms an hour ago, he simply asked him:

'Have you tried the far end? Can't we get out through the coal-faces?'

'Oh yeah, why not? They've collapsed, too, so we're blocked on both sides. We might as well be in a bloody mousetrap . . . But if you're good at diving, you can always go back down the incline the way you came.'

Sure enough, the water was still rising: they could hear it lapping. Their means of retreat had already been cut off. And he was right, it was like a mousetrap, a section of roadway blocked at both ends by massive rock-falls. There was no way out. The three of them were immured.

'So you'll stay?' Chaval asked in mock-cheerful fashion. 'Well, you couldn't have made a better decision. And if you don't bother me, I shan't bother you. There's plenty of room in here for two men . . . And then we'll soon see who dies first. Unless somebody comes to rescue us, of course, but that doesn't seem very likely.'

Étienne went on:

'What about tapping? Maybe someone might hear us.'

'I'm fed up tapping ... Here! You have a go yourself with this stone.'

Étienne took the piece of sandstone that Chaval had already half worn away and went to the coal-seam at the far end and beat out the miners' tattoo, that long sequence of taps with which miners signal their whereabouts whenever they are in danger. Then he put his ear to the rock and listened. He kept at it, tapping it out twenty times or more. There was no response.

During this time Chaval had been coolly affecting to set up home. First, he lined his three lamps up against the wall; only one of them was lit, the others were for later. Then he set his two remaining sandwiches down on a piece of timbering. It was his dresser; he could last two days on that little lot if he was careful. He turned round and said:

'Half's for you, you know, Catherine. If the hunger gets too much for you.'

She said nothing. For her it was the final straw to find herself caught once more between these two men.

And so their appalling new life began. Seated on the ground a few metres apart, neither Chaval nor Étienne would open his mouth. After a comment from the former, the latter extinguished his lamp; the extra light was a pointless luxury. Then they fell silent again. Catherine had lain down beside Étienne, worried by the looks that her former lover kept giving her. The hours went by: they could hear the gentle murmur of the water as it continued to rise, while heavy thuds and distant reverberations bore witness to the final disintegration of the mine. When the lamp ran out of oil and they had to open another one to light it, the fear of firedamp gave them momentary pause; but they would rather have been blown up there and then than survive in darkness; and nothing did blow up, there was no firedamp. They lay down again, and the hours began to tick by once more.

A sound disturbed Étienne and Catherine, who raised their heads to look. Chaval had decided to eat: he had cut himself half a slice of buttered bread and was chewing it slowly so as not to be tempted to swallow it whole. Tormented by hunger, they watched him.

'Sure you won't have some?' he asked Catherine with a provocative air. 'You're wrong not to.'

She had lowered her eyes, fearful that she might yield to
temptation as cramp gripped her stomach so hard that it brought
tears to her eyes. But she knew what he was asking. Already
that morning she had felt his breath on her neck; seeing her in
the other man's company had rekindled his former desire for
her. She knew that blazing look in his eye as he appealed to her
to join him, the same blazing look she had seen during his fits
of jealousy when he would beat her up with his fists and accuse
her of doing all manner of unspeakable things with her mother's
lodger. And she didn't want that. She was terrified that if she
went back to him she would be setting the two men at each
other's throats, here in this narrow cave where they were facing
death. My God! Could they not at least all breathe their last
together as friends!

Étienne would rather have died of starvation than ask Chaval
for a mouthful of bread. The silence grew heavier, and another
stretch of eternity seemed to go by as the minutes slowly passed,
the next one no different from the last, each without hope. They
had now been shut up together for a day. The second lamp was
burning low, and they lit the third.

Chaval started on the other slice of bread and grunted:

'Come here, you fool.'

Catherine shuddered. Étienne had turned away to leave her
free to go. But when she didn't move, he whispered to her softly:

'Go on, love.'

The tears that she had been holding back now poured down
her cheeks. She cried for a long time, neither having the strength
to get up nor knowing whether or not she was hungry, but
aching her whole body through. Étienne had got up and was
pacing up and down, vainly tapping out the miners' tattoo and
infuriated at having to spend the last remaining vestiges of his
life down here, cheek by jowl with a rival he detested. There
wasn't even enough room for them to die apart! Ten paces only,
and then he had to turn round and there he was tripping over
him again! And then there was the poor girl. Here they were
fighting over her underneath the bloody ground! She would

belong to whoever survived the other, and if he himself went first, Chaval would steal her from him once again. Time dragged by as hour followed hour, and the revolting consequences of their life at close quarters grew worse, with their foul breath and the stench of bodily needs satisfied in full view of each other. Twice Étienne lunged at the rock as though to cleave it asunder with his own bare fists.

Another day was drawing to a close, and Chaval had sat down next to Catherine to share his last half-slice of bread with her. She was painfully chewing each mouthful, and he was making her pay for each one with a caress, determined in his jealousy to have her once more, and in the other man's presence. Past caring, she let him do as he pleased. But when he tried to take her, she protested.

'Get off. You're crushing me.'

Étienne was shaking, having pressed his forehead against the timbering in order not to see. He leaped towards them in a fury.

'Leave her alone, for Christ's sake!'

'It's none of your business,' said Chaval. 'She's my woman. I can do what I bloody like with her!'

He grabbed hold of her again and held her tight in his arms, out of bravado, crushing his red moustache against her mouth:

'Leave us in peace, will you! Why don't you bugger off over there for a while.'

But Étienne, white-lipped, shouted:

'If you don't leave her alone, so help me I'll throttle you.'

Chaval was on his feet in a flash, realizing from the piercing tone in Étienne's voice that he meant to have the matter out once and for all. Death seemed to be a long time coming: one of them would have to make way for the other here and now. It was their old enmity showing its face again, down beneath the earth where soon they would both be laid to rest; and yet there was so little room to move that they couldn't even brandish their fists without grazing them on the rock.

'You'd better watch out,' growled Chaval. 'This time I'm going to have you.'

At that, Étienne went mad. His eyes clouded over with a red mist, and his throat bulged as the blood rushed to his head. He was seized with the need to kill, an irresistible, physical need like a tickle of phlegm in the throat that brings on a violent, unstoppable fit of coughing. It rose up and burst forth, beyond his power to control it, under the impulse of the hereditary flaw within him. He grabbed hold of a lump of shale in the wall, loosened it and tore it free. It was large and heavy. Using both hands and with superhuman strength, he brought it crashing down on Chaval's skull.

He did not even have time to jump back. He fell where he was, his face smashed, his skull split open. His brains had spattered against the roof, and a jet of purple was pouring from the wound like water spurting from a spring. A pool formed immediately, reflecting the hazy star of the lamp. Dark shadow filled the walled cave, and the body on the ground looked like the black hump of a pile of coal.

Étienne leaned over him, wide-eyed, and stared. So it was done, he had killed. The memory of all his past struggles came confusedly to his mind, memories of his long, futile battle against the poison that lay dormant in every sinew of his body, the alcohol which had slowly accumulated over the generations in his family's blood. And yet if he was drunk now, it could only be on hunger: his parents' alcoholism had sufficed at one remove. His hair stood on end at the horror of this murder and, though all his upbringing was against it, his heart was racing with joy, the sheer animal joy of a sated appetite. And then he felt an upsurge of pride, the pride of the fittest. He had suddenly remembered the young soldier, his throat slit with a knife, killed by a child. Now he, too, had killed.

Catherine had got to her feet, and she gave a loud shriek.

'My God! He's dead!'

'Are you sorry?' Étienne asked fiercely.

She was gasping for breath, at a loss for words. Then she swayed and flung herself into his arms.

'Oh, kill me too! Let's both of us die!'

She wrapped her arms round his shoulders and hugged him tight, as he hugged her; and together they hoped that they were about to die. But death was in no hurry, and they loosened their embrace. Then, as she hid her eyes, he dragged the poor wretch across the ground and pushed him down the incline, to clear the cramped space they still had to live in. Life would have been impossible with that corpse under their feet. But they were horrified to hear the body land with a splash. What? Had the flood filled the hole up already? Then they caught sight of it, overflowing into their roadway.

And so the struggle began again. They had lit the last lamp, and in its dwindling light they could see the floodwater steadily, stubbornly, rising. It reached their ankles, then their knees. The road sloped upwards, so they sought refuge at the far end, which gave them a few hours' respite. But the water caught up with them, and it was soon waist-high. Standing with their backs pressed against the rock, they watched it rise and rise. Once it reached their mouths, it would all be over. They had hung the lamp from the roof, where it cast a yellow gleam over the rippled surface of the fast-moving water; but as it faded, all they could see was its semicircle of light being gradually eaten away by the darkness, which itself seemed to increase as the floodwater rose; and suddenly the darkness engulfed them, the lamp had spluttered on its last drop of oil and gone out. They were in total, utter blackness, the blackness of the earth where now they would sleep without ever again opening their eyes to the brightness of the sun.

'God Almighty!' Étienne swore softly.

Catherine huddled against him, as though she had felt the darkness trying to grab her. Quietly she recited the miners' saying:

'Death blows out the lamp.'

Yet in the face of this new threat they instinctively fought on, revived by a feverish desire to live. Étienne began furiously to dig into the shale with the hook from the lamp, and Catherine helped with her bare nails. They carved out a kind of raised bench, and when they had hoisted themselves on to it, they found themselves sitting with their legs dangling and their backs hunched under the roof. The icy water now reached only as far as their heels; but gradually they felt its cold grip on their ankles, and their calves, and their knees, as the flood rose remorselessly, inexorably, higher and higher. They had not been able to level

the seat out properly, and it was so wet and slimy that they had
to hold on tight in order not to slide off. The end had come, for
how long could they go on waiting like this, exhausted, starving,
without food or light, and confined to this niche in the wall
where they didn't even dare move? But it was the darkness they
found the hardest to bear, for it prevented them from observing
the approach of death. There was deep silence. The bloated
mine lay perfectly still; and all they could feel beneath them,
swelling up from the roadways below, was the rising tide of its
noiseless sea.

Hour followed upon black hour, though they could not tell
how long it had been for their sense of time was now almost
gone. Their torment should have made the minutes drag, but
instead it made them race past. They thought they'd been
trapped for only two days and one night whereas in reality they
were coming to the end of their third day. They had given up all
hope of being saved; nobody knew they were there – in any case
nobody had the means to reach them – and hunger would finish
them off even if the floodwater didn't. They thought of tapping
out the signal one last time, but the stone was under the water.
In any case, who would hear them?

Catherine had leaned her aching head against the coal-seam
in weary resignation when suddenly she gave a start:

'Listen,' she said.

At first Étienne thought she meant the faint sound of the rising
water. So he lied, hoping to comfort her:

'It's only me. I was moving my legs.'

'No, no, not that! . . . Further away. Listen.'

And she pressed her ear to the coal. He realized what she
meant and did the same. They held their breath and waited for
some seconds. Then, far away, very faintly, they heard three
carefully spaced taps. But they still couldn't believe it; perhaps
their ears were making the noise, perhaps it was the rock shifting.
And they didn't know what they could use to answer with.

Étienne had an idea.

'You've still got the clogs. Take them off and use the heels.'

She tapped out the miners' signal; they listened, and once
again, far away, they made out the sound of three taps. Twenty

times they did it, and twenty times the reply came. They were crying and hugging each other, nearly falling off as they did so. The comrades were there at last, they were on their way. All memory of their anguished waiting and of the fury they had felt when their earlier tapping had gone unanswered was swept away in an outpouring of joy and love, as if all the rescuers had to do now was to open up the rock with their little fingers and set them free.

'How about that!' she exclaimed happily. 'Lucky I leaned my head when I did!'

'That's some hearing you've got!' he replied. 'I didn't hear a thing.'

From then on they took it in turns so that one of them was always listening and ready to reply to the slightest signal. Soon they could hear the sound of picks: they must be beginning to cut a way through to them, they must be sinking a new shaft. Not a sound escaped them. But their elation subsided. Try as they might to put on a brave face for each other, they were beginning to lose hope again. At first they had discussed the situation endlessly: it was clear the men were coming from Réquillart, they were digging down through the seam, perhaps they were making three shafts, because there were always three men digging. But then they began to talk less and eventually relapsed into silence when they considered the enormous mass of rock separating them from the comrades. They pursued their thoughts in silence, calculating the days upon days it would take someone to bore through so much rock. The men would never reach them in time, they could both have died twenty times over by then. Not daring to say anything to each other as their own anguish increased, they gloomily answered the calls by drumming out their signal with the clogs, not in hope but out of an instinctive need to let people know that they were still alive.

Another day passed, and then another. They had now been down there for six days. The water, having reached their knees, was neither rising nor falling; and their legs felt as though they were dissolving in its icy bath. They could lift them out for an hour or so, but it was so uncomfortable sitting in this position that they suffered terrible cramp and were forced to put them back. Every ten minutes they had to wriggle their bottoms back up the slippery rock. Jagged fragments of coal dug into their backs, and they had a permanent sharp pain at the tops of their spines from bowing their heads all the time to avoid the rock above. The atmosphere was becoming more and more suffocating, since the water had compressed the air into the sort of bubble they were sitting in. The sound of their voices, muffled therefore, seemed to come from a long way away. Their ears started buzzing with strange noises: they would hear bells ringing madly or what sounded like a herd of animals galloping through an endless hailstorm.

At first Catherine suffered horribly from the lack of food. She would press her poor clenched fists to her throat, and her breath came in long, wheezing, ear-splitting moans as if her stomach were being removed by forceps. Étienne, racked by the same torture, was groping round desperately in the dark when, right next to him, his fingers came on a piece of half-rotten timber, which he broke up with his nails. He gave Catherine a handful, which she devoured greedily. For two days they lived off this mouldy piece of wood; they ate the whole thing and were in despair when they finished it, scratching away till their fingers were raw in the attempt to start on other bits of wood that were still sound and whose fibres refused to give. Their torment grew worse, and they were furious to find that they couldn't eat the material of their clothes. Étienne's leather belt brought a modicum of relief: he bit off little pieces for her, which she chewed to a pulp and tried her hardest to swallow. It gave their jaws something to do while affording them the illusion of eating. Then, when the belt was finished, they started to chew their clothes again, sucking them for hours on end.

But soon these violent cramps passed, and their hunger was no more than a dull pain deep inside them, the sensation that their strength was slowly and gradually ebbing out of them. They would no doubt have died already if they had not had as much water as they wanted. They had only to bend over and drink from their cupped hands; and they did so continually, for they had such a burning thirst that even all this water could not quench it.

On the seventh day Catherine was leaning forward to drink when her hand knocked against something floating in front of her.

'Here, what's this?'

Étienne felt around in the darkness.

'I don't know. It seems to be the cover of a ventilation door.'

She drank the water, but as she was taking a second mouthful, the object touched her hand again. And she gave a terrible shriek:

'Oh, my God! It's him!'

'Who?

'Him. You know. I could feel his moustache.'

It was Chaval's body, which had floated up the incline towards them on the rising water. Étienne stretched out his arm and felt the moustache and the crushed nose; and he shuddered with revulsion and fear. Catherine suddenly felt terribly sick and spat out the rest of the water. It was as though she'd just been drinking blood, as though the deep pool in front of her was actually a pool of this man's blood.

'Hold on,' Étienne stammered, 'I'll soon get rid of him.'

He pushed the body away with his foot. But soon they could feel it bumping against their legs again.

'For Christ's sake, go away!'

But after a third attempt Étienne had to let it be. Some current must be bringing it back all the time. Chaval was refusing to leave; he wanted to be with them, to be right up close to them. He was a gruesome companion, and his presence made the air even fouler. All through that day they went without water, resisting the need and believing they would rather die than drink it, and only on the following day did the pain finally change their minds: they would push the body away each time they took a mouthful, but drink they did. They might as well not have bothered smashing his skull in if he was now going to come between them again, as stubbornly jealous as ever. Even though he was dead, he would always be with them, to the bitter end, preventing them from ever being alone together.

Another day went by, and another. With each little wave Étienne could feel the man he had killed gently bumping against him in the water, like a companion nudging him quietly to remind him of his presence. And each time he would give a shudder. He kept seeing him in his mind's eye, all green and bloated, with his squashed face and his red moustache. Then he couldn't remember any more and began to think he hadn't killed him, that this was Chaval swimming in the water and about to bite him. Catherine now cried constantly for long periods at a time, after which she would lapse, exhausted, into semi-consciousness. Eventually she fell into a deep sleep from which it was impossible to rouse her. Étienne would wake her up, and she would mumble incoherently before going straight back to sleep, sometimes without even opening her eyes; and he had now put his arm round her waist in case she slid off and drowned. It fell to him to reply to the comrades. The sound of the picks was getting closer, from somewhere behind his back. But his own strength was failing, and he had lost the will to tap. They knew they were there, so why tire himself out further? He no longer cared whether they came or not. The long wait had left him in such a dazed state that for hours at a time he would quite forget what it was he was actually waiting for.

There was one crumb of comfort. The water was going down, and Chaval's body drifted away. The rescue party had been at work for nine days now, and Étienne and Catherine were just taking their first steps along the roadway again when a horrifying explosion threw them to the ground. They groped for each other in the dark and then huddled together, terrified out of their wits, uncomprehending, thinking that disaster had struck once more. Nothing stirred, and the sound of the picks had stopped.

In the corner where they were sitting side by side, Catherine gave a little laugh:

'It must be lovely outside . . . Come on, let's go and see.'

At first Étienne fought against this delusion, but even his stronger head found it catching, and he lost all grip on reality. Their five senses were beginning to play them false, especially Catherine's, who was delirious with fever and tormented by the need to speak and make gestures with her hands. The ringing in her ears had turned into birdsong and the gentle murmur of running water; she caught the strong smell of trampled grass; and she clearly saw large patches of yellow swimming in front of her eyes, so large that she thought she was out in the cornfields by the canal on a beautiful sunny day.

'Oh, it's so hot today! . . . Come, take me, and let's be together for ever and ever.'

As he held her, she rubbed herself slowly against his body, chattering away in a happy girlish fashion:

'We've been so silly to wait all this time! I'd have gone with you from the start, but you didn't realize and just sulked . . . And then, do you remember, those nights at home when we couldn't sleep, lying there listening to each other breathing and desperately wanting to do it?'

Her gaiety was infectious, and he joked as he recalled their unspoken affection for each other:

'Remember that time you hit me! Oh yes, you did! You slapped me on both cheeks!'

'It was because I loved you,' she murmured. 'You see, I'd forbidden myself to think about you. I kept telling myself it was all over between us. But deep down I knew that one day sooner or later we'd be together . . . We just needed the opportunity, some lucky moment, didn't we?'

A cold shiver ran down his back, as though he wanted to banish such fond thoughts, but then he said slowly:

'It's never all over. People just need a bit of luck, and then they can start over again.'

'So you'll have me, then? Is this the moment at last?'

With that she went limp in his arms, barely conscious. She was so weak that her already faint voice trailed away altogether. Fearing the worst, he pressed her to his heart:

'Are you all right?'

She sat up in astonishment.

'Yes, of course! . . . Why not?'

But his question had roused her from her dream. She stared wildly at the darkness and wrung her hands as a fresh wave of sobbing overtook her.

'My God, my God! It's so dark!'

Gone were the cornfields and the smell of grass, the skylarks

singing and the big yellow sun. She was back in the mine with
its rock-falls and floods, back in the stench-filled darkness and
listening to the lugubrious sound of dripping water, down in
this cave where they had lain dying for so many days. The tricks
played by her senses now made it all seem even more horrific.
Once again she fell prey to the superstitions of her childhood
and saw the Black Man, the old miner whose ghost haunted the
pit and strangled the life out of naughty girls.

'Listen, did you hear that?'

'No, I can't hear anything.'

'Yes, you can. It's the Man . . . You know? . . . There, that's
him . . . The earth has bled itself to death out of revenge because
somebody cut its vein, and now he has come. Look, there he is!
You can see him! Blacker than the darkness . . . Oh, I'm so
afraid, so afraid!'

She shivered and fell silent. Then, very quietly, she went on:

'No, it isn't. It's still the other one.'

'Which other one?'

'The one who's with us. The one who's dead.'

She couldn't get the thought of Chaval out of her head, and
she began to talk about him in a rambling way, about the
miserable life they'd had together, about the one time he'd been
nice to her, at Jean-Bart, and about all the other days of cuddles
and bruises when he'd smother her with kisses having just beaten
the daylights out of her.

'Honestly, he's after us! He's going to have another go, he
wants to stop us ever being alone together! . . . It's his same old
jealousy! . . . Oh, send him away! Please! Keep me with you,
keep me all to yourself!'

She had thrown her arms round Étienne's neck and was
clinging to him, seeking out his mouth and pressing her lips
passionately against his. The darkness parted, the sun returned,
and she began once more to laugh the happy laugh of a girl in
love. And he, trembling as his skin felt the touch of her body,
half naked under her jacket and tattered trousers, pulled her
towards him, roused in his manhood. Now at last they had their
wedding night, down in this tomb upon a bed of mud. For they
did not want to die before knowing happiness: theirs was a

stubborn need to live life, and to make a life, just one last time. And thus, despairing of all else, they loved each other, in the midst of death.

Then there was nothing. Étienne sat on the ground, still in the same corner, with Catherine lying motionless across his knees. Hour after hour went by. For a long time he thought she was asleep, then he touched her: she was very cold. She was dead. And yet he did not move, for fear of waking her. The thought that he had been the first to have her as a woman, and that she could be pregnant, moved him. He had other thoughts, too, about wanting to go away with her and about the joyous things they would do together, but they were so vague that they seemed simply to stroke his brow like the gentle breath of sleep. He was growing weaker and could manage only the smallest movement, such as slowly raising his hand to stroke her cold, stiff body, making sure she was still there, like a child asleep on his lap. Everything was gradually fading into nothingness: the darkness itself had vanished, and he was nowhere, beyond time and space. Yes, there was a tapping sound just behind his head, and it was getting louder and louder; but to begin with he had felt so completely exhausted that he couldn't be bothered to go and reply, and now he had no idea what was happening and kept dreaming that Catherine was walking ahead of him and that he was listening to the gentle clatter of her clogs. Two days went by: she hadn't moved, and he stroked her automatically, glad to know that she was so peaceful.

Étienne felt a jolt. He could hear a rumble of voices, and rocks were rolling down to his feet. When he saw a lamp, he wept. His blinking eyes followed the light, and he couldn't watch it enough, in ecstasy at the sight of this pinprick of reddish light which barely pierced the darkness. But now some comrades were lifting him up to carry him away, and he allowed them to pour spoonfuls of broth between his locked jaws. It was only when they reached the main Réquillart roadway that he recognized someone, Négrel the engineer, who was standing there in front of him; and these two men who despised each other, the rebellious worker and the sceptical boss, threw their arms round each other and sobbed their hearts out, both of them shaken to

the very core of their humanity. And into their immense sadness
entered all the misery of countless generations and all the excess
of pain and grief that it is possible to know in this life.

Up above, La Maheude lay slumped by the side of Catherine's
body uttering one long, wailing scream after another in unceasing lament. Several other bodies had already been brought up
and placed in a row on the ground; Chaval, who was presumed
to have been crushed by a rock-fall, one pit-boy and two hewers
whose bodies had been similarly smashed, their skulls now
emptied of brains and their bellies swollen with water. Some
women in the crowd were going out of their minds, tearing at
their skirts and scratching themselves in the face. When they
finally brought Étienne out, having accustomed him to the light
of the lamps and fed him a little, he was no more than a skeleton,
and his hair had turned completely white. People moved away,
shuddering at the sight of this old man. La Maheude stopped
screaming and gazed at him blankly with huge, staring eyes.

VI

It was four o'clock in the morning. The cool April night was
warming with the coming of day. Up in the clear sky the stars
were beginning to flicker and fade as the first light of dawn tinged
the eastern horizon with purple. And the black countryside lay
slumbering, as yet barely touched by the faint stirring that
precedes the world's awakening.

Étienne was striding along the Vandame road. He had just
spent six weeks in hospital in Montsou. Still sallow-skinned and
very thin, he had felt strong enough to leave, and leaving he
was. The Company, still nervous about the safety of its pits and
in the process of carrying out a series of dismissals, had told him
that they could not keep him on and offered him a grant of a
hundred francs together with some fatherly advice about quit-
ting the mines, where the work would now be too hard for
him. But he had refused the hundred francs. Having written to
Pluchart, he had already received a reply inviting him to Paris

and enclosing the cost of the fare. His old dream was coming true. After leaving hospital the previous day, he had stayed with Widow Desire at the Jolly Fellow. And when he got up early that morning, his one remaining wish had been to say goodbye to the comrades before catching the eight o'clock train from Marchiennes.

Étienne paused for a moment in the middle of the road, which was now flushed with pink. It was so good to breathe in this fresh, pure air of early spring. It was going to be a beautiful day. Slowly the dawn was breaking, and the sap was rising with the sun. He set off again, striking the ground firmly with his dog-wood stick and watching the distant plain emerge from the early-morning mists. He had not seen anybody since the disaster; La Maheude had visited the hospital once but had presumably been prevented from coming again. But he knew that the whole of Village Two Hundred and Forty was now employed at Jean-Bart, and that she herself had gone back to work.

The deserted roads were slowly filling up, and silent, pale-faced miners were constantly passing Étienne. The Company, so he'd heard, had been taking unfair advantage of its victory. When the miners had returned to the pits, vanquished by hunger after two and a half months out on strike, they had been forced to accept the separate rate for the timbering, this disguised pay-cut that was even more odious to them now that it was stained with the blood of their comrades. They were being robbed of an hour's pay and made to break their oath that they would never give in; and this enforced perjury stuck in their throats with the bitterness of gall. Work was resuming everywhere, at Mirou, at Madeleine, at Crèvecœur, at La Victoire. All over the region, along roads still plunged in darkness, the herd was tramping through the mists of dawn, long lines of men plodding along with their noses to the ground like cattle being led to the slaughterhouse. Shivering under their thin cotton clothes, they walked with their arms folded, rolling their hips and hunching their backs, to which their pieces, wedged between shirt and coat, added its hump. But behind this mass return to work, among these black, wordless shadows who neither laughed nor even looked about them, one could sense the teeth

gritted in anger, the hearts brimming with hatred, and the
reluctant acceptance of one master and one master only: the
need to eat.

The closer Étienne came to the pit, the more he saw their
number increase. Almost all were walking on their own; even
those who had come in groups followed each other in single file,
worn out already, sick of other people and sick of themselves.
He noticed one very old man with eyes that blazed like coals
beneath his white forehead. Another man, young this time, was
breathing heavily like a storm about to break. Many held their
clogs in their hands, and it was hardly possible to hear them as
they padded softly over the ground in their thick woollen socks.
They streamed past endlessly, like the forced march of some
conquered army retreating after a terrible defeat, heads bowed
in sullen fury, desperate to join battle once more and take their
revenge.

When Étienne arrived, Jean-Bart was just emerging from the
darkness, and the lanterns hanging from the railway trestles
were still burning in the growing light of dawn. Above the dark
buildings a white plume of steam rose from the drainage-pump,
delicately tinged with carmine. He took the screening-shed stairway and made his way to the unloading area.

The miners were beginning to go down, and men were coming
up from the changing-room. For a moment he just stood there,
amid all the noise and the bustle. The cast-iron flooring shook
as tubs rumbled across; the pulleys were turning and paying out
cable as the loudhailer blared and bells rang and the hammer
fell on the signal-block; and then he found himself face to face
once more with the monster, gulping down its ration of human
flesh as the cages rose to the surface, took on their batch of men
and plunged back again, ceaselessly, like some voracious giant
bolting his food in easy mouthfuls. Ever since the disaster Étienne had had a nervous dread of the mine. These vanishing
cages turned his stomach, and he had to look away. The sight
of the shaft was simply too much for him.

But in the vast hall still cloaked in shadow, where the guttering
lamps cast an eerie light, he could not make out a single face
he knew. The miners who were waiting there, barefoot and

clutching their lamps, would stare at him nervously and then look down and guiltily move away. No doubt they recognized him but, far from feeling any resentment towards him, they seemed to be afraid of him and embarrassed at the thought that he might be blaming them for being cowards. This reaction made him feel proud. He forgot how the miserable brutes had stoned him, and began to dream once more about how he would make heroes of them all, how he would lead the people and direct this force of nature which all too often devoured its own.

A cage filled up with men and disappeared with its latest consignment; and as others came forward, he at last recognized a miner who had been one of his assistants during the strike, a good man who'd always sworn he would rather die than surrender.

'You too?' he muttered sadly.

The man turned pale, and his lips began to quiver. Then he gestured apologetically:

'What can I do? I've got a wife to feed.'

He recognized everyone now among this latest group of miners coming up from the changing-room.

'So you too! And you! And you!'

They were all shaking nervously, stammering out their replies in a strangled voice:

'It's my mother . . . I've got children . . . A person's got to eat.'

The cage had still not reappeared, and they waited there gloomily, so pained by their defeat that they stared obstinately at the shaft rather than look one another in the eye.

'And La Maheude?' asked Étienne.

They didn't answer. One of them made a sign that she was just coming. Others raised their trembling arms to show how sorry they felt for her: oh, that poor woman! What a terrible business! The silence continued, and when their comrade held out his hand to say goodbye, they all shook it firmly, putting into this silent handshake all their fury at having given in and all their fervent hopes of revenge. The cage had arrived: they got in and vanished, swallowed up by the abyss.

Pierron had appeared, with the open lamp of a deputy attached to his leather cap. It was now a week since he had been put in charge of the onsetters at pit-bottom, and the men moved aside to let him pass, for this great honour had made him stand on his dignity. He was annoyed to see Étienne there, but he came across and was eventually reassured when Étienne told him he was leaving. Pierron's wife, it seemed, was now running the Progress, thanks to the support of the kind gentlemen who had all been very good to her. But then Pierron broke off to reprimand old Mouque angrily for not having brought up the horse-dung at the regulation hour. The old man listened to him with hunched shoulders. Then, before going down, speechless with anger at being told off like this, he too shook Étienne's hand, and his handshake was like the others', long, warm with the heat of his suppressed anger, and quivering with the anticipation of future rebellions. And Étienne was so moved to feel this old man's trembling hand in his, forgiving him for the death of his children, that he watched him go without saying a word.

'Isn't La Maheude coming this morning?' he asked Pierron after a while.

At first Pierron pretended not to understand, for sometimes it was bad luck just to talk about bad luck. Then, as he was moving away on the pretext of giving someone an order, he said finally:

'What's that? La Maheude? . . . Here she is.'

And indeed La Maheude was just coming up from the changing-room, lamp in hand, wearing a miner's jacket and trousers, with the regulation cap pulled down over her ears. The Company, out of compassion for the plight of this poor woman who had suffered so cruelly, had quite exceptionally, and as an act of charity, permitted her to work underground at the age of forty; and since they could hardly have her pushing tubs, she had been given the job of operating a small ventilating machine which had recently been installed in the northern roadway, in that hell-fire part of the mine beneath the Tartaret where the air never circulated. And there, for ten back-breaking hours, down at the end of a suffocatingly hot and narrow road, she would turn the wheel while her body roasted in a temperature of forty degrees. She earned thirty sous.

When Étienne saw her, a pitiful sight in her men's clothes,

with her breasts and stomach looking as though they were distended with dropsy on account of the dampness in the mine, he was so shocked that he started stammering, unable to find the words to explain to her that he was leaving and that he had wanted to come and say goodbye.

She looked at him, oblivious to what he was saying, and then eventually spoke as though to a member of her own family:

'Surprised to see me here, eh? . . . Yes, I know, I was going to strangle the first person in our house that went back down, and now here's me going back. I ought to strangle myself really, oughtn't I? . . . Oh, I'd have done so before now, I can tell you, if it weren't for the old man and the little ones at home!'

And on she went, in her quiet, weary voice. She was not trying to make excuses for herself, it was just how it was. They'd all nearly starved to death, and then she'd made the decision, to stop them being thrown out of the village.

'How is the old man?' Étienne inquired.

'He's still as gentle as ever, and he keeps himself clean . . . But he's completely cracked in the head . . . He was never found guilty of that business, you know? There was talk of putting him in the madhouse, but I wouldn't have it. They'd have slipped something in his soup . . . But it's done us a lot of harm all the same, because he'll never get his pension. One of the gentlemen told me it would be immoral to give him one now.'

'Is Jeanlin working?'

'Yes, the gentlemen have found a job for him, above ground. He gets twenty sous . . . Oh, I can't complain. The bosses have been very good to us, as they pointed out indeed . . . The boy's twenty sous, plus my thirty, makes fifty altogether. If there weren't six of us, we'd have enough to live on. But Estelle's eating everything now, and the worst of it is that it's going to be another four or five years before Lénore and Henri are old enough to go down the pit.'

Étienne could not help groaning:

'Them too!'

La Maheude's white cheeks flushed, and her eyes blazed. But then her shoulders sagged, as though under the weight of destiny.

'What can I do? They're next . . . The job's killed everyone else, so now it's their turn.'

She stopped as they were interrupted by men pushing tubs past. Daylight was beginning to filter through the tall, grimy windows, dulling the lanterns in its greyish blur; and the winding-engine continued to shudder into life every three minutes, the cables unwound, and the cages went on swallowing the men.

'Come on, you idle lot, get a move on!' shouted Pierron. 'Get in, or we'll never be finished today.'

He looked at La Maheude, but she did not move. She had already let three cages go without her, and now, as though she had just woken up and remembered what Étienne had told her at the beginning, she said:

'So you're leaving?'

'Yes, this morning.'

'You're right. Probably better to go somewhere else, if you can . . . But I'm glad to have seen you, because at least you'll know now that I don't bear you any grudge. There was a time I could have smashed your head in, when everyone was getting killed. But then you think things over, don't you, and you realize in the end that it's nobody's fault in particular . . . No, no, it's not your fault, it's everybody's fault.'

She now talked quite easily about those she had lost, about Maheu and Zacharie and Catherine; and tears came into her eyes only when she mentioned the name of Alzire. She was once again the calm, reasonable woman she used to be, always able to take a sensible view of things. It wouldn't do the bourgeois any good to have killed so many poor people. Of course they would pay for it one day, the day of reckoning always came. There wouldn't even be the need to do anything about it, the whole bloody lot would just blow up in their faces, and the soldiers would shoot the bosses the same way they'd shot the workers. Underneath the blind acceptance inherited from previous generations and the inborn sense of discipline that was again bending her neck to the yoke, a shift had thus taken place, for now she was certain that the injustice could not go on, and that just because the gates of heaven hadn't opened this time, it didn't mean they wouldn't open one day and offer vengeance to the poor.

She spoke quietly, looking about her furtively as she did so. When Pierron approached, she added in a loud voice:

'Well, if you're leaving, you'd better come and collect your things from the house . . . There are still a couple of shirts, three neckerchiefs and an old pair of trousers.'

With a wave of his hand Étienne refused this offer of the few clothes of his which had not been sold off.

'No, don't bother about them. They'll do for the children . . . I'll sort myself out something when I get to Paris.'

Two more cages had gone down, and Pierron decided to summon La Maheude directly.

'Hey, you over there. We're waiting for you. Haven't you finished your little chat yet?'

But she turned her back on him. What was he being all zealous about, the bloody toady? It wasn't his job to supervise the descent, and anyway the men at pit-bottom hated him enough as it was. So she stayed where she was, clutching her lamp and freezing in the icy draughts despite the mild weather.

Neither of them could think of anything more to say. But as they stood there facing each other, their hearts were so full that they wanted to talk on.

Eventually, for the sake of something to say, La Maheude added:

'La Levaque's pregnant. Levaque's still in prison, and Bouteloup's been taking his place in the meanwhile.'

'Ah, yes, Bouteloup.'

'Oh, and did I tell you? . . . Philomène's gone.'

'What do you mean "gone"?'

'Yes, she's gone off with a miner from the Pas-de-Calais. I was worried she might leave her two kids with me, but no, she's taken them with her . . . Not bad for a woman who spits blood and looks as though she were about to breathe her last the whole time!'

She thought for a moment, and then continued in an unhurried way:

'And the things they've said about me! . . . Do you remember how they used to claim I was sleeping with you. Well, my God! After Maheu died, it could very easily have happened. Had I been younger, that is. But I'm glad it didn't, because we'd be sure to regret it now.'

'Yes, we'd be sure to,' Étienne simply repeated after her.

And that was all. They said no more. There was a cage waiting, and she was angrily being told to get in or face a fine. So she decided she'd better go, and shook him by the hand. He felt very sad as he watched her leave, so aged and worn out, with her bloodless face, and the mousy hair poking out under her blue cap, and the body of a fine specimen of a woman who'd had too many children, a stout body that now looked misshapen in its trousers and its cotton jacket. And in this final handshake he recognized once again the long, silent grip that promised support for the day when they would all try again. He understood perfectly, he had seen the calm faith in her eyes. See you again soon, and next time we'll really show 'em.

'Bloody idle woman!' shouted Pierron.

Having been pushed and jostled, La Maheude crammed into a tub with four other miners. The signal-rope was pulled to indicate that the 'meat' was on its way, and the cage swung from its keep and fell into the night. All that was left was the whirr of unwinding cable.

Étienne left the building. Down below, beneath the screening-shed, he noticed someone sitting in the middle of a thick pile of coal with his legs stretched out in front of him. It was Jeanlin, whose job was to 'clean the big bits'. He was holding a lump of coal between his legs and removing fragments of shale with a hammer. He was so completely covered in fine soot that Étienne would never have recognized him if the child had not looked up at him with his monkey-face of wide-apart ears and tiny green eyes. He gave a mischievous laugh, broke the lump of coal with one final blow of his hammer, and vanished in a billowing cloud of black dust.

Out on the highway Étienne walked for a while, deep in thought. All sorts of ideas were racing through his mind. But above all he felt the pleasure of the fresh air and the open sky, and he took deep breaths. The sun was rising gloriously on the horizon, stirring the countryside to a joyful awakening. A tide of gold was sweeping over the immense plain from east to west as the warmth of life took hold, spreading out in a tremulous wave of vibrant newness and youth that mingled the sighs of the earth, the songs of the birds and every murmur and whisper of stream and wood. It was good to be alive, the old world wanted to see another spring.

Filled with this spirit of hope, Étienne slowed his pace, gazing absently to left and right, taking in the gaiety of the new season. He thought about himself, and he felt strong, matured by his hard times down the pit. His education was complete, and he was leaving newly armed, a philosopher soldier of the revolution, having declared war on the society he saw around him and condemned. In his delight at going to join Pluchart, at going to *be* Pluchart, a leader who was listened to, he started making speeches to himself, rehearsing the phrases as he went. He considered how he might broaden his programme of objectives, for the bourgeois refinement that had taken him out of his own class had now made him hate the bourgeoisie even more. Discomfited by the workers' reek of poverty, he felt the need to raise them up to glory and set a halo on their heads; he would show how they alone among human beings were great and unimpeachably pure, the sole font of nobility and strength from which humanity at large might draw the means of its own renewal. Already he could see himself addressing the Assembly, sharing in the triumph of the people – if the people didn't destroy him first.

High above him he heard a lark singing, and he looked up at the sky. Tiny red clouds, the lingering mists of the night, were melting into the limpid blue; and in his mind's eye the shadowy figures of Souvarine and Rasseneur appeared before him. It was clear that everything went wrong when people tried to gain power for themselves. Hence the failure of this famous International of theirs, which was supposed to have changed the world but which was now weak and impotent because its formidable army of supporters had been divided and fragmented by internal squabbling. Was Darwin right, then? Would the world forever be a battleground on which the strong devoured the weak in pursuit of the perfection and continuity of the species? The question worried him, even if, as a man sure in the certainty of his own knowledge, he believed he could answer it. But there was one prospect which dispelled all his doubts and held him in thrall, and this was the idea that his first speech would be devoted to his own version of Darwin's theory. If one class had to devour the other, then surely it was the people, still young and hardy, which would devour a bourgeoisie that had worn itself out in self-gratification? New blood would mean a new society. And by thus looking forward to a barbarian invasion that would regenerate the old, decaying nations of the world, Étienne once again demonstrated his absolute faith in the coming revolution, the real revolution, the workers' revolution, whose conflagration would engulf the dying years of the century in flames as crimson as the morning sun which now rose bleeding into the sky.

He walked on, lost in his dreams, tapping his stick on the stony road; and when he looked round him, he saw the places he knew so well. Here he was at La Fourche-aux-Bœufs, where he had taken command of the mob that morning when they had stormed the mines. Today the same slave labour was beginning all over again, as dangerous and as badly paid as ever. Just over there, seven hundred metres under the ground, he could almost hear the steady, ceaseless clunk of picks as his black comrades, the very comrades he had seen going down that morning, dug away at the coal in silent fury. Maybe they had been defeated, maybe they had lost money and lives; but Paris would never forget the day that shots were fired at Le Voreux, and the life-blood of the Empire would continue to drain from that unstaunchable wound; and even though this industrial crisis was drawing to an end and the factories were opening again one by one, a state of war had been declared and there could be no more talk of peace. The miners had stood up to be counted, and they had tested their strength; and with their cry for justice they had rallied the workers throughout the length and breadth of France. This explained why their latest defeat had reassured no one. The bourgeois of Montsou might be celebrating, but deep down they felt the gnawing unease that accompanies the end of any strike; and in the heavy silence they kept looking over their shoulders to see if their fate was not already, ineluctably, sealed. They realized that the revolution would not go away, that it would return, perhaps tomorrow even, in the form of a general strike when the workers would all act as one and be able, with the support of strike funds, to hold out for months and on a full stomach. This time, like the last, a crumbling society had been given one more jolt, and they had listened as the ancient structure creaked beneath their feet. They could still feel the shock waves rising, tremor after tremor, until one day the whole tottering edifice would collapse and be engulfed like Le Voreux in one long slide into the abyss.

Étienne turned left along the road to Joiselle. This, he remembered, was where he had stopped the mob from attacking Gaston-Marie. Far away, in the clear morning light, he could make out the headgears of several mines, Mirou over to the right, Madeleine and Crèvecœur side by side. Everywhere things were humming, and the picks he thought he could hear beneath the ground were now tapping away from one end of the plain to the other. Tap, tap, over and over again, under the fields and roads and villages that lay basking in the light: a whole world of people labouring unseen in this underground prison, so deep beneath the enormous mass of rock that you had to know they were there if you were to sense the great wave of misery rising from them. And he began to wonder whether all the violence had really helped their cause. The smashed lamps and the severed cables and the torn-up rails, how pointless it had all been! What good had it done to go rushing around in a mob of three thousand people destroying everything in sight? Dimly he foresaw that one day the law might provide a more terrible and powerful weapon. His thinking was maturing, he had got the wild rage of grievance out of his system. Yes, La Maheude had been right in her usual, sensible way: next time they would show 'em. They would organize themselves calmly and without haste; they would make sure they understood each other; and they would band together in unions as soon as the law allowed it. Then one morning there they would be, millions upon millions of workers standing shoulder to shoulder against a few thousand idle rich, and that day they would take power and become the masters! Ah, what a dawn that would be, the new dawn of truth and justice! It would mean the instant demise of that squat and sated deity, that monstrous idol hidden away in the depths of its temple, in that secret far-away place where it fed on the flesh of poor wretches who never even set eyes upon it.

But Étienne was now leaving the Vandame road and coming out on to the cobbled highway. Over to the right he could see Montsou in the distance disappearing down into the valley. Opposite him were the ruins of Le Voreux, the cursed chasm where three drainage-pumps were now working nonstop. Beyond, on the horizon, were the other pits, La Victoire, Saint-Thomas, Feutry-Cantel; while to the north, from the tall blast-furnaces and the batteries of coke-ovens, smoke was rising into the pure morning air. He had better hurry if he wanted to catch the eight o'clock train, because he still had six kilometres to go.

And far beneath his feet the stubborn tap-tap of the picks continued. The comrades were all there, he could hear them following him with each stride he took. Wasn't that La Maheude beneath this field of beet, bent double at her work, her rasping breaths audible above the roar of her ventilating machine? On the left, on the right, ahead of him, he thought he recognized others, there beneath the corn and the hedges and the young trees. The risen April sun now shone from the sky in all its glory, warming the parturient earth. Life was springing from her fertile bosom, with buds bursting into verdant leaf and the fields a-quiver with the thrust of new grass. Seeds were swelling and stretching, cracking the plain open in their quest for warmth and light. Sap was brimming in an urgent whisper, shoots were sprouting with the sound of a kiss. And still, again and again, even more distinctly than before, as if they had been working their way closer to the surface, the comrades tapped and tapped. Beneath the blazing rays of the sun, on this morning when the world seemed young, such was the stirring which the land carried in its womb. New men were starting into life, a black army of vengeance slowly germinating in the furrows, growing for the harvests of the century to come; and soon this germination would tear the earth apart.

Notes

(For explanations of mining vocabulary see
Glossary of Mining Terms.)

PART I

CHAPTER I

1. *Marchiennes to Montsou*: Marchiennes, now Marchiennes-Ville, is situated east-north-east of Douai in northern France, in the Départment du Nord, just south of the border with Belgium and to the west of Valenciennes. Montsou is a fictional town, the name of which literally means 'mountain of sous'. With the exception of Valenciennes and Anzin (see below, note 6) the remaining place-names used to describe the area around Montsou are also fictional.

2. *Le Voreux*: This fictional name suggests the 'voracious' nature of the mine. See Introduction, p. xxi.

3. *fighting in America*: This war in Mexico lasted from 1861 to 1867. In 1861 Britain, Spain and France had sent troops to Mexico in response to the refusal by the recently installed President Benito Juarez (1806–72) to honour the country's foreign debts. Although Britain and Spain made peace in the course of the following year, France pursued its intervention, and the Emperor Napoleon III (1808–73), nephew of Napoleon Bonaparte (1769–1821), sought to impose the Archduke Ferdinand Maximilian (1832–67), brother of Emperor Franz Josef I of Austria (1830–1916), as the country's new ruler in 1863. After France was forced to withdraw by America in 1867, Maximilian was executed by firing squad on 19 March, an event strikingly recorded in a painting by Manet. The accompanying reference to cholera (see below, note 4) implies that the novel opens in 1866, when the French position in Mexico was becoming untenable.

4. *cholera*: Zola is here using a small degree of historical licence in that the cholera epidemic which gripped the Lille and Valenciennes region of northern France occurred several months later in 1866.

5.   *they called me Bonnemort, for a laugh*: Bonnemort means literally 'good death'.

6.   *Anzin*: A small mining town in the Denain coal-field, very close to Valenciennes, Anzin was the scene of several notable miners' strikes and was visited by Zola as he researched *Germinal*. See Introduction, p. xix.

CHAPTER II

1.   *Two Hundred and Forty*: These purpose-built pit-villages were indeed known by numbers rather than names, a fact which Zola highlights in order to stress the way in which mining companies treated their employees as faceless components in a mechanical process.

2.   *scrofula*: 'A constitutional disease characterized mainly by chronic enlargement and degeneration of the lymphatic glands' (*OED*). The condition could be identified particularly by the presence of hard lumps or sores round the neck.

3.   *cap*: In French 'béguin', a thin, bonnet-like cap usually made of cotton and worn under the leather cap, or 'barette', which miners wore to protect their heads.

4.   *till the fortnight's up*: During the nineteenth century mine-workers in both Britain and France were customarily paid fort-nightly. Since usually they did not work on pay-day, as we learn later in *Germinal*, weekly payment would have meant another day off.

5.   *nine francs*: In so far as the equivalent sum today can reasonably be calculated, one franc would now be worth in the region of £3 to £4, or approximately $5. At this period in the second half of the nineteenth century a sou, a pre-revolutionary unit of currency, was applied colloquially to a five-centime piece. It would therefore now be worth somewhere between 15p and 20p, or approximately 25c. See also Part II, Chapter IV, where La Maheude's purchases provide some evidence of what money would buy at the time: 7 sous for brawn (£1–£1.25); 18 sous for potatoes (£2.80–£3.60), which seems very expensive, although we do not know how many she bought nor how scarce they were. A beer cost two sous (30p–40p) (see below, Chapter VI, note 1).

6.   *five francs*: La Maheude uses the colloquial term 'cent sous' to mean a five-franc coin.

7.   *Emperor and Empress*: The Emperor Napoleon III and his Spanish-born wife the Empress Eugénie (1826–1920).

8.   '*piece*': In French 'briquet', because of the brick-like shape of the thick sandwich.

CHAPTER III

1.   *stealing the girls' bread out of their mouths*: As alluded to earlier in the chapter, the miners were keen for women and girls to be employed since it boosted the family's income.

CHAPTER IV

1.   *This particular seam was so thin*: So-called 'thin-seam mining' of this kind was particular to northern France and Belgium and required different systems of working. Zola highlights it both for documentary reasons and to dramatize the difficulty of the conditions in which miners had to work.

2.   *special token*: A piece of metal or leather stamped with the hewer's or putter's number or distinctive mark, and fastened to the tub he is filling or putting.

3.   *laundry-woman ... rue de la Goutte d'Or*: Gervaise Lantier, the central character in *L'Assommoir* (1877) lives and works as a laundry-woman in this slum area of northern Paris situated between Montmartre and the Gare du Nord. The plot of the earlier novel is briefly recalled in Étienne's reminiscences in the following paragraph. At this point in the fictional time-setting of *Germinal* (March 1866) Gervaise has not yet reached the point within the fictional chronology of *L'Assommoir* where she walks the streets and dies a squalid and lonely death; but the readers of *Germinal* would have known the outcome already.

4.   *the lesion ... harboured within his young, healthy body*: Principally on the basis of his reading of Prosper Lucas's *Traité philosophique et physiologique de l'hérédité naturelle* (1847–50), Zola was persuaded that alcoholism was inherited, and he used this as one of the main elements in his depiction of the degenerate Macquart branch of the family. Étienne's brother Jacques in *La Bête humaine* is similarly afflicted.

5.   *Pas-de-Calais*: The Department of the Pas-de-Calais is situated immediately to the north-west of the Département du Nord.

CHAPTER V

1.   *crosse*: This game, somewhat similar to golf, is described in detail in Part IV, Chapter VI.

2.   *ten years' service*: Horses were generally sent down the mine at

the age of four, ponies at the age of three, and the average length of service was ten years. Mules and donkeys had also been used but proved less co-operative.

CHAPTER VI

1. *beer*: In French 'chope', literally a beer mug or tankard. As Zola discovered on his visit to Anzin, a miner could buy a glass or mug of beer in three sizes: small, medium or large. The price was two sous, irrespective of the size. (See Henri Mitterand, *Zola. II L'Homme de 'Germinal' (1871–93)* (Paris, 2001), p. 725.) By translating 'chope' as 'beer' I have left the quantity drunk imprecise, as in the original French.

2. *asking the bosses for what was possible*: Rasseneur's political views equate to those of the so-called 'possibilists', members of the Socialist Party formed in 1879 (under the leadership of Jules Guesde (1845–1922)), who subsequently parted company from their more radical leader in 1882 and founded (under the leadership of Paul Brousse (1844–1912)) the Revolutionary Socialist Party, renamed the Federation of French Socialist Workers in 1883. Despite this temporary 'revolutionary' tag they were in fact opposed to revolution and favoured legislative reforms as the means to political and social progress.

PART II

CHAPTER I

1. *some forty thousand francs*: See Part I, Chapter II, note 5. Hence somewhere in the range of £125,000 to £150,000, or approximately $200,000.

2. *standard currency unit of the day*: Namely in the period before the French Revolution, after which the sou and the denier (and the écu) were replaced by the franc and the centime.

3. *for a derisory sum*: The State would have appropriated the land from Baron Desrumaux's heir during the Revolution.

4. *rejected by the Salon Hanging Committee*: The selection committee for the Salon annually arranged by the Académie des Beaux Arts for the exhibition of new work. The rejection of Jeanne Deneulin's painting, no doubt among a very large number submitted by amateurs and professionals alike, offers an ironic reminder of the furore created in 1863 (only three years before the fictional chronology of *Germinal*) when so many reputably innovative works (including Manet's *Le Déjeuner sur l'herbe*) were rejected

by the committee and the Emperor himself gave orders for an alternative Salon, the so-called Salon des Refusés, to be organized. This controversy in turn forms the backdrop to *L'Œuvre* (*The Masterpiece*), the novel which follows *Germinal* in the Rougon-Macquart series and which was published in the following year. The battle fought by its central character, Claude Lantier (Étienne's brother), to have his own work accepted illustrates the difficulties faced by the Impressionists as they, too, struggled for recognition – a struggle in which they were supported by Zola himself, who, as a journalist, conducted a vigorous campaign on their behalf in the press.

CHAPTER II

1. *poor mites ... bearing this brioche*: Zola may be intending an ironic reference to the notorious remark made by Queen Marie Antoinette (1755–93), wife of Louis XVI (1754–93), when, on being told that the Parisian populace were engaged in a hunger riot and demanding bread, she sought to solve the problem by saying: 'Qu'ils mangent donc de la brioche!', commonly but incorrectly translated as 'Let them eat cake!' See Part V, Chapter IV, note 1.

CHAPTER III

1. *having their end away, as they put it*: In French 'se jetant à cul', literally to upend each other roughly.

PART III

CHAPTER I

1. *the Tsar*: Zola's readers in 1885 would have been mindful of the fact that there had been a failed assassination attempt on Tsar Alexander II (b. 1818) at the Winter Palace in St Petersburg (on 17 February 1880) and that he had finally been assassinated in the following year (on 13 March).
2. *Poland*: Souvarine's choice of name reflects the anarchist's wry recognition of Russia's dominance over Poland throughout the preceding century. Within the fictional chronology of *Germinal* the suppression of a Polish insurrection in 1863–4 was fresh in the memory.
3. *International Association of Workers ... founded in London*: See Introduction, p. xviii.
4. *iron law of the irreducible minimum*: Originally formulated by

the British economist David Ricardo (1772–1823), this 'iron law' was described in E. de Laveleye's *Le Socialisme contemporain* (2nd edn, 1883), which Zola read. It had been given prominence by the German socialist Ferdinand Lassalle (1825–64) in his Open Letter of 1863.

5. *co-operative societies*: Co-operative societies were the brain-child of Pierre-Joseph Proudhon (1809–65). For him the founding principle of the new society was 'mutuality', a federation of small, semi-autonomous groups of workers supported by 'self-help' arrangements such as 'friendly societies' and the provident fund which Étienne will establish and run. See Introduction, p. xvii.

6. *new contracts*: In French 'marchandages', literally something acquired through bargaining.

CHAPTER II

1. *ducasse*: The name given to an annual celebration, lasting a minimum of three days, held (on their own chosen date) in towns and villages throughout the area now covered by Belgium and the north-eastern corner of France. The tradition dates back to pre-medieval times, and the celebration is characterized by fairs, processions and feasting.

2. *Prince Imperial*: Napoleon III's son Eugène (1856–79), who died fighting in the British army against the Zulus.

3. *Walloon*: The dialect of French spoken by those living in southern Belgium or the adjacent parts of north-eastern France.

CHAPTER III

1. *The Hygiene of Miners*: Zola himself had read Dr H. Boëns-Boisseau's *Traité pratique des maladies, des accidents et des difformités des houilleurs* [coal-miners], (Brussels, 1862).

2. *'social question'*: See Introduction, p. xxv.

3. *cards*: In French 'livret', a booklet. Since early in the century French workmen had had to have a booklet, which was stamped by their employer and certified by the municipality. The requirement was abandoned by a law passed on 25 April 1869. Having one's booklet returned was synonymous with being fired, as in comparatively recent British usage when a worker was given his or her 'cards' (bearing National Insurance stamps).

PART IV

CHAPTER I

1. *Prefect*: The administrative head of a Department in France, answerable to the Minister of the Interior, who at this time enjoyed very wide-ranging powers, including that of being able to deploy the army or the police.
2. *École des Mines*: France's national School of Mining founded on 19 March 1783.
3. *La Grand'Combe*: A small town in the mining area near Alès in the Languedoc.
4. *École Polytechnique*: Founded on 1 September 1795 as a national school to train young men for public service in various branches of civil and military engineering.
5. *longed for the days of Louis-Philippe*: Louis-Philippe (1773–1850) came to the throne following the 1830 Revolution and was deposed during the 1848 Revolution. He had acceded to power promising reform, but several of the liberal provisions of the Charter of 1830 were subsequently reversed under his increasingly oppressive rule.
6. *Emperor ... with his concessions*: From 1860 onwards, and against the advice of the majority of his ministers, the Emperor Napoleon III had introduced a series of constitutional reforms that represented a move away from government by decree towards real parliamentary democracy.
7. *'89*: 1789, the date of the French Revolution.

CHAPTER II

1. *contador*: A desk or bureau particularly designed for work with account books.

CHAPTER III

1. *Assembly*: The Assemblée Nationale, of which the Chambre des Députés was part.
2. *1848*: See above, Chapter I, note 5, and Introduction, pp. xxiv–xxv.

CHAPTER IV

1. *Lassalle's idea of co-operative societies*: See Part III, Chapter I, notes 4 and 5. Since the idea of co-operative societies was in fact Proudhon's, the 'muddle' in Étienne's mind is evident.
2. *Bakunin, the exterminator*: See Introduction, p. xviii.

CHAPTER VII

1. *Hainaut*: Formerly a 'county' within the Hapsburg Empire, Hainaut was divided when Louis XIV acquired the southern part of the territory under the terms of the Treaty of the Pyrenees (1659), confirmed by the Treaty of Nijmegen (1678). French Hainaut became the eastern part of the Département du Nord in 1790.

PART V

CHAPTER II

1. *bad air* – '*dead air*': The upper layer is firedamp, or methane gas; the lower is chokedamp, or carbon dioxide, which, being heavier than air, extinguishes flame.

CHAPTER IV

1. *We want bread!*: Zola uses this cry to recall two famous historical occasions on which it was used: (i) on 5 October 1789 when 6,000–7,000 women marched from the Parisian markets in the Faubourg Saint-Antoine and Les Halles to Versailles, later followed by some 20,000 men, and invaded the Palace of Versailles on the following day. As a result the royal family was obliged to return to Paris, where they were held virtual hostages in the Tuileries Palace (see also Part II, Chapter II, note 1); and (ii) when the Parisian populace demonstrated against famine and the government's economic incompetence on '12–13 Germinal III' (1–2 April 1795).

CHAPTER V

1. '*La Marseillaise*': Composed by Claude Rouget de l'Isle (1760–1836) in 1792 and so called because it was very soon afterwards adopted and made widely known by a band of Marseillais revolutionary volunteers making their way to Paris. It quickly became the anthem of French republicans and accordingly was banned under the Second Empire. It became the national anthem of France in 1879.

PART VI

CHAPTER I

1. *Cossacks*: See below, Chapter V, note 1.

CHAPTER III

1. *The writing was already on the wall for this mass movement*: Again Zola is using some historical licence since the rift in the International described here occurred over five years later. See Introduction, p. xviii.

2. *Only one man . . . destruction*: Namely, Mikhail Bakunin. See Introduction, p. xviii.

3. *the notorious nihilists*: See Introduction, p. xviii.

CHAPTER V

1. *served in the Crimea*: During the Crimean War (1854–5) Britain and France sided with Turkey against Russia in the struggle for this disputed territory. The Cossacks, originally a tribe of nomadic warriors, had settled in the Ukraine, and Cossack soldiers formed a distinguished corps in the Russian army, famously resisting British and French troops for a year during the Siege of Sebastopol (September 1854 – September 1855).

PART VII

CHAPTER II

1. *Darwin*: See Introduction, p. xxix.

2. *Annouchka*: Zola has in mind the Russian anarchist, Sophie Perovskaya, who was executed in St Petersburg with four others on 15 April 1881 after the assassination of Tsar Alexander II. Previously she had acted with another anarchist, Leo Hartmann, in an attempt to blow up the Tsar's train near Moscow on 1 December 1879.

Glossary of Mining Terms

In preparing to write *Germinal*, Zola undertook extensive research into the world of mining. He wanted his novel to be an authentic record of this world, but at the same time he did not wish to burden his readers with unnecessary information nor to alienate them with the excessive use of technical vocabulary. Accordingly he introduces us to this world gradually and unobtrusively, concisely explaining each new term or unfamiliar working practice as he goes along and generally only when he knows that they will be essential to an understanding of the story to come. The fact that his hero is, like most of his readers, entirely new to this world means that these explanations seem to arise naturally. We are not being given a manual on mining, and Zola so wrote *Germinal* that it could be read without notes.

In translating his novel I have had to find English-language equivalents for the terms he uses. Since mining technology in the second half of the nineteenth century was broadly speaking the same in France and Belgium as in England, Wales and Scotland (my research has not extended to mining practices in the United States or Australia and New Zealand), the search for equivalents was relatively unproblematic. On the other hand, English-language mining terms during this period varied from region to region far more than their French-language counterparts. The choice of an equivalent was therefore not straightforward. The Glossary that follows is intended to explain what the choices were and why a particular word has been used in this translation. If it incidentally offers an insight into the world of British mining, it should be remembered that that world was essentially the same as the one so accurately depicted in *Germinal*.

The following abbreviations are used for sources cited herein:
Bulman and Redmayne   H. F. Bulman and R. A. S. Redmayne, *Colliery Working and Management* (2nd edn, London, 1906 (1st edn, 1896))

Pamely   Caleb Pamely, *The Colliery Manager's Handbook* (London, 1891)

Penman   David Penman, *The Principles and Practice of Mine Ventilation* (London, 1927)

banksman In French 'moulineur', a term derived from the terminology of silk-working. According to Bulman and Redmayne, the 'bank' is 'the surface-land surrounding a pit's mouth'; 'the banksmen are stationed at the landing of the cage on the surface, and their work consists in "uncaging" the tubs – that is, taking the tubs out of the cage, and conveying them to the screens (where this is not done by mechanical power), putting the empty tubs into the cage, and giving the necessary signals to the engineman and to the onsetters. The latter, the onsetters, do similar work at the bottom of the shaft' (p. 96).

chimney Pamely records that 'as the colliers hew their coal it is filled into the nearest chimney, to be afterwards withdrawn from below by the putters, who bring tubs under the chimneys, and for a time remove the sluice, thus allowing sufficient coal to rush into the tubs to fill them' (p. 236).

coke-oven Coke is a form of fuel obtained by heating coal to high temperatures, a process which 'drive[s] off its volatile constituents, including all the smoke-forming elements, and leaving a fuel which is comparatively clean to handle, gives off no smoke when burnt, but generates great heat, and has a higher radiant efficiency than ordinary coal' (*The Mining Educator*, ed. John Roberts, 2 vols, London, 1926, vol. II, p. 1212). Hence its use in blast-furnaces as well as in the fire-grates of steam engines. When this process of 'carbonization' occurs naturally, the result is anthracite.

Davy lamp Sir Humphrey Davy (1778–1829) invented this safety lamp in 1815. It is so designed that the naked flame is protected by a piece of fine wire gauze, thus preventing ignition of the methane gas (or firedamp) which is found in so-called 'fiery' mines. According to Penman: 'If the workings are non-fiery, open lights may be used. These may take the form of spout lamps burning oil, animal fat or paraffin wax, and are carried on the cap of the worker, or candles' (p. 49). In *Germinal* the majority of miners have Davy lamps, but the deputies carry open lamps on their caps, doubtless because they did not work in the confined spaces where firedamp was likely to ignite.

engineman See **mechanic**.

firedamp Methane gas; see **Davy lamp**.

hewer In French 'haveur'. In British terms 'hewer' was by far the commonest term at the time. 'Pikeman', used in Havelock Ellis's translation, is a Staffordshire term (see Bulman and Redmayne, p. 406).

hopper A metal funnel in the shape of an inverted pyramid down which the coal passed from the screens into the railway wagons beneath.

loading-bay See **pit-bottom**.

mechanic In French 'machineur', a word now no longer used except in its sense of someone engaged in 'machinations'. The British equivalent would have been either 'engineman' or 'mechanic'. Bulman and Redmayne refer to 'joiners, fitters, smiths, masons, enginemen and other mechanics' (p. 70). According to C. H. Steavenson the job of an 'engineman' was 'attending winding-engine, hauling, pumping, fan, air compressors, electric generators, motors and locomotives', while the term 'mechanic' covers 'plumber, fitter, blacksmith' (in his *Colliery Workmen Sketched at Work*, Newcastle-upon-Tyne, 1912, pp. 24 and 26). For Bulman and Redmayne, therefore, an 'engineman' – which in some contexts we might call a 'machine-operator' – is a subcategory of 'mechanic'. Since it is not clear what Étienne's expertise or qualifications are (from his work in the railway workshop at Lille), nor those of Souvarine later in the novel (he is also a 'machineur'), the broader term 'mechanic' has been preferred.

overman The equivalent of an under-manager, the overman was in charge of the day-to-day running of the pit. He was assisted by deputies.

onsetter See **banksman**.

pit-bottom In French 'à l'accrochage', literally where things are hooked on or attached, and where the tubs full of coal are loaded into the extraction cages. Throughout the novel Zola refers variously to 'l'accrochage' or 'la salle d'accrochage': the former usually designates the pit-bottom in general and the latter more specifically the chamber or loading-bay hollowed out of the rock at the foot of the pit-shaft. Similar loading-bays were also situated adjacent to the shaft at intermediate levels in the mine.

pit-head In French 'la recette' (and later 'la salle de la recette'), literally where the coal is received. In British terms the pit-head, or the area at the mouth of the pit-shaft where the coal is unloaded.

putter In French 'herscheur'. Bulman and Redmayne refer to 'trammers, putters or hauliers' and describe them as 'big lads who convey the coal-tubs to and from the working places' (p. 47). Earlier in the century, as we learn from *Germinal*, most of these 'big lads' were in fact girls, or 'herscheuses' – that is, before the French passed a law in 1874 making the employment of women underground illegal. (This practice had been outlawed in Britain in 1842 when women – and children under ten – were thus protected. The age limit for children was raised to twelve in the Coal Mines Regulation Act of 1887.) None of the British terms distinguishes the sex of the worker. Since 'putter' seems to be the commonest term in the books that I have consulted, I have preferred it to the others, and on one occasion invented the term 'putter lad' where the sex of the putter is relevant and not otherwise identifiable.

roadway In French 'galerie'. Zola also uses the term 'voie'. Although he used the two terms for the sake of variety, and without there being any important distinction between them, I have almost always maintained his distinction by translating the former with 'roadway' and the latter with 'road'. These are both standard terms for a tunnel in a colliery pit: the word 'tunnel' itself is absent from standard late-nineteenth-century handbooks.

rope-works A factory which made not only ropes but also steel cables, which were known as 'wire ropes' at the time.

screening-shed The place where the coal was passed over screens to separate it from clay and small stones. The larger stones were removed by rake and hand.

shifter So called because they worked a shift, not because they shift rubble; 'a class of men who do the necessary *repairing and preparatory work* at nights, when the pit is not drawing coals – such as ridding falls of stone and setting timber, to make the pit ready for the following day' (Bulman and Redmayne, p. 95 (their emphasis)).

spoil-heap In French 'terri'. In British terms 'spoil' is 'earth or refuse material thrown or brought up in excavating, mining, dredging, etc.' and accordingly a 'spoil-heap' is 'the place on the surface where spoil is deposited' (*OED*). A 'slag-heap', on the other hand, is found beside a blast-furnace or smelting-works since 'slag' is 'a vitreous substance, composed of earthy or refuse matter, which is separated from metals in the process of smelting' (*OED*).

stonemen In French 'les ouvriers de la coupe à terre'. In British terms 'stonemen' belonged to the category of miners known as 'off-hand' workers (to distinguish them from those who actually dug out the coal, or 'coal-getters'). According to Bulman and Redmayne: 'their work, which may be termed the "dead" work of the mine – consisting as it does in a very great degree, if not entirely, of opening out and development – constitutes one of the most important branches of the underground department' (p. 83). 'Ripper', used in some translations of *Germinal*, was an alternative name for a stoneman (see Bulman and Redmayne, p. 406).

supervisor In French 'surveillant'. In British terms this person would have been subordinate to the deputies, themselves subordinate to the overman, and might have been either a 'master shifter', a 'master wasteman', or someone in charge of a particular area or activity. While the term 'supervisor' is not current in the handbooks of the period, I have used it for the sake of clarity and simplicity.

tippler The tippler, also known as a 'tumbler' or a 'kick-up' (see Pamely, p. 60), was a hand-operated or (later) mechanized device into which the tub was wheeled, allowing the banksman then to revolve and unload the tub with the minimum of effort.

tubbing The technical term for lining a shaft with wood (and later metal); akin to barrel-making.

ventilation doors The purpose of ventilation doors was to limit the passage of air in subsidiary roadways in order to direct the main air current to the 'ventilation roads' or 'air roads'. 'In its passage through the mine,' writes Penman, 'it is necessary to confine the air current to roads or places where men are to work or pass, and to conduct it by the shortest, largest and straightest road to the working faces, with as little leakage as possible. In many pits a considerable portion of the air entering the mine never reaches the working places. Care must be taken to block all roads but those along which the air ought to flow. This is done in three ways: – (a) By brick or stone walls (stoppings) ... (b) Hinged or sliding doors. These are employed when it is necessary for men or [tubs] to pass, and where at the same time tightness is desired. (c) Bratticing ... hanging sheets of cloth, nailed or tacked to props' (p. 181). Pamely notes also that 'when the road has to be used both for travelling and the passing of tubs, a different kind of door is required so as to allow the horses and tubs to pass. The framing of such doors should not be set quite upright, but sufficiently inclined for the door to fall and close by its own weight. A boy is stationed near to open it as required' (pp. 346–7). This boy was known as a 'trapper'. In *Germinal* the doors are attended to by pit-boys like Jeanlin as they accompany the trains of tubs.